Wendy Perriam

read History Honours
advertising and a succe
ranging from the bizarre
full time.

Her previous novels, wh   include *Absinthe for
Elevenses*, *Born of Woman*, *The Stillness The Dancing*,
Devils, for a Change, *Fifty-Minute Hour*, *Bird Inside*, and
Michael, Michael, have been acclaimed for their
exuberant style, their provocative mix of the sacred
and the profane, and their extraordinary power to
disturb, amuse and shock.

She is currently working on her twelfth novel.

WENDY PERRIAM

Sin City

Flamingo
An Imprint of HarperCollins*Publishers*

Flamingo
An Imprint of HarperCollins*Publishers*
77-85 Fulham Palace Road,
Hammersmith, London W6 8JB

Published by Flamingo 1994
9 8 7 6 5 4 3 2 1

Previously published in paperback by Penguin Books 1988

First published in Great Britain by
Michael Joseph Limited 1987

Author photograph by Ed Barber

ISBN 0 00 654623 4

Set in Bembo

Printed in Great Britain by
HarperCollinsManufacturing Glasgow

For Barbara,
last of the angels

1

St Joseph, are you there? Please hold me, hold me tight. I'm small. I'm very small. Just a tiny baby, like Jesus in the manger. I wasn't born in a manger, but in a hospital in Reading. My mother wasn't there. I was born to you, St Joseph, born to a father. You put me to your breast. Flat pale hairy man's breast. I'm suckling now, eyes shut, mouth pulling at your nipple.

Hold me tighter. So tight I can't see anything, just feel your chest pressed against my eyes. That's nice. Nice and safe. I like it. Your milk tastes of bananas. We never had bananas, not when I was small.

Afterwards, you bathed me. Warm water, hard green soap. You wore a plastic apron and I slipped and slid against it, free without my nappies. When you put them on again, I wet myself – felt the pee run down, hot and wet; soak into your robe. Old brown robe now stained with wet and me.

'Norah Toomey, you've wet your bed again. A great big girl like you. You'll wash those sheets yourself – and iron them.'

Heavy linen sheets which never dried. Nothing dried. St Joseph's was near a river. Damp stains on the walls instead of pictures. The iron was heavy, too, the ironing board too high.

I don't wet beds now. I moved from St Joseph's forty years ago. The nuns went back to Ireland, but they didn't take me with them. I was sent into a Home. It was bigger than the convent, not as quiet. Everybody shouted. I think it was a punishment.

Then I moved again. The new place wasn't damp. Small and cramped with shiny turquoise paint. I had to scrub the paint.

Then I went to Belstead where everyone was ill. There was a garden with real flowers, but you weren't allowed to pick them.

I forget what happened next. But I came here one December. It was bitter cold, with snow. The walls looked very high, and the snow was grey, not white.

I'm in the Day Room now. I sit here most mornings and every afternoon. The walls are green. The chairs are brown with lumpy plastic seats. The ceiling has two cracks in it. They're very long and wiggly. One day I think they'll meet.

Half the chairs are empty. All the younger patients have gone to see a film. I didn't want to see it. Films are always guns.

Ethel Barnes is talking to a man who isn't there. Annie's gone to sleep. Lil can't move at all.

It's still two hours till supper. It's salad on a Monday. Little cubes of beetroot with one leaf of purple lettuce underneath and some chopped-up peas and carrots mixed with salad cream. I like the pudding best.

The clock ticks very loudly. They had to choose a loud one because some of them are deaf. My hearing's good, but sometimes I still leak a bit. Sister says my bladder's fallen down, and I shouldn't cough or laugh.

Someone's just come in. That new nurse with the smile. They all smile when they're new, though not much later on. There's a girl with her. A pretty girl, fair, with nice blue eyes, and messy hair curling round her shoulders. She's smoking. They nearly all smoke here, staff as well as patients. There are ninety-seven burn-holes in this carpet. I counted just last week. And burn-marks on the chair-arms. Sometimes patients pester you all day. 'Cigarette, cigarette,' they wail even when you've told them you don't smoke.

They're coming right towards me, Nurse in front, the girl walking very slowly, as if she's frightened that the floor is made of paper and might not hold her up.

'Hallo, Norah. Know where Sandy's got to?'

'She's gone to see the film.'

'Oh, yes, of course. Clint Eastwood. Damn! I wanted her to keep an eye on Carole. Norah, this is Carole. Carole's new.'

Carole. That's a nice name. Prettier than Norah. I try to smile. It hurts. The girl looks very sad and very young. Sandy's young as well. Most people are old here.

2

'They've put her in your ward. She ought to be in Robson, but the ceiling's letting water.'

Our ceiling leaked as well once. They had to put three buckets underneath, to try to catch the drips. Carole has red shoes on. I've never worn red shoes.

'Carole, this is Norah. Norah Toomey. Norah's been with us over twenty years.'

The girl stares at me and swallows. She looks scared now not just sad.

Nurse pulls another chair up, next to mine. The seat is torn and some soft grey curly stuff is oozing out.

'Can I leave her with you, Norah? I'm wanted in the office.'

I feel frightened now myself. I won't know what to say to her. I'm not that good at words.

'Fred, get *away!*' screams Ethel.

Carole jumps.

'Fred isn't there,' I tell her. 'He died two years ago.'

The clock is ticking louder. Carole's looking round. I wish the room was nicer. They took the curtains down once and no one put them back. We used to have some goldfish, but they died. Two of them were grey, but Nurse still called them goldfish.

'It's supper in two hours,' I say. 'You can leave the pudding, but you have to eat the meat.'

She doesn't answer. I think she's going to cry. Her cigarette's burnt right down to the end. She lights another one. 'Cigarette!' Peg moans.

'Unless you're vegetarian,' I add. No one is. Not here. We had two vegetarians at Belstead, but one died and one was moved.

Carole blows some smoke out, puffs again. There's a ladder in her stocking. Suddenly she speaks. 'Toomey's Irish, isn't it?'

I nod. A lot of people hate the Irish. I expect she'll move away now, find another chair.

'You don't sound Irish, not at all. I went out with this Irish bloke and he was really broad. Quite a laugh as well. It didn't last, though. I only saw him twice. Where d'you come from? Dublin?'

3

'No. Belfast.' That's what they told me, but I don't know where it is. I've never been there; never been to Ireland. 'I was born in Reading,' I explain.

'*I* was born in Glasgow. I'm not Scottish, though – not really anything. My mother was just passing through. She ought to be a patient here, my Mum. She's more a mess than I am.' Carole laughs. The laugh is very sad. 'What are you in for?'

'I live here.'

'Yeah, but why? You can't just live here like it's some hotel.'

I've never been in a hotel. Sister Watkins went to one, in Spain, a huge one on a beach. She sent us a postcard of the beach and wrote on the back, 'I can see this from my window.' The other Sister pinned it up, but someone scrawled three black lines across it.

I ought to answer Carole, but I don't know what to say. I try to think way back. I can see the convent, very tall and quiet. I must have grown too big for it. I can see a mop and duster. The duster's soaking wet. 'I used to cry,' I say. 'Every day. All day, some days.' I tried to stop, but the tears came on their own.

'Oh, depression.' The girl flicks her cigarette. The long wobbly worm of ash collapses, powdering her skirt.

I nod. That's what the doctors call it when you cry. They give me pills which make my face stiff, so it's hard to cry or laugh now. Though the things which make me cry are still there.

'I've warned you, Fred!' shouts Ethel.

Olive's snoring. Peg has tipped sideways in her seat. There's a bad smell in the room. It isn't me. There are forty-eight toilets in this hospital. I've used them all, except the staff ones, which have proper towels and locks on all the doors.

I wish Sandy would come back. Or Alison, who talks a lot. Carole's saying nothing. I don't think she likes the room. There's nothing in it really, only chairs. There's a wall outside the window, so we don't have any view. There used to be a beech tree, but two men came with a lorry and cut it down. They tied it up with chains first. Then they cut its fingers off, and next its arms and head. It took them a long time. I think I heard it scream.

Carole's looking round again. There are bare spots on the walls. People pin things up, then rip them down again and the paint comes off as well. I shut my eyes and everything looks better.

'Would you like to see the library?' I suggest. The library is the best bit of the hospital, small, but very quiet. I've never seen a burn-hole in the library. It's the only room with pictures – proper ones in stiff black frames. The books have pictures, too, or some of them. I've looked at every picture in every book at least a thousand times. Mountains are my favourite. I've never seen a mountain, not a real one.

Carole shrugs. 'Okay.'

I walk very slowly in case Carole is on pills. Many of us are. It's a long way to the library, seems longer still this time, with neither of us speaking. The corridors are grey and very cold. Carole's shivering.

'Have my coat.' I wear it all the time indoors. It makes me feel there's more of me.

'No, thanks,' she says. 'I'm boiling.' Her voice is wobbly like the ash.

There's rain outside, sleety rain, and the sort of wind that claws, whining through a broken windowpane. I never go outside.

We turn a corner. There's a trail of number two across the lino, human number two. The smell is terrible.

'We're nearly there,' I say, to give her hope.

The library is empty. People prefer just sitting, or TV. Miss Barratt's there, of course. She always is. She's grey as well, but very very clever.

'This is Carole.' I try to keep my voice low. Libraries are like Church.

'Hallo, Carole. And what can we do for you, dear?' Miss Barratt wears glasses, but mostly round her neck. She wears them on a long gold chain which twitches when she moves.

'Get me out of here.'

'Come on now, it's not so bad, is it?'

'It's worse than bloody prison.'

Miss Barratt hates bad words, pretends she hasn't heard.

5

'Do you like reading, Carole?' She puts her glasses on, takes them off again, then puts a smile on, keeps it on. She's really trying. Miss Barratt always tries. Her dress is gravy-coloured, her feet are long and thin. 'How about a book, dear? Let me get your details down, then I can issue you with tickets. What's your other name?'

'Joseph.'

I hold tight to the bookshelf. 'Joseph?' I repeat.

Carole turns to face me. 'Yeah, it's Jewish. I'm only a quarter Jewish, actually, and I don't look Jewish at all, not even a quarter. My father's father came from . . .'

St Joseph must have sent her. Sent her specially when Sandy wasn't there. Sandy's her own age and should be looking after her. But St Joseph made it me. She hasn't got his eyes. St Joseph's eyes are brown – dark brown in all the pictures and the statues, and hers are blue, a greenish-blue with tiny darker flecks in them. Her hair is fair and wavy, lighter at the ends. Joseph's more like me. Plain and lined and getting on, with thinning hair which comes out on the comb. I always wear a fringe. Sister pinned it back once, but too much of me was showing. We don't have mirrors here, so I'm not sure what I look like. I've never been that sure. I'm on the inside and I look different from the inside. I tried to tell the doctor that, but he didn't understand.

Carole's staring at the floor, trying not to cry. She's been in tears already, I can tell. I think she's sad about her father. She started telling us about him, then her voice went dead.

Miss Barratt sits down at her desk, starts filling in a form. 'Norah's quite a reader, aren't you, Norah?'

I don't reply. I'm very slow at reading, but I like it for the quiet. Sometimes I read backwards, start books at the end. The important things happen at the end.

Miss Barratt shakes her pen. It isn't working. 'We've got some nice romances.'

'Romances?' Carole makes a face.

'Or Westerns. What sort of things do you like, dear?'

'Crime,' she says, fiddling with her hair. 'Horror stories. Death, funerals, suicides. Mass suicides.'

6

Miss Barratt looks quite frightened. I try to help her out. '*I like books with pictures in.*'

Carole swings round to the window. 'What's that noise?'

'Only the pump, dear.' Miss Barratt tries another pen, a black one. 'It's very old, so it makes that sort of roar, revs up every hour or so. You won't hear it once you've been here a few weeks.'

'I'm not staying a few weeks. No fear!'

I cough to fill the silence, feel a dribble from my bladder, try to hold it in. Miss Barratt's writing Carole's name on tickets. 'Joseph, C.' I've never heard of Joseph as a surname. There was a Joe in Belstead, but he died, and a female patient who called herself Josephina, but her real name was something else.

Carole walks towards a desk, puts her handbag down on it. 'Hey, can patients sit in here? I mean, if you've got some work and stuff, you can do it here?'

'Yes, of course.' Miss Barratt looks relieved.

'I'll stay here then, if that's okay. There's something really urgent I want to get on with, and that other lounge-place stinks.'

She sits down, tips out her bag across the desk-top, finds a sheet of paper with writing on it, scribbled small both sides. I feel excited. She's clever like Miss Barratt. I've stopped her crying. I've brought her to the library. She likes the library. It doesn't smell at all.

I find a chair, sit down very quietly so I won't disturb her writing. She's doing something urgent, writing very fast. She stops a moment, frowning, bites her pen, sneezes, starts again. Words are tumbling down a whole new sheet of paper, black important words. Her legs are twisted round each other. Her shoes are red, and dirty. Her hair is falling round her shoulders – wavy hair, lighter at the ends. She shakes it back, combs it with her pen. I keep my eyes down till she goes on writing, watch again. Her hands are small. She wears five rings, all silver, and a bracelet with a heart on. I'm glad St Joseph sent her.

Carole Joseph.

Joseph.

2

I smoke Players No. 6 because . . . I smoke Players No. 6 because . . . because they'll give me cancer, because they waste my money, make me cough. Stop it, girl, you've got to take this seriously. I smoke Players No. 6 because I'm dead keen to win this competition and you have to send three rotten cigarette-pack fronts with every entry form. I've never smoked them before and never would again – except I won't win if I tell them that. I smoke Players No. 6 because . . . because I've got to get away, got to have a break. They probably take my picture if I win, squeezed between two Names – maybe a DJ and a pop-star, or Miss World and . . . Imagine Miss Joseph and Miss World! 'Nice big smile for the cameras, girls. That's great, darlings. That's absolutely great.'

Blast. The pen's run out and I haven't got a pencil. I'll have to use my eyebrow one, which smudges. If I don't get on with it, I'll miss the closing date. October 16th. Only two days left now.

I smoke Players No. 6 because . . . because . . . I'm scared and broke and I hate this hospital. I've tried to kick the habit, but I started sweating, shaking, and I sucked so many fruit-drops I put on half a stone. Fruit-drops don't do much for you – not like nicotine. I smoke Players No. 6 because I love my fix. That rhymes. Perhaps I should do it in poetry. At least it would be different. Fix, kicks, six.

Six used to be my lucky lucky number until it let me down. It was September 6th they caught me. I'd noticed the first dead leaves, just that morning on my way to the supermarket, even picked one up, held it limp and faded in my hand. Yet it was summer still for all the normal world – girls in flimsy dresses, the ice-cream man in shirt-sleeves dishing out his Soft-Whip, the smell of rotting peaches. I didn't have a summer, not at all, not this year. I was crying in the shop, sniffling up and down the aisles without a Kleenex. It was Kleenex I took first – a mini-pack. I meant to pay, honestly. It was just that I had to use them straight away, to wipe my eyes. The other things I didn't even want. I don't know why I did it. I still feel frightened if I think about it – not just the police station and the court and the psychiatrist, but the fact it was me sitting on that bench, with a great burly policewoman beside me, in a room with khaki walls and a 'WANTED' poster just above my head – a smiling rapist. Imagine smiling in your 'WANTED' photograph.

All I took was a packet of Kraft cheese slices and a small swiss roll. The swiss roll was past its 'sell by' date, and marked down to half price. If I'd really meant to steal, then why take cut-price things, instead of caviare or gin or something? I love swiss rolls – unrolling them and scraping out the filling, eating it first with a spoon. I never did with that one. They caught me at the door. We had swiss roll at school every Tuesday dinner. Cold with tepid custard. I was Somebody at school – even did my A-levels. Then my father died, just two weeks afterwards. Molière and Hamlet, then a funeral.

I smoke Players No. 6 because my father died. That's true, in fact. He smoked himself, Rothman's Kingsize. We also shared noses and the same colour hair. (I'm nothing like my mother.) I'd been accepted by Southampton and he was so thrilled with me, so proud. His child at university! His nose and hair and mouth at university. They never went, in fact. I turned down Exeter as well. And Keele. I smoke Players No. 6 as a substitute for Keele. I smoke Players No. 6 because I loved my father best in all the world and he went and died of cancer, killed the summer. Died of Rothman's Kingsize. The doctor said perhaps I want to die as well, subconsciously. With Dr Bates, everything's subconsciously. I smoke Players No. 6 because they'll kill me in the end, help me join my father. Want a ciggie, Dad?

God! It's hot in here. Really sweaty hot. They could use it as a sauna if it wasn't for the boiler and those great fat lumbering pipes. It's even got the slatted wooden benches. I hide here every morning, use it as a bolt-hole. The library was hopeless. They wouldn't let me smoke there, and Miss Barratt kept tiptoeing up with books, dropping them on my desk like a dog with an old slipper. Next I tried the flower-room, which at least smelt better than the ward, but those stiff bouquets in cellophane reminded me of death again, and someone always found me anyway. Bathrooms are all right for half an hour, but after that, they always flush you out, make you clean the bath when you haven't even used it. This boiler-room is perfect, if you can stand the killing heat. It's down some steep stone steps, so you feel extra safe, and can use the slats to write on, or lie flat out and doze.

I just can't stand that ward. People wouldn't believe it if they saw the wrecks they keep there. Some of them have been patients since the early 1920s – except patients is the wrong word, since they weren't even ill when they came in. Martha Mead was frog-marched here in 1906 because she stole a loaf – just one loaf and eighty years in hospital. She's ninety-seven now. I could still be here in 2067, a dribbling hump like she is, with my tongue lolling out and my fingers bent like claws.

It was really only chance that I landed here at all. Jan went away for just three measly days, and the social worker chose day three to call. Okay, I'd let things go a bit, but I'd planned to tidy up that evening, do my washing, clear away the mess. And I only wasn't dressed because I haven't got a job. What's the point of putting all your clothes on when you've nowhere to go and nothing to get up for? Old Frog-Face just assumed that I was cracking up. I admit I cried and shouted, but if she hadn't come, I wouldn't have. I hate the way she pries, looks in all the cupboards, lifts up fraying edges in your mind. I don't think she believed in Jan at all. The other twice she visited, Jan was out again. It was just bad luck, but she thought I was lying, or confused. I'd hardly invent my best and oldest friend, one I went to school with, one who offered me a home when my father died and my mother went to pieces. If you can call Jan's bedsit home – a crummy room in Vauxhall.

Anyway, Frog-Face dried my tears and helped me mend the

Hoover, then went and ratted on me, reported back to someone, so I had to see the psychiatrist again and he suggested Beechgrove. Suggested, hell! You can't argue with psychiatrists. I did, in fact, for half an hour, but the more I ranted on, the more he said it proved I needed help.

Help?

I miss Jan, actually. It seems centuries since I've seen her, though it's only just ten days. She's frightened of the hospital, won't come near it, not a second time. She was meant to bring me in, but she panicked when she got here. She saw two patients just outside the gates. One was male, old male, with his flies undone. He had bought a paper, the *Sun*, I think it was, and he was slumped on the ground, not reading it, but tearing it in strips, very neat and careful strips, all the same shape and size and laid out in a row. The other was female – foreign, obviously, with white hair straggling down a dark and pitted face, and coarse hairs on her legs. The legs were bare. She wasn't doing anything. That was the trouble – there was nothing left of her. No mind, or thoughts, no hope. Just a framework toupéed with white hair.

Jan stopped, right where she was, started tugging at a button on her jacket. It was loose to start with and she'd been worrying at it all morning like a wobbly tooth. 'Carole, you *can't* come here. Over my dead body.'

'Don't be silly.' I sounded sharper than I meant to. 'Dr Bates is expecting me at ten.'

'Well, ring him up or something. Say you're ill. They should never have sent you to a place like this. They're all mad and old and . . .'

'What d'you mean "all"? You haven't seen them yet. Those two are probably staff.' With Jan, I'd always been the joker. It's hard to break a habit, even when you're about to join the dead.

Jan didn't laugh. 'Come on, love. I'll take you back. I'll even take the day off. We'll go to a flick or something – my treat.' The button had come off now and Jan was mauling it, poking it with a finger, chewing on it, flicking her nail against it with a maddening pinging sound. I snatched the button from her hand, cradled it in mine. It looked so weak and sort of hopeless, with

11

no purpose left, no longer one of four, a useful member of a team keeping out the wind; just a bit of bone hanging from a thread. 'Okay,' I said. 'The flicks it is. I'll just tell Dr Bates, though. He won't mind.'

Of course he'd mind, but I didn't want Jan's terrors (or an argument) on top of all the rest. I wasn't feeling all that bright myself. In fact, when those gates clanged shut behind me, all I could think of was my father's funeral – that really choking moment when the coffin slides downwards and the trap-doors close over it, and there's nothing left but floor-boards and the flames. I ran up Beechgrove's steps – ran for Jan's sake (I could see her watching anxiously from the iron grille of the gate), I even whistled, for God's sake. The whistling is a trick. You can't cry when you whistle. I've proved it scores of times.

I'm whistling now, I can feel that awful pricking in the eyes, my face unstitching, mouth loose on its hinge; that dreadful shameful feeling that if I don't hold tight, I'll just dissolve in floods again. It's stupid to keep snivelling, but I'm so scared of everything. I mean, how long will I be in here? And when I do get out, will Jan accept me back? Or go off me somehow, which she seems to have done already? And will I ever get a job?

Footsteps on the stairs. I sit bolt upright, snatch up my sheets of paper, pray it's not Nurse Sanders. She's the worst.

It's not a nurse, it's male – young good-looking male, with tattooed arms.

'Hallo, gorgeous. Lost your way?'

I grin. I'm not gorgeous, actually, but I suppose compared with what he sees around . . .

'No,' I say. 'I'm hiding. And you haven't seen me. Right? They'll kill me if they find me here.'

'You're not a patient, are you? Can't be. Not a cracker like you.'

I like him. 'No,' I say. 'I'm the heating engineer.'

He laughs, offers me a fag. I'm close to tears again. Just to be treated as a normal person, noticed as a woman. He's looking at my legs, admiring them. His own are long and thin. We don't have men in Florence Ward, though there's a woman with a beard and one who thinks she's Churchill.

I wish he'd hold my hand, call me Carole, invite me out for a coffee or a beer. I feel so horribly alone here. I haven't made a friend yet, hardly talk to anyone. They keep pushing me on Sandy, but we've nothing much in common except we're both eighteen. She frightens me, to tell the truth. She's been on dope and her eyes have great black holes in them.

'Hey wait!' I shout. He's checked the boiler and is making for the stairs again.

He stops. What in God's name do I say now? Take me with you? Hide me in your van? 'Er . . . have you any change?' I ask. 'Ten p's for the phone?'

He fumbles in his pockets, hands me three. I get my purse out, find it full of tens, pray he hasn't seen them, hold up a lone five.

'I'm sorry, I don't seem to have . . .'

'Don't worry. Have the call on me. Who's the lucky guy?'

'Pete,' I say. I've never met a Pete.

'I'm Paul.'

'Hi, Paul.' Perhaps he'll stay now. 'I'm Carole. Carole Joseph.'

'Ta-ra then, Carole. Don't burn your bum. Those pipes are bloody hot.' He laughs, takes the stairs in three huge leaps, is gone. I hear the door crash to.

I tip out all my change. I've got thirteen tens, counting mine and his; could hog the phone till lunchtime. Except I've nobody to ring. I try to flesh Pete out, turn him into Paul, but with no tattoos and darker hair, snuggle up to him. It doesn't work. He wouldn't want me anyway, not a chainsmoking cry-baby grizzling in a nuthouse. I mooch over to the boiler, examine my face in its shiny metal top. Am I really gorgeous? I always feel rather sort of ordinary and when people say I'm pretty, I never quite believe them. My face looks blurred, distorted, so I fill in all the details just from memory, frowning at myself. I suppose no one's really happy with their looks. Okay, my eyes are nice and my complexion's fairly decent and I go in and out at roughly the right places, but there are still a lot of things which aren't quite right. My left front tooth is just a fraction crooked, and my hair's the wavy sort instead of stylish straight, and you can't be really elegant when you're only five-foot two. I'd love to be a model, one of those half-starved ones who stand six foot in their stockings, yet still look frail and boneless. My father was quite small.

I trail back to the bench, spread out all the forms again. Safer to keep busy. I smoke Players No. 6 because they stunt you.

Steps again. It's Paul – come back. Come to ask me out, take me for a spin. I finger-comb my hair, prepare a dazzling smile.

'Carole, what *are* you doing down here?'

Nurse Sanders! Paul must have sneaked on me, called me gorgeous, then rushed straight to Sister's office.

'I'm . . . er . . . writing, Nurse, writing letters. Writing to my Dad.' She's not much older than I am. Thinner, though, and taller. Perhaps I'll start a diet.

'You should be in the Day Room, not skulking off in corners. I told you that last week.'

'I hate the Day Room.'

'We have to know where patients are. Can't you understand that? And Art Therapy starts in half an hour.'

'I don't like Art. I like being on my own.'

'You won't get better that way.' She's pouncing on my things, seen the competition forms.

'Hey, d'you smoke, Nurse?'

'Don't change the subject, Carole. You come back with me now.'

'If you had to give a reason why you smoke – you know, sort of official on a form, what would you say?'

'I *don't* smoke.'

'Yeah, but if you did, why would you?'

'I wouldn't. And nor would you if you'd worked on a cancer ward.'

'My father died of cancer.'

'And you're writing to him?'

'Mm.'

'Well, you can finish writing letters after Art. There's a nice big desk in that Crafts Room just next door.'

'Yeah, covered with jigsaw puzzles.'

'We can always clear them off.'

That's typical of Sanders. Those jigsaws are people's *lives*. Can't she understand that? A world where all the pieces fit, and where the picture you end up with is mercifully the same as the picture on the box, the picture you were promised. That's rare outside a jigsaw. Norah Toomey's doing one with five thousand pieces, all the same colour, more or less. She's been doing it for years. Someone lost the box-top, so she's forgotten what she's making. It could be anything.

I turn on Sanders. 'We can't do that! It's bad enough with people losing pieces. Or eating them. Or dropping them down toilets. Poor Norah's got great gaps in hers already.'

'You like Norah, don't you?' Sanders pushes me in front of her, up the steps and out. I blink in the harsh light.

'Not specially. I think she quite likes me, though. She's always hanging round.'

'Well, it's nice to have a friend.' Sanders is still marching me along. Right, left, right.

'I've got friends, thanks.' Have I? Jan could have come, just once.

'Not here, though. You've got to make an effort, Carole. You've been here a whole fortnight and you're still not cooperating.'

We've reached the ward now. Nurse Sanders heaves the door as if it's another bolshie patient who needs firm handling. I feel almost sorry for it as I walk on through; brave the now-familiar smell of pee and cabbage.

'Right, then, Nurse, I'll sit next to Norah in the Crafts Room and help her with her jigsaw.'

Darling Daddy, I didn't go to Southampton, but I got Honours in my Jigsaws. Hey, that might work! Players No. 6 are the last piece in your jigsaw, the jam in your swiss roll.

3

'Coffee, Carole?'

That volunteer again, the one in tweeds and Hush Puppies with a badge on her lapel saying 'Hospital Friend'. I wonder why she asks me? I always have coffee and she doesn't ask the others. They just get theirs, weak and sweet, pushed into their claws. The volunteers make it in the kitchen, mix the milk and sugar in a saucepan, boil it all up together with a liquid coffee essence, also sweetened, then pour it from a chipped enamel jug into stained brown melamine. They probably drink from Spode at home, grind their own coffee beans.

She passes me a biscuit, frowns when I take three. My jeans are so tight now, I can hardly do them up. Who cares? Norah gives me all her biscuits and saves me things from meals. She even bought me chocolates from the shop here, pricey ones, when she's hardly got a bean. She seems to really like me. God knows why. Actually, I've got quite fond of her. At least she's restful, doesn't keep on jabbering like Alison, or clutching me with bony hands like Peg. And she's not a nutter like most of the long-stay patients. She's also clean, which is saying quite a lot here. I mean, look at that woman with her dress on inside-out, coffee-stained both sides, and Ethel Barnes taking off her knickers in the middle of the room – white interlock and wet. No one even bothers. They've seen worse before, much worse.

I'm not that shocked myself now. I've been here six whole weeks and the pills have sort of numbed me. Might as well live here as anywhere. At least it's warm and the meals are free. I don't even cry for my father any longer, hardly cry at all. I suppose that's just the drugs again, but isn't crying human – proof you feel and care? He's been dead four months. Four centuries.

Another volunteer bounces over to take my empty cup. I haven't finished, but I expect she's keen to start the washing up, get back to her whist. She's the bossy one with Teeth who runs the letter-writing class. Norah dragged me to it once because she'd heard I was having trouble writing to my father. News spreads fast in Beechgrove. It's really meant for old folk and those who can't read or write, or who have forgotten who they are. But I went along in any case, just to kill an hour. I can turn out better letters than all those tweeds-and-twinsets put together, but I didn't let on; just acted dumb and let them write 'Dear Daddy,' on their prissy pale blue notepaper. They asked about my mother and would I like to write to her, too. I said yes, later please, though that would have been even harder than writing to a father who's just a jar of ashes on a mantelpiece.

My mother is in hospital herself, the other side of England. Drying out. Recovering from the death, when it was her who helped to kill him. She was always more concerned with him than me. In fact, I doubt if she remembers who I am. 'With love and kisses from your little Carole.' I wouldn't kiss her now. Her face is sort of loose, as if it's lost contact with the bone beneath. Her lipstick doesn't fit her mouth. Her hand shakes when she puts it on, so she ends up with four lips. She always wore too much make-up. Foundation like a mask and gunge and glitter on her eyes. Norah scrubs her face with soap. I'd like a mother like that. A face so clean and shiny you could see yourself reflected, recognize your features in it; feel that you belonged, were made of the same fabric, had actually curled up in her womb for nine long and cosy months, shared her blood supply. Sometimes, I think my mother grabbed me from a supermarket shelf, to avoid the pain of labour – probably never even paid for me, just slipped me in her pocket before the days of TV cameras watching from the ceiling. Mind you, it was she who got me off. A paralytic mother impresses them in court. The social workers *drooled*. My mother made the difference between prison and a hospital, though perhaps there's not much difference.

17

'Lil! Wakey-wakey, dear. Your coffee's getting cold.'

I jump as well as Lil. Those Friends have piercing voices and I was miles away. Lil is the headmistress. She used to run a private school in Hampshire for over a thousand girls. Now she dribbles both ends, asleep and awake. They ought to let her sleep. That's what I dislike about the Friends. They're so busy being bountiful, they can't see that oblivion is more precious than their coffee, especially for patients in pain. Lil has emphysema and osteoarthritis, as well as being senile. She frightens me the most, in fact. All that education couldn't help her, not even two degrees. You always think it won't be you. She thought that, no doubt, when she was taking Assembly in her cap and gown, or sipping Tio Pepe with the Mayor on Founder's Day. She's broken up her biscuits into a rubble of fine crumbs, dropped them in her shoes.

'Now be a good girl, Lil.'

That volunteer could have been her pupil once, carrying her books, cowering at her door. 'Yes, Miss Evans. No, Miss Evans', certainly not Lil. Lilian E. Evans (MA Oxon, FRCM) is dressed in a pink flowered cotton dress in mid-November, with thick lisle stockings wrinkling round her knees. Half of them wear summer frocks, with cardigans. Maybe it was summer when they entered, a hundred years ago. Winter ever since.

I think I'll go to Art. I can't take too much of Florence Ward, not without a break. The smell of lavatories, that woman who keeps chewing when there's nothing in her mouth, the one who pulls her hair out and has bald patches on her scalp. It's not that I'm superior – not like those damn Friends. That's the trouble, really. I know it could be me. It *is* me, isn't it? Six weeks, six years, six aeons. Or Norah. There's nothing wrong with Norah, not that wrong. Her mother was Irish, Catholic, pregnant and unmarried – a fatal combination. She ran away to England, had the baby (Norah – the name was pinned on to her shawl, with a tiny silver shamrock), left her on an English convent doorstep, and went back to another part of Ireland where she took a different name. They caught her in the end, but she cheated them by dying. It's like a fairy story without the happy ending. Nurse MacDonald told me the whole saga. She's been here almost as long as Norah has herself.

'Norah . . .' She's helping with the coffee, holding the cup for Lil, mopping up the dribble and the spills. She pauses, turns to face me. She may be slow, but she never says 'Not now', or 'Wait, I'm busy'.

'Fancy Art this morning?'

'I don't mind.'

Norah never minds. She's far too good for here. I want to weep sometimes the way she just accepts. I mean, even things like shoes. Those black and broken-down things belonged to another patient who conveniently died. I expect Staff Nurse cut the legs off, as well as nicked the shoes. They might have come in handy for an amputee. 'You should have refused to wear them,' I've told her twice already. 'They're not even your size, Norah.'

'I don't mind.'

She'd even look quite pretty if someone bothered with her, paid for her to have a perm or something, or newer glasses. Straight hair in your fifties looks wrong on anyone, but it's lovely silky hair and she's got that pale bone-china Irish skin which seems to last. I wonder what her mother was like – pale and mousy, or black hair and blue eyes? I wonder if she wonders.

'Come on, Norah. If you wait for Lil to finish, there won't be any decent brushes left.'

I quite like Art now. The girl who takes it is very nice and normal, married with two children and a golden labrador. She told me I had talent, which made me cry again because that's my father's talent, a present like his nose. I've never really used it. I did French at school, not Art. *He* was always painting, tiny fiddly things which wouldn't upset my mother or take up too much room. My mother hates hobbies, especially large or messy ones which can't be put away.

Norah takes my arm and we set off down the corridor. The corridors at Beechgrove are so dark and tall and narrow, you feel as if they're closing over your head. And at night time it's like walking through a tunnel. They're damp and sort of clammy, and if you shout, your voice reverberates. But at least I don't get lost now, and the porters always grin and call me 'love'.

The Art Room's in the annexe, which is newer than the main part of the hospital. Beechgrove proper is late Victorian with grim stone walls, built really high and thick so no one could escape. The annexe is prefabricated concrete, also grey, but lower, with a flat and damp-stained roof. It still looks makeshift, as if the workmen buggered off before they finished.

I hold the door for Norah and we enter to a smell of fug and feet. Coffee time again, though the coffee here is different – Maxwell House with sugar separately. I snitch a few more biscuits, slip them in my bag. Jan's visiting this evening, coming straight on after work, so she's bound to need a snack. Jan's a true friend, doesn't need it pinned on her lapel. Okay, so she chickened out the day she brought me here, but she waited two whole hours outside the hospital, even braved the gates, at last, but she got lost (like everyone) and landed up in Jude Ward, saw the stumps and junkies. She was so upset, she kept away for over two weeks, just phoned my ward and left pathetic messages, then a month ago, she suddenly appeared, loaded down with guilt and flowers and Lucozade. She's been coming ever since, though I know she loathes the place still. The least I can do is feed her custard creams.

Jan and I grew up in Portishead, just four short streets apart. We met at kindergarten, moved schools together, twice, both went on to grammar school at Bristol. We even lost our virginity together – well, not in the same room, but within a week. (She hated it. I didn't.) She left school a year before me, moved to London. I'd stayed with her a few times, when I had the time and fare, was secretly appalled that one cramped and gloomy room should cost so much. I never realized then that I might actually be sharing it, fatherless and futureless.

Cut the drama, Carole. You're better off than most here, as Nurse Taylor's always saying. She's right, in fact – just look around. Anne-Marie, wearing bovver boots with what looks like her nightie; Lady Macbeth Colin who sits hour after hour washing his hands in air; Dot screaming for more biscuits in a pre-school temper-tantrum – except she's forty-five. Someone gives her one. Might as well have chucked it in the bin. Dot vomits half she eats, deliberately. We all know each other's secrets through the Group. Dr Bates runs it, and another younger doctor, and all the nursing staff sit in, and the social workers sometimes. Norah never says a word. They let her off, I don't know why. But everyone else has to speak each time. Vomiting or stealing, nothing's sacred. Fathers, mothers – mothers in particular. There's always someone's mother being mauled to death.

Art is safer. We draw our mothers then, with horns and tails. Or fathers. I drew mine in a coffin with Rothman's Kingsize in a golden candelabra at his feet. I smoke Rothman's now myself, as a tiny tribute to him.

'Finished, Norah?'

Norah nods. Actually, I think she poured her coffee into Dot's cup. Dot would suck out Norah's innards with a straw if she thought they tasted good, sick them back again.

'Let's go, then. Bag some seats.'

It's funny how Art Rooms are always much the same – messy and untidy and sort of ripe and rancid. Even in a nuthouse they can't institutionalize them. The colours are too bright and the smells too interesting and the people who teach Art refuse to go grey or fit a mould. The Art Room at Beechgrove is almost identical to the one we had at school. I breathe in the scent of turps and linseed oil and blessed chalk-and-charcoal sanity. Dot's already there, deep in clay, modelling what looks like faeces, though perhaps they're rissoles, which are on the dinner menu for today. She likes to sit next to Teacher (Lynette Craig) and hog the limelight. Teacher's working, too – painting something abstract in shades of jungle-green. That's why I admire Lynette. Art for her is not just occupational therapy for the loonies, but something vital which is worth her time and effort as well as ours.

'Hallo, Carole, love. Hallo, Norah.'

Lynette has orange hair and magenta nails. She's only in her twenties and could have been a chum had I not been labelled Patient and she Staff. That chasm is unbridgeable.

'I thought we'd paint our dreams today – not the ones we have at night, but the ones we build in the daytime.'

'How d'you mean?'

'What we want. What we hope to be or do. Where we want to go.'

I slump down at the table next to Brian, who is mixing paint with coffee. I feel suddenly depressed. *I haven't won.* I stare out of the window. A grey and crosspatch sky, one skinny tree with two leaves clinging on to it. I hate November. It's the most hopeless of the months, especially this tail-end of it when the days are dark both ends, and everything is bare and raw and dying. It's summer on the radio, which is squalling on as usual – some phoney lyric about June and moons and honeymoons. They're terrified of silence here, have to fill it endlessly with wall-to-wall disc jockeys, vacuous love songs. I've never been in love. I was getting close with Jon, but he dropped me after the court case.

'And now we've got a request for Susan Andrews with love and kisses from her boyfriend, John. Are you listening, Susan, in Canbury Gardens, Hove, because John says he loves you more than . . .?'

'Can't we turn that off?'

Lynette turns it down, but I can still hear John and Susan swapping hearts. They're always John. Except mine was Jon without the h. Funny, really, Jon and Jan. I suppose I'm lucky to have Jan left. A lot of other friends were distinctly cool, and their mothers downright hostile.

I glance at Brian's dreams. They look more like nightmares, black with choking smoke. Last week, he painted his brain – at least that's what he said it was, though it was also black and seemed to be unravelling. There was a little Nazi figure at the bottom of the painting (well, just a head shaped like a swastika, and boots), pointing a gun at it. Brian often paints guns, or even guillotines. Anne-Marie is ruling lines, but then she always does. *Her* dream is to draw a line without a ruler, or even to dare a curve. She hasn't made it yet, not in eighteen months.

'Come on, Carole, aren't you going to start, love?'

'What's the point? I haven't any dreams.'

'Everyone has dreams.'

'Are those yours, then, the green ones?'

'Yup. It helps to choose a colour, hot and red, or cool and green.'

'All right, grey,' I say. Norah's painting a mountain, a very tall and thin one. Hers is grey as well.

I squeeze the tube of Payne's grey, pick up a balding brush. My mind is still on coffins. People's ashes must be grey, presumably, although I never saw my father's. They came in a brown pot with the lid cemented on.

I swap the grey for Vandyke brown, try to paint a pot. It comes out like a crock of gold. I've seen that somewhere, haven't I? On the competition form, spilling out gold coins.

'Any gold?' I ask.

'Gold?'

'You know, really glittery, like they put on Christmas cards.'

'We're doing Christmas cards next week.'

'I know. I need some now, though.'

Lynette always finds you what you want. I pick out a much fatter brush which looks vitamin-enriched, dip it in the gold. I meant to paint gold coins, but they turn into a palace, and the palace into two and four, and six, and twelve, until there's a whole metropolis of glittering golden palaces and a golden sky and shining golden people strolling down the golden streets.

Everyone stops working – even Brian – to stare.

'That's beautiful,' Lynette says.

I strike a match. Lynette fumbles for her Embassy. She always smokes when I do. Actually, I've left my ciggies in the coffee room.

I touch the match to the topmost of my castles. It flares gold on gold a moment, gorges a tower or two, then burns sulky-black across the golden street. Lynette says nothing, just fetches a wet rag and lays it on the paper. They're obsessional about fire here. If patients burn to death it gives the place a bad name. No risk of that in this case. My Shining Land of Dreams is just smudged and blackened dross. I'm terrified I'll cry. I can feel my face crumpling up, try desperately to hold it stiff, keep

23

swallowing and blinking. (I'm too far gone to whistle.) Norah notices. Her mountain is so high now, she's had to use a separate piece of paper to fit its pointed summit in. She puts her crayons down, clambers off her stool, takes my arm. She doesn't speak – I can't – and Lynette never says stupid things like 'Why did you do that?' She lets us go, in fact. If it had been the Group we'd have had to stay, control ourselves, or at least explain ourselves. It's funny, really, how they insist on explanations here, when nothing's explained at all in the outside world, not even what it's doing there whirling round in cold black space, or what we're doing on it.

We walk back along the corridors. There are seven miles of corridor at Beechgrove, counting all four floors. I'm shivering so much I make Norah shake as well. I like the way she holds my arm, rather like a courteous old gentleman who is out walking his sweetheart. We step round a patient lying on the floor. My first week here, I used to try to pick them up, but you soon stop bothering. Even the nurses tend to leave them there. They've enough to do for the upright ones, I suppose. We cross the courtyard into the second lap of corridor, pass the usual doors marked STORES, TOILET, BURSAR, BANK. I wonder what *I* should be marked – failure, loser, drop-out, thief? Ex-daughter?

I'm almost relieved to see the ward again. I'm beginning to understand how you could cower here all your life, refuse to venture out. It's not that long till dinner and I can smell liver now, drowning out the worse smells. Half the patients have their paper bibs on and two are banging their forks against the metal of their wheelchairs. We have a choice of menu. Minced-up pap for patients missing teeth, or things with lumps and grit in for those who like a challenge. Sometimes I have both.

'Norah! Over here!'

Sergeant-Major Sanders. She uses Norah as a workhorse – probably wants her to feed another patient or put the semolina pudding through a liquidizer.

'You've got a letter, dear.'

Norah looks frightened, backs away, folds her arms across her chest, hands lost under armpits. It's my turn to be the strong one. 'It's probably just a circular,' I soothe, trying to sound more sure. Would people waste their money circularizing mental patients? Perhaps they're selling straitjackets, or padded cells with all mod cons. I take the letter myself, hold it out to Norah who shakes her head, quickly slips her hands behind her back. It slithers to the floor. I pounce, stare at the golden letters bragging on the envelope. My whole stomach turns a sudden somersault. I glance behind me. Sanders is distracted – acting referee in a brawl between two over-eighty-fives.

'Norah,' I say. I try to keep my voice low, stop it leapfrogging. After all, it might still be a circular, selling plastic pants or bunion shields. 'Mind if I open this?'

'Yes, take it, take it, please. I don't want it. I never have letters. No one knows me. I haven't got an address.'

'I'll bring it back. It's just that I'd like to read it on my own, somewhere quiet and private. You see, I think it may concern me.'

I hold it white and heavy in my hand. Golden letters embossed across the stamp. That signifies. Gold towers, gold shining city. The whole thing must be meant. Lynette has been an agent, setting free my dreams. A sudden shaft of sunlight strikes the window, lasers through the glass. Even Florence Ward is gold now.

I stride towards the door, dodge the dinner trolley. Pig's liver smells of roses, Lynette's hot reds whooping from the ketchup.

'Back in just a sec,' I shout, slam the door behind me; run, dance, waltz along the golden corridor.

4

'You've won, Norah, you've won, you've won, you've won!'

'Won what?' I ask. I never go to bingo and they haven't had a raffle for six months.

'I used your name. For a competition. A holiday for two. You've won it. You've won the holiday. We've won it between the two of us. I filled the answers in and wrote the slogan.'

I try to find my voice. Carole's really shouting, whirling me round and round. I feel dizzy and confused.

'It was a crappy slogan, really, but they must have liked it. You had to send three empty cigarette packs – Players No. 6 – well, just the fronts; three for each try. I sent sixty-three – all under different names. Your name won.'

'But I don't smoke.'

'Look, we've won, chickenhead. What the hell does it matter whether you smoke or not? I only hope you drink, though. It's a champagne holiday with a champagne party every day. That's what it says here.'

'I've never had champagne.'

'Well, you'll have it now, even for breakfast, if you want. We leave just after Christmas – ten whole days including a New Year Party with more champagne and something called a Show Spectacular and . . .'

'They won't let us go.' I sink on to a pew. We're in the chapel. That's not right. It isn't Sunday and you shouldn't shout in chapels.

Carole missed her dinner. I haven't finished mine yet, but I expect it's thrown away now. It was semolina with jam and I always eat it slowly, make colours with my spoon – red, pink, pinky-white. The pink was still quite deep when Carole burst back in; said she had to speak to me in private. There isn't any private.

'Have a cup of tea,' I said. Sister always says that when anyone's disturbed. I tried to look for Sister, but she'd gone to tea herself and even Nurse Sanders had taken Martha to the toilet.

'Come on, *quick*,' said Carole. 'While nobody's around.'

She hurt me, actually, pulling me like that, but I didn't like to say so. It may have been the pills. Those pills can make you violent, even the ones which are meant to calm you down. Big Rita takes thirty-six a day and she punched the doctor just last month, gave him a black eye. Carole is still talking very loudly.

'What d'you mean, won't let us? It's not a prison, is it? I'm leaving anyway. I can't stick this place much longer.'

I clutch my spoon. I didn't know I had a spoon. I must have brought it with me from my dinner. I'd better put it down or they'll only say I stole it. I've never stolen anything, except a feather, once. I lay the spoon on a hymn book, try to stop my hand trembling. Carole mustn't go.

'You mustn't go,' I tell her.

'I doubt we'll have much choice, mate. I heard a rumour the place is closing down.'

I grab my spoon again; need something to cling on to. I try to speak, but no words come out at all. They've all been minced like dinner, lost their shape and strength. St Joseph's closed, and then the turquoise walls. Your home for twenty years a pile of rubble. I can see the huge blocks falling, hear the crash and roar. I don't want to move, don't want a holiday.

'They couldn't move us. Not seven hundred patients. Where would seven hundred go?'

'God knows! *I'm* going to Las Vegas.'

'Where?' I pick up the hymn book in the other hand. I feel stronger with a hymn book.

'That's where we've won the holiday. It's famous, really famous, like Blackpool, but with gambling. And it's hot.

There'll be sun there, even in the winter, and swimming pools and stuff. Look, if you don't want to come, I'll ask Jan instead. She'd jump at it. But I'll have to use your name. I mean, Norah Toomey won. So if I can be Norah Toomey . . .'

I open the hymn book. 'There Is A Land Of Pure Delight', I read. I'm very slow at reading. I shut the book again, feel the blue plastic cover sticking to my hands. Can someone else be me – own my hair and teeth, wear my clothes? Would I be Carole then? I stare down at my feet. Big black feet, not pretty. If I was Carole, I could wear red shoes. Small red shoes. I shut my eyes a moment, see different feet, brown and angry feet, clumping up the stairs. It's Miss Johnson with the key.

'No,' I whisper. 'Please don't lock me in.' She always did. She was frightened I'd turn violent. They sent me there because they closed the hospital – the one before, not this one. I hoped I'd move to Hillview, like Doris and the rest of them, but they sent me into lodgings in the town. You weren't allowed to choose. They just wrote it on your form – where you went and when. My room was very small, got smaller still at night when it was locked. 'And I don't want any *men*,' Miss Johnson said, the first night I was there. Her face was damp and very close to mine. She always came up very close and shouted. She thought I was deaf because I didn't say a lot. 'D'you get my meaning? I don't have men here, not at all. And it's no good saying you're engaged . . .'

I'm not engaged and I don't know any men. The doctor is a man, but I hardly ever see him. I couldn't sleep that night, not even with my pills. She unlocked the door at seven in the morning, but I didn't dare go out. I sat in the room all day, except for the evening meal. That was small, as well, and greasy, and served with the six o'clock news. Fried bread mixed with bombs. There was another patient there who believed she was expecting. She'd been expecting for five years, but she'd never had the baby. Babies. There were twelve, she said, all girls. Only dogs and cats have twelve, I told her, but she didn't answer. We were moved again in May. I don't like moves at all.

Carole's walking up and down. She's got plumper and

much quieter since she's been here, but she's not quiet any more. She's shouting like Miss Johnson.

'Listen, Norah, as far as they're concerned, I'm Norah Toomey now – d'you understand?'

'What about the doctors?' I enquire. They always know who you are, even if you say you're someone else, like Josephina. The doctors called her Pat.

'Oh, they don't matter.' Carole sits down on a bench, raps her fingers on the pew in front. 'It's the competition people, and photographers and stuff. At least they haven't seen me yet – or you. And this is my address as much as yours. I mean, Beechgrove's like a house name, isn't it? I didn't put "Hospital" on purpose, just Beechgrove, Milford Road.'

'All right,' I say. I try to make her happy if I can. I'm feeling almost happy myself that she wants to be me. No one ever has before. I'm not sure they'll believe it. She doesn't look like me at all. I'm taller and much scraggier with bigger feet and hands. And a different generation. I've never had a birthday, not a definite or official one, but I know the month and year.

I'm Carole – with a birthday, a proper one with candles and a cake. I've also got a friend. Her name is Jan and I save her all my biscuits. If they close us down, I'll go back home to Jan.

They called it home in the lodgings, but you couldn't make a cup of tea or keep biscuits in your room. It could have been far worse. Ella Cartwright slept on a bench on Hastings promenade. I like it in the ward. The beds have pale blue covers and you can pin up pictures on the piece of yellow wall above your locker. I've got a mountain, which I cut out of the *Mail*, and a Royal Lifeboat Calendar which Carole says is two years out of date, but the sea doesn't really change much.

'Christ!' yells Carole, suddenly. I jump.

'I'm late for my appointment with the doctor. And they fitted me in specially, so I could ask to change my pills. God! They'll kill me. Listen Norah, don't say anything to anyone. Not a word – right? I've got to think this out.' She's running down the aisle, almost at the door now. You shouldn't run in church. She trips on something, says a word that's not allowed, turns back to shout again. 'I'll keep the letter, okay? If nosey parker Sanders asks you what it was, say a circular.'

'A . . . a what?'

'Oh, anything. Just don't mention competitions, and least of all Las Vegas. They'll go mad.'

The door crashes shut behind her. I move to another pew, where the light is dimmer. I need to fade a bit, try to sort things out. Blackpool with the sun. I've never been to Blackpool, but Miss Barnsley went last year and didn't like it. And I've never liked the sun. It shows you up, takes away dark corners.

There was no sun this morning. I know that from the blackboard. Nurse Clarke always writes the weather up each morning, in yellow chalk; in very large capitals so the older ones can read it. 'A SUNNY DAY TODAY' or 'SNOW EXPECTED LATER'. It's kind of her to bother, since few of us go out. She also puts the day and date, and even the year, in case people have lost track of it. I remember all she wrote today. I always learn it off by heart so I know what to expect. I don't like sudden changes. 'TODAY IS 20TH NOVEMBER 1986. TUESDAY.' (That was underlined.) 'A COLD DAY WITH DRIZZLE.'

If Beechgrove closes, we won't have any weather. Or any Tuesdays, either. In the lodgings, the days were all the same, except supper was at seven o'clock on a Sunday, and cold. I'm cold myself, shaky-cold. I can see the hospital minced up very fine, bricks and walls oozing bloody from the mincer, huge trees mushed like peas; all the Homes and hospitals I've been in pulped sticky-grey like porridge; stiff white nurses now soft like mashed potato . . .

Carole said there'd be a second letter. Maybe from a landlady. That room I moved to had no proper curtains, so people just peered in. I could feel them watching me undress. I even turned the lights off, but I could see their eyes still shining in the dark. They didn't have whole heads, only yellow eyes which never closed.

I hardly slept at all until I was moved back to a ward. Beechgrove is miles away from any town, or even any street.

Nobody looks in. They couldn't if they wanted. The ward has no windows, not the bit we sleep in. The pale blue wall goes right up to the ceiling, shuts everybody out.

There are windows in this chapel, coloured ones with huge blue and scarlet people in them, which stops smaller paler people looking in (or out). I like the chapel, although it seems different on a Tuesday – more wood and fewer heads. There's a burn-hole on the bench in front and the hymn book has a deep scratch on its cover. It's sad how things get spoilt. I open it again. 'Come, my soul, thy suit prepare . . .'

I don't understand a lot of hymns, and I never sing in case I get the tune wrong. I'm not that good at tunes. I sang at the convent, but that was years and years ago. There was a hymn to St Joseph called 'Hail, Holy Joseph, Hail'. I don't remember any of the words, except for 'hail' which was repeated thirteen times.'

'Hail,' I say out loud, but Joseph doesn't come. He seems very far away and very faint. I close my eyes, try to draw him in my mind in strong black lines like those bright saints in the windows, creep back to his workshop.

I always choose a time when Mary's busy shopping and Jesus has gone out, or, better still, grown up. Then there's just the two of us. I crouch on the floor in the pile of soft wood shavings, trickling sawdust through my hands. Joseph saws. The sound goes back and forwards, back and forwards, calms me down. Joseph's always busy. He's got to earn our living – his and mine – but if I'm quiet and good, he'll put his saw away, wipe his hands, swing me up and sit me on his knee. I'm so light, I'm just a shaving, just a chiselled curl of wood. My hair is pale and pretty, pressed against his chest. My eyes are blue, greenish-blue like Carole's, with little darker flecks in them. My shoes are red, and tiny. He's proud of me. He loves me. His large rough hand is stroking across my head. I can feel the pee beginning to trickle down, staining us, joining us, hot and wet against his legs and mine.

'We've won, St Joseph,' I whisper, as his hand strokes up and down. 'Carole said so. We've won between the two of us.'

5

'Jan? Where are you? J-a-n!'

God! She isn't in. No, she must be. Her door's ajar. She'd never go out and leave her room unlocked. Jan just isn't like that. She's probably in the loo. I race along to the cold and spidery toilet which she shares with five other tenants in the house. It's empty.

'Seen Jan?' I ask the tall dark man clumping up the stairs. He's new.

'Who?'

'Jan Soames.'

'Never heard of her.'

'You must have. She lives here.' She can't have moved, can she? Not since Tuesday, when she came to visit, brought me a poinsettia. Supposing she's bolted back to Bristol, gone back home again to rejoin her three kid sisters? I'd be all alone in London then. And with Beechgrove closing, I'd have nowhere else to live. My palms feel clammy suddenly. I wipe them on my jeans. I wish I had a sister, someone sort of tied to me, who couldn't leave; who could share my father's death.

I can't go back to my home. It isn't home. It's empty. My mother's empty bottles, my father's empty chair. And what about his clothes and things? They're probably still just lying where he left them. I daren't trust myself to touch them, sort them out. Someone ought to, though, someone calm and sensible who won't start blubbing when they see his stamp collection, his baggy cardigans.

'Jan!' I yell again, to stop the ache.

Moira sticks her head out of her door. 'Hi, Carole. You back, dear? Jan's in the garden, if you want her.'

'The garden? But it's pitch dark and pouring.' I'm soaking wet myself; waited twenty squelching minutes at the bus stop, with no umbrella and this flimsy jacket which sops up rain like blotting paper.

I crash down the remaining flight of stairs and out into the back yard (which is more a junk heap than a garden), collide with Jan who's just returning to the house, carrying a few bare twigs and a sooty piece of laurel. Flower arrangements. Jan's training to be a florist in Mayfair, does homework in the evenings.

'Carole! What's the matter, love? What *are* you doing here?'

Suddenly, I'm crying. Jan sounds as if she cares – really cares – and I'd forgotten what that feels like. She walks me back inside, takes my sodden jacket, puts the kettle on, while I mop up rain and tears. I'm so relieved to see her – her short dark curly hair, her small neat nose and hands; everything about her small and neat; the way she bosses kettles, marshals mugs. Jan's quiet, but very firm, won't stand any nonsense, whether from droopy flowers or dozy gas rings. The kettle pants to a fast boil with her stern eye on it.

She passes me a mug of Cup-A-Soup: Chicken Oriental, with little shreds of noodle floating on the top. 'What's happened, Carole? You haven't run away, have you?'

I almost laugh. They'd have their tracker-dogs out if I tried. 'No, I'm meant to be at bingo. I was at bingo, actually. I even won. Two fat ladies – eighty-eight. I just slipped out for a pee – the longest pee in history. It's okay, Jan, don't look so worried. They won't know. Bingo goes on hours. I just had to see you. There's been this awful row, you see. This afternoon. They won't let her go.'

'Who?'

'Norah.'

'Go where?'

'On the holiday, you nut. Sister just refused point-blank, said it was absolutely ridiculous for someone who'd never spent a single night away, and whose longest journey in fifty-odd years was a day-trip to Littlehampton, to go waltzing off to the States.'

'Well, I see her point, love. I said much the same myself, if you remember.'

I do remember. Jan's really quite a pain at times. 'Look, Jan, if Norah doesn't take this chance, she'll never leave those four walls, except feet first in a coffin. You'd go nuts yourself if you never went out or mixed with normal people or saw a different view. There's nothing *wrong* with Norah. Okay, she's not exactly Einstein, but she's not mental either. The only reason she's in that place at all is because she's never had a home or proper parents. She's been in institutions all her life. One leads to another. You get caught up in the system, and before you know it, you're labelled "nut" or "case" or "halfwit".'

Jan says nothing, just sips her soup, face closed. She doesn't realize how much a matter of sheer chance it is, what you're labelled, or where you land in life. In her neat and tidy system, criminals go to prison and loonies live in mental homes. No mistakes, no botch-ups. No cases of bad luck or missing fathers.

She reaches for her laurel spray, shakes the cold drops off it. They sting against my face. 'Be honest, Carole. Why not admit you're simply furious that you won't be able to go yourself?'

I open my mouth to deny it, scald it with hot soup instead. Jan's right. Of course I'm furious. Frustrated, disappointed. Even when I had the row with Sister, a bit of me was disgusted with myself, championing poor Norah when all I really cared about was me. Okay, so I'm a hypocrite, and worse still, Jan sees through me, but it *is* my only chance to see America, have a bit of fun for once. And that stupid Sister Watkins says they've booked a lovely panto for New Year and we can go to that instead. Puss in fucking Boots.

Jan starts breaking up her laurel branch. Snap, snap, snap. 'You know it's crazy, Carole. I mean, how could Norah cope? She won't go places with you, or join in things, or be any proper company. And what are you going to talk about?'

'You're just jealous, Jan.'

'Jealous? I wouldn't want to go, thanks. A monster hotel with three thousand rooms and fifteen hundred slot machines. No fear! I'd rather have a cottage in Snowdonia.'

I flop back in my chair. I don't believe her, actually, but what's the point of quarrelling? Of course I'd rather go with her. If things had worked out better, she'd have been taking me. I entered in her name as well as Norah's, *and* her parents' names, and all three sisters'. And Norah won. Even so, I thought at first I'd swing it, borrow Toomey's identity and name, but take Jan as my friend. Except I'd quite forgotten vital things like passports. I can't be Norah Toomey on a passport. So it's either her and me, or not at all.

Not at all, said Sister.

Actually, she can't say that, not legally. I phoned a friend of mine who's reading Law at London University, a brainy girl I knew at school. She looked it up for me. Unless a patient is actually confined under various complicated sections of the Mental Health Act, you can't keep her in against her will, or forbid her going places. In fact, more than nine-tenths of those patients could discharge themselves today, just walk out, piss off, and no one would have any legal right to stop them, haul them back. The trouble is, they're all too drugged or scared to try. Once you're labelled patient, you become one – passive, apathetic, with no initiative; chained to a chair and a daily timetable, salivating when the meal-bell rings. Look at me. I've started building my life round those dreary Wednesday film shows, counting the days till Sunday because there's ginger cake for tea. I've been in bloody weeks now, yet I'm not exactly chafing to escape. I rarely see the doctor on my own and when I do, he never talks about me leaving, just assumes I'm there indefinitely. Okay, I know the place is closing, but if it wasn't, I could rot there till I die.

Jean Foster died last week, aged seventy-three. She was admitted in her twenties because she was pregnant and unmarried, just like Norah's mother. The baby was stillborn, so she was naturally upset. 'Clinically depressed' they labelled it – another label added to 'depraved'. She stayed depressed. No wonder, in a place like this. But like Toomey, she had neither home nor job; nothing and nobody to bail her out, offer an alternative. Sheer bad luck, or fate, not mental illness. All right, some of them are ill – schizophrenic, senile, even bonkers – and madness is infectious, just like measles, so if you're a patient long enough, you're bound to end up weird. But it's still inhuman to lump us normal ones with the zombies and the cretins. We haven't got a chance. I mean, take Di Townsend, who's really sweet, and used to run a chain of snazzy dress shops. She was only admitted because she got weepy with her 'change'. Now she says she's scared of ever leaving, feels she couldn't even run her home.

No one understands, though. Even my brainy friend, the barrister-to-be, was pretty scathing about what she called the nutters. I didn't let on that I was technically one myself. She might have refused to help. As it was, she was really very decent, said she'd get more details, look up all the books for me, type out what I needed. Once I've got her letter, got the whole thing clear, I'll march to Matron's office and confront her with the facts.

I spoon a few limp noodles from the bottom of my mug. Is it really worth the fuss? More rows and confrontations? To tell the truth, I'm feeling rather scared inside. In one way, I'm wild to go to Vegas, break out of my straitjacket, look forward to something more than ginger cake. And yet . . . Oh, I don't know. Winning's like so many things: it sounds wonderful until it really happens, or until you read the small print. The small print on this holiday is fine, in fact – exceptionally generous, with no hidden extras, as they say. It's the small print in my head which is causing all the problems, the secret doubts and fears. I've never won before; well, just a steam-iron once, and a game of Chinese chequers as a runner-up, but nothing big, nothing like a holiday. I didn't even know where Vegas was – America, of course, but I thought it was California, or maybe Mexico. Nevada sounds much duller, and it's not that hot at all. I looked it up. It's a furnace in the summer, but only fifty-five or so in winter. I'd rather have the furnace, so hot you'd just lie flat and think of nothing. I can't stop thinking since I won – or Norah won, I should say. That's the worst part. Supposing they find out she never entered, doesn't even smoke? It's like shop-lifting again, stealing someone's name. And I have to keep pretending so she won't refuse to go, pretending it will be fun and hot and wonderful and that we'll get on well together when she's miles older than I am and . . .

'Jan . . .'

'Mm?' She's talking to her flower-arrangement. If I were a birch twig or a spray of dwarf chrysanthemums, I'd have her full attention.

'Look, I'd take you if I could, Jan – if it was left to me, I mean. It would be something in return for all you've done for me. You know I'm grateful, don't you?'

'Yes, 'course. You've said it twenty times.'

She still sounds cross – no, not exactly cross, just on edge, as if she doesn't really want me there. She's wearing her best skirt and I've just noticed a fancy lemon cheesecake thawing on the side, which she hasn't offered me. Is she expecting someone? A bloke, maybe? And if so, why hasn't she mentioned him? We always confide about our boyfriends – or used to, anyway. I suppose she doesn't trust me any more. I'm batty, like poor Norah. Must be, mustn't I? Only loonies live in psychiatric hospitals.

I don't know why I came, really. I suppose I imagined she'd support me, back me up, sympathize at least. And I felt so overwrought, I needed to get out, confide in my best mate. Now I just feel flat, and in the way.

I glance around her room – three walls painted orange, the fourth one papered in blue and yellow squiggles. I suspect the landlord got both paint and paper cheap – offcuts or odd lines which no one else would buy. The chairs look reject too, faded cretonne poppies blooming over broken springs. Jan's done her best, prettied up the surface with ornaments and bits and bobs, hung a few small flower prints. The room looks bigger, somehow – perhaps because it's tidy, far tidier than it ever was with me there. My sleeping bag is rolled up in a corner, my books and knick-knacks banished to a box. It's as if she's parcelled me away, wiped me off like a greasemark on a table.

I watch her snip a stalk, ram it into chicken wire. She's brought a few flowers home, snooty hothouse things, purplish-pink, with sort of pouting lips. Are they really only homework, or something to impress her guy, her new Mr

37

Right who'll soon move in with her? There won't be room for three.

She repositions a flower head, moves back to admire it. 'Does Norah *want* to go?'

I shrug. 'Not really. I don't think she wants anything. When you've been in a place like that for years and years, you don't have any wants left. On the other hand, she's scared about the move. It's definite now. Everyone's discussing it. Patients like her who aren't batty or half-crippled or over eighty have to go into lodgings and she hates the very thought.'

'But how can a holiday change that? She'll still have to move, won't she, after the ten days?'

'Well, I suppose she thinks it's . . .' I swallow a last noodle, push my mug away. 'Longer.'

'Carole, you didn't *let* her think that, did you?'

'No, I bloody didn't. I can't help it, can I, if she refuses to read the bumph? She's had three letters now and hasn't glanced at one of them. She assumes all sorts of things without me saying a word – not just about Las Vegas, but everything else as well.'

'Look, Carole, she's obviously confused. There's just no point in going with her. She'll be a total drag. Or maybe worse. Supposing she goes funny, or has a fit or something? It's quite a responsibility, you realize, travelling all that way with a loony in your charge.'

'She's not a loony. I wish you wouldn't use that word.' I touch the squashy package in my pocket – a piece of mushroom flan wrapped in pale pink Kleenex, the pastry damp and blackened from the mushrooms. Norah saved it from her dinner, a treasure which had somehow missed the mincer, hoarded it for me. 'We do have loonies, sure, quite a choice selection. In fact, it could have been far worse. Imagine ten days in Las Vegas with Flora Thompson, who's got only half a face and less than half her brain cells, or Meg O'Riley, who thinks she's still in Ireland.'

Jan grimaces. I suppose she loathes the hospital because her life is prettying things. Exotic scented flowers to follow bloody tearing births or smelly sordid illnesses, or to patch up deadly quarrels. Even death itself strewn with coloured petals. Floral tributes, they call the wreaths in Mayfair.

My mother sent a wreath from both of us, a ghastly thing with silver lurex ribbons dangling from self-important lilies; wrote 'To Father' on it. He wasn't her father, only mine, and anyway I never called him that. I stole out later with a pair of kitchen scissors and snipped my name neatly off the card (which was vile itself – a white and silver cross with a disembodied hand held up in blessing). I scoured every money-box and hiding-place I'd ever used since I was a kid, tipped the pile of coins into a plastic bag (they were too heavy for a purse), and blew the lot on cheerful non-snob flowers – marigolds and cornflowers, sweet williams, scented stocks; spent all day clinging on to them. They were awkward to carry and the damp stems made my skirt wet, but I couldn't bear to leave them in that sapless crematorium, or slighted by my mother's fancy wreath. By evening, they were drooping. One marigold was just a stalk. I must have knocked its head off and not noticed. In the end, I left them on a bench, one Dad often sat on in the park, happy doing nothing – whittling sticks or patting dogs or exchanging words with strangers who walked by. (My mother never spoke to anyone unless she had a formal signed certificate – in triplicate – that they were clean, English, insured, and right of centre.) Perhaps someone picked them up, a dirty stranger or left-wing foreign tramp.

I hate the smell of stocks now – smell of death. Even the next day, I could still smell their sickly scent, as if it had seeped into my blood-stream, or was oozing from my pores.

'Carole . . .'

'What?'

'I wish you'd stop those pills, love. You just don't concentrate. I've asked you – twice – do you want an egg?'

'No, thanks.' I did miss supper, actually, but I hate to be a sponger. Jan doesn't earn too much and that lemon cheesecake must have cost a bomb, with those piped rosettes of cream on top and that ruff thing round the middle. I hope he likes it.

'You don't mind if *I* eat, do you?' Jan brushes bits of laurel off the table, removes them to the bin.

''Course not. Pig yourself. Aren't you cooking for him, though?'

'What?'

'Oh, nothing.' Jan's staring at me, frying pan in one hand, corn oil in the other. I think she suspects I'm going really nuts, keeps watching me for signs. It's spoiling our friendship. She doesn't quite trust me any more, seems always a bit wary and reserved. I've noticed it when she visits. We don't giggle like we used to, and sometimes there are actual silences, which we've never ever had in fourteen years.

I ease up from my chair, go and sprawl on her divan. I feel utterly flaked out, as if I've just lived through that funeral day again, carrying a corpse made of cornflowers and sweet williams. I'm also feeling queasy, the smell of cooking oil seeping through my stomach like greasy fish and chips through newspaper.

'Hey, mind that bedspread, Carole. I only washed it just last week. And look, please don't take this wrong, love, but could you phone before you come? I'm really pushed this evening. Once I've had my supper, I've got to have a bath and wash my hair and . . .'

'Go ahead. Wash it. Wash the fucking bedspread, if you like. I'm not stopping you.'

I'm really hurt. Jan's never turfed me out before, just because she needed to tart up. In fact, we always shared the bathroom, dried each other's hair, played our favourite records while we messed about with eye gloss. And why the paranoia about that cheap and tatty bedspread? I suppose she washed it in his honour, plans to lie there with him later, when I've gone. I can see the cosy pair of them, curled up in each other's arms; no room or thought for me. He might own a place himself, invite Jan to live with him, even propose. Jan's the type to marry early, settle down to some boring decent guy, raise her 2.5 children. I'd lose her then, completely. Married friends are different, don't need you any more; share things with their husbands, not with you.

I watch her crack an egg, neat again, the white a perfect circle. My fried eggs tend to run or break, or get little black bits on them. God! I envy her. Even at school, she was form captain, flower monitor, always wore her hat, had loads of eager girlfriends. Maybe it's not a guy at all, but a girl, another roommate, one who pays the rent this time, shares all the expenses, doesn't let the side down by nicking things, landing up in loony bins. Jan's probably learnt her lesson, found a different sort of friend; some high-powered career girl who needs impressing with clean hair and party food. Hell! She must be really greedy if she plans to polish off that cheesecake. I'm so empty, I can hardly bear to look at it.

I punch Jan's pillow, lean back on it against the wall. All my past is breaking up – first my father and now Jan. I've known her all my life, for heaven's sake. She's part of my whole childhood. Why should I lose her to some odd acquaintance?

'Hey, Jan . . .'

'Where's the pepper? Damn! I had it here a moment ago.'

'Shall *we* go away – just you and me? In the spring, maybe. Somewhere nice.'

'We can't afford it.'

'If I win, we can.'

'Win?'

'In Las Vegas. They give us these free gambling chips, stacks of them. It's part of the whole deal.'

'Okay, you can take me to Paris and we'll have slap-up meals each day. No more size-five eggs. But on the ferry, please. You know how I hate flying. God! I wouldn't want that journey. Eleven hours, isn't it?'

'Yeah. More, I think.' I close my eyes a moment to block out the orange walls (dying marigolds). 'It's odd, you know, that's the one thing Norah's mad about – flying – the only bit she ever mentions, actually. She keeps on asking questions. How high would we fly? Are there windows? Would we see mountains from the sky? She's started watching planes now – and drawing them in Art.'

Jan cuts a piece of bread in half, adds it to the pan, jumps back as it splutters. 'I'd like the gambling. You know, just to try it – see a real casino, have a giggle.'

I grin. That's more like the old Jan. Maybe the cheesecake's only homework, part of some new-fangled flower arrangement. Lemon cream poinsettias. 'A guy won half a million dollars just last week. I read it in the *Mail* – an ordinary sort of bloke, a house-painter, I think he was, no one special. He lived in Arizona and went to Las Vegas just for one weekend. He'd never gambled in his life before, yet he won the jackpot the Friday he arrived.'

Jan seems quite impressed, even turns round from the pan. I don't let on he lost it all again – and more – was stony broke by Sunday. Frightening really, sums as big as that. Losing them or winning, they're still enough to change you totally – not just your life – your self. 'Tell you what,' I say. 'I'll bet half my chips for you. Whatever I win on yours, I'll bring home and you keep.'

'That's generous, love, but since they're refusing to let you go . . .'

'I'm going.'

'Oh, Carole, don't be silly. How can you go, when Sister's put her foot down? And there'll be another row if you don't get back there now. It's almost nine, d'you realize?'

'Okay, okay, I'm off. But you just wait and see. I intend to get those chips down on the table, make my fortune – and yours – buy us a Mayfair mansion with a florist shop attached. Just keep your fingers crossed.'

'I can't eat with them crossed.'

I cross my own, collect my bag and jacket, rattle down the stairs, out into the dark. It's raining still, and cold. I unwrap Norah's damp pink mushroom package, bite into the pastry. It's cold as well, wet-cold. No cream rosettes, no fancy ruffs, but at least it fills the hole, and was given as a love-offering.

'Thanks, Norah. You're a pal.' I'm speaking to her flan, to a flabby chunk of mushroom. 'We're going, you and me, whatever Sister says. We're winners, right? So nobody can stop us.'

6

We're flying. Carole said so. It doesn't feel like flying. I'm strapped into a seat. I can't see out at all. I'm in the middle of a middle row. Carole is on one side and a fat man on the other. Carole says we're late.

I was very disappointed in the airport. You couldn't see the planes. I had expected hundreds of them with great shining silver wings. But there were only crowds of people and shops and stairs and everybody pushing. There weren't even any windows in the airport. We walked miles along a corridor and still didn't see a plane.

Then we turned a corner and went down a step and through a door and a lady in a uniform said good morning and our seats were on the left, further down. That was the plane. We were on it already, and hadn't even seen it. It didn't have wings. It was more like the coach we take to Littlehampton, but much bigger, with rows and rows of seats stretching back for ever. We kept on walking, past all these heads and heads, and then Carole said 'This is us' and we climbed in past the fat man and it was really quite a squash.

We had to be strapped in. I said I'd rather not, but the lady in uniform did the strap up for me, so tight that it was hurting. In a coach you can always see outside; always see the driver, even talk to him. Here, there isn't any driver, and the windows are quite tiny and very far away.

We sat there a long time, not moving, and they played nice music and then a man's voice boomed out of the ceiling. I couldn't understand the voice, but Carole said they were doing some repair. That made me really frightened, especially when two ladies in uniform stood in the aisles and started putting on

masks, horrid things like gas masks in the war. She said we'd
have masks as well. They'd drop down from above our seats and
we'd have to pull them on, right across our nose and mouth,
with the elastic strap pulled tight.

I hate things over my face. They choked me in a mask like
that when I had all my top teeth out. When I woke up again,
my face had gone a different shape and I couldn't speak or eat.
No one ever told me you wore masks in aeroplanes. I was so
afraid, I could hardly breathe at all, and I missed what they said
next.

It was something about vests. The lady said to unfold our vest
and slip it over our head. But my vest was on already,
underneath my dress. I checked it to make sure. When I looked
up again, the ladies both had jackets on, funny-looking yellow
ones with tubes and whistles hanging from them, and strings to
do them up.

'As you leave the aircraft, inflate your vest by pulling down
sharply on . . .'

'Why do we have to leave?' I whispered. 'We've only just
got on.'

Carole didn't answer. She was watching the two ladies who
were holding up their seat cushions, explaining how to take
them off the seats. I tugged at mine, but Carole said, 'Not now,
you nut. Only if we crash into the sea.'

'Crash?'

'Yeah. We float on them like rafts.'

Another lady was coming down the aisle. I stopped her,
clutched her arm. 'Yes, I *will* get out,' I told her. 'Right away.'

She said, Ssh, she'd help me later, but later never came. There
was only a loud roar, a really deafening noise which went right
through my whole body, and then I lost my body, so I thought
that I was dead, and then Carole said 'We're up' and that was
flying.

I've always wanted to fly. I was clumsy as a child, and fat, the
biggest girl in my infant school. I knew I'd be more beautiful with
wings. We did a school play once; a Nativity, they called it. The
prettiest girl was Mary and the cleverest boy was Joseph. I wanted to be an Angel, but they made me be a Tree. Angels fly.

I wish we could get up. We've been sitting here two hours, and we haven't had our dinner yet. Dinner's at twelve sharp in the hospital. Sometimes five past, but never later. It's nearly five past two now and there's not a sign of it. We didn't have any breakfast. Carole said not to because we'd have coffee and doughnuts at the airport. But we spent all the time queuing at a desk and after that we queued again, upstairs, and a woman touched my body, ran her hands all over it, up and down, so she could feel my stocking tops and vest straps. Even at the hospital, they never do that. The doctor examines you when you first come in, but only with his stethoscope. He doesn't use his hands. I think he's scared of germs.

We did have the champagne. A soldier brought it in a pail. It was cold and mostly bubbles. I was feeling cold already and would rather have had hot tea, but he said there wasn't any. We have tea in the hospital at six o'clock each morning, and three in the afternoon. And you can have it before bedtime instead of Ovaltine. Or any time at all down in the canteen, if you've got the money for it.

We didn't have to pay for the champagne. That was free. Once we get to Las Vegas, everything is free. Las Vegas means 'the meadows'. I like that name. I've got a book on it, a guide book from the library. I've only reached page twelve. It became a town because it was the only place with water. The mules used to stop there to drink, and eat the grass. A mule is half a horse, Sister said. I hope we see the mules.

I'd like to ride a horse. It would feel a bit like flying, proper flying. That voice in the ceiling told us we were flying at six hundred miles an hour, but I think he got it wrong. We're hardly moving – just sitting like we do all day at Beechgrove. And everybody's smoking, just the same as there. Carole's on her second pack already. She's nervous, I can tell. She's listening to the radio. She brought her own, but they wouldn't let her use it. The plane one's hidden in the seat and you have to wear headphones so you can't hear other things. I said 'Carole' once or twice, but she didn't seem to notice. Perhaps she didn't want to. The nurses are like that, pretending they are deaf.

The bubbles from the champagne keep exploding in my

stomach. I need some food to settle them. I've read the menu five times over. The food is very special and has long names. You can choose between something something chicken and something in French.

I think I'll have the chicken. At least it's English and I know what chicken is. They've even got a picture of it on the cover of the menu, a whole roast chicken with a bowl of fruit beside it, so full it's spilling out – apples, cherries, grapes and some fruits I've never seen. The grapes are huge and black and seem to shine. I've only eaten grapes once and they were green and tiny. Someone's son had brought them in as a present for his mother, but she had passed away a week or more before, and he didn't even know. Nurse Clarke was going to eat them, but an older Irish nurse said it was unlucky to eat corpses' food, so she gave them to us patients. She was right about the bad luck. Two days after that, they told us we were moving.

We had turkey yesterday. Yesterday was Christmas. I couldn't enjoy it because I was so scared about this trip.

I can smell the dinner now. It's coming down the aisle. Two ladies with a shining silver trolley, handing out the trays. Imagine dinner when you're flying! It must be special if it takes so long to cook. No one else seems hungry. The man beside me is asleep.

'Beef or chicken, madam?'

'Er . . . chicken.' No one calls me Madam. It didn't say beef on the menu. I'd have had it if I'd known. The chicken looks pale and rather ill, not golden-brown at all. I thought we'd get a whole one like the picture, or at least a large piece with a bone. There are just two tiny slices in a greyish gravy, two small white potatoes and a teaspoonful of peas. They couldn't fit more on because the plate's so small. It's not a plate, but the sort of plastic dish you put your soap in.

Carole's asked for beef. It doesn't look French, but more like the stew we have on Tuesdays, except there's less of it.

I touch her arm again. 'We haven't got a first course.' I was looking forward to it. It was written on the menu, four long words I couldn't quite spell out. I've never had a first course. There's only meat and pudding in the hospital.

'Yes, we have, silly.' Carole points to another plastic dish. It's wrapped in that see-through stuff the doctor keeps his dressings in. There's lettuce at the bottom, just a tiny bit, with one slice of tomato. I think I'll still be hungry.

'Where's the pudding?'

'There.'

'That's a cake.'

'No, it's not, it's pudding. Strudel Viennese.'

I don't know what she means. And I can't see any fruit, not even just an apple. Perhaps they got the picture wrong.

I eat the pudding first. It has wet stuff in it which doesn't taste of anything, and two small currants. The chicken has gone cold. At least they didn't mince it, but it isn't very filling. You can have seconds in the hospital, or fill up with bread and marge.

Carole's drinking more champagne. I mustn't drink, or I'll need to go. I need to go already.

'Excuse me, sir . . .' That lady called him Sir, the one who brought his dinner. He smiled at her. He's muttering at me. I think he's foreign. I can't understand the words. His eyes are very small, small and black like the currants in the cake. I can't get out. No room between his stomach and his tray. 'I'm sorry, sir, but . . .'

Three toilets in a row. I'll try the middle one. It's frightening locked in here. I should have left the door open, like they make us do at Beechgrove. I'm trapped in, like a prison. No room to move, no windows. A gust of wind is blowing from the ceiling, very cold. Maybe there's a hole in the plane and no one knows about it.

They have funny toilets here, metal ones which are noisy when you go. Can they hear outside? There isn't any chain to pull. I can't make the taps work, either, or the plug. That's my face in the mirror there. I don't look how I thought I did.

It's hard to stand. The floor keeps moving under me. There are lots of little cupboards with soap and paper towels in. The bars of soap are tiny. Perhaps they can't afford the large size. I slip one in my pocket. I've been in places where there isn't any soap, even in hospitals where they keep saying 'Wash your hands'. I'm not sure about America, but better to be safe. I also

47

find some sanitary towels which are useful if I leak. I don't have periods any more. They took a lot of things away when I moved to Beechgrove, including my insides.

I daren't disturb that man again. I think I'll stay in here. Except you're not allowed to hang around the toilets. Sister always comes to get you out. People smoke there sometimes. I tried a cigarette myself, just before we left. Carole asked me to. She kept worrying that I'd won the competition, yet never had a smoke. I cried first, then I coughed, but it made Carole happy, and I like it when she's happy.

'Norah? Are you in there, Norah?'

Someone's knocking. Sister. I'm not smoking, Sister, honestly, I'm not. I only smoked the once.

I open the door. It's Carole, come to get me. 'Are we there?' I ask her.

'Don't be daft. We've hardly started yet. I was just worried where you'd got to. Are you feeling sick or something?'

'Oh, Carole, look!'

'What?'

'The clouds.'

'What about them?'

We're flying, yes we're flying. It's true. We're right up in the clouds. They're so wonderful I must sit down and watch. There are two seats on their own, with no one sitting in them. I climb into the window one, press my face almost to the glass.

Clouds! So close we're right inside them. Flying clouds. Clouds with wings, great white feathered wings like those Angels in the play. Carole's right. I do feel sick, sick with happiness. I wish I had more words – words for happiness, words for all the clouds. Clouds like bandages, clouds like semolina. Some are flat and lacy, others thick and padded. Some are torn in strips, like we used to tear old sheets for curling-rags and dusters. Except they're not old, not at all, but very clean and fresh.

I'd like to smell them, touch them, maybe eat a bit of one. I think they'd taste like trifle. Trifle's very special. We had it yesterday.

I try to open the window, so I can lean right out and reach

them. It doesn't seem to open, so I take my glasses off instead. I feel shy without my glasses and things go strange and fuzzy, but I don't want anything between me and heaven.

There's an eiderdown! A white cloud eiderdown. I slept on one, just once. It belonged to another girl in Westham Hall, but she let me borrow it for a quarter of a night. I lay on top of it, not under it. It felt so soft and warm. Clouds must feel like that. I stole just one small feather before I gave it back, pulled it out and kept it, to remind me. Those clouds are full of feathers. I could lie on one for ever, with another one on top of me, pulled right up to my chin; feel the whole world soft and white, instead of hard grey stone.

'Norah . . .'

'Just a minute.'

'Look, do come back. We haven't had our coffee.'

I put my glasses on again. My eyes feel weak and dazed from being let out of their cage. 'Can't we have it here? Change our seats?'

''Course not, stupid. You can't see the screen from there.'

'Screen?'

'For the movie. You know – like TV. There's two films, in fact, one starting any minute. Do buck up or we'll miss that, too. It's a funny one, they said, quite a hoot.'

'You go.' I turn back to the window. 'I like it here.' The clouds have changed again. There are blue bits now, like lakes, between the white, and gold sprinkled on the top. I can't see the sun, but it must be very close because everything is shining. I knew heaven would be shining. I can feel my body gold inside. I fly.

A hand taps me on the shoulder. It isn't Carole's hand. 'Will you please return to your seat, madam. We're showing the movie now.'

I pretend I haven't heard. It seems rude to me that people should watch television when they've got this close to God.

'I'm sorry, but you'll have to move. We're closing all the blinds. And we like to keep those seats free, anyway, so as not to block the exit.'

I slide out of the seat. She sounds sharp like Sister Watkins, so

I dare not disobey. She leans over, snaps the blind down. Other hands pull other blinds all along the rows. It's dark now, really dark. This must be a punishment. I creep back to my seat.

The trays have disappeared, but Carole passes me a plastic bag with something grey coiled in it.

'Go on – put it on. It's the headset for the movie. Here, I'll do it for you, if you like.'

I hate things in my ears. At St Joseph's, they stuffed our ears with cotton wool in winter, so everything was muffled. If we took it out, they slapped us. This isn't cotton wool, but something harder. I can't hear at all, just a whispered roar which is different from the plane's roar. At least it's not a mask. At least I can still breathe.

I look up at the screen. A small thin man with a moustache is running in and out of rooms and climbing into wardrobes. His lips are moving so I think he must be talking, but I can't hear any words. Only roar.

I fiddle with the headset and everyone starts laughing – Carole and the fat man, the people next to them, and the whole row in front. I try to laugh myself, but I'm feeling rather scared. The laughs are getting louder, mixed up with the roar. I'm trapped in coils of laughter like barbed wire.

It's impossible to move. The fat man's stomach is shaking up and down. Carole's almost choking. I've never heard her laugh before, only cry. The two are not that different.

There's a boy behind me with a horrid jeering laugh. They laughed like that when I first arrived at Westham, forty years ago. I just stood there in the playground in my St Joseph's brown school tunic and the brown felt hat with its blue and gold striped ribbon round the brim. I couldn't see a lot because the hat was too big and came right down on my eyebrows. But I could hear the laughs all around me. There was glass along the walls at Westham Hall, broken glass sticking up from the topmost row of bricks, to stop us climbing out. Those laughs cut like the glass.

It was worse when they stopped, though, because no one said a word. The silence felt cold and thick like dirty snow. I moved my hat a bit. I could see a circle of feet, white plimsolls and black boots, edging slowly closer. I shut my eyes.

'What's yer name?' someone asked, at last. A boy, I think it was. There were no boys at St Joseph's.

'N . . . Norah Too . . .' I couldn't get the letters out. They had stuck to my teeth like toffee.

'What?'

'T . . . Toomey.'

They laughed again then, louder. Someone snatched my hat off, threw it in a tree. It didn't matter really. No one wore a uniform at Westham, and they always laughed at hats.

The second film is different. No one laughs at all. There are far more people in it who all look sad and frightened. I can't hear what they're saying, but I can see it from their eyes. Some of them are shouting, some crying with no sound. It seems sadder with no sound.

I'm very stiff and cramped. My head is throbbing and there's a pain all down my back. I'd like to move, stretch my legs, get some light and air, escape from all these people and the smoke. Even in the hospital you can sometimes get away, sit quietly in the library and walk up and down the corridors and think. And you don't have to watch TV. A lot of patients do, of course, but the set is in another room, so it's not forced on you, like here.

I've never sat so long before, in just one squashed-in seat and doing nothing. We have far more breaks at Beechgrove and we're allowed to move our chairs. Today is Boxing Day.

I don't like this low ceiling. I feel I'm all closed in and the world outside has flown away, disappeared for ever. You're not allowed to speak and Carole has forgotten that I'm here. A baby's crying just in front. It's been crying all the way.

I wish the roar would stop, the strange noise in my ears. I wish I could get out. A whole day has passed, at least, and maybe half a night as well. Boxing Day is over. We didn't have the carol singers, or cold turkey and mince pies. With Beechgrove closing, I may never have a Boxing Day again. You don't have them in lodgings, or on planes.

Carole's watch says half past eight, but she said that wasn't right. It should be dark by now. It is dark on the plane because the blinds are still drawn down, but they pulled them up for just ten or fifteen minutes before the second film, and it was as light and bright as summer. I got up to go number one, so I could see the clouds again. There was a long queue for the toilets (which were dirtier and smelt), so I only had a moment for the clouds. The sun was shining on the white and they were so clean and pure and beautiful. I could have watched them all my life.

I tried to ask permission to be excused the second film, so I could stand there a bit longer. But the lady said we were having drinks first, anyway, and would I go back to my seat please, because they couldn't get the trolley through if everyone got up.

Carole had a gin. They brought it in a tiny tiny bottle with a plastic tooth-mug full of lumps of ice. I said 'Nothing, thank you,' but the soldier gave me a little pack of peanuts with 'Enjoy your drink' printed on the wrapper. No one's ever done that at the hospital. I put it in my pocket with the soap. I was feeling rather hungry, but I didn't want to open it, in case I tore the words.

'Enjoy,' I whisper. Nice word.

They told us to enjoy our flight, but it isn't very easy. No one talks to you and there's nothing much to do. We're still going very slowly, slower than the coach. I wish they'd bring the craft box round. The clever ones do tapestry at Beechgrove, or knit, or make soft toys. I've got my big jigsaw. We never sit in silence in the dark.

I try a bit more film. Carole's frowning, screwing up her eyes. It must be something terrible. I still can't hear, but the man has got a gun now, a gun with silent bullets. Suddenly, I can hear. The screen goes black and a voice comes out of nowhere, a stern voice like the chaplain's. 'Will you kindly fasten your seat belts and keep them fastened. If you are not in your seat, please return to it immediately.'

'That's the captain,' Carole whispers.

'Where?' I ask. I haven't seen him yet. He's the most important person on the plane. Nurse Sanders told me that. I hoped we'd sit right close to him.

'Ssh! Do your seat belt up.'

I clutch her arm, afraid. 'What's happened, then?' I expect the masks will drop now. I won't be able to put mine on, shan't be able to breathe. There's not much air left anyway. Only cigarette smoke. My chest feels tight already.

'Nothing.' Carole shrugs. 'Just a bit of turbulence. Who d'you think did it, by the way?'

'What?'

'The murder, silly. Aren't you watching?'

I glance back at the screen. I think we're going to crash. The plane is shuddering, plunging down and down. I wonder if the sea is underneath. If it is, I'll die. I never learnt to swim and you couldn't float on cushions, whatever Carole said. She told me they had floating cots for babies. I can't see any cots, so that baby just in front will die as well. It's screaming even louder.

The people in the film look terrified. Two are dead already. I fumble for my hankie, wipe my face. I've been cold all through the journey. Now I'm sweating.

A long time passes. I know I'm still alive when Carole prods my arm.

'Stop fidgeting,' she whispers. She's very calm herself. I shut my eyes, try to do the exercises they teach in Relaxation. It seems to soothe the plane. It's quieter now.

I keep my eyes closed anyway, so now it's dark inside me, as well as in the plane. Last week, we had the Shortest Day, which means it's dark when you get up and dark again by teatime. It seems odd to block the light out when we get so little of it. It's summer just outside those blinds, yet we're sitting here in winter. Perhaps flying's like the war and light is dangerous. Or perhaps we're so high up, the sun could burn us.

I wish they had a shop here, so I could buy a bag of crisps. I think they've forgotten supper and I'm feeling very empty – empty everywhere, not just in my stomach. The Beechgrove shop is really just a room, not a proper shop with windows or a counter. It's run by two grand ladies who keep changing all the time, so they never know my name. You can buy bath salts there, and stamps, and bars of chocolate. I've never bought a stamp.

Carole said Las Vegas is five thousand miles away. I feel shaky when I think of it. Five thousand miles from Beechgrove and my bed. Carole says it's night-time back in England, which means that even if I did get off the plane, they wouldn't let me in. They lock the gates at ten.

I don't understand about the time, or why England is ahead of us. I think time must go more slowly on a plane. I asked if we'd catch up, but Carole said not till we returned, when we'd lose the time again. You can't lose time, or only if you have an operation. (When I had my op, I lost a day as well as my insides.) I don't like things to change. Even Christmas Day upset me because everything was different.

I'd like to be in bed now. I don't feel well at all. My feet and legs have swollen, and there's another sort of seat belt clamped tight around my skull. I'm strapped in twice, and the seat in front is like a padded wall. Always walls, everywhere I've been. I've never minded much before, never felt this trapped. I think they've locked us in again because I stole the soap. It wasn't really stealing. I was scared of germs, that's all. Sister says there are germs on everything: food, and people's faces, and especially toilet-chains.

Twenty years ago, they always locked the wards, not just the violent ones, but all of them, even children's wards. And they used to count the knives and forks after every single meal. We had to sit there, quiet in rows, and if just one small piece of cutlery was missing, they wouldn't let us move until they'd found it. A patient could kill them with a missing knife.

There's blood now on the screen, three men lying dead.

I'd better put the soap back. And the nuts as well. The nuts were mine. The soldier pushed them into my hand, but Sister won't believe that. I can't get out, though. Perhaps I'll just leave them on my tray, or give them to the lady when she passes by again. I wish she'd stop and say hello, ask me how my jigsaw's getting on.

Suddenly there's silence. Well, the roaring in my ears stops, though not the louder roar. People start shifting in their seats, rustling things or stretching.

'Great!' says Carole. 'Wasn't it? I never guessed the nurse, did you?'

'No.'

'I thought it was the brother. Gosh, they're serving tea already. That's quick.'

There are letters on the screen still, but they've put the blinds up now and are passing trays around. Carole's watch says ten past ten which seems late for tea, especially scones and jam and cheese which is what it is. Sister says cheese is bad for you at night, gives you dreams. I had a dream last night about a hospital. They blew it up with a bomb and there was nothing left at all except one tiny golden heart like the one on Carole's bracelet, lying at the bottom of the big black hole.

Carole saws her scone in half, digs her plastic knife into her tiny pot of jam — tiny like my tiny bar of soap, which I'm still clutching in my hand. I lay it on my saucer, put the nuts on top. They're small as well, just doll-size. Everything is tiny when you're flying.

Carole is talking through her jam. 'We'll be landing in two hours,' she says.

Two hours.

7

Hours and bloody hours have passed. Norah's taken her pills and gone to sleep. Lucky Toomey. I can't sleep at all. I feel more alone now she's got her eyes shut, as if I'm the only person still alive in this whole vast country, all forty-nine great States of it (or is it fifty?) stretching up to snows and down to sand, with mountains on both sides. There are people on this plane, but not that many – nothing like the first one – and they're all sitting further forward. We're stuck at the back in Smoking. I smoke Players No. 6 because . . . I don't, in fact. I changed from Rothman's to Marlboros at LA.

Los Angeles, City of the Angels. Norah liked the name. It's better than the place – though maybe that's unfair since we only saw the airport, which was drabber than Heathrow with longer queues. Lots of people were complaining about lost luggage. The airline quite surpassed itself, lost six separate cases and a bag of brand new golf clubs. The golfer chap was going spare.

Norah was upset as well, though quietly. Hers was one of the cases which was missing. Mine was merely crippled, came circling round the baggage-carousel with a bruised and dented side and a great scar across its face. We waited hours for Norah's, but it never came. It was a hospital case, cheap and cardboardy, so maybe it had burst apart en route. We wasted more time filling in reports and things (there was a queue for that as well) and trying to remember what the damned case looked like, since you had to tick the one it most resembled on the form. They all looked much the same to me, and Norah's not like any. Hers probably dated from 1888, like the hospital itself. The whole palaver took such ages I was scared we'd miss our second flight, but it was delayed, in fact, due to rain (torrential).

We sat out on the tarmac in this tinny little crate (which is very long and narrow like a passage), with rain streaming down the windows and stewards bringing paper cups of coffee, in the hope that we'd be too grateful to complain. I drank four cups to wake me up. It hasn't. I still feel absolutely frazzled, yet I'm afraid to close my eyes. I've got this feeling that if I shut them, even for a second, I'll simply disappear and maybe the whole of America will slide away as well. I suppose it *is* America. It's so dark outside it could be anywhere. Odd how we accept things. I've no proof whatsoever. Okay, so the stewards speak with a Californian twang, but they could be flying us to China or Siberia or Sumatra or . . . I check my watch again, do the usual subtractions in my head.

I tried to explain to Norah about the time difference, and she said, 'You mean, we have the time twice over?' She was right. We had a free gift of eight hours, to live again. If that had been on offer the day that I was nicked, I could have lived it differently, slept all day, or hung around the Job Centre, instead of pocketing swiss rolls. Or if I'd flown the other way, I'd have simply lost the time. No police, no court, no Beechgrove. Strange how ten minutes can make you Someone Else. When I walked into that supermarket, I was university material, a bright girl with a future – a future black-patched by a death, in fact, but still by no means a case. Now I'm 'depressive, hyperactive and unstable'. I saw it on my notes. My headmistress called me co-operative, responsible and a joy to teach. My father went still further: the best girl in all the world.

It's weird – it's my mother I'm missing at the moment, not my father. I can even see her, bits of her, her long white bony feet with their nail varnish chipped off; the flash of black lace bra-strap which always seems to be showing, as though to prove she's still got breasts, and sexy ones. Sexy Mum. Odd to call her Mum. It never fitted. Even when I was tiny, it sounded wrong. My father called her Kitty, which was worse. He used to call me sweetheart.

'Hey, sweetheart . . .'

I jump. My heart is racing, palms clammy-wet. Maybe I only dreamt the flight and I'm waking now in my bed at Portishead and I'll see my father standing there in his baggy Fair-Isle cardigan with my early morning tea. (Mornings had stopped happening for my mother.) I rub my eyes, hardly dare look up. No. A younger man, a steward. If disappointment had the power to kill, he'd be flat out in the aisle, cold and stiff already, instead of leaning over me with that silly flirty smile.

'If you wanna see Las Vegas, honey, just look down.'

I wipe the window with the paper serviette which came with coffee number four and has 'Good morning' printed on it, though it's almost ten to midnight, Pacific time. I gasp. Not all the paints in all the Art Rooms in every school and hospital in England or the forty-nine (fifty?) United States could ever make a show like that. Not just glittery gold, but glittery pink, scarlet, purple, turquoise, lime − neon colours, wild and throbbing-hot. It's a fairground, not a city, blazing out of darkness, welcoming us with a ticker-tape of lights.

I read in Norah's guide book that it's really quite a small town, just a few main streets. They're wrong. Those lights go on for miles, strings and strings of them, shimmering and twinkling like Christmas decorations. Christmas was a con this year, a non-event. But now I realize we haven't had it yet. That's Christmas down below − three-dimensional Christmas, tinselled and ballooned, a town in fancy dress. They're as wrong about the meadows as they were about the angels. Nothing so dull and green and squelchy as a meadow, which is a place for cows and weeds. This is a city made for parties, a razzle-dazzle city built of lights instead of concrete, and with fireworks for its stars. It's changing as I look at it, like a huge kaleidoscope which someone has just shaken, so that all the colours have shifted and re-formed − cyclamen, and peacock, a new electric green.

I'm so dazzled, so excited, I can hardly stagger off the plane. Norah's still a zombie, muttering about lodgings and Hastings promenade, slurring half her words. The airport's really wild. The first thing that you see (and hear) are rows and rows of slot machines, all tinkling out these catchy little tunes. There's a crowd of people playing them, even two in wheelchairs. We lurch along the carpet to the rattle of their coins – a red carpet, naturally, to welcome VIPs. We're all important people, judging by the decor, which leaves most airports standing. There's this amazing silver ceiling which snakes up and down in curves and looks really swish and space-age, and huge gold palm trees towering over tubs of jungly plants. It's nothing like Heathrow with its plastic glare and roar. Here, the lights are dim, and there's soft romantic music playing, and stylish fashion-shops full of alligator boots and slinky sequinned numbers trimmed with ostrich.

The smell of popcorn seems a bit incongruous, especially as it's really strong and sickly, wafting from a shop called Creative Candy Gifts. It makes me feel quite peckish, except I'm far too high to eat, and dare not stop for anything in case Norah just keels over. I try to keep her upright on the escalator, following the signs to the 'baggage reclaim area'. Even that is glamorous, with more gold palms and a great high ceiling, mirrored blue and silver, which reflects us upside-down.

I suddenly see two hundred kicking legs, two hundred naked breasts on top, a hundred scarlet smiles. I stop, watch open-mouthed, as a horde of topless showgirls dance a racy cancan. It's a commercial for Las Vegas, showing on a screen, a huge monster television, placed high above the baggage-carousels. No, *two* screens – one each end: four hundred fishnet legs now, four hundred bouncing boobs; at least two hundred decibels of music. The music's so infectious, I want to jig myself, start shimmying my hips, tossing back my hair. I leave Norah on a seat, go back to watch the screens. A deep male voice is speaking now, husky and seductive.

'Enter a world where seeing's not believing, where reality and fantasy entwine . . .'

Two fairy-tale princes, dressed in turquoise satin with swirling purple cloaks, leap on stage – a snarl of snow-white tigers snapping round their thigh-high silver boots. I watch, enthralled. These must be snippets from the famous Vegas shows – wild animals, magicians, dancing girls and strippers. A dancer's sawn in half before my eyes; a lion shoots from a cannon, and now wild green flashing laser-beams start criss-crossing on the screens, seem to explode out of the set, pierce right through my flesh.

'We'll transport you to a wonder-world of magic,' breathes the voice. 'On stage at the Gold Rush – New Year's Eve.'

The Gold Rush. *Our* hotel! This must be the Show Spectacular they promised in our package. Fancy all those marvels on one stage – our stage – two princes maybe staying in the room next door to ours, lions and tigers prowling in the grounds! I can hardly bear to tear myself away, keep craning my neck, watching over my shoulder, as I start the boring business of searching out my suitcase. I find it, still more dented, lug it back to Norah who's tipped sideways on her seat, seems unsure who I am.

'Hey, Norah, do wake up. It's so exciting here! Look at that kid in white fur dungarees. I'm sure they're mink or something, and he can't be more than three. And see that man in . . .'

Someone interrupts me. 'Miss Toomey and Miss Joseph?'

I jump, swing round. A girl is smiling down at me, a tall and leggy glamour-girl who looks as if she's just stepped off those screens. She's wearing a gold catsuit and her mass of golden curls is haloed by a round cap saying GOLD RUSH – that magic name again. I stare at her, start counting her gold bangles – ten, eleven, twelve – the gold rings on each finger.

'Miss Toomey and Miss Joseph?' she repeats.

I mumble 'Yes' for both of us, ashamed. We look plain and drab; unworthy, unbejewelled.

'Hi! Welcome to Las Vegas. I'm Cindy. Your limo's just outside.'

They had told us we'd be met, but I'd expected Nanny No One in a black and boring taxi, not this stunner in her hot-pink limousine. By the time I've recovered from Cindy herself (each three-inch nail is a different dazzling colour, and her hair's so blinding blonde, I need a pair of sun-glasses), I'm goggling at the longest car I've ever seen or dreamed of. I can hardly reply to all her friendly questions about England and the flight and was Norah sick or simply tired and had we travelled much before (etcetera), because I'm so knocked out by the way it seems to float along on water and by the velvet seats and phone. It's like a cocktail lounge inside, with a proper bar, and lights with frilly shades. (Pink lampshades in a car!) In fact, I quite forget to look where we are going, and when Cindy says 'We're here,' I feel as if the last half an hour has been running on fast-forward and I've missed it all except a whirring flash of colours.

Cindy helps us out. She needs to. Norah is still reeling from her pills and I'm so stunned by my surroundings, the ground feels none too solid. I haven't been abroad a lot. A week in Paris with our school, a long weekend in Guernsey with my parents – that's it – and a few cut-price Trust House Fortes back at home, coaching inns with ivy or new motels in raw red brick. This is a fairy palace, a serious fairy palace built to last; not gingerbread or sugar, but priceless marble, sparkling glass. The glass seems to ripple as it mirrors back the fountains. Yes, real cascading fountains thundering into pools with sculpted golden dolphins larking in the shallows. The pools and fountains are floodlit silver-blue, the grass is man-made and floodlit silver-green. There are palm trees made of lights and huge fluorescent flowers which keep opening up their petals, flashing through the spectrum from red to zingy violet, then closing down to green before they bloom again.

I force my eyes away, turn back to the palace. Its architect has ransacked every country in the world – barley-sugar columns, twisty-twisting up to bulging domes; minarets outflanking soaring spires. Reflections of reflections drown in glass and water, flash on gold and brass. I can see real flowers and palm trees behind pretend ones made of lights. Or *are* they real? My skin is glowing now red, now blue, now silver, in the never-ending light show. I can feel myself dissolving into brightly coloured petals, glistening drops of water. The only solid thing is Norah still slumped against my side.

I take her arm, steer her towards the towering golden arch in the centre of the building. We go from brilliance into gloom. There are chandeliers now, a whole ceiling made of crystal, but everything's so hushed and sort of grand, it's like we've entered some cathedral. There is even real stained glass. Not in the windows – there aren't any windows – but in panels round the walls, depicting holy naked women trailing feather fans. In place of shrines and altars are green-baize tables, spinning roulette wheels, more rows of gleaming slot machines, like those we've seen already at the airport. At every table stands a priest or priestess, dressed identically in white frilled shirts with brocaded gold and scarlet Lurex waistcoats and black satin ribbons at the neck.

My own crumpled skirt and blouse look suddenly blasphemous, like wearing shorts in church. I'd taken off my raincoat in the limousine. A chain-store mac with a snap-on fake-fur lining seemed unsuited to a cocktail lounge on wheels. I stare at a woman dressed in peacock-blue sequins with a tiny feathered hat. Nothing fake about her wrap – blue mink and yards of it; a matching iced blue cocktail in a knickerbocker-glory glass. She's all alone, seems sad, despite the towering pile of gambling chips in front of her.

Casino is merging into hotel foyer; high stools at gambling tables giving place to sofas and banquettes. I park Norah on a sofa, join Cindy at the desk. The two men and six girls behind it are all dressed in the same gold pantsuits, with GOLD RUSH on their hats. In a daze, I fill in forms, pass them back, and receive in return a huge golden key and scarlet padded book. A Bible, I suppose. My father told me once that some bods called the Gideons provide Bibles in every hotel room in the world.

'Welcome to the Gold Rush', I read on the first page. 'This is your passport to every pleasure you can dream of – and some beyond your dreams. Just pick up your room-phone and a genie will appear. Make your wish. His duty is to grant it, if he can.'

They must be taking the mick. No. I turn a few more pages, gag on the statistics: three thousand hotel rooms standing on a site worth a hundred million dollars, over seven thousand hotel staff, sixty thousand square feet of casino space, fifteen hundred slot machines, two Olympic-sized swimming pools, each containing two hundred thousand gallons of coloured perfumed water which laps around the shores of half a dozen palm-clad tropical islets. The islets come complete with gaming tables, so that even sunbathers and swimmers won't miss the chance of winning. If you prefer to gorge, there are seven separate restaurants, one with thunder and lightning while you dine, one with the longest wine list in the world; also six exotic cocktail lounges with two hundred different cocktails.

I look up from the Bacardis and the Gin Slings. My case has disappeared. A young lad (genie?), dressed like Cindy, except his suit has flies, motions us to follow, leads us to a lift. He presses a button and we ascend towards the stars. (A trillion trillion stars in half a billion separate galaxies.) We emerge into a passage lit by chandeliers, gold velvet on the walls, thick pile underfoot. I wonder about tipping. He looks so tiny and pink-cheeked, I feel I ought to press bubble gum or Smarties into his hand, instead of dollar bills. In the end, I give him English money, in the hope he'll think it's more. He doesn't even look at it. It simply disappears, as if by some process of osmosis.

He must have disappeared himself. I didn't notice, actually. I'm staring at our room. No, not a room, a suite, though even that is far too tame a word. It's white, bridal white, with one huge heart-shaped bed. The carpet is like snow, warm snow, the sort your feet sink into. The walls are ivory silk, etched with tiny silver hearts. Pictures everywhere – naughty pictures of naked gods and goddesses getting down to it: Jupiter and Danaë, Bacchus and his groupies, Venus with a Cupid looking younger than the bellboy. Their names are underneath, picked out in silver.

I leave Norah on a love-seat, peek into the bathroom. The bath is circular, pure white marble sunk into the floor, and big enough to hold a tribe. The swan's-neck taps look like solid gold, match the gleaming golden toilet seat and cistern. Beside it is a statue on a plinth – two white marble lovers embracing and entwined. I run the taps, surprised to see plain water gushing out and not hot and cold champagne. The soap is lily of the valley, gift-wrapped.

I close the door, sink into a white brocaded armchair in the bedroom. On the table, a huge bouquet of all-white flowers – carnations, iceberg roses and some exotic lily-things which smell whiffy like French cheese. My suitcase has arrived, its scuffed and shabby airforce-blue disturbing that luxurious sea of white. I'd better hide it, hide away myself. I open a cupboard door, stop in a shock as 'Here Comes the Bride' tinkles out from some hidden music-box. 'Shit,' I mutter, flop down on the bed. So this is the bridal suite. That explains the hearts, the wedding-white.

I glance at my bridegroom who is snoring on the love-seat, mouth open, thick lisle stockings bagging round her knees. She's spilt gravy on her suit, airline gravy, which has dried on brown and stiff. The suit itself is green, a sage-green Crimplene number which the WRVS picked out for her at the Beechgrove jumble sale. It even fits, though they were less fortunate with the shoes, which are brown and boat-like, gaping at both sides. Her coat was a present from a Friend, a cast-off in balding astrakhan and older than Norah is herself. The Friends all rallied round to help, once they'd recovered from the shock of a patient going anywhere beyond the day-trip to the coast which they organize themselves.

I lie back on the pillows, eight separate pillows, each a heart itself; see a tired and messy girl in a wrinkled denim skirt. Myself. The entire ceiling is mirrored, intended to reflect back the gymnastics of the honeymoon. The Gold Rush has its own luxurious Wedding Chapel. You can be wedded here, then bedded, with only a lift-ride in between. I reach out for the phone.

A bored girl answers, not a genie.

'Look,' I say. 'We're not the honeymooners.'

We must be. The computer can't be wrong. I point out we're both females, but it seems to make no difference. Las Vegas marries lesbians; it even marries dolls. There was a report in the (English) *Standard* which Jan had saved for me, about a clergyman from the American Fellowship Church joining two Cabbage Patch dolls in holy matrimony, in a Las Vegas Wedding Chapel. ('They were so in love,' he said.)

'Can you hold on a moment, ma'am? I'll have to have a word with . . .'

'Oh, forget it,' I tell her. It's hardly worth the fuss. I wish I hadn't phoned. I've got this horrid frightening feeling that we're just a computer error; that we didn't win the prize at all; maybe don't exist. Another girl's come on now, asking if I'm Mrs Rita Holdsworth from Ohio.

'No,' I say. 'I'm not Mrs anyone, but can we leave it till the morning? I'm really flaked. We've been travelling eighteen hours.'

In the morning, she'll probably send us packing, tell us to go home. Except there isn't any home.

I sit down at the dressing table which has a string of miniature light bulbs round the mirror, like film-stars have in Hollywood, and real porcelain powder-bowls. To tell the truth, I feel a bit uneasy, let loose in all this luxury. I mean, some poor sods in Vauxhall are living seven to a room, with mould on the wall instead of goddesses, and a smelly outside loo. Jan's place isn't bad, but it's still smaller than the bathroom here.

I can see Norah in the mirror. She's slumped right over, falling off the seat. I suppose I ought to haul her into bed, have a kip myself. Yet it feels all wrong to arrive somewhere so exotic and way-out and just tamely go to sleep.

'Fancy a quick flutter at roulette, Norah? Or a few hundred topless dancing girls?'

No answer. I wouldn't mind a drink. There's no sign of our champagne, though. It was promised in the package – a magnum of Bollinger awaiting our arrival. I presume the computer got that wrong as well.

'Norah, champagne or Ovaltine?'

Ovaltine's the magic word, seems to wake her up. She peers in my direction, head weaving like a silkworm's, makes a little moaning noise. I think I must have overdone her pills.

Sister Watkins gave me strict instructions, but poor Toomey seemed so anxious on the last part of the trip – refused to eat her scones, kept telling me she hadn't stolen them.

I lead her to the bed, heave her up on one half of the heart, try to take her clothes off. She's heavy, uncooperative. I remove her shoes, struggle with her suit buttons. For the first time, I admire the Beechgrove nurses. In the end, I leave her suit-top on, and a thermal petticoat in flesh-pink flannel stuff. She hasn't got a nightdress, hasn't even got a change of clothes until her case shows up.

I turn the satin sheets back, tuck her in. She keeps licking her lips and swallowing, seems confused and feverish. I stare down at her pale and sweaty face, brush the limp hair from her forehead. Although she's lying down now, I can still feel her weight around my neck. All the Beechgrove staff tried to talk her out of going, even after my marathon with Matron, whom I silenced in the end with my borrowed legal skills. My law-school friend even wrote a letter for me on paper stolen from a posh solicitor, pointing out Norah's legal rights. That may have done the trick, or maybe just the fact that with Beechgrove closing and everyone and everything disrupted, Matron had more vital things to fuss about. What if she was right, though, and Norah goes to pieces? I could even have poisoned her or something. Those drugs have side effects.

She's quiet now, deathly quiet, not even swallowing.

'Norah!' I shout. She opens her eyes. They look glassy and unfocused, but at least she's still alive. I thank God automatically, wish I were more sure that He existed. I feel horribly alone – alone in a hotel with five thousand inmates. That only makes it worse. I'm just a tiny fraction of some huge great tourist-camp, issued with a number as if I were a prisoner. Our suite is number 2024. The door is shut and bolted. Cindy advised us to keep it on a chain in case of break-ins (despite her boast that the Gold Rush employs twice as many security guards as the police force of an average town). There's no sound at all, no human voice or radio, no burst of music or passing car. The walls are soundproofed, insulated. A five-star padded cell.

I unchain the door, look out. No one. Just that stretch of ritzy corridor, and spiky shadows from the bowls of hothouse flowers. Even a mugger would be company, another human face. I suppose I could explore, whizz down in the lift again, stroll through the casino, order a meal with thunder-while-I-eat. I've lost all track of time – their time, our time – but the Gold Rush glitters twenty-four hours a day. That was in their Bible. Yet restaurants and casinos seem somehow still more threatening. I've never gambled in my life and waiters in those tailcoat-things always make me nervous. Anyway, how can I leave Norah? She's not used to sleeping on her own, might wake in pain or panic.

I close the door, pace up and down the carpet. The pile's so deep it's lapping at my feet, muffling any noise. I feel it's trying to stifle me, suck me into it. I'd better watch TV, find some serial or soap-opera, something comforting and witless which will act as a sort of sedative, lull me off to sleep. I press a button on the set which is white (of course) and mounted on a fancy stand with side-wings. A man in a dinner jacket with a red bow-tie and matching cummerbund is standing by a green baize table explaining double odds. I try to switch channels, but the red bow-tie keeps smiling, talking very fast. 'The same rule applies as if the shooter was making a first roll: if the next roll is seven, you win; if it's two, three or twelve, you . . .'

I feel confused, even slightly scared. They give us all those gambling chips, but what if I don't understand the games? Anyway, the whole prize thing is chancy now. No champagne, so maybe no chips either. Or free confetti instead. A computer could turn you into anyone – not just a bride, but a millionaire high-roller, or a bankrupt or cut-throat or a Sicilian mafioso. It could even lose you altogether, simply wipe you off the files. Maybe that's why Norah's weak and gasping – the computer is unplugging her, doesn't want her here.

I press another button. The red bow-tie returns. He's on to blackjack now. 'A tie is a standoff and nobody wins. If the dealer hits a . . .'

These must be the free gambling lessons offered in our rooms. I had imagined live ones, and certainly didn't realize they would hog every TV channel on the set. Perhaps the thing's fouled up, or I'm pressing the wrong buttons. I try again. The same tuxedoed smile, but different spiel – a free plug for Las Vegas. '. . . Biggest adult playground in the globe; entertainment capital of the world.' His eyes seek mine, seem to bore right into them. 'You owe it to yourself to try these games, try them all, make yourself a winner, change your life.'

That phrase again. Do I really want my life changed? I could win and still be lonely.

I turn him off, reach for the room-phone to ask how I get Dallas, and suddenly there's a hammering on the door, a really thunderous knock. I freeze. Full-frontal photographs of muggers, mafiosi, millionaire high-rollers who have mistaken our suite for theirs, flash lurid through my mind.

'Who is it?'

'Room service, madam.'

That could be a ploy. Easy to say 'room service' and then lunge in with a knife. I creep towards the door, glue my eye to the spy-hole. I can see a Christmas tree. I unhook the chain, open the door a centimetre. The tree walks in, on bellboy legs. A waiter follows, the frightening tailcoat kind, with an icebucket on a sort of silver pedestal. The Bollinger. Behind him is a waitress with a huge film-star bowl of fruit, and a second girl with two silver goblet things. I watch, amazed, as the procession files right past me, through a flush white door I'd assumed was just a cupboard, into another room I haven't even seen – a palatial sort of dining-room-cum-lounge. The four unload their goodies, and I'm suddenly a prize-winner, official and computer-certified, as the champagne cork explodes across the room and golden bubbles froth into the goblets. The bellboy is fussing with the Christmas tree, the white-gloved waiter shining up the fruit-knives. I smile at them, but their faces stay like masks.

I wish they'd stick around, make a little party. But it's like the hospital again – inmates versus staff – impossible to bridge the gulf. They're already at the door, bowing and salaaming, bidding me goodnight. It must be night (official) and they've turned it into Christmas with the tree. I feel touched and close to tears. It's such a glamorous tree – golden boughs with tiny golden birds on them, shining golden balls, gold star at the top.

My father always bought a real tree, the sort which sheds its needles and drove my mother mad. She made him stand it on a dust-sheet and kept hoovering around it, so that all the tinsel trembled and half the things fell off. We never had expensive decorations, only bits and pieces made of silver foil or milk-tops, and some wooden pegs Dad dressed in bits of lace and stuff as dolls, painting in their faces with smiling mouths and kiss-curls. Every December, from the time I was six or seven right up to last year, my mother said, 'Surely you're too old now for a tree?' I used to die inside, imagining no tree, no smiling pegs, no Christmas Eve wobbling on the ladder. But my father always worked the Christmas miracle, braved my mother's nagging.

It was a Beechgrove tree this year, Beechgrove everything. We had senile turkey yesterday and pre-sliced Christmas pudding, semi-cold; and all the staff wore tinsel on their caps and were fiercely and continuously jolly which made things quite a strain. (Though half the patients in Norah's ward didn't even realize it was Christmas. I envied them. I even envied Norah, who just ploughed on with her jigsaw whenever there was a break in all the whoopee.)

I sit stiffly at the table, goblet in both hands. It seems wrong to drink alone, especially with that second glass still spitting bubbles at me. I wonder if I'll ever have a honeymoon. I'd like to be a couple. It must be far less frightening to be joined and vowed to someone, one flesh and one heart. I've never been that close to anyone. Even with Jon, I felt awfully sort of separate. All the same, I'm missing him, feeling almost randy. All this crazy luxury sort of turns me on – satin sheets, fur rugs.

I have to smile when I think of Jon on satin. Once he'd moved into his lodgings, he never bothered with sheets and things at all – or pyjamas either, come to that – just a rumpled sleeping-bag rolled out on the mattress. I shut my eyes to see him in it: dark head and sturdy shoulders sticking out of the top, one hand flung across his middle, nails bitten to the bone; phone numbers and memos scribbled on the palm in smudgy ink. I watch him getting up: the four hairs on his tummy (he was very proud of those), the black shock lower down, his size eleven feet tripping over things. I still miss him quite a lot.

I wish he hadn't left me. I've been worrying ever since that it wasn't just the court case, but the fact I wasn't good enough in bed. That's something you can never really gauge. I mean, you can't compare yourself with friends, when it's such a private thing, and there are no official gradings, like for eggs or civil servants, so that at least you'd know you'd made it. It's not that I don't come — I do — but I'm always worried that other girls come better or more quickly, or take huge cocks down their throats and still don't gag, or have it twice a day. I've only done it eight times in my life — eight and a half if I count the Irish boy — and not at all since Beechgrove. The pills just killed it, even thoughts of it, damped down everything: grief, death, ambition, sex. I've stopped them now. Dr Bates said not to, but I didn't want a Vegas dulled with Valium.

I push my chair back, get up to inspect a statue in a niche — a naked Grecian boy with all his vital bits and pieces sculpted in. He's marble like the floor, hard and chilly marble. I walk up and down that floor, just to hear my footsteps, prove I'm still alive. It echoes and applauds. Wonderful. I stop at the window, push aside the curtain, gasp when I realize how high up we are. Below is the main street — what they call The Strip. Strip is such a small word — strip of paper, strip of lino, strip of sticking-plaster — crazy word for that huge great shining switchback of a street. Lights cascade like fountains, spin like catherine wheels; colours eat each other up, spit out showers of sparks. I can't see any people. I suppose I'm too high up to make them out, but it feels more as if they've all been marched away, locked up in their cells.

It's still completely silent. The cars have muzzled engines, thick padding round their wheels. I check my watch. It's stopped. Not much point rewinding it when I don't know what the time is. There isn't any time. I'm in a sort of limbo where it's dark and night for ever, and nothing's fixed or certain any more. I'm almost missing Beechgrove — the comfort of the timetable which served up time in small and easy portions; day and night always carefully divided into different pills and rituals; clocks ticking reassuringly so you couldn't lose your bearings. It must be worse for Norah. She's had timetables for over fifty years.

'Norah,' I say softly. I need to try my voice out, make sure they haven't gagged me. It seems ages since I spoke last, at least to anyone who answered. 'Jon,' I beg. 'Come back.' Or Jan. Yes, Jan, I'd like you here.

Jan went home for Christmas, a whole six days ago, wangled some extra time off. I'd love to have gone with her, if only for a day or two, but her mother doesn't invite me since the court case. My own mother is unwell, which is what she calls it when the Cure has failed (again) and the doctors re-admit her. She didn't even write or send a card. I felt really wretched yesterday. It was quite the loneliest Christmas of my life. The only thing which saved it was thinking of today – the holiday, excitement.

It's hard to feel excited on your own. I trail back to Norah, who is breathing very heavily, a hoarse and whistling sigh with every in-breath. Even if I wanted to share the bed with her, there wouldn't be much room, despite its size. She's sprawled right across the heart diagonally, lying on her face like a baby in its cot. I steal two pillows, ease the bedspread off, lug them into the other room, make up my own bed on a white velvet sofa with a white goatskin rug in front of it. I feel like some rejected spouse who's just had a quarrel with her other half. No one's meant to sleep alone in Vegas – brides with bridegrooms, gamblers with their moneybags, even the mafiosi with their molls. I'm beginning to wish I'd never come at all.

I get up to switch the lights off, but instead of blessed dark, there's a blaze of coloured light-effects, my own private light-show echoing the one outside. I blink as blue and silver breakdance on the ceiling, turquoise chasing pink. The damn thing won't turn off. 'Fucking hell!' I say, as I creep back to the sofa, hide my eyes. Even so, it's impossible to sleep. The sofa's sort of bony, and my waistband feels too tight. I peel my skirt and tights off, toss them on the floor. Some passing genie will probably pick them up. I haven't unpacked yet and my nightie's at the bottom of the case. Who wants nighties in this heat? I'd rather have a nightcap.

I pour out more champagne, raise my glass to the statue in the niche, the naked Grecian boy. 'Cheers!' I say. 'Nice to have you here.'

He's staring at my bush, one hip pushed towards me, mouth half-open, pouting. I touch a finger to his prick, shiver suddenly. I feel strange, hot, even though I'm half-undressed. I undo the fiddly buttons on my blouse. The boy's watching me, excited. I drape it round his shoulders, unhook my bra. It's a relief to take it off. I go up closer, press my naked tits against his cool white marble chest, feel my heart beating into his. I wish he had a real heart, real flesh arms to cuddle me. He seems to move, in fact, as the coloured lights keep flashing on his limbs, joining our two bodies. My nipples have gone stiff. I'm almost frightened. Can marble turn you on, or is it the champagne?

I take the bottle with me to the sofa-bed, lie back on the pillows, touch my breasts. Jon was always rather rough with them. He hated the word 'foreplay', was so keen to shoot his bolt, he hadn't that much patience for the slow-and-gentle bit. I stroke them sort of gingerly, then grope my hand down lower. I feel dry and out of practice, a genuine virgin-bride. I lick my finger first this time, try a dab of spit, but my mouth seems dry as well. I tip up the champagne, let a trickle run between my legs. It's stinging cold and shocks. I stifle a yell, then touch the rim of the bottle against my . . . my . . . I hate the word cunt. It sounds so brazen. But vagina is embarrassing and 'front passage' is pure hospital. Jan calls hers her starter-motor, and Jon christened mine Abigail, which I suppose is as good a name as any.

Abigail is moistening, though not from the champagne, which has mostly trickled off and soaked the bedspread. I keep jabbing with the bottle neck. It's cold and very hard. I have to stop myself from crying out – I daren't risk waking Norah, shocking her. She hasn't got an Abigail, was probably born without one, and even if she did have, those endless pills would have atrophied it by now. I'm beginning to understand about the pills. They're given for the staff's sake, not the patients'. Things like sex or anger, or even love and happiness, are all potentially dangerous, may result in noise or extra work. Best to lop them off, damp them down. I can see their point. I'm scared myself, feeling almost violent down below. A finger isn't long enough, or strong enough, and the bottle is too full. I shut my eyes. I can see all the pictures in the other room – Bacchus squashing grapes between his body and a nymph's; Apollo taking Cyrene from behind. I suppose they're meant to rouse the bridegrooms, give them new ideas, but if you haven't got a bridegroom . . .

I'm hot and restless still, can feel Apollo's nails digging into my shoulder as he slams against my bum; that tiny smirking Cupid biting both my nipples. I put the bottle down, fumble for the cork. It's time I gagged myself, shut up shop, before I go too far. The cork fits perfectly. I try it both ways up. Upside-down is nicer, the metal bit cold and hard and edgy against Abigail. It doesn't shut her up, though, only makes her greedier. I'd better be careful or the cork might disappear. Imagine ringing for a doctor and having to explain you've lost a cork inside you.

The bottle's safer, really, though still too full to manoeuvre very well. I daren't drink a whole magnum, and half of it is Norah's anyway. I drift back to the table, unstack the fruit bowl, pile peaches, lychees, mangoes on a tray (the pineapple's so perfect, it looks sculpted), then tip out the champagne into the bowl. I return to the sofa with the empty bottle.

It's much easier with it empty. I can move more, relax more, let both of us go wild. I pause for breath a moment, stroke its cool glass back. It's beautiful, that bottle, hard and smooth and heavy in my hands. I wish it had a voice, though. I try to make it speak, tell me it loves me and I'm great. I often do that when I'm all alone, imagine people – two or even more – all saying I'm sensational. It's safer really, just pretending. You can't disappoint them then, or risk a baby. I close my eyes. It's Jon's voice I imagine, but it comes out like my father's, deeper and more smoky.

'Sweetheart, you're sensational.'

'I'm *not*, Dad.'

I put the bottle down. The game is getting serious. I'm not

sure I want feelings, not at all. My top bit's close to tears, yet my bottom bit's still slavering. I'm also starving hungry. It's hours since we last ate, and drinking always makes me ravenous. I go and fetch some fruit, refill my goblet from the bowl. I'll have a little picnic on the goatskin rug. I sit crosslegged among the nectarines and mangoes, fur tickling my bare bottom; gulp some more champagne. I'm no longer quite a hundred per cent stone-cold clear-eyed sober. The bubbly's probably stronger over here, vitamin-enriched or fortified with hormones. And those flashing lights don't help, make me feel more pie-eyed than I am. I scoff three peaches, bite into a fourth. They're so huge and juicy, I'm almost full already. I giggle suddenly, uncross my legs, press the bitten piece of peach against Abigail. It feels cool and silky. Smashing. I move it round, so the downy velvet skin is touching her, tease it gently up and down her open mouth. She drools, begs for more. I try a lychee next. They're so small, they go right in, first scratchy and unskinned, then slimy peeled. (I'm glad they brought the fruit knives.)

I even try the pineapple, uncut. That's wild, really rough and prickly, almost hurts, especially the leaf bit on the top. 'Leaves!' shrieks Abigail. 'More like bloody loofahs.' She prefers the lychees. I peel a second one. It's moist and sort of squelchy like Abigail herself. Why don't they put lychees in the sex books? Or whole fruit salads? The grapes are good as well, especially cut in half. Bacchus should be here. It was his squashy purple ones which gave me the idea. Why not have a party, invite all the gods (not the goddesses) – Bacchus and Apollo, Mercury and Mars? At least we've got the strobe lights and the space. I dip a strawberry in champagne, slurp it down, stagger up to fill my glass again. I remove a rose from the arrangement on the table, stick it in my hair, admire myself in the antique gilded mirror. Yeah, Dad's right. I look sensational – breasts dappled pink and turquoise, silver nipples standing up.

We need more guests, though, more lovers to admire me; maybe all the other people from all three thousand rooms. This is Vegas, so they're probably all in action at this moment – three thousand couples screwing, or maybe more than couples, maybe orgies. I lie back on the sofa (the floor's too hard), close my eyes so I can see them all more clearly, join in with my finger – swarthy gangsters pawing long-legged show girls; reckless drunken bridegrooms splitting hymens; heaving bodies diluting hot jacuzzis with cold sperm. I'm giggling, can't stop giggling. Don't know why. Odd to giggle when you wank. (Jon used to call it 'wank', but I'm not sure if it's the same word when a woman does it.) Oh God! Oh Jon! – it's wonderful. Hold on a sec, I . . .

Oh Christ! Again. Fantastic. The sofa's really shuddering, its legs whining on the marble; the entire hotel swaying and vibrating, twenty thousand bed-springs gasping out in time with me. How could I be lonely with all those people, all joining in, all wanting me? I'm still not even tired yet, so why not more hotels? Cindy told us there are sixty thousand hotel rooms in Las Vegas, including all the small motels and annexes. Okay – let's have them all. And why stop at Vegas or even at Nevada, when there are all the other States, a population of – what did Norah's guide book say – two hundred something million? And how about the other thousand millions on the globe? I'm so hot, so gaping open, I've room for every one of them.

I'm panting, out of breath, as my finger takes the world with it – Indians, Chinese, Eskimos with fur-trimmed pricks. I'm slipping off the sofa. Oh, God! That fur's incredible. I'm coming. So's my Eskimo. Mutual orgasm. Not just me and him, but all the million millions coming with me, coming with one shudder, one cry which frightens God; makes Him wonder why He made sex in the first place. Such a stupid thing.

I rest my finger. Strange how quiet it is for a party of that size. Not a sound, except the frantic silent pounding of my heart. They must have all gone home – had their come and left me. That's typical of men. They shoot their bolt, then bugger off, fall asleep, lose interest. I suppose I must have shocked them. I've never been so wild before, so demented sort of greedy. It must be those damned pills – coming off them. They've been acting like a sort of chastity belt, keeping everything locked in, but now Abigail's unplugged she's gone berserk; determined to make up for all those doped and muzzled months.

I snatch the rose out of my hair, ram her with the hard and thorny stalk end. That'll teach her. I jab and jab until I'm actually in tears. The feelings are too terrible. Not just the thorns − they're nothing − but the misery and fury and the awful lonely greediness, and not knowing who I am and what I want, and disappointing people, and my father and my father and . . .

'Dad,' I whisper.

'Sweetheart?'

His arms are round me, strong and careful arms, fingers stained from a life and death of Rothman's. He's found a handkerchief. He always had clean hankies, big white coping ones. 'All right now, pet?'

I nod, wipe my nose, try to hide my face. I look awful with red eyes.

He helps me up. 'Shall we go and find a café, have a meal together? Share a curry?'

'Go away!' I shout. 'You're dead, you're *dead*. You can't eat curry. And you haven't got real arms. You're just like all the rest of them − paint and marble. Nothing.'

I blunder back to the bedroom. I've got to talk to someone, someone real. At least the lights are kinder there, two quiet bedside lamps casting soft blue shadows on the white.

'Norah!' I beg. 'Norah, please wake up.'

She doesn't, only murmurs. She's lying on her side, no longer sprawled diagonally, but curled up in one bulge of the heart. I creep round to the other side, slip between the chilly satin sheets. I stretch my arms right out − still can't touch her − turn on to my back. There's my second self, my other half, upside-down in the mirror on the ceiling, face blotchy-red, hair lank.

'Fright!' I mutter to myself. 'Stupid greedy slag.' My bridegroom mumbles something. 'What?' I say, edging a bit closer. It's difficult to hear her when she's got her back towards me, like a barrier.

'I didn't, Sister,' she whimpers in her sleep. 'Didn't steal the clouds.'

8

'Stop!' I yell. 'Go away. Get off. Get bloody off.' His truncheon is as big as a champagne bottle, his eyes are green glass goblets, his smile is a bow-tie.

'Get *off!*' I struggle up. Thank God they've sounded the alarm. I can hear it shrieking very loud and close. Someone ought to come now. I grope my hand out, unstick my gummy eyelids. I'm holding not a truncheon, but a telephone.

'What? Yes, that's right. Hallo. I'm sorry, I was dreaming. *Who?*'

The deep male voice repeats its name and title. Virgil Seymour Hackett. The Welcoming Committee and Assistant Vice President of Guest Relations. Phew! Can all that be one man? He sounds like more than one as he pours out words in torrents. Isn't it just great we won the prize? How thrilled the Gold Rush is to have us stay, and how he himself just can't wait to meet us both.

I hope he'll wait at least until I'm dressed. I tug the blankets up, conceal my naked body. I've got a nasty feeling he can see it anyway. American phones probably have those tele-screens inserted. I start tarting up a bit, combing my hair with the fingers of my free hand, smiling as I talk, in case he's watching.

'Yes, that arrived; yes, lovely. No, it's okay about the room. I told the girl actually, phoned down last night and . . . You'll move us? Well, it doesn't matter, really. We're quite happy. Oh, I see, you've got a lot of genuine honeymooners. Lucky them! Yes, thank you. Yes, you said. Yes, of course I'm thrilled I won.'

He must have won *his* prize for hype. He's said 'congratulations' six times and 'welcome' seven, and I've lost count of all the 'great's. Now he's back to moving rooms again. We're not to repack our suitcases, not to lift a finger. The maids will do it all.

I flop back on the pillows. I'm not feeling all that marvellous. 'Look,' I say. 'I haven't unpacked them yet, to tell the truth. And anyway, we've only got one case. My friend's was lost en route.'

Yeah, he knows. That's been taken care of. That's partly why he phoned. The clothes are on their way.

'Clothes?'

He starts explaining. The Gold Rush has its own exclusive fashion store, so if any guest needs anything from ski-wear to bikinis, the hotel can provide it.

'That's very decent of you, but my friend doesn't ski or swim. And I'm pretty sure she'd rather wear her own gear. She's not really into fashion. Hold on a sec, I'll ask her.' I hump over in the bed. 'Norah, would you like . . .? *Norah?*'

She's not there. What I took for Toomey is a pile of pillows, a humped-up bulge of blanket. I'm lying all alone in that huge deserted heart. I fight a surge of panic as I think back to last night – Norah's moans, her sweaty ashen face. Supposing she's pegged out? No. Even in my drunken state, I'd have heard the doctor come.

I slam down the receiver, sprint into the dining room, still naked. Half-eaten soggy peaches, the ripe smell of fruit and booze. No Norah. I try the bathroom next. The door is locked. Thank God. She's merely washing. Baths are scarce at Beechgrove, so she's probably making up for twenty tubless years.

'Norah?'

Not a sound. Fear knifes my gut again. I saw a movie once where a girl drowned in a bath. She'd been taking pills, slipped back, slid sideways and immersed her face. *I* dished Norah out her pills. Too many.

'Norah, let me in this minute.'

The door handle is moving, just twitching very feebly, but at least it is a sign of life. 'Are you all right?' I shout.

I can hear her muffled answer – can't make out the words,

but the fact it's words at all means her head and voice-box must be safely above water. I'm probably worrying far too much. I've never had a sister or a brother and the responsibility's beginning to get me down.

I drag back to the bed, change my mind halfway. Now I'm up, I'll stay up. We're meant to be at some Welcome Champagne Brunch, though the word champagne has already lost the glamour it had two days ago. Still, if it's free, we'd better drink it. I riffle through my case. What does one wear to a Las Vegas champagne brunch? I settle for a pair of dungarees and a sort of low-cut sparkly blouse on the grounds they can't both be wrong. It's gravy-stained Crimplene for poor Norah, unless they hurry with those clothes. I'm quite impressed, in fact. Virgil Whatsit Hackett said he'd contacted our airline twice already and would keep phoning through the day, but not to worry – anything still lost could be instantly replaced. I wish they'd kit me out as well as Norah. My dungarees have faded and there's a Players No. 6 burn on the pocket, though perhaps that's quite appropriate.

'Norah, don't get dressed. They're sending up some clothes for you.' I hate shouting through locked doors. 'Norah, can you hear me? And can you get a move on? I need a pee myself.'

She shuffles out, wearing her brown shoes and just the petticoat. Her face is pale, sort of greyish-pale like porridge made with water.

'Gosh, are you all right, love?'

She nods, then shakes her head. I slip past her to the bathroom. It stinks – a really bad smell, disguised with strong cologne. I pee as quickly as I can, return to her.

'Norah, have you been sick, or something?'

'No.'

'Are you okay? You sure?'

'Yes.'

'Honest?'

'Yes.'

'Ready for your brunch, then?'

She looks confused.

'Breakfast,' I explain. 'Plus lunch. Both at once.'

She shakes her head – twice – as if once for breakfast, once for lunch.

'Look, you've got to eat, Norah.' She's had nothing since that itsy bit of chicken on the plane. God, I wouldn't be a nurse. The strain.

There's a sudden knocking on the door. I've no worry left for muggers, so I open it quite brazenly, without even looking through the spy-hole. It's a Cindy double with the clothes. If I were feeling less hung over, I might have been excited. They're expensive clothes in those highly-strung materials which tend to sulk and tremble if you so much as rinse them through, let alone dump them in a launderette. The problem is they're totally wrong for Norah. I don't mean the size – they've got that right, remarkably right, considering that they only saw her as a slumped shape on a sofa. Even the colours are fairly reasonable – no scarlets or magentas. But a tracksuit and a cocktail dress, a pair of cream linen jeans with a leather belt and overstitching, a lace negligé and nightie set in pink, six pairs of camiknickers . . .

I suppose the tracksuit is the safest, but even that's got gold stripes down each leg and 'GR' emblazoned on the chest. The dress is quite impossible, at least for Sunday brunch – backless with bead appliqué-work. I leave it on the sofa, grab the tracksuit. Norah has disappeared again, re-emerges from the bathroom looking worse. It's not porridge I'm reminded of, but ashes.

'Look, love, why don't you lie down and I'll have brunch on my own. I can always bring you up a snack.'

'No, please don't go. Don't leave me.'

'Okay, keep your hair on. I just thought if you weren't well . . . By the way, we – er – wear tracksuits here for brunch.'

She lets me help her on with it. It's quite a struggle. I don't think she's worn trousers in her life and these are tightly ribbed around the wrists and ankles and don't have any zips. I'd lend her a skirt or something from my own case, but I'm a different shape completely and wear my things pretty short and tight.

She looks awful, sort of comic, and yet completely hang-dog miserable, standing very stiffly as if the tracksuit were a strait-jacket, but with her head drooping down.

'Ready, then?'

She doesn't answer, so I take her arm, unchain the portcullis of a door, and steer her along the passage to the lift. We hardly seem to move at all, but the lights are flashing down down down, from the two-thousands to just two. Two is the floor marked 'Restaurant' and we step out into gold and turquoise carpet and swoony music. We're in some huge anteroom, fierce with chandeliers; the longest queue I've ever seen snailing past rows and rows of slot machines. I treat the queue like a river, follow it to its source, where two men in dinner jackets are directing operations.

'Miss Toomey and Miss Joseph,' I announce, standing in front of Norah so that I hide, if not her head, at least her chest. Norah's chest is not the sort which needs attention drawn to it by embroidered monograms. 'We're the prize-winners,' I explain. My dungarees look wrong as well. Anything would look wrong against those swanky black tuxedos.

'I don't care who the fuck you are. You'll have to wait in line like everyone else.'

I'm really shocked. He swore. A Gold Rush top employee swearing at a prize-winner. 'Look, I don't think you've any right to . . .'

'Alberto!' The older man snaps his fingers and a security guard springs out of the shadows; a savage-looking gun in a holster on one hip and a truncheon on the other. It seems a bit excessive when I haven't even jumped the queue, not really. I trail back to the end of it, Norah tagging after. He's six foot six, that guard, and they probably shoot to kill here.

Norah has her eyes closed, so I prop her against the wall, and pass the time making up stories about all the different people in the room. A lot of them look really rather ordinary, and elderly – no more sequins like I saw last night, or bow-ties and cummerbunds. It's odd that the staff should dress more grandly than the guests. Not just those two tuxedoed Nazis, but even the girls giving change or nannying the slot machines are kitted out in dazzling gold and scarlet, with plunging necklines and very brief frilled skirts. Their black-seamed legs totter down to three-inch-heeled gold sandals, frilly scarlet garters on one thigh. Their glamour has rubbed off on the machines. I've played a few fruit machines back home – boring ones in tatty pubs. These are solid gold. Well, I suppose it's only brass, or fake, or something, but they look like gold, and there's so many of them you feel they're more important than the people. And each one has a matching seat, not just a stool, but a gold vinyl shiny seat with padded back and arms. No one expects you to suffer while you win.

Everybody's winning. I watch a woman so obese she overlaps two seats at once, fill two large plastic cartons with her loot. The cartons are stacked by each machine and look like giant-sized yogurt pots, except they're monogrammed like Norah. If you stay here long enough, you probably get branded with 'GR' right through to the flesh and end up like a stick of rock. Several men are halfway there already, wearing baseball caps with 'GOLD RUSH' printed on them, GR metal badges on their sweatshirts and GR plastic cartons in each hand.

The fat woman starts to play again, three machines in turn, stuffing them alternately. Maybe she's dieting herself and this is her indulgence. She certainly seems deprived, the way she crams the coins in, hardly waiting till they've dropped before she pulls the lever – two levers, three; greedy eyes on plums, oranges, fat and ripe red cherries. Her hands are black, black from filthy lucre. She wipes her face with them, leaving a grey streak. Coins are overflowing both her pots, but she's still not satisfied. She's a woman with three stomachs, three huge and gaping mouths. She'll faint if she stops stuffing, die from malnutrition. A waitress wiggles up to her, revives her with a cocktail, a long-legged glass with two striped scarlet straws and thick with ice and fruit. The cocktails are free here if you play.

Her hunger is infectious. I begin to feel weak and empty myself, long to cram and gorge. My hands are itching to pull those little levers, fill those plastic pots. And I've spotted something else now: 'The World's First Hundred-Dollar Slot

Machine' – it's written just above it – 'The World's First High Roller Slot'. I love that word 'high roller'. They explained it in the guide book. It means a gambler, one who really spends, pours out his money on the tables and the slots. Vegas courts high rollers, provides them with free suites, free meals, free cars; even lays on women for them; exotic showgirls who revive them if they're flagging.

I stare at the machine. It's huge, and self-important, lit up with coloured lights and with a sort of scarlet canopy above it, as if it were a statue in some Spanish church. You have to feed it great fat silver tokens, as big as last night's fruit plates. I watch it gobble twelve in quick succession, spit out nothing in return. If I played it now myself, I'd be bound to win. The law of averages. My money's all upstairs though. They warned us in our Bible to beware of pickpockets, suggested that we lock our cash and valuables in the special private safe provided in each room. Actually, the locks were so damned complicated, I couldn't make ours work, so I hid the cash instead, stuffed it under a cushion on the sofa. Shall I slip back and fetch it, leave Norah in the queue? It's moving so damned slowly, I'll have time to go twice over.

'Norah, listen, I need some money. Can you stay here while I . . .?'

'No, no . . .' She moves out from the wall, sways a little before slumping back again. 'No, please don't . . .'

'Okay, okay. But I hope you realize you could be losing us a hundred thousand dollars.'

Norah stares in horror. I'm probably exaggerating – I'm not sure how much those jackpots pay, but if she's going to be so *feeble* all the time . . . It's so exciting here – all that whirring, clicking, jangling, and the clatter of the coins as they cascade into the metal trays, and that romantic stirring music still playing in the background, which gears you up, makes you feel you can only dare and win. The machines play little tunes themselves and everybody's chinking coins and chattering, so that the human noise merges with the music and the whole room throbs and hums. My headache's disappeared. I feel light and white inside, a bride.

Forty minutes later, the whiteness is a little smirched. We're still starving and still queuing. In fact, it takes a whole hour and seven minutes to rejoin the two black dinner jackets, who don't look any friendlier. I'm beginning to wonder if this is just a simple brunch, or a queue for crack-troop training or military manoeuvres, the way they shout and drill.

'Right, two more. No, not you, sir. Get back in line and wait your turn. Okay, you girls, table number 207.'

'Quick march,' I add, but softly. No point in upsetting them when we've been cleared, at last, to pass the barricades, and are being press-ganged down the passage to the restaurant.

'This way, girls. Come on, make it snappy.'

No, I have to stop, I have to. I can't just be hustled to a table before I've breathed in all the splendour. I've never seen a restaurant quite so grand. It's more like a coliseum, fused with some gigantic greenhouse. The ceiling is a huge glass dome tangled with real grapevines. At least, I think they're real; the bunches of black grapes are so perfect, so highly-shined and burnished, they may be just pretend. There are plants all round the room, acres of them, all vibrant green and bursting with rude health. Now I understand why the Gold Rush needs two hundred indoor gardeners (which is ten times more than the number of psychiatrists at Beechgrove, and half of those are still training).

The food is the real show, though. It's all set out on tables in the centre of the room, which is lower than the sloping sides, and so really forms a genuine auditorium. Each table is circular itself, dressed like a bride in white, with lacy petticoats and a bouquet of pastel flowers. And the food – holy Christ! – the food! Where do I start, for heaven's sake? I don't mean eating, just describing it. It looks too beautiful to eat. There's a huge pink creamy salmon thing, shaped like a fish with silver fins and swimming on a sea of shredded lettuce, and a pâté which has been made into a peacock with real peacock-feathers rainbowing from one end, and an olive-eyed head and beak the other, and a ham with a paper crown on, and tribe-sized joints of meat being carved by tall white chefs, and every type of salad, cake, pastry, egg-dish, vegetable, and, oh, a meringue swan filled with strawberries, and more exotic fruits soaked in brandy and champagne. And the champagne itself, bubbling out of what looks like a garden hose which can fill twenty glasses in as many seconds and is attached to a sort of refrigerated cabin-trunk, with ten spare trunks lined up behind and . . .

It's no good, I'm being frogmarched on, past the food, past two hundred frothing glasses, past the cornucopia of fruits and *boulangerie* of croissants, to a scarlet-clothed table set with gold-medallion place-mats, and squashed so close to a swarm of other tables we can hardly squeeze in. There's a statue on the table – a white ram on its hind legs, curly horns wreathed with fresh green vine leaves.

'Bloody hell,' I say, which I know is hardly adequate. Norah's not much better. She hasn't said a word for half an hour. Jan would be delirious by now. Brunch in Vauxhall is usually baked beans, or two eggs instead of one.

'Good morning, ladies. What can I get you?'

A waitress has come gliding up to our table. Well, I suppose she's a waitress, though she's dressed more like a sultaness (or are they called sultanas?) in sort of silken robes with fake almond eyes (Max Factor) and dangling paper lotus flowers for earrings. The only problem is she's over fifty; looks quite grotesque with her crepey skin and crowsfeet contradicting all that Eastern Promise.

'Champagne for me, please.' I've got to drink some more, just so I can go back and brag to Jan. Two magnums in two days.

The sultana flashes Western-style false teeth. 'Just help yourself to that, hon. But if you'd like any other beverage, I can bring it to your table. We've got coffee, Sanka, Coke, hot chocolate, any juice you like, punch, root beer, tea . . .'

'Tea?' Tea is Norah's Bollinger, her first word in thirty minutes. Her face looks even eager for a moment.

'Yeah, sure, hon. Tea with milk, tea with lemon, herb tea, China tea . . .?'

'Just tea.'

Norah's enthusiasm is catching. 'Okay, tea for me as well,

please. Oh – and Coke.' Why not live it up a bit – tea, Coke, champagne?

'Right, two teas and a Coke, then. Diet Coke?'

'No, thanks.' I refuse to diet, not in Vegas. Vegas is for stuffing.

'Right, folks.' The sultana's terminology doesn't match her gear. I was Madam on the plane, not folks and hon. 'Just help yourselves to everything. The plates are down there with the food. Take as many as you like – no one's counting – and pile them up as often as you want. And listen, girls, those aren't just any plates. They're the largest in the world: a whole fifteen inches in diameter, specially ordered for the world's largest buffet. What we say at the Gold Rush is, "Imagine the biggest feast you can, then multiply by a hundred." Enjoy your brunch.'

'Thanks,' I mumble as she swishes off. Immediately, another girl snakes up. This one is much younger, and mostly leg and cleavage, with lashes mascara-ed so stiff and black they look like iron railings. 'Call me Barb' is written on her badge. She's carrying a clipboard and a sort of nosebag full of cash. 'Wanna play Keno?'

'Play what?' I ask. 'Barb.'

She starts explaining, pointing out the little racks with printed forms (numbered up to eighty) and crayons to mark them with, which are waiting on our own and every table, where the HP sauce and ketchup bottles would stand in boring England. Keno is apparently like bingo, but without the caller. You pick out your own numbers on a form (which Barb calls a ticket), and then, a few minutes later, twenty numbered ping-pong balls are drawn at the central Keno desk. If enough of your chosen numbers come up, you're a winner – and you can play as many tickets as you like.

Obviously time spent eating in Las Vegas is time wasted unless you're also making money.

'You ladies can win fifty thousand dollars on just one two-dollar bet.' Barb's teeth look false as well, but cosmetic false, not old-false. Her glossy scarlet lipstick has strayed on to the over-gleaming white.

'Damn,' I say. 'Our money's all upstairs.'

'Well, play after brunch then. The great thing about Keno is that you can play it wherever you are or whatever else you're doing. We have Keno runners in all our bars and restaurants, or we can bring your tickets and winnings to the slot machines or gaming tables. There's a new game starting every eight minutes, and that's twenty-four hours a day, seven days a week. And the Gold Rush has the biggest Keno lounge in all of Vegas, so if you'd rather play it there, we provide free cocktails, free hors-d'oeuvres, and special recliner chairs.'

'Okay,' I tell her. 'Later.' Just now, I want my full and undivided attention for the food. I wait until she's safely out of earshot, then, 'Come on, Norah. Charge!'

Actually, you can't charge. There are too many people and too many impediments in the shape of chairs, tables, plants and statuary (more rams and other mostly horned and horny-looking beasts). Still, it all helps to tempt the appetite, build up the suspense. I feel like someone in a fairy-tale. Will the magic feast vanish before I reach the golden dishes? Will a waiter wake me with a kiss?

Nothing's vanishing. There's more food now, if possible; the waiters far too busy to bother kissing anyone. They're sprinting back and forwards with great steaming trays of scrambled egg and so much bacon there can't be any pigs left in all the Western States. I ignore the eggs and bacon (even Vauxhall can manage those occasionally), help myself to pâté peacock, salmon, and King Ham, and as many vegetables and salads as I can cram on to the plate (which has 'GR' stamped across it, though hidden now by asparagus and palm hearts, green beans *amandine*, and seven variations on potato).

Norah is standing motionless staring at a jelly. The trouble with Las Vegas is that the words are all inadequate. Jelly is kids' party stuff, cheap and wobbly, and mostly boring red. This is a four-colour fantasy with chunks of fruit arranged in flower shapes, layered between the jelly, and shining with stars of white whipped cream. Norah takes a teaspoonful – not the cream or fruit, just jelly and just green.

'Norah, how about some protein first?'

'What?'

'You know, meat and stuff. That's pheasant there.' I couldn't tell pheasant from corned beef, but all the dishes are labelled, some in French: *Selle de veau à la francfortoise*; *galantine de dindonneau*. I take a portion of each, to improve my French. My plate looks full already until I compare it with the other plates, dipping and jostling around all the different dishes, and being dangerously overloaded by their owners. They haven't stuck to mere meat and vegetables, but have mixed sweet with savoury, swamped beef with trifle, ham with chocolate mousse. I glance back at our seats, dwarfed now in the distance, the intervening space jammed with tables, chairs and crowds. It would probably be more sensible to cut down on the trips, copy the locals and forget tedious distinctions such as first and second courses. I balance a piece of gâteau on my fish; sauce my beans with rum-and-orange soufflé; dip into the strawberries.

Norah takes a roll – the plainest simplest sort without icing, raisins, poppy seeds or cinnamon.

'Look, Norah, this is *free*.' Maybe she hasn't understood and is frightened that they'll charge for every item separately. (We'd be bankrupt if they did.) 'You can eat anything you like here, gratis and for nothing.'

She dares one pasta shell, six peas.

'Champagne?'

'No thank you.'

'Well, get some anyway. I can always drink it.'

The garden hose is still gushing into glasses. I pick out the two fullest with fewer bubbles and more body, entrust one to Norah, pick up my plate again and begin the journey back. Perilous! Crowds of hungry people are weaving through the tables in the opposite direction, colliding with Keno runners who are whisking back and forth, shouting 'Keno! Keno!' in full quadrophonic sound. I scatter 'sorry's' like confetti as I spill asparagus or soufflé on the hordes of stampeding starving. My plate looks much less brimming as I set it down, at last, on the gold medallion mat. A gold medal for persistence. My banana-cream gâteau is now soaked in vinaigrette and the hot things

89

have gone cold. Our tea is cold as well, and over-stewed. I remove the tea bag from my cup, drink a little – breakfast – before starting on the lunch.

Now I'm glad that Norah's silent. I want to simply eat, with no distractions. The last few months have all been make-and-do meals, eat-what-you're-given at the hospital, or eat-what-you-can-scrounge in the canteen. (I started chatting up the Beechgrove serving-girls who sometimes saved me buns and things which had gone too stale to sell.) I've got fatter from the stodge, but I actually feel weaker. It's time to change all that, to build strength like an athlete, strength to win – not just competitions, but jackpots, millions. There's some primitive tribe or other who eat their enemies' hearts and balls, so as to suck in all their strength. And in Russia they give ginseng to their crack troops, and pedigree dogs get Pedigree Chum. So what you eat is obviously important. I've become a patient by eating patients' food, sloppy stuff which takes away your backbone, puddings to make you puddingy, too much grease and suet so that you're wax in Sister's hands.

I start on the salmon. That's five-star food, kings' fare. And peacocks stand for glory, and strawberries in December put you in the winners' class. And palm hearts sound like palms which are emblems of triumph, and champagne's a victory drink. I eat and triumph, eat and glory, eat and win. I'm growing stronger by the forkful; my digestive juices are gleaming golden bubbles, my blood has turned to liquefied red carpet. Majestic coloured tail-feathers are sprouting from my chair-seat, paper crowns poised above my head. I'm gently gently swelling like a soufflé, rising, turning gold. It may be just champagne. I've drained both glasses now. I'm a very special vintage, château-bottled, full of fizz and grape.

'Carole . . .'

I look up. I'd almost forgotten Norah. If she sticks to rolls and jelly, she'll grow watery and feeble. I pass her a piece of peacock on my fork.

She doesn't seem to see it. 'Carole, I . . . I need to . . .'

'What? Oh, God, not the loo again. It's miles.' I'll have to go with her. She'll only lose her way or bag, or both. Well, at least I can get a fill-up of champagne. I seize both empty glasses, start the long trek down again. Maybe intimate little bistros have something to be said for them. Norah's legs are steadier than mine now. I use her to cling on to while I wait for more champagne. The hose-man grins at me.

'You don't need those glasses, honey. Just grab two full fresh ones.'

Nothing's rationed here. I love that. Rationing makes you mean and thin and bitter, like my mother who grew up as a war-baby. Even forty-odd years after VE Day, she's still trotting out her ration-books, mixing her dried egg – at least metaphorically.

I sip champagne as I saunter to the exit. Norah's walking faster. I think she must be desperate. A security guard stops us at the door.

'We're looking for the . . . er . . . loo.' What do they call it here? I try again. 'WC, lavatory, you know . . .'

No, he doesn't seem to know. 'I'm sorry, but you can't go out this way. It's an emergency exit only.'

'This *is* an emergency.' (Norah's doubled up.) 'We want the – ' I remember now – 'john.'

'You're looking for the restroom?'

'No, the john.' God, it's worse than French. Perhaps he speaks French. 'The . . . er . . . *toilette de dames.*' I add a bit more French. I'm only showing off now. Blame the French champagne.

He fingers his gun. Wrong again. He's obviously a francophobe.

'Can I help you, honey?' A woman has got up from her seat, elderly, but fighting it. Her hair is tinted pinkish-grey, her eyelids are blue and silver shutters; her smile is doubledecker, enamelled on. 'Are you gals French or something? My husband knows French – well, just a little. He was in Paris in the war. Harry!'

Harry's French is worse than mine. I stop him in mid-stumble. 'We're English,' I insist, though I'm beginning to have my doubts. 'My friend just wants . . .'

'Oh, you're English. We just love England, don't we,

Harry? We were in London this last summer – where d'you call it? – Maidenhead.'

'Maidenhead's not London.'

'Isn't it? I get so damn mixed up. It was just darling, anyway. We stayed in a hotel where your Lord Albert Tennyson wrote . . .'

'Look I'm sorry, but we've got to find the loo.'

'Loo! Remember "loo", Harry? We just died when we first heard that.'

'Well, Norah here's about to die herself unless we . . .'

'Norah? Hi, Norah. I'm Doreen. This is Harry. Harold Edward – two old English names.'

I don't think Norah cares much. She's clutching her stomach, moaning very softly to herself.

'Carole Margaret,' I say. If we get the introductions over, then maybe . . .

'So you gals want the loo? The *loo!*' she giggles. 'I'll take you if you promise to keep talking. I just love that English accent.'

She keeps chattering herself, which makes it hard for me to make the promise, let alone honour it. But at least she's outmanoeuvred the security guard who doesn't so much as blow his whistle. She links arms with both of us, prattles us along the passage towards a sign marked 'restrooms'.

'Oh, so you mean restrooms are . . .?'

Doreen holds the door for us. Wrong once more – it's not a public loo. She's brought us to her suite. There are three huge velvet sofas and the usual works of art and antique gilded mirrors hung on gold-weave linen wallpaper.

'Right, where's your bathroom?' It may sound brusque, but Norah's suffering, and if I give Doreen half a chance, she'll start pouring cocktails, or running her home-movies of Lord Tennyson in Maidenhead on the in-room video.

'Just through there, hon.'

Norah disappears. I follow. I don't want her peeing in a bidet or jacuzzi or upsetting Harry's shaving gear. I stop in shock. It is a public loo – john, toilet, *toilette*, lavatory – ten of them, in fact, with pink-veined marble floors and tooled bronze doors, and a mock-eighteenth-century oil painting in each individual cubicle, hung just above the toilet bowl. That's absurd. It looks quite incongruous to have heavy ornate frames rising out of twentieth-century toilet fittings, and you can't see the pictures anyway, once you're sitting on the seat.

I sit myself. I don't really need to go, but I like peeing onto porcelain flowers, and it makes room for more champagne. Actually, I feel a bit embarrassed pulling up my knickers with a bewigged and whiskered gentleman watching from his frame.

When I re-emerge, Doreen's disappeared. I feel a twinge of disappointment. At least she knew my name – the only one who does in all of Vegas, apart from Cindy and Virgil Whatsit Whatsit. You hear so much about Americans being friendly, inviting you to stay before you've even exchanged addresses, yet in a whole sixty-seven minutes of queuing, no one said a word to us (save one mumbled 'excuse me' when a man bumped into Norah). I peer in the mirror, try to see myself through strangers' eyes. I look better than I thought. There's no trace of the hangover. In fact, I could almost be an advertisement for some vitamin or something – cheeks healthy pink, eyes very blue and bright. I even seem slimmer, as if I've shed a few spare pounds, and that despite all the food I've stuffed. It may be just the mirror. Perhaps it's tinted, or specially angled, to make you feel good about yourself. Mind you, I'm still not tall enough and the dungarees lack class. I've always wished I was more the exotic type with high cheekbones and great smouldering tragic eyes, and my clothes designed by some wild Parisian genius with a torrid past. Or, if that's not on, I'd settle for a nineteen-inch waist, or floor-length eyelashes, or hair so startling-blonde that strangers stopped me in the street to beg for snippets of it. People call me blonde, but I'm really only fairish, and I've got this stupid wimpish dimple in my chin. Jon liked it, actually, said it turned him on, but then Jon liked freckles, too, so there's not much hope for him.

I return to Norah's cubicle, tap loudly on the door. The brunch finishes at three and there are a lot of different dishes I haven't even sampled yet.

'Are you coming, Toomey?'

'Yes. Well, no . . .'

God! Martha Mead would have been less trouble than dear Norah. Martha wears incontinence pads, does it where she's sitting. 'Norah, listen, I'll meet you back there – in the restaurant. Okay? It's just along the passage, you can't miss it.'

I have my doubts, in fact, so I wait another six or seven minutes, pacing up and down. There are three old biddies in the restroom now, reapplying make-up. I watch their faces brighten as they paint on youth and smiles. The attendant whisks away their dirty tissues, slings out age and frowns. She looks sad and old herself, a dark, foreign, brooding sort of woman, wearing a pale green nylon overall – the first work-clothes I've seen in this hotel. I'd like to talk to her, make conversation, anchor myself to someone – anyone. If it were England, I could murmur 'Awful weather', but I haven't been outside yet, haven't glimpsed the weather. Windows are the only thing on ration in Las Vegas. That dome in the restaurant is kept artificially sun-lit, even in the rain. I say 'Awful weather', anyway. She smiles – a genuine smile which transforms her face a moment, then the smile gives out and she is sad and plain again. I keep my own smile going.

'Look, could you do me a favour? My friend in there gets a bit confused. When she's finished, would you be an angel and point her in the direction of the restaurant, the big one – you know, where they're serving brunch?'

'You want brunch?' The accent is more foreign than the face.

I explain again, more slowly, and in simple Beechgrove-type words. With all this training, I could probably land a job there now.

At last the attendant appears to understand, so I leave Norah in her hands, dash towards the nearest set of lifts, soar up to my room. I can hear that 'Keno! Keno!' re-echoing in my head. Rule number one in Vegas – carry cash. Actually, cash may be a problem. The prize included some spending money as well as the free gambling chips, but it isn't all that much, and now

I've seen how greedy those machines are, and checked the minimum table-bets in our Gold Rush Gamblers' Handbook, I'm feeling rather worried. We're bound to win eventually, but it may take quite an outlay before we learn the ropes, get the hang of all the games. Before we left, Norah took out every penny she had in Beechgrove bank – a grand total of eleven pounds, six pence (her entire life savings). We've gone through more than half of that already, just buying a few items for the trip, and by the time I'd had a drink at LA airport . . .

Our suite door is wide open. I assume the worst – a break-in – no chips or cash at all now. Then I remember that they've moved us and my stint as bride is over. Yes, our things have gone and a maid is clearing up. I dash back the way I've come, passing signs en route to the Temptation Room, Santa Claus Suite and Fantasy Boudoirs. I try to imagine what our new room's like – a giant Players No. 6 pack for a bed, perhaps, with filter-tip cork pillows?

Before I find it, I pass a waterfall, an indoor waterfall, a great foaming chute of water cascading into a pool with floodlit rocks. There's a mermaid on the rocks, a jet of milk-white water gushing out of both her stiff bronze nipples. She looks obscene, one hand pushing up her breasts, one fondling her own tail.

I can still hear her thunderous breast-feeding as I insert my key into the carved wood door of suite number 436. It's so grand, it's almost frightening. There's a downstairs salon carpeted in crimson and panelled in mahogany, with a spiral staircase leading to a balcony and other rooms upstairs. Fluted Grecian columns soar up to the ceiling, a cocktail bar beneath them with blood-red padded stools. The stained glass in the window fits neither garish modern bar nor Ancient Greece. It also cuts down any light. There are two huge velvet sofas in the same oppressive red, guarding a gold table with lions' paws as its legs. I like red if it's cheerful – pillar-boxes, robins – but this is a real gory red, reminding me of smashes on the motorway, abortions, operations, the first day of the curse. There's more red round the walls, oblongs of red velvet inserted in the panelling. Each oblong frames a picture – gods again, but Victory Scenes this time; gods crowned with laurel wreaths reclining on Olympus, winning battles, deciding Destinies. My own nicotine-stained victory seems puny in comparison.

I walk slowly up the spiral stairs, admire the little balcony with its gleaming golden rails, then push the door in front of me. The entire floor space is taken up by an Olympus-sized jacuzzi (red again), surrounded by a jungle of evil-looking ferns. Next door is the bathroom, which is mercifully pastel. The bath is raised, not sunken; raised on golden lions' paws like the table in the sitting-room, with golden lion-head taps. There must be a lot of spare lion parts around – unwanted tails and torsos.

Two maids look up as I slip into the bedroom. Both are small and dark. One seems just a child still, the other sad and worn like the lavatory attendant. The elder one's unpacking my old suitcase, untangling screwed-up tights and jeans, mopping up spilt face-cream from the jumble at the bottom.

'Look, *I'll* do that.' I wrest a shoe from her, blush when I see the state of it, the toe scuffed and stained with face-cream, the heel worn down. 'I should have cleaned them, shouldn't I? And found a mender's. There wasn't time. You see, we had to . . .'

The woman backs away. She looks terrified, kneading her hands in a kind of silent prayer.

'You understand?' I ask. 'I'm just no good at packing. You're meant to fold things, aren't you, and put tissue in the folds and wrap shoes in plastic bags.'

Her face is taut with fear. She disappears a moment, returns with all my money, a pile of dollar bills and traveller's cheques, which she thrusts into my hands. I can't understand her flood of foreign words, but I can hear the pain in them, the near-hysteria. Does she imagine that I'm accusing her of stealing, about to call the management, demand she be immediately dismissed? I note the thin gold wedding band. Perhaps she has a brood of hungry children. That girl could be her eldest, sent out to work too early, to help pay all the bills. I could land up like that myself. Okay, so I've got three A levels, didn't cut my schooling, but what jobs are there for untrained eighteen-year-olds with psychiatrists' notes black-pencilling their life-reports? If I don't strike lucky here, I could find myself making beds and cleaning loos in some second-rate hotel in the back streets of King's Cross.

'Look,' I say. 'I know you didn't steal it. It was a stupid place to hide it, anyway, when you're bound to plump the cushions up. In fact, it only shows how well you do your job. I should have phoned reception, asked someone to come up and explain that wretched safe.'

She doesn't understand. She's still pleading with me, begging, in that shrill and desperate jangle. I peel a crisp ten-dollar bill from the top of the pile. 'Here,' I say. 'Take this. God! I feel like a damned superior capitalist pig handing out sops to the exploited.' I'm talking to myself, but still out loud. They must assume it's some mere variation on 'Awful weather', since the cringing terror has changed to cringing smiles. I hate myself. For staying in a $600-a-night suite when six hundred dollars would keep their entire (extended) family for a month or two; for acting like a Beechgrove Friend and feeling smug about it. I stuff the rest of my money in my handbag, have trouble shutting it. Now I'm doubly determined to win – just so I can stalk back here and hand them fifty thousand each. And a few cool thousand for that lavatory attendant. I'll win so much, I'll hire a helicopter and scatter hundred-dollar bills all along the Strip, marked 'Maids and workers only. Hands off filthy rich, especially all psychiatrists and magistrates.'

'Listen,' I say. 'This could be the last day of your lives you ever make a bed or scrub a floor.'

The smiles bob back again, though I suspect I could be saying 'chicken soup and noodles' for all they understand. Actually, they must think I'm dismissing them, because they're bowing to me, leaving, tripping down the stairs. Once they're gone, I glance around the bedroom, which I've hardly taken in yet, except the fact it's red and grand again, and with so many mirrors, I can see at least a dozen Caroles. I've obviously been cloned and these are my reserves. I grin at them. They all grin 'back. I'm feeling stronger all the time. Twelve of me to win now.

I'm also relieved to see twin beds instead of one huge double – though, once again, the language needs upgrading. 'Beds' is fine for our narrow two-foot-six affairs at Beechgrove, with their iron frames and thin and lumpy mattresses. These are thrones, or altars; raised up on sort of platform things, and made even more imposing with velvet hangings, carved and gilded wood surrounds, and crowned with swanky shields. Winners' beds.

I close the door, walk slowly down the stairs again. Winners all around me in those gloating gods. Don't *I* deserve a laurel crown? I won that competition out of thirty thousand entrants. That's not bad. And I plan to go on winning.

I touch my finger to Zeus's wreath as he sits preening on his throne on the top peak of Olympus. 'Bring me luck,' I pray.

9

I make straight for the champagne. Winners need fuelling first. The crowds are even thicker in the restaurant now, which reminds me of Wembley on Cup Final day, combined with Harrods' sale. The bubbly shows no sign of giving out, though a chain of empty canisters are lying like beached whales. Once my glass is full, I heap my plate, concentrating this time on the array of Chinese foods. I hesitate a moment over Dim Sum (dumplings) and deep-fried prawn balls, both oozing grease and calories. But a glance around the tables reassures me. I'm actually quite dangerously thin, at least compared with most of the women here. A party of seven blue-rinsed matrons (whose combined weight must top the hundred-stone mark) are gorging cakes and pastries, fat fingers scooping cream off treble chins; spare flesh dangling from vast upper-arms or oozing over chair-backs. And it's not just the women. The man beside me looks eight months gone with twins. I feel very frail and puny in comparison, help myself to five prawn balls (the pregnant man takes eight); some crispy duck, sweet and sour pork, and Hung Shao Yu because I like the name.

Our table is still miraculously free, though there's no sign of Norah yet. Did that attendant understand, or is she marching Toomey to the health spa or solarium, or booking her a private gambling lesson? I put my plate down, remove a Keno ticket from the rack. I'm here to win, not to worry. If Norah can negotiate the miles of Beechgrove corridor, then a few yards of Gold Rush passage shouldn't faze her. She's always slow, in any case, likes to take her time.

I stare down at my ticket. Can that flimsy bit of nothing, badly printed on cheap and dingy paper, really change my luck?

Yes. I must have faith. The Bow-Tie Man said luck is a great lady who rewards those who believe in her. I crayon '$2' in the upper right-hand corner, try to decide which numbers to pick out. Perhaps I'll concentrate on ones – 1, 11, 21, and so on. After all, I'm on my own, basically, so I'd better learn to like it, look after number one, as Jon's mother used to say. Jon . . . I chew my crayon. I wish I could forget him. Okay, I know he wasn't right for me, but at least he made me real. I existed in his head (and bed), as well as just in mine. I tear the ticket up, take another. Who wants ones? Lonely feeble failures.

This time I mark the twos – 2, 12, 22, etcetera – Jon-and-Carole, Virgil-and-Carole, Zeus-and-Carole – and I up my stake as well – five dollars instead of two. Risks are part of winning, and the sooner I win, the more we'll have to spend for the rest of the ten days. It's economic sense. I take another ticket – one for Norah. If the numbers are drawn just as she returns, she may feel out of things. She's been a loser all her life. Time she won, or at least participated. I decide on threes for her. This is my third ticket and threes are always lucky. I cross through 3, 13, 33 . . . No – not 13 – I score that out again, continue with 43, 53 . . . Whoa! Not too many. I think you win more cash with fewer numbers. Actually, I'm not that clear about the rules. They say Keno's very simple, but by the time I've read the (so-called) explanatory leaflet in the rack, I'm totally confused, not just by odds and numbers (and combinations of numbers), but also by special deals such as the Catch-All Rate, the High-Five Special, and the Fifteen-Dollar Combination ticket, which looks the best, since it's starred in red and printed extra large. I call the Keno girl, ask her to explain it.

'Well, honey, you pay just fifteen dollars, which gives you as many as fifteen different possible ways to win, using four groups of two combinations. Let me give you some examples . . .'

She starts showering me with dollars – dollars in hundreds, thousands, tens of thousands. All I have to do to win them is group the numbers I've already marked in twos, circling them with my crayon. I do the same on Norah's ticket. Must be fair.

'That'll be thirty dollars,' the girl says, checking both the tickets.

'Thirty?'

'Yeah, fifteen each.'

Even I can work that out. It's just the sound of it which scares me. Thirty dollars is almost a week's dole, a skirt or pair of jeans, a hundred tins of Heinz baked beans, at least two hundred eggs.

'Look, I'm not sure if . . .'

'Ya don't have that much time, honey. This game's closing in three minutes.'

I hand her six five-dollar bills, gulp my champagne, start stuffing in my food. I need courage, instant strength. Thirty dollars is *not* a load of groceries, or a few cheap chain-store clothes. It's an investment, a down payment for the future. I shovel in a piece of duck, using just my fork. The fingers of my other hand are crossed. 'Win,' I whisper between mouthfuls. 'Believe.'

The Keno girl returns with copies of both tickets and a dazzling smile. (I suppose her dentist cost so much, she's keen to show him off.) 'Good luck,' she whispers huskily.

I nod, continue eating, though I hardly taste the food. My eyes are fixed on the Keno board which is set up on the wall (several of them all around the room, so you can see one from wherever you are sitting). The numbers drawn at the central desk flash up on these boards in coloured lights, so there's no need to leave your seat. I check my watch, which I suspect is jet-lagged, actually, since I've never known it quite so slow and sluggish. Even the second-hand seems drugged. 'Come on,' I urge, swallowing my Hung Shao Yu, which could be plastic Keno-board itself for all I'm relishing the flavour. It's numbers that I'm eating, not mere food, sucking Norah's threes, spinning out slow delicious mouthfuls of my own twos and twenty-twos.

Oh, God! They're coming up now. A 48 is winking on the board, followed by an 8. I push my plate away, put the tickets in its place, use my fork as a pointer. It hovers over 22. I check the board again. No. Damn. It's 26, one I didn't mark. I glance back at the board. A 4 comes up and then a 70, a 13 (unbelievable), a 7. I cram a prawn ball in my mouth, whole, hold it there, not chewing. My stomach is a war-zone. Not one of mine or Norah's has come up yet, not one single one. But wait – more numbers – flashing up so fast now, it's difficult to check through both the tickets.

Relax, girl. If you get so damn uptight, you'll miss them when they do come up. I force the prawn ball down. It sticks halfway. I try a gulp of Coke. It tastes bitter, poisonous bitter like the fact that neither I nor Norah have marked a single number on that board. I check once more, try to concentrate. I'm new to this, and with all the noise and clatter in the restaurant, the babbling voices, clash of cutlery, not-so-background music, I could be missing things. I start at 1, go slowly down to 80, up and down each line. No – I'm right – not one. Near misses, yes: 34 instead of 33; 1 and 21, both of which I marked originally. I should have stayed a single, looked after number one.

The screen is dead now. No more flashing lights. Just twenty numbers mocking there, wrong numbers. The odds against that happening must be absurdly, unfairly high. It can't be mere bad luck – more like spiteful fate. I wasn't meant to win. I must be programmed as a loser, another Norah. My life was fine (well, bearable) until just last summer. I had a father and a future, a boyfriend and a home. All vanished now. Okay, so it's only one game, and a silly game at that, just a distraction while you're eating, not a serious distinguished game like baccarat or blackjack. All the same, it hurts. I trusted, I believed, and still it let me down. I stuffed myself with kings' food and ended up a lavatory attendant.

I push my plate away. Kings' food, hooey. Soggy batter oozing oil, mounds of slimy rice. How could I have eaten all that greasy fattening rubbish when I'm already a fat slob? I glance around me: a dumpling of a woman dressed in shiny pink, cramming in eclairs as if she's stuffing a silk cushion; a Japanese baby being force-fed by its mother, spewing out creamed spinach both sides of its mouth; an ageing gangster ripping up a chicken breast, sinking yellow china teeth into young white flesh. The noise is terrible. Not just jangling knives and forks, but the yelp of plates as the cleaners scrape and clear them, the groan and slurp of wasted food cascading into pig-bins. No pigs left – just carcasses and bones. Calves and lambs slaughtered in their thousands, pheasants shot in droves, salmon bloodying whole rivers – and all to feed us fatsos.

The background music has changed from a victory march to Christmas carols. 'Silent Night.' The 'Rest in heavenly peace' is drowned by raucous shouts of 'Keno! Keno!', a sudden bray of laughter from the table opposite. They're drunk. I ignore my own glass, fumble for my bag. I feel sick with stuffing, sick with lies. I push my chair back, struggle down to the exit, past all the loaded tables in the centre. Norah's jelly has collapsed into a multi-coloured mess; the meringue swan has a broken neck, the fish is skin and bone.

I return to the restroom. No sign of Norah, and a new attendant – a gigantic black woman wearing pink rubber gloves to match her overall.

'Norah!' I shout, as I dash through to the cubicles.

The woman follows. 'You lookin' for you friend?'

I swing round again. 'Yes, I am. Where's she gone? There was another woman here before – Mexican or something. Did they leave together?'

'No. Ramonda's gone to lunch. You friend's in here.' The woman raps a door. 'In trouble.'

'What d'you mean, trouble? What's happened?'

'She got the runs.' The attendant heaves with laughter. 'Got 'em bad. She come out, yeah, but back she go again, three times. I say to her: "That somethin' you ate, hon?" but she didn't get me. Where you friend from?'

I don't bother to reply. I'm talking to Norah, hammering on her door. 'Why didn't you *tell* me you had diarrhoea?'

Okay, so Norah's shy, fastidious, but I feel somehow hurt, left out. Friends are meant to share things, even grotty things like bowels. Jan and I discuss our bowels (and periods), breathe on each other before important dates, to check we don't need Listerine, borrow each other's laxative or tampons – or used to, anyway.

I slump against the wall. I can hear Jan's voice saying 'Bon Voyage', see her walking out as Sister rings the little bell which marks the end of visiting-time. Once she'd left – really left, for Bristol and for Christmas – I felt another awful pang (the worst one yet, in fact) that it was me and some near stranger jetting off, not me and my best friend. The feeling surges back as I bang on Norah's cubicle again. 'Are you still bad?' I shout.

She mumbles something indecipherable. The fact she's in there still is reply enough. I feel a monster dragging poor old Toomey to a sixty-five-course banquet with champagne, when she should have stuck to water and dry toast. But how was I to know? It's usually her bladder, not her bowels.

'You best get her somethin'.' The attendant has followed me again, and is listening in, hand on hip, head cocked. She's obviously enjoying this diversion, this rest from swabbing floors. 'Diar-Aid's real good. Don't clog you up for days like some of them things do. An' it's jus' a small white pill, so you friend won't have to swallow all them pints of chalky goop. There's a drugstore jus' three blocks away. You go out the back of the hotel – not the main front entrance – an' take a right, then cross the street an' . . .'

I try to follow her directions, get lost before I've even left the hotel. It's so huge, so overwhelming; too much crystal, velvet, bronze, to dupe the senses, too many attractions and distractions to trap me, hold me up. Cul-de-sacs which end in cocktail lounges, stairs which lead to bars or balconies instead of to the street, vast mirrors which confuse and duplicate, taped music to make me moon instead of march. I'm on the ground floor now, at last, drifting past a long arcade of shops. I stop, peer in a window. Perhaps there's a drugstore here in the hotel and I shan't need to brave the streets. The window glares with jewels – greedy boasting diamonds; emeralds, amethysts; great chunks and chains of gold. I walk on, past a kiddies' fashion shop selling tuxedos for toddlers and spangled plastic pants, and an Eastern bazaar offering everything from yashmaks to alligator boots – but nothing for loose bowels.

It takes me ten more minutes to locate the exit, and then it's the front one, not the back, which means about-turn and another hundred miles of daunting carpet. No one seems that eager to direct me to the back. I understand why when I finally stumble on it for myself. It's the Cinderella exit, the ugly-duckling cat-flap. Instead of golden palace portals opening on to palms and plashing fountains, this is a furtive sort of doorway, flanked with dustbins. I stare in shock. Rain, puddles, litter, an overflowing drain. This can't be exotic Vegas. All the brochures show it sunny with blue skies. This sky is the colour of smudged charcoal. Even the clouds look stained and tatty, ragged round the edges. My 'awful weather' has become a dismal fact. A waste of car park stretches on both sides. I cross the concrete, find myself in a side street, but looking towards the Strip. *Can* it be the Strip? It's a different place entirely from the Magic Colour Show of after-dark. The glitter and the sheen have disappeared. No peacock-blues, no fairy-pinks. Only drab grey pavement, ugly posters, a petrol station, a huge sign shouting 'LOANS'.

I struggle on, huddled against the rain, pass a cheap motel built of plasterboard and signs ('Lowest Rates in Vegas', 'Fourth Nite Free'), and a Woolworth's-type shop spilling its goods on to the pavement – curvaceous coffee mugs with red-nippled breasts as handles, Las Vegas tee shirts ('I Lost my Ass in Vegas'), toy fruit machines made of tin and plastic.

'Wanna fun-book?' A man steps out from the entrance of the shop, presses something in my hand. I barely glance at it, stick it in my pocket. It's too wet to stop. I'm soaked already, had forgotten I would need a coat – not just coat, but umbrella, gloves and snow-boots. It's colder than back home. Shouldn't I have crossed the street by now, and which street did that woman mean, in any case? I try to re-run her directions in my head, but they're drowned out by the drumming of the rain, the cough and belch of traffic. I stop at the lights, watch the cars flash past. Judging by the empty pavements, everybody drives here. Only losers walk. There are two huge hotels in front of me, a gap between them like a missing tooth, a vacant lot piled with builders' rubble. I cross over, take a look. I can see the desert struggling to break through – sand beneath the rusting strips of iron, grey-leaved scrubby plants pushing up between girders and old pipes. Beyond me rear the mountains: brown, bare, jagged, desolate.

I break into a run, to try to outwit the rain, but it follows, cold and sullen, slams against my back. Where in God's name is that drugstore? I've hardly seen a shop at all, except those cheap bazaars stuffed with souvenirs. No supermarkets or grocery stores, no friendly little corner-shops selling life's essentials such as bread and aspirin, milk and cigarettes. All you can buy are huge great ugly clocks with their figures made of dice or cards, naked-female playing cards, roulette-wheel key rings, nesting pairs of dice – and every type of instant meal and snack. I pass a Diet Centre wedged between 'Frankie's Foot-Long Frankfurters' and 'Have a Whopper – Visit Burger King'. I'm completely lost by now, though at least the rain is easing. I remove the soaked fun-book from my pocket. I'm not sure what a fun-book is, but it may include a fun-map. I separate the pages, print smudged from the wet. 'Thirty-nine-cent breakfast; Big Six Wheel of Fortune; craps 3 for 2 Match Play; your own personal Jackpot Photo taken next to a genuine slot machine.' No fun Diar-Aid, no free dry toast.

I've reached another set of lights. The pedestrian sign says 'STOP'. I'm glad to stop – I'm tired – jet-lagged maybe, or just fed up with trying to walk in a pair of squelching court-shoes. The rain has stopped as well. I lean against a newsstand to remove one shoe, peel off my sodden sock, squeeze the water from it. There are these little perspex newsstands at every junction, with magazines and newspapers inside. No vendors, as in England, shouting '*Standard, Standard*!' or 'Twelve killed in Armagh'. Here, you help yourself. DON'T BE ALONE IN LAS VEGAS' is printed across one stand. They must know how I'm feeling.

I open the flap, remove a magazine. 'FREE', it says, 'Take one. Adults only.' I leave my shoe and sock off, eyes on stalks as I skim through the first page. 'Classy lasses (or lads) direct to your room. Golden girls and guys available twenty-four hours a day. Call our sensual, sensational Vegas play-pals.' I stare at the pulsing bosoms, the pouting lips, the lace and whalebone corselettes, the micro g-strings. 'Call Angie Ample – the girl your mother warned about'; 'Brigitte Bardot look-alike gives French lessons – very strict with naughty boys'; 'Mistress Marilyn, experienced in bondage'. My hands are trembling. I feel disgusted, yet horribly excited. Classy Carole. Champagne Carole. Experienced in . . . The pedestrian sign says 'GO' now.

I pick my shoe up, step forward automatically, eyes still on the print. 'Double your pleasure. Two blondes are better than one. Let Blue-Eyes and Bombshell work on you together.' 'Call Dawn – prettier than a sunset . . .'

'God! I'm sorry. I didn't hurt you, did I?'

I've collided with some guy, dropped my shoe and sock. The magazine is face down in a puddle. I blush as he retrieves all three, hands them back to me. The light has changed to red again. I dither, dart back, forwards, back again, as an Oldsmobile bears down on me with hungry scarlet jaws.

'Oh, Christ!' I shout, confused by all the curses and the honks. Another car is panting on my legs, some Goliath of a driver winding down his window to add to all the uproar. Someone grabs my arm, hauls me back to safety.

'Gosh, thanks,' I say, glancing up at him. It's the same guy I bumped into – tallish, middle-aged, with greying hair, and wearing a black mac. I look straight down again. Men in macs have a frightful reputation. My mother was always warning me about men in dirty raincoats (or was it dirty men in raincoats? I don't recall. Anyway, I freeze).

'On your own?' he asks.

'Er . . . no. I'm with a friend. Just waiting for her – him.' He'll know I'm lying. I'm really scarlet now. I hate it when I blush.

'Oh, are you an escort girl?'

'No, no. I'm not. Of course I'm not. I'm just a visitor, a tourist.' I'm back by that damned newsstand and still brandishing that girlie magazine. He must assume I'm a demonstration product, a sort of on-the-spot free sample. I'm disproving all their advertising – not a golden girl in whalebone and black lace, but a drenched and wringing wreck wearing a plain white cotton Marks and Spencer bra (one strap safety-pinned), beneath mud-splashed dungarees. The Brigitte Bardot double probably looks appealing in a sack. I need props and help, and preferably dry hair. I've still got one bare foot. I stop to put my sock on, overbalance, almost topple over. The black arm is there again, steady as a rock.

'You okay?' His turn to ask me now.

'Yes, fine.' I think I must be pissed still, reeling from champagne. I don't feel pissed, just scared of him, but I suppose he's sort of saved my life, so I force a smile, let him act as prop while I ram my shoe back on.

'You must be from England with that accent.'

'Mm.'

'London?'

'Mm.'

'I've never been to England. I had a trip planned once, but . . . Hey! Watch your step.'

I'm so keen to get away from him, so clumsy from sheer nerves, I've just tripped again on on a broken piece of paving stone. He must think I'm some spastic, or completely paralytic drunk. He steadies me, steers me round the hole.

'What's your name?'

'Er . . . Jan.' I keep staring down. So many hazards to avoid.

'Nice to meet you, Jan. My name's Vic.'

'Vick?' My mind's on drugstores still. Vick to rub on chests.

'Well, maybe Victor, if you're English. I had an English buddy once and he was Edward, never Ed. Though I guess Jan's short for something, isn't it?'

'Yeah, Janice. But no one calls me that.' Too right they don't. I'm impressed, despite myself. Victor's just the name to have in Vegas. Careful, though. He may be Victor Capone.

'You look cold, Jan. Want my coat?'

'No. No, really. . .' It's the old old story. They give you sweeties (coats), then lure you into the woods. Actually, there's hardly a tree to be seen, only garish hoardings and a sign saying 'Breast sandwiches' which makes me fear mutilation as well as just plain rape. Perhaps I ought to wear the coat. My blouse has gone transparent in the rain and my own breasts may be outlined in full uncensored detail – red rag to a bull. Anyway, he's already struggled out of it and is draping it round my shoulders. Probably just an excuse to feel me up. I side-step, mumble 'Thanks', steal another glance at him.

He looks quite different in his suit, which is almost boring in its dull and formal grey, but what my father called superbly cut, and obviously expensive. I should guess he's pretty rich.

He's got a diamond in his ring, another in his tie-pin. Okay, so men in diamonds aren't my style, but this is Vegas, and half the men I've seen so far wear so much jewellery they clank. His at least is tasteful. I saw one guy with a great 3-D crucifix dangling round his neck, the dying Christ picked out in dazzling rubies.

Victor turns and smiles at me – a nice smile, shy and honest. I really like his eyes. They're a brilliant blue and very kind and gentle, not rapist's eyes at all. In fact, it was only that black mac which made him seem so sinister. I slow my pace a bit.

'Are you a tourist, too?' I dare.

'Kind of.'

I think he prefers to put the questions himself. 'Where are you staying?' he asks, before he's really answered me.

'The . . . Tropicana.' Best be careful still. 'What about you?'

'Caesars.'

'Caesars Palace?' Now I really am impressed. According to the guide books, Caesars Palace is the one hotel in Vegas which comes anywhere near the Gold Rush, both in opulence and sheer lunatic expense. He must be loaded if he's staying there, and without Players No. 6 to foot the bill.

'Do you know it, Jan?'

'Well, no, I don't. But . . .' I've seen the pictures, read about the place. Caesars is as famous as the London Ritz.

'I only come to Vegas for the poker. I've just played a big tournament Downtown, but I prefer staying on the Strip. The tourney finished a whole week ago, but Caesars Christmas sounded kind of fun, and I'd won a few bucks, so . . .'

I stop dead in my tracks. 'You're a *gambler*, a high roller?'

He laughs. 'Oh, no. I just like playing poker.'

'But if you play in tournaments and win and . . .' My voice tails off. Surely poker players don't look so . . . so ordinary? In movies, they wear hats – cowboy hats or huge sombreros, or have scars across their faces and narrowed flinty eyes, and puff on fat cigars, and carry guns.

'I like to win – who doesn't? – but it's not so much the money, more the game itself. It's fascinating, poker. It can be thrilling, or infuriating, or dangerous, or boring – sometimes all those things, and more, just in one hand. D'you play at all yourself, Jan?'

I shake my head. Helping Norah with her patience is about the limit of my skills.

'I used to have a weakness for blackjack, but it depends too much on luck – just sheer blind chance. Poker needs skills, quite a few different ones, in fact, which makes it more of a challenge. Yet luck still enters into it, and can make or break anyone. There's always that element of risk. And . . .' He grins. 'I guess risk is exciting.'

'Gosh,' I say, still staring at him. Have I missed a scar, a hidden holster? 'I've never met a poker player, never in my life.'

'Well, I'm afraid I'll disappoint you. I only play for fun. The world-class players are something else entirely. I met them at the tournament. Some of them are real flamboyant characters, but for a lot of them, there's nothing in their lives beyond the poker table, or some other form of gambling. In the end, nothing really grabs them unless they're betting heavy money on it – a hundred thousand dollars, say, on just one hole of golf, or one Sunday football game.'

'You're kidding.' I try to imagine a hundred thousand dollars, all the things one could buy and do and be with it; then losing every cent just because the Redskins beat the Rams.

'That's gospel, Jan. Their world gets so unreal that money means everything and nothing. I saw one player tip a cocktail waitress a thousand bucks, just for bringing him a Pepsi.'

'Wow!' I let out a low whistle.

'Even recreational players can get totally obsessed. Poker's like a gaol sentence for some of my old friends. They never leave the table, never breathe fresh air or see the daylight, are hardly aware there's an outside world at all. And "friends" is the wrong word. They don't have friends, not really. They play for blood. One guy lost so much he was forced to sell his kidney.'

'His *kidney*? Why?'

'It was a rare one, real valuable, and the only way he could pay his gambling debts. He'd sold everything else he owned – his house, his car, his business – even his wife, according to the rumours. And another guy I knew jumped from a high bridge, smashed himself to pieces because he'd lost a pot. It wasn't just the money. He couldn't face the fact he'd lost at all.'

I fumble for my cigarettes. I need a smoke to calm me down. Damn. I haven't got them, must have left them in the restaurant. 'Do you smoke?' I ask.

'No, I'm afraid I don't, Jan, but how about a drink? We could go to Caesars, if you like, and I could show you round the place – if you've got the time, that is.'

Carole, stop. Be careful. All you'll see of Caesars is Capone's suite. 'I'm sorry, no. I'm worried about my friend. You see, I . . .'

'Bring her along, Jan. I'd really like to meet her.'

'*Him*,' I start, then turn it into a cough. I can't make Norah male. It's too damn complicated. Already I keep looking round for Jan.

'She's . . . not too well at the moment.'

'Gee, I'm sorry. What's the trouble?'

'Sort of stomach.' I can suddenly see Norah clutching at the waistband of her tracksuit. I'd assumed she was just busting for a pee, not wracked with griping pains and voiding half her gut.

'In fact, I really must get back to her. I only slipped out to buy her some medicine. She'll wonder where on earth I am.'

I know he thinks I'm lying. Odd that he accepts the lies, disbelieves the truth. He looks not just disappointed, but quite genuinely hurt. Perhaps he's lonely, too, a single, on his own, forced to spend Christmas in hotels. I'm sure he's not a gangster and certainly not a homicidal maniac. I'd get different vibes if he were about to split my skull. He seems really rather decent, and certainly not pushy. 'If I like', 'If I've got the time'. And he's obviously dead keen, leaning towards me while we walk and hanging on my every word as if they're made of diamonds and have to be saved from dissolving in thin air. That makes me feel important.

Mind you, we must look pretty weird together – he so smart and me a sodden mess. I'm rather touched by the way he's tried so hard with his suit and jewels and everything, and those new calf-leather shoes in pigeon grey. It's his face which lets him down, though. It's too old for the shoes, and even for his eyes which are really vibrant blue – a young man's eyes. The face looks pale and tired, as if it would prefer to retire to some nice quiet English suburb and grow roses or breed dogs, instead of impressing girls in Vegas, or playing tournaments.

I can see him watching me, like a tail-down dog himself, dejected that its precious walk is over. I throw him a small bone. 'Look, maybe you can help me. I've been searching for a drugstore. That's how I got lost.'

'There's one just a block from here. I'll show you.' Tail wagging now, ears pricked.

'Thanks.'

He takes my arm again to guide me round a puddle which has flooded half the pavement. The drainage in Las Vegas is nowhere near as impressive as the food. I see a woman tutting at us. 'Arm in arm and old enough to be her father.' I grin. Perhaps he *is* a father whose beloved daughter died. Perhaps he's mourning her, wandering round the lone streets choked and desolate. I keep hold of his arm, even when we're safely past the puddle. We're almost at the drugstore. I don't want the idyll soiled with Diar-Aid. I'd rather he recalled me as a golden playgirl than as a frowsty shopper rooting through the medicines. I let go his arm, step briskly back.

'Right, I'll have to say goodbye now.' I shrug his raincoat off, fold it neatly before I hand it back. If I'm Jan, I'm tidy.

He doesn't take it. 'Hey, what about our drink?' His voice sounds almost panicky and a cloud has rolled across his blue-sky eyes. He looks deprived and shamed and hopeless all at once. My Ma could make my father look like that. I weaken, taken a deep breath in.

'Maybe . . . later?' I suggest.

I've handed him a diamond, not a damp black mac – one larger than his ring. He's almost on his knees to me. I feel a heady sense of power. Mistress Janice Dominant. I should have chosen some really dynamic name – Delilah or Sapphira, or even Aphrodite. Jan is far too tame.

'Thanks, Jan. That'll be just great. Any time you choose. In fact, if you make it after nine, we can have a drink on Cleopatra's Barge.'

'What's that?'

'Oh, just one of Caesars' swanky bars – a real Egyptian barge like Cleopatra sailed in – well, a replica, I guess, but with oars and sails and floating on real water. They have a band on board and the boat sways back and forth. We can dance there, if you like, then maybe hit the casinos around midnight. Do you gamble?'

I feel a shiver of excitement. He'll teach me, teach me how to win. He must have won a packet if he can afford Christmas week at Caesars. All that stuff about playing just for fun could be just a smoke-screen. I mean, he probably thinks I disapprove of gambling and wants to make me like him. I bet he risks fantastic sums of money. He said himself that risk made life exciting. And what about his job? If he's had all that time off, then perhaps he hasn't got one, wins enough to live – and live it up. I saw one film where the poker-playing hero needed two whole suitcases just to lug his winnings home. He played three short hours each day, and the rest of his life was lotus-eating – sleeping in till noon, lolling by his swimming-pool until the sun went down, then drinking in exotic bars, or toying with a pound or two of caviare. God! It must be great to live like that, never having to bother with footling things like pension schemes or clocking-in, or all that soul-destroying nine to five. My Dad worked nine to six, including Saturdays, and even then he hardly had a bean to spare. In that way, I'm unlike him – a gambler, not a slaver, at least in mind and spirit. It's just that I haven't been initiated. (Keno doesn't count.)

'I'd love to learn,' I say. 'The only problem is I don't think I'm too lucky at the moment.' There's another problem, actually. I'm under-age. You have to be twenty-one in Vegas, not only to gamble, but even to buy a drink. Crazy, isn't it? In fact, it was just as well that Norah, and not me, was the official competition winner, or they might have made a fuss, especially with all the free champagne. I'm not sure how strict they are, or whether Victor cares a fig or not, but I'd better say I'm twenty-one, just in case he's paranoid. And I'll have to dress to look like it. No more dungarees; something more mature.

'What?' I say. Victor's speaking, but I'm miles away,

rethinking my whole image – new hairstyle, older make-up.

'I just said "luck can change".' He leans forward suddenly I flinch. I'm still half-expecting a flick-knife or a gun. But all he does is trace that stupid dimple on my chin. His hand feels very gentle. 'I'll pick you up at the Tropicana, shall I?'

'Oh, no, not there,' I say, a bit too quickly. 'I'll meet you at Caesars I only hope it's not too far to walk. My money's pledged to Lady Luck, not taxi drivers.

'Okay. How about the main hotel reception desk? It's less crowded there and I don't want to lose you in the crush. Does 9.30 sound okay?'

'Yes. Fine.'

'See you later, then. You . . .' he pauses. 'Won't let me down, will you, Jan?'

'No.' I make it cool. I really do have power. This is quite some guy – probably a high roller, despite all his denials, yet I could reduce him to a gibbering wreck, diamonds, tournaments and all, by simply failing to turn up. He's still left me with the raincoat. I suppose he imagines it will bond us, remind me of our date. I press it firmly into his hands. I may as well enjoy my power – the first time I've ever had power – keep him guessing.

'Goodbye, then, Victor.' His whole face brightens when I use his name. I shall have to ration it.

'Bye, Jan. I'm really looking forward to tonight.'

I flash him what I hope is an enigmatic smile, turn into the drugstore. 'Victor,' I repeat, once I'm safely on my own. Yeah, I like the name.

10

Life is tougher, gettin' rougher.
Prices aren't the same.
Insure with us.
Be sure with us.
Phoenix is the name.

'Feast your eyes. One fresh egg, bacon and sausage, and your choice of these super sizzlin' pancakes. The truly special extra special, only at your International House of Pancakes.'

'See Snoopy as he roams the park. You can even shake his paw . . .'

I wish they wouldn't go so fast. Everything's mixed up. I liked the Snoopy, but now there's fighting. Bombs. The man with the big smile says two hundred people died. I can see them on the screen, lying very still in pools of blood. Some of them are crying. The man's not crying. He's smiling now again, telling me to spoil myself.

'Go ahead, indulge. Cut a slice of Sarah Lee's all-butter cake. There's nothing like it, is there? Buttery and moist.'

I shut my eyes. I can't eat when there's blood, and that cake is very greasy. They keep begging me to eat. First Shredded Wheat, then Shrimp-Bites, then Bubble Yum, then Jube Jels. Carole told me not to eat, only water and dry toast.

I've been to the toilet (number two) nine times since this morning, made four bathrooms smell. I hate that smell. They won't want me to stay here. This is a very special room for very special people. A doctor's room, I think. Or maybe Matron's. I don't know why we're in it when we're only patients. I expect they'll move us soon. They've moved us once already. I don't

115

mind. I'd feel less worried in a different room, one with fewer things in. Everything is very new here and cost a lot of money. If I spill some water or crumple up a cushion, they'll probably make me pay.

'A car that brings the road alive. Put the key in, put the top down, let her go . . .'

He's driving far too fast. I expect he'll have a crash. I've seen a crash already on TV. One man lost a leg, and they said he ought to use a new shampoo.

My own hair's gone quite limp. I'd like to wash it, but I mustn't spoil their bathroom, and Carole said don't move. I haven't moved for two hours fifteen minutes. I'm sitting in the bedroom. I don't like the room downstairs. Everything is red downstairs and there are men without their clothes on watching from the walls. Here, the walls are mirrors. I'm in all the mirrors, looking at myself. I'm not sure which one is me.

Carole's out. She went to a palace for a boat-ride, but she wouldn't let me come. I expect she's angry that I made those toilets smell. The saints don't smell, not ever. They don't go number two. That's why they're called saints. And the Virgin Mary never had a period, not one in her whole life. She's the only person in the world who had no germs on her at all. They told us that at St Joseph's. There was a statue of St Joseph in Reverend Mother's study, but I only saw his foot. You weren't allowed to raise your eyes when you spoke to Reverend Mother.

St Joseph feels very far away. He didn't come to Las Vegas. I shouldn't have come myself when Sister told me not to. Now I'm being punished. But Carole cried when I said no, and I don't like her to cry.

'Tell her you're the greatest with this diamond love-knot ring . . .'

It's very loud, that television, but I mustn't turn it down. Carole said not to touch the set. If I do, I'll get the gambling lessons. Everybody's shouting. The man who bought the diamond ring just asked her if she'd marry him, really screamed it out, so everyone could hear.

I'd like to go to bed. I'm already in my nightgown. It's a pink lace one, with frills, stiff and rather scratchy. I always wear pyjamas in the hospital. They're warmer and don't itch. They found me an almost new pair at the WRVS bazaar, pale blue with darker cuffs. Two buttons had come off, but they bought a 5p blouse as well, just to get the buttons.

'Free MacSwivel-razor with egg MacMuffin sandwich . . . Only from McDonald's.'

A lot of things are free. They get terribly excited, even when it's something really small. There was a free transfer in a cornflakes packet, just a sticky label with a tiny picture on, but they sang a hymn to it.

The weather man has said goodnight and gone. He always laughs, even when it's rain. It's rain again tomorrow. He told us to have our umbrellas ready for the morning. We didn't bring umbrellas.

I can't see any weather. Someone came in hours ago and drew all the curtains in all our different rooms. She wasn't a nurse, though she was wearing a blue uniform. I tried to talk to her, but she only shook her head. She also took the bedspreads off our beds. I expect she thought we'd spoil them. I looked out once, before she drew the curtains, but it was very high and dizzy. I don't like such big windows.

With smaller ones, things can't get in, things like sun or germs.

We had bars on all the windows at Westham Hall. I had a window just above my bed, a small one with six bars. I gave each bar a name. I wanted Irish names, but I didn't know any, except my own and Patrick, so I asked the lady who cleaned the dormitories. She was Irish herself – Miss O'Something – I can't remember now.

Miss O'Something used to scrub us sometimes, when she'd finished scrubbing floors. The bathrooms were cold and the ceilings very high, so if anybody shouted, it echoed round the room. She shouted quite a lot.

There weren't any plugs, so she stuffed dirty socks and dish-rags down the hole, but the water still leaked out. Sometimes she was called away, and you had to sit there naked, with no water left at all. Once, she lost the bath-brush and did me with the brush you clean the toilet with. It was very rough and hurt. I didn't cry. I just shut my eyes and imagined it was my mother who was washing me, very very gently with white satin hands and soap that smelt of flowers.

We have flower soap here, but I didn't like to use it, and I left my hands all wet because I was scared to touch the towels. The Beechgrove towels are very stiff and thin. They were white once, long ago, but they've been washed and washed to grey. 'GOVERNMENT PROPERTY' is stamped across both ends. I don't know why governments need towels.

The Gold Rush towels are red and very furry, as if they are alive. There are ten of them, all different shapes and sizes, the biggest ones so big they're more like blankets. I think they expected more of us to come. That's why they gave us all these phones and televisions, and three rooms instead of one.

I'm frightened I still smell.

There's a doughnut on the screen now, one with legs. It's singing very loud. People in America eat much more than we do, not just at meal-times, but almost all the time. My stomach must be different from the stomachs over here. I think I've got more tubes and things inside me, so there's less room for the food. One woman in that restaurant ate thirteen cakes and ten large chicken legs. I couldn't eat at all. I even left my jelly, though nobody was cross. Sister says it's wicked to waste food.

There's a war on at the moment, a very loud and noisy one with guns. I think I'll shut my eyes again. I shut them quite a lot here.

When I look again, it's a different war, with planes. Then a man comes on and says the air is poisoned. I don't know which air he means – just here or back in England, but it can't be all that bad because people start to dance and sing on a golden beach with palm trees. Then a young man appears, not on the beach, but sitting at a desk in proper clothes and says they've dropped a bomb in . . .

I didn't catch the name, but I don't think it's an atom bomb because I'm still alive.

I wish Carole would come back. Even when she shouts, it's

nicer with her here. She spent two hours getting dressed. She put on five different blouses, before deciding on a frock. She's got something called a paintbox with a little brush in it. She kept brushing colours on her face, then scrubbing them off again with spit and paper tissues. She even changed her hair, put it up on top. I didn't like it. It made her look older and somehow sadder. Then she sat, just frowning at herself. I think she was scared about the boat ride. She shouted at me, twice, and she shouts when she's afraid.

There's an important Message coming up. The young man just said so. It may be about the bomb. I sit up very straight. I'm not allowed to lean back in my chair in case I spoil the velvet. I think they watch us here. There's a spy-hole in the door so they can check that we're not stealing or messing up their things. And they have television men hidden in the ceilings.

'Make your cat a happy cat. Happy Cat stays moist and meaty-tasting all day long . . .'

I've never had a cat. Everywhere I've lived, pets have been forbidden. I'd like a bird, a coloured bird that sang.

'Hey, you're gonna be a happy cat . . .'

I think I've missed the Message. It's only cats, not bombs. Everyone is happy on the television. They keep laughing all the time, even after wars. I think it's just the time of year. You have to be happy when it's Christmas or New Year. They keep mentioning New Year. They've wished me a happy one fifty times already, and it's still four days away.

Years are never really new. And this next one won't be happy if they move me into lodgings. Miss Johnson hated cats.

'Do your hands crack in the winter?'

'How long since you had ribs?'

They keep on asking questions, but there's no time to reply.

'Are your headaches tension headaches? Do you take your job to bed?'

I used to have a job, putting string in carrier bags at Belstead. They closed the workshop years ago. They said we were too slow at it, and stealing jobs from other, normal people.

'My headache's gone!' the woman shouts. Pills in England never work that fast. Sometimes they don't work at all. Tom

119

Bryden was on fifteen pills a day, but he still cycled down to Eastbourne and jumped off a cliff.

The woman with the headache is playing with her children. Everyone has mothers on TV. And they're mostly all dressed up, even when they're hoovering or feeding cats and dogs. I take my glasses off, rub my eyes. My shoulders hurt from holding them so stiff.

There's a church now on the screen. It's a very faint church which I think is going to fall. The doors are opening and I can see a flowerbed singing hymns. I put my glasses on again. The church stops trembling and the flowers grow faces. I like the hymns, try to sing myself.

When we've finished, a man in a white suit climbs up on a platform, shouting, 'Glory glory glory glory . . .' I think he's wearing lipstick.

'You, *you!*' He points his finger right at me. His face gets larger and larger until it's filling the whole screen. I can see black hairs in his nose.

'Are you ready to die?'

He's asking me. His eyes are staring into mine, wild eyes like Tom Bryden's before he went to Eastbourne. My heart is beating very fast. Doris Clayton died and she was only fifty. They took her away on a trolley, covered with a sheet. I could see just half her hand which was trailing down one side. Tom said he saw a finger move, but she was cremated just the same.

'You're a sinner.' He's still talking to me. 'A deep-dyed wretched sinner.'

I stare down at my laces. I haven't any slippers, so I've put my outdoor shoes on. I was a sinner at St Joseph's. Reverend Mother said so. She said God had punished me by taking away my mother. At Westham Hall we didn't have a God. At Beechgrove, He came back again, but only on a Sunday. Today is Sunday still.

'The end of the world may come tonight – this very evening. Are you prepared?'

No, I'm not, I'm frightened. What if it ends and Carole isn't back? He's throwing up his arms now, pacing up and down.

'God has warned you through His Prophets. You!' he

screams again. He's reading from a book now, a big white padded book with coloured ribbons. ' "The Day of the Lord is at hand, a day of fury, a day of ruin and desolation, a day of gloom and darkness . . ." At hand means *now*. TODAY!' He hits the book, slams it really hard. 'Don't think you'll be spared. You won't. How can you, when the Lord said . . .' He turns the page – ' "I will bring such disasters on mankind that their blood will be poured out like water and their corpses will lie rotting on the ground?" '

I'm so scared, I block my ears. I can't hear him now, only see his teeth bared, his eyes screwed up, his finger pointing, pointing. Then he disappears and the figure 6 flashes on the screen, followed by a row of noughts.

I remove my fingers from my ears. He's talking about money. He says he needs six hundred thousand dollars. I don't know why he needs it if the world is going to end. The noughts keep getting bigger.

Suddenly, he's back, falling on one knee, stretching out his hands. He's got rings on both his hands, diamond rings and gold ones. He says his church will have to close if I don't help. If I send him just a hundred dollars, Jesus Christ will double it.

I can't follow all the words, but he says how can I refuse with all God's angels looking on? I can't see any angels, but maybe they're above him, in the sky. He's taking up all the space himself, just his face again. He hasn't got a body, only eyes. His eyes are very violent. I think he needs his pills. He says for just ten dollars, he'll send me a gold pin with 'Jesus, Friend of Sinners' on it, and for twenty dollars, I'll get a Bible bound in white, with coloured pictures.

He's crying now. I hate people to cry and the tears look very close. If I send the money, he promises to pray for me by name. 'By *name*,' he sobs again, so loud I jump. He says he writes the names of all who send him money in a special gold-clasped book which he keeps on the altar, close to God. God reads the names each morning. I'd like God to read my name and I'd love the coloured pictures. There might be one of St Joseph.

I cut him out once, years and years ago, from a book in St Joseph's convent library. He was only small and I cut round him very carefully. I didn't take the Jesus or the Mary, and there were lots of other pictures left, but Reverend Mother was so angry she went white. She said I was a vandal and a thief. I don't know what a vandal is.

They've written the address now where you have to send your money. It keeps flashing on and off. You've got to send it now, not wait until tomorrow. The man says God may take away tomorrow.

I fetch a pencil from my handbag, copy down his name. He's called the Reverend Arthur M. O'Toole. I remember now, that was Miss O'Something's name – O'Toole. She didn't have a first name. My insides heave again. Miss O'Toole would be dead and cold by now, but perhaps she sent him.

I'm very slow at writing, but I complete the final e and start on the address which disappears before I reach the town. The postman probably knows it. The Reverend looks very rich and famous. I don't think Jesus wore white suits, or rings.

My money's in the safe. Half of it is mine. More than half, because Carole's already taken some of hers. The safe is locked. It's difficult to open. Even Carole couldn't do it. She had to phone and ask a man to show her. If I wait for Carole, I could land up in Hell. The Reverend said he knew a sinner who promised to send his money in the morning, once he'd had a good night's rest. He went to sleep and woke up dead in Hell.

I pick the phone up. A voice says 'Yeah?', a girl's voice. I ask her about the bomb first, to make sure I've got some time left, but she doesn't understand. They don't speak proper English over here. At last, she sends a man up, a very big and tall one with a gun.

'Right, where's the bomb?' he asks. He's come to search my room. He didn't knock, just burst into the downstairs room and came crashing up the stairs. He's squeezing under furniture, throwing all the blankets off the beds. I think he's angry with me. He hardly speaks at all, until I explain about my money and the church. Then he unlocks the safe for me and even hands me paper from a sort of padded folder which I hadn't dared to touch. The paper's very grand, with gold round the edges. The envelopes have crowns on.

I ask about a stamp and the man says not to worry, he'll take care of it. He seems much nicer now and calls me Ma'am. He even turns the television down. I try to count the notes so I can work out how many half is, but I've only got to six when he asks me where I come from. I say 'Beechgrove' and then 'Belfast' because I'm not sure which he means, and then he says he's Irish, too, from way back, and maybe we're related. He doesn't look like me at all, but I say 'yes' to be polite. I wish he wouldn't talk. I can't count with him talking.

I'm not used to counting money and this is foreign money. The man is standing very close, asks if he can help. I know Carole wouldn't like that, so I just divide the notes into two big piles, put one back in the safe and the other in an envelope with crowns on.

I write my name, very big, in the middle of the large white sheet of paper, then add Carole's name underneath. I want our names very close together when God reads them in His gold-clasped book. The man's so keen to catch the post, he tries to take the envelope before I've sealed it up.

'Just a minute. I've still got the address to write.'

He hands me his own pen, a slippery silver one which makes my writing slower still. I copy down the street name, ask him if he knows the town. 'Yeah, sure,' he says, but he doesn't write it on, just locks the safe again and says 'Goodnight, ma'am.'

I hear the downstairs door slam. I'm all alone again. The Reverend's gone as well. There's a fat man on the screen now, telling jokes. He's whispering, not shouting. Whispering makes me nervous. I always think they're whispering about me.

I press some switches by the door and cold air starts to blow. I can't seem to turn it off again, so I put my coat on over my nightdress, and go back to my chair. Soon it's very cold. My hands and feet feel chilled and very heavy, as if they're made of cold white china like the chamberpots at Belstead.

Perhaps I'll go to bed. When I moved into my lodgings, I spent a lot of time in bed. There wasn't any heating in my room.

I'll have to take the lace off. I don't think it's for sleeping, just for show. I haven't got a waist, but the nightdress has a tight one with elastic, so it's hard to get it off, especially on my own. It's colder with no clothes on. The jet of air is blowing on my back, disturbing all my hair. I fetch my vest and petticoat and a pair of thick lisle stockings. My hands are cold and clumsy, so it takes me quite a while to put them on. My fingers have gone bluish round the nails.

I don't know how I'll sleep with the television on. A grey-haired lady is whispering to her daughter down the phone. She says they live five thousand miles apart, but I can see them both together, both with phones. She's whispering to me now. 'We're still so close,' she smiles. 'Even though my daughter's moved away. Save sixty per cent evenings and weekends. Simply dial 1 and your long-distance number.'

Perhaps I could phone Beechgrove, ask Sister what to do about the pains. It's evening and weekend now, so it wouldn't cost that much. I dial the 1, then stop. I'm trying to remember the Beechgrove number which I think starts with a 6 and is very long and complicated. A man says 'Room Service', so I put the receiver down and start again. The same voice answers.

'Room Service. Can I help you?'

I pretend I haven't heard. Perhaps I shouldn't dial the 1 at all; I start with 6 this time. A different voice says 'Barber Shop.'

'I'm trying to phone the hospital,' I explain.

'Are you sick, ma'am? We have a doctor on call, twenty-four hours. I'll connect you.'

I put the phone down quickly. You're not allowed to see the doctor unless you're really ill. It's to do with bombs again. Sister said if they spent less on bombs and more on health, every patient could see a doctor regularly and she'd have less to do herself.

I remember now, the number's 6-3-something, so I dial the 6 and 3, hear a lot of buzzing and a sudden louder click.

'This is a recorded message. The main swimming pools are closed at present due to unusually low temperatures. Should you wish to swim in our luxury indoor heated pool, then please . . .'

'Hallo,' I say. 'Is anybody there?'

The same message starts again. 'Closed at present due to unusually low temperatures.' I'm shivering already. That cold jet's getting colder, blowing like a wind. I try another switch to turn it off. Loud blaring music fills the room. There's music on the TV set as well, but different, quieter music – a woman and three men whispering with a band. The two musics get mixed up, keep colliding in my head. I put my hands over my ears to try to block the noise out. I'm shivering so much, my ears shake with my hands.

'Carole, please come back.' I'm talking out loud, but nobody can hear me. I can hardly hear myself. Perhaps Carole's gone for ever, left me here alone. I've got to speak to Sister, ask her what to do. I pick up the other phone, the red one by the bed.

'Should you wish to swim in our luxury indoor heated . . .'

I mustn't cry. The tears will stain the sheets and Carole says they're satin like Marilyn Monroe's. I don't know who she is.

Perhaps I'll write to Sister. There were postcards in that folder, postcards of the Gold Rush. I think they're free. Sister pins her cards up on the notice board, so they'd see my name every time they passed it, the patients and the nurses. I couldn't disappear then.

I fetch my pencil and a card, but I don't know what to write. I've never written to anyone before. In the end, I just put 'We've arrived.' The card looks empty still.

My writing's very wobbly as I sign my name. The pencil's shaking with the cold and you need smaller hands to write well. I've never liked my hands. They're rough and badly shaped, as if nobody had time to smooth them down or finish off the fingers. Carole's hands are plump, but very small.

I'd better go and look for her. I can't stay here alone, not all night, not when it's so cold. I could also post the card.

I think I'll put my Crimplene on. I feel safer in a frock I bought at Beechgrove. It makes me feel it's not so far away. I button up my coat, fetch my other shoes, the brown ones from the jumble sale. I like the Beechgrove jumble sales. They always have a Cake Stall with every sort of cake.

I close the bedroom door, take the stairs quite slowly. I can't feel my feet at all now, and I wouldn't want to fall. It's so quiet outside, it's like a shock. I stand in the corridor, trying to hold the silence in my hands. I'm not so frightened now, without the noise. There's nobody around, but a sign says 'elevator' and I remember that's a lift because Carole wrote it down for me, and also 'restroom'. There's a lady in the lift and I ask her where the river is.

'River?'

'Yes, my friend's gone on a boat ride. I've got to find her.'

We've reached the ground floor now. The doors are opening and the lady's walking through them without answering me at all.

I ask again, but only for the exit. Once I get outside, I'll probably see the river for myself.

No . . . I can't see anything but lights. I'd better stop. I'm blinded. They're so bright, it's like the daytime, except the sky is black. There's not a lot of sky left. It's mostly filled with buildings, very tall and grand ones, which keep flashing and blurring as if I've left my glasses off again. My eyes hurt with the colours, which are changing every minute. There are signs as well, and letters, but I can't read what they say because they're shivering and spinning and I'm not sure if I'm ill or not. Sometimes with the pills, you see lights and even pictures which the doctors say aren't there.

I stand by a palm tree, hold on very tight. I mustn't start walking until things have settled down. I take a few deep breaths, but the signs and colours won't keep still. I think they're really there. I'd better find a side-street, somewhere quieter.

I take a few slow steps. It's very cold, almost colder than the bedroom, and I haven't any gloves. Carole must be frozen on a boat.

I walk on down the side-street, see a lady standing in a doorway.

'Excuse me, please. I'm looking for the boats.'

'How d'ja mean, boats?'

'Well, my friend said a boat. I think she did,' I add. If I'm ill, I may have got it wrong.

'Did she mean the Paddlewheel?'

'Is that a boat?'

'It sure looks like one, yeah. It's a big entertainments centre –

you know, hotel and casino and all the kiddies' rides – skeeball alleys, video games, carousels – all that sort of thing. Or she could have meant the Showboat. That's built like a model of a nineteenth century riverboat – real cute. It's quite some way, though. You'd better take a taxi.'

I thank her and walk on. I haven't any money and I'd feel frightened in a taxi. Walking warms me up a bit and the streets are very empty, once I've left that big one with the lights. I'm looking for a pillarbox, but there doesn't seem to be one. Perhaps they don't have them over here. They may even read your letters first, like they used to do at Belstead.

It's snowing.

No, it can't be. I must be seeing things again. Carole said Las Vegas has no winter and the summers are so hot you can't go out after ten o'clock in the morning or you simply frizzle up. She said they don't have snow and not much rain. But it's been raining since we got here and now it's turned to snow. I can feel the flakes falling on my face, see them filling up the sky. Perhaps it's artificial snow. I wish they'd turn it off.

I start to run, back the way I've come. My shoes keep slipping off and my fingers hurt with cold. At last I see the lights again. Everything is whirling – snowflakes, colours, letters and my head. A huge hotel is glittering on one corner, silver letters written on the glass. I try to spell the words out: 'PEACE', 'JOY', 'GOODWI . . .' I choose the door with 'PEACE' on it, push it open.

I'm hot now, boiling hot. I'm in a huge big room with crowds and crowds of people playing all those games we saw before. Everybody's smoking like at Beechgrove, but fat cigars which smell. There are lots of different noises in my head, clatterings and clangings, constant whirrs and buzzes, horrid jangly music. I've never been this bad before. Perhaps I need new pills.

There's hardly room to move, but I find a corner, press myself against the wall. It must be a party because everyone's dressed up. There's a woman in an evening dress and a black man in a white fur coat which goes right down to the ground. My coat is fur, the Friend said, though it's rubbed away in patches and the fastening doesn't work. I brush the snow off, edge along the wall. I'll never find Carole if I stay in this one corner.

The music's getting louder. Perhaps it's the music from my room which I've brought with me in my head. I squeeze through all the people, reach another room. A band is playing on a stage – five men and two blonde girls. No, one. The one girl doubled. I shut my eyes, blink hard before I open them again.

Still two, exactly the same in every little detail; not just their silver dresses and their scarlet shoes, but their hair and mouths and noses, their shape, their height, their hands. I feel very scared. I think I'm seeing double. That happened once before, because I changed my drugs. Everything was blurred, but always two of it. These two girls aren't blurred, though, but very clear and sharp.

I'll have to see a doctor, not here, but back in Beechgrove. They may send me for shocks. We all had shocks at Belstead, even children. A Dr Asif gave them. He wasn't well himself. I used to hate the shocks. When they wake you up, you're someone different, but you can't remember who.

Someone's speaking to me. I think it's someone real, though I may be hearing voices. A face looms up, a kind face.

'Aren't they great? They're absolutely identical, you know. They were born like carbon copies, but it takes some work as well. I mean, they both have to diet and make sure they stop at exactly the same weight, and if one goes to a beauty parlour, the other has to follow and have just the same deal – same shade of colour-rinse or same half-inch off the ends. They say they've both got a mole on their right inside-thigh – exactly the same size and in exactly the same spot. Isn't that something? I've seen twins before, of course, on stage, but never two as similar as that.'

'Twins?' I say. I feel a little better. We had twins at Beechgrove once, in Carlton Ward – Joan and Vera. They said Vera wasn't ill at all, but they refused to be split up.

'Can I get you something, ma'am?'

A waitress has come up to me. She's forgotten to put

128

her skirt on and is wearing just her tights with a jacket on the top. I walk away, so I won't embarrass her. I've got to look for Carole.

It's very hard to look. There are too many people and a lot of them just push. One man almost burns me with his lighted cigarette. The slot machines keep spitting out their coins. The noise goes through my head. There isn't any air, only smoke. Coloured lights are circling from the ceiling so that people have green hands and purple faces. 'Win a car!' the signs say. 'Win a colour TV set!' 'Win ten thousand dollars!' I'd like to win, so I could give them all to Carole. She feels stronger when she wins things.

I walk all around the lounge, but I can't see any sign of her. I find another exit which leads into the street. It isn't snowing now. Perhaps it never was. There are puddles, though, with lights and pictures in them, and a tall glass building which bends and trembles as shadow-cars drive right through the glass. There are quite a lot of real cars splashing me with water as I walk along the street. The street is made of lights. Some of them have broken and spilt out on to the pavement in fizzy pools like Lucozade. I wish I weren't alone.

Suddenly I stop.

CIRCUS CIRCUS CIRCUS CIRCUS CIRCUS CIRCUS CIRCUS CIRCUS.

It says 'CIRCUS' eight whole times in different places. I'm counting all the letters, white letters and pink letters and huge red ones, higher up. My heart is beating very fast. I found a book called *Big Top* once. It was lying on a table in St Joseph's. I don't know how it got there because we weren't allowed books like that, not happy ones with pictures and no prayers. I didn't steal it. I just looked at all the pictures – elephants and tigers, acrobats and clowns. I liked the clowns the best.

There's a clown in front of me, so huge he's like a giant, taller than the buildings. The palm trees only reach his waist. Each foot looks bigger than a car. He's holding a lollipop which is like a big red wheel. He's made of lights and his body is a notice board. 'FREE CIRCUS ACTS' it says. Circuses cost money. That's what grown-ups always said when I asked if I could go. 'FREE', I spell again. The clown is pointing to a pink and white striped tent. No, it's not a tent. It can't be. It's far too big and solid.

I walk up to the entrance, which is very grand with flags. There isn't any queue and no one's taking tickets. I hope I'm not too late.

I push the doors, look around. It's no different from the place I've just been in. The same flashing lights and rude machines, the same pale and angry people sitting at the tables playing games. I rush up to a waitress. This one has her skirt on, but it's the shortest skirt I've ever seen, not decent.

'Circus?' I gasp out. I'm so worried that I've missed it, I can't form proper sentences. 'The clown . . . Big top . . .' I start again. 'Free circus acts, it said. Out there on that . . .'

'Yeah.' She points. 'Up on the first floor.'

The escalator has broken, is jammed with people walking up. I join them, step off at the top. I can't see anything. Only heads and heads and heads. Guns are firing all around me. It must be war again. I struggle to turn back, but I'm not me any more. I'm just a crowd, a crush of fighting bodies. A pushchair-wheel runs over my left foot. I swallow tears of pain. I trip on something. Impossible to fall. Too many people pressing round me like a wall. Nobody is whole, though, only feet and backs and elbows; bits of broken faces, gash-red mouths, sockets with no eyes in.

'Let me out,' I whisper.

No one hears. Everybody's pushing. There isn't any circus, only humans with clown faces, eating eating: bags of crisps exploding in their mouths, popcorn showering from a chute, black ice cream foaming into cornets.

'Help,' I say. 'Please help me.'

A little boy with monkey eyes is staring. I try to smile, but my face is stiff and dry. If I smile, it might crack and split apart. I may simply smash to pieces like a cup. Now he's got a gun, the monkey-boy, a gun as big as he is. I think he's going to shoot me. I shut my eyes, hear the bangs. No pain.

A long time passes.

When I look again, things are clearer. It wasn't war. The guns are only toy ones; guns for shooting dolls off stands, guns for smashing clowns. There are darts to throw as well, and balls to roll, and hammers to hit moles with when they pop up from their holes. I watch a man kill seven moles. He's laughing as they die.

'Carole . . .?' I say it very softly.

There's no Carole here, no river. There is a stage with wires and a trapeze, but it's dead and dark and empty, and everything costs money, even killing moles. I pass a mirror, stop. I've shrunk – gone very short and squat, as if someone's squashed me down and I'm oozing out both sides. I take a step towards the glass. An ugly dwarf waddles up to meet me, face flattening like a tea-plate.

'Go away,' I say.

The mirror-mouth is speaking, a squashed and bleeding mouth. Its feet are huge, bigger than its head. I back away, and suddenly I'm tall and thin, so tall I bend the mirror. Somebody is laughing, someone even taller, in the mirror with me. I turn around. He's tiny. Tiny children should be tucked up safe in bed.

I wish I was a child. Not tucked in bed, but sitting at the circus. Under the Big Top. Sitting next to Carole. I don't think I'll ever find her because I've forgotten what she looks like. I feel very odd and tired. I've also lost my card, the one I should have posted. They won't know I've arrived now, may forget who Norah is.

I sit down on the ground, shut my eyes. There's too much noise to rest; bang-bang-bang of guns, screams from dying moles. I try to change the noise, turn it into circus noise: bells instead of bangs, bells on silver ponies, children clapping clowns.

I force my eyes to open. I can feel something on my knee, something hot and damp. It's a hand, a man's hand, dark, with long black hairs on.

'Hi,' he said. 'You sick, ma'am?'

I wish he'd take it off. He's an old man, rather fat, with a bald and shiny head and a brooch pinned on his coat. The brooch says 'JESUS SAVES'. He must be a godman. Not the Reverend kind in suits, but a shabby one like Jesus.

'What's the matter with ya?'

I'd prefer to think, not talk, but I explain I've lost my friend and I couldn't find the circus.

'This is Circus Circus.'

I don't know why he says it twice. 'Yes, but where are all the clowns?' I ask. 'And acrobats?'

'You want clowns?'

I nod.

'Follow me,' he says.

We go down the escalator and past all the games again, and along a corridor and up a lift and down another passage. Then he unlocks a door and pushes me in front of him. It's a hotel room, his room, but nothing like as big and grand as ours. 'You want acrobats?'

I don't say anything. I'm frightened now. He's sitting on the bed, undoing his old trousers, just the front.

'I'll show you acrobats,' he says. 'Hold this.'

I don't want to hold it. It's very red and swollen, especially at the end. 'I'll go now, please,' I say.

He grabs me, tries to kiss me on the lips. I keep my mouth tight shut. You make babies if you kiss.

'Get your hands round that.'

I shake my head. He's holding it himself now. It looks raw and very puffy. I think he may be ill. He's not talking any more. His eyes are closed, his face screwed up in pain. He's making moaning noises.

I don't know what to do, so I stand still in a corner. 'Hail,' I whisper silently. 'St Joseph lily flower. Eden's peaceful hail.' The words are coming back now, but all jumbled up together. I go on saying them to drown the other noises. The moans are getting louder.

'Word made hail flesh husband of hail Mary chaste . . .'

When I dare to look again, he's gone. I think he's in the bathroom. I can hear the water running.

I creep towards the other door, the main one. It opens, just like that. St Joseph always hears you in the end.

I tiptoe out. I'm shaking. 'Hail,' I say again. It takes me quite some time to find the street. It's raining, heavy rain. It doesn't rain in Vegas, doesn't snow.

A siren howls. Another. An ambulance screams past; a red and rattling fire engine, a white police car. Sirens all around me now. Alarm bells, flashing lights. I've got to cross the road. It looks safer on the other side, darker, with more room to hide. The sign says 'STOP'. I daren't stop, dash between two cars. It doesn't matter if I'm killed. Everyone will die, the Reverend said. I'm a sinner now, a real one. I think the germs got in. If you open your mouth even just a crack, they fly right in and crawl down to your stomach. Then you grow a baby.

'*Are you prepared?*'

No. I keep on running. I saw a picture once of the End of The World. It was in St Joseph's library, but I didn't cut it out. There were clouds of thick black smoke and great high flames and devils in the flames with toasting forks and all the graves were opening and corpses stepping out in long white night-gowns. Corpses smell.

I stop to block my ears. Sirens, sirens, sirens. Fire engines won't help. You can't put the fires of Hell out, not even if you used every drop of water in every sea and river in the world. There aren't any seas or rivers in Las Vegas. Carole didn't know. I'll have to stop. It's hurting when I breathe. I lean against a wall, shake water from my hair, dry my glasses on my petticoat. When I put them on again, a sign appears. I think it's real, but the words are very long.

'GUARDIAN ANGEL CATHEDRAL.'

It takes me quite a time to spell it out, and when I have, I don't believe it. It wasn't a circus and it won't be a cathedral. A cathedral is a church, a grand one with a shop which sells colouring books and cards. There's one in Canterbury. We went by coach to Canterbury with the Friends, and had tea in silver teapots and cakes you ate with forks.

The sign is pointing to the left. I run that way because it's darker, and further from the sirens which are starting up again. I need to go – not number two (the pains have gone), just number one. Rain and nerves always make it worse. I can't see any toilets and if the End Of The World is starting, everyone will see me if I do it in the street, because God comes down to earth then, with all His saints and angels.

There's an angel right above me, hanging in the sky. No, it's not, it's hanging from a roof, a huge pointed roof towering over me. You don't see guardian angels very much. We had them at St Joseph's, but not at Westham Hall. One of the Catholics in my ward at Belstead said hers followed her about and she could hear its wings flapping just behind her, but every time I looked, it hid. I think they're shy, like birds.

I'm standing right beneath him now. The nuns said to call them 'hims', but they're not real men at all. I'm glad. They have wings above, instead of red and swollen things below.

It *is* a church, though it doesn't look like Canterbury and there's another sign above it saying 'Bali Hai Motel', which they wouldn't have in England. The door opens like a real door, and there's the shop with postcards (closed now, but I can see them through the glass), and another door in front of me. I open it, step in.

It's very grand inside with great tall stained-glass windows and rows and rows of wooden pews and real carpet on the floor. I've never seen a carpet in a church. I don't think you're allowed it back in England.

A sign says 'Restrooms', which Carole says means toilets. You don't have toilets in cathedrals. You're not allowed to go in church at all. I follow the sign, and find some real white toilets, very new and clean. I use them both to show I'm grateful and wash my hands, twice, in both the basins.

I can still hear the sirens, but they're fainter now, shut out. It's quiet in here, much safer. If the world is going to end, the best place to be is in a church. During the war, we always went to chapel during air-raids. I wasn't frightened because the nuns prayed out loud to drown the noise, and they said if we were killed, we'd all go straight to heaven because we'd died in God's own house. Then I moved to Westham, where they didn't have a chapel and the bombs were always louder.

The American God must be bigger because His house is twice the size. I walk to and fro a while, just to feel the carpet, but stay down near the doors. The altar is where God sits, and if we hadn't sinned, we could see Him, really see Him, just like a real person with hands and hair and legs. The nuns knelt near the altar because they're holier than children, and if you'd made your First Communion you could go right up there and eat Him. I never made mine.

They said I wasn't ready. I still wasn't ready when they moved me to the Children's Home, where we had castor oil each morning, not Communion.

There's nobody about, no men or priests or nuns, so I creep up to the altar. It's very beautiful, with white lilies in a vase and golden candlesticks.

Then I see him. St Joseph, in his long brown robe. He's standing by the manger. St Joseph never sits – he's not allowed to. He looks far too rich and grand. All the figures do. The Mary's like a princess in her expensive blue silk frock. And shepherds wouldn't wear such fancy clothes, not for working in the fields with muddy sheep.

Mary's got her eyes closed. The Jesus looks so big, He must have split her coming out. He's lying on green velvet, not on straw. And all around the crib are silver Christmas trees hung with fairy lights and big expensive plants. They didn't have fairy lights in Bethlehem. Or plants with satin bows on top and ribbons round the pots. It was just a poor dark stable where an ox and ass were sleeping. There's no ox nor ass in this crib. I expect they were too messy for the velvet, or would have dirtied Mary's frock.

St Joseph hasn't seen me. He's staring at the floor. He's been up all night, looking after Mary. He didn't put his germs in her. She made Jesus on her own.

I lie down on the carpet. It's brown and very thick. I don't want to make a baby. I'm only a baby myself. I'm lying in my manger on a soft brown bed of straw. St Joseph is my mother – my own St Joseph, not the rich and grand one. He's taking off his robe, tucking it around me. It's old and warm and shabby; smells of sawdust. He's smiling now, rocking me to sleep.

He didn't want a boy.

He wanted a girl, a little girl called Norah.

11

'Gamblin' requires brains, Jan. It requires a lot of work. It requires talent, it requires thought, it requires intellect, it requires foresight, it . . .'

If he says 'requires' again, I'll shoot him. Right here in this rotten cocktail lounge. They're all the same, these gamblers, totally obsessed, like Victor said himself. Except Victor's just as bad. I only landed myself with *this* jerk because I was sick of Victor's poker.

'Now, listen to me.' (I'm listening. I haven't got much choice.) 'We didn't invent these games here in Vegas, honey. Absolutely not. The Greeks invented craps, the Italians invented roulette, the Chinese invented Keno, the Egyptians invented slot machines, the French . . .' The heavily ringed hand (three diamonds, two rubies and a garnet) gropes for its Pepsi glass.

That's five 'invented's already and more to come, post Pepsi. At least I'm good at counting. I might be good at gambling if we ever get around to it. Snake Jake's been talking non-stop for one and a quarter hours. It's my own fault for playing truant from the poker room, sneaking off when Victor wasn't looking. Victor's *not* as bad. Nothing like. He didn't even want to play; said he had enough of cards all year, and he'd prefer to take me out. We've been out two whole days, in fact; hardly parted since that first exciting drink on Cleopatra's Barge – except for boring things like sleep. We got on really well, had a ball, as they all say over here, but I was keen to see some poker, watch the guy in action, so to speak. He warned me I'd be bored, but I took no notice, nagged him into playing, simply overrode him, like Jake's overriding me.

'The first gamblin' device on this planet was a slot machine. It's recorded in history, Jan, five thousand years ago.'

God! History now. We've already had geography (the layout of casinos), psychology (the psychology of winning), biology (my tits), cardiology (his heart condition), simple mathematics (counting cards) and religion – his – (gambling).

The briefest pause, for olives. He starts again, still chewing on a stone. 'An Egyptian Pharaoh had a wheel and he used to spin that goddam wheel and whatever symbol it stopped on gave him his horoscope for that day. If it stopped on a diamond, he was gonna find money. If it stopped on a heart, he was gonna fall in love. If it stopped on a club, it meant big trouble, and if it stopped on a spade, it meant hard work. Then he started bettin' on it. That's all we're doin' today, hon, bettin' on a slot machine, bettin' on a wheel – except it's three wheels – and instead of hearts and diamonds, it's got cherries, plums and oranges.'

I try to interrupt. I've lost enough on those damned sour fruits already, but his voice submerges mine.

'The real pros in Vegas play slot machines fifteen hours a day, Jan. And some of them have been doin' it for thirty or forty years. Thirty *years*, Jan. And if they're husbands and wives, they may play teams. He'll come in and play eight hours or so, then she'll relieve him while he goes home and sleeps and showers and eats, then he comes back and plays the next eight hours, while she . . .'

'Eats and showers and sleeps,' I say, wondering who does the shopping and the laundry. At least there wouldn't be any kids to take to school – no time to conceive them.

'Right. You've got it, Jan. That's dedication. That's professionalism. That's . . .'

'Craps,' I say. I dislike the word. It's worse than cunt and with Norah's bowels still playing up . . . 'You promised to teach me craps, Jake.' That's how all this started. I'd been sitting in that poker room for what seemed like eternity, when I heard a lot of racket just behind me. It was coming from the crap table – a crowd of people cheering, groaning, laughing – a really welcome sound when poker's so damned silent. (No one says a word except 'check' or 'raise' and a few mumbled 'shit's and 'fuck's, and they're afraid to move a muscle or show the slightest flicker of emotion in case they give anything away.)

Snake was fairly dripping with emotion, making prima donna faces, shouting out his numbers, rocking to and fro. I couldn't take my eyes off him. The poker crowd had been a definite disappointment – a bunch of fogies, mostly, and mostly over-weight, dressed in dreary polyester, or ghastly tasteless tracksuits, not a hat or gun amongst them, save those stupid baseball caps which Americans seem so fond of, and which make them look like pensioned-off schoolboys.

Snake's hat was sensational – a wide black stetson with a jewelled python round the brim – ruby tongue, flashing emerald eyes. His own eyes were hidden by dark glasses, which themselves looked pretty dashing, and he had this amazing satin shirt (black to match the hat) with dice and chips and cards embroidered on it, all in brilliant colours. Well, of course I was attracted, and the fact he left the game for me (which Victor hadn't), even though he was winning, and had these high-heeled cowboy boots on . . .

The boots are total sham. He was born in the Bronx (Jack, not Jake, and his mother kept a corgi, not a python), and runs a chain of dry-cleaners in New England, so there's nothing wild or Western about him at all. And he was only wearing glasses because he's got a touch of conjunctivitis in one weak and watery eye. (We spent a whole ten minutes on his eye problems.) Actually, once he'd taken off his glasses and his hat, his whole image just went phut. He looks ordinary and boring, with floppy sandy hair and funny ears. Victor's not an Adonis, but at least he's honest in his dress, honest generally. He's also very generous, buys me strawberry daiquiris instead of rotten Coke. And he always lets me talk. Snake's hardly paused for breath.

'It's okay, honey, I haven't forgotten craps. Craps is on our list. Just hold on a moment, will ya? I wanna clear up blackjack first.' He grabs another olive, includes it in the lesson. 'Now we've covered blackjack, right? You remember about countin' cards?'

I nod. We've counted cards three times. No – four – I've just set him off again.

'Okay, so it's a lotta work, countin' cards. And there's no damned law that says the deck has to go accordin' to your count. No, hon. Just because you've worked out that a lotta tens are left in the deck, it doesn't mean that the two cards comin' off the top are tens. No, no, no, no, no. They may be threes or twos, or eights, or nines, or fours, or . . .'

'Fives,' I say.

'Yeah, dead right, hon. Fives. And if they're goddamned fives, it's no good gettin' mad. You gotta keep your cool. Now remember this, hon: the best time to make money is when the dealer's got a six showin'. A six, a six, a six, a six, a six. Got that? And how can you make money? I'll tell ya. Number one, don't hit a breakin' hand; number two, you either split or double down. Splittin's easy. When you're dealt a pair . . .'

We did splitting half an hour ago. ('Always always always always always split a pair of aces.') I gulp my drink. There's only ice left now, flavoured ice, but it helps to cool my aggro. 'Look, Jake, I asked you about *craps*.'

It's craps I want to play. I don't know why, except it looks the most exciting game and it doesn't seem as passive as the rest. You stand instead of sit, and you can throw the dice yourself, change your own luck, whereas in blackjack or roulette, the dealer spins the wheel or turns up all the cards. They're really neat, those dice. (Neat's American. They use it all the time for anything they like.) They're made to even higher precision than a space programme – Jake told me that. And that gambling guy on television said craps was the easiest game to play and you could learn it in two minutes (he didn't know Jake, obviously) – at least the basics, and since it's an international game, you can play it round the world, or on a boat in the middle of the ocean, or in the army. It all seems less convincing now. I'm not likely to be sailing round the world or joining up. In fact, Victor warned me *off* craps. He said I'd always lose in the long run because the house percentage works against even seasoned players with mathematical skills, let alone beginners. Actually, all the games are beginning to sound like a pain. Jake makes such heavy weather of them, and we haven't played a card or thrown a dice yet. We're still sitting in this murky bar, mugging up the 'theory', while Jake draws illustrations on paper serviettes. (He's got through half a packet.)

'Right, craps.' Jake fiddles with a cheese-ball, puts it down, uneaten. 'See this pair of dice, Jan?' He produces them, a conjurer, from the back pocket of his jeans. I perk up a bit. They're red with bright white spots, like those mushrooms which elves sit on in children's picture books, but which are really hallucinogenic, turn you on. I need a high, for God's sake. It's one hour twenty minutes now. I'm timing him. And I haven't won a cent yet.

He throws the dice, which come up three and five. He rolls them over so they're showing one and one. 'How many ways to make a two, Jan?'

'Two,' I say. I'm not really listening. I'm still thinking about Victor, worrying now, in fact. I must go back to him.

'No – *one*. Only one way to make a two. I can throw these goddamn dice for ever, but if they don't come up one and one, there's no other way to make a two. How many ways to make a three?'

'One.'

'No, two, hon. It can be two and one, or a one and a two. There's two ways to make a three, all right?'

'All right.' Mind you, Vic may not even have realized that I've gone. That's partly what upset me – the fact he seemed so engrossed in those damn cards. And poker lasts such hours. For all I know, he could be sitting there till morning – or all week. One guy he knew played three days and three nights without a break, and he was eighty-three. At least he won't be missing me. If I stayed away till midnight, he probably wouldn't notice, would still be slumped there, piling up his chips.

I'll go back all the same. It's the least I can do for him when he's been so good to me. It isn't just his money (though be does drive a Thunderbird and took me to a restaurant which served twelve-inch steaks on solid gold). He's a really decent person, doesn't boss, or boast, or interrupt, like most men do, or have to put me down (like Jon did, just to prove who was top dog). He makes everything I say special and important, almost sacred, as if there's nothing in the world beyond my mouth and his two ears. Most people never listen. They're either longing to jump in themselves, or glancing round the room to check they're not missing something better, or hearing what they want to hear instead of what you're saying, or working out their schedule for next day.

I jump. Snake's just thumped my arm. 'You're not concentratin', Jan. Now, how many ways to make a four?'

'Three.'

'Yeah, great! That's it. You're learnin'. Remember, one way to make a two, two ways to make a three, three ways to make a four, four ways to make a five, five ways to make a six, six ways to make a seven . . .'

'Seven ways to make an eight,' I say. I could just leave, simply dash away, say I'm feeling sick.

'No no no no no no no *no*, Jan. *Five* ways to make an eight. It goes back the other way, see? Five ways to make an eight, four ways to make a nine, three ways to make a ten, two ways to . . .'

'Is this craps?' I interrupt.

'Sure it's craps. But I wanna make certain you understand the odds. That's all I'm teachin' you, Jan – the outline, the basics, the structure of these goddamned games. I'm not tellin' you how to gamble, hon. No, no, no, no, no.'

I crane my head towards the poker room. Victor's not that far away. I could almost see him if there weren't so many gaming tables filling in the space between us, and all those fancy pillars. This casino's fairly small – at least compared with giants like Caesars and the Gold Rush. It's a new one, called Last Chance, pretty grand, but compact. Victor only brought me here because they run these weekly poker tournaments with higher stakes than most. I was keen to see a world-class game like those he'd played Downtown, but there were none in his league, nothing big at all. This place was just a compromise. Victor warned me all along that weekly tourneys are never all that special, but I didn't take it in. I was still hyped up on television cameras, players flying in from round the world, crowds of tense spectators; all the things he'd told me about his previous tournament.

Of course it was a let-down when I found a scene not that different really from Jan's mother's little bridge evenings, but it was totally my fault for living in a dream. I feel rotten walking out on him when he tried so hard to scotch the whole idea. If I hadn't been so stubborn, I could be sitting now in some nice romantic restaurant, or learning to drive that steel-blue Thunderbird, instead of trapped here by a snake.

'Don't let anybody tell you how to gamble, Jan. Not your boyfriend, not your mother, not your uncle, not your pastor, not your room-mate, not your . . .'

'No, I won't. I promise. In fact, now you mention my room-mate, I really ought to . . .'

'Nobody. D'ya hear me, Jan? Gamblin's personal, like gettin' married. It's your money, your luck, your life, your hunches, your goddamned chips down on that table. Now listen, hon, pair of fives you don't have to split, because if you get a ten or a jack or a queen or a king or a nine or an eight or a seven or . . .'

'. . . told her I wouldn't be late. Doesn't like being left all on her . . .'

'Pair of aces? That's different. Always split a pair of aces. Always always always always . . .'

I'm gone. I've run. My heart's beating like all hell, but I've got away. He won't find me in the Ladies' Room. I'll stay here fifteen minutes, till he's buggered off himself, then return to Victor and the poker room. If Victor's even noticed that I've left – which somehow I still doubt – I'll pretend I just popped out for some air, or was feeling faint and had to have a lie-down.

I re-do my make-up first. I like to make an effort when Victor's so appreciative, calls me beautiful, though I'm less bothered now about trying to look older. I told him I was twenty-one and he just accepted it, and no one else has so much as raised the issue. Mind you, I do look quite sophisticated. I'm wearing a tight black skirt with a rather racy slit one side, and a clingy sort of sweater with little buttons down the front, and I washed my hair in True Blonde, which made it go fairer and more fluffy.

I undo my top two buttons, spray my breasts with scent, sling my new cream raincoat round my shoulders. Victor bought me that. It's the frightfully snobby trench-coat kind with a belt and epaulettes, which *très chic* females wear in foreign films. I was teasing him about his rapist's mac – the black one he was wearing when I met him – and he asked me would I help him choose a new one, then bought me one to match. He even suggested buying something for Norah, so I had to explain her horror of new clothes.

He was really sweet with Norah, and also concerned about us leaving her alone so long, so yesterday we took her out with us. I was a bit annoyed at first, didn't want a threesome or a chaperone, but Victor was so kind to her, even made her laugh (which is quite a feat itself), that I was really rather touched. He took us to a chocolate factory, which is one of the attractions here, where you watch the chocolates being made and the squiggles put on top. Norah was confused at first. All the factory workers wore white coats, so she assumed they were doctors and that we'd moved to some new hospital. Actually, he must think Norah's far worse than she is, because every time she called me Carole, I hissed 'Jan' at her and glared, and poor Toomey just went silent and looked hangdog.

I suppose I should confess about the Carole, but he's called me Jan so many times by now (Americans use your name far more often than we English, so you begin to feel you really do exist), and anyway, I feel safer being Jan. Jan never lands in trouble (or in psychiatric hospitals), or screws up her own chances. She wouldn't have left the poker room, to start with, or got involved with Jake, or grabbed that hundred dollar bill. I was really had, there, wasn't I? I imagined Jake was giving me a hundred bucks to try my luck at craps, until I turned the damn thing over and found it was a business card, printed with his name the other (plain white) side, 'Snake Jake' – that's all it said. No boring surnames. Well, I was disappointed, naturally, but also quite impressed. I mean, snakes are sheer sex, aren't they, what with Eve and Freud and everything, and Snake Jake sounds incredibly exotic after standard names like Jon. I felt quite apologetic about my own name, which I had to keep as Jan, since Victor was within spitting distance and for all I knew, the two might know each other.

God! I'm horrid. Waltzing off with Snake under Victor's very nose, giving up on him when he's done everything my way the last two days. Two days? It must be longer. I feel I've known him half my life. We talked so much, did so many things. Both days were wonderful, didn't rush us, let us take our time, spun themselves out into two dramatic sunsets, two dazzling starlit nights. I actually felt happy, not wild or drunken happy, just surprisingly content.

I stride towards the door. I'm going back to him, not waiting fifteen minutes. If Jake's lurking just outside, too bad.

He's not lurking. He's not even playing craps again. I squeeze past the wild crowds at the tables into the solemn hush of the poker room, which is not a separate room at all, just a group of tables beneath a carved and gilded ceiling in one corner of the main casino.

Victor's gone.

He can't have. I check all the different tables, all the groups of people watching or just lounging, scan the tiny bar. No Victor anywhere. I rush back to the table he was playing at – three players still in action. One was sitting next to him, a small man in a turquoise satin tracksuit drinking milk instead of cocktails.

'Excuse me, but do you know where Victor is?'

'Who?'

'You know, Vic. The guy in the grey suit.'

'He left.'

'Left?'

'Yeah. He just steamed, sluffed off his chips and ran.'

What's that supposed to mean? That's the trouble with this game. It's all double Dutch to me, not just the jargon, the whole thing. No wonder I got restive when I don't understand the rules, and everyone's so surly. I mean, this pinta chap isn't even listening. I try again.

'Look, I'm sorry, but I've got to find my friend. It's urgent.'

'The way he looked, I'd leave him on his own.'

'What d'you mean?' I'm scared now. Did Victor see me with Snake Jake and walk off in a huff; or did he lose his game, lose a lot of money; or has he simply gone to have a pee?

'Did he say where . . .?'

'Gimme a break, will ya? I'm tryin' to play, not run a datin' service.'

'All I want to know is . . .'

'Get lost. And if that's not clear, fuck off.'

I storm back to the bar, buy myself a daiquiri. Christ! They're rude in Vegas. I gulp my drink, try to calm my rage, calm down generally. If Victor's playing still, he'll be back in just a second, and if he isn't . . .

He can't have seen me, can he, with his back turned and his eyes glued to his cards? And even if he did, what's so terrible about exchanging names with a passing stranger? Jake and I weren't kissing, for God's sake. All these guys are far too keen on gambling to waste precious time on clinches. No, Victor's gone to find me, obviously, and so long as one of us stays put, we'll meet up in a moment.

I drain my glass, join the few spectators by his table. Best for him to find me there, not loafing in the bar. I'm ashamed now that I was bored. The other player's girlfriend is still in harness, so to speak, boosting his morale. She's been there hours, yet still looks quite content. She's called a 'sweater' – another jargon word, but one which Vic explained: someone who sits behind their partner and 'sweats' for him or her, supports them, roots for them. They may be financial partners who've both put money up and have arranged to split the winnings. More often, they're just women – wives or girlfriends, submissive passive females with no part in the action, but who just sit tight and wait.

This one's brought her sewing and looks the picture of tame womanhood, plying her needle while the Big Guy does the winning. I must admit, it bugs me. It's like those Japanese wives who walk three steps behind their husbands, or these stupid cocktail waitresses who are simply sexual turn-ons for the men. One's wobbling past me now, her micro-skirt slit right up both sides to show her black lace knickers. It'll be the twenty-second century before Women's Lib hits Vegas.

I'm a sham, though, aren't I? I don't believe in Lib; am desperate for a man, don't feel real without one. I only picked up Jake because Victor seemed so distant, completely changed from the kind, devoted admirer he'd always been before. Once he sat down at that table, his face went cold and closed; mouth set hard, eyes steely. I was scared that was the real Vic, and that the indulgent tender one was just a play-act.

It all seems stupid now. Of course you've got to concentrate if you're a high-powered poker player, risking next week's caviare or next year's winter cruise. If I weren't so paranoid, I'd have just sat back and enjoyed it. It's nothing like the bridge-evenings. Am I blind or something? They don't have dealers in red frilled shirts and bow-ties – not in Portishead; or men in diamond bracelets (one who's lost three fingers); or way-out female players like that gigantic blonde in frills, who's brought her teddy bear and appears to be explaining all her hands to it. This is really living. It'll be a lot more boring back in Florence Ward, watching Ethel Barnes cheat at snakes and ladders.

No, it's Carole who's the patient – and I've decided to be Jan – placid, happy Jan, drinking it all in, waiting for her guy who'll be back in just three seconds . . .

Half an hour later, I'm still standing there without him. I'm really panicked now. He's left me, abandoned me, paid me back for my own disloyalty. He told me himself how casual people were in Vegas, how friendships never lasted, how the folks you met were mainly 'transients', passing through, passing on. Yet didn't he regret that, seem to want me as a friend? He never took his eyes off me, for God's sake. Perhaps he's ill, came over faint or something, and went back to his hotel.

I snatch my coat up, dash towards the exit. Dolt I am, hanging around this table like a ninny. I never even thought of his hotel.

'Caesars Palace, please, as quickly as you can.'

The cab streaks along the Strip, past the Sahara, Riviera, Circus Circus, Stardust, Sands, the Imperial Palace, all trying to outdo each other with their attractions and their light effects.

Caesars wins hands down – more fountains than the Gold Rush, more lackeys than the Ritz. It reminds me of Versailles with its dramatic sweeping entrance, its floodlit pools and trees, though its official theme is ancient Greece and Rome. There are Carrara marble replicas of all the classical statues, mostly over life-size and made at frightening cost – the Venus de Milo, Venus de Medici (and other assorted Venuses I've never even heard of); the winged Victory of Samothrace (which has neither head nor arms), and a score of naked gods doing nothing whatsoever to hide their private parts.

The Rape of the Sabine Women stands right outside the entrance – another blow to Women's Lib. I avert my eyes from the struggling shrieking victims, enter into gloom. The more exclusive the casino, the lower the lights. Here, you almost need a guide dog to find your way at all. I blunder past bronze sphinxes, alabaster Pegasuses – almost blasé now about the overkill. They're exhausting, these casinos. All that luxury seems to weigh you down, as if the bronze and marble is pressing on your skull; the hothouse air drying up your juices. And there's always so much noise – dance bands playing; gab and shrill from crowds of foreign tourists, the constant maddening jangle of the slot machines.

At least it's quieter by the hotel reception desk. I join the queue of people waiting to check in, gaze around at the dozen Christmas trees, the 1920s white Rolls-Royce tethered on the carpet to advertise some show. It all looked so exciting when I saw it first with Victor. I was mad to sneak away from him.

'Can I help you, ma'am?' The impatient female clerk is tapping a red talon on her desk. I've wasted a whole second of her time.

'Er, yes. I . . . wish to contact one of your guests. Could you please phone up to his room, or get him paged.' I'm glad I've got the trench coat on. It gives my words some class.

'What name is it and what room number?'

'Victor . . .' I say, then stop. Victor who? Victor what? I must know. He told me, didn't he? And if not, wouldn't I have asked him? You can't spend two whole days with someone, have them paying court to you, telling you you're beautiful and still not know their surname. Anyway, surely I'd have seen it on a credit card, a driving licence? An initial even, on a wallet or a pocket. Americans love monograms.

The girl grooms one sleek eyebrow with her pen. She manages to combine extreme heroic patience and politeness (she's even stopped her tapping) with a hint of sheer contempt. I rack my brains, gallop through the alphabet. Victor Ace? Victor Barnes? Victor Zebedee? Mind you, he didn't know my surname, or even Jan's. Names were a dangerous subject, one I deliberately avoided.

'Look, I . . . um . . . can't quite recall his other name. The first name's Victor. Vic.'

'If you have his room number, that will be enough, madam.'

Madam doesn't have it. Madam is horribly embarrassed now, blushing and muttering, trying to explain to some supercilious desk-clerk that she's really bad at numbers and it's just slipped her mind. Perhaps I should guess a room, pick one out like a Keno number. But I haven't exactly proved my skills at Keno and there are only eighty numbers on the Keno board, not one thousand seven hundred. (Fifteen hundred rooms and two hundred suites at Caesars. I read it in my guide book.) The girl must imagine I'm some out-of-work hooker or a rejected Other Woman. Her expression suggests both at once. She's right. I am a failure. I haven't even seen his room. It didn't seem that strange at the time. We were so busy driving, dining, talking, playing, sightseeing, why sit around in stuffy hotel suites? Anyway, he's far too old for bed and I'd have simply slapped him down if he'd suggested it. He did stroke my hair and squeeze my hand, but that was different, not really sex at all. It made me feel – well – precious, which sounds soppy, but it's true. All my wild and greedy feelings had somehow all calmed down, and I felt just happy, mind and body.

Now I feel like grot. Victor didn't fancy me – that's obvious – even though I'm twenty-odd years younger. I just didn't turn him on. He mistook me for an escort girl, but a true Las Vegas escort or Brigitte Bardot look-alike would have been stripped off in his suite that very evening, not playing slots and stuffing steak, then sleeping in separate beds in hotels a mile apart.

Another complication: Victor still thought I was staying at the Tropicana; even drove me there both nights, said his chaste goodbye downstairs in the foyer. Both nights, I waited till he'd gone, then took a cab straight back to the Gold Rush. Oh, I know it sounds plain daft. Why couldn't I have explained, for heaven's sake, owned up about the lies; said I'd only made things up because I feared he was a mugger? But that's not exactly flattering, and anyway, I should have done it straight away, not let him get to know me as Jan, aged twenty-one, training as a florist, staying at the Tropicana. All lies.

More lies, as I try to fob the desk clerk off, answer her bang-bang-bang of questions. Am I a friend, or business contact? Can I leave my card? Do I remember where his room was – in the tower, or . . . ?

I've no idea. All I know is he didn't want me in it. I sniff my fingers, back away. Perhaps I smell of nicotine. Victor doesn't like smoke, so it might have put him off. I can only smell Wild Musk, which the blurb says drives men wild. I'd sue them for false claims if I didn't feel so miserable.

I slink back the way I've come. Victor's trench coat seems to drag me down now. Forget the fact I didn't turn him on. I've lost him as a friend, as I lost Jon in the summer. Men don't like me, do they? I'm too bossy, too impatient, can only take, not give. I pass a troupe of nymphs, ten pairs of perfect breasts in non-sag marble. I hate this place. You can't walk a step without some Model of Perfection showing up your own flab.

I've reached the shops now. All the big casinos have their own boutiques – sometimes strings of them. I peer into the toyshop. Even Caesars' dolls are dressed in mink. One has diamond earrings – real ones. I press on to the casino, wander idly up and down, bumping into people. Caesars' slot machines spell out little messages to encourage you to play.

I stop in front of one. 'Quick! Play me now,' it says. 'I'm easy.' I just stand there doing nothing, so it tries again. 'Cash in on your luck. You look like a winner.'

'You're joking,' I tell it. 'I couldn't stop Jon going and now I've lost Victor.'

'When you're hot, you're hot.'

'Victor didn't *want* me hot. That's what made it so relaxed. I could just be me and . . .' Well, actually, I couldn't. I doubt you ever can. You must always keep pretending if you want to keep a man. I should have played the sexpot, or the impassioned poker addict.

'Don't quit now,' the machine begs, trilling out its little tinkly tune.

'I haven't much alternative. He's gone.'

'Columbus took a chance.'

'Oh, fuck you!' If I'm reduced to conversation with a slot machine, it proves I've got no friends.

No friends but Norah. Christ! Norah. I've totally forgotten her, left her hours ago, still feeling weak and ill. She needs me. I need her. She's my only link with England, the only one who seems to really like me, even when I'm vile.

I rocket to the exit, call another cab. It's Victor's money I'm using for these cabs. He never gave me money – wouldn't be so patronizing – but when we played the tables, he laid all his bets for me, and every time he won, he insisted they were my winnings. It was me who'd brought him luck, he said.

'Luck!' I snort, over-tip the driver, dash towards the lifts. Norah may be fast asleep. It's nearly midnight. Selfishly, I hope she's wide awake.

I find her with her eyes closed, but on her knees; kneeling on the carpet in our bedroom in just her thermal petticoat, one bare arm outstretched, palm held flat against the television set. For one ghastly moment, I assume she's gone quite gaga. Las Vegas can do that, so Victor said – drive people over the top. Then I see the godman. She's got her hand pressed against his own. He's dressed in primrose yellow, with obtrusive gold back teeth which keep flashing as he smiles. He smiles a lot. He's telling us to keep our eyes tight shut, keep our hands pressed against the screen and to say out loud with him, 'I expect a miracle.'

'I expect a miracle,' says Norah.

I don't move a muscle, just stay motionless, watching her in silence from the doorway, torn between pity and sheer fury. She's already wasted half our precious money, sending it to preachers who are already filthy rich and so blatantly commercial that Jesus would have whipped them out of the temples, overturned their God-wares – Jesus-printed tee shirts, Holy Spirit brandy glasses. They don't even preach in temples, but in huge great stadiums bristling with microphones and thick with hothouse flowers – God's pop stars playing to their groupies. The whole thing's just a racket. They're preying on the fears of mugs like Norah, frightening them or conning them, so they send off all their cash.

I was furious when she told me what she'd done. Victor was there, too, which was just as well, since I'd have probably lynched her otherwise. I admired him, actually. He never raised his voice, yet calmed us both down, said what was done was done, and pointed out (later, and very tactfully and gently) that since I'd used, and lost, all Norah's gambling chips the very same evening, then maybe we were quits. He also made it up to us – gave me his own chips and all his winnings and bought Norah the prettiest box of chocolates in the chocolate factory shop, slipped some ten-dollar bills beneath the coffee creams, then replaced the wrappings and the ribbon, so she'd think all the boxes came complete with cash.

The memory makes me smile. It also stops me yelling. If Victor can be decent, so can I. 'Norah,' I say quietly.

She opens her eyes, stares at me in shock, as if she imagined God Himself had called her, and was expecting the Divine Countenance, not my freckled own.

'Norah, they don't want money, do they? Not again.'

'No,' she says. 'The miracles are free.'

'Miracles?'

'It's the year of miracles – this next year, he said, coming in just two days' time. Everyone can get one if they ask.'

I could do with one myself – Victor at my side, still doting and devoted. I turn the set down. 'Norah, you don't remember Victor's name, do you?'

'Vic,' she says.

'No, his other name, you nut.'

'Robert.'

'Was it? Did he tell you? Was that his surname or just his second name?'

Norah looks confused. 'Can I call you Carole now?'

I hesitate. She seems to hate to call me Jan, keeps glancing at me anxiously, as if she's scared I'll change my face and whole identity, as well as just my name. I'm sick of all the sham myself, the stupid complications, yet if I do find Victor and immediately explain I'm someone else, he may conclude I'm crazy and disappear again.

'No, better not,' I say. 'I'm sorry, love, but keep it Jan, will you, just for the moment?' I know we're on our own, but Norah gets so muddled and if I let her call me Carole now, she'll only go on doing it with Victor there.

'Do I call Victor "Robert"?'

'No!' I shout. 'You don't. Just try to remember what he said. Was it Mr Victor Robert or Victor Robert Something-else?'

She's frowning to herself, mumbling both alternatives, yet still sneaking furtive glances at the television set. I turn it up again. It may help her to remember – all that grace and God-stuff. The Reverend Primrose has brought on his whole family, who are now singing with the choir, beatific smiles on all their faces: two white-haired aged parents, a dazzling younger sister and an elder brother who looks a shade like Victor.

Could Victor be a godman, just softening me up before he started waving Bibles or spouting holy texts? That would explain why he never made a pass. I know it sounds ridiculous, but the whole of America's crazed about religion. Las Vegas has more churches per head of population than any other city in the world. They advertise with lurid lighted signs like shops or restaurants, or offer special deals to lure you in. Perhaps Victor was employed by some Big Brother organization to pick up teenage girls and turn them into Jesus-freaks. Or perhaps his speciality is converting escort girls and that's why he was loitering near those newsstands – sort of Friend of Mary Magdalens. He could even be a member of that television Church, the one Norah sent her money to, and all he did was hand her back her own ten-dollar bills. Okay, I'm joking now, but religion in America's gone far beyond a joke. I read about one Reverend who runs live Sunday sex-shows for his congregation. And there's another one – a woman – who's been divorced five times and was once Miss Arizona. She's written a book called *How To Get More From God And Bed*. I saw her on TV – forty-inch hips crammed into skin-tight snakeskin jeans and that sort of white-blonde hair all piled up stiff in curls like shop meringues. You can really take your choice with these television God-shows – lean clean young men with crew cuts, or fifteen-stone blonde bombshells, or happy Holy Families, like this one.

I flop back on the bed. I'm feeling really drained. 'Norah, did you hear me? Is it Victor Robert, or Victor Robert Something?'

'I don't know.'

'I mean are you sure he said Robert in the first place?'

'No.'

She's hardly even listening. Usually, like Victor, she hangs on my every word. I'm losing all my power. I glance back at the screen. That's where all the power is – a congregation at least four thousand strong, a huge choir of gorgeous females, colour-matched in shades of rose and beige, backed by a full orchestra, all wearing black tuxedos. That choir have changed their outfits twice in just ten minutes. Think of the expense. All those frilled Victorian dresses and lacy petticoats, the hours of cosmetic dentistry for those rows of perfect teeth. They must be competing with the Las Vegas Show Spectaculars – twenty costume changes, thirty different sets. The camera cuts from their glowing Pan-sticked faces to fields of summer flowers, golden beaches, little babbling brooks. It's all so pretty, so innocent and safe – the smugly beaming family (no fathers hiding gin bottles, no mothers throwing up); the clapping cheering crowds. I feel a sudden longing to join in, to be part of God's great tribe, have someone to believe in. Jesus wouldn't leave you in a poker room, desperate and alone, wouldn't hide His surname. These girls are all in love, all praising their Beloved in some weepy of a hymn. 'I surrender, I surrender, surrender to my Lord.' No prickly tricksy things like Women's Lib – just submission and obedience in return for constant love; a man who'll never leave you, who'll die for you. (He did.)

The frail old father now takes the microphone, his halo of white hair newly bleached and polished at the beauty parlour.

'This New Year will be your Year of Destiny; your year of miracles; your year of holding up your head and seeing all the stars.'

It sounds so beautiful, I half-believe it. His slender, fair-haired daughter is standing just beside him. They exchange real lovers' smiles. I turn away. 'Stand up!' he shouts suddenly, raising both his arms. The congregation stands, then disappears as he fills the screen himself, addressing us directly, all those million million viewers tuned to him at home.

'Everyone out there, watching in your bedrooms or your living rooms, or in bars or cafés, hotel rooms, get up on your feet now. Stand up to show your faith, and say with me, "I expect a miracle!" Shout it real loud.'

We're standing, me and Norah, holding up our arms, shouting out, 'I expect a miracle, I expect a miracle!' It's crazy, yet it feels so good, so powerful. We're part of that whole extended family, joined to all America. I feel quite different now – confident and hopeful. Of course I'll find Victor. I didn't try hard enough, that's all. I should have stayed longer in the poker room, or checked the Tropicana, where he'd probably gone to search for me. And now I have his surname, Caesars can locate him for me anyway. I squeeze Norah's sweaty hand.

'Victor Robert, wasn't it, you're sure?'

She nods, face shining, eyes still on the screen.

'Right,' I tell her. 'Put your clothes on, Norah. I want my miracle now, and you can help me get it.'

12

'Mr Victor Robert?' Norah asks.

I can hardly hear her. I'm lurking in a corner, concealed behind a Caesars' Christmas tree. Thank God I brought her with me. It's the same contemptuous desk clerk as before, still tapping her red nails. If I came grovelling a second time, she'd shred me into coleslaw. She's not exactly beaming at poor Norah. I can't make out her words, but I'm already losing hope. This is our last try. We've scoured the Tropicana, hung around for ages in the blasted poker room. Is it even worth it? I mean, if Victor can't be bothered to come and look for me, why hunt him down like this?

I try to sound unmoved when Norah returns, babbling on about two Mr Roberts, one French and one J. A. No Victors. I suppose I was too greedy for my miracle. It's not the New Year yet, our Year of Destiny.

'Who cares?' I shrug. 'How about a cocktail, Norah?'

She shakes her head.

'What d'you want to do then?'

'Is there a . . . circus here?'

'Bound to be. *And* a zoo. And probably replicas of Disney-land and Longleat rolled together.' They've got everything in the world at Caesars Palace, except one stupid boring man. 'But I'm sorry, love, I couldn't face the clowns, not now.'

'Could we go to bed, then?'

'No!' I shout. 'We couldn't.' I'm damned if I'll trail off back to bed. I'd never sleep anyway, with all this mix of guilt and disappointment and resentment, and Norah can't be tired. She's been in bed all day, sleeping off her tummy-bug.

A fully-armed sheriff is moving in on us, alerted by my shout. The security at Caesars is more suited to Alcatraz than to a mere resort hotel. It even makes the Gold Rush seem quite lax. Besides these hulks in uniforms there are swarms of steel-jawed plain-clothes men lurking in dark corners, electronic eyes scanning lifts and car parks, and maybe Special Squads to eavesdrop on eighteen-year-olds, snap them into handcuffs at the mere mention of a dangerous word like 'cocktail'.

I steer Norah to the exit. I daren't take any chances when I'm under-age. I was pretty safe with Victor. His own sober middle age and bulging wallet were like a shield, protecting me. I need a guy, for God's sake. You're in danger on your own here.

I feel suddenly very small and frail. Some show has just ended and people are pouring out in droves towards the doors. I'm swallowed up in other people's arms and legs, other people's laughter; people talking over me as if I don't exist; their sweat and scent curdling in my nostrils. I fight back through the crowds to rescue Norah. She's hemmed in as well, looks pale and really drained. Why don't I do the decent thing for once, take her back to bed? Okay, if I can't sleep, I can always read some soppy magazine – a love story where the guy adores the girl, or at least doesn't hide from her on purpose.

'Okay, Norah. Bedtime.'

I refuse to join the queue for cabs – all those smug and laughing couples, hand in hand. If we start walking along the Strip, we're bound to find one free. I link arms with Norah, and we plod, heads down against the rain. Yes, rain again. It's been the wettest-ever December in Las Vegas since 1940-something. I heard it on the news. Just our luck. And the first time they've had snow in years and years, though at least that didn't settle, just flurried down, then melted.

Every cab I wave at is either blind or deaf or both. You need a guy for getting cabs as well. Some big bloke snaps one up with just a waggle of one finger, while I'm standing right beside him, shaking my whole arm off. I glare at him, but he's already settled back and in the dry.

The Strip is jammed with traffic, the whole town filling up for New Year's Eve. That's the big deal here – New Year.

Everyone's pushing it, proclaiming it, and nothing else is mentioned on TV – re-runs of old New Years, previews of this coming one; New Year offers, New Year forecasts, hopes. It's a bit like gambling, I suppose. A new year may make your fortune or land you in the gutter; see you rich and famous, or skint and shunned. That's why people get so hysterical about it. Even people who've had a run of rotten years still cheer and dance and open the champagne. It's like someone's put a bet on them, given them another chance of winning – one which could wipe out all their previous losses at a stroke.

Thinking about champagne reminds me that I've missed three Champagne Receptions in a row – all free and part of our prize deal. They didn't seem important at the time, not compared with Victor. Now, I'm not so sure. If I'd gone along, I might have met some really young and gorgeous man. No – not too young. I prefer them older, when they're kind, and know the restaurants, and want someone to look after, and are rather sweetly grateful for nothing much at all. Victor was like that. Victor . . .

Damn Victor. It's his fault I've wasted all this time. He just led me on, let me think he liked me, so it would hurt more when he went. I suppose all men are like that, relishing their power. And yet I know I need one. I just don't feel important on my own. And sometimes hardly real. I stop a moment, turn my collar up against the drizzle.

'Norah?'

'Yes.'

'Don't you ever mind being, you know – single – on your own?'

'I don't live on my own. I never have.'

'No, but when you were – well – younger, didn't you ever think you'd like a man?'

'No.'

I say nothing after that. I suspect that I've upset her. She's walking sort of heavily and flatly. God! We're stupid, both of us. Here we are on the Trip Of A Lifetime, yet both looking as if we've been sent off into exile.

We're forced to stop again. We've run into another crowd,

jostling round the entrance of a big casino. Some bloke dressed as a pilot in goggles and a helmet is handing leaflets out. 'WIN A HELICOPTER ON OUR PROGRESSIVE SLOTS!'

'Hey, Norah, look at this. If I won a chopper, we wouldn't need a cab.'

She doesn't seem convinced, follows only sluggishly through the doors of the casino. I think it's the wrong one. We've found the dollar slot machines, but no sign of any helicopters. They usually park the prizes right there on the spot – James Bond speedboats or jet-set Cadillacs – to encourage you to play. Here, there's hardly room – slot machines packed tight in rows and rows; shoals of gambling tables which look as if they've spawned themselves. The ceiling is wild purple, starred with silver lights; more silver on the cut-out cardboard trees. It's hard to see the walls at all, when they're three foot deep in punters. I hand Norah some dollars, find two free machines. Now we're here, we'd better have a flutter. If we don't win a helicopter, we may well win our cab fare, and at least we're drying off.

I sit back on my stool, start feeding my machine. It's wonderful the way it calms you down. Pulling that huge lever mops up the adrenaline and you can really ram the coins in – bang bang bang bang bang – Jake's dead; Victor's dead; that man who grabbed my taxi's dead; all shrinks and social workers are dead dead dead dead dead. I'm not winning, not at all, but I don't care – it's great. Anyway, if you lose, it gives you an excuse to thump the damn machine. No one seems to mind. They're all too busy with their own concerns – winning, losing, drinking. Norah's played just one lone coin and is still sitting there, staring at her two lemons and a plum.

'Let's move,' I say. 'Try the quarter machines instead. These dollar ones are probably rigged. They're losing us a bomb.'

I call the change-girl over (more black-lace thigh and cleavage), change a wodge of dollar bills for quarters. I fill two plastic pots with them, entrust the lighter one to Norah, coax her to another stool.

'Go on, love, have a bit of fun for once. See if you can win us both a fortune.'

I start shovelling in my own coins, pulling the handle harder for each one. I'm losing losing losing losing losing. Luck can change, though. Victor told me that himself. Just last year, an unemployed divorcee who'd lost a breast to cancer won one million, two hundred and fifty-seven thousand, four hundred and thirty-two dollars in the Hilton Super Pot of Gold Slot Championships. That so impressed me, I remember all the figures, even down to the last two dollars. I cross my fingers, lose. Lose again. Lose, lose, lose. It's just not fair. I must have won by now, on any law of averages. I try another machine. Some of them are definitely unlucky. I heard a woman swear at one in The Four Queens, Downtown, even kick and punch it. She was dressed like a queen herself, in a designer gown and diamonds, and little white kid gloves so she wouldn't get her hands soiled handling coins; but you should have heard her language. Filthy dirty.

'Let's go back,' says Norah. She's breathing down my neck, and still has all her quarters. I just don't know what's wrong with her. She won't eat in the restaurants, won't risk a nickel on the slots. It's as if she feels nothing's really hers. She'll be punished if she swallows half a pea, damned in hell for losing that one buck. Even now, she's handing me her pot. I play her quarters for her, losing every time, really zipping in the coins because I know she's tired and dying for her bed.

'Slow down,' warns the woman next to me. 'If you play so fast, the machine can't pay, even if you do win. It takes a few seconds for the coins to drop. You might have won a jackpot, but you played right through it; didn't give it time to show, or give the bell a chance to ring.'

I stare at her in horror. Victor told me just the same. He laughed, in fact, because I was so keen to get the coins in, I forgot to pull the lever. There are just four quarters left in Norah's pot, none at all in mine. I've poured all Victor's money down the drain, whereas if I hadn't been so stupidly impatient, I might have made myself a millionairess. I play my last coins very very slowly, give the machine all the time it needs to ring and win.

It loses.

A bell *is* ringing, very loud and shrill. I glance round, see people rushing over to the progressive dollar slot machines which we've just left ourselves. 'Quick!' I say to Norah. 'Someone's hit the jackpot.'

A dumpy balding man in a short-sleeved nylon shirt and pea-green slacks is in a clinch with his slot machine, stroking it, caressing it, feeling up all its bumps and curves. 'We got it!' he keeps yelling, as he turns back to his friends. 'We got it! We got the son of a bitch.' Now he's hugging all his friends, whirling them around, doing a sailor's hornpipe solo on the carpet. I edge a little closer. He's won twenty thousand, six hundred and eighty dollars. The figures are lit up and flashing on and off, the bell still pealing out, the old crone playing next to him yelping with excitement, crowds of strangers pushing, shoving, 'aahing'. The whole casino seems to have come alive. Security guards appear from nowhere, tower above the little chap. He's a winner now, worthy of protection. Already he's handing out largesse – ordering drinks for everyone, tipping the waitress before she's brought a thing, calling up champagne, cigars.

More people scurry over. Two men in dark blue jackets pump him by the hand, ask for proof of his identity, pass him pen and paper. He starts filling in some form or other, still not concentrating. He keeps pummelling his own chest, mock-wrestling with his buddies, yelling out 'Oh, boy!' and 'Jeez!', as if he's just too freaked and high for longer words.

There's no sign of any money yet, though I hear him say he'd like some of it in cash, instead of one big cheque. I wait, breathless and keyed-up, almost as excited as if I'd won myself. He's just a nobody, a Mr Something Jones – I missed the Christian name – and yet he's made it. Twenty thousand dollars just like that. Sheer luck, that's all it was. I'd better stay around. Luck's infectious. The drinks have come now, scores of them. He hands me a tall glass, thick with ice and fruit. At least he's noticed me. I'm the only under-thirty female in the swelling crowd around him. Some aged harridan is pushing to get closer, but I block her way. Gotta be tough in Vegas.

Norah's out of it, drooping by a cardboard tree right over by the wall, but glancing at me anxiously, as if she's scared she'll lose me in all the press of bodies.

'Come over here,' I mouth.

Suddenly, there's a ripple through the crowd, like a strong breeze blowing through a wheatfield; then wheat changes into water as it parts like the Red Sea. I've no eyes for Norah now. Every head, including mine, is turned towards the uniformed official who is striding through the gap just opened up. The money – on its way!

The official hands it over, not to Mr Jones, but to the sultry carousel girl with liquorice hair and eyes who stands above the row of slot machines. She gives him first the cheque, then counts out the cash very carefully and solemnly – an impressive pile of hundred-dollar bills. There's almost total silence now, save for the swiftly rising figures of the count. This is a sacred moment and the casino's congregation reverence it. Never before have I seen so much money in one small and dirty hand.

I glance behind me, terrified that some hit-and-run man may be waiting to dart in. No – they've thought of that. Three security guards are already hovering, fingering their guns. The final eighty bucks is paid. The crowd lets out its breath. They've all just won that jackpot in their minds, and half of them are spending it already. There's an orgy going on while young men test-drive Porsches, women overheat in minks, old crones move their cats and budgies into luxury bungalows with live-in nurses. I've bought a house myself (twelve bedrooms and an indoor swimming pool), and I'm just strolling through the stables inspecting my thoroughbreds and telling my chauffeur I prefer the white Rolls to the silver one, when Jones picks out two hundred-dollar bills and hands them to the carousel girl. She murmurs 'thanks', as if they were two mere lousy quarters. Two hundred dollars just for counting out the cash, and she's not even all that struck! I vow to take a job here, write in for an interview tomorrow. I'm desperate for cash. Norah and I have got through all our money in just four days, not to mention Victor's.

People are swarming up to Super-Jones, shaking his hand, clapping him on the back, making little jokes. He's kissing two change-girls now, has his arm around the waitress. He's only about five foot five (and that's in Cuban heels), has age spots on his hands, and a roll of fat between his collar and his neck, and yet he could be a top rock-star for all the adulation he's receiving. I suppose money makes you tall and handsome, as well as just plain rich. He's never going to notice me, with all those crotch-length skirts and wired-up cleavages. I step out of the crowd.

'Thanks for the drink,' I say. It was quite some drink – a tumbler-sized cocktail with at least three different liquors in it; must have given me new courage.

'Say, you from England, honey? I just love that accent.'

They all just love that accent. Being English here is like having a gold American Express card; it opens doors. I murmur a few words, trying to sound more Princess Di/Sloane Ranger than Portishead – though I doubt if most Americans have a clue about the difference.

'Where you from?'

'London. Just off Sloane Street.'

'Great to meet you. I'm Milt Jones.'

'What Jones?'

'Milt. Short for Milton.'

'Like the poet?'

'Poet?'

'You know, *Paradise Lost*. John Milton.'

'No, I'm not John. Milt's my first name. Milton Sherwood Jones. Jones is Welsh. My great-great-grandfather came from Wales. And my grandma came from Ly-cester.'

'Leicester.' I correct his pronunciation.

'What?'

'Oh, forget it.' I feel a nervous tugging at my sleeve. 'Er – this is Norah.' I wish now I'd left her safe in bed. I can see Milt's friends eyeing her with a mixture of distaste and curiosity. Her Crimplene's really filthy now, the jacket buttoned up wrong, and the rain has done nothing for her hair.

'Hi, Norah. This is Gabe. That's Eddie in the stetson. Wayne's the ugly mug, and this tree-trunk here is Shorty.'

We all laugh save Norah, who looks scared out of her wits. I say 'hallo' for both of us, save my broadest smile for Wayne, who's actually quite dishy. Milt hands me a new drink, another whopper.

'What did you say your name was?'

I didn't. Names are still a problem. Will Norah call me Jan and land me in it? I'm sick of Jan, to tell the truth. She's only brought me trouble. Yet Carole's so damned dull.

'Er . . . Atalanta,' I blurt out. God knows why. Blame three different liquors. I can't even remember who she was, except definitely a goddess and extremely beautiful. I think she won a golden apple; won something, anyway – and I like the names of winners.

'That's some name, kid.'

Kid, when I'm a goddess! 'My father chose it,' I say nonchalantly. 'He was a Professor of Ancient Greek.'

I can see they're impressed – not just Milt, but all the friends and hangers-on as well. (My father sold shirts and ties and handkerchiefs in an old-fashioned menswear shop, where he worked for twenty years. The only Greek he knew was 'hummus' because when my mother was too bad to cook, he bought it from the Cypriot take-away and we had it on Ryvita with a pot of tea and Kit-Kats.) Anyway, it's worked. I've been admitted to their circle, two arms linked in mine now, Wayne's eyes on my skirt slits, which he obviously approves of. He offers me a fat cigar. Why not? I'm down to my last Marlboro.

I sip my gin, puff out clouds of smoke. Life's looking up, no doubt about it. I just wish Norah didn't seem so jumpy. These guys won't eat her, for God's sake. A rather sweet old grandpa-type with silver hair and glasses is even trying to talk to her. I flash him a big smile. If Norah's happy, I can relax a bit myself. Milt's still playing winner, mopping up more fans, dishing out the drinks. Their fawning seems to turn him on.

'How about some dinner?' he suggests. It must be two AM at least, so they've probably eaten, most of them, but this is swinging Vegas. Why stop at just one dinner?

'Great idea,' I say, pushing right up front again. I don't want to lose this wonder-guy, though it's a shame about the trousers. That green's okay inside a pod, or jazzing up boring pie and chips, but not on human legs. If he'd done his shopping at my father's store, he'd have been persuaded into quiet grey serge or sensible brown worsted. Never mind. I feel exceptionally forgiving at the moment, and also rather peckish. 'Yeah,' I say, waving my cigar. 'A celebration dinner. Fabulous!'

A strand of Norah's dripping hair snails across my cheek. I turn to face her. 'What?' She's whispering in my ear and I can't hear a thing for all the whoopee.

'I'm not hungry, Jan. I'm not allowed to eat.'

'Yes, you are, love. That was just the first two days. In fact, you ought to try to eat now, or you'll start keeling over. You can always order something plain.'

'It's not dinner-time. It's bedtime.'

'Ssh,' I whisper back. If Milt's just won twenty thousand odd, this may be the most expensive lavish dinner we've ever seen or dreamed of. Norah shouldn't miss it. She's missed too many things in life already, always cowering in a ward or shut away. This is her chance to live it up for once, build some memories, before the walls close in again. Okay, I could take her back, or put her in a cab, but she's been cooped up in the Gold Rush all damned day.

'Look, just have some soup, love, or just one course or something. I'll sit next to you – okay? – tell the waiter you're not feeling all that great.'

You can't have soup or only just one course. It's a Moroccan feast, ten courses, and a chef who gets insulted if you don't have second helpings of them all. And I'm not sitting next to Norah. I tried my best, but Milton split us up, insisted he sat next to me; then Wayne flopped down the other side, with Gabe and Eddie opposite. No one's sitting, actually – not on chairs – there aren't any, and no knives and forks or spoons. You eat with your fingers and recline on silken cushions. It's part of the attraction. The restaurant is a sultan's tent, a replica, with no boring inessentials like ceiling, walls or windows, just purple silk billowing in folds. The floor is spread with oriental carpets and there are gleaming copper kettles dotted all around.

When we first came in, a sort of Moroccan-style Lolita picked up a kettle and went all round the table, pouring warm rose-scented water over everybody's hands, then dried them with pink towels. It took her ages. There are thirty in our party.

Once he'd won, Milt was like a magnet, his cash attracting groupies. I'm the number one, though, all his own kudos spilling over on to me. The two of us are sharing one large cushion at the far end of the knee-high coffee table, his bulging wallet swelling out his trousers like a trophy, badge of rank. It's strange how it attracts me. I keep looking at it, checking on it. It's not just cash as such – it's power, authority, my power as well as his. Waiters are kowtowing to me, Moroccan nymphets simpering, dusky youths plying me with wine.

It's a Moroccan wine, called Sidi Mustapha, which is the same name as the chef. (Well, not the Sidi bit, just the Mustapha.) He's a sweetie, Mustapha, keeps lumbering out of the kitchen in his tall white hat and apron, hugging guests at random, begging them to eat more, praising his own cooking to the skies. He was really upset because Norah wasn't eating, wouldn't touch his couscous. She wasn't all that keen on scooping up a soggy mess of chickpeas with her hands, and she doesn't fancy raisins mixed with meat. It's even worse trying to eat salad with your fingers. We had this huge great bowl of it, with a really oily dressing which dribbled over everything. I swilled down three big helpings before I discovered there was something called *cilantro* in it – Chinese parsley, an aphrodisiac. It's affected me already, or maybe it's the booze, or hunky Wayne, who keeps leaning over, asking me to wipe my greasy fingers on his jeans.

I move my knees nearer to his crotch, glance around our table. There's quite a lot of talent – at least six or seven really classy men, and that rather adorable oldie who's sitting next to Norah, still struggling hard to get a word from her. The women aren't that great, though – a tedious redhead who answers to the name of Misty and keeps talking about her osteopath; a female wrestler in polyester leopard, with her depressive younger sister, Merry-Lyn, and a few nondescript fatsos who obviously resent the fact I'm younger, slimmer and Milt's Elect.

The waiters are all darling – lean and dark with peat-bog eyes and dressed in baggy scarlet pantaloons and gold Moroccan slippers, pointed at the ends. The whole atmosphere's exotic, with the swaying coloured lamps and the wild impassioned music blaring from the stereo, with its sudden dramatic pauses and crescendos. Ed says it's a ninety-nine-stringed Kanoon, whatever that is. Ed's been here before. He told me it's a tourist place, quite a favourite spot for celebrations. Well, you'd need to win a packet just to foot the bill. Dom Perignon costs two hundred dollars a bottle – I saw it on the wine list. Milt ordered some for me, but I must confess, I prefer the Sidi stuff, which is sweetish and sort of aromatic. I push my glass across, offer him a sip. He's drinking Seven-Up himself.

'No, alcohol's a stimulant and I'm not allowed to get pepped up. Doctor's orders, honey. That's why I drink this stuff. It's got no caffeine, see? Like they say on TV – "Never had it, never will".'

It sounds a pretty dreary claim to me. I wouldn't go round boasting that I'd never had it, but then poor Milt's off a lot of things – has to watch his calories, his cholesterol count, his daily fibre intake, and something called his EFAs. Misty's not much better. She's describing a recent trip to Europe's capitals in terms solely of her bowels: bunged up in Amsterdam, fast and loose in Paris, laxatives in Athens, griping pains in Rome.

Wine's a laxative, I've heard, so I put my own glass down, squeeze Milt's chubby thigh, my eye still on that wallet. I'm its bodyguard, its watchdog, protecting it from pickpockets. No danger at the moment – except from Mustapha, who is bearing down on us with a gigantic sort of pastry thing, bigger than a car-tyre and snowed with icing sugar. The pudding? No. We've got five more courses still to go before we reach dessert. Mustapha is beaming. This is the *pastilla royal*, which in his native Casablanca is made to honour royalty. Milt is king, so Milt must break it open, let the aromatic steam escape. Mustapha's English leaves a lot to be desired, but I understand the gist of it. He's babbling on about the importance of this ceremony, which I gather is symbolic, and how the ingredients of the dish itself are loaded down with meaning – fertility, virility, friendship, immortality. It all sounds pretty heavy for what is basically a gargantuan cream puff.

No. Wrong again. There's no cream in it at all – everything else except. I see Norah's face fall further as he starts listing all the fillings: honey, almonds, chicken, scrambled egg. I doubt if she could face them singly, let alone all mixed and mushed together. Milt looks dazed as well, though he's trying hard, up to his wrists in grease and icing sugar as he tears apart the gigantic ring of pastry. The steam escapes, the waiters cheer, the ninety-nine-stringed whatsit adds its wail of triumph. Then we all dip in, yanking off great hunks which smell sensational, but are impossible to eat. The strudel-type pastry flakes and breaks to nothing, dollops of the filling drop on laps and cushions, icing sugar wafts in sneezy clouds.

I feed Milt with a sliver. It's probably on his no-no list, but if he doesn't at least sample it, he may risk friendlessness, sterility, impotence and death. Wayne is feeding *me*, dribbling honey down my cleavage, which gives him an excuse to lick it up. His tongue is in the pro class, though it distracts me from the taste of the *pastilla*, which is really quite extraordinary, very sweet and cinnamony, yet with sudden shocks of salty egg or spicy chicken jarring on the palate. I glance at Norah, who can't eat anything, since she's bandaged both her hands in her soft pink Turkish towel. (We were all given these pink towels, which seem to be the Moroccan equivalent of paper serviettes, and much more useful when there's so much grease and gunge about.) I ease up from my cushions, *pastilla* chunk in one hand, wine glass in the other.

'You've just got to try this, Norah. It's power-food, quite amazing. You won't get *this* at Beechgrove. And have a sip of wine, love. You can't keep drinking all that boring water.'

The sweet old guy who's sharing Norah's pouffe looks quite relieved to see me, squeezes up one end to make room for me as well.

'Is your friend hard of hearing?'

I nod, suppress a giggle. His accent is deep South. Poor Norah probably hasn't understood a single word. Suddenly, Mustapha's huge belly is wobbling over us. He pulls Norah to her feet, whisks her through the curtains of the tent. God! What now? Norah needs a nursemaid and I'm too unsteady on my pins to fit the role. I stagger after them, catch my breath as sultan's tent gives way to steamy kitchen – the hottest, busiest kitchen I've ever seen; grills and gases flaring, whole tribes of dark-skinned boys stirring, chopping, kneading; sweat pouring down each face. The smell's delirious – cardamom and garlic mixed with buttered honey; sharp astringent mint. The boys all nod and smile as I slink in. I mutter a hallo, but the word's completely lost in the clash of pans, the whir of liquidizers, the chef's own voice lashing out at Norah.

'You no like our food? You no think our kitchen clean? I show you kitchen. Kitchen *very* clean.'

He picks up shining saucepans, gleaming ladles, shoves them under Norah's nose. He's obviously upset. Ed told me that it's an insult in Morocco to refuse your host's food and that anything under six or seven courses is considered parsimonious, hardly worth the name of meal at all. I'd better make sure I never win a holiday in Agadir or somewhere – or not with Toomey as my table-mate. The chef is close to tears.

'I cook for royal palace. I cook for Shah. I cook for Princess Anne . . .'

'My friend's not well,' I soothe him. 'It's not your food at all. She was feeling lousy anyway.'

'Nothing lousy here. My food good, very good. I buy myself. I get up at blast of dawn . . .'

By the time I've calmed him down and reassured poor Norah, and we've all three made it up with huge bear-hugs and free samples from the battery of pans, our party is two courses on, and Misty and a man called Doc (who's nothing medical) are fighting a mock duel with their two-foot-long kebab skewers. Wayne has saved me a kebab and starts wooing me with chunks of pork and mushroom.

'Where did ya get to, honey? I was worried you was throwin' up or somethin'.'

I can't speak for charcoaled pork, so I shake my head, then nod it, to show I'm quite okay. Wonderful, in fact. He's sort of massaging my mouth with a warm and buttery mushroom cap, running it round the insides of my lips. I lick his fingers as a small return. They taste delicious – honey-roasted he-man with a hint of spice and sweat. I just wish Milton wasn't watching. I like the guy, but he's not exactly a ball of fun. His seventh course is not kebab, but indigestion tablets – two Tums washed down with water. I suppose he likes the Tums commercial too: 'Do without the heartburn *and* the sodium.'

He returns the carton to his pocket, pulls out something else – an airline ticket – starts to crumple it up.

'What you doing, Milt?'

'It's no good now, honey. The damn plane left six hours ago.'

'You mean you . . . missed it?'

He drains his Seven-Up. 'I was shootin' craps. I'd had a real good run and was all psyched up; didn't want to interrupt my luck. Just as well. In the end, I lost at that damn crap table, but if I hadn't stuck around and started playin' the slots, I'd be twenty thousand grand the poorer now.'

I stare at him. He didn't *know* he'd win. He could have lost his bankroll, lost his shirt, be stranded in Las Vegas without even the fare for a Greyhound bus, once he'd let that plane go. Or maybe you can swap plane tickets over, re-book a later flight. In which case, why tear up the ticket? It must have cost a bomb. He lives miles away, way up near Chicago.

'But couldn't you have changed the ticket, Milt? Used it tomorrow or the next day?'

He shrugs. 'Yeah, I guess so, but it ain't worth the hassle.' He removes an ice cube from his glass, cools his forehead with it. 'I've missed a lotta planes, hon. If you're on a winning streak, you can't live your life round airline schedules. You have to be ready to drop everythin' and jus' go with the flow.'

I'm really quite impressed. I'd put Jones down as Mr Ordinary, but maybe he's the real McCoy high roller I thought I'd yet to meet. I mean, I was wrong about Victor, imagined him swanning round Las Vegas, living off his winnings, when he's an engineer or something rather dull. I feel a sudden pang. Victor wasn't dull. He knew a lot of things, was always so . . . No. No regrets. Victor doesn't want me – he made that pretty clear tonight – and those guys do. In fact, the feeling's mutual. I need them. There's no one else I know now in this whole hardhearted town.

I edge a little closer to Milt's bulge. He's having quite a turn-out of his pockets, looking for another unused plane ticket, so he can illustrate his point. He turfs out aspirin, low-sugar breath-mints, salt-free chewing-gum, a whole concertina fold-down of credit cards, and a larger card with a pink flamingo entwined around his photograph.

I pick it up. 'What's that?'

'My VIP guest card. I've got a big credit-line with the Flamingo, so they look after me. It's like – well, a free pass, I guess. I don't pay for my room, or meals.'

Wayne's playing snap, has produced one of his own, this time from the Golden Nugget. Someone else is joking about the last free suite he had which was called Old Masters and had a mini Sistine Chapel ceiling in the bathroom.

'I cricked my neck keep lookin' up at all them dingers. I could have had a "Cave Man" room with real rocks and a fake-fur bath-robe, or "Tarzan" and a jungle, but I guess I felt too old to start swingin' from the trees to find my Jane.'

We all laugh, except Norah, who appears to be mesmerized by a blue-rinsed fatso lecturing her on the nutritional dangers of the Beverly Hills Diet.

'We just can't live on avocado, hon, or kiwi fruit. If God had meant for us to do that, He wouldn't have made doughnuts, especially not cream ones.'

I stretch right out, head in Milton's lap, feet nuzzling Wayne's right thigh; reward them both with dazzling smiles as they fight to light my cigarette. I'll make it up to Norah in the morning. For the moment, I intend to have a ball. These guys are true high rollers – free suites, free passes, missed planes, the lot. If they accept me into their circle, even for just a week, I could win enough to change my life. I've got to escape from Beechgrove, escape from dole queues, dead-end jobs, and I need cash for all of that. I shan't be greedy. Once I've got my basics like my mansion and my Rolls, I'll give the rest away. God! I'd really love that – writing out cool four-figure cheques to Martha Mead and Ethel Barnes; buying mink-trimmed incontinence pants for Lil; setting Norah up with her own private circus and her own portable super-loo which she could tow along behind her. I'd give massive bribes to governments to abolish all psychiatrists, or make cigarettes free-issue like infant orange juice. I'd buy a chain of florists, then offload them on to Jan, with the one small proviso that she despatch a lorry-load of marigolds to my father's grave each week. I'd . . .

'You're not drinkin' your champagne,' says Milt. 'Would you prefer the sweeter sort, hon?'

I nod. What's another two hundred dollars among friends? I like these friends. They don't keep counting every penny like my mother always did, or waste precious time and energy worrying about rainy days, or acts of God, or accidents, and all that other dreary, cautious, life-negating stuff which kept my poor father in its grip. His life was so damned dismal. Twenty years of working overtime, crawling to his customers, smiling when his feet hurt, getting out a hundred shirts or sweaters for some swaggering tin god who then walked out with nothing; folding them all up again till lunchtime, then spending his short break running errands for my mother, or eating a Spam sandwich on a bench. And any measly pound he saved went straight into some piggybank or death insurance policy, was never splurged on fun-things.

Sometimes, I worry that I'll turn out like my parents. I mean, genes are powerful, aren't they, and I'd hate to hem my life in with Post Office savings books, or long-service awards where they reward you only for dying still in harness. Men like Wayne and Milt don't bother with all that. They're free to win, free to buzz off where and when they want, free to waste their money, tear up airline tickets. Free to live.

The eighth course has just arrived: *Poussin à la Casablanca* – honey-basted, garlic-roasted hen, served with prunes and apricots. I dip my bare hand in the dish, relish the greasy warmth as I fish around for fruit. Who wants forks? Who wants clocks? There's enough of those at Beechgrove, ticking out the steel-toothed timetable. No one gives a fig here. It must be three AM at least, but new guests are still pouring through the door, the music even wilder now, the new champagne cork popping. I think we're all affected by the drink. Misty's pawing every waiter she can reach, the female wrestler nibbling at Gabe's ear, as if it's a last and special course, and two old boys are almost nodding off.

Suddenly, there's a click of castanets and six Moroccan belly-dancers burst into the room, their naked stomachs undulating to the fanfare of the music, their fringed skirts whirling out to reveal honey-basted thighs. The whole restaurant is applauding, clapping to the beat. The plumpest of the dancers shimmies over to our table, offers her hand to Norah's dear old gent. Up he gets and joins them, trying to writhe his barrel stomach as deftly as their taut ones. Next it's Eddie's turn. Some black-eyed Jezebel scoops him on to the dance floor, shows him how to snake his hips. Merry-Lyn leaps up on her own, untucks her satin blouse, displays her bare and wiggling belly to rapturous applause.

'Come on, doll!' shouts Wayne, lurching to his feet with his mouth still full of prune and trying to drag me with him. 'Let's boogie.' I hesitate, glance around the table. Both Milt and Norah have the same crestfallen faces. I don't want anyone unhappy, anyone left out. I prise Milton from his cushion, then wobble round to Norah's pouffe.

'Toomey, now's your chance! All those PE classes must have taught you something. Up you get! You need some exercise after all that sitting watching telly.'

I'm amazed to see her follow me, though perhaps she's just relieved to escape from all the food. I leave her with a dancer in a spangled, feathered yashmak, go back to fetch the gorgeous guys at the far end of the table, whom I've hardly exchanged a word with yet. Now we're all up – Misty and the wrestler, Gabe and Shorty, a drunken Doc still brandishing his skewer, even the fatsos showing off their flab. We dance a sort of conga, weaving in and out of tables in a long and snaking line, the belly-dancers leading us, the other guests applauding, the waiters stamping their feet to the rhythm of the dance.

Suddenly, two strong arms are round my waist and I'm lifted right up on the table, Milt deposited beside me. We stare at each other in a sort of shock, then move towards each other, join hands, both hands, start dancing down the table, which is groaning under our weight. Everyone is cheering. We're the royals, the king and queen, higher than the rest, receiving all their homage. Mustapha cooks for royals. Yeah, he's there, too, doing his obeisance, clapping his fat hands. The music spins faster faster faster as we dance up and down, round and round, until I'm not me any more, just a two-headed whirling blur with a bulge in its back pocket and a pounding thudding heart.

13

'What'ja say your name was, kid?'

'Ata. . .' No. I can't pronounce it. Milt probably couldn't either. It's only now I realize that he hasn't used it once, not through all ten courses or our Royal Progress to his room. His room! I was so stupidly naïve I assumed we were whizzing to the rooftop bar.

'A . . . Abigail,' I stutter. I've got her on my mind. He'll expect to see her, expect to take my clothes off, throw me on the bed. No, not bed. Not now. I'm too hung over.

'Gale?'

I nod. Gale will do. There's quite a strong one blowing through my head, a sickening sort of churning in my stomach. It started in the lift. I realized then I was trapped with him – alone. Not Milt-and-Wayne-and-Ed-and-Gabe-and-Shorty, who was glamorous and witty, sophisticated, dishy, but one small balding man with sweaty hands. It was worse still when the lift doors glided open and I saw, not bar or disco, but rows and rows of bedrooms. I should have said 'no' then, but I was in a sort of daze, and by the time I'd worked out what to do, his key was in the lock and he was ushering me in, hot arm around my waist. 'Go right ahead, honey. There's the light. Hey! Watch your step.'

Yes, I was so uptight I tripped, sprawled headlong on the carpet. I tried to laugh it off, but the laugh came out all wrong, sounded close to tears. He seemed nervous, too, helped me up, offered me a brandy. I shook my head. I've had enough – too much.

We're still standing by the mini-bar, saying nothing in particular, but a bit too close for comfort. I back away a little, try to gain some breathing space. He doesn't look that well himself. His eyes are dulled, with puffy swollen lids; his headache stamped in frown-lines.

Suddenly he moves. I jump.

'Mind if I take a bath, Gale?'

I shake my head, though I'm not sure what he means. Am I to share the bath, get in with him, scrub his back, soap his private parts? I kick one shoe off, ram it back again. What in God's name am I doing? If I don't look out, I *will* land up in bed, and won't know how I got there. I sidle to the mirror, start fiddling with my hair. I need more time, time to make excuses, time to cure my gut-ache. I shut my eyes, as a sudden wave of sickness rolls across my stomach. When I open them again, Milt has disappeared. I hear a key turn in a lock, the roar of running taps. He's locked me out.

I sink down in a chair. I should be glad he's gone, and doesn't need me as his bath-attendant, but I feel somehow still more jumpy on my own. The room's not the sort which makes you feel at home. It's very high and formal, done up all in browns, with that chilly, solemn air you get in some museums, and a silence as thick and heavy as the carpet. Milt's turned the taps off now and I can't hear anything except the odd complaint and gurgle from my stomach, the repeated nervous clearing of my throat. Odd for him to shut me out. Perhaps he was just desperate for a pee, or wearing dirty underclothes and preferred to peel them off in private. Or maybe simply shy. I feel shy myself, stupid, tied in knots. One part of me wants to run away; keep running till I'm safely back in England. The other part's so woozy and laid back, I hardly care what happens. I was all right in the restaurant. So long as we were one big crowd, I was as bouncy as the music, as bubbly as the champagne. Now bubbles, grease and panic are curdling in my gut, warning signals throbbing through my head.

I get up again, weave across the room, sit down the other end. A different stretch of mid-brown hessian wall stares blankly back at me. The pictures are all brown as well; old prints of vintage cars. God! It seemed exciting when we were whisked into that limousine, a chauffeur-driven Cadillac (not vintage,

175

spanking new) which had been summoned to the restaurant by King Milt. I wasn't even sure where we were off to – maybe to a night club, or for a spin beneath the stars. It was enough that it was me – yes, Carole Margaret Atalanta Joseph, swaggering out on Milton's arm, watched by that whole admiring crowd: dancers blowing kisses, waiters bowing, waving; Mustapha pressing sweetmeats in my hand. A Moroccan girl dashed forward, looped garlands round our necks. The king and queen betrothed, sent cheering on their honeymoon.

I rip my garland off, a flimsy thing of coloured crepe, toss it on the floor. I should have stopped the car, made up some excuse: I was tired, or sick; just married. How could I, when I've been so wild all evening – gorging, boozing, flirting – leading poor Milt on, syphoning off his power? Didn't I owe him something in return? And if I hadn't paid him back, some other female would have leapt to take my place. Merry-Lyn was eaten up with jealousy, Misty planning murder. I could see their green-eyed glances as that limo purred away. That's partly why I went. It's so heady to be envied, to be playing star for once, instead of just an odd face in the crowd scenes. Now, I'd gladly swap with them. Misty's probably tucked up safe in bed, Merry-Lyn enjoying a last quiet filter-tip.

I need a smoke myself. I search my handbag. Damn! The packet's empty. I've been smoking Wayne's Superkings all evening, with the odd cigar thrown in. I shut my eyes, feel Wayne's rough tongue again, prowling down my cleavage. He was half the trouble. His throaty voice and greasy fingers were a constant kind of foreplay, rousing me, seducing me, until I was delivered hot and ready into Milton's den. Everything was working on me – the wine, the food, the music; those dark romantic waiters, the other gorgeous heart-throbs in our crowd, who danced crotch to crotch with me, told me I was wonderful.

All vanished now. No music, no champagne, no giggly whispered compliments. Just dumpy Milt and me. No – wrong. Just me. I check my watch. He's been ages in that bathroom, and there's still no sound from it: no water gurgling out, no reassuring shout to say he's almost through. I could just sneak away. It seems a God-sent chance – just three steps to the door and out. He wouldn't even see me, and I'd be safe downstairs before he realized that I'd gone. But then what? I've no money for a cab, feel far too flaked to start trudging back on foot.

I pace up and down, fingers twitchy, desperate for a fag. Milton smokes. He shouldn't. It's top of his Forbidden List, but he said he had to keep one vice to cope with all the other damn restrictions. He's probably got a pack or two stashed away somewhere in this room. Dare I take a look, check the drawers? Better not. He must be finished soon, then we can sit and have a smoke together, cool the whole thing down. I could say I'm underage. I am for drink and gambling, so why not sex as well? No, he'd never swallow that, when I've been drinking more than anyone all evening, and made everybody laugh recounting my fiascos at the gaming tables.

I fidget to the window, pull aside the curtain. We must be at the back of the hotel, or stuck down some side alley. Everything looks dark and almost sinister. I shiver, move away. Ten more minutes crawl. What can the guy be doing in that bathroom? Perhaps he's shaving, wants to be smooth and silky for the kiss. I feel a sudden rush of panic. I don't want a kiss. Well, I wouldn't mind if it were nothing more than that – just a kiss and cuddle as payment for the meal, to set my conscience straight, but not the rest, not the whole seduction bit. If I'd had more experience, I might know what to do. I mean, am I crazy to stay jittering here, when I've got this chance to leave? If I don't fancy walking back, I could always hide downstairs, try to snatch some sleep in a bar or lounge or somewhere. If I don't act now, this instant, he'll be back beside me, breathing down my neck, and I'll kick myself for dithering. Anyway, I ought to check on Norah. She hurt her leg dancing. It didn't look much, but you never know with Norah. I put her in a cab – should have gone back with her.

I snatch my coat and bag up, dart towards the door, grab the handle – stop – body facing one way, head and eyes the other. It seems so mean just to ditch the guy, run away without an explanation, without even thank you or goodbye. He paid for Norah's cab. My hand slides from the handle, my coat slips to the floor. I leave it there, continue with my pacing. It's hard to make decisions at the best of times, let alone at this godforsaken hour, which is neither night nor morning, and when I'm feeling sick and groggy and can't concentrate on anything except blessed cigarettes. I'm nothing but a craving now, just got to have a fag.

I cross the brown expanse of carpet to the chest of drawers, ease the top drawer open. It's empty. I ram it shut again as I hear a sudden rattle from the bathroom door; stay pressed against the chest, pretending to examine the picture just above it – a brown Bugatti with a biscuit-brown chauffeur, brown half-moon, brown clouds. My heart is like a hammer. Stupid fool I am. Of course I should have left. Supposing Milt's stark naked, grabs me, goes too far too fast? I can hear his footsteps now, closing in on me. Anything could happen. After all, I hardly know the guy. He could be sort of weird – even violent or perverted or have some deadly thing like AIDS. Christ! I never thought of AIDS, and after all those grisly warnings about going to bed with strangers, avoiding casual sex . . .

I swing round to fight him off. He's not naked, nothing like. He's wearing pyjamas, the sort my father sold, in no-nonsense thick striped blue, with a Black Watch tartan dressing-gown on top. They look quite wrong together. The colours clash and the stripes upstage the tartan. The pyjama legs are trailing, fall in folds around his feet. What hair he has is wet, and plastered to his head. His hands are dirty still, despite the bath. Money stains indelibly, I see.

'N . . . nice bath?' I ask.

'Yeah. Had some trouble with my plumbing, though.'

'Oh?' What *does* he mean? His bladder? Or has he got the runs like Toomey? What's wrong with this damned country? Everybody's got the runs: Norah, Misty, Milt.

'I've been mixin' all my pills, Gale. Real dumb. I could kill myself like that.'

'Yes?'

'Like a bath yourself?'

'No thanks.' I've had two today already. Jon hardly bothered with washing – he was too keen to get stuck in. Milt seems slightly dazed. He's not even looking at me, just staring at the wall. Does he fancy me, or doesn't he, plan to make a pass or not? The suspense is almost worse than the seduction. My own insides aren't right, still burbling and protesting. My whole body feels off-keel, as if someone's taken it to pieces and put it back all wrong. I wriggle on my chair, chew my thumb, chew my hair, try to think of some big momentous subject which will totally distract him from minor things like sex.

'It's . . . er . . . quiet up here, isn't it?'

'Yeah. Sure is.'

Perhaps he's inexperienced himself. No, he can't be – not a high roller with free girls. Maybe that's the trouble. They do all the work and he's waiting for me to slip off the dressing-gown, undo the pyjama cord . . .

I can't. I daren't. Those AIDS advertisements have all come screaming back now – gruesome tombstones inscribed with four dire letters; posters plastered everywhere: 'Don't Die Of Ignorance!'

If I'm going to die, I've got to have a fag first – though I suppose I'll have to earn it, like those fawning call-girls do. I smooth my skirt down, force my mouth to smile, make my voice sound husky. 'Milt, I'm simply gasping for a . . .'

Help! He's taking off his dressing-gown himself. I freeze. He's blundering towards me. I cross my arms, cross my legs.

'Which way do you sleep, Gale?'

'I beg your pardon?'

'Facing the wall or facing the window? I like face to wall, so if you choose face to window, we'll be back to back. That's not friendly.'

'No,' I say. 'I suppose it's not.' I take a deep breath in, try to sound less panicked. 'Look, Milt, why don't we just . . . ? I mean, I'm not that sure I really ought to stay. My friend . . .'

He's yawning. Honestly. He's not even trying to disguise it, turn it into a cough or gasp of passion. I can see the gold fillings in his far back teeth. Another, lesser yawn and now he's climbing into bed, face to wall.

'I'm sorry, kid, but I'm not feelin' all that great. I gotta get some shuteye. Okay?'

No, it's not okay. I know I don't fancy him, but to be

dismissed like that, rejected . . . *I* was the one who was meant to say 'No, thanks'. All right, he's ill – I'm sorry – I'm not feeling all that wonderful myself, but does he have to just crash out? Couldn't we be ill together, swap sympathy and symptoms, chat a while, at least? I can't just switch off like a robot, settle down to sleep in a strange bed with a strange guy, and with these hurt and angry feelings curdling in my head. Who does he think he is, for heaven's sake, in those unspeakable pyjamas and so boorish and insensitive that he can simply shut me off? I should have stuck with Wayne, or be safe in bed with Norah. More fun to sleep with her than some insulting hypochondriac. I mean, the way he calls me 'kid', as if I'm some silly little chit.

I stalk into the bathroom for a pee, stay sitting on the toilet-seat, trying to calm down. The guy's old, unwell, harried by his doctors, and has just swallowed half a chemist's shop of pills. Why should it surprise me if he can't or won't perform? I didn't want him anyway, should feel sheer relief. I'm let off, reprieved, rescued from a tight spot, maybe even rescued from my grave. So why be so upset?

'Victor,' says a voice inside my head. That's the reason, isn't it? The fact that Victor didn't want me either, the feeling that I'm just not – well – desirable. Oh yeah, the guys all chat me up – Wayne, Milt, Vic himself, but when it comes to the crunch, the real nitty-gritty, they don't seem to want to know. I glance in the mirror, half-expect to see some hideous old frump, the sort of draggy bore men yawn out of their beds. Or a brat in socks and pigtails, with braces on her teeth. In fact, I look my best: super-sexy outfit, hair just washed and blonded, clever bra which pushes up my breasts. Yet Victor ran away, and Milt couldn't wait to get to sleep – alone. There must be something really wrong with me. Or them.

Yeah, why not them? They're probably just incapable, Milt as well as Victor, can't get it up at all. Men make such a thing about their pricks, see everything as cock-shaped – buildings, sports cars, rockets, even lipsticks – and all those girls in the commercials licking lollipops and comets, who are really sucking them. Yet, half the time, their tower-blocks have collapsed, their rockets crashed to earth, their Ferraris out of juice, their raspberry ripples melted. If we girls had pricks, we'd make much better use of them. Girls are just as sexy – it says so in the textbooks – but most men can't accept that, keep trying to deny it, or belittle it with words like nymphomaniac. There ought to be a transplant scheme: all idle half-cock pricks lopped off and grafted on to females.

I jump up from the toilet. Who wants a prick at all? I'd rather have a cigarette – another phallic symbol, according to the men. At least Marlboros don't go limp. Or yawn.

I grope into the bedroom. It's pitch dark now, all the lights put out. My voice sounds loud, intrusive, in the gloom. 'Milt, I'm sorry to disturb you, but I'm dying for a smoke. Can you tell me where you keep your fags, before you go to sleep?'

Too late. He *is* asleep, breathing very hoarsely through his mouth. He's not a snorer, not in Norah's class, just a shuddering sort of wheeze. That's the bloody limit, to switch the lights off, fall asleep before he's even said goodnight, or asked if I'm all right or want a drink or something. I'm going, walking out. I haven't got my cab-fare, but I'll have to help myself, take it from his wallet, leave an IOU. I won't take much, just one five-dollar bill. That should pay the taxi. No, two – enough for cigarettes as well. He owes me cigarettes. After all, it's his fault that I'm stuck here. In fact, why should I pay him back? If he'd been a normal sort of guy, well-mannered and attentive, he'd have put me in a cab himself, laid a hundred kingsize on the seat beside me, and told me where he'd pick me up tomorrow.

I'll take twenty, damn it. What's twenty mingy dollars when you've just won twenty thousand? Peanuts. I check that he's still sleeping (the breathing hasn't altered), creep back to the bathroom. I know he left his clothes there – I saw them in a crumpled sweaty pile. Yeah, there they are: a pair of paisley boxer shorts, a limp and off-white vest and those unspeakable green trousers. That green should have been a warning to me right from the beginning. Any guy who could choose a shade so vile, so utterly uncouth . . .

I make straight for the back pocket. Empty. Flat. Deflated. Damn! He must have moved his wallet, put it somewhere safe.

I suppose that's only natural. He'd hardly leave all his precious money spilling on a soggy bathroom floor. It's in here somewhere, must be. That bulge was still in evidence when he went to have his bath – the last thing I saw of him, in fact. He returned without it, in just his dressing-gown.

I check all the bathroom cupboards, find a whole dispensary of pills – pills for heartburn, constipation, travel sickness, insomnia; pastilles for sore throats, a spray for stuffed-up noses, a salve for aching joints. I replace a carton of glycerine suppositories; try the larger cupboard. It's full of towels, hotel towels. I rummage through them, looking for a lump. All smooth. I go down on my knees, crawl around, peering under everything. Senseless. High rollers wouldn't stuff their winnings behind a toilet seat. They'd have a safe, a proper one, and probably concealed. That painting, for example, may swing out from the wall to reveal a hidden cache. No. It's hanging on a simple picture hook and there's nothing behind it except a little dust. So Milt's outwitted me, stowed his cash away in some foolproof hiding-place where I wouldn't think of looking in a hundred years. He didn't trust me. I was just a pick-up, some brazen little floozie on the make. He couldn't even leave me with a pack of cigarettes in case I nicked those too.

He was right though, wasn't he? I mean, here I am, rifling through his cupboards like a petty thief. I grab the basin to steady myself. I'm shaking, really shaking. I *am* a thief. I'd planned to take a twenty-dollar bill. That's stealing. Even twenty cents is stealing; even one cent. My father taught me that; my father, who was so genuinely good he never filched a penny in his whole sad and saintly life – not a safety-pin, not a rubber band. I remember once, one of his customers left a biro on the counter – not a Parker or a silver one, just a cheapo plastic thing which anyone else would have nicked or thrown away. Not Dad. The trouble he went to trying to trace the man and give it back.

'Stealing's stealing, sweetheart. Okay, so it's just a needle, but why not two next time, or the whole packet, or the scissors, or that solid-silver thimble?' He's right. I pocketed a mini-pack of Kleenex and now look where I am – trapped in a room in the early hours with a guy I hardly know. My father would be doubly shocked. He was never prudish, always welcomed Jon, but he taught me to be careful. Not for silly reasons like what the neighbours thought, or obvious ones like the fear of getting pregnant or catching something ghastly, but because he told me I was precious and should save myself for a man who'd value that.

Precious! If he could see me now, see the miles and miles I've fallen. I stare at my reflection in the glass. Who cares if my hair's clean or I'm wearing sexy clothes? Underneath, I'm foul, and men can probably sense that, see beneath my clothes, see how mean I am, how money-grubbing, selfish. My mother was like that – avaricious, crawling around influential people, never satisfied. It's *her* genes I've inherited, not my darling father's. I'm even like her in the way I criticize. Pitching into Milt when he'd already wined and dined me, drowned me in champagne. He didn't owe me anything, didn't even know me, yet he let me join his party, share his celebration. Okay, so he went to sleep a little prematurely, but I didn't even want sex, and anyway, he's probably really ill. I just shrugged off his symptoms, cared more about my own hurt, didn't give a damn. And – oh, Christ! I want a fag.

I sink down by the dressing table. I'm stuck here now, with neither cash nor transport, and no hope of cigarettes. Serve me right! I'll have to make the best of it, think of Milt for once, instead of just myself; pay him back as night-nurse rather than as call-girl. He may need me in the night, wake up feeling worse, want me to ring room service, call a doctor, send out for more pills. I'll stay until the morning, make sure he's in good hands, then bugger off – for good. And after this, I'll give up men completely. If I need cash or kudos, I'll have to earn them for myself, take the Women's Lib line. Or perhaps I'll find a different sort of man. I'm not quite sure how different, but I'll know when he turns up. The rest have all been wrong. Jon was just too young and immature, Victor far too old. Jake was quite unspeakable, Milt . . .

I start as he turns over, pray he won't wake up yet. No, the wheezing's still quite regular – those steady snuffling in-breaths, followed by the little gasping moans. I envy him his sleep, his comfy bed. I'm dead tired myself, and these chairs are really hard, covered in some wet-look stuff which feels clammy underneath you. I could just lie beside him, keep my clothes on, but make myself more comfortable, try to get a bit of kip myself.

I remove my shoes, take off just my skirt, tiptoe over, peel the covers back. Milton grunts and murmurs. I wait till he's quite still again, then slip between the sheets. I close my eyes, try counting sheep. Sheep are hard to picture in Las Vegas, so I switch to counting dollars – all those swiftly mounting hundred-dollar bills showering into Milton's outstretched hand. It doesn't work, just reminds me what a gold-digger I am. Would I chat up Jack the Ripper if he won enough? I feel rotten about Norah, too; keep hoping she's asleep and not waiting up and worrying, with a painful swollen leg. I should never have dragged her to that restaurant, kept her up so late.

I start counting cigarettes next, packs and packs and packs of them. Soon, my head is like a giant tobacconist's, every shelf and display-rack piled with kingsize, yet not one mingy roll-your-own between my lips. I'll never get to sleep without my bedtime smoke. It's become a sort of ritual, a soothing lullaby, and without it I'm a screaming fractious baby. My bra's too tight as well, impossible to sleep in. I push my sweater up, fumble for the hooks, let my breasts spill out. Milton wheezes on. I wish he'd turn the other way, to face me. He said back to back's unfriendly, but breasts to back is not that marvellous either. His back is like a barrier and his heavy breathing only makes the silence worse.

I touch my breasts, sort of vaguely and for comfort; keep my hand nestling there between them. It must be strange to be a call-girl, the kind that Milton's used to – in and out of different beds all week. Do they ever sleep at all? Feel guilt, or self-disgust? *'Angie Ample, the girl your mother warned against; Mistress Marilyn, experienced in bondage.'* Victor even mistook me for a call-girl. I shut my eyes, see myself in a black lace corselette and matching g-string, like those pictures in the escort magazines. I'm brandishing my whip, snaking a feather boa between my thighs. I turn my fingers into feathers, stroke them very lightly up and down, in and out. It's nice. Except I'd rather it were someone else's fingers, some gentle loving guy who really cared for me, wasn't ill or rude; knew my name.

A tear runs down my face. Sheer self-pity. I slap it off, use the other hand to jab between my legs. The tears keep coming, the hand keeps jabbing. I can't stop either of them. My face is wet; Abigail is wet. Soon, I'm really sobbing, yet heaving and jerking to the rhythm of my sobs. Milton shifts an arm, mutters in his sleep. I tense. It's agony to stop when I want to just let go, let go of everything – tears, fears, remorse, and Abigail. But that's selfish, isn't it, waking Milton up, disturbing him when he's ill and needs his rest.

I creep out of bed again, back to that damned bathroom. My legs feel shaky and my eyes are blurred with tears, so I'm stumbling like a drunk. Once I've got the door shut and am stretched out on the carpet, I let them fall unchecked, use my hands to comfort Abigail. Great shuddering sobs shake through my whole body. I'm scared – scared of all these feelings. How can I feel sexy when I'm crying; or change so suddenly from dead beat and drooping to feverishly on heat? I should never have come off those pills. They've changed my mood, changed my personality, so every feeling's far too strong and wild. I'm insatiable for everything: men, thrills, money, booze. Yes – booze. Had I forgotten that my mother likes the drink? That's probably in my genes as well. I've hardly stopped tippling since I've been here. If I'm not careful, I'll become another Kitty – drying out, relapsing, shaming all my friends.

I'm swallowing my tears now; salt taste in my mouth, eyes swelling up and smarting, and that glutton of an Abigail still throbbing and demanding. Perhaps it's not the pills, but all those aphrodisiacs. The whole meal was awash with them, or so the waiters claimed: honey and shellfish, garlic and *cilantro*, hot and lethal spices. I shut my eyes, slink back to the restaurant. Wayne's stretched out beside me, trickling olive oil between my legs, tonguing softened apricots from his mouth into mine. It's wonderful. Fantastic. Oh, Wayne, oh, Wayne, I . . .

Shut up, you fool. You can't shout Wayne, when it's Milton who's next door. I turn over on my stomach, use the carpet as a gag. Even now, I can't lie quiet. The soft brown pile is touching up my breasts, tickling against my bush, starting all the feelings off again. I half-kneel up, use my hands more roughly. Wayne has disappeared and Snake Jake just slipped in – well, part of him, a disembodied python's head with a flickering ruby tongue. I can feel that tongue forcing deeper, deeper, into Abigail, the scratchy rubies hurting, the wild wet tip scouring round and round. She's shuddering and gasping, heaving up and down. She's coming, but it's awful – sort of shaming and too violent, and the sobs are cries of pain now. I bite my hand to stop myself from yelling. I mustn't wake Milt up, or let him see me like this. He'd be horrified, despise me. I despise myself, especially when I glimpse my sweaty face grimacing in the mirror, my features all screwed up, as if I'm being tortured on the rack. I go on wanking, watch myself with fascinated horror – teeth bared like an animal's, lips stretched back and open; fingers tensed, then clutching at thin air; even my toes sort of splaying out and jerking. I'm sure other, normal girls don't go through such contortions. Men would hate it; jeer, or walk away.

I flop down on my front again, mouth full of carpet fluff, tears running down my neck. I'd like Milt to wake up – have him comfort me, hold me in his arms, tell me that everything's all right. Just to hear another human voice would make me feel less miserably alone. I wonder if he's married. Maybe there's some sad and dumpy woman waiting up at home for him, cold in bed without him. I doubt if *I'll* get married. Nobody would want me, not when I'm so vile. I admitted once to Dr Bates that I'd like to settle down, be secure and wanted, have someone care for me, and he saw it all as neurotic fear and over-compensation. 'Don't you understand, Carole, you may be using men to seek the nurturing your mother couldn't give you?' God! He made things complicated with all his analysing. Another time, he warned me that I might start choosing partners who would merely confirm my own low opinion of myself. If I listened to all that psycho-stuff, I'd never dare go out with anyone, let alone get hitched. It must have been much simpler in the old days, when women married almost automatically, without being labelled repressive or regressive.

Slowly, I roll over, ease my aching legs. My cunt's sore, my eyes smart. I'm utterly exhausted. So shut up and go to sleep then. I can't, still can't – can't stop crying and can't stop Abigail. My fingers aren't enough. Too small, too feeble. I want to be entwined with someone, wild with someone, have them bang and bang and bang . . . Victor, please come back. Hold me, Victor, stroke my hair. I didn't mean to walk out of that poker game. I liked you. I liked you such a lot. I felt safe with you and right with you and . . . Oh, it's great, it's great, it's terrible. Oh, Victor!

Got to stop! Out of breath. Hurting. Fingers tired, leg muscles seized up. I lie flat on my back, arms folded across my chest. I can feel my heart pounding through my hands, nipples sticking up like two spare clits. My neck is really painful. I need a cushion, something to rest back on. I reach for Milton's clothes, fold his trousers, shirt and vest to make a pillow, slump back on it, spread my legs again. What's wrong with me, for God's sake? Even now, I don't feel satisfied, or sleepy, or all those things you're meant to feel in sex books. There's a hole between my legs, a deep and endless hole, an ache so bad it feels as if nothing and nobody could ever really fill it. I turn over on my side, curl up very tight so I'm just a child; shut my eyes, hide them with my hands. When I was a real child, I used to think that nobody could see me if I kept my eyes tight closed. 'I'm not here, Daddy. You've got to try to find me.' He always played the game, searched my room from top to bottom, crawling under the bed and chest of drawers, hunting through the wardrobe, calling out my name. I'd almost choke, lying in my bed, trying not to breathe; wait until he was well and truly frantic before I resurrected, opened my eyes and shouted 'Here I am!' He was so surprised, so utterly relieved, so happy that he had me still.

Open your eyes, Daddy, open your eyes.

Stop crying, stupid. What's the point of crying? Your head hurts as it is, and you're soaking Milton's clothes. I grip the bath to help me up. Slowly, very slowly . . . I feel as if I'm recovering from an illness – light-headed, short of breath, with tissue-paper legs. The mirror adds swollen puffy eyes, red blotches on both cheeks. I splash my face with water, check Milton's store of pills. There's nothing for my symptoms, so I gulp two sleeping pills. At least they'll stop me thinking. I daren't sleep naked, though. My bra is somewhere in the bed and I can't even remember where or when I took my pants off. I slip on Milton's limp white vest instead. It feels clammy, damp with tears, but at least it makes me decent. I limp back to the bedroom, clamber in once more, still face to wall, like Milt. He's muttering in his sleep, must be dreaming: a dream about a girl he found, an Ugly Sister – sad as well as ugly – who woke up in the morning transformed as a princess. A real princess with golden hair (not True Blonde), beautiful and chaste, who never drank or smoked or craved sordid things like money (and was just a little icy like the Snow Queen, so she wouldn't go too far), and was happy, truly happy, so she never cried or hurt her eyes again, and . . .

I'm feeling slightly better now, quieter, even sleepy. Those pills must be fast-acting ones. I dare to edge an inch or two towards Milton's blue-striped back, close my eyes, hear my breathing deepen.

. . . and who fell in love (true and lasting love) with a pea-green frog who changed into a Prince when he woke her in the morning with a . . .

I smile, let myself sink down.

. . . with a kiss.

14

'Want to fly?' The woman at the desk is smiling at me, handing me a form.

I nod. I can't speak at all, not even 'yes'. I'm too excited. I'm going to fly, really fly. Not just in a plane, but on my own. You *can* fly now. It says so on the poster. 'MAN CAN FLY LIKE A BIRD.' It's written in capital letters so it must be true. Important things are always put in capitals.

There are pictures round the walls – people flying – men with wings and helmets; women, too, and children, soaring through the air. There's a poem pasted up, a long one with long words. It took me hours to read it.

I turn back to the notice board, spell out the last verse again. I can't follow quite a lot of it, but it's so beautiful, it makes me want to cry.

> *Up, up, the long delirious burning blue*
> *I've topped the windswept heights with easy grace*
> *Where never lark nor even eagle flew*
> *And while with silent lifting mind I've trod*
> *The high untrespassed sanctity of space*
> *Put out my hand, and touched the face of God.*

'The face of God.' Maybe I can touch it. Even if I don't, just to be that close . . .

The woman's calling out. She wants my money. It costs fifteen dollars, which isn't all that much for the chance of touching God. The plane cost more than that, much more. Victor gave me money in my chocolate box. I like Victor. Carole's with him now, I think. She lost him for a while and I had to help her find him.

We found another man, a Poet called John Milton who took us to a restaurant. I didn't like the restaurant. Someone had stolen all the knives and forks. It's rude to eat with fingers and everyone was punished for it. We had to get up and dance round and round the room while they played this loud and painful music. If you stopped, or went too slowly, or tried to find your seat again, they dragged you back and the music played still faster.

I hurt my leg, so I was allowed to leave before the others could. Carole ordered me a taxi, came right out to the street to say goodbye; told me not to worry if she was late.

She's not just late – she hasn't come back at all. I'm not sure what the time is, but it's been morning for some while. It may be even twelve o'clock and dinner time. I did worry, quite a lot, even went out looking for her. She didn't like the Poet much. I could tell that by her face. Vic's the one she really likes; the one who makes her happy. I think she must have found him in the end; got her miracle. That's why she's still out.

I got my miracle as well. When I went to look for Carole, I found this place instead, saw the notice tacked outside the building. 'Soar like an eagle, float like a butterfly.' I shall, in just a moment. I'd rather fly than have my dinner. I'd rather fly than do anything at all.

I go back to the desk. I've lost my place in the queue now. There are a lot of people lining up, mostly little boys. I hope I'm not too old to fly. It says 'safe for all ages' on the poster, but I ask the lady, just in case.

'It's nothing to do with age, honey. Just yesterday we had a great-grandmother of ninety-one come in, and the day before, a fifteen-months-old baby. They had a ball, both of them. If you want to fly, you fly. So long as you're fit, that is.'

I nod. I'm hardly ever ill. And of course I want to fly. I've been waiting all my life for it. I just wish I was smaller. There are two grown-ups in the queue now, but they both look small and thin.

'I'm not too heavy, am I?'

The lady really laughs. 'Heavy? You should see some of the tubs who walk in here. We had a prize-fighter the other day who weighed three hundred and eighty pounds and he floated like a feather.'

A feather! I can see whole wings. Angels' wings. The lady's counted out my money and is handing me a form, which she says I have to sign. There's too much print, small and hard to read, with some things underlined. I don't like the beginning. The words are very difficult and there are lots I've never heard of. I start again, halfway down. The word 'INJURY' appears several times in big black capitals, so I don't read that bit either.

The bottom is the best part. There are just blank spaces where you write your name, address, and driving licence number. I print 'N. TOOMEY, GOLD RUSH'. I don't know the address and I haven't got a driving licence, but the lady says it doesn't matter and would I sign there and there and . . .

My arm is getting tired and I'm so excited the letters look like squiggles. The lady gives me a slip of paper, waves me up the stairs. I climb them shakily, until I reach a door marked 'FLIERS', at the top.

Fliers. That's me. That's Norah Toomey. An eagle and a butterfly. An angel. I push the door, walk in. It's just an ordinary room. I can't believe it! I thought I'd see a great hall full of sky, with the rushing noise of wings. The only noise is giggling boys and a man on the radio telling me to drive a Ford. There's nothing much to see at all, except rows of metal lockers like we had at Westham Hall and a padded bench to sit on. The girl behind the desk hands me out a locker key and tells me to take my coat off and the jacket of my suit, and also my shoes and any jewellery. I haven't any jewellery, except my silver shamrock, which I never ever wear because if I lost it I'd lose the last trace of my mother.

I don't like to take my jacket off with young boys in the room, so I just remove my coat and shoes and put them in the locker. I have to wear a flight-suit, which is a bright shiny red with a zip right up the middle. I like clothes which come in halves − top and bottom, skirt and jumper, pyjama legs and jacket. This is just one-piece and not easy to put on. It's too short in the body and too long in the legs and my skirt gets in the way and then the zip sticks.

The boys are getting ready too, chattering and joking with each other. No one talks to me, though one lad points and laughs. I wish we had curtains like we do in Florence Ward. They could only see my feet then.

I sit down to put my shoes on, though it's hard to bend with the suit zipped up, and my feet seem a long way from my hands. The shoes are white, the sort of shoes which people wear on tennis courts, except they don't have laces. I'm not sure how you do them up. They're too small anyway. The girl asked what size I wore and I whispered 'eights', very very softly, because I'm ashamed to have big feet. I don't think she heard me right because they're pinching at the sides and there's no room for my toes.

I hobble to the mirror at the far end of the room. I don't look like an eagle. Or an angel. I'd rather fly without the suit. I don't know why we need suits. Or white shoes. Birds don't wear white shoes.

I hope we start soon. I think it must be one by now, or even quarter past. No one's moved at all. I slip behind the last locker in the row, so that nobody can laugh. I look very large and red and bulky, as if someone's blown me up.

I stand there quite a while. Then a tall man in a tracksuit opens a door I haven't seen and says, 'Right, fliers, come this way.'

Fliers! Every time I hear that word, my stomach jumps a bit, as if I've got the pains still, but happy pains this time. 'Fliers,' 'Fliers . . .' I say it once or twice. Nobody can hear me. I'm saying it inside.

We follow the man into another smaller room, which is very dark and stuffy and has all the curtains drawn, as if it's night-time. We couldn't fly in there. It's far too small and poky. He tells us to sit down, then switches on the television. There must be some mistake. I don't want to watch TV. I've been watching it all morning.

'Excuse me sir, I want to fly.'

'You'll fly, ma'am. When you're ready. We have to brief you first, instruct you what to do. We've made this special pre-flight video which shows you how to fly, and – more important – how not to fly. Right, just watch the screen and I'll be back in twenty minutes.'

He shuts the door, leaves me in the dark with all the boys. There's a sudden noise from the television screen and I see a big fat figure in a scarlet suit like mine falling on his face. This must be the wrong film. Nobody is flying, only falling. A girl in a blue suit crashes down, followed by a little boy who bounces as he falls. There isn't any sky or space at all, just a sort of cage. Perhaps they couldn't take pictures in the sky – it's probably far too high or the sun would burn the camera.

A voice is speaking very loud. I think it's speaking English, but it's not the same as ours. It's hard to understand it, but I try to concentrate. Flying isn't easy. There are lots of things you mustn't do, but I don't think I'll remember them because they're rushing by so fast. Everybody's falling still.

The boys are laughing, pointing at the screen. I expect they'll laugh at me. I can't follow it at all. I wonder how birds learn.

The voice becomes a head and smile, then the head gets smaller, to make room for the body on the screen. The body has bare legs. It isn't wearing a flight-suit, just a pair of shorts. Men's shorts. He must be very cold. He asks us to stand up and check our own suits. He says they should be comfortable and not pulling anywhere. Mine is pulling under the arms and between the legs. I try to tell him, but he's saying something else now – how dangerous it is to leave anything in our pockets or to wear a ring or bracelet which might spin off and injure someone. I begin to feel quite frightened. I check both my wrists and all my fingers. I never wear rings or bracelets, but I'd hate to injure someone.

The man has turned into a bird, a large white bird flying through a bright blue sky with little fluffy clouds. It flies very high, right up close to God. It hardly moves its wings. It's just gliding like the angels do, not crashing down or clumsy like those people in the suits. There's music now, very gentle music. The music flies as well. I close my eyes, flying with the music, with the bird. I think I was a bird once, long ago. I remember flying. I was very light and white and I flew across great white shining spaces, never fell.

193

The man's voice pulls me back, tramples down the music. He's bending his knees, leaping in the air. I shan't watch any more. They only make it stupid on the screen, pretend flying's very difficult and dangerous. I try to see the bird again, make it fly inside my head, but the voice keeps frightening it, scaring it away. It's telling us to check our pockets, take off any jewellery. It's said that once already. I don't think it's a good film.

'And if anyone wears dentures, it's essential you remove them. They could shoot out of your mouth in the force of the wind and cause an injury.'

I open my eyes, and stare at him in horror. All my teeth aren't false, just the top ones. A dentist took them out once. I don't know why. They weren't decayed, or hurting. He was going to remove the bottom ones as well, but he died on the Tuesday and my second appointment was the Friday afternoon.

I'd hate to take my denture out. I never do, unless it's really private. I even leave it in at night, now Carole's sleeping next to me. I don't want her to know I've got false teeth. People laugh at them.

The voice is still speaking, but I can think only of my denture. It's very dark in here, so maybe I could slip it in my pocket. No. You're not allowed to put things in your pockets, not anything at all. The tall man in the tracksuit has just come in again, and is switching on the lights. The film has ended, the boys all standing up. I stay sitting where I am. I feel very very heavy, as if I'm made of iron. I don't think I can fly.

'Are you all right, ma'am?'

I could do it now, ease it out while he's standing there blocking me from view. At least the boys won't see. But my mouth will go a funny shape without it, and I'll sound odd when I speak. I try to speak, but my voice has flown away. It does that when I'm frightened.

'It's quite normal to be nervous, ma'am. A lot of folks feel scared when they haven't flown before. Once we start, you'll be just fine.'

I nod. It's easier to nod. He leads us into a passage, hands us each a helmet and a pair of green foam ear-plugs, and some things called goggles which he says protect your eyes. The boys all put theirs on. I don't. He checks the other helmets, then stops in front of me.

'You'll need to take your glasses off. Just leave them on this windowsill and you can pick them up after your flight. Okay? The helmet goes like this.'

He's trying to explain, but I'm feeling very strange now. Everything has blurred without my glasses. He's very big and close and very blue.

'What's the matter? Can't you manage? Here, bend your head. That's it.'

He's putting on my goggles for me, making sure the helmet fits. It feels very hard and heavy, weighing down my head, and there are metal bars across my face, as if I'm in a cage. I can't hear with the ear-plugs in, and my voice has not come back yet. All the boys are ready. They're whispering and giggling, looking back at me. One of them has lovely eyes like Carole's. I'll feel dreadful if my teeth fly out and hit him.

'I . . . I . . .' It's no good. They can't hear me. I can't even hear myself. I'm shut in like a locked-ward dangerous patient in a tiny padded cell, with no windows, only bars, and strapped into a straitjacket with a blindfold and a gag.

The man in the tracksuit is still standing over me. I can't hear what he's saying, but it's something very angry. He's pointing to my feet. I bend over, stare down at my shoes. They're still undone. I feel too weak to try to do them up, so I simply walk away. I think he's shouting after me, but I don't turn round to check.

I've found another passage where there isn't anyone. I see a door marked 'TOILET'. They don't have toilets in America. I walk in, shut the door. I'm trembling now, all over. I'd forgotten about toilets, forgotten my weak bladder. Sometimes I need to go very suddenly and quickly. I couldn't in this suit. I'm trapped in it, closed in by the zip. I've got to take it off. I start pulling at the helmet. My head is throbbing with all the fear and worry, and the metal hurts my ears.

At last I tug it off, remove my goggles and the ear-plugs. I can hear noises now, the dripping of a tap, footsteps down the passage.

The steps are coming nearer. Someone's at the door, rattling the handle, trying to get in.

'Everything okay in there?'

It's the man in the tracksuit. I recognize his voice. I stand up very straight, close my eyes.

'I can't hear what you're saying, ma'am. We're waiting for you. Are you nearly through?'

I don't say anything. I pretend I'm just my feet, sink down into them, curl up in the pain. My toes are all squashed under, so the pain is very bad. I can hear time passing, ticking very loudly in my head. I think the man has gone now. I open the door as softly as I can, eyes still on the ground.

'My friend,' I say, in case there's someone there. 'I'm going to go and fetch her. Her name's Carole, Carole Joseph. She's small. She only wears size threes. And she doesn't have false teeth. *She'll* be able to fly . . .'

'God! Am I cheesed off! He left me, Norah, just like that. I woke up in the morning and he'd gone. Not a note. Nothing. I rang down to reception and they said he'd checked out two whole hours ago, had to catch a plane.'

'Victor didn't fly here. He's got a car. He drove here. He told me that. He said he . . .'

'I'm not talking about Victor. I'm talking about Milt. Milton Sherwood bastard Jones. Fine for *him* to fly first class and leave muggins to walk back. All that Big-Guy talk last night about missing planes. Well, he should have missed another one, bought us both some breakfast, before buggering off like that or at least ordered me a cab. I traipsed the whole way in these rotten fucking shoes, from his hotel to ours. I hadn't got a cent left for a bus, let alone a taxi. Hey Norah, you can't spare me a few dollars, can you?'

I fetch my chocolate box. There's not much money left and only two lime creams.

'Where's the rest?'

'I ate them. Just now. I'm sorry. I didn't have my dinner.

Or my breakfast.' This is the first day I've felt hungry. I couldn't eat before, not even at the restaurant where that fat man got so cross.

'I don't mean the chocolates, silly. The cash.'

'I . . . I spent it.'

'What d'you mean, spent it? What on?'

'I got lost, Jan. I had to take a taxi in the end. A lady told me to. She said I'd never . . .'

'*Carole.* My name's Carole.'

'But you said I had to call you . . .'

'Not now. I'm not Jan any more. Jan's unlucky. Jan's a stupid little fool. And Atalanta's worse.'

She's almost crying. I feel very sad myself still, but I'm glad she isn't Jan. When I called her that, I felt I'd lost my friend. Jan is Carole's friend, not mine. I've never had a friend before.

'Carole,' I say carefully. I hope I don't forget and call her Jan again. I spent a long time practising; said Jan a hundred times before I went to sleep, so I wouldn't make her angry.

'Have a chocolate.' I pass her a lime cream. I wish I'd bought those chocolates with the wine in. Wine always makes her better. I hate it when she swears. She doesn't mean it, though. Inside, she isn't happy, so she swears instead of crying.

'I don't want a fucking chocolate. I want some cash. Look, how did you get lost, Norah? And why did you go out at all, when I told you to stay in and wait for me?'

'I did wait. I only went to look for you, not far. And then I saw this place where you can fly.'

'Oh, don't start that again. Not now. I've got a splitting headache.'

'Everyone can fly now, except people with false teeth. It cost fifteen dollars. I didn't know you'd mind. You said Victor was rich and he'd won some money for us.'

'If you mention Victor again, I'll . . .' She bites into a chocolate, puts it down, suddenly grabs me by the arm. 'Norah, you haven't just spent fifteen dollars, have you?'

'Well, yes . . .' I hand her all the brochures. That lady gave them to me when I said I was going back to get my friend.

Carole stares at them, sinks into a chair. We're in the

downstairs room, the one that's ours, but very red and grand. I prefer the bedroom.

'Good God! You really can fly.'

'Yes,' I say. 'You can.' I shan't explain about the teeth. She might not be my friend if she knows I've got false teeth. She's found that form now, the one I had to sign.

'Norah, you didn't sign this, did you?'

I nod. She's very angry.

'How could you? You're meant to swear you're not taking any drugs or seeing any doctor or . . .'

'I haven't seen the doctor, not for months.'

'You're a patient, Norah. Permanently. Which means you're under a doctor all the time. And you know you're taking drugs. And you've got high blood pressure and . . .'

'No, the tablets keep it down.'

'Yes, *more* tablets. You could have killed yourself. And what about your leg? You said you couldn't dance last night, and now I find you flying. You must be stark raving mad!'

'I . . . I didn't fly.'

She crams in the last chocolate, turns on me again. 'Why say you did then and frighten me to death?'

'I didn't say.'

'Yes, you did. A whole fifteen-dollars-worth of flying. We've got to be really careful with our money. You've already wasted most of yours on that stupid fucking church. I mean, they're rich, those preachers, filthy rich, with vast great mansions and killer dogs to guard them and Cadillacs and private planes.'

She told me that before, but not so loudly. Victor was there and she didn't shout with Victor there. Victor made her happy. I wish I could make her happy. I did her washing for her and tidied all her things, but she doesn't always notice things like that.

'I mean, d'you imagine Jesus drove a Cadillac or had a bloody great Alsatian baring its fangs outside his $500,000 carpenter's shop?'

I shake my head. I think St Joseph had a dog, but probably a mongrel, something plain and ordinary which slept with him at night.

She sucks a smear of chocolate off her tooth. 'It's not just the luxury – some of these religions are really sick, and they're all commercial rackets. Remember that Reverend in a tracksuit selling Jesus Jewellery – lockets with Christ's hair inside, or rings which change colour when God hears your prayer? I mean, it shouldn't be allowed.'

I don't say anything. I liked the rings. I was going to send away for one, but the address went off before I'd found a pencil.

Carole snatches up her jacket which she's only just flung off. 'We're going back,' she says.

'To England?' My voice stumbles with excitement, with relief.

'No, you chump. To get a refund. Even if you did fly. I'll say you didn't understand the form.'

'I didn't fly,' I say again. My voice is limp and grey now. I thought she meant back home. If we left immediately, I could be sleeping in the ward tonight, and help lay breakfast in the morning. We have sausages on Thursdays. Sometimes they're not cooked inside, so I only eat the cornflakes. There's a bird on the packet, a bright green cockerel with a scarlet comb. I don't think it can fly. It hasn't any wings, only a head and beak.

Carole gets my coat, locks the door behind us, calls the lift. The sun is shining when we reach the street. It makes me look bright and far too big. My shadow is enormous and keeps trembling. At least we don't get lost. Carole has a map and is walking very fast. She's talking about Milt and how she only got his vest. I'm not sure who he is.

There's a long queue at the flying place, but Carole takes no notice, marches right up to the desk. I stay by the notice board, spelling out the poem.

I've wheeled and soared and swung high in the sunlit silence.
Hovering there, I've chased the shouting wind along and . . .

'Norah! It's okay. They've given me the money back. I didn't even have to argue. The girl said they always give a refund if you don't actually fly, or if you change your mind or something. She thought you'd be gone only a few minutes and would be coming back with me.'

'Well, yes. I . . .'

'Mind you, it does sound quite a lark. I wouldn't mind trying it myself. Did you actually see them flying?'

'No.'

'You should have done. It says on the form you're meant to have a dekko first. You could have gone up to the flight chamber and watched them fly for free. Now we'll have to pay. It costs two dollars for spectators – that's four between us, just to have a peek. Hang on, I'll twist her arm, ask her if we can nip up there for nothing. She seemed quite decent and if I say we both may fly . . .'

All the excitement is creeping back again. Carole flying. Norah flying. Two white birds winging past each other. Perhaps I could get different sort of teeth, the type that don't come out.

'Great! She says we can. Just a quick look and not to breathe a word, otherwise half the queue will want to watch for nothing. Come on, Norah, quick!'

I follow Carole up the stairs. I'm so excited, I keep tripping and half falling. I could explain about the teeth, take them out first thing, when you remove your coat and shoes. Even if she laughs, it would be worth it just to fly. I close my eyes a moment, lean against the wall. I can hear that white-bird music soaring through my head. We're soaring with it, both of us, Carole just in front, drifting through the clouds. We're clouds ourselves, white and light and floating. We're . . .

'Get a move on, Toomey. There's another flight of stairs yet.' Carole's running now. She's passed the door marked 'Fliers', gone straight up.

'Here we are.' She's stopped.

I can't see any clouds, only still more stairs winding round and round. Perhaps they lead up to the sky.

'Don't go any higher, love. You can see okay from here.'

She's standing by a lift. I didn't know they had one. It comes up through the centre of the curving stairs. Carole's pointing, peering down.

I go and join her. No. It's not a lift, it's more a padded cage, like the one I saw on the television where everyone was falling. A cage with windows in. I look down through the windows. They're still falling.

A man in a flight-suit crashes to the ground. He doesn't fall very far because the cage is rather cramped and all closed in. There isn't any sky, only padded walls. There's a wire grille on the bottom which makes him bounce a bit. The tall man in the tracksuit tries to pull him up, grabs him by one leg. He falls again. He's just a child who hasn't learnt to walk yet and keeps collapsing on his face. Except he's not small, not at all, but very big and clumsy. They're all big and clumsy, the five fliers in the cage. Their suits have swollen up, so they have great fat arms and legs, and gas-masks on their faces with iron bars to hold them on.

The man is lying still now, lying in a heap. He may be a woman. It's difficult to tell. They all look just the same, very bulky and puffed up, more like huge great rubber toys than human beings. Their suits are flapping in the wind. The wind is very strong and too loud for them to speak. The man in the tracksuit is making signs to them, stretching out his hands, dashing after them. I think he's getting cross. He's shaking his head, jumping up and down.

The roar is getting louder. I can't seem to block it out, even with my hands across my ears. It's far worse than the plane's roar, impossible to speak. I thought it would be peaceful when you flew: just the brushing of a bird's wing, the breathing of the clouds. I imagined you'd escape the noise of earth, and soar right away into silent empty space. But here the noise is frightening, booming all around us. Even Carole's got her fingers in her ears.

I turn back to the fliers. Another man is falling now, sprawling on the padded bench which goes right round the cage. It's bright blue like his flight-suit, a horrid plastic blue, not pretty like the sky. The whole cage is lined with plastic. It's scuffed and dirty, even torn in places. There was sky in all the pictures on the notice board downstairs, not plastic or a cage.

'Fliers' is a lie. None of them are flying. They're only

toppling down and falling, landing on their heads, bouncing on their bottoms. The wind throws them up, blows them down again. They smash against the sides, thud into the wire. One man turns a somersault, bumps into two others. I can't tell which is which. They're just a tangled pile of bright blue flapping limbs.

Bang! Another fall. That one crashes on his back, doesn't move at all. He may be dead. Carole's laughing. I can hardly hear her laugh. The roar's too loud. She has to shout above it, really yell.

'If that's flying,' she splutters, 'I'm Henry VIII. "Experience the thrill of sky-diving" – that's what it said. And all you do is nosedive. Or break your bloody neck. Oh, look! He's got her by the seat of her pants.'

The man in charge is holding one of the fliers by her trousers, running round and round with her. He's got his hand right between her legs. You shouldn't touch a girl there. It *is* a girl. I can see her pigtail jerking in the wind. I had a pigtail once, a very long and thin one. I never had a ribbon on it, only rubber bands. Oh, let her fly, I pray, please let her fly.

The man is still dragging her along, still clinging to her suit. He suddenly lets go, throws her up above him. She's flying. Yes, she's flying, soaring on her own, the pigtail flying with her, streaming out. Oh, please, don't stop, don't stop her! Let the roof open, let her float right through it to the sky. Let her feel the clouds, white and soft as feathers, rushing by her, let her see the face of God. St Joseph, when you meet her, send her back to me with some message, some small present – a scrap of blue, a feather . . .

She's falling. I shut my eyes, can't look. I feel my stomach fall and smash inside me as I thud down to the floor. Everything is falling – clouds, birds, sky. The world goes black.

When it's grey again, the girl is on her back. She tries to struggle up, feeble arms waving in the air. She flew for just five seconds – five brief seconds, when she had longed and prayed to fly for twenty years. *Fly like a bird*. She was just a baby chick, a clumsy chick, which hadn't grown its wings yet, falling from its nest.

Carole grabs her bag, buttons up her jacket. 'Come on,' she shouts. 'It's getting boring. We've got better things to do than watch people falling on their fannies.' She keeps her mouth right close to my ear. Even so, it's hard to hear. 'Do you realize, Norah, not a single person's flown yet?'

I'm forced to shout myself. 'That girl just did. *She* flew.'

'No, she didn't. She was just blasted up by that propellor thing, and then plonked straight back down again. And Macho Man kept hold of all the others. I mean, it's hardly flying if some twelve-stone bully grips you by the arm or leg and whirls you round his head like a lasso.'

Suddenly, her voice sounds very loud. I jump. They've turned the wind off, so she's shouting over nothing. We stand quite still a moment, listening to the silence. Silence feels so strange.

'Thank God for that. I was just about to sue them for damage to my eardrums. Oh, look, Norah!'

The big and bulky fliers have all gone thin and limp like burst balloons. It was only the wind which kept them puffed up. They creep out of the cage, suits flapping now in folds around their feet. Carole checks her watch.

'Is that all the time they get? Five mingy minutes between the lot of them? Thank God we didn't waste our precious money. Gosh! I'm starving. We've missed lunch as well as breakfast, which means more cash down the drain. Fancy an ice cream?'

I nod. I should be feeling hungry, but the hole inside is more a sort of pain now. Pain because I didn't fly. No one flew.

The sun glares at me as we walk off down the street. We find an ice-cream shop with eighty different flavours. I don't know which to have. I like plain vanilla, but there's nothing plain at all. I hate deciding things. At Belstead, we had to choose our meals the day before; tick a piece of paper with the dinners written on it. It used to take me hours. Sometimes I ticked liver and they gave me cottage pie.

'You choose,' I say to Carole.

I sit down at a table while she queues. You have to queue for everything. She comes back with two spoons and just one glass. The glass is very full. It isn't just ice cream. I can see sponge, as well, and nuts, and some squashy bits of fruit, and they've poured Bisto gravy on the top. Carole bangs the spoons down.

'All that gunge cost extra and I didn't even ask for it. And look at the false bottom on the glass. This place is full of cons.' She picks out half a peach, goes on talking while she chews it. 'I mean, I was walking back this morning, starving hungry, when I saw this sign, "Free Breakfast". Well, of course I stopped, went in. Turns out they only serve it between midnight and five AM. Who'd want breakfast then, for heaven's sake? It wasn't breakfast anyway, just coffee and a doughnut. Then I saw "free tee shirt" – and I charged right in to get you one, but they were only toddlers' sizes, more like dolls' clothes. Hey, Norah . . .'

'Yes?'

'I'm sorry.'

'What for?' I wouldn't want a tee shirt. I never wear them. They make your chest look rude.

'You know – shouting, sounding off, being such a pain when I got back. I'm horrid sometimes, Norah. I hate myself, even while I'm doing it. I don't know how you stand me. I'm going to change, though. It's New Year's Eve tomorrow and that's the perfect time to change. I've never bothered much with New Year resolutions. But this year – you just wait. I'm giving up shouting, swearing and smoking for a start.'

'Smoking?' She's just bought cigarettes, used the money from the refund.

'Mm.' She puts her spoon down, lights one up. 'Well, I'll have to smoke this last packet, obviously. No point wasting money. And talking of money, that's another resolution. I'm going to make some for myself, not rely on other people's. How about you? Do you make resolutions?'

I never have before, but I try to think of one. I've never smoked and I don't want money because there'd be more things to decide then. I'd love to fly, but now I know I can't. I'd like to be smaller, with tiny hands and feet, but you can't make resolutions to change your size and shape. You can't make resolutions about a lot of things.

I don't reply. The ice cream is melting. The gravy has gone pink.

'It's important, Norah, don't you see, especially this year. We've got to have new lives. We can't rely on Beechgrove if it's closing. If we both made money somehow, then I wouldn't have to take some rotten boring job, or try to manage on the dole, and you wouldn't have to move out into lodgings. We could buy a flat, a nice one, do what *we* want, not what they decide.'

My hand shakes so much, I slop pink all down my skirt. I don't want to buy a flat and I hate to think of lodgings. I don't like change at all.

Carole's crunching nuts. 'I mean, even that old Reverend on the box said this New Year was special, a Year of Destiny. He could be right, I suppose.'

I say nothing. I thought we'd got our miracles already – Carole back with Victor, me with wings. It's more difficult to hope now, when I feel so sad and clumsy.

'Don't look so tragic, Norah. We're dead lucky, actually. Las Vegas is the one city in the world where you really can make money. I picked up this leaflet in the Hilton. It had a crock of gold on the cover, with loads of money spilling out, and inside were rows and rows of little photos. They were all the winners, Norah, people who'd won *millions*. Not nobs and snobs and hardened gamblers, just normal sort of people – housewives and shopkeepers and old age pensioners.' She crams her mouth with ice cream, wipes it off her chin. 'Some of them were ugly, old and bald, or even with buck teeth, but they all had this enormous smile. They'd changed their lives, you see. We've got to do the same. The trouble is we need money to make money and we've got . . .' She pauses, checks her purse. 'Ten dollars and two cents. That's not enough, not unless we win immediately. Mind you, we've got to get lucky pretty quick. It's New Year's Day on Friday. That leaves tomorrow and this evening. Come on, let's drink to it. New Year, new start. New Norah and new Carole.'

I shiver. It's cold in the café with the sun shut out. 'We haven't any drinks.'

'We'll toast it in ice cream then.' She passes me my spoon again. I'd put it down after just two mouthfuls. I still find it hard to eat.

'Dig in. Take that great big strawberry. Go on, Norah, aim high for once.' She loads her own spoon, a pink pool overflowing on the table, clinks it against mine.

I force the strawberry down. It feels too big and scratchy for my throat. 'New Norah and new Carole,' I repeat.

I don't want her to change.

I don't want anything to change.

15

'How's everyone feelin'? Is everyone feelin' pretty good? Any winners out there? Did anyone win money today? You, sir? How much did you win? Right – you can lend me a hundred bucks to pay my speedin' fine.'

The fat man on the stage yelps with laughter, does a little soft-shoe shuffle with the microphone. 'Is anyone out their havin' a birthday? What's your name, beautiful? Eunice. Let's give Eunice a big hand. She's twenty-one today.'

Laughter from the crowd now. I laugh myself. Eunice is white-haired. There are quite a lot of women in the audience. They've come for the male strip show which is held after the (female) naked dancing, and before the wet tee shirt competition. Far more men, though – crowds and crowds of fellers packed into the club, thronging round the bar, blocking all the exits, jostling elbows, spilling drinks. There's such a babel from the voices, the whole place sort of roars, as if we're in a dark and murky cave, with an underground waterfall thundering down just outside the entrance. It is a basement, actually, and I feel rather claustrophobic, and keep wishing we were sitting nearer a door. There's not a window to be seen, and the only lights are dim red-shaded ones hanging from the low black ceiling, which seems to press right down. The fat man on the stage has kept up his patter all the time, screaming through the mike above the uproar, making people laugh, telling dirty jokes. He's at it now again.

'A guy walked into a whorehouse and said to the Madam, "I'll give you a hundred bucks for the worst bit of ass you got in the house. No, I'm not horny, I'm homesick."'

They love it. I'm not sure I do. I feel a bit uncomfortable and some of the jokes are really crude. I'm only glad Norah isn't here. She'd be deeply shocked – if she even understood them, which I doubt. Anyway, she'd have hated all the noise. The music is so loud it's hard to talk at all. I've mouthed a few things to Angelique, who shouted back or nudged me if a famous face came in. I'm really thrilled I've met her. She's English, the first English person we've seen so far, amazingly. She's not a tourist – she lives here now. She came over for a holiday and stayed. Her story's like a fairy-tale. She was plain Angie Evans back in England, vegetating in a neo-Tudor semi in Watford, with her widowed mother and a handicapped elder brother; worked nine to five as a clerk in an insurance office. Now she's Angelique, drives her own Mercedes with AE on the numberplate, owns fifty pairs of shoes. (Fifty! She told me. She wasn't boasting. Her wardrobe's so big it's like a separate room.) She got her break by winning an amateur nude dance contest. She'd never even danced before, but it was how she took her clothes off. I was a bit put out at first when she said it just like that, but there's nothing crude about her. In fact, she's obviously refined and very elegant, with high cheekbones and the sort of auburn hair you call Titian, rather than common red or ginger, and very cool grey eyes. She's twenty-three – that's only five years older than I am, yet she's so stylish and sophisticated, she makes me feel as if I've only just crawled out of my eggshell and am still wet behind the ears.

We talked for hours. I met her at the free champagne party, the first one I'd attended. It was all part of my New Year resolution thing – take my chances, get about. Norah wouldn't come. She seemed so upset about that flying place, she simply went to bed – at six PM. Actually, I was feeling quite self-conscious, standing on my own in a vast ballroom with no ball, not even many people. So when Angelique came up, I was terrifically relieved, especially when I heard her English accent. I hadn't realized how cut off I'd felt. Because we speak the same language, we presume Americans are like us, stamped from the same mould, but actually I suspect they're more foreign than the French. Angelique said she'd never change her accent. It helped to get her jobs and guaranteed a better class of boyfriend. Her current man is a pit-boss at the Gold Rush, which was how she'd wangled an invite to the party. (I'm not sure what a pit-boss is, but I didn't like to ask.) Anyway, we stood there chatting about cosy things back home like C & A and Wimpy Bars and golden syrup. (Angelique said the only English things she missed were golden syrup and milkmen.)

Once she'd told me her story, I entrusted her with mine (with certain bits left out), and she said if I wanted to make money and was so good at competitions, then why didn't I copy her example and enter a nude dance contest? I almost choked on my champagne. I can't dance for toffee and as for taking all my clothes off in front of half a million people . . . Then she suggested a wet tee shirt competition, and said they had one every Wednesday at a club called Ritzy's, with a male strip show first, to entice the women in – just ordinary working girls who didn't mind a lark, or wives and girlfriends of men in the audience who were game for a bit of fun.

'It's Wednesday today,' she said. 'Let's go.'

I started to object. I didn't like the sound of men emptying pails of freezing water over girls in tee shirts to make their breasts stand out, show the outline of their nipples, and anyway, I was wearing not a tee shirt but an expensive blouse I didn't want to spoil.

'Oh, come on, Carole, be a sport.'

'Are *you* going to enter, then?'

'I don't need the money. You do, obviously. There are lots of prizes, all in cash, and even if you don't win a thing, the guys in the audience all shower you with dollar bills, just to cheer you on.'

'No.' I shook my head. One of my New Year resolutions was to stop acting so impulsively, landing up in situations I regretted. I was also worried about Norah, who seemed really quite depressed.

'Ritzy's *is* Las Vegas, Carole. You've got to see it. You don't have to enter anything, if that's what's bugging you. We'll just go along and watch, have a ball.'

I didn't want her to write me off as a spoilsport and a wimp when I'd only just met her and I needed a real friend, so I downed my champagne to give me courage and five minutes later we were streaking along the Strip in her Mercedes. Well, not quite streaking. With one day to go till New Year's Eve, Las Vegas is bursting at the seams, hotels as well as streets; 'No Vacancy' signs flashing everywhere and the Strip a traffic jam. There's a convention going on as well (maintenance engineers), which means ninety thousand extra visitors. Ninety thousand spare men with spare parts, as Angelique put it.

I was rather disappointed when we eventually drew up outside the club. It looked shabby, almost sordid, a low one-storey building, with a balding palm tree shivering outside. Beneath the palm was a tiny group of demonstrators – just three beleaguered females holding up placards saying 'WOMEN SAY NO TO PORN', and 'SISTERS, WHY BE SEX OBJECTS?' All three were plain, one with heavy glasses, one with frizzy hair, the youngest in a boiler suit, with a pale and piggy baby on her back. Yet all had principles, cared enough to stand there in the cold, risk ridicule and worse. I tried not to meet their eyes, felt a sort of traitor as I slunk past them through the door; almost bolted out again when they asked me for a twenty-dollar entrance fee.

Angelique pushed forward. 'Don't worry. I can get us in for nothing. They know me here.' A smile, a whispered word or two, and we were squeezing through the bodies, being ushered to a table. Angelique pointed out her friends – the tall black brawny barman, two rather gorgeous waitresses, and a sultry dark-eyed dancer performing up on stage.

'Alexis Lovejoy – well, Mary Brooks to you and me. She's quite a girl.'

She looked it. Her spangled satin sheath-dress was Durex-tight, her long legs tapering down to three-inch heels. She was pouting in a spotlight, peeling off her elbow-length lace gloves – teasingly, provocatively – finger by erotic finger. I watched, amazed. She couldn't have been more than twenty-one, yet again she was so confident, so elegant, so utterly assured and in control. I couldn't help comparing her with the three denimed frumps outside, felt ashamed to realize I'd rather have her glamour than their principles. Soon, we were sitting right up near the catwalk, so close that we could touch her if we wanted (several people were – the men, at least). I don't know how we got the seats. The place was packed.

Alexis seemed more a stripper than a dancer and was taking off more clothes; really involving the audience, bending forward so that a man could undo her zip or unlatch her bra, draping her black stockings around another fellow's neck, tickling him with her scarlet feather boa. I felt a bit uneasy, even squeamish. These guys were total strangers, yet she was kissing them on the lips, taking their hands and stroking them against her naked breasts, pushing her buttocks right into their faces. I've never seen a stripper before, except once on television, and she stayed up on stage, strictly out of bounds. With Alexis, it was no holds barred. Men were reaching out to fondle her, touching any flesh that they could reach, really slavering. She stopped in front of one guy, removed his spectacles, slipped them down inside her g-string, then rubbed them up and down against her crotch. He ground his face right into her breasts, used both hands to knead and pinch her bum. Slowly, she took the glasses out again, replaced them on his nose, stayed pressed up close against him, legs open, tongue flicking in and out. I could feel myself blushing. I don't know why. Everyone else was cheering and applauding, including Angelique. I stole a glance at her – the stern grey eyes, the prim and high-cut blouse. Did she dance like that herself? I couldn't picture it, somehow didn't want to. For the first time in my life I felt a prude, almost wished I could join those three brave girls outside.

There were quite a lot of dancers and they all went just as far – or even further – Cheryl and Miranda and a tattooed one called Tyger, two Orientals and a gorgeous black girl who looked six feet tall and called herself Delilah. Angelique said they almost always changed their names and quite frequently their shape as well, so that sometimes they were more silicone than flesh. I couldn't take my eyes off them. Although I was shocked and slightly repelled, there was also that hot and creeping excitement I'd felt when reading the escort magazines. These were women like I'm a woman with the same curves and holes and slits, yet they were making money from it, parading their bodies, not hiding them away. Why are we ordinary girls so modest and so private, when we could display ourselves for profit? Is it really all that wrong to be a sex-object? It's easy to say yes when you've got some other asset – brains or skills or influence – but for a lot of girls it's their bodies, or oblivion. I felt really quite mixed up: disgusted when a dancer went down on her hands and knees and started tonguing a man's bare and hairy paunch; admiring when the whole ecstatic audience cheered her in the cancan. *I* was cheering too, felt a weird sort of tingle when I caught glimpses of a cunt, or watched naked boobs bouncing up and down. That worried me as well. Why should other women turn me on? Was something wrong with me, something else (and worrying) to add to my fat pile of Beechgrove case notes?

I was really quite relieved when they announced an interval. I didn't like the thought that I actually wanted to stare at women's breasts and fannies, and could get a thrill from it. I sat sucking ice-cubes to try to cool me down.

I'm still sucking ice-cubes. The interval has lasted half an hour, though the fat man razzles on, cracking jokes, or shouting out to members of the audience. 'Is that your wife, sir? Send her home! Bringin' your wife to a joint like this is like bringin' a dildo to an orgy.'

'Hey, you, sir, with the beard. You're not queer, are you, sir? A lot of queers wear beards to hide the stretch marks.'

I'm blushing again, right down to my feet. I'm not sure I like this place, and it's getting frightfully late. It's too dark to see my watch and I don't really want to check it, in case Angelique assumes I'm bored. It's just that I'd promised myself an early night, so as to save my stamina for New Year's Eve tomorrow. We're going to that show – the one with lions and tigers and God knows what else besides. And after that, there's another champagne rave-up, the biggest yet. If they don't buck up a bit here, I'll be going straight on from wet tee shirts to wild beasts, without a wink of sleep between. We haven't had the male strip yet, let alone the tee shirts, and there's no sign of any stirring from the wings.

Mind you, I don't think I could get out if I tried. The crowds are so thick they're jammed solid round the table, ten-deep round the bar. The waitresses are amazingly good-tempered, squeezing between bodies and stepping over legs. The blonde one brings us two more piña coladas. I think they're free as well. I hope so. They cost three pounds each in England, which is why I've never tried one. They're delicious, all frothy, like milk shakes, with little coloured paper parasols stuck into the froth, and lots of ice. We need the ice. It's stifling in the club with all this press of people. They're squashed so tight in some spots, you can't quite tell whose arms or heads are whose, except there seem too many hands spare – hands grabbing, waving, snatching, pointing, groping. I've already had three separate hands explore my knee; someone's elbow keeps knocking into mine, and I can't hear Angelique for the brays of beery laughter or garlic-flavoured guffaws blasting in my face.

There's a sudden fanfare from the band, as clarinet and trumpets shrill above the din. 'This is it,' mouths Angelique, as the curtains on the stage swing down, rippling red and silver in a burst of coloured lights. 'The guys are coming on now, and the women just go wild.'

I can already hear excited screams as the fat man reappears, no longer in his shirt-sleeves, but wearing a purple velvet jacket, straining at the seams.

'Good evening, folks, again. Welcome to Ritzy's All-Male Strip Revue. Our strippers are sheer dynamite. How many girls out there wanna see our guys strip down to their muscles?'

Shouts of 'yeah, yeah, yeah!' and not only from the girls. Angelique told me they get a lot of gays here, and also straight men who want to see how they compare for size. It's odd how men are so obsessed with such a tiny part of them. If a six-foot man has a six-inch prick, that's only 8.3 per cent of him, yet he probably spends half his life fretting about its length, breadth, stiffness or performance. I'm not that sure I'd want a prick at all, whatever Freud's supposed to have said. Why have something dangling there which worries you so much?

'Ladies and gentlemen, put your hands together and make a lot of noise for our first great guy, the one and only, the incredible Mr Nude Universe.'

Lights and music go hysterical, followed closely by the crowds. The curtains swoop apart and a hugely muscly bodybuilder struts on to the stage, dressed in a red satin jacket, matching satin shorts and red laced boots, with a wide white satin sash draped across his body, as if he's just been crowned Miss World. He takes up several different poses, showing off his physique, turning this way and that, so that everyone can admire him from every different angle. He then removes his sash, tosses it behind him and throws himself into an energetic workout, as if this were his private gym rather than a nightclub. Sweat pours off his face as he works through sidebends, leg-swings, squats, touch-toes. He mops himself with a scarlet towel, then prances down the catwalk, stops in front of a small and rather mousy girl, who giggles nervously.

'How come all you girls in the front row have your legs crossed?' cackles the fat man from the wings. 'What's your name, hon? Brenda? Brenda's bin here since three o'clock this afternoon, waitin' for this guy. Brenda, do you wanna see Mr Big strip down? Do you wanna see his muscle-tone?'

Brenda nods, seems too keyed up to speak. Mr Universe is easing off his jacket, inviting Brenda to help him, stroke his naked chest. She does so, between another bout of giggling. He stands over her, one foot on her table; takes up another swanky pose, tensing all his muscles.

'Isn't he a hunk?' the fat man shouts. 'Don't you girls all love him?'

Obviously they do. They're all shouting and applauding as he prowls back to the stage to fetch his sash. He's so well developed he has mini breastlets – well, not so mini, actually. Some girls I know would swap with him, if it weren't for the coarse black hairs around the nipples. He drapes his sash over each nipple in turn, wiggling them alternately, making the sash flick and twitch, without ever falling off. The crowds go wild, though I refuse to clap. He pinched that trick from the dancing girls. Cheryl did it first, and better – not with a sash but with her sheer black stockings, rotating each breast individually, so that the stockings seemed to dance themselves. I must admit it got me quite excited. She had smashing tits, really full and round, and everything she did was so sensual, yet graceful. She pulled one stocking taut and massaged her nipple with it, up and down, round and round. The nipple went quite stiff and hard. I noticed that particularly.

This man's breasts are really only rolls of fat, tangled with hair and shining with a film of sweat. His lips are full and sullen, his eyes bulging with his biceps. I'm the only one who's not a fan. The other girls are salivating and even the fat man has come down off the stage to dance attendance.

'You girls can get your dollars out and stick them down his g-string. Some of these guys can even give you change without using their hands.' He shakes with laughter. 'And they all accept Mastercharge or Visa cards.'

There are titters from the girls, who begin fumbling for their purses, taking out wads of dollar bills and stuffing them down the scarlet shorts and boots. I watch, astonished. What's he done, for heaven's sake, to earn that sort of cash? He can't dance and he hasn't even stripped yet. He's just a hulk of sweat and muscle, getting girls to fawn on him. He swaggers up to another giggling pair, orders each of them to unlace a scarlet boot; preens and prances while they grovel at his feet. Beads of sweat are falling from his face onto their expensive lacquered hairdos.

He's now standing in his socks and shorts. He drapes himself against a table, pulls a sock off, wiggling his whole body. He's copying the female strippers again; except when they removed their seamed black fishnet stockings, at least it looked provocative, whereas he just looks plain daft, especially when he flings his sock into the audience. Net stockings turn men on, but why should a sweaty sock in navy wool and nylon make any woman slaver? Socks are dirty washing – a woman's chore. I used to get mad with Jon because when he moved out into lodgings, he expected me to take on his doting mother's role and supply a laundry service.

Hell! I'm ranting on like a full-fledged Women's Libber and Mr Universe is marching right towards our table. The fat man yells encouragement. 'That's it, girls. I wanna see everyone out there gettin' into the act. We're gonna have a grab-bag here tonight. Just grab him, girls, grab him where it counts. Wow!

Those underpants are tight. They're like a cheap hotel – no ball-room. Ha ha ha! Go on, girls, give the guy a break – drag his shorts down.'

Angelique obliges, cheered on by the rest.

'What's your name?' the fat man keeps repeating. I look round. Who's he asking? *Me*, for heaven's sake!

'Carole,' I blurt out.

'Go on, Carole. Untie that g-string. Help yourself.'

My cheeks are really flaming. Everybody's watching me, men as well as girls. Arms are jostling mine as females wave their dollar bills. 'Stop!' I want to shout. 'Keep your rotten money.' I force a smile instead, pull at one side of the g-string, clumsy with embarrassment. You can almost hear the tension. What will be revealed? Will I have to touch it? Wrap it round with bank notes?

Nothing is revealed. Mr Nude Universe isn't nude – not yet. He's wearing a second g-string snug beneath the first. He looks quite small, in fact, hasn't built his muscle-tone in that particular spot. No one else appears to mind. His second g-string is already fringed with dollar bills, and he's collecting up still more from all along the catwalk. He disappears a moment to stow them somewhere safe, returns to pluck a woman from the audience, carries her on stage, pretends to have it off with her, jerking his whole body, making thrusting movements. The audience goes mad, clapping, stamping, yelling. This girl isn't even shy, but is joining in, moving under him, shrieking with excitement, echoed by the fat man's.

'Go on, Tarzan, give it to her. She's really hot for it. Kiss her on the lips, kiss her right on the lips.'

Mr Universe turns her upside down, kisses her on the crotch. The laughter gets wilder and more vulgar. 'What's your favourite position, hon? Wow! She likes it from behind, folks. It's okay, darlin' – you can swallow it. It's very low on calories.'

The audience fall about. The girl is overweight, great fat arms and thighs. At least the two are matched for size. I can hardly bear to watch, though. They're making sex so crude and rude and animal. They're *all* sex objects – guys as well as girls. And it's almost prostitution, the way that fat man keeps touting for more money. I expect he gets a cut.

'Now, I want everyone here to give this marvellous guy a dollar. It's still Christmas, still the giving season, so everybody give. That's right – just throw your money on the stage.'

When Mr Universe finally bows out, he's clutching rolls of dollars in both hands, and can't even wave goodbye. There's another burst of fireworks from the music, another exploding rainbow from the lights.

'Ladies and gentlemen, put your hands together for our next amazing guy – a real fantastic dancer – Guiseppo, the Italian Stallion.'

I doubt if he's Italian. He looks more Mexican with his black eyes and oily skin, his agile wiry body. He's dressed in a pure white suit and shirt, with a cream straw hat and natty little gloves. At least he can dance a bit, does high kicks and pirouettes while the band plays 'Arrivederci Roma'. When at last he braves the catwalk, the girls mob him quite spontaneously, clambering out of their seats to unbuckle his belt, unlace his two-tone shoes.

'Take 'em off. Take 'em off,' encourages the fat man. 'How many girls wanna see this guy really strip down to basic Adam?'

Guiseppo shrugs off his jacket, copying Cheryl and the girls again in all his sexy poses. That's what bugs me, somehow. Why can't the men work out something different, something more suited to their gender and physique, instead of just imitating women? Female strippers have spent years and years perfecting their techniques, then men come along and do just the same routines, when they've got completely different bodies and equipment. Don't they realize they look comic and embarrassing, wiggling their non-existent hips like that? Those gestures all shout 'female' while their muscles and their body-hair shout 'male'. Guiseppo is exceptionally hairy. He's taken off his trousers now and is gyrating round and round. Even his buttocks are covered with dark hairs and his chest is like an unmown lawn. He still has his gloves on, and when he does get round to removing them, it's just a take-off of Alexis. There he is, stroking each butch and hirsute finger and expecting us to drool. Most of the females do, in fact, but I feel just pissed off.

His underpants are shaped like a miniature dress-shirt front, with a row of little buttons, two black lapels and a tiny red bow-tie, to match the one he was wearing higher up. There isn't any back, just two thin strings to hold the thing in place. He goes around the audience pushing this white shirt front into female faces, or sidling his bare and hairy buttocks on to laps. He doesn't even smile, just looks sullen, even bored; though he's pretty quick to gather up the loot – dollar bills stuffed right inside his pants. He can't have much else down there if there's room for so much cash. I'm beginning to wonder if these guys have pricks at all. You can hardly call it stripping if they won't take off their g-strings. Another con, I suppose. You can see bare male chests or hairy legs on any boring beach, without paying a twenty-dollar entrance fee, plus all those bribes and tips.

I'm going to call their bluff. If this is called a strip show, then the men should strip. After all, the females did. Okay, I admit I recoiled a bit at seeing all those Abigails really flaunted and exposed (and pubic hair trimmed and shaped like ornamental hedges), but at least they had the guts to go the whole hog. Why should it be different for the men? When Guiseppo comes this way, I'll do what the fat man told us, have a grab. He's coming now, shimmying his hips. He stops by Angelique, takes her hand, strokes it up and down his nipples. I grab, while he's still busy. There's nothing there – well, almost nothing. The stallion is a gelding.

'Watch out!' the fat man shrieks. 'Young Carole's goin' wild. Didja see what she just did? I can hardly believe my eyes. Okay, get the lights down and let her do her thing. Give the guy a dollar, Carole. He deserves it. Yeah, just push it down.'

I can't give him anything. I'm paralysed. He's sitting on my lap, pressed up right against me. I can smell his sweat and hair-oil, and his greasy hair is dangling in my face, as he pretends to grind his pelvis into mine. It's all pretence. He doesn't like me – I'm pretty sure of that – and *I* feel almost sick. Yet the audience is cheering us on, shouting out 'Bravo', 'Encore', and other ruder things. Now he's including Angelique, doing the splits across both our laps, his naked sweaty legs sticking to our skirts.

'That's right! Two at a time. Goodness gracious, those girls are hungry for it! They've been waitin' all their lives for a real hot Latin lover.'

The Latin lover is rocking backwards and forwards on our laps, kissing us in turn, fat wet lips smearing all our make-up. His breath smells of cumin seeds, overlaid with mouthwash. I can't stand any more. I push him off. Angelique is reaching for her purse, extracting dollar bills, paying for our pleasure. I'm so hopping mad, I hardly notice the next stripper coming on – Mr Fantasy. He's black. Dressed in a lilac spangled boilersuit, which he eventually strips off to reveal a g-string trimmed with fur. 'Real mink,' shouts the fat man. 'The most expensive cock in the house.'

The white-haired birthday girl is straining out of her seat, darts on to the catwalk and throws herself between the two black legs.

'Oh my goodness, Grandma's goin' down on the man! This is more fun than cookies and milk, isn't it, Grandma?'

Grandma doesn't answer. Mr Fantasy has scooped her from the floor, and rushed off through the curtains with her. We can only hear her squeals.

'They're going off to make chocolate chip cookies, together. No! they're back already. That was quick, Eunice. Eunice likes it black and quick.'

I'm getting bored. Yes, really. It's just vulgar jokes and sham. Okay, so all the acts are different – Tiny Tim with his thumb stuck in his mouth and cuddling a teddy bear, which I suppose is meant to appeal to our maternal instincts, and Dr Probe with his Master's degree in Sexology, who enters wearing nothing but a jockstrap and a mortarboard; Dangerous Dave who snarls on stage looking really frightening, dressed like a punk in studded black leather with lots of zips and chains, and one final guy got up like an airline pilot who looked better in his braid than in his pale white flesh.

I'm actually longing for my bed, alone, without any man at all. Perhaps I'm still hung over from Milton's sleeping pills. Or there's something basic wrong with me – the only female in the whole packed room not having fun. The airline pilot is squeezing between the tables, picking out the girls, pawing, snogging, smooching, aiming his pelvic thrusts at every female lap. One girl has snatched his hat off and is stuffing it with cash; another is stroking dollar bills down the whole length of his damp and sticky body, inching them slowly and provocatively past his throat, chest, belly, until she finally secures them in his g-string.

I'm still amazed at all the contact. I never thought that strippers would actually get that close, let themselves be groped, or touch and grab themselves – and all with total strangers. Everyone else accepts it, even revels in it, but I can't help being shocked. I mean, if one of those men had VD or AIDS or something, or hadn't washed after what Norah calls going number two, he could spread his germs, pass on his infection. After all, their buttocks are completely bare and they've been grinding them into any willing crotch, or slipping their hands down inside their g-strings, then fondling female faces. I'm not normally obsessed with germs – that's Norah's thing. Perhaps she's influencing me without my realizing. God! I hope not, or I'll end up celibate, or carrying Dettol in my bag instead of scent. Funny, though, I miss her. She'd loathe it here, of course, but I feel better when she's with me. I can be myself with Norah, whereas with girls like Angelique, however nice they are, I somehow feel I'm not enough; have to make an effort, put an act on.

She's turning to me now, offering me a Virginia Slim. She *would* smoke those – they're elegant and skinny like she is herself. 'Are you all right, hon?' she asks.

'Yeah, fine.' Well, what else can I say? I don't want her to label me a prude.

She reaches for her lighter. Every time I see her hands, I want to hide my own. Her nails aren't just painted, they're works of art – each one transformed into a glossy golden heart, with a tiny A nestling in its centre. They do that over here: sculpture nails, reshape you toe to finger. The lighter, too, is gold and monogrammed. She lights both cigarettes.

'It's the finale next,' she tells me, pausing for a drag. 'All the guys at once and all completely starkers. No more g-strings. It's quite a sight.'

I stop griping and sit up. I'm intrigued, despite myself. I haven't seen that many pricks – hardly any, really, if I'm honest, and I must admit I am quite curious. The band is playing expectant trills and fanfares, the fat man almost choking with excitement.

'Stand back, girls. Don't all rush at once. This is the moment you've been waitin' for. Sit down, Grandma, you'll need all the strength you've got.'

The curtains open and out rush the seven strippers – all well and truly stripped now, right down to the skin, though sporting various minor props such as hats and gloves and sweatbands. I ignore the props, glance lower. I don't know quite what I expected, but after all that build-up, the excitement and the foreplay, the simulated fucking, the thrusts and heaves and gasps, I'm primed for an erection – seven erections.

I keep staring at the seven dangling droops. Tiny Tim's doesn't even droop. It's too small for that, just a little bud, hardly visible at all between his thighs. The airline pilot's is pointed at the end, pointing down. Mr Fantasy's is large, but just as limp. Mr Nude Universe has bigger bulges higher up. The seven men strut and plume, rippling their muscles, puffing out their chests. It's only now I understand why I've been feeling so cheated and resentful. A soft prick is a put down, the clinching proof that the man is feeling nothing, limp and dangling nothing. These seven guys have spent the last two hours panting and frothing with a desire which isn't there. They probably just despise us girls, see us as a source of easy cash.

Oh, I know you could say it's the same with female strippers, that Alexis and the rest of them feel nothing either and are just feigning their excitement and their turn-on, but you can't actually prove it with a female. There's no clincher, as with men, so that at least you're free to imagine they're genuinely aroused, which just saves the thing from insult.

They're taking their bows now, still pulsing with mock passion, blowing kisses, striking erotic poses, while those seven

221

floppy misogynists declare the whole thing a sham. I turn away, can't look.

'Enjoy it?' Angelique asks.

I nod, wonder if I dare explain about the pricks, and see if she feels the same. I try to point out how hollow it all seems – sex without the x, without the charge and thrust, all posturing and façade. I fumble for the words. I've only just met the girl, don't want to offend her.

'Oh, come on, Carole. What d'you expect? Erections every week and on demand? It's just a job, for heaven's sake.'

I don't reply. It's obvious I'm the only one dissatisfied, the only sourpuss. The other girls are still squawking with excitement, swapping high points from the show. I remember something Dr (Beechgrove) Bates said: 'You're angry with your father, Carole, for dying, so you take it out on all men, want to punish them.'

Bugger Dr Bates! He always made things so involved. I'm confused enough already. Those females with the placards object to porn as porn. At least that's fairly simple and consistent, whereas what I'm saying is (I think) that I want porn to be professional, porn for real. No, that's ridiculous. I object to porn myself, and yet . . . Oh, I don't know, but those female strippers seemed so glamorous, so suave. I'd rather look like them, earn their sort of money, than parade in a dirty boilersuit with nothing in my purse but skimpy principles. Yet I must admit I'd like to have a cause, something to believe in beyond mere cash and clothes; to be part of a group who cared enough to fight. I've always felt ashamed that I didn't join the peace marches, or chain myself to railings, or cut the wire at Greenham. Instead, I used to criticize their gear, those awful woolly hats and nylon anoraks.

I excuse myself a moment, pretend I need the toilet. I really need a break, a rest from all the noise and razzmatazz. The music is still ear-splitting, a sort of jangly yelping wail, amplified to pain. I fight my way to the exit, dodging chairs, tables, and randy men who grope me as I pass, shouting out, 'Hi, gorgeous! On your own?' I fend them off, squeeze through the mini soccer crowd still gathered round the bar. The foyer is mercifully deserted. It smells of curry, strangely, since they don't serve meals, only snacks and sandwiches. A broken doll is lying in one corner. I pick it up. Perhaps a family live here, above the basement. I've hardly seen a child in all Las Vegas. They don't belong. It's not a family place.

Adults only. And 'adult' means something slightly sordid here. Adult movies, adult entertainment.

It's funny – I longed to be an adult, dared trial-runs when I was only twelve or so, larding on the blusher, buying dangly earrings, stuffing out my chest with tissue paper. Now I've made it: breasts for real, mascara and jewellery no longer hidden in my piggy-bank, yet it's all a disappointment. I thought it would mean more – much more – that I'd suddenly feel different, less confused, receive some insight or enlightenment, know what I believed in. But my eighteenth birthday was really much the same as all the rest – my father buying cakes and crazy presents, my mother nagging about crumbs and waste of money; a few jokey cards from friends. Perhaps we need something like the Jewish bar mitzvah, some solemn celebration to make the thing dignified and real, to convince ourselves we really are grown up.

I walk round and round the foyer, the doll cradled in my arms. Nice to be a kid again. Or would it? Even then, you're pressurized, have to keep up with your crowd, know what's 'in', what's yuk; follow trends and styles. I only started smoking because that was clever, daring. Now I'm hooked.

Las Vegas is a bit the same. You have to be a swinger, keep on Having Fun. 'Enjoy, enjoy!' everyone insists. It's their favourite word, written on the menus, shouting from advertisements, in the mouths of all the staff – waitresses and barmen, Keno girls and hostesses. They say it when they bring your food, bring your change, find you tables, mix you drinks. 'Enjoy, enjoy, enjoy.' To tell the truth, I'm feeling a bit sated. I've drunk too much, gorged too much, and I'm getting almost blasé. If there aren't a hundred courses, or two hundred dancing girls, a glade of marble nymphs or a pride of gilded lions, then the place is second-rate.

I slump down on a bench. A television set is playing to itself.

223

Two soldiers run for cover in a burst of rifle-fire. I can hear the fat man's laughter as background to the guns, amplified and booming from the other room. Then Israel (or wherever) gives place to sunny Spain – bronzed and leggy lotus-eaters throwing beach balls, sipping Coca-Cola. 'It's the real thing, the real thing . . .' Actually, it rots your teeth, so next we get a toothpaste ad: Plaque Control with Fluoride. They're Having Fun again – skiing, surfing, sunbathing, flashing ice-white teeth against white snow, white surf, white rum. They're always drinking in the ads: Bacardi in Jamaica, bourbon in log cabins, and everything is Fun, even things like dandruff. You don't actually see the itching or the reddened flaky scalp, just Golden Girls floating in slow motion over silver sands, their sheeny hair streaming out behind them, and blissful smiles again. They ought to do a combination ad – shampoo, toothpaste, Coke, Bacardi – just one beach, one big grin. Perhaps that's why my mother drank, to find the missing Fun. There weren't a lot of laughs in Elm Close, Portishead. My father did his humble best, but the house was cramped and damp, and the immersion heater was always breaking down, so if you washed your hair it meant boiled kettles or cold water, not hot springs in Jamaica.

They're back to guns and bombs now, so I walk on down the passage to the restroom. I'd better use it now I'm here, though it's cramped and filthy dirty, with a crate of empty bottles in one corner. (Budweiser, not Bacardi.) I pee as quickly as I can, wash my hands in a trickle of cold water. There's a contraceptive machine above the basin selling Super-Sex French Ticklers. 'Only Super-Sex offer the ecstasy of colour, with improved raised spirals which combine total stimulation with maximum sensitivity.' Great. If I had a guy to wear one. I don't want a guy, though, do I? I'm hostile to them, fixated on my father. Oh, Dr Bates, where are you? No, I couldn't cope with him.

I'm tired now, really tired, wish I could just leave. But that would be unfair to Angelique, and in the absence of a bloke, she's my only friend. Well, Norah, of course, but even though I feel relaxed with Norah, there are still a lot of things we can't discuss – men, pricks, French ticklers, even resentment. If I were Toomey, I'd be burning with resentment towards everyone, from her non-existent father (who was too drunk or wild or careless to even bother with a tickler), to bloody Dr Bates, who more or less ignores her. And instead she loves the world – or at least accepts it, and her place at the bottom of the pile, with the poor, the sick, the sexless.

I dry my hands on my skirt (the towel-holder is empty), and return to the fray – which is easier said than done, since the wet tee shirt competition is just about to start and more men are pouring in to see the fun – Fun. (It has to have its capital.) When at last I reach our table, Angelique is talking to a foreign-looking man, tall and rather striking.

'*No*, Reuben,' she's saying. 'No, I'm sorry. I've told you no ten times.'

I'm intrigued. Is he propositioning her, trying to wean her from her pit-boss? I suddenly feel jealous. This man has some quality I've never seen before – an intensity, a seriousness, a sort of fire and passion which has nothing to do with sex. You can see it in his eyes, which seem too large for his thin and sallow face, staring fiercely out of it, burning up everything they light on. He can't be more than twenty-five or so, but he looks older because of the expression in those eyes, one of suffering, oppression. He's wearing ordinary blue jeans and a matching denim jacket, except they don't look ordinary on him, but daring and original, especially in this setting, where most people are dressed up. He's very thin, as if he's burnt up all spare flesh in action and conviction. His hands, too, are long and lean, and he uses them a lot, gesturing, appealing, stroking back his thick dark hair, rubbing at his chin. He hasn't shaved for a day or two and his chin and jaw are shadowed, which makes him look not slobby, but somehow vulnerable.

Angelique hasn't introduced me. Some girls are like that – they don't want the guy themselves, but heaven help you if you try to snap him up. Actually, they're both ignoring me, still deep in conversation. Angelique seems angry, almost scared. I can feel her vibes affecting me, making me not angry, but restless and excited. I bang my glass around a bit to remind them both I'm there. At last, he seems to see me, turns in my direction. I smile. He doesn't, just keeps his eyes focused on my face. I can feel myself flaming. His glance is fire, reducing me to ash, burning away all pretence and affectation. Angelique is silent, so I introduce myself.

'I'm Carole,' I say, unsteadily. 'Carole Joseph.' I no longer need to change my name. I want to be myself.

'Jewish.'

He isn't asking, merely stating. His voice is very low, intimate and urgent, as if we're sharing in some secret, or he's telling me the password. I don't say 'just a quarter', as I usually do. He's obviously Jewish himself with a name like Reuben, and those deep brown burning eyes, so why make myself three-quarters different from him? I simply nod.

He rubs his chin. 'From England.'

'Yes,' I say, though it wasn't a question, just another statement.

'Staying here or visiting?' His voice is very deep. The American accent is barely noticeable, and is overlaid with something else. He seems to have pared down the language to its shortest simplest components, as if he's short of time, doesn't want to waste it, or is used to giving orders.

'Visiting,' I answer. For the first time in five days, I wish I could say 'staying'.

'How long?'

'Ssh,' says Angelique. 'It's starting now.'

I long to escape, sneak out with Reuben on my own, creep away from the racket and hysteria, have him to myself. This man is something special – I know that in my veins – the unique and different man I knew I had to find. He's talking about Israel. I can hardly make the words out, but I can hear the fervour in them, see the passion and conviction in his face. Those other guys like Jake and Milt were playboys. I just clutched at them because I was feeling lost and lonely. Reuben's in a different class entirely – young, good-looking, serious, obviously intelligent, and concerned with things beyond mere greed and gambling. He's questioning me again. I crane forward to hear, but his words are scuppered in the fat man's spiel.

'Now, any of you lovely girls who wanna get involved in our tee shirt competition, all you have to do is come up here and give me your names. Don't worry if you haven't got a tee shirt. We'll supply one. We've got hundreds – big, small, very big. We love the big ones, don't we, guys? There's a prize for the biggest, don't forget, but also for the smallest, the cutest, the best shaped nipples and . . . Sit down, sir. There's a security guard standing right behind you and you should see where he hits. You'll be the winner of the next no-ball prize.' (Screams of raucous laughter, including the fat man's own.) '*My* name's Leroy. That's a black's name, isn't it? No, I'm not a black, but my mother loved 'em, couldn't get enough. Ha ha ha! Anyone out there with a wife or girlfriend who's a little shy, just push her up on stage. We'll wet her down and show everyone her titties. Look at all those horny guys sittin' in the front row. Smile if you're horny, guys. Great! Every goddamn guy is smilin'.'

I feel embarrassed for Reuben. He's not smiling, hardly seems to be listening at all. He's still sitting next to Angelique (though she's turned her chair away), and is scribbling on a folded bit of paper, his brows drawn down, his profile sad and stern. I think Jesus would have looked like that. I know the pictures show Him as a wimp, with long blond curls and clutching little lambs (or lilies), but He was obviously dark if He came from Palestine, and I'm pretty sure He looked haunted and oppressed when you think of all His problems.

Angelique is nudging me. 'Go *on*.'

'What?' I say. I'm so obsessed with Jesus-Reuben, I think she means take his hand, solve his problems, join his Church.

'Get up there and give Leroy your name, hon. This is your big chance!'

I shake my head. I'm even more opposed now. I want Reuben to regard me as someone cool and dignified, an apostle, a disciple, as serious as he is. They're anything but serious on stage. They've dragged on a children's plastic paddling pool and are handing out tee shirts and bikini bottoms to a troupe of giggly entrants.

Leroy is bawling through the microphone again. 'Hundreds of girls want to be in showbiz. Well, this could be your break, girls. Look at that great audience out there – impresarios, theatre owners, motion-picture producers, all pantin' to spot new talent, snap you up. And even the regular guys will be rootin' for you. Come on, guys, get your wallets out, unroll those dollar bills. I wanna see you all go crazy tonight. It's the first time for most of these girls and they're nervous as all hell. I hope we get some pretty ones, but we take on anyone. We can't say no. Last week, the winner had only one tit. We gave her the prize for most original. Ha ha ha! Right, who wants to see some action?'

Screams of 'yeah', wolf whistles, glasses banged on tables.

'The first girl to appear in our contest is' – he consults his list – 'Dolores. Everyone clap Dolores. Isn't she a looker?'

No, she's not. She's rather plain and scraggy with the sort of thin straight thighs which have a gap between them at the top. Her hair is pretty, granted – long and fair and curly – but it's breasts, not hair, which count, and hers are barely pushing out her tee shirt. She looks pale and numb with fear, cowering at one corner of the stage, still clutching an old brown handbag and her shoes. Leroy takes them from her, shoves her forward.

'Say "Happy New Year", Dolores.'

'Happy New Year.' Her voice is just a whisper, choked and swallowed up.

'Everyone say "Happy New Year, Dolores".'

'Happy New Year, Dolores.' We chant it after Teacher.

'Where you from, curly?'

'Connecticut.'

'And what d'you do in Connecticut, Dolores?'

'I'm a secretary.'

'That's a very noble profession. How many guys out there would like Dolores as their secretary?'

More shouts, whoops, 'yeah yeah's.

'Ever seen a place like this before, hon?'

'Er . . . no.'

'Well, we're gonna wet you down. The guys do that. In fact, they have to fight for the privilege. See this bucket of water, hon? We auction it to the highest bidder and he gets to throw it over you. Okay? It's not cold, I promise, only melted ice. Ha ha! Once you're wet, you have to dance around, okay – really show your titties off. We'll play some real fast music to warm you up and you get shakin', hon. Right? Now, who'll start the biddin' for the chance of gettin' in the act with Dolores here? You can go back home, guys, and brag to your friends that you threw a pail of water over the new James Bond girl, or the future Miss World. That's what happens to the girls who win at Ritzy's. They go on to make the big time – names in lights, legs insured for a hundred thousand bucks. You, sir? Right. Are you from the convention? How many guys here from the convention? Put your hands up. Great! Welcome to Ritzy's. You gotta bid against each other, you convention members, really screw up the excitement.'

I'm shocked. It's just a way of extorting cash – more cash. They've rooked the girls, now they're fleecing the guys. Mind you, the men don't seem to object. They're bankrupting themselves just for the chance of pouring water over an underdeveloped high-school kid who hasn't shaved her legs.

Five dollars, ten, twelve, fifteen, eighteen, twenty . . . At last the bidding stops. An old greyhead in a stetson frolics on to the stage, his buddies yelling obscene encouragement. Dolores looks terrified, begins to murmur something, when – WHOOSH! – she's just a dripping, choking, miserable drowned rat; water streaming from her nose and eyes, running down her thin white legs. Even the fair curls have disappeared. Her hair is dark and straight now. You can see her nipples standing out very sharp and clear as the wet fabric clings to them. The breasts themselves are hardly there. Perhaps she'll win the smallest, or the shyest. She's turned her back, is trying to shake off both water and embarrassment.

'Come on, Dolores! This is your big night. All these folks here wanna see your titties, wanna see you dance.'

She dances – well, makes a stab at it. A few men throw dollar bills, but the bulk of them are obviously disappointed.

'She entered once before,' Angelique whispers to me. 'Didn't win. Not a hope in hell. I think she's desperate for the cash, though. She's only a kid, still lives at home with her parents. Her mother gambles and her father's out of work. They're all losers in that family.'

I watch with new compassion. Yes, the girl looks defeated

and defensive even while she's dancing. Leroy tries hard to encourage her.

'Work that body, girl, work that body! Come on, do it for Leroy. You guys out there gotta give her more support. Or d'you wanna go home to your wives and fifteen kids? That's right, sir, make it worth her while. Now, how many guys wanna see Dolores take her top off?'

The shouts increase in volume now. I almost spill my drink, claw at Angelique. 'You mean they have to *strip*?'

'Some do, yeah. It's nothing, just a bit of fun.'

I watch, astonished, as Dolores struggles out of her wet and clinging tee shirt. Her breasts look even smaller with it off, though the audience are cheering and applauding, much freer with their money now. Dolores collects up all the bills, stuffs them in her handbag, gives a hasty bow, gallops out. That's it.

Leroy is already introducing the next girl. No, not a girl – it's Grandma – Grandma Eunice. I can't believe my eyes. She must be sixty-five at least, yet she's changed into mini-shorts and a tee shirt with an Aladdin's lamp emblazoned on the front, and the words 'RUB GENTLY' spelt out across her breasts. They're quite some breasts, in fact – large, well-shaped, imposing.

'Say "Happy New Year, folks", Eunice.'

She really shouts it out. She's obviously a pro, flirting with Leroy, pushing out her tits, tweaking at the nipples.

'Eunice tells me she may have a little snow on the rooftop, but her furnace is still burning down below. You bet it is! Now, are there any Orientals in the house? We get a lot of Japanese in here. Actually, they don't give a shit about the girls. They're just missin' their cameras. Ha ha ha! Look at that one, stickin' out his tongue. D'you like Orientals, Eunice?'

Eunice grins, shakes her head.

'No, she don't like Orientals. Too small pee-pee. Ha ha ha ha ha!' Leroy goes near hysterical, slapping his fat sides. 'Grandma likes 'em big and black, don't you, Grandma? This is black night. Any blacks out there wanna drench our Eunice? We're gonna need a fire-hose to wet her down. She's got a lot of titty and she's got a lot of guts. Right, get movin', guys. Grandma loves you.'

The bidding goes much higher, right up to fifty bucks, but it's a Japanese who wins, not a black. He looks scared to death, peering through his thick-lensed glasses as Leroy leads him up on stage; a tiny trembling guy in a formal pinstriped suit, complete with waistcoat and silk handkerchief, standing next to Eunice in her beach-gear. I have to laugh.

'Come on, get in closer, Shogun. You can't see from there. She won't eat you. Well, maybe she will. This lady likes cock more than cookies. Now watch it, sir. No honourable karate chops or any of that kinda shit. You're here to wet her down, not make her.'

In the end, the Japanese pours only half the water before ducking back to the safety of his seat. Perhaps he's scared a ten-foot black will lynch him. At least Grandma's breasts are wet and looking huge, their outline and the nipples clearly visible. The men go wild, throwing money on the stage, wolf-whistling and cheering, Leroy louder than them all.

'Isn't she great? She says she's got seven grandchildren, but she still likes makin' babies herself. Ha ha ha! Work that body, Eunice, swing it round. How many guys wanna see her take her top off?'

All of them, judging by the noise. I'm appalled. Eunice is at least twenty-odd years older than my mother and she's going to take her top off. And not just her top. She's actually stepping out of her shorts, parading naked-chested in just her black lace panties. Black lace on a grandma! Her breasts don't droop at all, though. She must have had surgery and silicone. But the rest of her is flabby – wobbly thighs, folds of slack flesh drooping from her upper arms, more flab on her back. The men don't seem to mind. All eyes are on her breasts still. She shakes and swings them, squeezes them together, prances down the catwalk, pushing her nipples right against male faces. The cheers crescendo.

'How many guys wanna see her take her panties off?'

'*No!*' I gasp it out aloud, hardly realize what I'm doing. Her hair is white and thinning. She has seven grandchildren. She can't, she simply can't.

She does, she is. She moves like Cheryl, like Alexis, wiggling her whole body as she eases off her panties. Her pubic hair is sparse, not white, but mousy brown. Everything is old, except her breasts, saggy-old and drooping. Perhaps she needs the money for more cosmetic surgery – on her hips, bottom, face, eyelids, arms. Even her hands are a give-away, the veins too prominent, the fingers slightly stiffened from arthritis. Yet she's jigging and cavorting like the youngest of the strippers, thrusting with her hips, rotating her whole pelvis, gasping out her passion. The music pants along with her, a love-moan from the saxophone, a slow roll to climax from the drums; the lights drape her nakedness; now red, now blue, now silver. Several men have joined her on the catwalk, and are touching up her nipples, even licking them, stroking her bare flesh, showering her with dollars. Finally, she more or less collapses, gives one last heavy-breathing wiggle, then totters off, hugging all the cash.

Leroy stops cheering to check his list. 'Right, Wanda's next. Anyone seen Wanda? No, Wanda's wandered off. Ha ha! Okay, we'll have Marie. Where's Marie?'

No Marie. No Wanda.

'They've chickened out,' says Angelique. 'They often do – lose their nerve when it's actually their turn. Why don't you go up instead, hon? You've seen the standard – not that marvellous, is it?'

Actually, I was thinking just the same. If those guys could be so generous to an old age pensioner, then . . . No. I've said no and I mean it. Those demonstrators are probably still outside, starving now and freezing, yet committed to their cause. How can I let them down, make myself a sex object, betray what they'd call my sisters?

I watch Eunice swank back to her seat. She's my sister, too, and her bag won't shut for all the dollar bills. You could say she's got guts, sense enough to grab her chances, cash in on her assets. I mean, a fortune just for taking off her clothes. Aren't I crazy not to try it? After all, it's no great deal. They're topless on most European beaches now, and I needn't take the rest off. Funny, though, I want to, in a way. One crazy little bit of me is panting to go wild for once. You never can at home. There's always somebody you know disapproving, or holding you in check. Here, I don't know anyone – well, Angelique, but she's all in favour, anyway. In fact, she told me that what she really likes about the States is that people are much freer than in England, ready to have fun and let their hair down, less governed by convention and what's 'done'. Why should some concave-chested spoilsport and a flabby over-sixty-five have all the men slavering and applauding, while I moulder here with no one even noticing I've *got* tits?

Reuben's scribbling still, deaf to the music, blind to the stage, deaf and blind to me. At least if I got up, it might distract him. And would he really be so shocked? After all, he'd hardly come to a place like this if he were prudish and straitlaced. And if he's a friend of Angelique, then he's used to dancers, girls who flaunt their bodies. Okay, I know he looks like Jesus, but even Jesus was broad-minded, went around with Mary Magdalen, who did worse than simply dance.

I check the stage again. There's another woman up there and I haven't even noticed, despite the crashy music, the dazzle from the lights. She looks rather shy and nervous, with a shawl wrapped round her shoulders and her arms hugged right across her chest. She isn't even wearing shorts, let alone bikini bottoms, but still has her creased old denim skirt on and short white high-school socks. Socks at a strip joint – crazy! The bidding's pretty slow, sticks at fifteen dollars, which I suppose reflects her unerotic gear. If you're allowed to keep your skirt on, then mine would be ideal, very tight with two high slits, and I'm wearing stockings and a suspender belt. That would turn them on, judging by the dancing girls, who all wore suspenders and made a great play with their stockings.

Even White Socks isn't doing badly, dollar bills already thrown on to the catwalk, though all she's taken off so far are her shoes and woolly shawl. She's wearing her own tee shirt, a limp and rather grubby one, which says 'Love me – I'm adorable.' (I doubt it.) Her breasts are actually quite big, but so is all the rest of her – calves, thighs, hips, behind. She looks like one of those advertisements for Weight Watchers (the 'before' picture where the girl always has lank hair and dreary clothes as well as being simply overweight, as compared with the 'after', when Vidal Sassoon and Zandra Rhodes have obviously spent all week transforming her from kiss-curl to high heel).

Angelique has slipped out for a moment. I slide into her chair, pull it round till it's facing Reuben's. He's more important than any stupid contest. I've decided not to enter. I'm bound to make a mess of it – trip or blush or something, or get my head stuck in my tee shirt and blunder off the catwalk. I'd like this guy to notice me, but not flat on my face. I lean forward, touch his arm.

'Excuse me. Have you got a light?'

I know he's a smoker. He accepted one of Angelique's Virginias. I'm glad. Non-smokers are so often prigs. I bet Jesus would have smoked if they'd invented cigarettes by then. In fact, the Gospels might have been different if He had. He'd have been less concerned with food to start with (bread and wine, loaves and fishes), and with a Marlboro to calm Him down, He probably wouldn't have got so mad with those buyers and sellers in the Temple, or gone around cursing barren fig trees.

Reuben's bending over me, shading the flame with his hand. Both hand and lighter are impressive – the hand slender and artistic, the lighter heavy, black, and slightly ribbed in texture like those ticklers in the contraceptive machine. I try to spin the moment out: our two heads bent towards each other, the leaping flame reflected in his dark and watchful eyes, his cupped hand circling mine. I don't know how I'll ever give up smoking. It isn't just the nicotine, it's all these heady rituals, especially with a new important man. I let my fingers brush against his own, just to steady them, nothing more, nothing blatant. His hand feels cold. Strange, when the club's so jungle hot – lights, music, drinks, crowds, all seeming to increase the temperature. My own hand is damp with sweat, my whole body hot and shaky. I think it's simply nerves. I take a drag on my Marlboro, inhaling the smoke right deep down, as if I'm breathing in Reuben, filling all my lungs with him. I want it to be mutual, want him to suck me in.

'Cigarette?' I offer.

He shakes his head. He's put his pen away now and is glancing at the stage. Fattie's got her bucketful and is well and truly drenched, looking still more bulbous as wet fabric clings to bulges and spare tyres. Reuben shrugs, dismissing her, then turns back to me.

'Aren't you going to enter, Carole?'

I stare.

'You're beautiful. You'll win.'

I'm dumbfounded. I'm beautiful. He's used my name, remembered it. 'No, I thought I'd better not.'

'You enter.'

It's an order. Whispered, but an order. I sit there, still half-paralysed. What about my principles, my scruples? I try to find my voice. 'But I've never . . . I mean, I don't think I approve of . . .'

'I'll bid for you. Go on.'

I drain my glass, drain Angelique's as well. They're only froth, those piña coladas. I stagger to my feet, turn to look at Reuben. Did he mean it?

'Good luck,' he murmurs. His eyes are so intense, I could be going to fight a Holy War or spread the Gospel. I can feel the full force of his conviction wrapping me around, giving me courage to walk up to that stage, whisper to Leroy that I want to enter and I hope I'm not too late.

'Never too late for a stunner.'

I'm beautiful. I'm stunning. I'm also boiling hot. It's a relief to take my blouse off, unhook my bra, put on just a tee shirt. I've been pushed behind the curtains, left with the girl who fills the buckets, kits us out with clothes. It looks a lot less glamorous from this side of the stage. The girl passes me a pair of shorts, yellow ones, frayed around the hems.

'No, I'll leave my skirt on, thanks.'

'You'll get it soaked.'

'That's okay.'

I daren't take anything else off. I'm shivering already, sweltering and shivering at once; curse myself for being such a prat. There must be some escape. I glance round quickly, searching for a door, even a low window; feel a hot hand on my back, stern fingers digging into my spine.

'Go on, hon. They're calling you.' The girl's marching me

straight back, pushing me towards the spangled curtains. 'It's your turn now. You're *on*.'

'No, don't. I can't. I'm sorry. I've changed my mind. I've got to leave. I . . .'

My words are drowned in a fusillade of music. Everybody's firing. Bang bang bang. Booming cannon. Ricochet of bullets. Lights as well, fierce and blinding-hot, circling over the battlefield, searching for the casualties. I'm a casualty myself. Paralysed. Legs shot off, voice clogged up, sweat beading on my forehead. No, it's not a battle, it's a zoo. Pack of wild animals closing in around me, yawping, yowling, bellowing. Feeding time. White fangs, scarlet claws, roars of maddened hunger.

Damp and heavy pressure on my arm. Leroy. He's walking me downstage, right down near the animals. He's making jokes. They're laughing. Cackling jackals, hysterical hyenas.

'Say "Happy New Year, folks", Carole.'

'Happy New Year, folks.' I'm an animal myself, a talking parrot.

'Donja just love that accent? Where you from, beautiful?'

'London.'

'London, Ontario, or London across the ocean?'

'London across the ocean.' An English parrot: hot and heavy feathers, flaming face.

'Carole's come all the way from England, folks, just to enter our contest. Isn't she cute? Give Carole a big hand.'

War again. Bombing. The whole room exploding as they clap. I wince against the blast, dodge the flying shrapnel. Leroy grabs my shoulder. 'Now, listen, doll, this is your debut in the theatre. You're in Vegas, baby, so this could be the start of something big, the biggest night of your life, the night you become a star. Look at this great audience. At least three of them have jobs. Ha ha! How many guys out there like the looks of this girl? She's got a great body, hasn't she? How many of you guys like English girls? How many guys want to wet a girl from London?'

The response is quite amazing. The animals have faces now, mouths open, teeth bared. They're not snarling, they're smiling, roaring with approval. They like me, yes, they like me – or maybe they like England. I reward them with my most dazzling English smile. There are mirrors round the walls and on the ceiling. I'm everywhere – three of me, four of me – grinning blushing me, trying to prance round a bit, show my body off. My boobs look bigger than they are. The tee shirt is too tight, straining over them. The bidding's started, jumped straight to twenty dollars. I can't hear Reuben's voice, but l try to pick him out from the jammed and jostling bodies, dance for him alone.

I skip along the catwalk, puffing out my chest, wiggling my hips – all for Reuben's benefit. I hear him yell 'Bravo' through a hundred throats and larynxes, clap wildly with his thousand hands. I pout and simper, copying Alexis. I've more right than those male strippers to copy what the dancers did. I'm a female, same as them, a natural mover. And beautiful – Reuben said. He's wolf-whistling and cheering, bidding higher, higher, in fifty different voices. I'm worth a lot of money. All those guys are proving it, all trying to buy the chance of getting near me.

I listen to the figures. Fifty dollars, sixty, eighty-five. I can't believe it. I'm valuable. I'm going up and up, I'm a Titian now, a Rembrandt. I prance some more, feeling newly confident. The bidding goes still higher, soars way above a hundred. I've broken all the records. I whirl. I pirouette.

'Any advance on a hundred sixty-five?' Leroy sounds dazed himself.

I hold my breath, feel the perspiration prickling on my back.

'Two hundred,' shouts a deep male voice, one I haven't heard before. The room is strangely quiet now. You can almost hear the tension. Most bids go up in fives, not in thirty-fives, and no other bid this evening has gone above that fifty bucks for Eunice. Two hundred! I simply can't believe it. Just to fling a pail of water over a dropout on the dole. Two hundred dollars would buy the most fantastic high-tech camera, or quarter of a motorbike, or a dozen Sunday brunches at the Gold Rush, or a whole week in a deck chair on some perfect golden beach, or . . .

'Going . . .' shouts Leroy.

I can hardly bear to listen. It was probably just a joke. That fellow didn't mean it, has already bolted out and is speeding down the highway to New York or San Francisco.

'Going . . .'

I keep jigging like a lunatic to try to hide my fear. What a fool I'll look when Leroy screams 'Gone!' and there's no punter with the cash.

'Gone!'

The word is swamped in a tidal wave of clapping. I'm being hugged, I'm being kissed, I'm being squeezed to glorious death. A huge six-foot-six joker with a handlebar moustache has come to claim his prize. I smell whisky, sweat and aftershave in roughly equal parts, feel bristly beard tickling on my mouth, metal belt-buckle digging in my ribcage. 'Thanks,' I whisper to his Adam's apple. He's saved my face, my reputation.

'Ha ha ha ha *ha*!' Leroy is quite ecstatic. 'Here's a guy that can eat and sweep at the same time. Do you like moustaches, Carole? Yeah, Carole loves moustaches – she can't put this guy down. Are you from the convention, sir? What d'you do? Electrical engineer. Right – you can give Carole here a charge, light her fuse.'

I open my mouth to make a risqué joke myself and suddenly I'm spitting out not steamy words, but ice-cold choking water, blinking it from my eyes, shocked with it, soaked with it, struggling, drenched and gasping. How could so much water fit into one small pail! I scream, fight, wriggle, shake my dripping hair. Three more crazy girls do antics in the mirrors, girls with transparent breasts, nipples sticking out like the sticks on ice lollies. Everybody's laughing. I jig and shake some more. I like them laughing. It warms me up, makes me feel hot and good inside. The lights are hot as well, flashing on and off my body, wild and scorching scarlet, peacock blue. I try to move in time with them – dance, spin, circle, arabesque. Leroy yells encouragement.

'What a girl! We love her. That's it, Carole. Work that body, swing it round, shake those great big boobies. This girl's got some tits. Tits are like potato chips. You can't have just one. Ha ha!'

Men are rushing up to me, pressing dollar bills into my hands, sneaking them down my neck, sticking them in the waistband of my skirt, kissing me, stroking my wet breasts. I'm making them all wet as well. They don't care. They can't get enough of me. They're emptying out their wallets. Bank notes whirling through the air. I catch the notes, kiss them, kiss their generous owners. I've got to earn this cash. Okay, you guys, you'll get everything I've got. Watch me, Reuben. Watch me, Daddy. Watch me, everyone! I'm dancing, I'm dancing for my Daddy. I'm so light and free, it's easy. I'm all froth like those piña coladas, all bubbles, bubbling over. I think they had some rum in them, as well as just the froth. I can feel the rum, helping me, supporting me, strong and sweet and just a little dizzy. The music's laced with rum as well, swoopy boozy music, going to my head.

'Boy! This one's really somethin'. How many guys wanna see her take her top off? Not so loud, you'll scare her. Carole's never ever in her life taken off her top in front of a whole bunch o' people. Is that right, Carole? Yeah, Carole says that's right. She's English, don't forget. They're very shy in England. You'll have to give her some support. Now, everyone, get up off your asses and make all the noise you can – really make her nipples sit up! Hear that clappin', Carole? They're goin' crazy out there.'

I suddenly spot Reuben. He's looking straight at me. His eyes are on my breasts. He wants to see them naked. Okay, Reuben, I'm easing off my top. I'm doing it for you, no one else. There's only you and me. We're alone and I'm stripping off to please you – slowly, very slowly.

'Oh, my goodness gracious, look at those! Real big English titties. See that smile on Shogun's face. The Japanese are goin' wild down there. Give it to 'em, Carole, let 'em have it.'

I shan't. I won't. I don't like Japanese. I'm doing it for Reuben, only Reuben, fondling my bare breasts, squeezing them together, pulling at the nipples – all for Reuben. I dance right down the catwalk, so I'm nearer him. Men are reaching out their hands, touching me, stuffing money up my skirt – Reuben's Jewish shekels, Reuben's long thin hands. I stop in front of a table, pick up an empty glass, cup it over my right breast, hold it in place while I do a sort of tap dance. I learnt that trick from Tyger, and another one as well. Tyger grabbed a beer bottle, stuck her nipple in the top and poured beer across her

239

breasts. I'm wet already, so a bit of beer won't hurt. I flounce up and down again until I spot a lager bottle, snitch it for my party-piece. The beer feels icy, snailing down my breasts. Men rush up to lick it off. Cold beer, warm tongues; Reuben's tongue more sensuous than the rest. I've lost him again in the blur and smudge of faces, but I know he's watching still, clapping till his hands ache. I'm loving it, loving this applause, all these people thinking I'm fantastic. I *am* fantastic. I'm a dancer, a professional one, who's trained for years and years. Watch me do the splits! They're watching, more and more of them, still pouring in at the door, fighting for a seat. The word's got round: there's a new fantastic English girl at Ritzy's. Drop everything to see her. Even the music's getting quite aggressive – war drums, jungle trumpets, making them sit up.

'What a body, huh? What a girl! How many guys wanna see Carole raise her skirt?'

Reuben does – they all do – so I raise it. Got to please them. Got to earn my money. They go wild at the suspenders. Okay, if they want to see suspenders, I'll take my skirt right off. It's soaking, anyway – uncomfortable and tight. Slowly, Carole, slowly. Do it like Alexis. Don't forget your training. Right, Reuben, look at this! This is how the pros strip. Inch by panting inch. I'm dancing in my stockings now, stockings and high heels. Wish I had a g-string, instead of Marks and Spencer pants. At least they're brief, though, brief and black, and the men all seem to like them, judging by the bank notes. I've got to pick them up, stow away my tips. It's all part of the act. Alexis did it, and Cheryl, all the dancing girls. They didn't make it blatant, but sexy and provocative, pressing bills against their naked breasts, holding them between their teeth, playing with the loot a bit before darting off backstage with it, freeing their hands to receive the next instalment. I try my own variations, squeezing my tits together with a wad of notes between them, stroking dollar bills down each leg in turn, first down the outside, then up the inside thigh. The men join in, stuffing generous contributions down both my stocking tops.

'Strip her down!' a black man shouts. 'Strip her to her skin.'

I suddenly feel nervous. Too many rough and eager hands

stretching out towards me, too much raucous noise. I remember Dangerous Dave, the stripper with the whips and chains – all that male aggression threatening us mere women, reminding us who's boss still. These guys could lynch me, rape me. I'm one against the lot of them, small and almost naked, while they're huge and fierce and hairy, stamping in their heavy boots, armed with belts and beer-bottles. I can feel my body running down, feet turning into wood. I stand paralysed a moment, until a female voice shrills above the crowd. Angelique – cheering me, reviving me, keeping me on course.

I snatch up a whisky glass from the table nearest me, gulp a burning mouthful. It's bitter, very strong, but it gives me courage, hypes me up again. I take another swill, feel it scorching down my throat. My hands are busy with the glass, so I let the guy who owns it unfasten my suspenders. That's only fair payment for his drink. He tries to grab my stockings, but I wrest them firmly back. I'm a dancer, so I need my props, must use them like Alexis did. I toss my suspender belt into my crowd of eager fans, watch them battle for it, men doing rugby tackles to try to get their hands on it. They'd be fighting for my toenail clippings if I got my scissors out.

I know now why girls are strippers. It's not the thousand bucks a week; it's the attention, adoration, being centre-stage with a thousand men mobbing and desiring you. I hang a sheer black stocking from each nipple. Okay, Mr Universe, if you can do it, so can I. I concentrate, hold my breath, then try to move each breast in turn. Miraculously, it works. The stockings jig and swing, one first, and then the other. My English teacher said we all had talents and abilities we simply weren't aware of. She's right. I've had those breasts since I was thirteen-and-a-half and I never knew I could move them individually, never realized stiff nipples had some use. They are stiff. I feel quite worked up, in fact. I think it's just the atmosphere – the lights and music and maybe all those cocktails, and the healing shot of whisky and the sense of my own power – oh, and Reuben. Yes, Reuben, Jesus-Reuben, why hasn't he come up here, like all my other fans? I'll make him come, don't worry. I snatch a stetson from one of the young cowboys sitting near the catwalk, put it on my own head, then go down on my hands and knees, crawling like an animal, tossing my wild mane of hair, making roaring noises. Tyger did the same – acting out her name, playing dangerous.

'Oh my goodness gracious! Carole's goin' crazy. This girl's got the hots, guys. Keep back, now, or you'll trample her to death. It's no good, Carole, they wanna see your pussy.'

No, Leroy. That they simply can't. Not Abigail. She's private. I turn over on my back, slip my hand down, make sure she's there. She is. I retrieve my stocking from the man with the moustache who has it draped across his face, stretch it taut as Cheryl did, rub it between my legs. Abigail approves. So do they. In fact, there's so much money piling up, the catwalk looks as if it's been re-carpeted not with scarlet matting, but with blue-green dollar bills. I've got to earn this money. The male strippers were just cons, collecting up the cash, but keeping on their g-strings. I stare down at my pants. Aren't I doing just the same? I'm a fraud myself, a sham. In fact, if I were really generous, I'd not only take my pants off, I'd masturbate for real. After all, I'm good at it, get a lot of practice, and that English teacher said we ought to use our talents, not let them go to waste. Jesus said the same.

Alexis and the rest all touched themselves (pretended), but it didn't convince me for a single second. Oh yes, they gasped and groaned and panted and appeared to be pressing all the right buttons and ringing all the bells, but I knew it was just fake. Their hearts and souls weren't in it. They were probably working out their tax returns or composing angry letters to their landlords about leaky roofs or overflowing dustbins. I know I could do better. You have to keep your mind on it, give it your total concentration, not care if you look stupid or make faces. Every night since I arrived, I've been touching myself up, alone and bloody miserable. Last night was worst of all. All those tears, and feeling such a failure. I'm *not* a failure. They love me here, adore me. I don't need aphrodisiacs. I'm good at it, a natural, came seven times last night. Why hide away in bathrooms, sobbing and ashamed, with only Milton's snores to cheer me on, when I can do it here on stage to wild applause? These guys deserve to see me come – yeah, seven swaggering times.

They've made me a celebrity, a star: music playing for me, lights trained on my body, every eye turned in my direction, every throat gasping out my name.

'Take 'em off, Carole. Take 'em off!'

I will, of course I will. Just let me have another tiny drink to stop my heart pounding quite so hard. Thank you, sir. You're sweet. It's a liqueur this time. Delicious. Amber-coloured, and very strong and warming. I dip my fingers in the glass, stroke them down my breasts. I can see eight breasts in the mirrors, all with stiffening nipples, all glistening with liqueur. My fingers are quite sticky now, so I lick them one by one, very very slowly, swirling my tongue around the tips, then up and down, up and down, lingering on each one. I like the taste of that liqueur, the pressure of my tongue. Men are milling round, sticking out their own tongues, going near-hysterical. Lazily, teasingly, I move my hand lower, slide it beneath the waistband of my pants, use my other hand to ease the wisp of nylon down. No rush. Take my time. I'm not quite naked – not yet, not completely. I've still got the stetson on, and the lights are veiling me, discreetly draping private parts – peacock breasts, rainbow bush. My pubic hair isn't trimmed or shaped. No one seems to mind, though. Applause is roaring round me, fusing with the music, the entire room spinning, booming.

I shut my eyes, shut everything out, as I slip my finger down and in. Right in. I'm doing this for Reuben – only Reuben. It's his finger I can feel: slender foreign finger, probing deeper, deeper, his free hand on my breast. I let myself cry out. The music cries as well. I've never done it with music or with lights before. It makes it more exciting, more exotic – silver on my fingers, scarlet in my ears. I open my eyes a moment. I'm surrounded. Men are pouring up on stage, trying to touch me, on their knees, imploring. Why be mean? Why reward just Reuben when all these other guys adore me? I love them all, love the world like Jesus did. I want to give myself to them – all of me, all of them. Why restrict myself to Reuben when he hasn't even bothered to come up here? No – this for the Japanese, the Mexicans, all the men from the convention, the guy with the moustache, the security guards, the barmen, the car park attendants out there in the cold and dark. This is for Leroy and Snake and Milt, and for darling darling Victor, and for all the old and bald and ugly, and the lost and sad and lonely, and also for the beautiful – for Alexis and for Cheryl, for Tiny Tim, Guiseppo, Mr Universe. I'm almost there. Don't stop! Don't stop cheering, everyone. I love it, love your fingers. I want all your fingers, male and female, all your long and clever fingers. Yes, cheer me, cheer me, cheer me, cheer me, C-H-E-E-R. Oh, my God! Oh, Christ! Oh, Reuben!

16

'Norah, wake up. Wake *up*. I'm getting married. Today. Tonight. At midnight. You can be the bridesmaid. Norah, did you hear? What are you doing sleeping in the middle of the day? You ought to be outside. It's gorgeous. The best weather we've had yet. Blue sky and sun and . . .'

She opens her eyes. She's lying on her bed, fully dressed, even with her lace-ups on. The curtains are drawn close, the whole room gloomy, airless.

'Are you all right, love?'

Slowly, she sits up, rubs her eyes, rubs her forehead. 'I . . . I had a headache.'

'Oh, bad luck. I'm sorry. Did you find the aspirin? Jeez! I'm so excited, Norah. He's wonderful. You'll love him.'

'Milt?'

'Of course not Milt. Milton's in Chicago. No, Reuben. Reuben Avraham Ben Shmuel. He's Jewish. We're going to Israel for our honeymoon. Well, not our honeymoon. He's got to fight. It's a sort of . . . mission. He wants me to go with him and become a Jew. I've already got some Jewish blood. I've never really thought about it much, but he said if I converted, it would completely change my life, give me something to hold on to.'

'Where is he?' Norah's groping for her glasses. I think she expects to see my spouse-to-be looming over her bed. I *can* see him, actually. He's imprinted on my mind, reflected in my eyes; my body's wet with him, my heart thumping out his name. Reuben Avraham. He took that name just a year ago to reaffirm his Jewishness when his father had denied it. His father called himself Sam Lee when he moved from the New York ghetto to

LA. He was really Samuel Litovski. That's why Reuben chose the surname Ben Shmuel, which means son of Samuel. Reuben himself started off Dick Lee – Richard. The only thing he kept was the initial R. Reuben was his grandfather's name, the one born in Lódz. Avraham is more symbolical: the Father of the Jews. No hope of explaining all those names and ancestors to Norah. I was pretty much confused myself when Reuben started on his lineage – not just the Polish grandpa and Russian grandmother (who both fled to New York to escape the pogroms), but also his slightly older and more famous forebears – Isaac, Jacob, Moses, Abraham himself.

Norah's polishing her glasses, peering round the room. 'Did you bring him?'

'Oh, no – he's got a hundred things to do. So have I. It's such a rush, you see. We're hoping to get married at the stroke of midnight, and we haven't got the licence yet.'

'Tonight?'

'Yes. New Year's Eve. Just as it moves into New Year's Day. Isn't that fantastic – after all I said myself about a new start and a new year and everything, that he should feel the same? He didn't want to wait at all. Not even till tonight.'

Norah flops down from the bed, takes a few dazed steps. 'I thought we were going to the show tonight.'

'Show? What show? Oh, you mean the Show Spectacular. God! So we are.' I do a few lightning calculations in my head. Too much magic in one night – fireworks, show and wedding. I can't let Norah down, though. I read her all the spiel about the show, made her quite excited by leaving out the topless girls, concentrating rather on lions and tigers, elephants and princes.

'That's okay, we'll fit it in,' I tell her. It doesn't start till ten, so we'll have to miss the end, and also miss the actual New Year rave-up when the clock strikes twelve, but Norah won't mind that. We'll be in the chapel then, with any luck, me exchanging vows with Reuben, while she acts as our witness. I still can't quite believe it, that things have moved so fast. He said as soon as he set eyes on me he *knew* . . .

'Don't worry, love, we'll see most of it, I promise. And once you've met Reuben, you'll understand the way I feel. He feels the same for me. He's twenty-six and still not married. He's been waiting all these years, you see, for a woman who could work with him, share in his ideals, fight along beside him.'

'You're going to . . . fight?'

'Well, not in the army. Though women can, actually, in Israel. Maybe I will later. I'm not too sure.'

'Israel?'

I wish she wouldn't interrupt, keep parroting my words. I don't think she's too well. She looks very pale and drained, keeps swallowing and blinking. I hope to God she's not going down with something.

'Israel?' she asks again. It sounds completely different when she says it. Reuben made it glitter. I march over to the window, fling the curtains back – which takes some doing, since there are at least three sets of ruffles, drapes and nets. Reuben had no curtains in his room, and only one small and smeary window, looking over dustbins.

The sun floods in, gold-leafing my arms. 'Yes, Israel,' I breathe, shining up the word again. 'We're going to settle there. Reuben says it's our spiritual and political home.' Well, not strictly speaking mine. I'm not Jewish yet at all. It doesn't count on your father's side, only on your mother's, and my Ma's very much an Anglo-Saxon Protestant. Reuben says you're either Jewish or you're not – you can't be just a quarter. I was quite upset about it, but he said it didn't matter: once we've lived in Israel for a while, I can become a Jew, legally and wholly. I love that word 'convert'. It sounds so dramatic, offers me the chance of becoming someone else, someone with a purpose, a conviction.

Norah's face looks paler still, as if all the blood has drained from it. Her mouth is opening and shutting like a fish's, but no sound comes out at all.

'Norah, love, don't think I'm deserting you. I begged for you to come as well. I said you'd be no trouble, but Reuben's quite difficult to argue with. He knows so much, you see. He's incredibly clever and has read almost every book on almost every subject and runs workshops and action groups, and his room is full of leaflets he's distributing, or posters he's designed or . . .'

I sink down on the sofa, shrinking from the velvet, ashamed now of the luxury preening all around me. It seems vulgar and excessive after Reuben's shabby bedsit, which is smaller than our bathroom here, and dirty. He said it didn't matter, that things like food and furniture were mere distractions and ephemera, and we should be ready to give everything to a higher cause or calling. I gave him all my prize money and the great wad of dollar bills which all those men had thrown at me, or stuffed into my stocking-tops or bra-cups. I didn't even count them. Nor did he. It wasn't really giving because what's his is mine now, whether money or a cause, and he also made me see that by donating it to something more important than myself, I benefit as well, since I'm part of a community, a People. And anyway, he's got to buy our tickets to Tel Aviv and a whole mass of other things.

God! It was so incredibly exciting. Not only did I win, had my photo taken for the *Las Vegas Sun* and *Mirror* and was the toast and star of Ritzy's (and so loaded down with money I couldn't even fit it in my handbag – left the place with two bulging plastic carriers), but Reuben slept with me. No, not slept. That's such a boring sluggish sort of word, completely wrong for our wild electric night together, and we didn't sleep at all. There wasn't time, and anyway, we were both far too high and happy to close our eyes even for a moment.

I close mine now. I want to re-run that stupendous sacred scene. I'll never forget it, not ever in my life. All my fears about being odd or over-sexed or hostile to men or fixated on my father simply flowed away in Reuben's sweat. That sounds wrong as well. Why are words so crude? Reuben did sweat, but it was like a Baptism. I lay under him, on his thin and scratchy rug, and I felt these warm wet drops falling on my breasts, my face. At first, I couldn't understand it. I was still a bit hung over and thought the roof was leaking. After all, his pad was pretty slummy. Then I realized the man was sweating out his lifeblood in my service. We'd been going at it for over an hour by then and his whole body was covered with this film and sheen of sweat. I didn't feel put off. He wasn't some vulgar muscle-man like Mr Universe. This was spiritual sweat.

Reuben made love to me with the same sheer wild unstinting passion as he gives to his chosen country Israel. I was no longer just a stranger, some odd English girl, a hanger-on of Angelique's. I was Woman, Sexual Woman, Political Woman, his helpmate, henchman, midwife to his cause. The sex simply clinched it. It wasn't something separate or different. With most ordinary men, everything's in compartments: eight hours work, an hour or two drinking with the lads, another hour or two for sport or snooker, then a brief ten minutes' sex before eight or nine hours' sleep. Reuben sleeps for just four hours – no more. He says man must evolve until he doesn't need much sleep; must use the extra time for struggle, revolution. He doesn't bother at all with sport or recreation, and work and sex are both aspects of the cause, both energy, commitment.

Energy, my God! He came four times in one night. I didn't know that men could even do that. I mean, four real times with all the build-up and the heaving, and when he came, he cried. Yes, really cried, each time. I've never seen such feeling. Jon would give an embarrassed little gasp, then push off to fetch a beer or have what he calls a leak, or start making Marmite sandwiches, doorstep ones, with stale bread cut all crooked. Reuben stayed – right there on that rug – the tears still running down his face and saying all these marvellous high-flown things, using words I hardly understood, dazzling words more suited to religion. He simply wasn't bothered with boring things like eating, or swilling down Black Label from the can. He just kept talking talking talking, stroking me, adoring me, sharing all his plans. It made me feel tremendously important. I could see he really trusted me, needed me to help him in his work.

It's so wonderful to *have* work; to have met a man who's so absolutely certain; knows exactly what he wants, where he's going, what's important and what's not. All my own confusion, my seesawing from one view to another, my sheer muddle as to who I even am, simply seeped away. I'm Reuben's bride, his soul mate.

'Carole . . .?'

I open my eyes. Norah is standing by the sofa, still dressed in that depressing green, which by now is like an archaeological record of our trip: airline gravy overlaid with Sunday champagne brunch; Victor's chocolates merging into spilt Moroccan couscous; strawberry ice from yesterday, and a new anonymous stain to bring us up to date. They haven't found her case yet. I've got to put a claim in, dig out our insurance forms, but I've been so busy I haven't got around to it. She won't touch the Gold Rush clothes. It's as if she's clinging to security, still hanging on to Beechgrove via her Crimplene.

'Are you really getting married?'

'Yes, of course.' I try to avoid her haunted frightened eyes. If it weren't for Norah, I'd be over the moon. Of course it hurts to leave her. And I can't help feeling worried. I mean, how will she get back, or manage on her own? Actually, I'm still hoping Reuben will change his mind, agree she can come with us. I've got to work on it – and fast.

'Norah, you haven't got a bit of Jewish in you, have you? Somewhere far far back, perhaps? I mean, you never heard that . . .?' I break off. How could she have heard anything when she knew neither of her parents, and never had a relation in her life? That really chokes me. I mean, how d'you cope when you've nobody at all? It's bad enough for me, with my father gone and no brothers and sisters, but I've always had aunts and cousins (and even second cousins) and two rather distant grandparents. Norah's on her tod. *I'm* her sister and her cousin, her mother and her daughter, and I'm walking off, orphaning her again. No, I'm not. I can't. I'll really plead with Reuben. After all, if Norah is our bridesmaid and our witness, then she's someone very special, part of the whole marriage.

I pat the cushion beside me, try to coax her down. 'Norah, you will be bridesmaid, won't you?'

She doesn't say a word, just shakes her head. She really does look awful, sort of agonized and grey: still keeps swallowing, as if something sharp and jagged is sticking in her throat.

'Why not?' I take her hand and squeeze it. It's cold, clammy cold, feels rigid, unresponsive, as if that hand had died and is just beginning to stiffen.

She doesn't answer. She's staring down and blinking. I think she's close to tears, but is trying desperately to hold them back. I want to weep myself for all the complications. Angelique said 'no' as well. She'd have made such a stylish bridesmaid and been an extra tie with England, but I suspect she's cut all ties, after our one short night of friendship. I phoned her just this morning from Reuben's place, to tell her about Israel and the wedding and she was really weird – cool and rather distant and yet sounding scared as well, scared and angry. She was much the same last night, in fact, when I left to go to Reuben's. She kept telling me to leave the guy alone and not get involved in things I didn't understand. Reuben says it's merely jealousy. Apparently he slept with her as well, once, and she was so uptight and frigid, she didn't come at all. He says she's probably guessed we'd be wonderful together and simply couldn't face the contrast. I felt a whole conflict of emotions – a red rush of jealousy that she'd ever been to bed with him; regret that I'd upset her when I'd hoped she'd be a friend and might even come and see me when she was visiting her mother back in England: and a sneaking satisfaction that I was better in the sack than a trained exotic dancer who was considered worth a thousand bucks a week.

I stride into the bathroom, start stripping off my clothes. They're sweaty, creased and oily and I've got to look immaculate. I've things to do, people to impress. Norah follows. She's usually so modest she always keeps her distance when I'm changing clothes or washing, but today she seems nervous like a child, clinging to my skirts in case I disappear again. I remove my pants and stockings, put them in the basin to soak. So many men have pawed them, they must be alive with germs, almost crawling on their own into the water. I blush as I remember. Ritzy's seems a hundred years ago, instead of just a morning. I think it's because I grew up in those last few hours with Reuben, received the sacrament of adulthood, was touched and quickened by some higher power. I swing round, give Norah a great hug. I want to share my joy with her, my triumph; heal her misery, transform her from a cold and trembling spinster to a radiant bride.

'Norah, you must be at the wedding. It's vital. You'll be our

251

witness, you see, which makes you part of the whole thing, writes you into it.'

She pulls away, starts tugging at her hair, mumbles something about not liking crowds of people.

'What d'you mean, crowds? We're not inviting anyone. Reuben said not. Just him and me and you. You only need one witness in Las Vegas.' I feel a sudden pang. I'd always imagined a large romantic wedding with a pink and white marquee, and big shots in morning dress swanning around a rose garden, and a six-tier cake, and page-boys in white socks.

'And I haven't got a dress.'

'Yes, you have – that Gold Rush one. It's perfect. You'll steal the show, in fact. It's me that hasn't got a dress, not anything remotely suitable.' I glance down at my naked legs, my bare and grubby feet. Reuben said it didn't matter. He told me it's the vows which count, the ceremony, and not to get hung up on the trimmings. All the same . . .

I sluice myself with water, put on clean pants and tights, start sorting through my rail of clothes. Nothing long, nothing white at all, and absolutely nothing like that wonder-gown I saw in the wedding chapel shop just half an hour ago. I know it's stupid to be dreaming of a dress like that – the flowing train, the layers of lacy petticoats, the scalloped neck, the sprigs of orange blossom embroidered on the skirt, but it really was sensational. Toomey's got to see it.

'Hey, Norah, would you like to see the wedding chapel? I've just come on from there. It's rather sweet, made of wood and painted like a gingerbread house. I've got to go back, actually. They were fully booked, you see, for all the hours round midnight, but the guy in charge said if I kept on trying, they were bound to have a cancellation. He said I could just phone, but why don't we go together and I'll show you this really gorgeous dress?'

'Dress?' She's started parroting again. God! It's so awful being happy when she's so obviously upset. I'll have to try and distract her, make her change her mind, involve her in my plans. It's a long hike to the chapel, but I can show her things en route, or we can walk halfway, then catch a bus. Even a few stops on a bumpy Route 6 boneshaker is quite a treat for Norah.

'Yeah,' I tell her. 'They've got their own shop at the chapel which sells absolutely everything you need for a wedding – dresses, veils, rings, bouquets, photo albums, even suitcases. It saves time, you see. Most people in Las Vegas are getting married in a hurry. It's the only place where you can marry with no banns or anything. I mean, you can meet someone at ten and marry at ten past, so long as there's no queue at the Courthouse – that's the place you get the licence. Anyway, I saw this dress. It was really beautiful, like something in a film.'

'Is Milton going to buy it for you?'

'*Reuben*. Norah, honestly. You haven't heard a word I said. What's wrong with you? Milt's nothing to me, no one. And Jones is not a Jewish name, it's Welsh. Can't you even listen?'

'I . . . I am. I did. I heard it all. You're going to fight. In Israel. Reuben's going to buy your dress.'

'He's not. It's too expensive.' I stop, bite my lip. I could have bought it myself, twice over, if only Reuben had relented. It was my money, after all. Forget the veil, the rings, the flowers, the photo albums, but just to have the dress . . . You can hire them, actually, but the ones for hire were nothing like as special as that one with orange blossom. No. I've got to see it his way. Dresses are just frippery and swank. He wasn't keen on any of the frills; said what mattered was our tie with one another, our commitment to one cause, not empty finery.

He wouldn't even come and see the chapels, left all that to me. I tried to take his line, pick one with a pin, or phone around for the cheapest and the quickest, but it simply didn't work. I just had to see a dozen, spent a whole two hours this morning (the minute that I'd left him) swanning round Cupid-bowers and rose-gardens, comparing costs and decor. It was really quite a giggle. Some of them were ghastly with polystyrene cherubs and these awful lurid signs. 'Fast and cheap!' screamed one. 'Five-minute weddings. No hidden costs, no extras. Lowest price in Vegas. No waiting – walk straight in.' I walked straight out, in fact. The place was like a garden shed, and stood right next to a gas station, so that the Shell signs and the petrol smell overpowered the cupids. Okay, we want to keep it simple, but there's such a thing as dignity.

Another place was offering three free rolls of nickels to play in the casinos to every happy couple, and six free raffle-tickets for what they called a 'Love-Boat Cruise'. I ask you! I was much more taken with a rather swanky joint which had six chapels in one, all done up in different period-styles, so you could play Scarlett O'Hara in flounces and a crinoline, or Calamity Jane carrying your six-shooter instead of a bouquet. The last of the six chapels (the twentieth-century one) had ten instant colour-changes, done with lights and lasers, so any bride could colour-match the decor to her dress. They even had a honeymoon motel attached, with rows and rows of bridal suites and a special high-speed travelator which whisked you straight from pew to satin sheets.

I couldn't see Reuben dressed as Deadwood Dick in buckskins and a hat, or making vows to Scarlett, so I dragged myself away, settled for something smaller and more ordinary. Which is what I'd better do about the dress. I slam a mental door on lace and tulle, content myself with British Home Stores viscose – a floral skirt and toning blouse, which I put on for the moment. I'll pick out something later for the wedding, something plain and simple.

Norah is still tagging after me, shadowing every move I make. I try to change the subject, cheer her up a bit with a (highly censored) résumé of last night's rave-up at the club, but I can see she's hardly listening. She's in some other world, a dark and frightening world where every exit from the maze is a dead end.

'At least it's nice and sunny,' I say brightly. Wrong again. Norah is screwing up her eyes against the glare, doesn't like the sun. I think she sees it like a searchlight in a prison.

I take her arm, lead her down a passage to the lift. While we wait for it, I read the list of rooms and services, floor-by-floor attractions: roof garden, play deck, health spa, Imperial Suites, Bridal Suite. *Bridal Suite* . . . I trace the letters, marvelling. That computer was right – a little premature, but right in essence. It was like a sign, a portent. Reuben believes in signs, believes everything is meant: our meeting, my Jewish name and blood, even his futile childhood in LA, which formed his revolutionary ideals, his need to fight, to break away from his parents' trashy fashion business, and their attempts to be accepted as all-American secular materialists. He calls America New Babylon – and Israel home.

God! He's going to hate the show. That's materialism gone mad, Babylon on stage. It cost eleven million dollars just to put it on. Eleven million dollars squandered on tit-and-arse and light effects, with a few big cats thrown in. Reuben could redeem the world with eleven million bucks. Perhaps he'll come just as a favour, our last big splash before the solemn rites. I smile again, at nothing. It's not easy to be solemn when I'm all candy-floss inside.

It's pretty gorgeous outside. Once we reach the street, I see that spring is in full stride – a truly golden day, sun burnishing the pavements, flowers in bloom in all the hotel flowerbeds, frothy white tulle clouds. I pick a flower, twine it in my hair. However much I try to keep my mind on serious things like saving worlds, or marriage vows, it keeps doubling back to orange blossom.

'You know that woman in the shop?'

'No,' says Norah.

'The wedding chapel shop. She was really quite a character. And she told me such a lot. I mean, she knew the reasons for all our wedding customs – why we throw confetti or old shoes, or put marzipan on wedding cakes. Well, actually she got it from a book; a really pricey one with all these glossy pictures. She kept trying to flog it to me, said it would give my wedding a whole new depth and meaning, but I just didn't have the money. I asked her about orange blossom and she looked it up for me, said it stood for happiness and fruitfulness, and also for innocence because the flowers are white. And she said if the bride wears it as a wreath, that's a sort of funeral thing as well – dying to your old life and entering a new one. I was all ears, of course, since it fitted in with all the stuff we'd talked about – you know, the death of the old year, and a new start and everything. When she'd gone, I had a dekko at the book myself and it kept on mentioning death, which seemed a bit peculiar.

But it said that in Greece and China, white was the colour of the spirit world and always worn at funerals. And I mean, when you come to think of it, all corpses wear white shrouds.'

I shiver a moment, despite the sun. Marriage *is* a sort of death, particularly this marriage. I have to die to my own country and background, even to my language, die to Jan and possibly to Norah; to all I know, all that's safe and easy. And the word death is still my father's shroud. Oh, Daddy . . . He should be there tonight, walking down the aisle with me, my orange-blossom dress symbolizing his happiness, my fruitfulness, the dark Jewish grandchildren he'll never even see. I squeeze Norah's hand. My father would have liked her.

'Norah, you must come to Israel. If I have kids, I want you to be their grandma, or their godmother or aunt or something. We've got to stay together. This whole trip was meant, I know it was. I'm meeting Reuben later and the first thing I'll mention will be you.'

Well, not quite the first. We'll kiss first, I expect, and then he'll tell me how incredible I was last night and how I'm naturally and wildly passionate and how he intends to use that passion, harness it, develop it.

I try to shift the smug smile from my face, concentrate on Norah. 'Listen, Norah, you can become a Jew, you know, even if you're born a goy.' I use the word self-consciously. Reuben taught me my first words of Yiddish in the bath this morning, including some highly private lovers' words which he said not to repeat. 'I mean, it takes a while, of course, and you have to be accepted and go through various rituals and so on, but I'd be there, as well, going through them too. And Reuben's made me see how vital a religion is, something to work for and believe in, and a community and heritage and . . .' I break off. Reuben made it vibrant and exciting. I need him here to inspire and rally me again, to provide me with the rousing words, to change Norah's whey-faced stumbling to a victory march.

'Oh, look!' I shout. 'A wedding chapel.'

There are dozens of these chapels in Las Vegas, so I suppose it's not surprising if we pass another one: one I hadn't noticed on my morning's recce. No great loss, in fact. It's horrid – despite the flashing sign which boasts 'Featured Internationally on Network Television!' The chapel doors swing open as we watch. A bride and groom are just emerging, though they're not even arm in arm, but looking in opposite directions – he staring at the ground, she dodging the confetti being hurled by a fat and sullen adolescent girl. His child? Hers? They're both old enough to have a teenage daughter. He's bald, she's greying, and neither of them has bothered to dress up. They're both wearing jeans and she's carrying a heavy leather handbag which looks quite wrong with her corsage of white flowers. I wish they'd smile. I wish somebody would smile. The child looks close to tears. No wonder. Kids are outcasts in Las Vegas.

I sidle up behind them, peer into the chapel. It's tiled – yes, honestly, just like a public toilet, except the tiles are mauve and flowered. Actually, there's a toilet bang next door, exactly matching, even down to its pale mauve loo-paper – handy, I suppose, for Big Day nerves, but really a bit off. Everything is heart-shaped, even the wastebin in the chapel, the guest-soap by the basin, and the lilac-coloured stepping stones which make a cutesy little path up to the door.

I sneak back across the stones before Norah sees the toilet and starts begging for a pee. She's picking up confetti, grovelling on her knees for paper hearts and petals. They used to throw rice in the old days – so that lady in the shop said – as a symbol of fertility again. I'd be getting a bit worried about fertility myself, if Reuben hadn't used a . . . a thing. That proves how much he cares. I mean, most men never bother, or say it's like making love in waders. He made it quite exciting, got me to put it on – not just one, a packetful, by the time we'd finally (reluctantly) got into our clothes again.

Half of me is still back on his floor. Undressed. I just can't help myself. It really was so special – our wedding night, our honeymoon. Yeah, we're married already, in the most important sense. Reuben was right: we didn't need rings or even chapels, just our naked passion, naked skins. I close my eyes. I want to keep those memories for ever, my own free wedding album – not coloured photos, smiling-stiff and posed, but black and white in the moonlight on the rug, humping, thrusting, all ways up, always in slow motion. I can feel his hands again. I'm sure he had more than just two hands, more than one hot mouth. Hands and tongue, hands and teeth, hands and . . .

'Where's the dress?' Norah's asking.

'Oh, not here. They haven't got a shop here.' I open my eyes to a gigantic 3-D frankfurter (which looks like a stiff prick complete with yellow mustard sperm) circling round and round outside a take-away. What a sight to greet you as you step out of the chapel – an ejaculating sausage! And the reek of grease and onions blasting out your orange blossom. I turn my back on it, help Norah to her feet. (She's brushing off the dirt from paper horseshoes.)

'No, ours is prettier than this, much prettier. It's called the Veil of Peace – you know, a sort of pun: veil as in wedding veil.'

Norah looks confused again, so I take her arm and march her on. Actually, the names are quite a hoot. There's the Hitching Post and the Happy Ever After, and the Chapel of the Hearts and Flowers (which has a huge red heart outside proclaiming 'Cupid Lives Here', then, smaller: '10 per cent handling charge on photographs. All cheques OK. NO PARKING') and the Wee Kirk o' the Heather, which has tartan decor, and even one called We've Only Just Begun. There were nearly sixty thousand weddings this last year in Vegas. If we're lucky, ours will be the very first for the *new* year – if we get that cancellation. The guy seemed fairly hopeful. He said the couple who booked the midnight slot have cancelled and re-booked three times already and he's pretty sure the girl will call it off again. Gosh! She must be in a state – worse than me. I'm not really in a state, just excited. And scared a bit. Scared and thrilled. Scared and worried. Scared and gloating.

You don't have to have a chapel. There's this special service called Wedding on Wheels – 'Have minister, will travel'. The Reverend travels anywhere. He went to Circus Circus to marry a couple sitting tandem on a roundabout-horse, and another on a real horse, halfway up a mountain. (They were married naked, which should appeal to Reuben. You can't get much more basic than your birthday suit, and think how much you'd save.)

He's even tied the knot in county jails, when a bride or groom was doing time; or at airports when they're changing planes and have only got five minutes, and one homely couple he married on a bus.

We'd better catch a bus ourselves. Norah's flagging. I take her arm, jog her to the bus stop, and fifteen minutes later we're alighting at the Veil of Peace. I'm somehow disappointed. It looks smaller now, as if Norah's fears have shrunk it, even spoilt it. Was the paint so faded, the sign so garish? It's also far more crowded, people queuing to be married, mostly foreigners – Mexicans, Koreans, Japanese. I suppose their own native countries' marriage laws are stricter. The only white-skinned bride-to-be is dressed in a full-length Lurex evening gown. The effect is rather spoilt by dirty white gym shoes showing underneath and the fag-end stuck between her lips.

I vowed to give up smoking, but perhaps I'll wait now till we've settled down. After all, marriage is quite stressful. So is emigration. Though I've got to see the good side, remember Reuben's point about a second chance. LA is called the City of the Second Chance, and it *was* for Reuben's parents, compared with their ghetto in New York. They made it in LA – though Reuben despises what they do there: the phony shallow fashion trade and his mother's sideline, haute couture for dogs. He also hates Los Angeles itself – its lack of history, lack of culture, the importance of possessions and facades, the fear of growing old, the frenetic keeping up. He's not that keen on Vegas, damns all Nevada as a barren poisoned state, good for nothing except testing missiles and dumping nuclear waste. *His* second chance will be in Tel Aviv. And mine.

I can start again in Israel – wipe out that shoplifting offence, pretend Beechgrove never happened, work for an ideal. Israel! Land of Milk and Honey. How beautiful that sounds. (Reuben called me milk and honey on the rug last night.) And home to both of us. He said when you enter Israel as a Jew, the immigration people hand you out a badge which says, simply, 'I've come home.' I haven't got a home now of my own, with my mother still in hospital and preferring gin to either milk or honey. I'll be free at last, free of her and the fear of growing up like her, free from social workers and Jan's bad-tempered landlord, free from scrounging or the dole. Reuben says they give you food and lodgings for absolutely nothing if you work in a kibbutz.

Norah needs a home as well, the first she's ever had, a second chance after all those years of hospital. She's got to be included. I know she's not that young or fit, but there are lots of things she'd do quite well, have the patience for looking after children, for example. They could use her in a kibbutz where all the children live in common while their mothers work. She could be mother to my own kids while I'm out working with my husband.

Husband. The word sounds strange still, almost foreign to me, like that very foreign bridegroom just emerging from the chapel, his new wife hugely pregnant. She looks a child herself, barely seventeen. I feel scared for her, scared for me and Norah. New lives mean pain and labour, blood and sweat. I turn away. I'll go and find that lady in the shop. She was kind – plump and motherly, called me 'Carole honey' as if she'd known me all her life, sold marriage like ice cream, as something sweet and nourishing.

'Come on, Norah. Let's go and see the dress.'

The dress is there, but not the lady; only her assistant, a brittle supercilious girl who says Martha's gone to lunch and can she help? I shake my head, feeling stupidly upset. Martha seemed the only stable thing in a day of avalanche. I cheer myself by paying homage to the dress again. Norah seems quite awed by it – *and* its price. I tour the shop with her. She keeps stopping at the rings.

'I love the matching ones, don't you? His and hers. That book said rings mean union – two people pledged to one another, completing one another.' We did complete each other on that rug, he joined to me, joined everywhere: fingers linked, tongues entwined, skin sweating into skin. I dart back to the book, read out just three lines to Norah, in the hope they'll change her mind.

'Listen, Norah, rings are a royal symbol. You see, in lots of different countries a bride is seen *as* queen – queen for the day, at least. That's why she wears a train and has ladies-in-waiting to hold it up for her. Well, bridesmaids, anyway.' I catch her eye. 'See how important bridesmaids are? You've got to be my bridesmaid. You won't be holding up my train, alas – not at that price. But you can hold my ciggies, if you like, and a Gold Rush marble ashtray.' I'm trying to make her laugh again. Every time *I* feel good, her misery reproaches me.

The salesgirl is watching us, hawk-eyed. Are we going to buy the book? A ring, perhaps? An outfit? She strides purposefully towards us, hard-sell smile in place. 'Is your mother looking for a dress? We've got some very nice two-pieces.'

'She's . . . not my mother.' I stare down at the floor and Norah's lace-ups – scuffed at the toes, worn down at the backs. My mother crams her feet into teetering stilettos, wears fishnet tights at forty. No – Norah's not my mother, but we've got to stay together. I'm certain of that now. She'll never have a daughter or a husband. Which is why I won't desert her. I shan't beg or plead with Reuben; I'll simply tell him, straight. He understands conviction.

Norah has moved to the far end of the shop and is spelling out the words on a Certificate of Marriage in the shape of a huge slot machine which is hanging on the wall. It's written in a curly purple script and framed in gold, with a frieze of dice and playing cards. I start reading over her shoulder. 'These partners in wedlock have agreed that their marriage will be based on honesty, faithfulness and devotion. As husband and wife, they will enjoy the pleasure of sharing the warmth of each other's touch, the joy of each other's smile and the comfort of each other's nearness . . .'

I was ready to scoff, but the words are really beautiful. I read them out again, aloud, as Norah's getting stuck. My voice is drowned by the chiming of a clock.

'Good God! Is that the time? I'm meeting Reuben in just two hours and I haven't done a single thing he asked me yet – not even seen the guy who takes the bookings. Come on, Norah – quick!'

The guy greets me with a victory sign. Yeah, the couple cancelled – or at least the woman did; yeah, he's put us in instead; yeah, the stroke of midnight. I stutter out my thanks. I'm beginning to understand what Reuben means by destiny. This was meant. It must have been. Even the rabbi is available, which means a proper Jewish wedding. I'll be joined to that great family, the greatest people in the world, so Reuben said, who survived all persecution, produced sons like Christ, Freud, Einstein, Moses, Marx, and a lot of other names I'd never heard of.

I check my watch. Ten past two. Less than ten hours to midnight and our marriage. I'll never do everything in time, especially now that Norah's coming with us, which means new plans, another airline ticket, maybe complications – not to mention that damned show. I'm meeting Reuben at four o'clock at the Marriage Licence Bureau. He said he'd come and find me in the queue. You even have to queue to get a marriage licence, especially on New Year's Eve, which is the busiest day for weddings out of the entire three hundred and sixty-five (except for St Valentine's, when apparently the whole place goes berserk).

I'll just have to take a chance and trust Norah with some errands, the simplest ones like shopping. At least they'll distract her, stop her agonizing, and Reuben will have proof that she's some use. I steer her from the office, start explaining what I want. What Reuben wants, rather, since it was him who made the list. My money, though, he's using – part of my wet tee shirt prize. It still hurts a bit to have lost it quite so fast. This is just a fraction of it. He's got all the rest.

Norah takes it warily and I make a little joke about not sending it to God-men. She doesn't smile. In fact, I've never seen her quite so limp and wretched.

'How about a pee first?' I suggest. She's like a child in some ways, has to be reminded to relieve herself and not to lose the purse.

I take her to the restroom door, hold it open for her. 'I'll wait out here, love. Don't be long.'

There's a tiny courtyard just outside, a square of sun and shadow with a wrought-iron bench. I lie full length along it, face-up to the sun. I had no sleep at all last night, and the night before I took those sleeping pills. I feel rather strange and dizzy now, hung over from my cocktail of Mogadon, excitement and white rum. I long to sleep, or at least sink down and do nothing for a while, try to take in all that's happened, stop it exploding in my head. But there are things to do – things to do for Reuben, errands to run, promises to keep. He'd despise me if I simply nodded off. I've got to try to train myself to manage with less sleep, follow his example, ignore petty things like hunger and exhaustion. Thank God I'm seeing him at four. I need him like a pep pill to revive me and recharge me.

I close my eyes, the sun scarlet on my lids, scarlet like the hot red lights at Ritzy's. I'm on that stage again. I've won. They judge the winners not by writing names down or even by a show of hands, but simply by the volume of applause. A jet zooms over, providing the applause. Except the plane has droned away now, while the applause goes on and on. On and on. I'm a winner. I'm a star. Alexis and the rest have come back on stage for the finale, and invite me to join in. Cheryl lends me her scented body oil, whispers what to do with it. I'm naked save for all the lights, their fierce glare tigering my skin; the scent of musk, spicy and exotic as I start rubbing in the oil, stroking it across my breasts, up and down my thighs, until my whole body is shimmering and glistening. Men are mobbing me, rushing up to press dollar bills against my sticky shining flesh, rubbing in the oil themselves. And suddenly it's Reuben's hands I feel. He's there, at last. He wants me. Now. Won't wait.

I don't remember how I put my clothes on, or how many clothes I bothered with, but I know I was still sticky underneath – and hot: hot with sweat, hot for him, hot in the cold clean purging night, which scoured away the fug and fume of Ritzy's as we left the club entwined, our two cigarettes red pointers in the dark, and a new thin-smiling moon starting its new life with ours, and the silence velvet-deep after all the raucous music.

He's stopped. He's kissing me. Wrong word again. It isn't just a kiss. His lips, tongue, teeth and soul are in my mouth. And my mouth is opening deeper than it ever has before. He's given me a new mouth, wider, wilder, more grown-up.

At last, we stumble on, his arm around my shoulders, his taste still on my lips. My mouth feels bruised and stretched. He stops again, leans over, kisses it, just a brush of lips this time, as if to heal and salve it. The slice of moon is suddenly outside now, outside Reuben's window, looking in. We're standing in his room together – dull green walls, grey rug. He lies down on the rug, pulls me down beside him, between the piles of books. Slowly, he undresses me. No rush. His hands need time to praise each part of me. My skin is still sticky from the oil. I can smell the tang of musk again, mingling with his own smell, some faint aftershave, overlaid with smoke. He still has all his clothes on. He keeps them on, kneels over me, starts licking off the oil. His tongue goes everywhere, starting at my top end – soft across my eyelids, coiling in my ears, down a little across my neck and throat; then shoulders, armpits, the inside of each elbow; down further, tracing crooked circles round my navel. All my parts are merging, so that I'm not ears or throat or navel any more, but only one sensation, one crescendoing excitement as his mouth goes lower still.

His strong hands push my legs apart and suddenly his tongue is right inside me, pushing up, circling round and round, soft and rough at once. It's wonderful, exquisite. He stops a moment. I yelp with disappointment, but he's only moved his tongue to somewhere still more private – forcing, shocking into it, giving me the wildest strangest feelings.

'No,' I gasp, frightened that we've gone too far, that he shouldn't lick me there – not there. My own body contradicts me. It's shuddering and moaning in time with his wild tongue. Go on, it says. Go *on*.

He does, until I'm frantic with the feelings, and know I'm almost coming. I try to hold it back. It somehow still feels wrong. Wrong and wonderful. His tongue won't let me stop, continues probing and insisting until I'm yelling, coming, yelling – coming twice, three times.

He stops, kneels up, face dripping with me, slimy. He doesn't speak, just watches as I bite my fingers, thresh from side to side. Then, slowly, I calm down a bit, still breathing hard, still sticky-hot; lie back in a haze of musk and triumph. For the first time in my life, my whole body has been recognized and worshipped; no inch of it left out, no part rejected as dirty or too private. He's still kneeling there, in front of me, as if in homage to his queen. Queen for the day. I don't need any ring or crown to prove it, only his daring rough-tipped tongue.

He's naked now himself, though I don't remember him undressing. No fumbling zips or clumsy buckles. He makes a pillow with his clothes, slides back down, me on top of him. His shirt looks very white against the dark hair on his body. Dark hair everywhere – on his toes, his thumbs, his bottom, even on his balls. I kiss his balls. He asks me to. I'm nervous, never done it, but he guides my head down, tells me to be careful with my teeth. His balls are cool, cooler than the rest of him, feel strange and rather lumpy in my mouth. Then he turns me round again, slips his fingers between my lips, makes me suck them, one by one, right down to the knuckles; then slowly up again, the right hand, then the left. He lies upside-down on top of me. He's big now, very big, too big for my mouth. I gag.

'Breathe,' he whispers. 'Take a deep breath in.'

I breathe, relax. His own breathing deepens to a gasp. I'm frightened that he'll come. I know you're meant to swallow it and I'm scared I won't or can't. He doesn't come, just eases out, sits up. It's as if he's teasing me, refusing actually to fuck me until I'm on my knees and begging.

'Reuben, Reuben, *please . . .*'

Oh, God! At last. It's wonderful. He's taking it so slowly, still tantalizing, pulling back, coming almost out, then inching in again. I shut my eyes, want nothing to distract me. A police car sirens past, drowning out my cries. He comes just as it passes, comes just after I do, but still stays stiff inside me. Then he takes my hands, holds them very tight, braceleting the wrists, runs his teeth just across the fingertips, and . . .

No, that was later, wasn't it, much later, when his knees and elbows were rubbed raw by the floor, and my own back and neck were aching, and we stopped a while and talked and stroked and talked again, and I felt Woman there beside him – Eve, Venus, Israel – and knew I was important, and I kissed his knees and elbows very very gently, as he'd taught me, and bit by bit, the darkness in the square of window faded, from smoky blue, to grey, to dirty white, and suddenly the sun came up and there were hot gold fingers touching up my body and scarlet on my lids.

My eyes drift open. Yes, the sun is very bright, but it's Norah, though, not Reuben, shaking her wet hands. I ease up very slowly. My neck and back are aching from the bench.

'There wasn't any towel,' she says. 'Or soap.'

17

It's cool in the cathedral. Very quiet. No one here at all. The stained-glass windows shut the sun out. I still feel very hot, though. Hot and frightened. Carole said I've got to do some shopping, but I'll have to have a rest first. There's a banging in my head and my chest feels very tight.

Carole's getting married. She can't get married. Not so soon. People get engaged first. Sometimes they get engaged for years and years. Nurse Willis got engaged seven years ago and she hasn't married yet. She's saving up. You need a lot of money to get married. Carole hasn't any.

I sit down on a bench. My legs keep trembling still. Carole's getting married. Not in a real church, but in a shop. *This* is a real church, high, with strong stone walls. Those wedding chapels are only paste and cardboard. Everything costs money there, even things like organs and a choir. Sister Agnes played the organ at St Joseph's. She didn't charge for it. Carole can't get married in a cardboard church. She can't get married anywhere. She hasn't got a dress.

I take her purse out, squeeze it. That's Reuben's money. If Carole marries, she'll have to change her name. I don't like Reuben's surname. I can't pronounce it, can't remember it. Joseph is a nice name. So is Carole. If I want to stay with Carole, I'll have to go to Israel.

There are bombs in Israel, bombs and wars. You see it on the television, all the time, even over here. Carole may get killed. I may get killed myself. I wouldn't mind. It's peaceful when you die. When Doris Clayton died, the vicar said that a funeral was your wedding with the Lord. That's why the corpse is dressed in white and you have hymns and flowers and those little rolls with chicken paste inside. Carole said the same. She said white was for death, and orange blossom wreaths for funerals. She read it in that book.

I'd like to buy the book for her, buy the dress as well. The dress was beautiful. It cost four hundred dollars. I never knew a dress could cost so much. If I had four hundred dollars, I'd buy it straight away. She'd shout then, with excitement, whirl me round and round. I like it when she does that, even though it hurts my back. She hugged me in the bathroom just this morning. No one else has ever hugged me. Ever. Or squeezed my hand. She won't hug me when she's married. She'll be ashamed of me.

I fumble for the purse again, count out Reuben's money. I'm very bad at counting, so I do it twice. The first time it's fifty-seven dollars. The second time it's only fifty-three, so I start again a third time. Now it's fifty-five.

That's a lot of money, the most I've ever seen in just one purse. But it's not enough to buy the dress. I couldn't even buy a ring, not the ones she liked. Matching rings – his and hers. I'd like to buy a set for me and Carole. We'd be joined for ever then.

I walk down to the altar, to the crib. St Joseph is still staring at the floor. He doesn't wear a ring. He isn't Mary's husband, not her real one. And he isn't Jesus's father. I think he's often lonely.

Carole said St Joseph was a Jew. I don't believe it. She said he lived in Israel. I think Reuben made that up, just to make us move there. Our Lady's not a Jew. Jews don't have blue eyes. This Mary's got her eyes closed, but they're always blue in England. Blue like Carole's. Carole's not a Jew. A quarter doesn't count. Miss O'Toole said Jews were very wicked, and put Jesus on the cross.

I think I'll light a candle. The girls with parents lit them at St Joseph's. They cost a penny each, so you needed parents. If you lit one, God heard your prayer immediately, because the smoke went up to heaven and He smelt it. These ones don't have smoke, or even flames. You just put your money in, and they light up like a lamp.

I used to like the flames. The way they always moved, the shadows on the floor. The wax made funny shapes as it dripped down on the stand. The shapes had faces sometimes, and watched you while you knelt there. God was watching too. If a flame started flickering, that meant He was angry and wasn't going to give you what you'd asked. And if the flame went out, you'd die. These ones *can't* go out, which is why they cost so much – a dollar, not a penny.

I put my dollar in and the red light flashes on. You have to say your prayer then. It's like a wish at birthdays when you shut your eyes. I pray and wish together. I can see the dress if I shut my eyes. It has little sprigs of flowers all over the white skirt. Orange blossom. Which means you'll have children and be happy. I'd like Carole to be happy. She says she's happy now, but she isn't, I can tell.

I don't think you're allowed to pray for money. Not four hundred dollars. You have to make money for yourself. Carole said that yesterday when she bought us our ice cream. She said you need money to make money.

I've got money, Reuben's money, fifty-seven dollars. I get it out again, kneel down by the candles, wipe my face. I'm feeling very faint. Miss Barratt in the library said gambling is a sin. I count the money one last time. It comes to fifty-eight now, yet I've already spent a dollar. Perhaps I'm lucky.

That man who sat beside me in the restaurant said luck is a Great Lady and if she calls you, you must follow, give her everything. *He* didn't think gambling was a sin. And the man on television gambles all the time, night and day and night again. He has a special programme where you learn. They wouldn't let you learn if it was wrong. I think Miss Barratt meant a sin in England. They have different sins in England.

I wish someone would come in. The cathedral's far too big to hold just me. And if I fainted, I might lie there for hours. People look silly when they faint. Their mouths drop open and they show their underclothes. There's no one here at all, just rows and rows of empty wooden benches.

I go back to the crib. At least St Joseph's someone. He and Mary never had a wedding. That's why he was shocked when she said she was expecting. An angel had to tell him not to worry. They had more angels then.

Suddenly I stop, stare up at the huge great stained-glass window on the right. There are buildings in the glass, tall buildings and a road. I move a little nearer, polish up my glasses on my skirt. I've seen those buildings before. I've even been in them. They're the places where you gamble. Yes, some have got their names on, or half their names. STARD . . . That's the Stardust. Carole took me there. And H for Hilton. That's the great big curving one where all those smiling people win Crocks of Gold.

So it's not a sin. It can't be. Not if they have gambling in cathedrals, in holy windows, underneath the saints. I think they're saints. It's difficult to tell.

'You're admiring the stained glass then?'

I jump. Someone has crept up on me. A man.

'Unusual, isn't it?' His voice is rather high.

He's not a man. He's wearing a black frock. 'Y . . . yes,' I say. I'm scared. I haven't seen a priest for years and years, not a Catholic one. The Beechgrove Catholics go to Mass in a little wooden hut, and if they're really ill, the Vicar sees them. He doesn't like the Catholics.

'This one is my favourite.' The priest is smiling, edging up beside me. 'Where're you from?' He sounds like Meg O'Riley, not American.

I don't know what to say. Carole told me not to mention Beechgrove. 'Belfast,' I say softly.

'Irish!' The smile gets bigger, shows his teeth. 'Great to meet a fellow countryman. I'm a Dublin man myself. You must be one of us if you've come to say your prayers here.'

I don't say anything. It doesn't matter really because he goes on talking himself. 'I've been over here a month now, and, do you know, you're the first Irish person I've met. The Americans are different, take my word for it, very different. What's your name?'

'Norah.'

'Grand to meet you, Norah. I'm Father McKenna. Mac, they call me here. They're very casual here. It's "Father" back in Dublin. I'll be home in just two weeks. Can't wait to be back. How long is it you're staying here?'

'Ten days,' I say. We've had five of them already. It seems more than five. More like weeks and weeks.

'Ten days! That's a lot for Vegas. Most people stay only three or four, and I've known some poor souls head for home after just a few unlucky hours in one casino.'

Casino. That's the word. Those places where you gamble. I point towards the window.

'Yes, surprising, isn't it? Casinos in stained glass. Some people take exception to it, say it's not right in a church. I said the same myself until I met the Sisters here. D'you know them?'

I shake my head. I only know the Sisters back in Beechgrove and I mustn't mention them.

'Sister Anne's my favourite. She's a character. Irish by extraction. She told me all about the glass. It was done by these two women – foreigners, they were, from Hungary, or somewhere Communist. They got out, fled to freedom. Well, they say there's freedom over here. I'm not so sure, are you? I'd rather be in Dublin, tell you the truth. Anyway, they do a lot of glass, and they always like to gear it to the actual place it's in. So if it's stained glass in a steel town, they show steelworks or whatever in the church. I'd prefer just saints, but there you are. That's foreigners.'

He keeps pulling at his frock. It looks too tight for him. I think he must have borrowed it. Perhaps he lost his suitcase.

'There's no steel in Las Vegas, no industry at all, except for gambling, so . . .' He shrugs. 'They had to put casinos in that window. Fair enough, I suppose. Sure most people here do work in them, and they've not forgotten the other sorts of jobs.' He takes my arm, moves me closer in. 'Up there you'll see the farmer with his wheat sheaves, the nurse and her patient, right there in the middle, underneath the teacher with his book. And that's a poet on the right, the tall fellow with the harp.'

I look up where he's pointing. The poet's neck is very thin and scraggy. He doesn't look like Milton.

'I think Sister said a poet, though I've never met a poet in Las Vegas. Only gamblers. Eighty per cent tourists we get here on a Sunday, and they've all come to Vegas to get rich. You should see the collection plate. It's not just money they drop in, but casino chips as well, all colours of the rainbow, and some worth fifty dollars. Father Jude has to cash them in each week. He's been doing it for years. He calls it the "Casino Chip Run", says he's the only one in Vegas who comes out of a casino with as much as he took in.'

His laugh is grey and thin. (He is plump and black.) I'm too surprised to laugh myself. A church with gambling chips. A priest in a casino.

He checks his watch. 'I'd better be on my way. I've got some calls to make.'

I ask him what the time is.

'A little after three.'

'Oh, dear.' I've wasted half an hour. Carole will be cross. I ought to have started on that shopping. The list is very long. But if I spend the money, there won't be any left to make some more with. I've got to make some more. I know it isn't wrong now.

'Are you running late? I can offer you a lift if it's any help. It's not my car, it's Sister Anne's, but she always gives me the loan of it, God bless her. Father Jude is never out of his – never walks a step. He'd drive up to the altar if he could. Which direction are you headed?'

'The. . . Hilton,' I reply. Of course it's not a sin. I remember now, that Reverend on the television said God approved of gambling. This Reverend does as well. And Father Jude. I don't know who he is, but he must be quite important if he never walks.

'It's on my way. I can drop you right outside. What did you say your name was?'

'Norah.'

'Ah, yes. Lovely Irish name. I miss Ireland, to tell you the truth. It's not the same here, is it, dear, not the same at all. I'm only glad it's not the summer. It's murder in the summer, so they say. Have you been here in the summer?'

'No,' I say. 'I haven't.' I wish he wouldn't talk. I'm trying to work out what to do, how to make the money.

He keeps on asking questions, even in the car. He doesn't want the answers, so I don't say much at all, just sit up nice and straight. I feel very grand to be driving in a car, driving with a Reverend. He pulls up outside the Hilton, helps me out, still talking. The hotel's so big and frightening, I almost change my mind. It's also very ugly. Not a palace like the Gold Rush, just rows and rows of windows stretching up so high they hurt my neck.

I take a few steps forward, see the Crock of Gold. It's gleaming in the sunshine and full of golden coins. I have to crane my neck again. It's set high up on a tower, which is standing in a garden with a blue pool underneath it, and painted like a rainbow.

It *is* a rainbow. I stand and stare at it. I had a book once about a Crock of Gold. You find them at the end of rainbows, but only special people ever get there and there's a lot of pain and sadness first. It's different at the Hilton, though. You can be old or bald or ordinary and still win a million dollars. Carole said so. She showed me all the photos. Some were really ugly. One man was eighty-three. I wouldn't want a million, just four hundred.

A lot of taxis are drawing up outside, with people jumping out of them. I follow three fat ladies through the heavy double doors. Inside it is a palace, with those huge lights made of glass, and flowers in golden pots. It's also very crowded. I keep bumping into people or tripping over cases. Everybody's arriving in time for New Year's Eve. They all look very rich, in furs and jewels. I'm scared they'll make me leave. I don't think you're allowed here if you're poor.

The whole ceiling shines and sparkles, though it's only afternoon, and there are more lights in the mirrors, and Christmas trees hung from top to toe with shiny coloured balls, and a great stuffed camel, bigger than a real one, and the Three Wise Men holding three more Crocks of Gold. The camel smiles at me. No one else has smiled yet. The third Wise Man is pointing to a notice. A very special notice, one for me. 'Free gambling lessons,' it says. 'TODAY, 3.30 PM. Ask for Tony.'

It's because I lit that candle. God couldn't smell the smoke, but He heard me just the same. He must have done. I ask the time and it's half past three exactly. That proves it.

Then I ask for Tony, and I'm taken to a table with a brown dish at one end of it and lots of coloured numbers on the bright green tablecloth. A lady and two men are sitting on high stools. All of them are smoking and wearing their best clothes. The lady has pink hair, and earrings which reach right down to her shoulders and keep twitching when she moves.

Tony shakes my hand. He's all dressed up in one of those black suits with stiff white shirts and black bow ties which men wear when they play in bands on television. He has diamond rings on both his hands and his teeth look very new. I didn't know you dressed up to play cards.

It's not cards, he says, it's roulette he's going to teach us. I say I've never played roulette, only snakes and ladders, and patience on my own. He laughs and says I'm not to worry, roulette is very simple and a child of five could play it.

It isn't simple, not at all. He uses words I've never heard, and talks faster than my brain works. There's less time in America, so everyone talks fast. The lady with the earrings is very kind and whispers things to help me. She also whispers where she lives and what she's called and what she did today, so the red and black and numbers get all mixed up with names and places.

'I'm Sally-Ann,' she tells me. 'Sal to friends.' I knew her name already. It's spelt out on a necklace made of letters. I tell her my name, which I think she likes because she uses it a lot.

She must be fairly old, but her face looks younger than her hair and hands, as if it belongs to someone else. She has long red shiny nails and a red bow in her hair like children wear. She hasn't any children, but two husbands and three homes. She says she always spends the winters in Las Vegas because it's warmer than her other homes back East.

'I'm bored to tears, though, Norah. There's not a thing to do here, except eat and drink and gamble and see shows. I've seen the show at Caesars a hundred times at least.'

'A hundred?' My own whisper is a gasp.

'Yeah. That's nothing, hon. A friend of mine's been to see *Star Crazy* three hundred and twenty times. The three-hundredth time they gave her a gold watch, a real fancy one with diamonds on the strap.' Sally-Ann shakes her head. The earrings shake as well. 'Lee don't want a watch. She must have half a dozen, and, anyways, what's the point of knowin' what the time is, when you've got damn all to do and all day long to do it in?'

'Ssh,' says the tall man sitting next to her. He doesn't like her whispering. He frowned at her before.

She takes no notice. 'Know why I come here, Norah? No, it's not the lessons. I don't need no lessons. I know all these damned games backwards.' She puts her face right up close to mine, giggles in my ear. 'I got the hots for Tony, that's for why. Isn't he a hunk? The cutest thing on two legs.'

The tall man turns on her. 'Look, if you wanna talk, go find a bar or somethin' and spare the rest of us. We're here to learn the game.'

Sally-Ann winks at me. 'My first husband, Herb, was always gettin' mad at me like that. That's what killed him in the end – hollerin' and shoutin'. He dropped dead at forty-one.'

'Right,' says Tony. 'We're going to try our luck now. I'll give all you folks some chips, and you get them on this table. Don't worry – we're not playing for real cash. This is just a practice, to give you confidence, so you can march up to these tables tonight and know exactly what you're doing and how to win.'

I *don't* know what I'm doing, but Sally-Ann stops whispering about funerals and starts explaining red and black again and Tony smiles and says he'll talk us through it. I watch the others for a while and realize all I have to do is put my chips somewhere on the tablecloth. I'm not sure where, but I wait for Sally-Ann, and wherever she puts hers, I place mine on the number right next door. I feel close to her like that.

We all have different coloured chips. Hers are pink to match her hair. Mine are blue. Blue's my favourite colour. It's Our Lady's special colour, so the nuns said.

Tony throws a little ball which spins round and round the dish, round and round, and everybody watches and stops breathing. Even Sally-Ann is silent till it stops. Then Tony calls out 'Twenty-three' and gives me some more chips, which means I've won.

It's a good thing I like blue because I keep getting more blue chips. Soon I have three big piles of them. Tony says I'm on a lucky streak. Our Lady must be helping me because I don't know how to play. I just follow Sally-Ann, wait for her to choose a square, then take the one beside it. She's getting rather angry. I pray I'll start to lose soon, so she'll go on being friendly.

I win again.

'Shit!' says the tall man. 'If snakes and ladders makes you so damned lucky, I'll stay at home, for chrissakes, and play it with the kids.'

People are crowding round our table, watching, whispering. Some of them must think it's a real game because they start throwing money down, trying to join in. Tony has to give it back. I begin to feel excited. It *is* a real game. We're playing in a real casino with real chips and real live people. There isn't any money, that's the only difference. I'm still winning more than anyone. Even more than Sally-Ann, who's been coming to Las Vegas every year for twenty-seven years. And more than those two men who look very rich and clever and wear proper suits like doctors.

The people standing round keep pointing to my piles of chips. I feel very grand and special, like I did in the priest's car. I'm a winner. I'm on a lucky streak. Tony says I'll probably win all evening. He says lucky streaks often last a day or two, especially with beginners. 'Beginner's luck,' he smiles.

'Okay, folks, that's it for today. Tomorrow there's no class – New Year's Day. Next class Monday morning, ten o'clock – baccarat. But between now and then, get on these roulette tables. Now you know the basics, try your luck – especially Norah. When you're on a lucky streak, you've got to get your money into action. Get it out of your pocket or your purse and put it on the tables. That applies to all of you. You're all winners in Las Vegas.'

I start collecting up my chips, my hands still damp and shaky from excitement. Tony used my name, called me Norah. He smiled at me again, just me. He's got a lovely smile, like Carole's, which goes right up to his eyes. I open up my handbag, pour the chips in.

'Hold on, madam. Those aren't yours to keep.'

'But I thought you said I'd won?'

'Yeah, you won, sure you won, but the chips stay here with me. You buy your own chips, right? Just go up to any table, put five dollars down and you'll be given twenty chips, each one worth a quarter like I said. Okay?'

He's frowning now, not smiling, checking all the chips as I tip them out again. I hope he didn't think that I was stealing. He called me madam and madam means they're cross.

'Right, folks, thanks for coming – and remember what I said: find a weakness in the game and attack that weakness. Don't forget your corner bets, your combination bets, or if you want to keep it simple, just bet red or black, or odd or even. But above all, get your money on a table.'

I can't get it on a table because Sally-Ann's linked her arm through mine and says how about a drink. I'm so glad she's friends again, I let her lead me to the bar. I don't know why it's open when it's only afternoon, and I thought she meant a cup of tea, not cocktails. I try to force mine down because it's not polite to leave it when she's paid. She's not whispering now, she's talking very loudly about coffins, and how much it cost when her second husband died.

'That was the only time he didn't bawl me out for over-spendin' – at his funeral. Have you been married, Norah?'

I shake my head. I wouldn't like a husband. They always shout a lot and you'd have to share your bed. I'd like to wear a ring, though. A ring means someone wants you. Sally-Ann has rings on every finger. If I won enough, I could buy a ring, as well as just the dress.

My straw makes a rude noise in my drink. I wipe my mouth, stand up. 'It's my friend who's getting married,' I explain. 'I'm going to buy her dress.'

Sally-Ann asks which stores I'm trying and I tell her how I

have to win the money first. She laughs a lot and chokes into her glass. Then she says if I really want to gamble, to start Downtown, not here, because the pace is slower, and the minimum bets are lower than on the Strip.

I'm not sure what she means and I'm feeling rather dizzy from the drink. I lean against the wall, ask her where Downtown is.

'You've never been Downtown, hon? God! You gotta see it. They call it Glitter Gulch and – jeez – it glitters! You get right down there, Norah – take a cab. You'll love it. The dealers are less smart-assed than here, so it's easier to ask for help and if you make mistakes, well, no big deal – not like these swell joints where they freeze you off if you so much as open your mouth. I'd come with you, Norah, honey, but I've got a date – a guy from Michigan. Don't worry, you'll be fine.'

She digs into her handbag, passes me a long and speckled orange thing, like a snake, but soft.

'Norah, honey, I'd like for you to have this.'

I back away, don't really like to touch it. I don't know what it is.

'Don't worry, it won't bite. Not that end, anyway.' She laughs again, then starts to cough, finds us both a cough sweet. 'It's a lucky Tiger's Tail. You only gotta stroke it and you get four hundred times more luck. Go on, honey, take it. I've got two dozen more the same. They were half-price in the store. Discontinued line, they said. I don't know why. We all need luck, for God's sake.'

The earrings sway and jingle as she staggers up. She's kissing me. She's really kissing me. She smells of powder. I can feel her corsets. She pulls away, pats my hand. 'Now remember, honey, if you're ever in Washington, DC, or Dover, Mass, just call me up, okay?'

She likes me. I've made another friend. She's given me a present, four hundred times more luck. She kissed me, called me honey. Tony called me honey. I'm lucky. I'm a winner. I'm going to see Downtown.

She walks me to the door, tries to call a cab for me, but I

want to change my clothes first. You have to be dressed up to play roulette. I try to run, past the taxis, out into the street, but that drink I had has leaked into my legs. It takes me quite a time to find the Gold Rush.

It's crowded like the Hilton. The whole downstairs is blocked with queues and luggage, and the passage to our room is filled with those men from the convention who stay up half the night and make so much noise you can't get back to sleep. I'm so scared I drop my key. A big man picks it up for me, but I knock first anyway, in the hope that Carole's there, though I know she's meeting Reuben somewhere else.

She isn't there. I take my Beechgrove suit off, wash my face. I'd like to have a bath, but there isn't time. I sniff my hands and body. I smell of Beechgrove, even in Las Vegas, so I put a lot of talcum powder on, and then the Gold Rush frock. I've never worn a cocktail frock before. This one has no back, but rows and rows of little beads sewn on to the front. My brassiere is showing quite a lot. I dare not take it off because then my chest falls down, and anyway, it's rude.

I put my old green cardigan on top, which hides the brassiere, but also hides the beads. The shoes look rather odd. I wish I had red party shoes, instead of big brown lace-ups. Sally-Ann wore lipstick, bright and shiny red. A streak of it has come off on my cheek. I rub it in, spread some on the other cheek. My face looks better, pinker. I've never worn lipstick in my life. I could put some on my lips, but I'd have to borrow Carole's, and Reverend Mother said borrowing is stealing if you haven't asked beforehand.

I replace my glasses, comb my hair. I'd like to put my coat on. I always feel safer in a coat. But you couldn't see the frock then. And you're not allowed to play roulette in coats. I'll carry it instead, with my bag and gloves, and a plastic bag for the wedding dress, in case it rains and I need to keep it dry.

I'm ready. No, I'm not. I go back to the wardrobe, reach right into the back, unwrap the towel and then the layers of tissue until I reach the silver shamrock. My mother gave me that. She pinned it on my shawl when I was born. Shamrocks mean good luck. They come from Ireland. A man called St

Patrick drove away the snakes with them. There are no snakes left in Ireland now, not even in the zoo.

My shamrock's really lucky because it's the only thing which no one's ever stolen. I've always had to hide it, but the other things I hid were stolen just the same. I think my mother guards it. She may be still alive, or gone to heaven. I don't know what she looks like, but I imagine her as pretty with red shoes.

I put the shamrock in my purse, in the compartment where you're meant to keep a photo. I've never had a photograph. I'd like one of my mother, with me sitting on her lap. I'd like to see her eyes and touch her hair. Perhaps I'll even find her now. A Tiger Tail and shamrock both together probably mean a thousand times more luck.

There are no stairs in America and all the lifts are full, then I waste more time waiting for a cab. I'm frightened of the cab drivers. I think they all have guns. But I don't know where Downtown is and Sally-Ann said take one.

'Where shall I drop you off, ma'am?'

I don't say anything. I'm staring out of the window. Downtown is ugly, very ugly. The streets look old and poor, and there are lots of poky little shops and horrid cheap motels with dirty faces. There are no trees or flowers or green, just dead grey pavements with flashing signs above them which seem to shout and scream.

The cab drives on a bit. Now there are casinos, not grand ones like the Gold Rush, or huge ones like the Hilton, but smaller ones, all squashed together, with crowds of people pouring in and out of them.

'Okay here?' the driver shouts.

He's stopping anyway. He tells me what the fare is. It sounds too much. I'll have to take the bus back. The driver seems quite cross, swears as he drives off.

I'm standing in the middle of the pavement with people pushing past me. A lot of them are eating. Hot dogs, ice-cream cornets, plastic pots of popcorn. There are food shops all around. I can smell doughnuts mixed with onions. I tread in dog's mess by mistake, try to scrape it off against the kerb. I'm not sure where to go, so I cross the road because everybody else is, then cross back again.

A big black sign says 'HAPPY BIRTHDAY JESUS', but I can't see any church, only a film called *Take My Body* and a picture of a lady wearing just her boots. I turn my back. It's rude to look at people when they haven't got their clothes on. I see another sign: 'World's Largest Gift Center'. It isn't big at all, just a squashed-in building with pink paint peeling off it.

It's difficult to walk fast because of all the crowds. A lady stops me, smiles. She's wearing long black boots like that lady on the poster and a very short red skirt. Her smile is red as well and looks wet as if she's licked it.

'Welcome to Coin Castle.'

I can't see any castle, just a building like a cinema with slot machines inside.

'Your fortune in the stars,' she says. 'Free gambling horoscope done on our computer while you wait.'

I don't know what she means. And it's difficult to hear her because there's music blaring out, and other girls are shouting things and there's a lot of noise and clatter from the coins.

'Step right in and find out what the stars say. It's real scientific. We combine computer-age technology with all the ancient wisdom of astrology. You get your own personal print-out with your special lucky numbers, and whether you should play today or wait till a luckier time, and where you should put your money and . . .'

I step inside.

They ask me for my birth date, which I've never known exactly, so I give them the month and year, and the day which Reverend Mother used to put on forms, which is the feast of St Sylvester. I don't know who he is. They say I'll have to wait a while as the computer has a fault.

There are several girls in bathing suits, sitting up above the slot machines. They keep calling out, begging me to play. I can't play yet, not without my horoscope. I stand quietly in a corner and try to think of black. They do that in the Relaxation Classes. Black is the quietest of the colours because sleep and night are black – and soot, which creeps from

281

chimneys very softly. Red is noisiest. Screams are red, and fire engines, and nearly all the lounges in the Gold Rush. Nothing here is black. The colours are all bright and hot, and keep flashing on and off.

My horoscope is yellow when it comes, yellow paper folded like a card with purple stars dotted on the front. The print inside is very small and all the o's are missing. It calls me N rah. 'Y ur sec nd name is Luck, N rah. And thank y ur lucky stars it's Thursday because Thursday is y ur extra lucky day. N rah, riches can be y urs t day.'

Riches. Riches would buy dress and veil and wreath. Riches would buy wedding photographs. I'd stick them in a padded satin album with white doves on the cover. We saw those in the shop. I'd give them all to Carole, keep just one for myself, to put in that compartment in my purse. I don't want Reuben in it. Only Carole.

'Y ur lucky numbers, N rah, are 5, 8, and 23.' I stare down at the card. Twenty-three. It's true. That was the first number I won on at roulette. I also won on five.

I go on reading, though the words are very hard. 'N rah, y ur charming and dynamic pers nality will attract a stranger wh can change y ur life. Y u will travel t a fascinating c untry far away.'

Israel . . . My heart is beating very fast. A stranger. A new start, like Carole said.

I walk out into the street, casinos all around me. The Pioneer, the Golden Gate, the Plaza. The computer didn't say which one. It told me to play the dollar slots, but I don't know what they are.

I'd better play roulette. I'm good at roulette. On a lucky streak. Sally-Ann said find a small casino, a homey one, one I feel in tune with. I pass a tall and frightening one, walk on.

I cross the street, turn a corner, stop. Right in front of me is a bright red flashing heart, all lit up and moving, and above it 'LADY LUCK' in huge gold letters, changing now to blue. Lady Luck. I've been looking for her ever since that evening in the restaurant, when the man said to follow if she calls me. There isn't any picture of her, but I know she's beautiful. I shut my eyes and see her. She's wearing scarlet shoes, and an evening frock right down to the floor, and a tiny silver shamrock round her neck. My second name is Luck. It said so in my horoscope, so this may be my mother. Or everybody's mother, like Our Lady. I can feel her arms around me as I walk slowly in, beneath her beating heart.

Inside, it's rather shabby with none of those glass lights or golden flowers. It smells of cigarettes, and there's popcorn on the floor, all trodden in and dirty. No one is dressed up. Most people wear jeans and a lot of men have hats on, cowboy hats or funny caps with letters round the brim. A lady in a wheelchair is talking to a slot machine. I think she's foreign because her hair is wild and black, and the words are more like babble. Beside her is a man. Or maybe it's a boy. He has a tiny stunted body with a grown-up's head on top, which looks far too heavy for it. He comes up to my waist, but his face is very lined, so I'm not sure if he's old, or just a child. It's rude to stare, so I walk the other way.

I find a roulette table, but it's very crowded with no free seats and lots of extra people standing round. The man who throws the ball isn't dressed like Tony and he doesn't smile at all, not even with his mouth. His name is Hans. It's written on his brooch.

I get my Tiger Tail out, stroke it once or twice. It works, because a lady leaves the table and I climb into her seat. People turn and look at me. My coat is in the way, so I clamber down again and put it under the seat with my gloves and plastic bag. The man beside me frowns and mutters something.

I unzip my purse. Tony said to put five dollars down, but the notes all look the same. Everybody's smoking, and my glasses have steamed up. I try to find a five. My hands are shaking. My mouth feels very dry. I'd better hurry. They're short of seats. Hans may shout at me, tell me to get down and go away. I take all the notes out, hold them very tightly in both hands. I can see the dress. Carole in the dress. Orange blossom. Happiness. I put the money on the table, all of it. The more you play, the more you win, Tony said.

Hans is passing me some chips, a huge great pile of them. I

touch them with a finger to check they're really there. I never thought I'd get them. I thought something would go wrong, or he'd say I was too old to play, or dressed wrong.

I try to count them, keep on getting muddled. It doesn't matter really. I've got more than anyone. I can see that just by looking. I pick one up and smell it. It doesn't smell of anything. I can still smell orange blossom, but that's up in my head.

The chips are red, not blue. Red for shoes. Red for Lady Luck. My second name is Luck. N rah Luck. They took the o's away because o's are holes, empty lonely holes. I'm going to meet a stranger. There are lots of strangers here, but they're mostly very ugly. One has lost a finger and another has a scar across his face.

Everyone is playing, hands reaching past me, elbows knocking mine. Hans is throwing chips across the table. Then he throws the ball. It goes really fast, rattling round and round its little dish. No one speaks at all now. They all look very frightened. Someone coughs. Someone strikes a match. The man beside me bites his thumb. His shirt is half-undone and long black hair is showing through the gaps. I think I'm too dressed up. I button my cardigan to try to hide the frock. The wool is thick and matted, feels itchy on my neck.

The ball has almost stopped. The man opposite is frowning and his eyes have disappeared. Hans passes him more chips. Orange ones. Orange blossom. I've got to play myself. I wish Sally-Ann was here, to make me brave. There's no one like her. The only other woman at the table has a twisted mouth and red blotches on her hands instead of rings.

I touch my silver shamrock, stroke my Tiger Tail, then put a little pile of chips on number twenty-three. Lucky twenty-three. Hans is taking money, giving people chips. His hands move very quickly, but not his mouth. Even when he speaks, his lips hardly move at all.

'No more bets,' he says. Tony said that too. You're not allowed to put chips down on the table once the ball starts slowing.

It's slowing now. I can't see where it goes because I'm

down the other end and I haven't cleaned my glasses yet. I take them off to polish them. All the faces blur. When I put them on again, my chips have disappeared.

I stare down at the table. Number twenty-three is bare, without its tall red crown. My hands feel damp and a piece of steel is pressing on my head. It's because I didn't watch. Tony said you have to watch the action all the time. I put some more chips down, place my eyes on top of them this time. I choose twenty-three again, my number in the stars. The ball is quite excited, whirls so fast I can hear it bouncing, skidding in the dish. It stops at last. I hold my breath. Hans puts a little pepper-pot on number seventeen. 'Seventeen, black,' he says.

'No,' I say. 'That's wrong.'

Everybody stares. I don't think you're allowed to talk. It's like Beechgrove after ten. I close my eyes, pretend it wasn't me. When I open them again, things are going far too fast, like those films we had at Westham Hall where people always ran instead of walking. Everyone has more than just two hands and all the hands are jerking, reaching out. I can't see any numbers. They're all covered up with chips now. Orange, pink, yellow, green and blue. No red. I haven't got mine down yet. Quick! He's thrown the ball. I pile them on a nought. It's the only one that's free.

I watch the red, listen to the ball. Now the film is running in slow motion. The ball won't stop, goes on and on, round and round, teasing me and everyone. It's such a tiny ball, a small white egg, a little spinning marble. But everybody's watching it, begging it to choose their special number. I don't think it can hear. It makes an angry rattling noise, as if it doesn't like us.

Now it's quieter, slowing, maybe getting tired. 'No more bets,' says Hans.

I squeeze my Tiger Tail so tight, my hand begins to ache. Four hundred times more luck. My other hand is tight around the shamrock. A thousand times more luck. I'm smiling when the ball stops.

'Thirty red,' says Hans, banging down his pepper-pot. He sweeps my chips away. I watch them go. Noughts are only holes. I search for eight. I like the number eight. At St Joseph's, we had something called the Eight Beatitudes which all began with 'Blessed are . . .' Seven is blessed too. There are seven sacraments and seven Holy Angels and seven dwarfs and God made the world in seven days and seventh heaven is when you're happy here on earth.

I put some chips on eight and some on seven. The ball is really angry now, banging round its dish. I pray this time. To Lady Luck, St Joseph, to the stars. The saints turn into stars when they die and go to heaven, so they can shine down on the earth and make the nights less dark.

I'm praying so hard, I don't even hear the ball drop, but Hans already has his pepper-pot on number thirty-three. Everything starts spinning in my head then. The ball, the chips, the colours, the whole room. I fumble for my handkerchief, wipe my face and hands. I don't feel well. There's a ra-ra in my ears like the babble of that lady in the wheelchair, and the man beside me is breathing very fast. I can feel my chest panting in and out with him, his dark rough hair prickling on my skin.

I try to edge away, touch a shoulder on my other side. The shoulder growls. More people are pressing up behind me, someone's elbow digging in my back. I'm surrounded on all sides. People watching, jeering. I can even feel the saints' eyes, staring down from heaven, cold and cross. Stars have eyes, silver ones, which only close in daytime. And Lady Luck has crept away, left me on the doorstep. I can see another baby in her arms. A pretty girl, with tiny feet and hands.

I try to swallow, wish I had a drink. My throat is scratchy like the cardigan. My hands are swelling as I look at them, so clumsy now I can hardly hold the chips. I haven't many left. Every time the ball spins, more have gone. Only seven now. They must feel very lonely. Only five. Five's my lucky number. They were wrong about the eight, or perhaps I read it wrong. The print was very faint, so it may have been a three.

I put the five on five, hold my head. My head is a brown dish and the ball rattles round and round inside it, round and round. It's hurting. My eyes and mouth are holes, holes with numbers on. Number five.

'No more bets,' says Hans again. I can't bet any more. I've no more money, no more chips at all.

The ball begins to slow. Suddenly it drops. In my stomach. In my bowel. Somewhere dark and low which hurts a lot.

Hans calls out a number. It's very close to five. But it isn't five. It's six. Lucky six.

I sit a while, staring at the table. It's very pretty, really. All the different colours are like flowers. Yellow flowers and blue flowers. Orange, pink and blue ones. Every flower but red. I don't like red. It's noisy. Fire engines and screams. I put my purse away, close my handbag, slip down off my stool.

'Goodbye,' I say, to no one.

18

I walk out into the street. It's a completely different street.
It's night, not day, though it's brighter than the daylight.
Everything is moving, even tall great buildings. I can feel the
pavement breathing, hot between my legs. The whole night is
ill and hot. Sweat is running down the walls, running down my
face. Coloured sweat which burns. There isn't any moon. Lots
of little suns are shining, spinning round and round.

The moon is pale like Norah. An empty O like Norah.
There's nothing pale Downtown. The stars are scarlet mouths,
screaming in the sky. The trees are coloured lights. The lights
flash on off on. My eyes hurt with the glare.

'Keep still,' I whisper. 'Turn off all those lights, please.'

No one listens. Nobody has ears.

I need a drink. Something safe and kind. A glass of milk. A
cup of tea like Sister's with two sugars in. There are cafés everywhere, closing in on me. I can smell onions on their breath.
They're serving words, not food. Sizzling words spitting in
my head. BIGGER, BURGER, LIQUOR, EAT, HOT, RIB. I push
a door. More words. 'TWENTY-FOUR-HOUR BREAKFAST.
CHEAPEST EATS IN TOWN.' I step in, blink against the noise.
There's music playing. Music like a pain.

'A cup of tea, please.'

It doesn't look like tea. It's very dark and black, with
something floating in it. I can't see any sugar. I wish I'd asked
for milk. Milk is pale and quiet. They give it to small children.
It's made of grass and munching. They don't have grass
Downtown.

'That's fifty cents.'

I fumble for my purse. It feels very limp and thin, like a small brown animal which no one's fed. There's nothing in its stomach, not even fifty cents. I leave my tea, walk out. I can hear the woman shouting after me. A lot of people shout here.

I check my purse again. No, it's not my purse, it's Reuben's. That was Reuben's money. I don't like Reuben and I only borrowed it.

Borrowing is stealing if you haven't asked.

A thief, a petty vandal.

A deep-dyed wretched sinner.

Gambling is a sin.

I sit down on a step outside a shop. The shop is empty, boarded up. The step is very cold. I've lost my coat. I don't know where I put it or why I took it off. I never take my coat off. That Friend who gave it to me had it since the war. I've also lost my gloves. They'll say I'm very careless and they don't know why they bother. The gloves weren't quite a pair. They were both dark blue, but one was fuzzier. I've never needed gloves before. I don't go out at Beechgrove. It's safer to stay in. You can't lose money then, or lose your clothes.

A boy and girl have stopped outside the shop. They're kissing. It's a long kiss, very long. Sally-Ann didn't kiss like that. She told me to phone her, but she didn't leave her number. I haven't got a friend now, not even Carole. I've lost her money – Reuben's money, stolen it. They won't let me come to Israel. Not a thief.

Another couple are walking arm in arm. Their hands and sides are joined like one person with four legs. You're one person if you're married. It says so in the Bible. Joined for ever. Carole will be Reuben. Reuben doesn't like me. Even before he met me, he said I couldn't come.

I get up off the step, walk slowly down the street. No one is alone. They're mostly all in families, or couples. There are also gangs of frightening-looking boys, throwing coloured streamers at each other. Some are swaying, shouting, drinking out of bottles, kicking empty cans. They're waiting for the fireworks. They set them off Downtown, a great show at nine o'clock. It can't be nine o'clock yet, though it feels very late and dark inside my head. They may put me into prison if they find me.

Bars on all the windows like at Belstead.

'Hey, lady, wanna hat?'

A man has stopped me. He's holding out a golden crown, and a hat with orange feathers on. Other hats are piled up on his stall. He takes a step towards me, slams the hat right down on my head. 'Happy New Year' is written on the brim in coloured letters.

'For you, lady, three dollars.'

I take it off again. I haven't got three dollars and nothing will be happy any more.

A wheelchair is blocking half the pavement. There's a man in it, a beggar. He hasn't any legs. A woman throws a bank note in his dish. He bends to pick it up and I see he's lost his hands as well. His wrists just end without the fingers. Half of him is missing. He's a stump.

I turn away. I'm a stump myself. A lot of me is missing. I feel very light and weak. I think I may be hungry. I haven't eaten anything all day. Food is lying in the gutter: a piece of bread, half a fat brown sausage. I ought to pick them up, save them for my breakfast. I peer down at the bread. There's lipstick on it; teeth-marks on the sausage.

I walk on, pass an open door. Tables, chairs, a counter; people eating clean food without lipstick on, or germs. I haven't any money, but at least I could sit down. I limp in, find an empty seat. There are great big coloured pictures on the walls. Food again. Potato chips piled on plates like firewood; chocolate cake so huge you can see its pores. The real cake looks quite small, and rather dry.

'Can I get you something, madam?'

'I'm waiting,' I reply. 'Waiting for my friend.' The waitress walks away.

I lean back on the padded scarlet bench. Red again. Too loud. All the different noises go round and round my head. Knives and forks keep quarrelling and something in the kitchen is roaring on and on. Someone laughs. A sneeze fires like a gun. There's a steady chewing-chewing noise, much closer than the rest.

I open my eyes. (I don't know why they closed.) A woman's

sitting next to me, chewing on a bone. She's eating with her fingers, reading while she eats. Her newspaper is propped against the ketchup. I read the other side of it. There are a lot of bombs and shocks. 'Blood Bath', 'Gas explosion', 'Big Blast New Year's Sale'. I can see a picture of a crash. The larger car is lying upside down. I think it's dead. The woman turns the page. 'Baby found in trash.'

I rest my forehead in my hands. I'm very tired. I'd like to go to bed, back to our hotel. But Carole might be there. And Reuben. Waiting for his shopping. Waiting for the change.

The woman's just got up to pay her bill. She's left her chicken, left her newspaper. There's a little pool of ketchup on it, which looks like Carole's blood. I wipe it off. Newspapers are useful. When Ella Cartwright slept rough on Hastings promenade, she wrapped her feet in newspaper to keep them warm. I try to fold it up.

'FREE FUNERAL', I read, in big black letters. 'The Eden Funeral Parlour offers a free funeral to anyone who plans to drink and drive this New Year's Eve.'

I'd like to die. It's peaceful when you die. You wear white because it's your wedding with the Lord. I'd be a bride like Carole, wear orange blossoms, be joined to God for ever.

I go on reading. All you have to do is sign a piece of paper which says you'll agree to drink and drive on New Year's Eve.

'In return, we offer you an antique silver sealer-casket, lined with moss-pink satin, and a polished granite grave marker in our beautiful memorial park.'

I'm not sure what they are, until I see the photos. There's a coffin with its lid up, a very grand expensive one with silky stuff inside. And a gravestone with a lily on, and two whole rows of writing. 'Up to ten inscribed words,' it says. 'Plain or Gothic script, your choice.'

If you die at Beechgrove, the coffin's very plain. The State pays, unless you've got money of your own, and the State is very poor. You don't get a headstone, or silky stuff inside, and sometimes you're buried in a grave which belongs to someone else. It's cheaper if you share. The other corpse is often very old, only bones and worms left. You don't get many flowers. Doris

Clayton had plastic flowers. Green ones with blue leaves.

I'd like flowers which smell. And a polished granite headstone with ten whole words on it. It would be hard to choose the words. I think I'd have Carole's name put on, instead of mine. It's prettier, and I'd have the Joseph then. *She* won't need it any more. She'll be Mrs Reuben's Name.

Funerals cost pounds. Like those weddings in the wedding chapels where everything is extra. If you're really rich in England, you can even have an angel on your grave. I saw a huge one once, with white marble hair right down to its shoulders and wings which kept the rain off. I'll never get an angel.

If Beechgrove's closing, I won't get any funeral at all. The vicar buries people, and you never see the vicar once you've moved out into lodgings. I read about a woman who was just stuffed into a dustbin-bag and buried in the garden with no coffin and no clothes. They found her later, some of her, when her dog was digging for a bone.

There are bones in front of me, that woman's bones, pale ones, tiny ones, some with flesh still on. I push her plate away, get up. The waitress hurries over.

'My friend didn't come,' I tell her.

I find myself outside again, right out in the street. I'm not sure how I got there. I'm just wandering round and round. It's colder now, much colder, though all the suns are shining still and the lights won't let the night in. A band is playing, plays right through my head. The noise turns into Reuben's voice, calling me a thief. The voice gets louder: thief, thief, thief, THIEF! Suddenly, a bomb explodes. The sky turns pink, then silver, and sparks fly everywhere. I crouch down in a doorway, block my ears. I don't want to go to Israel.

Perhaps it's not a bomb. It may be a Sign from God that He's about to end the world. One Reverend on the television lives in California. They have earthquakes all the time there, and floods and storms as well. They're Signs, he said. Signs that God is angry. And a punishment for sin. There's more sin in California.

I walk on very carefully, waiting for the storm. I'm so cold,

I've lost my hands again, and my stomach's still a hole. I stop outside some big glass doors. They open, just like magic; slowly close behind me. It's warm inside, safer if it floods.

'Free margaritas,' says a sign. I don't know what they are, but maybe you can eat them. I join the queue. It's very long and noisy, and only moves in shuffles. When I get up closer, I can't see any food. Just tiny plastic tooth-mugs with stuff like water in them. I almost walk away, but it may be wine, and wine can make you better. Carole's always happier with wine.

'Carole,' I say softly. I'm missing her a lot. I may never see her in my life again. I haven't said goodbye. I haven't said a lot of things. I don't know how to say them.

At last I reach the counter. I try to take a glass, but a big man grabs it back.

'Where's your coupon, lady?'

'I thought the drinks were free.'

'Yeah, but only with the coupon from your fun-book.'

'Book?'

'Jesus Christ!' he mutters, wipes his face. 'You can get one over there.' He's pointing to another queue, so long it winds in circles and hasn't got a beginning or an end.

'Move ya butt now, will ya? You're holdin' up the rest.'

I join the second queue. It's slower than the first one, so I close my eyes and pretend that Carole's with me. We're sitting at a table eating bread and butter. Just the two of us. Reuben's gone to Israel. On his own. The bread is new and fresh. It's not margarine, it's butter, and there's jam with strawberries in.

I've eaten fourteen slices, chewing very slowly and with a wait between each one, before I get my fun-book. The lady stamps each coupon, writes the time on them.

'Do I have to queue again to get my drink?' I ask. I wish it was free bread and jam instead. The drinks looked very small and very cold.

'Yeah, I'm afraid you do, ma'am. We're real busy New Year's Eve. But you have to wait an hour first. I've stamped the time right here, see? When one hour's up, you can claim your margarita.'

'An . . . hour?'

'Don't worry – these coupons give you three-for-two match play on all the table games. So you can spend your hour makin' lots of money. This is how it works. Say you wanna play roulette, well, you just tear out this coupon, bet it with two dollars, and if you win, you'll get three bucks instead of two on even money bets.'

I don't know what she means. I don't want to play roulette. Not again. Not ever. 'No,' I say. 'No thank you.' I'm talking to myself, walking past the long long queue, right out to the exit. I can see the stump of beggar just outside. He's following me, he must be. His lips are moving. He's going to give me a Message. I think he's come to warn me. There are lots of beggars here. They lie on bits of cardboard in the gutter. Some were very rich once. Victor told me that. He said they lost their money playing cards.

'FREE DONUT.' 'FREE HOT DOG.' I don't take any notice, just walk past. Nothing here is free. 'WE SELL HAPPINESS.' That's outside a flowershop, but there's nothing in the window and the shop is locked and barred.

'WIN A CAR!' I stop this time. It's a great big shiny yellow car, parked right inside the window, and hung with yellow flowers. The flowers are only paper, but the car is real. I don't know how they got it in. It's wider than the doors.

I press my face against the glass. If I won it, I could drink and drive. Then I'd get the funeral. If the End of the World is coming, then I'd rather die before it comes. Quieter and less frightening. Without the smoke and devils, or all the other corpses wailing in their nightgowns. It's peaceful when you're dead. You don't feel tired or hungry. You don't lose gloves or coats. You're just white inside, like clouds.

'This new-model Tornado can be yours for just one dollar. Simply play four quarters on our . . .'

No. It can't be mine. I haven't got four quarters. I haven't got just one. If you haven't any money, they bury you in dustbin-bags.

I walk away. I don't know where I'm going, or what to do. There are more cars in the street. Shiny ones. Scarlet ones.

I could borrow someone's car.

Borrowing is stealing.

I stop. It won't be peaceful. Or white inside like clouds. Hell is red and hot. Tom Bryden set himself alight once and burnt half his skin and flesh off. He was in hospital six months. But the flames of hell go on and on for ever and they don't give you injections or antiseptic dressings. The Reverend said if we imagined the worst pain possible, then multiplied it by a hundred thousand million, that would be just half an hour in hell. I can't multiply, but it still made me very frightened. I couldn't sleep that night, even though I took my pills. Every time I tried to close my eyes, the blankets caught alight and I could hear the flames licking at my skin.

If I paid Reuben's money back, I wouldn't be a thief, wouldn't burn in hell. I'd be white again like clouds. There's money all around me. The slot machines are choking with it and it's piled up on the stalls. I watch people buying hats, people buying doughnuts. There's sugar on the doughnuts. I can feel it on my tongue. Sweet, and melting slowly, trickling down my throat. You die if you don't eat.

A gang of boys, all dressed the same in black with silver skulls, is marching right towards me. I run across the street to hide, watch the boys pass by. They keep chanting the same words, on and on and on. I don't understand the words. The tallest boy throws an empty bottle in the air. It goes right across the road, crashes into pieces at my feet. They all cheer, then march on.

I stare down at the glass. I can see bits of Carole in it, broken now and bleeding. She has only one eye, a cold and staring one. Her mouth is a red horseshoe, hung the wrong way up. Her luck is pouring out of it. She hasn't got a dress.

A huge gorilla with fat pink lips comes swinging round the corner. I turn and run. I can hear it roaring after me. Its shadow catches mine. My legs hurt. My feet don't fit my shoes. My heart is going faster than my legs. The lights keep playing tricks on me. I'm bumping into rainbows, running over ponds. The water's gold and silver, splashing round my feet. I glance behind. The gorilla is still there, a gorilla with blue denim legs. It snatches off its headdress. It's a man.

I stop. I'm panting. I don't know where I am. There are

no casinos here, only small and dirty shops leaning on each other, as if their legs have given way. 'WORLD'S LARGEST PAWNSHOP' says a sign across the road. Everything is largest in the world here. I don't think they really measure. I've never been inside a pawnshop, but I know what they are. Ella Cartwright went to one in Hastings. She pawned her watch to buy a doll.

'GOLD, SILVER, JEWELRY' says the sign, then – larger – 'READY CASH.'

Silver. I could pawn my silver shamrock. It's not the same as selling. They give you a ticket, so you get it back again. I couldn't sell it. Ever. It's the last bit of my mother. She may have worn it round her neck on a tiny silver chain. It may have touched her skin, listened to her heartbeat.

I cross the road, so I can look in the window. I've never seen so many rings and bracelets. They're piled in bowls, spilling out of boxes. There are two pink necks which haven't got their bodies, but are hung with diamond necklaces. And dead pink hands with rings on. And lots of different watches set to different times. Dead and staring clocks. Cameras with no eyes.

I can see a man inside, an ugly man with tattoos all down his arms. He's watching me, and smoking. He must be very rich. He's wearing rings himself, three or four big gold ones. He hasn't got a shamrock, though. Not one single shamrock in all that crowded window. Shamrocks are lucky, luckier than horseshoes. He might pay me for that luck, pay a lot.

I'm not sure what to do, though. What to say, how to get the money. Another man is watching me as well. A smaller man in a grey mac and a hat. He's not inside, he's outside, standing in a doorway. I feel nervous with his eyes on me like that. I tug at my cardigan, wish it was a coat. Coats hide more of you. I could buy a coat if I had Ready Cash, a cheap one, secondhand, add it to the list of Reuben's shopping.

I try the pawnshop door. It's locked. The man inside looks me up and down again, puts his cigarette out, lets me in.

There's so much stuff inside, I have to walk all round it. It's piled up on the floor. Guns and lamps and furniture, and at least twenty different televisions. Some of them are very old and dusty. Two are still alive and shouting very loud.

I go up to the counter, pass my shamrock over. The man picks it up, but doesn't even glance at it. I wish he'd wash his hands. They're stained with oil and biro. He's looking at the television. Some men in helmets are playing with a ball.

I cough, to prove I'm there.

He turns his head, picks up half a pair of glasses, puts them in one eye, then holds the shamrock right up close to them. He's peering at the tiny silver letters.

'They're not a Message,' I explain. My mother didn't leave a Message on the shamrock. I wish she had. Ten whole words in Plain or Gothic Script. I wish she'd told me where she lived. Or even put her name. I'd like to know her name. I used to try to guess it.

The man says nothing. I think he likes the shamrock. He puts it on a little scale, then holds it in his hands again, closes them around it.

'How much d'ya wanna borrow?' He talks with only half his mouth, like Hans.

I don't know what to say. I haven't worked it out. I must pay Reuben back. That's fifty-seven dollars. And some money for the bus to take his shopping back. And I'd better have some tea, to stop me fainting. Fifty cents. And another dollar to try to win the car. And if I'm going to buy a coat . . .

'How much?' he asks again. He's sounding cross.

'I need four hundred dollars.'

I don't know why I said that. I saw a coat, a cheap one, secondhand, lying on a stall. Then I saw a dress. Not cheap at all. A wedding dress. It stepped down off the stall with Carole in it. Carole smiling, hugging me, whirling me round and round, so I was spinning with the dress, white myself and frothy.

The man is laughing. The laugh is sharp and cruel, claws my face.

'I'll give you twenty.'

I clear my throat. My voice is hiding in it, has curled up in a prickly frightened ball. I try to drag it out. 'It . . . it's worth more than that,' I tell him. 'St Patrick blessed the shamrock, Miss O'Toole said.'

297

'Twenty-five,' he says, picking at a nail. 'That's my final offer. Take it or leave it.'

I lean against the counter. My mother might be angry if I took just twenty-five. She may be watching me. She'll say I'm ungrateful and she can't think why she bothered. She could have kept the shamrock for herself, worn it in her coffin. Twenty-five wouldn't even do the shopping. Not all of it. I'd still be half a thief. I shut my eyes, count the scars on Tom Bryden's arms and legs, try to multiply them by a hundred thousand million. The flames of hell start roaring in the shop.

'No,' I say. 'I'm sorry.'

The man shrugs, gives me back the shamrock. Halfway to the door, I stop, dig down in my bag again.

'I've got something else,' I tell him.

He doesn't answer, so I take my Tiger Tail out, pass it over. 'If you stroke it, you get four hundred times more luck.'

He throws it, really throws it. It falls on to the floor. I leave it there, walk out. He's right. It wasn't lucky.

He bolts the door again. The bolts sound very angry. I stand there on the step. The small grey man is watching still, though he's moved out of the doorway, taken off his hat. He starts edging up towards me.

'Short of cash?' he asks.

I nod. Perhaps he knows another pawnshop, maybe even owns one.

'How much you lookin' for?'

I start explaining about Carole's wedding and how I want to buy the dress for her, but he interrupts me, jerks his thumb towards the 'READY CASH' sign. 'No luck?'

I shake my head, let him see the shamrock, ask him what he thinks it's worth. He weighs it in his hands, bites his lip. He's still looking more at me than at the shamrock, staring at my dress. Perhaps he thinks I stole it. It doesn't match my shoes or cardigan, and all those beads and ruffles must be worth a lot.

'What's your name?' he asks.

'Norah.' I don't say Toomey. He may laugh.

'English?'

'Yes.' They all ask that. They like you to be English.

'Come with me,' he says. 'I think we can do business.'

I'm feeling rather frightened. His face is thin and bony, greyish like his mac. The skin around his eyes is very wrinkled, as if someone creased the fabric when they sewed them in. His hair looks flattened by the hat. He didn't give his own name. I ask him what it is. He doesn't answer. A police car sirens past and he jumps and pulls me with him, down behind a wall.

'Call me Al,' he says, at last, as he lets go of my hand. His voice is very shaky and he's dropped the hat. He leads me through a dark and narrow alleyway into a tiny room with crates and boxes piled all round the walls. Three men in dirty vests are sitting at the bar. Al goes up to them, talks with them a while. I can't hear what they say. I wish there was another woman there. I'd feel safer with a woman.

Al returns with two glasses on a tray. The glasses are so small he must be short of money. There isn't even room for ice cubes. I'd rather have had something hot like tea. With an extra lump of sugar. Sugar stops you fainting. The drink is cold and brown and tastes of tar. It makes me choke. He keeps shifting in his chair, glancing at his watch.

'Norah,' he says, leaning down to face me. 'How'd ya like to do a little job for me? Earn yourself some cash?'

'No,' I say. 'I couldn't take a job. English people aren't allowed to work here.' Carole told me that. 'Anyway, I won't be here that long.' My own words frighten me. Where *will* I be? We're meant to return to England in just five days. But if Carole goes to Israel . . . I try to cough my drink down. 'I need the money now,' I tell him. 'Tonight. The wedding's booked for midnight.'

'Yeah. You said. You need four hundred bucks. That's a lotta money, Norah, a fuckin' gold mine. More than this job's worth.'

He shouldn't use rude words. I stare down at the table, pretend I haven't heard.

'Are you listenin' to me, sister? Hell! I'm trying to save your ass as well as mine. If you help me, then I'll help you – okay? You'll get your fuckin' dough right away, all of it. The job'll take five minutes – maybe less.'

'Five minutes?' I stare at him. 'You'll give me all that money for five minutes?' I hold on to my chair, I'm not sure if I'm dreaming. Perhaps I've fainted. I used to faint a lot. Perhaps Lady Luck's come back. The most I've ever earned before was two-and-six an hour for putting string in carrier bags at Belstead, and that was more than twenty years ago.

Al drains his glass, wipes his mouth. One side tooth is missing. 'Look, Norah, let me put you in the picture. Okay? It's my . . . er . . . mother. She's real sick.'

'Oh, I'm sorry. What's wrong with her?'

He doesn't answer right away. I wish I hadn't asked. It may be something private or embarrassing.

'Heart attack,' he mutters. 'And a stroke.'

'*Both?*' She must be dying. 'Is she in hospital?'

'No. She's . . .' He pauses, drums his fingers on the table.'She's in trouble, Norah. Before she had the stroke, she borrowed money – a shitload. The shark who loaned it wants it back. Like now. If she doesn't pay him back tonight, he'll send his heavies over. They could kill her, easy – an old lady on her own, half-paralysed.'

'Yes,' I say. 'They could.' I push my glass away. I'm too upset to touch another mouthful. She should be in hospital with nurses and a doctor. It's frightening to be ill at home. Vi Miller had a stroke and she couldn't move at all. Or speak.

Perhaps she lost the money on roulette. That could bring a stroke on. Sister says they're often caused by shock. I feel very sorry for her, but I don't know how I can help. I'm not a nurse, and I can't lend her any money. Perhaps he wants my dress for her, to sell.

'I haven't any money. None at all. And this dress . . . It isn't mine. I didn't steal it. It's because I lost my suitcase.'

'It's not the money, Norah. My Mom's got the dough all right. It's sittin' in her fuckin' bank. That's the trouble. She's gotta get it out. I'd do it for her, but she's gotta go in person, sign for it herself. Well, she can't, can she, when she's lyin' sick like that?'

'No,' I say, shocked to even think of it. 'Anyway, the banks are shut by now.'

'She don't need no bank. She's given me her plastic.'

'Plastic?'

'Her card. Credit card. American Express. There's a place at Caesars Palace which gives you cash on them. It's open till seven, weekdays.'

'It's nearly nine,' I tell him, very gently. He must be so upset about his mother, he's lost all track of time.

He looks down at his watch. 'Six thirty.'

'That's wrong,' I say. 'It's stopped.' I've been wandering round Downtown for hours and hours. I lost Carole a whole day and night ago.

'Bob,' he yells. 'What time you got?'

One of the dirty vests takes a watch out of its pocket, shines the face up. 'Six thirty.'

Al shrugs. 'We got thirty minutes, Norah, to make the other end of town. We'll do it easy in my car. Now, all you gotta do is walk into that office and pass this card across. Okay? You'll need her chequebook, too. Just give them to the girl and say you want five thousand dollars.'

'Five *th . . . thousand*?' I can hardly get the word out. His mother must be desperate if she lost five thousand dollars on roulette.

'Yeah. It's a gold card. They let you have five grand on a gold card.'

'Gold?' I whisper. Everything is gold here, even all the names. Gold Rush, Golden Nugget, Golden Gate.

'Don't worry. They won't ask no questions and you don't say nothin' unless they speak to you. That's real important. You just sign my mother's name, okay? Mary Haines.'

'But I'm English. They'll know I'm not your mother.'

'No, they won't. She gets her money from a lotta different places. They don't know her by sight.'

'But I'm single. And she's married. And . . .'

'It's okay. I thought of that.' He pulls a ring out of his pocket, a wide gold wedding ring, slips it on my finger. I stare at it in shock. I'm married. I'm a bride. The ring feels hot and heavy, weighing down my hand. I fumble for my drink again, drain the glass.

'Here's my mother's signature. She writes small but neat, see? Can you copy that?'

I'm very slow at writing, but my writing's always neat, and fairly small. 'I'll try,' I say. My voice and hand are shaking.

Al uncaps his pen, finds a scrap of paper. 'You'll have to practise first,' he says. 'But make it quick. The traffic's always hell on New Year's Eve. If we don't get there tonight, we're fucked. It's a holiday tomorrow and the fuckin' office is shut all day.'

I take the paper from him, pull my chair up closer to the table. 'Anyway,' I say. 'It's tonight they're coming, isn't it?'

'Who?'

'Those men?'

'What men?' He looks suspicious.

'The . . . er . . . heavies.' I've never heard the word before, but it frightened me a lot.

'Yeah, sure they're comin'. We've gotta save her, Norah. They're shits, those guys, won't stop at nothin'. Here, take the pen.'

I turn my sleeves up, push my hair behind my ears. I've got to concentrate. I draw the first stroke of the M. I'm glad her name is Mary. Our Lady's name. Perhaps Al will let me meet her. I could sit with her, be her friend, bring her tea with sugar in. I'd like a friend called Mary.

The M is finished now. It looks quite nice, though Al seems very jumpy and on edge. I show him the whole 'Mary', once I've struggled with the y, which is different from mine, with a longer fatter tail.

'Not bad,' he says. 'But get your ass in gear. Do you always write so fuckin' slow?'

He shouldn't talk like that, use all those wicked swearwords. I'm trying, really trying. I make my hand go faster. The H looks faint and ill.

I can hear Al muttering, tapping with his foot. I think he's ill as well. Drops of sweat are bulging on his forehead, yet the bar is very cold – damp and dark with a stone floor like a cellar.

'Look, you'll have to practise in the car. We gotta leave now.' He's unbuttoning his raincoat, passing it to me. 'Put this on.'

'But . . . But why? It's a man's coat and . . .' My voice just disappears. I'm a man. I'm Mary Haines. Mrs Mary Haines. My legs won't hold me up. I sit down again, too quickly, hold my head.

'Get up.' He yanks my arm. 'What the fuck's the matter with ya?'

'I don't want to go. I can't.'

'Don't fuck with me. You gotta go. My mother could be dead this evenin' if we don't get that money for her.'

'But I'm no good at the writing. The H went wrong and I can't do the y's like that, with tails.'

'Sure you can. You did real great. Just practise some more and by the time we get to Caesars . . .'

'No,' I say. 'I don't like Caesars Palace.' That's where Carole went with Victor. She may take Reuben there. I'll meet him. He'll shout 'Thief!'

Al puts his face very close to mine. 'Five hundred,' he mouths. His breath smells of the drink, and something else – something strong and sour.

'Five hundred what?' I ask. I'd like to go to bed. I don't believe it's half past six. It's midnight.

'Five hundred bucks, you stupid broad. You get me that cash and five hundred of it's yours. No questions asked, okay? Now put this coat on.' He's dressing me himself, forcing my arms into the sleeves, doing up the buttons.

I'm too amazed to help. Five hundred. I can buy the dress, buy wedding albums, wedding flowers, do all Reuben's shopping, even give him change.

Al pushes me in front of him, keeps hold of one wrist, tight. 'Okay, Mary, move!'

'I'm Norah,' I object. He's hurting quite a lot. 'Norah Toomey.'

'No, you're Mary Haines from now on. You gotta think Mary all the way to Caesars. We'll run through it once or twice, okay? Right – I'm the chick in the office. You walk in. I smile. Now what do you do, Mary?'

'I . . . I sign my name.'

'No, you English fuck,' he yells. 'Not *yet*, for chrissakes. You give her the card and cheque.'

'I haven't got them. You didn't give them to me.'

'You'll get 'em, fuckwit. When it's time. You'll also need her driver's licence.'

'But I don't drive. I'm not allowed to. I'm on these pills and . . .'

'Shut the fuck up and listen. We're short of time. Right, you've handed them over. Now what?'

'I don't say anything unless they speak to me.' If I had a driver's licence, I could drink and drive. Then I'd get the pink silk coffin and the headstone. Perhaps he'll let me keep it. His mother couldn't drive now, not when she's so ill.

'Great! You got it, Mary. Now listen to me, okay? They *will* speak. They'll ask you how you want the dough.'

'How I want it?'

'Yeah. All you say is "Gimme a thousand dollars in hundred dollar bills and the rest in . . ." '

I close my eyes. 'A thousand dollars in . . .' I'm trying to remember, learn it off by heart, store it in my brain. My hands and feet are big, but not my brain.

'Okay, Mom, we'll go over that some more in the car, make sure you got it straight. Now, about the cheque. I filled it out, but you gotta sign in front of them, right there at the desk.'

I'm getting rather scared. There's so much to remember. The mac feels clammy on my skin. It's very new and smart, but I don't like wearing men's clothes. He's pulled the belt too tight. I try to let it out a bit.

'Hey, Norah! You're not listenin'. Now what did I just say?'

'The . . . cheque,' I whisper hoarsely. He's still got me by the wrist.

'Yeah. I said they'd have to phone, okay? Don't worry, all they're doin' is checkin' my Mom's credit. It only takes a second. You just act real cool – file your nails or pick your nose or somethin'. But keep your fuckin' mouth shut. Right? We don't want no talkin'.'

I shake my head. I don't think I could talk. My voice has crawled away again.

'Now, when you sign the cheque, take your fuckin' time. Don't panic. But don't be too slow neither. I'll be watchin' just outside. In fact, I may call up the office when you're about to sign. That'll distract the girl a minute, give you space, get her off your back.'

I'm beginning to feel excitement as well as just the fear. His voice is very urgent. He needs me. I'm important. I've changed my name like Carole did. Like Reuben. I'm married, with a ring. A ring means someone wants you. Joined for ever. Mary had a Son. I have a son. He loves me, called me Mom. He's going to save my life, get my money for me, save me from the heavies.

'We're lucky that it's New Year's fuckin' Eve. Those girls will be all dyin' to get off. They'll be thinkin' of their parties, not their job. I doubt they'll notice nothing. And if they've had a drink or two . . .'

We're in the street. I can hear the cough of traffic, feel cold air on my face again. It's still quite dark. I think they've put the lights out. The street is very narrow, closing in above us. We pass three dustbins which have sicked up all their rubbish on the pavement. Empty beer cans. Rotting fruit and greens.

'Get in,' says Al. He's standing by a car. It isn't long or shiny, and someone's punched it in the side. He slams the door. I hear a second slam. Suddenly, we're moving. Very fast. I think we're almost flying. Through the air. It's impossible to write, but I try the M again, just trace it with my finger on my lap. M for Mary. St Joseph lives with Mary. St Joseph loves her. He'll help her get the money, help her do the y's right.

I clutch a handle as the plane swings round a corner in the sky. I try to remember what I have to ask for, how I want the money. I remember something else instead, some other words I stored up in my brain. 'The warmth of each other's touch, the joy of each other's smile, the comfort of each other's nearness . . .'

I touch the ring and smile. 'St Joseph,' I say softly, hear him whisper 'Mary' as he nestles close.

19

I'm a queen. I am. Queen for the day. No, queen for the night. It's a cold night, steely-blue, with a duvet of grey cloud softening the jagged mountain-tops. Each star has been individually polished and re-hung; the whole sky smells of flowers. My flowers. Lilies, roses, freesias, soft green fern like babies' hair. The bouquet feels strangely light as if the flowers were only scent and petal – no stalks or leaves, no thorns. Everything is light. The dress looked quite bulky in the shop, with its full flounced skirt, its layers of petticoats. Now I have it on, I seem to float. I feel completely different in it – no longer Carole Joseph, but Mrs Ben Shmuel. I'm taller, more important, even beautiful. You couldn't not be beautiful in a dress like this. Once I'd zipped it up, all the greedy, grasping, shameful bits of me simply fell away, as if the dress had magical powers to transform anyone who wore it.

I'd actually decided on my honey-coloured dress, neither new nor very special, but the nearest thing to white in my rather scanty wardrobe, and quite pretty in its way. I'd laid it on the bed with lace stockings, a lacy bra and pants, gone to run my bath. It was quarter to eleven, time to change. I'd just stripped off all my clothes when I heard a scuffling outside the door. I stuck my head out. Norah. We stared at one another. She looked absolutely knackered, trailing a grey raincoat I'd never seen before; terror in her eyes, a smudge of dirt across one ashen cheek, and loaded down with an enormous plastic carrier and another bulky bag – Reuben's shopping, I presumed.

I snatched off my bath-cap and went to steady her. She looked about to topple, bags and all.

'I . . . I couldn't find you.' Her voice was hoarse and scratchy, as if someone had stripped its gloss off, rubbed it down with sandpaper. 'You weren't at the fireworks. Or the show.'

I could feel myself blushing, not just my face, the whole of me. The blush clothed me like a body-stocking, head to toe. 'No,' I muttered. 'I'm sorry, Norah. We meant to come, honestly we did, but . . .' My voice tailed off in shame. How could I have let her down like that? It just didn't seem important at the time. Nothing seemed important – neither Norah, nor an eleven-million-dollar Show Spectacular. The only thing which mattered was Reuben's body joined to mine again. God! Love makes you selfish. Poor Norah, all alone with dancing girls and catherine wheels while I set off sparks in Reuben's bed. The blush deepened as I recalled the things he said. He taught me a few Hebrew words, as well as just the Yiddish. Both languages sounded so exotic – sort of passionate and breathy and very complicated. I suspect he was showing off a bit – but so was I. We both perform for one another, and I don't mean just the languages.

Even now, I'm back with him in bed, when I should be on my knees to Norah, begging her forgiveness. It's not easy when I've nothing on. I try to hide my bare boobs with my arms. Norah's really hung up over nakedness – hers or anyone's. I think she was probably born with all her clothes on, struggled out of the womb in a Crimplene Babygro and Damart thermal nappies. She's staring at the wall, looking at if she's holding back the tears. I apologize again, call myself a rat, a louse, a rotten faithless friend. She doesn't say a word. I coax the raincoat from her, use it as a fig leaf.

'Shall I phone down for some tea or something? You look all in.'

She shakes her head, sinks slowly into a chair, one bag across her lap like a monster child. She removes her glasses, shines them up. Her naked eyes look weak and dazed like pale blue shellfish which have lost their homes.

'Well, did you enjoy the show?' I ask her, trying to sound bright. She must have left it early. It's still dazzling on downstairs. I could hear hysterical applause booming from the showroom when I passed it on my way up here, just fifteen minutes ago. Even then, I didn't give a thought to her, just floated down the passage with nothing in my mind but Reuben, Reuben. I really am a swine. She must have felt quite awful sitting there alone, with everybody else romantic couples or happy laughing groups. In fact, it's quite a tribute to what I feel for Reuben, what he makes me feel and do in bed, that we preferred to stage our own private Show Spectacular, than attend the one the posters call a miracle. There won't be any shows like that in Israel – with pumas and white tigers, walls of fire on stage, waterfalls, real cannonfire . . .

Yet Norah has no words for it. No smile for the princes, no whisper for the elephants, no gasp of admiration for the world's biggest stage, which had to be totally remodelled to fit its cast of hundreds, its behind-the-scenes menagerie, its forty different set-changes. The miracle has simply left her cold. She looks as if she's just come back from shock treatment, not from the most lavish extravaganza ever conceived in the whole hype and history of showbiz.

I try again, crouch down on the floor beside her chair, take her hand. 'How about the fireworks? Were they fun? And the balloons? You saw them, did you, Norah, found the square all right?' Norah loves balloons, and these are really something, according to reports. Thousands and thousands of them are released into the sky from the top of the Union Plaza, and float slowly up and up, until the whole night is filled with drifting coloured spheres. Angelique urged me not to miss it, said it's almost more impressive than the fireworks.

Norah continues shining up her glasses, seems unaware she's doing it. Her hands move like automatons, her eyes aren't focused properly. To tell the truth, I'm losing patience with her. I admit I'm in the wrong, but does she have to rub it in, keep up that stubborn silence? I mean, she could say it's okay and let me off the hook, instead of piling on the guilt like this. And she'll make us late if she just sits there looking tragic, staring into space. I'm pretty tense already, with the minutes ticking by and still not dressed or anything. I don't get married every day, for God's sake.

308

'Look, I'm sorry, Norah, honestly. I've said so twenty times. Can't we leave it now?'

No, obviously we can't. I drag myself up from the floor, stand stiffly by the mirror. Weddings are quite stressful without all this extra aggro. Can't she understand that? I just don't know what to do. She's never been like this before, seemed quite so strange and silent. I can see her face, mask-like, in the glass, her shoulders hunched and tense as if she's expecting to be whipped.

She clears her throat, swallows once or twice. 'Are you and Victor still getting m . . . married?' she asks.

'Me and *Reuben* are, yes.' I'm so miffed that she can't even remember my fiancé's name, I fling her coat off, march back to the bathroom. Both taps are thundering still, angry water belching through the overflow. I turn them off, put one toe in. Hot! 'Reuben,' I whisper to myself. If the most romantic and exciting name in all the world means nix to Norah, then I'll lock her out, wallow in my bath, re-run our private magic.

Tap-tap on the door.

I pretend I haven't heard, start humming a rousing Hebrew tune which Reuben had been singing in *his* bath. Actually, he hasn't got a bath. We had to go two floors down to the one he shares with fifteen other people. A bath to me has always been a simple (and private) exercise in washing, with perhaps a little reading or choir-practice thrown in. This was something else entirely. I smile as I remember, feel myself relaxing. Stupid to be cross. Why spoil my one Big Day? Norah probably needs her pills. I'll get them in a minute. Meanwhile, I'm going to have another bath with Reuben.

I close my eyes. He's soaping me, all of me, the inside bits as well as just the outside. He turns the shower to 'fierce', aims the jet right between my legs. We're giggling, both of us, and now he's sort of thrusting down on top of me, water splashing everywhere. We both slide forward, so I can feel the taps hot and hard, digging in my back, and . . .

Louder tapping. Norah never interrupts me normally. She's too well-mannered, hates to make a nuisance of herself. I suppose she must be busting for a pee. (Reuben peed in front of me. I wasn't shocked. I liked it.)

'Can't you hold on just a sec? I'm in the bath.'

'I . . . I bought the dress.'

'I won't be long, I promise. Pee in the flower-vase if you're desperate. Okay?'

No answer.

'Norah?'

Silence.

I'm worried suddenly. She's fainted. Ill. Terribly upset. I yell her name, really loud this time. It echoes round the bathroom, but no answer from outside. Perhaps she's just walked out, had enough of me. I won't have any witness then, or bridesmaid; no loving batty friend to take to Israel.

I leap out of the bath, unlock the door, barge into the bedroom, dripping wet. 'Norah, please don't go. Don't leave me. I know I'm horrid, but . . .'

I stop. I clutch the wardrobe. I'm the one who's dizzy now. The Dress is laid out on the bed. It looks alive, the silky fabric rustling, the full skirt swelling slightly in the breeze from the air-conditioning fan. A bouquet of hothouse flowers has appeared from nowhere and is blooming on the pillows, supported by a huge great book on weddings, and a padded satin photo-album with two white doves cooing on its cover.

Norah's sitting crying. Yes, crying. Her handkerchief is twisted through her fingers, a box of confetti in the other hand. I fling my arms around her.

'Oh, Norah Norah Norah Norah *Norah!*'

I'm soaking her. Her tears are soaking me. No, she's not crying any more. She's sniffing, blowing, smiling, and I'm hugging her and shouting and asking questions and not waiting for the answers and dancing her round and round the room until we both collapse exhausted on the bed (the other bed). By then, I'm dry enough to dare to touch the dress, hold it up against me. We're both silent suddenly, because this moment's somehow sacred – not just the wonder of the dress, but the fact that Norah bought it, did that for me, cared enough.

I still don't understand how on earth she found the cash. The story was so garbled and centred around some poor old thing called Mary whom Norah hoped to meet, but her son dashed off so fast, he didn't even wait to get his coat back. Norah was so concerned about the coat, so frightened that he'd say she'd stolen it, we spent more time on that than on the amazing feat of her swelling fifty-seven dollars to five hundred (which puts the loaves and fishes in the shade). I kept pumping her and pumping her and she began to look quite wretched and embarrassed, and it crossed my mind that perhaps she'd let this 'son' take her to his room and do something quite unspeakable. Surely not? Not Norah. And why should any rich guy proposition a grey-head in scuffed lace-ups, when Vegas is bursting with young talent? In the end, I left it. I was still wild with curiosity, but time was getting really short and I hadn't tried the dress yet.

It's a little long, in fact, but there wasn't time for shortening hems. In fact, we were almost late by the time we'd finished with the bride and started on the bridesmaid. I glance across at Norah. She looks transformed as well. I somehow managed to wrest off her old cardigan and cover up the bra-hooks with a lacy stole from *my* case and I also lent her stockings (sheer ones, not thick lisle), and she even dared a dab of lipstick and a hint of eyeshadow. I catch her eye and smile. We both keep smiling like a pair of loons. She's so thrilled she's coming with us. I talked Reuben into it, said I couldn't leave her. I'll really make it up to her in Israel, pay her back, make her someone special. I love her. Now Reuben loves me, it's easier to love. It's like money making money. All these hostile feelings I had towards my mother, or the irritation I felt with Dr Bates or Sister Watkins have simply disappeared. I can include them in my love now – them and everyone. I love the Jews, the whole great race of Jews, even the Shylocks and the Fagins. I love the Arabs. Reuben says I have to hate them as the Enemy. I can't.

I check my watch again. Ten to twelve. A restless breeze is ruffling my skirt, the clouds fidgeting above me; everything impatient. The other waiting couples are all inside, in a cramped and stuffy room which smells of cheap cologne and hair-oil. I'd never fit in there – not just my flouncy petticoats, but all my layers and layers of happiness, my flowing train of elation and excitement. Anyway, I want to be outside with the cold and clouds and the huge miraculous night. I've hardly seen the Vegas sky before. The man-made lights are so brilliant and obtrusive, they quite eclipse the real stars. Not tonight, though. Tonight they're like confetti, flung in handfuls.

I glide towards my bridesmaid. I love the swish my dress makes – swish and rustle. 'Norah, you're not too chilly, are you?'

'No,' she smiles, smoothing down the gooseflesh on bare arms. Her stole has fallen off. I pick it up, drape it round her shoulders. I long to warm her with my own warmth, shine down on her cold world, thaw it like the sun.

'Happy?' I whisper.

She nods, though her smile has slipped a little, like the stole. 'He's late.'

'Don't worry. He said he might be – just a fraction. He had such a lot to do and I held him up a bit.' More than just a bit. I smile again, a private smile for Reuben.

I loop my skirts up, rustle to the corner where I can see the big main street. Hordes of people, streams of cars, their headlamps steady golden eyes against the ever-changing tangle of the rainbow lights. I couldn't make out anyone, not in all that glare. The place looks like a film set. Crowds of New Year revellers are swarming in the streets, singing and dancing between the hooting scrum of traffic, marching arm in arm along the pavements, smashing magnum bottles against the parking meters, so that champagne foams like Omo in the gutters. I feel they're all my guests – dressed up in my honour with paste-and-tinsel tiaras, or funny hats and paper flowers; drinking my champagne, tramping out my wedding march. There's even a full orchestra. They've bought those things called noise-makers, which I saw this afternoon on all the stalls. It's such a happy noise. One guy's got a whistle; another blows a trumpet, shakes his little bells: wedding bells, fanfare for the bride. 'I love you all,' I whisper, as I skitter back to Norah. I can't just walk. My feet are too excited; my body wants to float.

The chapel doors are opening, the couple booked before

us emerging hand in hand. They're young, both very handsome
– Mexican, I think, dark and sultry-looking, with that coarse
strong hair which reminds you of a horse's mane. I smile at
them, but their world stops at each other's eyes. It's obvious that
he's wonderful in bed, licks her front and back. She'd only look
at him like that if they'd gone pretty far together. Love bonds
you. People only call it lust or sin when they've never done it,
or had cold or clumsy lovers.

Oh, hurry, Reuben, hurry. I want your eyes on me like that;
your hands against this silky dress, so you'll know I have nothing
on beneath it, only shoes. I take my watch off, hold it in my
hand, as if that way I can control the time – and Reuben. Two
minutes to go. The chapel director has come out of his office
and is flapping round us. If a bride or groom is late, he says, then
he's sorry, but the couple lose their slot. He's booked solid as it
is, and if he hangs around for us, he'll make everybody else late.
But not to worry, he'll fit us in later, between bookings, as soon
as my friend shows up.

Friend. Reuben's not my friend. He's my flesh, my cause, my
life.

'We've still got fifty seconds,' I say, as coolly as I can. Sweat
trickles down my back, contradicts my voice. I can hear the fifty
seconds hammering in my head. Ten to go. Seven, six, five,
four, three . . .

'Happy New Year,' I say to Norah, looking past her as I hug
her, so I won't miss even a second's-worth of Reuben. The
time doesn't matter, actually. It's just a fiction. They said
'Happy New Year' at the fireworks and that was only nine
o'clock. (We heard it on the radio, in bed.) Nine o'clock in
Vegas is midnight in New York, you see, and since they show
the Vegas fireworks on eastern-time-zone television, they have
to stage them three hours in advance. It's like they move the
New Year forward here, to fit in with New York. Television
rules, okay? (As usual.) The whole time thing's frightfully
complicated. There's a place near here, on the Colorado River,
which stands between two time zones, so you can cross back
and forward from the old year to the new; cling on to the past
for one hour more, or leap into the future at eleven. It makes

me feel quite weird; more so when I think of Jan in England. Her New Year started hours and hours ago, whereas people in Tahiti or Hawaii have still two hours to wait.

I'll decide my own time. My New Year can only start with Reuben. The clock will strike the moment he arrives. *This* midnight means nothing much at all. It's merely local custom, a convenience for other, simpler people like the couple after us who've just been summoned from the waiting-room to take our place. They both look really scruffy; he couldn't find his razor, she didn't iron her shirt. I loathe them. They're smiling, shaking hands with the minister. He looks wrong as well – no robes, no flowing vestments, just a loud blue suit with two-tone shoes, like some vulgar flash tycoon. Has he really taken orders, learnt his Bible, or was he simply borrowed from the nearest business school? And where's our Rabbi? I suppose he's late, like Reuben, or did his price go up for New Year and we were twenty dollars short?

The chapel doors close behind the three of them, almost in my face. I'm tempted to wrest them open, yell out 'Wait your turn!' How can I, with no Reuben? I stare dully at the wood (fake wood). There's a notice on the doors: 'PLEASE – no food or beverages. No bare feet. No chewing gum.' That's ridiculous, uncalled-for. Brides are hardly likely to march in barefoot with a double strawberry cornet instead of a bouquet, or bridegrooms smuggle in Kentucky Fried. Why ruin everything, remove all the dignity of marriage? And look at that really hideous drinks machine, stuck right outside tbe chapel, with dirty paper cups littered on the floor. If they had to put it there, couldn't they have chosen something tasteful, without that massive-breasted cowgirl holding out her Coke to us and winking one green eye? The place looks like a bar-room, not a church.

A new couple wander up. I think they're only tourists, gawping at my dress, but the chapel director is already muscling in.

'Wanna get married, sir?'

He makes it sound like some cheap souvenir. 'Wanna baseball cap? Free hot dog, free wedding?' Hardly free. Every time I've been into his office, there's someone writing out a cheque or handing over money. Marriage is a cash transaction here.

I follow his expensive gold-trimmed loafers back into the office. It's the only place that's warm. A radio is blaring. A bomb attack in Phoenix: ten dead and fifty hurt. A fire in Reno – three children and a baby burnt to death in bed; a madman on the loose in Salt Lake City; pile-ups on the freeways everywhere. The newscaster signs off: 'Happy New Year.' Yeah, *very* happy.

The chapel doors re-open and the two slobs shuffle out. Their wedding took under seven minutes. The basic chapel fee is fifty dollars, which must work out at not far short of eight dollars a minute.

The director darts back to check on me again. He's wearing a red carnation like a groom himself, a strained and harassed groom.

'No,' I say. 'He hasn't come. Not yet. Yes, of course I understand. Go ahead – marry anyone you like. Mustn't waste a minute. That's eight whole dollars.'

I hate this place. Everything is fake. Fake ministers, fake grass (they've bought it by the yard); fake stained glass (it's perspex); fake candles (all-electric); fake flowers (dye and plastic); even fake marriages. I bet half these couples are only here because they're semi-sloshed, or had a big win at the tables and decided to get married just on impulse. It happens all the time. The director told me so himself when we had our chat this morning. He seemed to rather like me (he doesn't now), offered me coffee, sugared it with funny (tragic) stories about a guy who married ten times in succession, after nine quick-fire divorces, and another chap who turned up at this chapel with a girl he'd met just half an hour before. They divorced as well. Hilarious.

He stays open twenty-four hours a day, seven days a week, so he can catch every passing drunk, cash in on every instant lust or whim, keep his till ringing round the clock. He's pretty fake himself, with his hair so glossy dark it's either dyed, or stick-on, like his regulation smile. Does he have to bare his teeth at me when he's obviously pissed off?

I escape into the waiting room. It's far too cold to hang

around outside now. Anyway, it's really rackety. I don't know why these chapels are all built near busy roads – brakes screeching, throb of engines, whoops from passing drunks. Norah follows like a spaniel. There are no spare seats, so I slump against the wall, Norah fussing with my dress. The next couple are summoned, get up, hand in hand. Japanese. He's in just his shirt sleeves, she in a simple cotton skirt. I'm overdressed – that's obvious – dolled up for St Paul's Cathedral or Westminster Abbey, when this chapel's hardly bigger than a shack and not much more substantial. How could I have chosen such a dump? A painted plywood gingerbread-house for the most important ceremony of my life. Except it isn't going to happen, by the looks of it. It's a wonder no one's laughing. The only real traditional bride, three foot deep in tulle and outswanking all the rest, with just one small thing missing – the bridegroom. I laugh myself. Ha ha. Norah jumps.

'Have you seen him?'

'No,' I snap. 'Do you imagine I can see through walls?'

Norah looks ludicrous as well, the Blue Pearl on her eyelids smudged into blue bruise, her varicose veins showing through sheer stockings, and that stupid beaded dress with its white bra-back. I drag her outside again. I can't keep still, can't stay in that room with all those smug and smirking couples. Everyone in couples. A few doting mothers, giggly friends. Anyway, maybe Norah's right. Maybe Reuben has come.

I use my eyes like searchlights, sweep them over chapel, shop and street. A huge jacuzzi-limousine is drawing up, all forty foot of it. You can hire that for a hundred dollars extra – book a half-hour champagne-tour of Las Vegas. There's a hot tub in the back, with mink-upholstered seats, and black glass in the windows to ensure your privacy. I'd rather have Reuben's cracked enamel bath with its badly fitting plug – so long as he was there.

He isn't.

Maybe he's been held up by the crowds, even hurt. They're getting really vicious, judging by the racket. I trudge back to the corner, so I can check on the main street again. The bright and happy New Year has already turned to ashes. The crowds aren't dancing any more, but fighting and rampaging; smashed bodies in the gutter now, not just broken bottles. Policemen are hitting out with truncheons, clawing bloody louts apart. A girl vomits down her black ranch mink. A desperate baby howls and howls, abandoned in a pushchair looped with streamers. The pavements are ankle-deep in litter; burst balloons, spent rockets, limp and dirty flower-garlands adrift on pools of beer. I can still hear all the noisemakers – screeching whistles, shrill and jangling bells. Music for a nightmare, not a wedding.

I feel a cold hand on my arm. It's Norah, come to find me. She looks haggard, terror-stricken. She also needs a pee. I take her to the toilets, mooch out into the tiny square of courtyard where I waited before, just this afternoon. Then, I was with Reuben, sprawled out on that wrought-iron bench, yet really in his bed – one with him, joined to him. Now I'm all alone, grown old in half a day. I pace up and down, up and down, trying to think of nothing, grey and faded nothing. Ten minutes later, Norah joins me. Her stole has slipped again. Her teeth are chattering. Her eyes stray to the bench as well, then look away. I try to whistle, but no sound comes out at all. Norah breaks the silence first.

'He's not coming, is he, Carole?'

'He *is*!' I want to scream. 'Of course he is.' How can she be so *dim*? 'He's got things to do, that's all. He's a busy man. Important. Important people are often late for things.'

He was late before. This afternoon. He said four sharp at the Courthouse, then turned up at twenty past. Those twenty minutes were deliberately sadistic, spun out each cruel second like an hour. It was horrid in that queue, especially on my own, with everyone else in brash and cocky twosomes. Some were really foul, pissed and pushy, or reeking of BO. Even after Reuben joined me, I didn't feel too bright. He seemed terribly on edge and sort of snappy. I assumed he was just tired after our wild and sleepless night together, or maybe simply anxious about all he had to do still, when the queue was only moving at a snail's pace.

Now I realize he was probably trying to tell me that he'd changed his mind, but couldn't pluck up courage. Simpler just to go through with the licence, then do a bunk, buzz off.

It's probably the whole Jewish thing. I'm not a Jew – he told me so himself, and though I can convert, it's not the same. He said it didn't matter, but obviously it does now. Most Jewish men wouldn't touch a *shiksa*.

I sink down on to the bench, remembering the other words he taught me – lovers' words, private words. Norah sits as well, but leaves a gap between us, as if she's scared I'll shout again. She stares down at her hands. They're trembling, blue with cold. I feel a rush of shame. She waited all the evening, not just twenty minutes. I can see her suddenly, loaded down with shopping, walking round in frantic hopeless circles, jostled by the crowds. Or deafened in the showroom, hemmed in by cackling strangers. I let her down, left her on her own. Yet she didn't complain, didn't hurl abuse at me, or demand an explanation. *I* was the one who got angry and unreasonable.

'Oh, Norah . . .'

'What?'

'I feel so awful.'

'He'll come. He's very busy.' She's returning me my words, doing everything to comfort me, shaking out the stole, swathing it round my shoulders when her own are gooseflesh-bare.

'No, I don't mean Reuben. You, Norah. You waited hours and hours for us and . . .' My voice just peters out. God! I'm vile. And then I dare to say I love her, swan around beneath the stars boasting that I love the world. I don't know what love is. She does. Even now, she's looping up my skirt, trying to keep it clean.

'Shall we play "I Spy"?' she says. 'Just to pass the time till Reuben comes.'

An aeroplane kindly fills the silence. I know what we're both thinking. My face starts crumpling up. I force it back to normal. 'O . . . okay,' I stammer. 'You begin.'

'I spy with my little eye something beginning with . . . with . . . with D.'

I shiver. It's really raw now, the iron bench cold and hard beneath the tulle. D for damp. A randy wind is groping up my skirt. It knows I've left my pants off. No one else will. D for desertion. D for dark, depression, dastard.

'D for dog,' I say instead. I can't see any dogs, but we've played 'I Spy' before and Norah sometimes spies things no one else can.

She shakes her head.

D for drunks, I wonder? No, they're out in the street, with a lot of other D's. Danger and destruction. Damage, deathblows, debris. 'D for drains,' I try.

'No.'

'D for daisy?' I bend down to pick it up. It's a lump of chewing gum, well-sucked and dirty grey. I hold it in my hand – my daisy in the dark – feel tears splash warm and stupid on my fingers.

'Give up?' asks Norah. She likes it when I give up in 'I Spy'. I nod.

'D for *dress!*'

Of course. D for Dress. The most expensive lavish dress I've ever owned – and all for thirty minutes' empty vanity. No wonder Reuben hasn't come. He tried to show me there were more important things than clothes. I sit in silence.

'Your turn,' prompts Norah.

I mop my face, grateful for the dark. 'I spy with my little eye something beginning with...' I pause, leap up. Someone's calling me. '*R!*' I shout. I can't spy anything, but I can hear him.

'Wait here!' I yell to Norah. 'Hold my flowers.' I toss her the bouquet. R for roses, rapture, sheer relief.

I run, trip, recover, bunch my dress up, hurtle on.

'Reuben, *darling* . . .' I'm crying, laughing, both at once. I knew he'd come. He's kissing me, and the entire world's clocks are chiming midnight in our mouths, all the bells ringing out New Year; rockets, golden rain, coloured streamers . . .

He pulls away, and I see him for the first time – his crumpled denims, scuffed and dirty sneakers. I hoped he'd wear all white, like Jewish bridegrooms do, or at least a clean white shirt. He looks tired and really drawn. He probably had too much to do – just couldn't fit it in and still have time to change. It doesn't matter. He's here – and that's enough.

319

The director scurries over. I almost kiss him too. Yes, of course we'll wait ten minutes. I'll wait for ever now Reuben's here beside me. There's no sign of the Rabbi. That doesn't matter either. The minister can marry us. I was far too hard on him. I *like* his suit. It's smart. And the shoes are quite unusual. He escorts an elderly couple into the chapel.

They're beautiful. I love them. White hair, bridal white. Six thin unsteady legs, their witness even older and more doddery.

Witness. Norah. Shivering on that bench. We need her and my flowers. 'Don't go away,' I call to Reuben. 'I'm going to fetch the bridesmaid.' I dart back to him, whisper in his ear. 'Will you kiss her, Reuben? Just for me. A really lovely kiss, one she'll treasure always. Don't scare her. Make it very gentle, but . . .'

He nods, seems nervous, keeps glancing at his watch. I think he's still upset about being late, impatient to make up for lost time. I'm impatient, too, impatient to be married and then to be alone with him – back in bed for a few snatched private hours before our flight. I'll let him rest first, really sleep, revive. I hate to see him quite so tired and tense. Oh, he's wonderful. I love him. Oh, Norah, Norah, Norah, just wait until you see him.

She's still sitting on the bench, eyes down, bouquet gripped stiffly in her hands, big brown feet turned out. I'm worried suddenly. What will Reuben think of her? He's used to girls like Angelique and Cheryl. I tried to explain that Norah's fairly simple and not that young, and . . .

'Norah?'

'Yes?'

'Look, don't say too much, will you? I know you never do, but don't go on about the hospital.'

She looks hurt and almost frightened. I lean over, hug her and the flowers. God! It's difficult. Perhaps she won't approve of Reuben either. Norah doesn't go for jeans, and she'll see they're frayed and dirty. I just wish he had a tie on. I know it doesn't matter, but . . .

I smooth my own dress down. 'He's . . . not dressed up, Norah. He doesn't care about that sort of thing. He thinks it's unimportant and we ought to . . .' I wheel round. I can hear shouts and running feet, a sudden piercing shriek. Those ruffians in the street must have got into the chapel, the drunken New Year rampage spread as far as here. I grab Norah by the hand, drag her after me. We'll be safer back with Reuben if there's going to be a shindig.

We pound up to the chapel, stop in shock. The doors are open. A vase has been knocked over, plastic flowers tangled on the floor. The white-haired bride is sobbing, the minister and bridegroom dashing out. Three policemen armed with guns and truncheons are hurtling down the street. They're chasing someone. A lout, a tramp, a tall dark shifty figure still streaking well ahead of them. I shade my eyes against the fusillade of lights. It's Reuben.

'No!' I yell. 'You're chasing the wrong man. That's my husband, not a criminal. *He* wasn't drunk or fighting. He hasn't done a thing. Stop! Please stop them, someone.'

No good. They're catching up with him. One huge cop draws level, trips him up. A police car screeches round the corner. He's bundled in.

'No!' I scream again – or try to scream. It comes out as a whisper. They must have gagged me, tied me up. My legs won't move at all now. All the churning, sickening motion's in my stomach; sirens in my stomach, blaring out as the police car speeds away. Two red eyes growing smaller smaller smaller in the dark. It's very dark. I think it's just a dream. Norah's in the dream. I can hear her voice, feel her ice-cold hands on mine.

'He's here,' I say. 'Don't worry. He's come. We need the flowers.'

Someone's crying. I touch my cheeks. They're dry. Little knots of people are gathering on the pavement, more cars sweeping up. One I've seen before. A red Mercedes. The driver's door swings open and a girl gets out, dashes over, grabs my arm, drags me with her back towards the car. I can smell Anaïs Anaïs. That's Angelique's perfume. And her voice.

'Carole – quick! Get in.'

I try to struggle. Even if I'm dreaming, I've got to be with Reuben, save him, kill those brutal cops. 'Get away! You're hurting, Angelique. You're only jealous. You slept with him, I know you did. He told me so. Get off!'

She slaps me, hard, and suddenly everything is red – the car, the night, the speed; the lights flashing flaring past us as we hurtle down the freeway, the pounding music painful in my head.

I shut my eyes and red slumps slowly, dully, into black.

20

Carole's dead, I think. She hasn't said a word. There's just some music playing, very loud. I can still hear sirens. The police caught Reuben, but they were really after me. They thought I'd stolen the raincoat and the ring. I meant to give them back, but Al rushed off too fast. He said he had to catch a plane. He shouldn't have done that when his mother was so ill. I think we're flying now. You can fly in cars. We did before, in Al's. I wasn't frightened then. I'm frightened now, very very frightened.

Carole's in the front with Angelique. I can only see her head, and that's bent over. It reminds me of a flower-head, a dead one on a broken stalk. I keep reaching out to touch it, hoping it will move. It doesn't.

There's someone else beside me in the back. I'm not sure who he is. He doesn't speak at all and when I said 'hallo', he only stared. I edge away from him, jerk forward once again, stroke Carole's hair.

She stirs and moans. I'm so happy. I start laughing. Right out loud. Angelique turns round.

'What's wrong?'

'She isn't dead.'

'Who?'

'Carole.'

Carole hears her name, turns round herself. Her face looks very pale, her eyes half shut. I don't think she remembers who I am.

'Norah,' I remind her. 'Norah Toomey.'

She doesn't smile or say hallo, just turns back again. I dropped her wedding flowers, left them on the bench. She's probably very cross.

Angelique starts talking to her. I can hear their voices, but I can't make out the words. Then Carole starts to cry, really sob. Her tears are on my own cheeks, running down. I wipe them off. I mustn't make a noise or they'll tell me to get out, leave me all alone again, like I was Downtown when they set off all those fireworks. I don't think they were fireworks. That was Israel. They were blowing up the town. I saw the ambulances, and there were policemen everywhere. The police in Israel all have guns. And carry long black shiny bombs. The bombs went off, all of them at once. It was the loudest noise I've heard in all my life.

I can hear it now, again. Black holes in the sky, tall buildings falling down. I try to run. I'm trapped. Heads and bodies pushing shoving round me. Yellow eyes which never shut. People singing foreign songs. Crashes, showers of sparks.

The birds are terrified. Pigeons flapping round and round the sky. They're trying to escape. They can't. No one can escape. I can feel their wings beating in my chest. The police are very angry. They're punching people, even those who've died. I can see the dead ones bleeding in the street. One man has no face. Only bruises.

Everyone is screaming. My throat hurts with their screams. My ears are full of sparks. An ambulance roars up, almost runs me over. The ambulance men throw people in like luggage. I'm frightened they'll throw *me*. I crouch behind a door, hide my eyes. Someone kicks my back. I can hear a woman being sick, sobbing in between.

It's cold. It's very cold. I dare not wear the raincoat.

They'll say I stole it, stole the dress. The dress is heavy, weighing down my arm. I took it back to the hotel, but Carole wasn't there, hadn't left a note. I thought she'd be in Israel, but there were only more loud bangs – coloured bangs, pink and blue and gold. All the pavements trembling. Echoes in my head. I saw Reuben, though, in Israel. His eyes were burn-holes and he was wearing dirty jeans. Forty of him, fifty, pressing up against me. I could smell his smell: hair oil and fried onions. He opened his mouth and a siren started wailing. On and on and on.

Quick! Out of bed and into the air-raid shelter. Miss O'Toole is running; heavy feet clattering on the stone. 'Hurry, children! Get your gas-masks on.' The sky is red and grazed. I can hear the planes. German planes. We stumble down the cold stone steps. A big boy pushes past me. I trip, get up, limp on. Both my knees are cut. I can't see the blood, only feel it slimy. It's very dark and gloomy in the shelter. Wars are always dark. They put blackout on the sun. We don't eat in the shelter, only cups of cocoa. That's dark as well, with skin on.

We sit there hours and hours. I wet my knickers. No one sees. The stone is damp already, damp and hard. Someone reads to us. The children in the story have real parents and a dog. Miss O'Toole's not listening. She's talking to herself, or maybe to Our Lady. She's scared. Bombs blow you into bits. They don't always find the bits, so when you go to heaven, parts of you are missing.

I think we've died already, gone to hell. I can see the flames, real flames in the showroom; devils dressed as acrobats jumping through a fire; red and orange dancing-girls holding lighted torches. Dancing flames. I'm frightened. The noise is hot and crackling. We had a fire at Belstead and two patients burnt to death. There's a lot of smoke choking from the stage. Pink smoke. It can't be hell. The smoke is black in hell and people don't keep clapping.

There's more smoke all around me. Cigars and cigarettes. The Belstead fire was started by a lighted cigarette. I'm a long way from the exit. There's music playing which is too big for the room and is screaming to get out. I must get out myself. I'm hot, I'm catching fire. I struggle to my feet, pick up all my parcels. I'm still carrying Carole's dress. I think it's only ashes. Four hundred dollars for a bag of ashes. White for funerals. It costs less to bury corpses than to burn them.

'Sit down,' says someone. 'I can't see through your head.'

I sit. I start to cough. 'Ssh,' says someone else. The cough won't ssh. It needs a glass of water. Everyone is drinking, but it isn't water. I gulp my own drink. The waiter brought me one, though I didn't ask him for it.

I'm cooler now. It's raining on the stage and all the dancing-girls have taken off their clothes and put up gold umbrellas. I shiver. The rain is gold as well, and turns into a storm. Claps of thunder, music terrified. The lightning flickers right across the room. No. It's worse than lightning. It's green, and cuts like knives, cuts me right in half. I'm bleeding thin green blood. I crouch behind my shopping, but it pounces on me there, shoots right through my eyes. I close my eyes. It's safer in the dark.

It's thundering again. I can't see anything, but I can hear the bangs and crashes, hear the rain still beating beating down. I feel my arms. They're dry. I think I must be ill. You don't have storms inside. I fumble in my handbag, find a pill, force it down. I swallow smoke as well, and music, but at least it makes the thunder stop.

Four elephants walk on. They have red bows on their ears like Sally-Ann. They stand on their back legs and turn slowly round and round, so all their private parts are showing. Everybody laughs. I don't. It's not nice when people laugh, especially at your body.

They don't laugh at the tigers. The tigers are angry, showing all their teeth. You can't hear them roaring because the other roar is louder – the people roar, the clapping roar. I'm feeling worse. I'm far too near the tigers. Their mouths are caves, with scarlet at the back. Their eyes are yellow glass.

I think I took the wrong pill. It may have been a fruit drop. I'm seeing small white birds now. A man in a black suit has taken off his top hat and put it on a table. It's covered with a cloth. Every time he moves the cloth, another bird flies out. Then he waves his wand and the birds all disappear. The clapping gets so loud, I block my ears. The birds have all flown back again and are circling round the stage.

I think I'd better leave. You need stronger pills for birds. All I saw before were coloured lights. There are more of those, far more, spangling all the curtains, turning people's skin blue. We haven't had the Princes yet. I think they died in Israel.

I pick my parcels up. People say 'Ssh' again, 'Sit down.' They're angry like the tigers. I keep bumping into them, tripping over tails. Angry swishing tails. It's pitch dark in the showroom, once I've turned my back, but I can see their yellow eyes. I stop a moment, glance back at the stage. It's full of angels, angels with bare bosoms. Their wings are red and purple, their hair is silver-green. More and more of them, flying down the golden stairs from heaven, filling the whole stage. They're singing holy songs. They have feathers on their heads as well as wings, and great long shining trains.

The music changes. It's not holy any more, but very fast and wild. They're kicking up their legs. Angels don't have legs. Or big white wobbling bosoms. I turn and run. They're running after me, coming right down off the stage. The tallest has a snake wrapped round her body. A real snake, very long. I can see it moving, see its flickering tongue. Snakes are dangerous. St Patrick drove them all away. I wish they had him here.

I can't get out, can hardly move at all now. My legs have turned to feathers, and there are all these seats and people in the way. I can hear shouts and roars behind me; tiger-roars, people-roars. They're after me, like Reuben. Angry sirens, policemen firing guns. I'm not inside, I'm outside, back Downtown again. More fireworks – bombs – exploding all around me. Showers of sparks. Huge bangs from the music. Everybody screaming, like before. This time I'll be killed. I turn a corner, fall between two buildings, lie face-down in the street.

'Norah, what's the matter with you? Can't you keep still there in the back?'

I get up from the showroom floor. It's not the street – not Downtown at all. It's moving. Moving very fast. It's turned into a plane.

'You're pissing Angie off, Norah. She says if you don't sit still, she'll make you drive yourself.'

That's Carole's voice, her laugh. She was crying earlier on, but I think that was a dream. She's drinking. From a bottle. A tiny one. Things are always small on planes. She's holding out the bottle. Angelique grabs it, tips her head back. She's drinking while she's driving. It's New Year's Eve, so she'll get a funeral.

I'd like to drive, but I haven't got a licence now. Al took that away, with the money and the card. He only left the ring. I'm Mrs Mary Haines. I'm very old and ill. My head is polished granite with ten words written on it. The writing's very wobbly. I think it's had a stroke. The y's have swollen tails.

'Norah?'

I can't answer.

'Norah, we're going to a party.' Carole laughs again. I don't know why she's laughing. Perhaps she's glad she isn't dead.

'A New Year's party.' She's found another bottle, a bigger one this time. She giggles through her drink. 'Happy New Year!' She kisses Angelique, who slaps her off. 'Happy New Year, Toomey-in-the-back.'

'Happy New Year,' I say. She never calls me Toomey now, not since we've been friends.

'Happy New Year,' she says again, to no one. I wish she wouldn't say it. They said it at the fireworks, shouted it out loud. People kissed me. Strangers. And the kisses smelt of beer. One man tried to strangle me. I don't like being kissed. Then everybody danced, right there in the street. I was holding two hot hands – men's hands, black men's hands – and they dragged me round and round. It was difficult to dance because my feet kept falling over things: broken bottles, dirty cardboard crowns. I said I'd like to stop, please, but no one seemed to hear. So we went on round and round. Round and round. Miss O'Toole said the earth spins all the time, but before I'd never felt it.

'Hey, Norah . . .'

'Yes.'

'See that guy beside you?'

'Yes.'

'That's Angelique's big brother. Say hallo to Angelique's big brother.' They both laugh then, Angelique as well.

'Hallo,' I say, again.

He doesn't answer. Carole laughs instead. 'Today's his birthday. Say "Happy Birthday", Norah.'

I don't say anything.

'It's not a birthday party, it's a really special do – a rave-up. Guess where they're holding it.'

'On a . . . boat?'

'No, you nut.'

I don't think she's my friend, not any more. I can hear it in her voice. Angelique's her friend. She kissed her, called her

Angie. She's shouting at me now, turning round and shouting.

'Scotty's Castle, that's where! I thought Angelique was kidding, but she's not. It's a real castle in the desert, built by this guy who pretended he'd found a gold mine when he hadn't.'

She thinks I stole the dress. I couldn't tell her how I earned the money. Al made me swear I wouldn't. He said if I breathed a word to anyone, I wouldn't have a mouth to speak at all. He used a lot of swear-words, horrid words. I've said too much already; told Carole about Mary. If Al finds out, he'll send his heavies over. I know what heavies are now. I saw them in the streets.

At least I hid the ring. I'm more scared about the ring than anything. It's gold, real gold, so they're bound to say I stole it, even Carole. I'd like to give it back, but I don't know where Mary lives. I put it in my pill bottle, the empty one I keep for ladybirds. Then I wrapped the bottle up and pushed it through the lining in my handbag. (The lining's torn already. I didn't make a hole.)

They may still find it if they confiscate my bag. So I crossed out 'Norah Toomey' on the label, 'Three times a day with meals', and wrote 'MARY'S RING' instead. They'll know it isn't mine then, and that I meant to give it back.

'You're not listening, Toomey. We're going to a castle for a binge. It's very grand with eighteen fireplaces.'

That can't be true. It's very hot in deserts, so you wouldn't need a fireplace. I've seen pictures of the desert in my library books. And there are deserts in the Bible. I think St Joseph lived in one. Or near one.

'And fourteen bathrooms. Scotty's buried there. Not in a bathroom.' Carole laughs and hiccoughs. 'His grave is up a hill. His real name was Walter Scott. Not the Ivanhoe one.' A hiccough takes her voice away, then back it comes again. 'He was called Death Valley Scotty.'

'Why?' I ask. I feel too tired to talk, but it's rude if you say nothing.

'Because that's where he lived – where he built the castle.'

'Where?'

'Death Valley.'

I don't say anything. I know we're going to die now. Angelique turns round.

'It's famous, Norah – a huge great National Park, with a hotel and a ranch and lots of things to see: old borax mines and ghost towns and museums. Scotty's Castle is a museum now itself. The party won't be there, not in the main house. It's full of all this precious stuff – you know, chairs and rugs and curtains which Scotty chose himself. They guard it with their lives.'

Carole interrupts. 'Where's it going to be, then? On the roof or something?'

'Could be! They got pretty wild last year. Some guests even broke into the basement where the ghosts are said to walk. No – it's at the Hacienda. That's the guesthouse in the grounds where the unit manager lives. He's a pal of mine, invites me up each year. Mind you, I've never been as late as this before. They'll be well away by now.'

'Angie had to work late, didn't you, Angie?' Carole nudges her. 'D'you know what Angie does, Norah?'

'She's a dancer,' I reply. Carole told me that already.

'No, Angie's not a dancer. Angie's . . .'

'Shut up, Carole. And put that gin away. You've had enough.' Angelique glances back at me again. 'It's quite a drive, Norah. We cross the boundary into California soon.'

California. That's where God is angry. Where they have the storms and earthquakes. I clutch the seat. I wish I could get out.

'I know this road backwards. Another of my friends is a ranger in the park, and I go visit him a lot – well, not in summer. You frizzle to a cinder in the summer. It's the hottest driest place in the whole United States.'

'Hot?' I say, alarmed.

'Yeah. The hottest in the world maybe. Some years, there's not a single drop of rain from December to December. You can die there in the heat. I came across a grave once – a rough cross made of stones with this guy's name scratched across it and RIP. Another time, I almost walked into a dead coyote, just a heap of bones, bleached white in the sun. And birds die, scores of them. Just last year, a flock of geese mistook the salt flats for a stretch of water. They flew in to rest.' She laughs. 'Eternal rest! And the first whites who ever came here mostly died of exposure, or exhaustion. Then the gold prospectors followed and . . .'

'Angelique,' I say. 'I . . . I need to go.'

'What?'

I'm too shy to say it twice. I wish I had a house with fourteen bathrooms, all with toilets in.

Carole stops drinking, wipes her mouth. 'Norah's busting for a pee. You'll have to stop. It's probably only nerves. You're frightening her.'

'I can't stop. Sorry, Norah, but we're late enough already. Anyway, I'm scared the cops are after us. Now they've got Reuben, he may say anything, really drop us in it. I don't intend to take my foot off the gas until we're safe at Scotty's.'

I cross my legs and try to hold the nerves in. Carole starts to sing, a sad song, very sad. I can feel the wet trickling down my legs.

I edge up to the window, as far away as possible from Angelique's big brother. He isn't big at all. I heard her call him George, which used to be a king's name. His face is squashed and his eyes are very small and hiding in it. The wet has reached my shoes. Some has gone the other way, so even my vest is damp. My face is hot with shame. I'm glad it's dark; dark outside as well. The road is angry. It's put out all its lights and is running very fast to catch us up. There are no other cars or buildings, just black and blurry shapes like huge policemen crouching down, waiting to spring out.

I've stained the beaded dress. It isn't mine. I may have stained the car seat. They'll make me pay, make me iron the sheets. I haven't any money. This evening I was rich. I can see the gold card shining in my hand, the jangling gold bracelets of that woman in the office; the gold ring on my other hand. They'll ask me where the ring is, why I took the raincoat.

I stare out at the dark. A big lighted sign is looming up. Gold letters in the black. 'WELCOME TO CALIFORNIA, THE GOLDEN STATE.' We seem to fly right through it, gold on both my hands again, gold on Carole's hair. I shut my eyes to block it out.

I don't like gold.

331

21

Those are mountains, real live mountains. They *are* alive. I saw them stretch and smile. And they spoke to me. 'Don't go,' they said. 'Stay here.'

I'd like to stay. I'm happy. I knew I'd love the mountains. They're so tall they can see God. They're not like the pictures in the books. Those were sharp and jagged, with ice and snow and Christmas trees on top. These are brown and bald. I think St Joseph lived here. The land looks very old. Its face is lined like his is, and it wears his colour, brown.

It's not hot, not at all, just cool and fresh and clean. No party smells or people smells. Not even any flowers. There's nothing bright or green. Just sandy-brown and grey-brown, and a little quiet blue mist. Angelique was wrong about the tourists. She said they came to visit. There's no one here. Just me. The silence is thick and padded like an eiderdown. I wrap it round me, smile.

I'm the only one who has a morning. Everyone at Scotty's is asleep. The party went on all night, all day, and then another night, and then the sun came up and people went to bed.

I came out here instead. I don't like parties and it wasn't a real castle. Everybody laughed too much and drank too much and one man tried to touch me on my chest. I couldn't drink myself. I knew I'd need to go, and no one ever told me where the toilet was. In the end, I had to do it outside and I disturbed two men kissing in the dark.

The gardens were quite big and there were lots of people in them, playing games and laughing, or creeping into bushes and taking off their clothes. Some kept all their clothes on, but jumped into the pond. They came out slimy wet, with green stuff in their hair. They didn't dry themselves, just went on laughing, drinking.

Carole disappeared. I only saw her once. She had taken off her wedding dress and was dressed in Angelique's clothes. They didn't fit her. Nor do mine. I'm wearing George's jeans. I don't like jeans, but there's nobody to see me. No mirrors to make three of me, then laugh at all of them. No cars or lights or music. It's like the chapel name – vale of peace. Not even any birds. The Beechgrove birds sometimes screech rude words.

There's more room in my head now. It's often full of soft grey lumpy stuff which sticks to all my thoughts. But today the air's got in. Desert air. I feel better in the desert.

I sit down on a piece of rock. I've brought my breakfast with me. They don't have meals at Scotty's, not proper ones with knives and forks or chairs. I took an apple and a roll. It wasn't stealing. A man said 'Help yourself.' I asked if he was Scotty, and he laughed and said he hoped not, or he'd be well over a hundred and it was bad enough being fifty-three. None of them had names.

I break a piece of bread off, chew it very slowly. It tastes of morning, dry and plain and clean. The morning stretches very long and wide. I've never seen such space before. There are always walls in England. Corridors.

I reach both arms out, as far as they will go. They don't touch anything. I laugh out loud, get up from my rock and run. I haven't run for years. Not since I was small. It makes my body shake. I stop. I'm out of breath.

I think I lived here once, long ago, when I was very small. Lived here with St Joseph. They had a Bible in St Joseph's library with coloured pictures in it. The pictures looked like here. The ground was rough and stony. There wasn't any grass. Just a few small bushes, not green like English bushes, but grey and plain like I am. One picture showed St Joseph. He was standing by a bush. His eyes looked straight at me.

I remember walking with him through the quiet brown peaceful pictures. He used to hold my hand. St Joseph's not a Jew. He doesn't live in Israel. There are no bombs or sirens here. No fighting or policemen. No noise at all. Just peace.

I look up at the sky. The clouds are like lace petticoats cut off from a wedding dress. I've seen those clouds before. On the plane. They must have flown on here. They didn't like Las Vegas and there wasn't room for them. The sky is full of buildings there, and lights.

The balloons may fly here, too, the New Year's Eve balloons. I've never seen so many all at once. I tried to count them, but I only got to twenty, and there were thousands floating past me. They flew up, up, up, so far, they were like confetti in the sky. You have balloons at parties. If they fly on here, I'll catch them, have a party all alone.

I've never been alone before. I like it. It means they trust you and you're not on any pills. I don't think I need pills now. I feel very quiet and white inside, not grey. The mountains make you quiet. I think they're sleeping.

I'm tired myself. You couldn't sleep at Scotty's. They did have beds, but only three or four, and there were people in them, girls as well as men.

I stretch out on the ground. It's rough and hard. I like that. It makes me feel that someone's holding me with strong brown arms.

I look up at the mountains. They're talking in their sleep. I strain my ears to hear.

'Enjoy,' they say. 'Enjoy.'

Sand.

I've never sat on sand before. I didn't see the sea until I was nearly thirty-nine. And then we had to stay up on the promenade. Sea is dangerous. There isn't any sea here. This sand was mountains once. The ranger told me that. Great solid stony mountains. But wind and rain ground them down like nutmegs. I know what nutmeg is. We had it on rice pudding at St Joseph's. You don't see it any more. The rice pudding comes in tins.

Everything keeps changing, even here. There was a lake here once, but the water all dried up. And two hundred million years ago, Death Valley moved to here from somewhere else. I didn't know land moved. The ranger said it did. He said mountains walked about, and lands and oceans crashed like cars, and bits of them broke off and flew around.

I think he said two hundred million years. I may have got the numbers wrong. There wasn't room for all the millions in my head. It made me quite excited. He told me about floods and storms and earthquakes, but it wasn't like the Reverend. The world wasn't ending. It was only just beginning and there wasn't any sin.

I like the ranger. I think he's quite important. He wears a uniform with a special badge and tie. He came to fetch me in his jeep. He said Hi, his name was Bernie, and Angelique and Carole were unwell, so he was looking after George. I asked him what was wrong with them and he laughed and said nothing that sleep and Alka Seltzer couldn't cure. He drove me through the park. I don't think it's a park because there were no trees or grass or benches and we hardly saw another car at all.

He told me lots of names. I stored them in my mind. I'm better now, so there's more room in my mind. The names were nice. Wild Rose Canyon. Warm Spring Canyon. Hidden Valley. Jubilee. Reverend Mother had a Jubilee. It was the only day she smiled. I liked that name the best. He said Jubilee was full of flowers in springtime. It feels like springtime now. The sky is blue.

I put my hands flat down on the sand. It's rippled like the sea; seems to move in waves. Bernie says the land still moves. It keeps shifting under us and even great big mountains twitch and fidget. He said you couldn't feel it, but it goes on all the time. He said in another million years, Death Valley might not be here at all.

I hope it stays. I like it. And I think it likes me, too. Most places don't. They'd prefer it if I left.

This is my real holiday, the first one I've ever had. I won it. Norah Toomey won it. It said so in that letter in gold print. Ten days in Death Valley. Not Las Vegas. This is the first day. I've still got nine.

There's always sand on holidays. A beach. This beach isn't flat like the one at Littlehampton, but goes up and down in hills.

Some of them are high, as if God had built a sandcastle. Others are just curves like the one I'm lying on.

I fill my hands with sand, let it trickle through my fingers. It's very fine and pale, as if the hills have burnt to ash. Some of it is blowing up like smoke. I can't see any wind. The mountains are still there, though they've walked away a little and look more blue than brown.

It's afternoon, and warm. I've had my dinner. Sandwiches and cake. The ranger gave them to me with some real dates from a date tree. I've still got all the stones. He said he had some calls to make, but if I liked, he'd leave me at the sand dunes with a picnic. *If I liked.* I kept repeating it. He didn't ask if George liked. George was told.

I didn't eat the cake. You're not allowed to eat too much in deserts. You have to save the food, and ration water. The bighorn sheep who've lived here for thousands and thousands of years nibble just the tops of plants. They never stuff and gobble like the people in Las Vegas do. They'd die if they did that, because there'd be nothing left to feed them. The land would die as well.

I'm happy in the desert. I never eat a lot. That's why I belong here, like the sheep. That cake was far too big. I ate the peace instead, took bites out of the clouds, filled myself with space. I'll give the cake to Bernie. He's fetching me at four. He trusts me, left me on my own without a nurse. He didn't give me rules, or tell me not to do things, or warn me he'd be watching me. Nobody is watching.

I don't feel frightened. I don't even feel alone. I can see the tracks and trails of things. Small and creeping things. Lizards, spiders, and something called a circus beetle. I like that name.

I peer down at the trails. They look like the embroidery the nuns did at St Joseph's. Crawling stitch, running stitch, chains of legs and feelers.

The ranger showed me footprints. A pack-rat and a kitfox. I don't know what they are and he said I wouldn't see them. They live in holes and burrows, come out just at night when it's quiet and safe and cool. That would suit me too. I like the cool, and nobody could see me in the dark.

I get up from the ground, follow two tiny tyre-marks in the

sand. They're not real tyres. You don't have cars up here. Only shadows. Dark blue shadows, the same colour as the mountains. I feel very high. I can almost touch the mountains with my hands. They look very worn and twisted. I think the land has suffered quite a lot. I can see the purple bruise-marks and the scars. The ranger said great earthquakes bent and broke it, and then wind and rain kept wearing it away. It's too tired and old to grow things, too weak to hold up trees.

Once, it was all green. So long ago, my head hurts when I think of it. There's still some water left, but it's mostly salt, like tears. We saw it earlier. The ranger stopped to show me. He told me it was lower than the ocean, one of the lowest in the world. I don't think I heard him right because it still felt high, like heaven, and God was very close. There were two of everything. The clouds and sky and mountains were shining in the sun and shining in the water. There was white snow on the mountains and white salt on the ground and both were all mixed up with the clouds. White clouds. There was a cloud across my own face in the pool. I felt us float together.

The salt looked just like water. Salt can kill things. If you pour it on a snail, it shrivels up. Bernie said some pioneers had died here, long ago, and the salt embalmed their bodies. I asked him what embalmed was and he said it meant their corpses didn't smell. I'd like to be embalmed.

I listen to the silence. At Beechgrove, they keep talking and playing radios. And in Las Vegas, it's never quiet at all, not even in the night. It's so quiet here, you can hear the silence breathing in and out.

There's more room for it to breathe. The sky is very tall here, so there's more space in between. The space stretches back to when everything was sea. You can't go back at Beechgrove. It's one day at a time there, the day which Sister chalks up on the board. The other days are dead. There's no room in your head for them. The drugs take all the room. Here, they're still alive. You can feel them all around you and they're stored up in the rocks. Bernie said the rocks are like a calendar.

I walk very slowly, up a hill and down again. It's hard to walk on sand. It keeps moving with you, pulling at your shoes. I'd love to take them off, but I don't think that's allowed. My shoes make tracks themselves. I turn back and stare at them. I'm a big brown creeping thing which lives in a brown burrow in the shade.

I walk on again, hoping someone else will find my trail and wonder what I am. There are other marks shining in the sand. A name. Someone's traced the letters with a stick. I spell them out. M-A-R-Y.

My heart is beating very hard. *Mary.* Al's mother couldn't come here. She's far too ill and weak. There's no one here, nobody at all. Our Lady must have written it. I walk all round the letters. They're very straight and clear.

I pick the stick up. I want to write my own name next to hers. I start the N, and stop. I wish I had another name, a king's name like George, or a pretty name like Carole. 'Norah,' I say softly. 'Norah Toomey.' No one laughs. I say it louder. 'NORAH TOOMEY.' I can hear the mountains whispering it themselves. I think they like the name. It sounds better than it ever has before.

I write it – all of it – put a fat tail on the y. It takes me a long time. When I've finished, the Mary looks quite small. I'm bigger than Our Lady, even neater. I'm getting good at writing.

I kneel down, trace a J. J for Joseph. I make his name the biggest, huge letters guarding mine. The sand is blowing slightly, grains from Joseph falling on my N. Pale like pollen. I take a stick and draw a circle round us. Not Mary, she's outside.

I want to dance. I've never danced, not ever in my life. I think my mother danced. Danced all night in a room which smelt of flowers, in a white silk dress and scarlet shoes. I glance around. No one's looking, except the sky and mountains. They won't mind. They like me being here.

I take a step, a hop. Dancing isn't easy. My legs feel strange. Too heavy. I sit down, undo my laces. I'm not wearing any socks. My feet have yellow gristle on the soles. Carole's feet are soft and white, like the bread in Bernie's sandwiches.

I try again. I'm lighter. My feet are clouds. I'm dancing like the white clouds on the pool. I stretch my arms, make waves.

'Norah!'

Someone's shouting. Bernie. I force my shoes back on, hide the stick. You're not allowed to dance, or write on sand.

'I . . . I'm coming.' I'm out of breath. I don't think he can hear me. He's only a black speck, a circus beetle crawling up towards me. I run down as he walks up. We meet.

'Hi,' he says and smiles. He isn't cross at all. His feet are very big, make a deep ridged trail beside my own. Two by two. Two by two. I'm a creature with a mate now.

George is in the jeep. He never talks. The ranger talks instead. He told me what a jeep is. He's clever like Miss Barratt in the library.

'Like to see Keane Wonder Mine?' he asks. He keeps asking would I like things. No one has before.

'Yes, please,' I say. I don't know what it is.

We drive along together. I'm sitting in the front. George is in the back. Important people always sit in front. I think the ranger likes me. He passes me a sweet. 'Take two,' he says, and smiles. George gets one.

The mountains follow us. They're always there, however far you drive. They have shadows on them now. But the sky is very blue still.

We turn off the road on to a rough and stony track. The van bounces on the stones. George shakes like a sack. It's only four o'clock, but the moon is out. Just a tiny moon, a young one, newly born. It's shining one side and the sun the other. You don't see that in England, so it may be a miracle. That Reverend said expect a miracle.

The rocks are bare and dry. Some of them have fallen, broken into pieces on the road. There's not one blade of grass, not one patch of shade. I'm glad it's not the summer. Bernie said it's so hot here in summer that if you eat a jelly, it melts on your spoon before you've even got it to your mouth. He called it jello with an o. I'd like to eat a jello with an o. The dry rocks make me thirsty.

Bernie stops the car. 'We have to walk the last bit. It's kinda steep. Can you manage, Norah?'

'Yes,' I say. 'Of course.' He didn't even ask George. George stays in the jeep.

339

Back home, I never walk much, except up and down the corridors, but Bernie said I'm good at it. He said I had strong legs. He talks to me a lot. Not many people bother.

We climb the stony path. I can't see anything, except more brown rock and a lot of rusty iron and rotting wood.

Bernie shades his eyes, looks round. 'This is where the mill was. See the old machinery? The mine is further up. Eighty years ago, they were crushing eighteen thousand tons of rock a month. Imagine the noise! Twenty huge machines grinding great jagged lumps of gold ore into powder.'

I listen. It's so silent now, I can hear a lizard chewing. Powdered gold. I'd rather have the sand.

'WONDER,' says the sign. Underneath is a pile of broken bottles, an empty oil can, a piece of twisted piping. Perhaps people danced here once, barefoot in the gold-dust.

We climb some more. The mountains climb with us, always higher.

'They're the Funerals,' says Bernie.

'Pardon?'

'The Funeral Mountains.'

I shiver in the sun. Everything has died here. Gold and men. Machines.

Bernie stops, turns round. 'It's too far to the mine, Norah, and we ought to check on George. Anyway, there's nothing much to see – just a heap of wood left, half a rotting bedstead and a pile of rusty cans.'

His face looks sad. He says men lived there once. Men with dreams, who lived on cans of beans.

We stand in silence. Dreams are always sad.

Bernie helps me down. 'All gold mines in Death Valley had short lives. I guess it's like Las Vegas. You pour cash in, in the hope you'll get more out. But mostly you go bust.'

He bends down, picks up something glinting at his feet. An empty sardine tin. 'Some sharp guys sold mining stock when all they had was a few holes in the ground without a trace of ore in them.' He drops the tin, steers me down the slope again. My feet keep sliding. Everything is brown.

I trip on something – half a broken chamber pot without its

handle, blue roses round the rim. I pick it up, wipe the dirt off with my handkerchief. Someone rich owned that, used it every night. Las Vegas may be ruined soon, the Gold Rush just a pile of marble toilets, broken into bits. Golden taps shining in the rubble. It's desert underneath the Strip. I saw it pushing through. Just a patch of it, where they'd pulled a building down. Sand and stones instead of gold. No meadows. No casinos.

I look back to the mill. Bare brown rock, a few grey thorny bushes. Bare brown silence.

The jeep disturbs the silence. Bernie starts the engine, slams the doors. We bump off down the track. It's cooler now, much cooler. The light is fading. The hills are stony, seem to close us in. Some are shaped like faces, faces without noses or with empty holes for eyes. They're all pale and very tired.

We drive in silence. There are no cars on the road, no birds in the sky. The little thorny bushes look like hedgehogs. Sleeping hedgehogs. The mountains have dark rings around their necks, as if a giant has tried to strangle them.

The road begins to struggle. The hills are steeper now, and it's panting up and down them. We've reached the snow, small patches of it, icing on the brown. Suddenly, everything is high. And very grand. The mountains spread right out each side, so far my eyes can't reach. I've never seen such space before. I can feel the space inside me, huge and clean.

The sun is going down. It's like an orange ball, balanced on the mountains. The sky is gold behind it. On the other side, it's pink. Soft pink on the snow. It's time to eat again; eat pink and gold and orange. I can feel them slipping down my throat, shining through my body. I'm licking the gold sky, spooning in pink snow. I start to sing, silently, inside.

George is just a bundle. I think he's gone to sleep. He sleeps a lot. Many patients do. I'm not a patient any more. I haven't any germs left. There are no germs in Death Valley.

The road is flatter now and very straight. Bernie swings sharp left. The sign says 'RHYOLITE'.

'This was the real big strike, Norah. A guy called Shorty Harris first found gold here. Know how he celebrated? With the world's greatest eggnog. Yeah – no kidding. He wired the LA

341

railroad for a carload of whisky and another full of eggs. When the train steamed in, he and his buddies smashed the whisky barrels open with their axes, threw in the eggs, shells and all, stirred it with their shovels – and – whoopee!'

Everyone drinks whisky here. I've never tried it. I'd like an egg, though. Soft-boiled in an egg cup. You can get egg cups in Las Vegas with your name on, or with legs. We don't have eggs at Beechgrove, and we've missed most of our free breakfasts at the Gold Rush. Carole likes to sleep late. She's sleeping now. I miss her. I hope she hasn't forgotten who I am. I've got some things for her. A stone which shines. A beetle. A piece of pickleweed. I'd like to save this sky for her, put it in a matchbox.

We drive along an empty pitted road. Half a house has fallen down. An old car has split open and is showing its insides. Bernie slows.

'This was a real fine city, can you believe, a wonder in its day, a boom town of ten thousand people where there hadn't been a white man within fifty miles. They built to last, Norah, in stone and concrete – big three-storey offices, banks and churches, a school, a fancy opera house. There were twenty-four hotels, fifty bars, a stock exchange and dance halls . . .'

I shut my eyes to see it in my mind. I can't see anything. Just black. I strain to hear the dance tunes, but the gramophone's run down.

Bernie points through the window to a pile of crumbling stones. 'That was once the biggest bank of all – in Golden Street. The walls were thirty inches thick and each vault door weighed a good four tons at least.' We drive on slowly past. I see a rat dart across the stones. 'By 1922, there was just one person left. The millionaires were lining up for hand-outs someplace else, or begging for free soup. They'd spent some seven million dollars winkling out three millions-worth of gold. Crazy, isn't it? The biggest boom-and-bust that ever was.'

He pulls up with a jerk, lets me out. An old mattress is lying in the ditch. I pick my way through rusting tins and pipes.

'I'll have to leave you, Norah. There's this guy I got to visit. He's ninety-three years old, but still a real live wire. He remembers Golden Street when it was crowded with prospectors who ate, talked, breathed and sweated gold. He found some real old snapshots when he was going through a drawer, and I'm hoping I can buy them for our records. Can you amuse yourself? I won't be long. Why not go see the Bottle House? It's built of fifty thousand beer bottles. And there's a heap of stuff to look at. They've made it into a museum.'

He checks on George, who's still asleep, tucks a rug around his legs. It's getting cold. I walk across a little patch of snow. It scrunches. The land is mostly brown again, just a few white rags of snow. The sun has disappeared.

Sad grey clouds are lying on the mountains, with twists of golden ribbon threaded through them. There is soon more grey than gold. All the colours fade. I'm fading with them.

This is called a ghost town, Bernie said. I can hear the ghosts, thin and very pale, limping after me. They don't speak. Nor do I. There is no one else, no one still alive. Or maybe only one. The one he's gone to see, who's ninety-three. He'll die soon. Bernie said families still live here; live in the museum, run a coffee shop. I think he was just joking.

I pass some ruined houses. The windows are blind eyes. One last ray of sun pokes its finger through an open door. The houses have no roofs. The stones are gardens.

I walk on, down the hill, find the Bottle House. There is rubbish all around it, bits of car, dead and cold machines, overflowing dustbins. It can't be a museum. Museums are neat and clean, with lots of rules and men in uniform who take your money, and let you in and out.

'Hallo,' I call. 'Hallo-o.' I make it louder.

'Oo-oo,' the mountains copy.

The door is open, so I walk inside. There are three small rooms, all dark and very poky. Things are jumbled on the floor, or pinned up on the walls. They're grey with dust, and mostly very old. Old clothes. Old snakes. Old furniture. The floor itself feels gritty and is covered with little bits of different coloured lino, with gaps where they don't meet. A broken drum is cooking on an old iron stove. It's rusty. Everything is rusty. Rusty saucepans. Rusty guns.

I jump. I've seen a skeleton. A whole one in a coffin with its lid up. The skull is smiling at me. The photos smile as well. Dead and smiling photos all around me, asking who I am.

I go a little closer. A dry black bat is pinned beside a woman's white lace glove. My mother wore white gloves like that. These could be her things.

Better not to have things. They only rust and die.

I touch a rocking-horse. It whines and starts to move, bumps into a sailor-doll, which falls onto its face. I leave it there, creep out again. The pale ghosts point their fingers. The mountains move a little further in.

I'm cold. I'd like a cup of tea. I walk down to the coffee shop. It doesn't look like one. It's all alone in the middle of a wasteland. A sign says 'Open', so I push the door. It's locked. I knock. A dog barks. On and on. It may be a ghost dog. No one comes.

I walk on down the track. I'm thinking of my mother. Her white lace gloves. Her skull.

I come to a wire fence. I don't know why it's there. There's nothing much inside it. Only stony ground and a few brown and thorny bushes.

I squeeze in through the fence, find some wooden graves. They're very old. Just piles of stones, or humps, with pieces of plain wood sticking up each end. The wood is rough and stained. No gothic script, or lilies, like that funeral place I read about. No beautiful Memorial Park. No grass at all. No flowers. Poor men's graves. Men who lived on beans.

Some of them have wooden cages round them. The cages are all broken, falling into bits. Millionaires begging for free soup, locked for ever in broken wooden cages.

I walk back the way I've come, stand outside the coffee shop again. I knock, I call hallo. Oo-oo-ooooo. Still nobody. Just the tiny frightened rustle of a ghost-rat. I don't think God wants people in the desert. They'd only spoil it. It belongs to Him. It says so in the Bible. God is very big and needs the space. If men lived there, they'd fill it up with buildings, make a lot of noise. God likes quiet brown peace, not coloured lights. He doesn't eat or drink, so He wouldn't waste the food or mind salt water.

344

God made sky and mountains before He made us. I think we're less important. That's why I like it here. It's so dark now, I can hardly see the path. The blue mountains have dissolved into blue night. I'd like to be a mountain. Then God would climb me, St Joseph lie on me.

I find a rock, look up. The sky is full of stars. They're very special stars here, much bigger and much brighter than in England. There are no windows in the ward, so I hardly ever see them back in England, but when I do, they're tiny, just small dots.

Bernie said there are ten thousand billion stars. That's more than two hundred million. Much much more, he said. He told me there were whole worlds in the sky. Cold and shining worlds, so far away you could spend your whole life getting there and still be nowhere near them when you die. They don't look far away. They look quite close. I think they can see me.

The stars have names, like plants have names, or mountains. The names were very hard. I remember one, just one. Pegasus. That's a horse with wings. I'd like to be a horse with wings. Flying with the stars.

I keep looking at the sky, trying to find the horse. The sky is shiny black, as if somebody's been polishing it all day. The stars look polished too. Polished with that very special silver-polish, which the nuns used for holy things like chalices, not common things like forks.

My neck is aching, but I keep on looking up. That Reverend told us to. He said: 'This New Year will be your year of miracles; your year of holding up your head and seeing all the stars.'

Year of miracles. I'd like a miracle. To stay on in Death Valley. Live here with St Joseph and with Carole. Have her as my friend. Joined for ever. I don't want Angelique.

I close my eyes and wish. A star jumps in the sky. Horses jump. It must be Pegasus. I think he heard me, heard my wish.

'Thank you,' I say softly.

22

'There's the sign,' says Angelique, as she turns left off the highway, following the arrow. The party's over, Death Valley just a haze of gin and headache.

'Silver Palm Brothel,' I spell out silently. I turn away, feel sick. Up till now, I haven't quite believed it – that Angelique, my friend, my rescuer, is a . . . a . . . All the words are so repellent: whore, hooker, scrubber, tart. She calls it working girl, says she's simply going back to work. Work! Getting paid for letting any freak or pervert hire her body, use it like a punchbag or a rubber doll.

She kidded me she was a dancer (stripper). She was – for eighteen months. But prostitutes earn more, much more. Which is why I'm going with her. Yes, Carole Joseph, apprentice prostitute. It should have been quite different. Carole Ben Shmuel, Zionist, new wife. My Jewish bridegroom spent the wedding night in jail. He's still in jail. His idealistic work for the Land of Milk and Honey turned out to be robbery, extortion, even accessory to murder. Oh yes, he loved the Jews. He kept nothing for himself. All the loot was sent to Tel Aviv. The murdered man was Arab. It's God's work to murder Arabs, God's work to steal for Israel. A petty thug with high ideals.

I don't believe it – not a word of it. I keep thinking of his hands, blood on them, handcuffs round the wrists, touching me, exploring me, going everywhere. I've had nightmares. His black prick cocked and loaded like a gun. Blood instead of come. My wedding dress embroidered with black bullet holes.

'Angelique . . . ?'

'Yeah?'

'I'm sorry. I feel sick. Can you stop?'

'Sure.'

She pulls up by the roadside. We're in a no man's land. No fields, no houses, just a yellow-brown parched landscape with jagged mountains closing in around us like some prison fence.

I scramble out, looking for a tree or bush, something to be sick behind. There's not a tree for miles. Just a few bare rocks sticking up from stony barren soil. I crouch down on the ground, knees pricking on the grit. Throwing up is the most lonely thing on earth. You're nothing but a heaving stomach; a shameful smelly outcast. I want to sick up everything – my misery, my shock, the whole jumbled battleground of fury, guilt, horror, disbelief; leave it here in this shrivelled landscape, drive on somewhere new and green.

I spit out a slimy trail of mucus, nothing else. I keep coughing and retching to try to bring the rest up, but all I do is hurt my throat. I can't even be sick. 'Daddy,' I mouth silently. He always held the sick bowl. My mother couldn't cope.

I mop my face on a corner of my skirt, walk slowly back to Angelique. She's flicking through a fashion magazine, looks up from the new Italian spring-knits.

'You okay?'

'Yes, thanks.'

'Coffee?'

'Please.'

Angelique unscrews a Thermos. I drink too fast, scald my mouth. Simple sorts of pain block out the deeper ones, at least for a few minutes.

'Look, I'd better drive you back, Carole.'

'No.'

'You haven't said a word since we set out. You must be ill.'

I force a smile. 'I'll survive.'

'You can still change your mind, you know. I could probably wangle you some other sort of job. Jack Stein needs a waitress.'

'No.' Waitressing won't earn two air fares back to England, two sets of clothes, a suitcase. All our stuff is stranded at the Gold Rush, out of bounds.

I daren't return there. The police may be waiting for me, ready to arrest me as soon as I walk in. Oh, I know I haven't

347

done anything, but I don't want to be questioned, labelled an accessory myself. They may find out I've already got a record. Okay, stealing a swiss roll is not exactly a big deal, but once you're in their hands, they can blow things up, make them sound much worse, especially in Las Vegas where crime appears to be the local industry.

They may even have our passports. I gave them both to Reuben. He said he had to have them when he changed our tickets over from London to Tel Aviv. Perhaps he didn't change them, just sent them on to Israel as another sort of loot, invented the whole story of our new life on a kibbutz. But then why did he turn up for the wedding? Even Angelique can't understand that. If he's the crook she says he is, he should have grabbed the goods, then done a bunk, disappeared completely, not put himself at risk by appearing at the chapel. Would he have gone through with the marriage, caught that flight to Israel? God knows. I keep asking myself questions which don't have any answers; going round and round in circles. Did he have the passports on him, or had he left them in his room? Or had he already doctored them, passed them on to someone? I'd feel a lot less frightened if I just knew where they were: on their way to Tel Aviv, in the Las Vegas Police Department, or totally destroyed?

Angelique was horrified I'd lost them; even changed her tune about the cops – said I should report the theft, tell them all I knew, ask their help in getting back to England. No. I can't betray my husband. Almost husband. It wasn't theft, in any case. I gave them to him freely. I'm sure he meant it at the time – that we'd marry, fly to Israel. He was probably forced to change his plans. Some threat, or plot, or blackmail, by a member of some gang; someone much more ruthless who had him in their power. Reuben wasn't ruthless. Okay, so he stole from other people, but not to make himself rich. And whatever else they say he's done, they're not crimes at all in his mind. If you believe in something passionately, you have to override the law. Even Christ was called a criminal.

And yet . . . Oh God, it's awful, but my own doubts keep creeping in. The thing's so complicated. I've run it and rerun it in my head – his ideals and his vision, and then what Angelique said, or read out from the newspaper: how he'd been in jail before, jumped bail, was a disturbed and violent drop-out who seized on the whole Jewish thing as an outlet for his own aggression. She said she wouldn't even glamorize him with the name of terrorist. He didn't have the guts or dedication. He's also been in a mental institution – yes, that as well as jail. She hinted he was really quite unhinged. That upset me more than anything, except I still can't quite believe it. You can land up in a loony-bin through sheer bad luck, or just with minor problems like worry or depression. Don't I know that from my own case, or Norah's, or Di Townsend's? If Angelique's still jealous, she could be blackening him on purpose. She told me she first met him in the brothel, as a client. Whose money paid for *that*, I'd like to know? Or is it just a lie? Another lie. As a child, you accept most lies as gospel. Being older means you never know, can't tell friends from jealous bitches; unhinged crooks from husbands.

Angelique refills my cup, extracts a cigarette from her initialled silver case, lights it for me. She's acting like a friend, has done since she first showed up, providing everything – clothes, food, smokes, a place to stay.

'Angelique . . .?'

'Mm?'

'You . . . know I'm grateful, don't you?'

'What for? Turning you over to a life of vice, corrupting your young innocence, acting the procuress?'

'Shut up.'

Angelique laughs, swings her glossy hair back. 'Look, love, you're intelligent. You don't have to take the standard view of brothels. They're a service.' She shrugs. 'A social service. Providing sex for those who can't get it elsewhere, because they're too busy or too old or shy, or their wives are sick – or selfish – or their girlfriends too uptight to give them what they want. Okay, some of them want the way-out kind of stuff, but so what? It's not doing any harm. Better to do it safely with a girl who's trained to handle it, than break a marriage, or go out and rape some kid. A brothel cuts the risks all round. No pimps, no threats of blackmail, much less chance of catching a dose. We're checked, you realize, every week. The doctor's quite a sweetie, laughs and jokes with us, stays on to have a drink. It's all quite civilized. Okay, so we charge. But everything costs money. Why not sex? You could say it makes it better. People only value what they pay for.'

Angelique stows away the Thermos, reapplies her lipstick. I say nothing, simply watch her lips change from palely prim to scarlet. I keep wondering what that glossy mouth has done, where it's been, how much it earns.

She blots it, twice, smiles at her reflection in the mirror. 'Our clients aren't just nerds, you know. In fact, I've met a better class of person here than I'd ever meet back home in boring Watford – attorneys, film producers, top businessmen, high-ranking physicians – you name it. Some of them work sixteen hours a day. They haven't time for dating, so they come to us instead – get exactly what they want and what they pay for – then straight back to their desks. No need for smoochy phone calls, lavish presents, wining, dining, dressing up.' She crumples up her Kleenex, smooths her skirt.

'Others are just lonely. They may spend six or seven hours with us, but only half an hour or so on sex. They want tea and sympathy as well, someone to confide in, someone they can trust. Some are handicapped, or have lost an arm or leg, or even both. One poor sod I saw last month had been smashed up in a car crash and still had all the scars. Other are too ugly to attract a girl, maybe very short, or hugely overweight. One guy who comes quite often – drives all the way from Utah – weighs three hundred and thirteen pounds. We need a winch to get him on the bed.'

Angelique is laughing. I'm appalled. Bad enough to think of normal clients, but dwarfs and amputees, Billy Bunters, cripples . . .

'We're doing them a favour, Carole. They crawl in here feeling like they're failures, and if we're any damn good at our job, they ought to swagger out. We're twenty girls in all, okay? Three of those are ex-nurses and two ex-social workers. One was a psychotherapist with her own private practice. Carl picks girls like that deliberately. Okay, we've got to be reasonably attractive, and ready to open our legs as well as just our arms, but if we're not kind and sympathetic and good listeners, then better stick to stripping.' She sheathes her lipstick, starts the car.

I say nothing. Who's she kidding? Does she need to see herself as a Florence Nightingale, can't face the sordid facts? Or is there some real truth in all that spiel? Is it any worse for Reuben to call robbery and murder Holy War than for Angelique to turn whoring into social work? Don't ask me – I don't know. I know less and less with each new day, in fact. All the uncomplicated values which my father taught me, or my school spelt out, seem too naïve and simple for the real world.

'We're lucky really, Carole. Carl insists on standards. He calls his place the Caesars Palace of brothels. And he's right, you know – at least compared with some of the dumps round here.' Angelique screws up her face, makes a spitting gesture. 'They're the pits. The girls all have to haggle, and sell their own used panties, the smellier the better. They even sell used rubbers. No, you don't have that word, do you? What do we say in England? My mind's just gone a blank. It's weird how I forget my own damn language sometimes.'

'Condoms,' I tell her. 'Balloons. French letters. Durex.' Reuben taught me 'rubbers'. Of course he's not unhinged. He showed he cared, proved he . . .

'Yeah, of course. French letters. I always wondered how they got that name. Anyway, some girls do a trade in them, wet and full and dripping. It makes you puke, doesn't it? Carl wouldn't hear of such a thing. He's got class, finesse. And I know I've got a future with him. He's got these big expansion plans, you see – wants to add a golf course and a health farm, even riding stables; have clients stay here, like they're on vacation, but with girls as the main attraction.'

I try to look impressed. What a future. The final hole for golfers, the softest saddle.

'It's not a bad life, Carole, if you can only clear your head of all the shit, all that stuff about nice girls not doing it. Our girls *are* nice. You'll see that for yourself. Okay, there're a lot of hard-nosed sleazy hookers on the game, but Carl won't touch

351

them. He's even a bit wary about girls who've been working on the streets. He says they often learn bad habits and get careless about hygiene.'

I mumble some response. I can't sit dumb for ever. Why is she such a fan of Wonder-Carl? Does he screw her, pay her double?

'Anyway, where else can you earn so much so quickly? The money's damned important – course it is. Why not? Our whole society's geared to making money, except it's usually the guys who are stashing it away. No, I'm not a feminist, it's just a basic fact that in most ordinary jobs we girls can't seem to make it. There's too much stacked against us – wombs and kids to start with. I mean, what other job can earn a girl a hundred thousand bucks a year, with no training, no college education and no rich Daddy pulling strings?'

'A hundred thousand?' Now she's kidding, must be.

'Sure. If she's not too squeamish, does anything she's asked, takes on all the weirdos and the masochists. *They* pay more, of course, and they're often the top brass. It's a funny thing, you know, Carole, it's always top tycoons or judges, guys who spend their lives controlling other people, who want to be tied up, or beaten, or crawl around like slaves.'

I swallow, shut my eyes, but I can't shut out the pictures in my mind. Sordid frightening pictures. Worse than cripples.

'Yeah, the money's really good, though a lot of girls just waste it. There was this silly bitch last year – saved a good four thousand dollars in just a couple of months. She wanted to get out, start her own small business, buy herself a dress shop. And what does she do? Drives down to Vegas and plays four hands of blackjack at a thousand bucks a hand, loses the whole lot. She was back here the next morning.' Angelique waves a hand, dismisses her. 'That's not the way to do things. And she had three kids, kept moaning about the fact she never saw them.'

'Kids?'

'Oh yeah, a few of them have kids. And some are married with husbands who regard it as just another job. They're the honest guys. There's too much hypocrisy in this game. Men who pay you, then despise you.' Angelique leans forward, adjusts the air conditioning. 'By the way, you mustn't call them "tricks" or "Johns". Carl objects. He's very hot on language. It's part of his whole standards thing. We're "ladies", not just girls. He even calls us courtesans. Okay, it's fancy, but who gives a shit if it attracts the richer blokes? Have I told you how the system works? Carl splits our takings fifty-fifty with us, then charges us for room and board. *Over*-charges, Suzie says, but she's a born complainer. It's fair enough, I reckon. I mean, the cooking's pretty good and all the housework's done for us, and for some of the girls, it's the first decent home they've ever really had. There's this kid, Desirée, arrived six months ago. Her father was a brute, roughed her up. And Beth was bawled out by her parents for getting pregnant, told never to show her face at home again. We get the Pill, and steak three times a week, and we've got Uncle Carl to run to with our worries and . . .'

She swerves to avoid a pothole in the road. She's smoking, a ring of scarlet lipstick on her slim white cigarette. No, it's not a cigarette, it's a stiff white prick, branded with that same brilliant lipstick. She has a whole silver case of pricks, each one stamped with her initials on its tip. She glances at me, sideways, then eyes back to the road. 'So you're still not saying anything? I might as well have saved my breath.'

'Yes. I mean no. It all sounds great, but . . .' I can taste come in my own mouth – come and vomit. When Angelique first told me what she did, I could feel myself shrinking from her, literally, as if she had leprosy. How can she call them 'nice girls' when I've seen the list of things they have to do? It's called the 'menu' – appetisers, entrées, à la carte, desserts. Specialities of the House. They're the worst. I don't even understand them, half of them. Angelique said not to worry, she'd explain. She can't seem to wait to break me in. It's as if I either join her, or stay an enemy, a critic. She reminds me of those fatsos who keep pressing cream doughnuts on their friends in Weightwatchers, because slim girls show them up. Or divorcees who have suffered, and console themselves by hitting out at marriage, trying to separate any happy couple left.

No – that isn't fair. She went to quite some trouble finding me a job. It wasn't easy when I haven't got a work permit, and no hope of getting one. At the Silver Palm, I'll be simply 'helping out', officially not there. They're always specially busy at New Year, so she managed to arrange a deal. They're short of girls, I'm short of cash. If I say nothing, he'll say nothing. One favour for another. Good old Uncle Carl. Not a madam, but a male. He's called the overseer. He does see everything – like God – on closed circuit TV. It's for our own security, like the four Alsatians, the two armed guards on duty round the clock, the emergency switches in each and every room, wired directly to the Sheriff's office. It sounds like Reuben's jail.

I stare out of the window. Still no green, no other cars, no houses. Just bare brown scrubland stretching to the mountains. We're in Nye County, where brothels are permitted. They're illegal in Las Vegas, some eighty miles away. A million miles away. It's stupid, but I miss the lights and glitter, even miss the crowds. There's nothing here at all. It's as if every living thing has crept away to escape the contagion of the brothel.

It was like that in Death Valley. No trees, no crops, no homes. Not a mingy sparrow or a cat. To tell the truth, it scared me; made me feel like nothing, just a speck in all that empty space. It was okay at the party (though I felt so shocked and weepy, it might just as well have been a funeral), but once the guests had gone, everything went quiet and sort of deathly, especially yesterday. Bernie drove us miles through all this bleak and lonely scenery, which looked barren like a moonscape, or some science-fiction movie where everything had died. It was even worse at night. The stars were too damn close, seemed to stare at us like spies. There was no other light to dim them – no street-lamps and no neon – and they went right down to the horizon as if the night had shut us in. I couldn't bear to live there: nothing to distract you, nothing sort of human-scale or snug.

I turn back from the window, start jigging on my seat. As Norah says, I need to go. These last few days, I've been on the run one end or other. I've had stomach upsets, headaches, crying fits, cystitis. Normally, I'm hardly ever ill. It's as if I'm breaking up.

Angelique pulls in again. If she swears, it's only silently. She is my friend, a true one. Which means that Reuben is a . . . No. Not necessarily. She could have got her facts wrong, be merely passing on some ugly gossip. A lot of people hate the Jews. I feel hate myself, mixed up with the love. Hate because he made me doubt; gnawing hate which keeps crumbling into guilt. I can't stop fretting about that mental hospital. It's like we had the thing in common, yet both of us concealed it from the other. Was he really a bad case; psychotic, schizophrenic? He couldn't be – not with his intelligence, his passion. I should realize, more than anyone, how easy it is to get labelled and locked up, how passion can be diagnosed as mania, or fervour as hysteria.

I should have got in touch with him, written him a letter, done some small thing to show him I still cared. I tried. I really did. I kept telling Angelique I couldn't just desert him. I didn't even believe the things he'd done; had crazy plans at first to try to rescue him, or even share his cell. I kept begging her to drive me back, leave that stupid party; or use her influential friends to try to get him off. She refused point-blank, said if I ever made a single move to contact him, she'd drop me, just like that. She didn't use threats normally, she said, but I was putting her in danger – not to mention Norah. I shut up after that. I felt bad enough already dragging Norah with me into all this mess. I was scared myself; still am. Yet ashamed of being scared.

I suspect even Angelique's a bit on edge. When we crossed the border out of California, back into Nevada, she glanced around her sort of nervously, and I half expected the police to suddenly close in. And she was driving like the clappers when we first set out this morning, as if she felt exposed and on the run; couldn't wait to bolt back to her sanctuary, Fortress Silver Palm.

I bunch my skirt up, pull my pants down. Not mine, Angelique's. Real silk pants, real linen skirt with a designer label sewn into the back. Nice to own clothes like that myself, drive a red Mercedes. Is that why I agreed to work with her? Greed again? Envy of her lifestyle, her second home (her first one is the brothel), the maid who keeps it clean, looks after George, does all the grotty chores? After all, if I've got so many scruples, why don't I change my mind, inquire about that waitress job instead, ask Angelique to drive the other way? She offered. I said no.

Greed is bad enough; revenge is worse. Yes, revenge. I want to get my own back. If Reuben was a client at that brothel, poured out all his skills on prostitutes, then I'll go one better, work there, turn every client into him, then cheat on them in some way, do them down.

See? I'm horrible. My urine stings and burns as if to punish me. I glance down between my legs, remember Reuben's mouth there. I can feel other tongues probing into me – furred and coated tongues; paraplegics dribbling down my thighs; kinky crawling judges; old men, men who smell, stumps of men with neither arms nor legs. God! I envy Norah. She's never had it, never likely to. I ignored her in Death Valley. Now I miss her. A beetle crawls across my shoe. I pick it up. It's red with silver wings. Exotic. She saved me one like that, put it in a matchbox as a present. I hardly even looked at it, just told her I felt lousy, begged her to shut up and go away. I can feel the beetle frantic on my palm, weaving round and round in circles, flustered and disorientated like Norah. Poor Norah. I miss her now, already. There's a matchbox in the car. I'll take this crawly back for her.

Except we're not going back, not for two whole weeks. Angelique's used up all her leave. The beetle will be dead by then, and I'll be . . . well – if not dead, then hardened. Numb. I'll have to anaesthetize myself if I'm ever going to do those blatant things. They're written in a dreadful jokey prose to make them sound cute and good clean fun. Flavoured Pussy Party, Two-Piece Snack Box, Hot and Cold French, Water Sports, Japanese Quickie, Passion Chair Profligate. I feel my stomach heave again as I run through the hors-d'oeuvres; imagine those top brass being tied down to the bed, spanked until they snivel.

I pull my pants up, slouch back to the car. 'Angelique, I . . . I've changed my mind. I do want to go back.'

'Well, I wish you'd said so earlier. We're almost there. I'll be late now, if I drive back all that way.'

'Okay, okay. Go on, then. I don't care.'

'What *do* you want, for chrissakes? You've changed your

mind twenty times already. Last night you said you were absolutely sure. That's why I phoned Carl, confirmed the whole damn thing. He's relying on you now.'

'I was pissed last night.'

'No, you weren't. We stuck to orange juice. I hid the gin deliberately.'

I don't remember orange juice. To tell the truth, I don't remember much at all. And if she hid the gin, why have I got this awful nagging hangover, the worst one yet? Perhaps it's from the night before. I've been drinking for the last few days just to drown things out. Not to feel. Not to think. Not to blame or hate or doubt. It doesn't work.

'Look, Carole, we either turn back now and forget the whole idea, or we go on and you act professional, honour your commitment. Right?'

I nod. She sounds like Sister Watkins. I'm scared, though, really scared. If she leaves us in the lurch now, then Norah and I are totally alone in a foreign country without money, friends or passports. Without even a roof above our heads. I'm lucky to get any job. You need a permit to wash dishes or sweep streets. A lot of people do land jobs without one, wangle them illegally, but I daren't take any more risks. I'm in enough mess as it is. It's so frightening the way that things just happen, through random chance or fate. I mean, winning this whole trip was only really luck, and then meeting Reuben, who's mixed up with all those horrors and nothing like he seemed – maybe even dangerous or mad. Then landing up a . . . a whore, when my father hoped to see me a nice respectable teacher or a safe conventional wife. It's like gambling in a way – your whole life changed by the spin of a wheel or the throw of a dice.

Angelique is still waiting for an answer. 'Okay, Carole, which is it going to be?'

I hesitate a moment longer, see Norah and myself sleeping on cardboard like those beggars in Las Vegas, see policemen closing in. Their questions fire like bullets; questions about Reuben, grilling about passports. 'Go on,' I whisper, doing up my seat belt.

'Great!' she says. 'Have another fag. Calm your nerves. It is just nerves, you realize. I was just the same myself – kept worrying about my Mum and what she'd say.'

My hands are trembling on the lighter. 'What did she say?'

'Nothing. She doesn't know. She thinks I'm still a dancer. The Swan Lake sort of dancer – tutus rather than titties. She'd die, if she found out. That's the trouble, really. I'd like to bring her over, give her a break, a decent sort of life after all her years and years of making-do, but how can I? That's one advantage with dear George. Even if he guesses what his sister does, he can't let on.'

George is deaf and dumb. It amazes me the way Angelique accepts. Accepts her job, her mutilated brother, her father dying when she was only three. And still stays cheerful, paints her nails puce-pink, wears citron-yellow playsuits with gold boots. She ought to be a bitch with looks like that, cash like that. Yet she spends half the money flying George out here and back, so her Ma can have a rest from looking after him. And she took in me and Norah. Norah's sitting in her house this very moment, with the maid to wait on her, three television sets, a Burmese cat. I ought to stick with Angelique. At least she's sorted out her life. 'Yes – as a well-dressed wealthy leper,' a little voice whispers in my head. I try to shut it up as we rattle on again, through leper-land. Still no grass or trees. They're scared to take root here.

I'm wrong. We've passed a tree, a bare and stunted one, but still a tree. We even pass a house, a normal cheerful house with washing on the line, two small children playing in the garden. To think that whores have kids! I mean, who the hell looks after them, and what are they told when they ask what Mummy does? I crane my head back, keep looking at the toddlers – blue tee shirts, orange shorts – the first bright colours I've seen for miles and miles. I've never felt so utterly alone. No kids myself, no husband, no safe and happy home, not even any Norah; another move to somewhere strange; a new anonymous room with nothing of my own to put in it. I keep thinking of my gear, shut up in the Gold Rush. We were meant to leave tomorrow, so maybe they'll just sling it in a box, shove it in Lost Property, if it's not with the police. I hate to think of all my things ill-treated. They're precious, part of me – the striped dress from my father, the checked shirt pinched from Jon, the black-cat brooch I've had since I was ten. All gone. Even that smart coat which Victor bought me. It cost a bomb and I wore it just three days. Now I've got to start again from scratch. Borrow things, scrimp and save to buy them. Even my toothbrush is hard and unfamiliar, and so new it makes my gums bleed. And real silk pants feel strange. I've lost the cheapo pair with hearts on which I bought with Jan in Brighton.

'See the sheep,' says Angelique.

They're so still and grey they look like greyish stones, but at least they're living things. Sheep mean farmers. Farmers are real people, not lepers, gaolers, pimps. I can even see some grass, yellowish and parched, but welcome none the less. The sun is really warm now. Blue sky, puffy clouds. It's like May back home in England. But that's only on the outside. It's November in my head – bleak and cold, things dying, shrivelling up.

We drive on for another half a mile. No more sheep or houses. Just blistered brown, ash grey. Then suddenly there's red. Red! Red for danger. A huge red flashing arrow pointing to a high wire fence with barbed wire coiled on top.

'That's it,' says Angelique. She stops, gets out, comes round and helps me out the other side. She needs to. It's like the moment when I first walked into Beechgrove, the same liquid stomach, paper legs. I stare in shock at the grey one-storey building spreading out untidily beyond the wire; the pile of lumber, the clapped-out fridge stranded on its back. The Caesars Palace of brothels? Christ Almighty! It looks more like a Portakabin, or a Salvation Army shelter for the homeless and deprived. I'm not sure what I expected, but if the Vegas tourists come here, then they're used to glamour, opulence. This is simple grot.

We pick our way between a few grey straggly bushes. No flowers, no silver palms. Dogs are barking, angry dogs. I've got so used to the silence of the road, the noise sounds still more frightening than it is. I can't see the dogs – or anyone. There's not a soul around. I read the notice on the fence: 'WARNING! These premises are protected by electronic and radio security. Unauthorized visitors will be liable to arrest and prosecution.'

I'm half-expecting sirens to scream out as Angelique presses the buzzer, speaks into the intercom.

The first gate opens, but there's still another gate and two more doors, all locked. It's worse than Norah's stories about Belstead. I follow Angelique through the last wired door, and suddenly we're standing in a normal cheerful room. The jail, the shack, the mental home, has turned into a hotel lounge in Eastbourne, or a schoolfriend's parents' best front room. There's a sofa and two easy chairs, a nice thick cosy carpet, a few fringed lamps, a coffee table with a pile of magazines. (*House Beautiful*, not *Playboy*.) Absolutely nothing to suggest a knocking-shop.

I'd imagined naked statues, leopard skins draped across red velvet, the heavy scent of musk. Or maybe something sordid. Dim lights and poky rooms, discarded Durex. Everything is squeaky clean and smells like a commercial – pine polish, lemon Flash. There are spring flowers on the sideboard, roses on the cushions, more flowers in the prints around the walls. Two girls burst in, give Angelique a hug. It's like first day back at school. They even look like schoolgirls – straight hair, no make-up, casual clothes. One's wearing dungarees, the other just a simple skirt and blouse. They can't be prostitutes. Perhaps they're Carl's nieces, or the maids or . . .

'Meet Kathy and Desirée,' says Angelique, offering round her pack of cigarettes.

I take one in a daze. Desirée. The one whose father roughed her up. She looks about my age. Not glamorous. Not anything. Sort of girl-next-door-ish. Mousy hair, nice smile. Kathy's a bit older, in her twenties. Fairish. Nothing special. I'm astonished. Pictures of the girls in those escort magazines have been floating through my mind since Angelique first told me where she worked. Bleached and blowsy blondes with satin skirts split halfway to their navels, lashes like iron railings, cascades of hair. Kathy's skirt is denim, her eyelashes so pale they're barely visible, hair cropped short.

'Kathy plays the fiddle. She used to be a professional violinist before she came to work here. If you don't behave, she'll make you listen to Bartok's Violin Concerto. *We* all run away.'

Everybody laughs. Bartok? I was prepared for nurses, social

workers, but not for culture. I suppose classical musicians are pretty poorly paid, though; can earn more whipping judges.

'Come on,' says Angelique. 'I'll show you round.'

I follow, dumbly, as she walks through into the kitchen, a sunny yellow room with Sugar Puffs and Frosties on the shelves, a row of Snoopy mugs hanging on the scrubbed pine dresser. A middle-aged woman in a nylon overall is rolling out pastry at the table.

'Hi, Peg,' says Angelique. 'This is Carole.'

Peg gestures with her rolling-pin. 'New girl?'

Angelique says 'yes' for me. I say nothing. I want to stay a visitor.

'Well, I'm glad you're not a scraggy one. I like to see an appetite. D'you want a cup of coffee and a cookie?'

'Thanks, Peg.' Angelique helps herself to apple slices from the peeled and glistening pile. 'I'll continue with the guided tour while you make the coffee.'

'Yeah, sure, sugarplum, but leave me some apple for my pie, okay?'

It's all so . . . cosy. The little jokes, the banter, the home-made apple pie. I keep being reminded of commercials: puppies selling toilet-paper to distract you from the fact you wipe your bum on it; prepubescent girls who never bleed drifting through cornfields wearing super-plus tampons; old-fashioned whole-some brothels without a man in sight. I can't see one, any-way; neither Carl nor any client, nothing to remind me where I am. Do guys pay all that cash for cookies in the kitchen, violin recitals? Another ample lady is hoovering the passage. More introductions and a kiss for Angelique. It's all one big happy family.

Angelique leads me out the back. 'That's the airstrip,' she explains. 'A lot of guys fly in by plane. There's a special package deal – two hours here, flights both ways, and a film show of the brothel on the way, introducing all the girls and services. That saves time for new clients in a hurry who may not know who or what they want. The soundtrack's dubbed in seven different languages, including Japanese. We get a lot of Japs. Their own brothels are horrendously expensive and most

Japanese businessmen have unquestioned expense accounts, so they can use their credit cards. We take Mastercharge and Visa here.'

How convenient. Do the wives back home ever see the slips, wonder where their busy tycoon husbands bought a Beaver Platter, or why they spent a fortune on a Back Door Screw? If I'd married Reuben, is that what he'd have done? Betrayed me on Mastercharge?

The runway is deserted. Angelique shades her eyes against the glare. 'Bob's just left, apparently. He's our pilot, seen it all. The men with James Bond hang-ups do it on the plane.'

'You're joking.'

'No, I'm not. It costs them, though – what with Bob's time, and the gas, and the loss of the aircraft for half an hour or so. You'll like Bob, he's a sport. I'll introduce you later. He's gone to fetch a load of guys from Vegas. In fact, I'm wanted soon. I'll have to go and change. I'll leave you with Desirée. She's got the morning off.'

We turn back to the house. Angelique points out the swimming pool. 'That's for our use only, not the clients'. They've got three jacuzzis, including a huge group one. By the way, be careful if you plan to swim. The temperatures can really plunge, even on a sunny day like this. I've seen icicles some mornings on that roof there.'

I'm shivering, though not with cold. Sex in a plane, sex in a jacuzzi . . .

We return inside. Two more females greet us in the passage. One is Asiatic – Malaysian maybe, with long black hair and one of those coy and tinkly giggles which never seem to work on English girls. The other is much older, almost forty, judging by her skin. She reminds me of my mother, the same determination to be young, contradicted by the lines, the sag. Angelique mentioned job security, but what happens after forty? I'm introduced. Sudchit and Joanne. Sudchit is one of seven daughters and grew up in Bangkok. Joanne is an ex-investment counsellor. There's the answer to my question. She'll retire from the brothel back to the world of high finance.

The house is much larger than it looks from the outside,

sprawls in all directions. We continue down the passage to what they call the 'cat-room', the girls' own lounge where they relax and watch TV. It's more untidy than the public lounge, a pair of dirty sneakers gaping in a corner, torn pop-posters on the walls, half a stale cheese sandwich doubling as an ashtray. Three girls are watching *Popeye*.

'Hey, Desirée,' Angelique calls. 'I'm working from eleven. Can you look after Carole?'

'Yeah, sure.'

'Peg promised coffee. Why don't you go get it, take it back to your room, and answer any questions Carole's got?'

She waves at both of us, strides off down the passage, disappears. Working. That means fucking. Being fucked. Letting all those workaholic Japanese fit in her body between a conference and a sales briefing. Tying up the managing directors, torturing the top executives. I still can't quite believe it. Someone's slipped a plastic cover over me, as if I were a car-seat or a book, so nothing touches me directly. The same thing happened the day my father died. The doctors and the nurses and that dreadful empty bed all stayed outside my tough protective coating – though only for the first few hours.

Peg doles out the coffee, tops it with cream and a little joke apiece. I tag along behind Desirée, carrying my mug, set it on the table in her room.

'Sit down,' she smiles. 'Make yourself at home.' She throws me a cushion, squats beside me on the rug. It looks like Jan's room back in Portishead – the same flower-sprigged walls and pretty white lace bedspread, the same knick-knacks on the dressing-table – china figures, photo frames. I'm really choked, terrified I'll cry. Cry for Jan and me. Both little kids, both innocent; bossing our poor dolls about, planning for a future full of no school and free sweets. I hadn't realized how much I've missed her room – not the child's one – the tatty Vauxhall bedsit. Okay, it's pretty basic, but it's full of bits of her: the photos of her sisters, her collection of glass animals, the toy giraffe she's had since she was three. It seems ages since I've slept with things like that around me, opened my eyes to something real and human. The Gold Rush was all cold impersonal luxury; my Beechgrove cell just a sixteenth of a ward, curtained off and bare.

I force my stupid tears back as I stare down at the bedspread and a furry face. Yes, Desirée's got her toys as well – a gigantic teddy bear hogging half the bed. Does Teddy watch his mistress, or is he turfed out when she's got another bed-mate? Do men come here at all, or are they taken to some other fancy room?

'If you've any questions, shoot.' Desirée bites into her cookie, spraying crumbs.

Any questions! I've so many she'd need a week to answer them. And I don't know how to phrase them. It sounds so rude to say 'Do you do it *here*?' or ask her advice on what I do if a man can't get it up, or hasn't got his legs or . . .

'I . . . I like your room,' I say.

'Yeah, cute, isn't it? I've never had a room that's all my own before. Back home I had to share with three kid sisters. The youngest was just five, so it was hell. How old are you?'

I have to think quite quickly. I've been twenty-one this whole last week, and now I've lost my passport, I suppose I can be any age I choose, since there's nothing either to prove it or deny it; no official Carole left at all. What's the point of lying, though, when it's quite legal to be a hooker at eighteen? Crazy. You can sell your body, but you still can't buy a beer. That's Nevada.

'Eighteen,' I say. Odd to shed two and a half years so fast. I feel rather insubstantial altogether, as if I'm losing not just years, but vital cells and organs.

'I'm nineteen and a quarter, so that makes you the youngest now. Great! I was getting kinda sick of being babied.'

'Babied?'

'Yeah. Peg's always trying to mother me and Carl treats me like I'm just a seventh-grader.'

And how do the clients treat you? Another question I can't ask.

She passes me a biscuit. 'Is Carole your real name?'

'Yes. Why?'

'We mostly change our names. I'm Deirdre really.'

'Do I call you Deirdre, then?'

364

'Oh, no. Deirdre's dead and buried. She wasn't happy and her father didn't like her. I chose Desirée not just because it's French and glamorous, but . . . well – I wanted to be wanted. Right? De-sire-ed.' She makes the word three syllables. 'It was a new start when I came here, a completely different life – new friends, new home, new me.'

I stare at her. New start. The phrase I used myself, just five days ago, and which seems to mock me now. The same spiel as Angelique's. Are these girls simply programmed? Is it part of their job to sell the service, plug the whole ideal, recruit anyone they can, like Moonies or evangelists?

'So are you going to stick to Carole?'

I don't answer for a moment. My mother chose Carole, not my father. It hasn't got me far. But then neither did Jan or Atalanta.

'What d'you think?'

'Oh, change. It's fun! And it helps you in the work. You can leave all your old prejudices behind – you know, that you should earn your living as a secretary or hairdresser rather than a hooker. Deirdres don't. Desirées do. And Desirée's prettier than Deirdre ever was. Her skin's zit-free and she's a whole inch bigger on the top.'

I laugh. 'I can't afford to put on inches anywhere. I seem to be the fattest here, as well as just the youngest. All the girls I've met so far are Twiggys.'

'Wait till you see Clare.'

'Who's Clare?'

'Our heavyweight. The guys go wild for her. Tons of fun, they call her. She's busy now with a big blond Swede. I really dig that guy. You can see the clients through a one-way mirror when they first come in, and that one – wow! Yes, please.'

'You mean, you actually *like* . . . ? You want . . .?' The words give out. I'd somehow assumed the whole thing was a penance, or a duty, that you serviced all the men through gritted teeth, or only survived the whole ordeal by lying back and thinking of your pay cheque.

'Sure I do. Why do a job you hate? Okay, some of it's real boring, and sometimes you're just bushed, or stuck with guys who bug you. But that's the same as any other job. Like, I mean, I used to work in a store and you got all kinds coming in. The bullies and the bores, and the ones you warmed to right away and would get out half the shop for, or the little guys who had no confidence and needed your advice, or the loudmouths who went pfft if you big-talked back.'

My father said the same about his shop. My father . . . If he saw me here it would break his heart.

Desirée drains her coffee. 'So what about your name?'

'I'll change it. Definitely.' Be someone else. A girl without a father. Without a surname, or a past.

'What grabs you? Something French like mine?'

'Okay.' I return to school, ransack my French text-books. Phèdre. Andromaque? No. I don't want to be a chilly righteous heroine. I want to be loved, adored. I want a Reuben in my life, one who's normal, one who'll stay, a father who won't die. 'I know,' I say. 'Adorée.'

'It's too like mine.'

'No, it's not.' Any tart can be desired. Adored is different, special.

'Anyway, it's kinda goofy, isn't it? We don't want guys to rib us.'

'Goofy?' I don't like this girl. If anything is goofy, it's Desirée, when it belongs to that straight hair, those childish freckles.

'Hey, don't get sore. You're English, so I guess you'll get away with it.'

'What d'you mean?'

Desirée shrugs. 'Forget it. Right, now clothes. We provide our own gear here, even special costumes – you know, stuff like nurse's uniform, school kid, SS guard. Maybe rubber, if you like. It's up to you. The guys soon find out who's best at what.'

She's ripped my plastic cover off. I feel sick again and scared. I might just manage something simple like hot oil massage, or even Crème de Menthe French, but not SS guard – not ever, not on principle. It's sadistic, horrible. I long to be back home, even back in Beechgrove. Our Las Vegas trip is really almost over. Norah and I should be packing in our hotel room, or buying our last souvenirs. I'm missing Norah, badly. She's my only link with England, with the real safe simple me.

Desirée is riffling through her wardrobe, tossing outfits on the bed, negligés and party gear, a full-length evening dress in slinky black.

'That'll probably fit you. At least we're the same height. Go on – try it on. Carl likes us to wear evening gowns after six or so. He's all for class, really bawls us out if he finds us with our nails and hair just anyhow. We can take the plane to the local beauty parlour, if Bob's got room and time. They give us special rates. And there's a great new place for sculptured nails, just opened. Here – let me see your hands.'

I hold them out, reluctantly. I've never bitten my nails, not consciously. Let's say they just break off.

'Jeez! Carl won't pass those. You'd better come with me tomorrow and they'll fix you up with false ones. It'll take an hour or two and set you back fifty bucks at least. You earn a lot in this job, but you have to spend a lot, as well, just looking good. Know how much this dress cost?'

'No.'

'Four hundred.'

I turn away. My wedding dress cost that. Torn now, stained with booze and sweat, bundled in an old brown paper bag.

'What's wrong? You homesick, Carole?'

'No.' I can hardly be homesick when I haven't got a home.

'I was. Real dumb, wasn't it? My Mom was always nagging and my Dad was real mean, yet I still missed them when I came here. I cried the first few days. It takes a while to settle down. Don't worry. I'll look after you. You stick around with me. Okay?'

'Okay.' School again. Best friends.

'What size shoes d'you take? Hell, the sizes aren't the same in England, are they? Try this pair, anyway. They match the dress.'

The shoes slip at the heel and the dress is straining everywhere. I don't look bad, though – really rather ritzy. I rarely wear all black. It makes me look much older, more sophisticated. The neckline is cut low. Desirée adds a sparkly diamond choker, stands back to check the effect.

'Yeah, that's great. I just love clothes and stuff, don't you?'

I nod. I daren't say 'yes' out loud. It's as if Reuben's listening still, trying to wean me off such trivialities.

'Here, try this red one.' She slings me a crimson sheath dress, slit right up both sides, starts stripping off herself. 'I'll dress up as well, show you my new catsuit.'

We *are* at school – best friends – dressing up, showing off, trying out new make-up, giggling, fiddling with each other's hair. I was wrong about Desirée. Okay, she's a bit naïve, but she's also very generous.

'Go on, Carole, keep it. Yeah, for real. I've got loads of bracelets and I never wear that one. Oh, and have this blouse. It looks real cute on you.'

We've turned her room into a dress shop. Half the stuff is on the bed or floor, drawers pulled out, wardrobe just a row of empty hangers. We're both modelling cocktail gear at eleven-thirty in the morning, with rainbow-coloured eyes and three-inch heels; my broken nails enamelled scarlet now, my hair swept up on top. All the things Reuben disapproved of – frippery and fashion, froth and tinsel.

I stare in the mirror. I hardly know the woman who looks back. She is a woman, not just some odd kid – glamorous, seductive, and more important than I realized. Men have to pay to touch her, pay for every minute of her time. Not *any* men. Why do work I hate? They won't give me the ugly ones, the cripples, or expect me to do sadistic things like whipping. I'm a special case, a new girl, who'll be treated with kid gloves. Angelique told me I'd be popular – English and the youngest, and with tits. Whatever Desirée said about gaining an inch on top, her boobs aren't exactly obvious. She's got courage, though; she must have. It takes guts to do this work at all. A lot of girls would be simply too conventional, or too feeble and straitlaced, or say they disapproved of it because they were really just too plain to get the chance. I've been negative myself, seeing all the bad things, ignoring all the good. If a nineteen-year-old with mousy hair and a 34A chest can buy herself expensive gear like that – a dozen evening gowns, a whole row of cocktail dresses, diamonds (fake maybe, but huge), thirty, forty blouses, and enough belts and bags to stock a leather shop – then the pay must be fantastic. Money makes you powerful. Even Reuben taught me that. I don't have to fritter it away, blow it all on clothes. I can also change the world with it.

Suddenly, the whole room shakes and rattles, and a throbbing roar drowns Desirée's voice. 'Whatever's that?' I shout.

She waits until it stops. 'Only Bob. It's a real old crate, his plane. He bought it cheap, fourth-hand. You get so used to it in time, you hardly hear it.'

I peer out of the window, but it faces front, not back. I can see only barbed wire fence. I strain my ears to listen. I can hear tramping feet, a laugh. Clients. Rich ones, who can afford a private plane. Attorneys and physicians. Film producers.

Desirée checks her watch. 'It's lunch in twenty minutes. We'd better put this stuff away.'

I leave my hair and eyes exactly as they are. I want to stay Adorée. I swap my dress for a pair of leather trousers with zips both back and front. They're so tight, it's hard to eat.

There are just five of us for lunch. Which means the place is full of men. And still I haven't seen one. No one even mentions men – nor anything you couldn't say quite safely at a Women's Institute coffee morning or a Conservative Women's Luncheon Club. It's just clothes (again), and holidays, and a bit of local gossip about the man who runs the gas station. Peg serves lunch and another jolly lady passes rolls and butter and pours out jugs of milk. Yes, milk. Nobody drinks wine, or even beer. The food is good and homely – a chicken casserole with jacket potatoes and lots of healthy vegetables. Desirée sits next to me, and the other girls make sure I'm not left out, give me double carrots, ask me about England, say they like my hair.

The apple pie's delicious. I lean back in my chair, lick sugar off my lips. It's ages since I've had a home-cooked meal, sat around a table with a group of friendly girls instead of psychiatric patients. Even before Beechgrove, meals were pretty miserable. My mother wouldn't cook and if she deigned to join us, there were always rows and sulks. I understand better now what Angelique meant about a home. Her own meals back in Watford can't have been much fun. I've seen her brother eat – or try to eat. She said her friends refused to visit, were too appalled by George. Just her and him, silent at the table, while her widowed mother got on with the chores.

Peg removes my empty dish, offers coffee, tea. I'll get ruined if I'm waited on like this. I keep feeling I should help, or do the washing up. I accept a cigarette instead, blow smug and lazy smoke rings.

A car draws up, a door slams. More rich clients?

'That's Carl,' says Kristia, a Swedish girl with fantastic hair but rather podgy legs. 'Late for lunch as usual.'

I tense. Carl. The overseer. God. Supposing he doesn't approve of me, sends me packing?

He's small, with gingery hair fading into grey, and a pallid doughy face. You'd call him ugly if it weren't for his clothes, which are plain but very elegant. He's dressed like an accountant or a lawyer in a dark grey business suit, expensive shirt. His eyes are on me instantly, detective eyes, missing nothing, taking in the evidence. I can feel them measuring my hips, sneaking down my cleavage, up my legs. Should I stand up, or smile, or say hallo, or put my cigarette out?

'You're Carole.'

I nod.

'Hi.'

'Hi.'

'I'm Carl.'

I nod again.

'Settled in?'

'Yes, thank you.'

'Love the accent. Where you from?'

'Portishead.'

'Where?'

'London.'

'Great city.'

'Yes.'

'Wanna see me in my office?'

'Er, yes. When?'

'Now. Bring your coffee with you.'

It's tea this time. I'm so nervous, half of it slops into the saucer.

I'd somehow pictured Carl as big and butch. And young. He's old. Quite lined and with one of those high foreheads where the hair is disappearing, thinning into shiny scalp. I wobble after him, wish I'd worn a skirt, something less constricting. I can feel apple pie and fear leaking through the zips.

His office is just that: a desk, a swivel chair and several metal filing cabinets. I suppose running a brothel is just another business; the same problems of client satisfaction, marketing, PR. He's good at the PR. I recognize some of Angelique's hard sell. Carl goes further; tells me how the Silver Palm ploughs back money into the community, keeps it prosperous, how the girls support the local stores, the local charities, raise funds for senior citizens.

There's a mirror on the wall and he keeps casting furtive glances in it, straightening his tie, or smoothing down his hair, admiring his crowned teeth. His nails are pink and glossy. He must have had a manicure. He's as vain about his brothel as he is about his person, gives me all the Caesars Palace spiel. It's getting a bit boring third time round.

'If a guy comes here and asks about the competition, or is scared he's missing something better someplace else, I always tell him "Go right ahead and check it out. If you find a house with more class, more style, more exciting girls, you stay right there, sir." ' He shrugs, taps the desk with his slim gold-plated pen. 'They all come back.'

He then moves on to pay and rules. I can see the martinet now. I keep nodding, mumbling 'yes' and 'no' on cue. He makes it very clear that he's doing me a favour, not vice versa.

'You're lucky to be working here, you know that?'

I nod again. He's crossed one leg over the other, the foot right up on his knee. I feel somehow threatened by that foot, the black ridged sole squared up to my face; the immaculate grey trousers straining over slightly plumpish thighs; two television monitors framing his chair like blank-faced robots.

'I got girls lining up to work for me – high-class girls – some of them with PhDs or fluent in six or seven different languages.'

I say nothing. Angelique told me he was short of girls. Anyway, I can't see how a PhD would help.

'I turn down more than I take on. I've had hysterics, bribes – the lot. It makes no difference, Carole. If they haven't got that something, then it's "Good day, ma'am".'

I'm tempted to give him a good-day myself. I loathe what he's doing – building up my insecurity, so I'll never dare demand a better deal, keeping me grateful and enslaved. There's a sudden silence. I can feel his eyes still on me. I look up, look away again, start chipping at the polish on one scarlet nail.

'Right, get your clothes off.'

'*What?*'

'I can't hire you without giving you a look-over. It's not fair to our customers. You might have scars or birth-marks, or some hidden disability. And you'll have to see the doctor for a check-up. Okay, other places hire girls over the phone, but that's not the way I do things here. I prefer to see the goods I'm buying, inspect the merchandise.'

He laughs. I don't. It's not a joke. It's monstrous.

'Come on now, I haven't got all night. Another girl just called me for a job – an ex-movie star from Hollywood.'

I'm just too shocked to move. I never knew I'd have to strip, assumed Angelique had vouched for me, guaranteed my lack of scars. Carl's been talking all this time as if I've got the job already, been accepted on his payroll. Now I could be shown the door. Oh, I haven't any birth-marks – no marks at all, except a tiny mole the size of half an ant on the back of my left thigh, but Carl may well be checking something else. Like have I got a really sexy body, some instant oomph which turns men on? The answer's no. It must be. I mean, Milt and Victor didn't want to know, and Reuben's panting compliments were probably only lies, like all the rest.

I stand there with my shoulders hunched, my whole mind in a fret of fear and fury. Why should I submit, be inspected like a cow or a piece of horseflesh? And supposing I don't pass? Do I hitch a lift back to Norah and the maid, become a char myself, end up sweeping floors and scrubbing toilets?

I undo one button of my blouse, curse Desirée's trousers with their double zips; inch the front one down a bit, fumble with the back one. Carl says nothing, absolutely nothing. His silence makes me clumsy as I fight with four more buttons, claw at stubborn bra hooks. My boobs spill out at last, but I immediately try to hide them with my hands. I'm not even stripped yet, but I've never felt so naked, so totally defenceless and exposed. It's even worse once I've pulled my trousers down; stand there barefoot on the carpet in nothing but Angelique's brief and flimsy panties.

Carl jerks his thumb at them, wants those off as well. He takes a step towards me as I slip them off. I flinch, freeze. Is he going to touch me up, put me through my paces? I'm not sure he even goes for girls. Angelique was cagey when I asked, hinted he was gay, but Desirée told me airily that he'd slept with a thousand different women, tries out all his 'ladies'. God knows which is true. I just wish he wouldn't come so close, peer at me like that; his eyes right in my navel now, then running round my groin.

'Turn round.'

No 'please'. No 'Would you mind'. What do I expect? You don't say please to horseflesh or to cows. It's worse still with my back to him. I can't see his face, can't see what he's thinking, keep expecting his hot hands to land on my cold back. They don't. He doesn't touch me, doesn't speak at all. The suspense is really awful. I want to scream with nerves.

'Okay,' he says, 'you'll do. Get your clothes back on.'

I'll do. I'll do. How dare he? I'd like to order *him* to strip, go up close to view his saggy stomach, his puny little prick, ask him to turn round, go down on both his knees; then say sorry, no, he's failed. Instead, I drag my clothes on, sit down when I'm told to, accept a cigarette, answer all his questions about what he calls my 'work experience'. He knows I haven't any, but he still wants all the intimate details of my personal likes and dislikes, my repertoire, my special skills and preferences. He's slumped back in his chair now, feet spread wide apart so that his trouser-straining crotch is facing directly towards me; head thrust forward, lie-detector eyes watching every ripple on my face. It's even harder to stay cool now he's viewed me naked. It's as if he can still see me – see my nipples and my bush, the crease between my buttocks, that mole on my left thigh. I can feel myself blushing through the layers of make-up; hear my voice, too shrill, saying the wrong things. I drop a trail of ash, stoop to pick it up, bang my head on something sharp. I try to smile away the pain, answer Carl's last question.

'Well, no, I haven't ever actually . . .'

'Okay, kid, relax. You'll learn. And if you don't, you're out. What about a professional name?'

'Yes, I've thought of one. Adorée.'

'What kinda name is that, for heaven sakes?'

I bristle. 'It's my own name. My father chose it. It means adored. My Dad was very fond of me.'

'Must have been. So why the Carole then?'

'My . . . mother called me that. She's dead now.'

'Angelique said your Pa was dead. They're both dead?'

I'm almost crying as I nod, not because I've made myself an orphan, but because I can't stop lying. I don't know why. It's as if I'm never quite enough just as I am, but have got to be more tragic, more dramatic.

'Poor kid.'

There, you see, sympathy already. He's smiled for the first time. I simper back, start flirting with him; despise myself, continue.

'Well, Carole, I think we'll get you working right away, okay? See how you make out. Like to start this afternoon?'

I stare at him, my own smile frozen now. I'm speechless. I haven't even seen my room, or met all the other girls. Angelique promised they'd break me in gently, give me time to settle in.

'Don't worry. All I want you to do is look after a wife.'

'A wife?' I'm catching Norah's habit – parroting. But I'm so confused I can't manage more coherent words. Does he mean some sordid dykey thing? I can't. I won't. I was never told this brothel serviced lesbians.

'Sit still, Carole, can't you? You're so darned twitchy, you're driving me up the wall. Where was I? Yeah, this couple. They're coming in at three o'clock. It's the guy's birthday and his visit here is a present from his wife – her own idea, in fact. She did the same last year, drove him all the way from Barstow, then waited while he did his stuff. That's where you come in. I

374

just want you to sit with her, make her feel at home, okay? Have a cup of coffee with her, tell her about England – anything you like. She's a real nice woman – friendly – you won't have any problem. Then, afterwards, you can help pass round the plates. We've made the guy a cake, a huge one, seventy candles.'

'Seventy?'

'Yeah, he's older, actually, but men are just as vain as women when it comes to birthday candles. He was seventy last year. And the year before, no doubt. Right, any questions?'

'Er . . . no.'

'Good girl. That's it for the moment, then, until I've called the doctor. He won't come up till later. Go find Kathy and ask her to show you where your room is, sort you out any stuff you need. You've met her, haven't you?'

'Mm.' The violinist. Maybe she should wife-sit too. Provide some background music, divert the wretched woman from what her husband's doing. An old boy of seventy-two. Has he got his legs, I wonder? Will he need a winch? Perhaps she's older still, can't do it any more, has to hire a substitute, a treat just once a year.

All my anger comes seething back again – anger with the couple, with Angelique, with Carl; with the whole stupid crazy set-up. Is that all Adorée's good for, sitting with some pensioner, making instant coffee, small talk? I kick my chair back, close the door behind me more loudly than I need, fumble for a Kleenex as I walk back along the passage, start scrubbing at my face. I don't need all that make-up or come hither eyes. And I may as well change back into a simple skirt and blouse. Skin-tight leather trousers aren't exactly working gear for a geriatric social worker.

23

I pace up and down the room, up and down. It's huge, what they call a VIP lounge, though it's not a lounge, not really, since the only furniture is an enormous water-bed. You can't count the chair – that's metal, and described in the brochures as an adult monkey bar. Don't ask me what it's for – I don't know, don't want to know. There are a lot of things that go on here which I've simply turned my back on, blocked out of my mind. The dominance and bondage, the slave training, spanking lessons, the video-taping service which immortalizes customers in any sado-masochistic mayhem that they choose.

I've been here two whole days now, and they've gradually lifted up the corners, let me see what's there beneath the roses and the Pine-Fresh. I'm no longer scared and sickened, though I tend to cringe a bit when I hear Carl use his favourite words – 'standards', 'class', and 'style'. Okay, he's achieved them, as far as externals are concerned. Dress and meals and decor are all elegant enough, but what about the clients and the other sort of menu? Is a fantasy dungeon 'classy' (complete with rack and thumbscrew); a torture-chamber 'stylish'? I haven't seen those yet, hope I never do. I prefer to forget the more outrageous things, pretend they never happen. Some of them I can hardly quite believe – the guys who pay to have a girl shit in their mouth, or be dragged around the room with a string tied to their tongue. I try to stop my ears to those, act deaf.

We do that all the time in what we call the real world. I mean, last night's news on television – a kid of just fifteen strangling himself with the bed-sheets in a children's home; a trusted babysitter molesting a six-year-old; a Chicago street gang with a thousand members buying double-barrel shotguns with their profits from the dope. I was watching it with Kristia and Joanne. We switched channels, didn't we, preferred to listen to a jingle for Diet-Aid Dream Topping. Diet-Aid, when half the world is starving.

There's a commercial break now. The huge TV set above the bed is advertising itself: '. . . elegant oak-grain cabinet, infra-red remote control, and a fifty-inch diagonal screen with the sharpest clearest picture you can . . .'

I switch it off. It's only there to show the adult movies. (I still don't know why 'adult' should mean porn.) I don't think my client will want porn. He's a virgin, and probably underage. You have to be eighteen to use the brothel, and with an identity card to prove it, but some boys borrow older men's ID's, and Carl says if they've got the cash, why probe? I suspect Carl chose me purposely for this lad. As someone who is working here illegally, I'm not likely to tell tales on him. And if he's inexperienced, he won't be too demanding, can't make unfavourable comparisons. Actually, I feel a bond with him. He's Korean, a foreigner, and I'm a foreigner myself. I don't mean being English. The twenty girls who work here are by no means all American and include some dusky skins and unpronounceable names. No, it's because I don't belong yet. The girls are very matey still, but it's only superficial and I can sense a lot of rivalry bitching on beneath the smiles. The cosy happy family isn't what it seems. Desirée said she liked the work. That's rare. Most of the girls endure it as a duty, the only way they know of making money. Some of them resent the men, even hate their guts.

I mean, I had this talk with Naima, who was really bitter. She's half-Moroccan, escaped from some whorehouse in Casablanca where the madams and the cops worked hand in hand, took away everything she owned – her passport, all her papers – so she was completely in their power. She often worked fifteen hours a day, got through over a hundred clients in that time, which works out like those quick-fire Vegas weddings – eight minutes apiece. She never left her room, rarely had a second for a sit-down or a fag. Okay, it's a palace here, in contrast, but she said she's still basically a fucking-machine who can't choose or vet her clients, has to service anyone who comes. 'We're just beds for them to lie on, Carole, or chairs to sit on. They get on, they get off, they get dressed, and it's next please.'

Then she started pitching into men – what pigs they were, what garbage; top brass maybe, but creeps: either cruel and ruthless louts or weak submissive slaves. I didn't want to hear. Okay, she's seen men at their worst and in the raw, but there must be some guys left who are decent normal types. Desirée thinks so, anyway. It was quite a relief to escape back to her room from Naima's savage tongue. I can't think how Carl ever took her on, though I suppose he values her experience. Five years on the game in Casablanca (which must add up to umpteen thousand men) is like those PhDs he brags about – a doctorate in fucking.

I prefer Desirée, who believes in pleasing men. Or Angelique, who's kept her sense of humour, counts her blessings. The other girls are much less open with me, so I'm not sure what they feel. They're friendly, yes, but guarded, as if they're still a little wary. I can hardly blame them really, when all I've done so far is eat their food, try their clothes, take up their free time. Perhaps things will be better once I've started work, made myself one of them officially.

This boy will be my first, which is why I'm so afraid. I keep glancing at my watch. Still twenty minutes to go. If they crawl as slowly as the last half hour, he'll be greeting an old crone. I'm no longer scared about it being wrong. Maybe I've been brainwashed, but selling sex seems normal now, even sensible, convenient. Well, I can't defend the sadist stuff, or the way-out kinky things, but I shan't be touching those. And when it comes to simple screwing, I can think of other jobs far worse – writing lies for those commercials, for example. What I'm frightened of is failing.

I lie back on the bed, suddenly leap up again. Reuben could have lain here, on this very counterpane, with another girl – more than one. I've never quite accepted it before, that he walked into this brothel, picked his fancy dishes from the menu, maybe paid for them with money which he'd stolen for the

Jewish cause, sold my passport to buy himself a Three Girl Show, or what they call 'Fantasy and Fetish'. And then he dared use words like principles, integrity; tricked me into believing in the Utopia of Israel when he'd already flogged my only means of getting there; let me praise him for his kindness in including Norah, too, when all he was doing was picking up her loot – a second passport, a second airline ticket – enough for an All Niter with the most expensive hooker here.

Hold on. He only had those passports for a day – our wedding day. He'd hardly spend his precious time driving to a brothel, fucking whores, least of all when he'd come four times already – with me, the night before; more than four, if you count our morning session. And if he was going to sell our passports, he wouldn't waste the proceeds on another round of sex, then turn up for the wedding bold as brass.

He was late, though, wasn't he; not bold at all, but very strange and nervous. Another voice pipes up: of course he'd be nervous if he was working with some gang, planning theft and murder, known to the police, risking his skin by showing up at all. So why did he show up, then? Madmen don't need reasons, scoffs a third voice. If you're psychotic or deranged, you're capable of anything. Shut up, I tell it furiously. That's tattle, even slander. He could just as well have come because he loved me – come to warn me or explain. So why did he say nothing then, and why did . . .? The voices fight and wrangle, contradict each other. None of them makes sense. I'm back to where I started – with that sick and senseless image of Reuben lying naked on this bed.

I've got to get him out. I'll never please another man while I'm so involved with this one, still torn to pieces over him. He didn't book this room. I push him off the bed, march him to the door. 'And don't think I believed those lies you told me – how you'd never met a girl like me before. I suppose you used those Hebrew words to all of them . . .'

I'm shaking as I stride back to the bed, walk round and round it. Reuben's over. Finished. The only man in my life just now is my ten o'clock booking. I've got to be – professional, got to be relaxed for him. He'll be shy himself and nervous. Angelique warned me about virgins, how I'll have to work harder, take much less for granted. She didn't seem that keen on them herself – more work for less return was how she put it. And Carl gave me a pep-talk about the importance of a man's first time and how it was my concern to make it memorable. I suppose what he's really after is new business, repeat bookings, but all the same, I feel burdened with my twin responsibilities – to the client and to Carl.

Client. God! It sounds so formal. I keep picturing him, wondering what he's like. Perhaps he's picturing me, and just as scared. First time for both of us. And yet it's really very simple. All I've got to do is what they call a straight lay, which means sex in the missionary position. Normally, we're meant to discuss the menu with our customers when they first arrive, go over all the items, push the most expensive ones, play tough and steely salesgirl before we switch to tart. But for some reason, I'm not doing that this morning. It's all arranged already, though I've been told as a general principle to try to entice clients into buying extra time. There's a pinger in each room, a sort of sexual egg-timer which goes off when your time's up. The best girls keep resetting it. There's good profit in the drinks as well, especially champagne. We're meant to really flog it, yet not get pissed ourselves. The girls often drink carbonated apple juice, but served in a champagne glass and charged to their clients at vintage champagne prices.

I check the drinks again, polish up the ice-bucket, put a piece of ice into my mouth, hold it in one cheek. The guy may change his mind and want Frappé French. (That's ice-cold oral, brandy-flavoured sometimes, if the client wants a double jolt.) I'd better practise now, and not be thrown. My gums are tweaking with the cold, but I keep the ice in place for two whole minutes. Another seventeen to go until I'm needed.

Ten AM seems a most unerotic hour to go to bed. Cartoon time on the telly, coffee time with Peg, the sound of hoovering. I can even hear a baby crying. That must be Peg's new grandchild. She was passing round the photos only yesterday, had half the girls drooling as if they were broody hens instead of hardened whores. I suppose they *are* frustrated, some of them, all maternal urges just stamped down. A few have kids, but they don't get to see them often. A lot have had abortions, so Angelique confided, but still long for babies and a normal happy home – well, those who aren't completely disillusioned. Naima would murder any husband or male child, serve up all the corpses in a pie, and Joanne's pretty bitter about families and marriage. She'd hardly said a word to me until I happened to remark about how many customers I'd seen walk into the parlour wearing wedding rings. That really got her going – on and on about how married sex was often just an empty ritual, with wives lying there like boards carrying out their 'duty' because they're paid, if not directly, then some other way.

'And then they have the nerve to bitch at us, slam paid sex because there's no real feeling in it. And husbands are as bad, Carole. Loads of them stick in rotten marriages because they're fed or mothered or get their laundry done, or don't want the stigma of divorce or the risk of losing half they own. We get them here in droves. They tell their wives they're working late; book a hot oil massage and a sixty-nine, then back to home-cooked dinner and another nice clean shirt.'

I didn't answer. Joanne never married and she's pushing forty, so perhaps it's just sour grapes. I'd rather be a Peg, simple and soft-hearted, with a cuddly caring husband, four daughters and two grandsons. I can hear her now, singing to the kid to stop it crying. 'Rock a bye baby.' I didn't know they had that in America. It seems so English, makes me want to blub. 'When the wind blows, the cradle will rock . . .'

The baby in my own arms is still that damned Korean. Sixteen endless minutes still to go, but I can't put him down, even for a second. Whatever else I think of, he keeps popping up again and taking over. I've got two more clients, actually, booked this afternoon, but they're simply hazy names. All my nerves, all my hopes and fears, are concentrated on this all-important first one. He's like a sort of test case. If I can cope with him, send him out eager to return, then I'll take it as a sign I'm meant to work here. If not, then . . .

Fifteen and a quarter. Unless he's late. Or early. God! Not early. I'm not ready. Oh, I'm tarted up all right – wearing what

Desirée calls her playsuit, with a red lace g-string underneath, but I'm still unprepared inside. If you peered in through my navel, you'd see not just organs and intestines, but a whole bubbling ferment of fears and worries, resentments and confusions. I don't feel like a hooker – not cool enough or tough enough, not even glamorous. I'm still Carole, not Adorée. The name never quite took on. The girls all call me Carole, lump me with Desirée as a kid. Desirée hangs around a lot. I like her, I admire her, but we can't be really friends. That's my fault. I've told too many lies, wanted her to see me as more special than I am. Now the lies get in the way, stop her knowing me.

With Angelique, it's still more complicated. She doesn't know me either, and I'm not sure I know her. She's full of contradictions: seems to like her work, defends it, except suddenly she'll blow, show a different side – bad-mouth all her clients and the entire male sex; Carl of course excluded. God knows what's between them, but I feel a bit uneasy that she's so much hand in glove with him. Sometimes I even see her as a spy. Yet she's also a good friend – I can't doubt that. I mean, the way she took in Norah, hasn't charged a cent for three meals a day and maid service.

I'm missing Norah terribly. I never thought I would, and it may sound plain perverse when I've complained she was a drag. But she accepted me as me. She knew about the shoplifting, she'd met me in the hospital, so I didn't have to hide things. She's seen me howl, seen me looking grotty without a scrap of make-up, heard me shout and swear. And didn't run away. I know she cares. These girls don't. Why should they?

I've phoned her once or twice, but the conversation was so hesitant, so stilted, I felt even more removed from her than if I hadn't tried to get in touch at all. Norah loathes the phone, regards it as a trap, is never sure whether the voice she hears is real or simply planted. I kept asking how she was. There were long nervous silences, and even when I'd convinced her it was me, she still wouldn't talk about herself, but asked me how I liked my job. Since I'm meant to be a dancer (and a touring one, to explain my two weeks absence), I was forced to change tack and move on to the weather. Warm for January.

'Is it?' she replied. 'I haven't been outside.' Which made me worry. I hope she isn't ill. She wouldn't tell me, even if she were. No doubt Beechgrove are worrying as well. I only wrote yesterday to tell them we're okay. It was the hardest letter I've ever had to write. What in God's name could I say? I didn't want to scare them, or they might start checking up on us, set up some inquiry. They could easily phone the Gold Rush, and be told we've disappeared, leaving all our stuff there. They'd really start to panic then, imagine we'd been kidnapped, even murdered.

In the end, I cobbled up some story about being invited to stay with a large and friendly family who live just out of Vegas, and how I was earning my keep looking after little boys. No lies there. I told them we'd be staying just a few more weeks; then scratched out 'weeks', put 'months'. I can hardly solve the problem of passports in just weeks. Unless it's solved for me – some midnight swoop, police raid. No. The cops won't find me here, when they're looking for two swanky Gold Rush guests. Which is one of the reasons I agreed to take the job. Odd to think I'm safer in what's called a house of vice. It is a sort of refuge, with its barbed wire fence, its high security, its total segregation from any other house or human being. Uncle Carl protects us – at a price.

Beechgrove would go spare, especially Sister Harding, who equates all sex with sin and would call Carl a second Satan. I told them not to worry; made sure to say that Norah was just fine; didn't want their 'told you so's'. I only wish I felt more sure of it, had seen Toomey for myself. The weekend after next I've got some time off. I'll take her out then, just the two of us. No Angelique, no George, no men at all.

No men! I must be joking. I'll be crawling with their fingerprints, dripping with their sperm; will have probably worked through scores of them by the time I get to see her – with a few wives thrown in as well. (Some book threesomes.) That first wife wasn't bad, the one I had to chat to. We talked about corgis and the Queen. She brought her knitting with her, purled and plained while her husband had his birthday treat with Suzie, who joined us for the cake. It was what they called

383

a Fun Cake, in the shape of two huge breasts with glacé-cherry nipples. Suzie got both nipples – popped into her mouth by her flushed and grateful client. I don't like Suzie much. She's bitchy and sarcastic. I wondered why he chose her, actually. Or perhaps the wife did, to put a little sting into all the saccharine.

Thirteen minutes. Damn this watch. It's slow. I'll go through to the lounge now, the 'get-acquainted lounge'. We're meant to greet our clients there, put them at their ease, make them feel they're visiting a normal friendly home. 'Class' again and 'standards'. In some low dumps all you get, apparently, is a mattress on the floor and no preliminaries – straight down to it the minute any man walks in, straight out again while he's zipping up his flies.

I adjust my outfit in the mirrors. Yes, mirrors all around me, even more than in the Gold Rush. The sales of glass in this state must be pretty staggering. (We never saw a mirror back at Beechgrove. I suppose glass is dangerous – not just because of smashing it, but because it gives you an identity, a face.) I take one last prowl around the room, checking all my props. I pray they won't be needed. Keep it simple, please, I beg him in advance – for both our sakes. I shut the door, prepare my smile. Halfway to the lounge, my whole face aches, as if the smile belongs to someone else, doesn't fit my mouth. I let it slip when I see he isn't there, start to panic. He's changed his mind, doesn't like the sound of me. I'll be booked with someone else – some pervert, paraplegic, one of Naima's brutes.

I walk on to the parlour, stop outside, where that one-way mirror reveals the clients to the girls, but not vice versa. There's a line-up just beginning. I've watched loads of those already, so I'll know the score when I join in myself tomorrow. Yeah, tomorrow. I'll be thrown in at the deep end then, have to parade half-naked in a leotard or body-stocking, or, after six, in cocktail gear. I hate the very thought. The hostess leads us out, and we have to say our names in turn, simpering and smiling. 'Hi, I'm Kathy.' 'Hi, I'm Carole.' Then walk up and down like animals, turn around, show off all we've got.

I watch the girls perform, hips wiggling, sexy pouts in place. There are four men sitting watching – three youngish, one quite ancient – sizing up the talent: judging the wobble on a pair of boobs, or picking out the biggest bum. They all look rather scruffy, but at least they're quiet, respectful. Some guys crack rude jokes, or make personal remarks, right out loud so everyone can hear. 'My Uncle Herb's got bigger boobs than Blondie there', or 'That one needs a diet, not a dick'. You have to keep on smiling, however rude or crude they are, wait until you're chosen. I don't know which is worse, being chosen, or rejected. And imagine being passed up three or four times running. It happens. I mean, these line-ups go on all day long; the whole charade repeated for every customer, unless he's booked a regular, or made some prior arrangement like my Korean.

Christ! I'm late for him, and after all that twitchy clock-watching. I sprint back to the lounge, find Laura there, the strictest of the hostesses, frowning at her own watch. She doesn't tell me off. She can't – she's not alone – though her fleshy figure almost hides the pocket Oriental cowering in her wake. He's tiny, looks as if he's eaten nothing more substantial than bean sprouts and bamboo shoots since he was weaned off his four-foot-nothing mother's watery milk. Laura introduces us. His name is Kyung Tae Chung. I can't pronounce it. My fear spreads like a rash.

'We were just wondering where you were,' says Laura coldly.

I mumble an apology, but she's already at the door, on her way to Carl, no doubt, to report my negligence. The door clicks shut behind her. Kyung Tae and me are on our own.

My blue eyes meet his brown ones for one naked panicked second, before we both switch on smiles again.

'S . . . sit down,' I urge.

He sits, seems to shrink still further, be swallowed up in the sudden deathbed silence.

'Er . . . have you driven far?' I ask. Crazy when I know he's come from Vegas and a taxi driver brought him.

'Please?'

Christ! He hasn't understood, can't speak English. No, he must do. 'Please' is probably just a courtesy. I wish I knew more about his country. Isn't it Korea where yes means no and no means yes? God! I hope not. It could cause complications later on.

I try again. 'It's . . . quite a place, Vegas, isn't it? I come from London – well, Portishead, but no one's heard of that. Have you been to London?'

He keeps on smiling. He's obviously polite. 'London,' I repeat, slowly, very clearly. Those with meagre English can often pick up place names.

He doesn't. I try his own name. 'Do I call you Kyung?' I ask. 'Or Mr Chang?' (*Was* it Chang, or Ching?) 'Or Chung, or . . .?'

There's no start of recognition, no nod or gesture to confirm either variation. Maybe I pronounced it wrong. Or perhaps it's not his real name, but a false one like Adorée which he gave to Carl to protect his true identity and has now forgotten. Or a name on an ID card which belongs to someone else. I can feel both our selves blurring into nothing, tipping into void.

I start talking very fast, to pull me back again, anchor me to solid things like birthday cakes or corgis; try tackling the same subjects which succeeded with the Wife.

He looks bewildered. 'Sorry?' At least he knows two words. Please and sorry. We won't get far with those.

'It doesn't matter. Really.' It does, though. He's sitting very straight, one hand trembling on his knee. I've failed, failed already. He's more nervous than when I first came in.

'Well, shall we . . .? I mean, we might as well . . .?' I stand up, take his arm, steer him through the door. Anything is better than trying to relax a man who can't make out a single word you say. They should have given him to Angelique. At least she's good at sign language, had years and years of practice with her brother. I long for her – or anyone – just to help me out. The private room looms and brags around us. This man is far too small for it, far too small for me. Thank God he's booked the missionary position and not girl-on-top, which might do him an injury. I realize now why everything was negotiated in advance. He must have done it through an interpreter, unless Carl speaks Korean, which I doubt. I remember reading somewhere that Korean has no relationship to any other language in the world. The thought is somehow terrifying, cuts me off still further.

Those dark slit eyes are looking round, taking in the huge and glacial bed, the naked-lady lamps, the dildos and vibrator on the table. I should have sneaked him into my room, a cosy child's room with a simple wooden bed and bluebird walls. But the VIP lounge costs more, much more. Have I forgotten this is just a business? The whole 'happy family' thing which Carl keeps stressing is all geared to extra cash. Give the guys a niche in the bosom of the family, offer them a permanent relationship. Permanence means profit.

So what am I doing dithering at the door? I've got to sell myself (and Carl), turn my client on. And I also have to check him before we actually get down to it. I loathe the thought of that. It seems so calculating, so cold and clinical, but Carl insists. Every guy has to be inspected, for his own protection, not to mention ours, then swabbed with disinfectant. I've been trained to do it, but it's completely different giggling with Desirée over a set of written rules, than actually peering at a cock, pulling it around, dousing it with Dettol — or whatever that vile stuff is they buy in gallons here. With any English-speaking client, at least I could explain, ease the whole procedure with a joke or two, or a little sexy talk. In Kyung's case, I'm tempted just to skip it, but supposing Carl's watching me through that closed circuit TV? The thought makes me so nervous, I feel a wave of almost panic, want to run away, bolt out of this prison back to England. How? Have I forgotten the little matter of five hundred dollars for a one-way ticket? A thousand for two fares. I can't leave Norah as another dependent sibling for Angelique.

I sit down on the bed, coax Kyung down beside me, take his hand. He pulls it away. I feel hurt, offended, until I realize he's delving in his pocket with it, wants to show me something — a photo in his wallet. Please God, not his girlfriend, some schoolkid I'm betraying because her parents would disown her if she did what I'm about to do. He edges a bit closer, passes me the snapshot. It *is* a female, but an ancient one, his mother, maybe, even grandmother. Her greying hair is scraped back from a flat and yellowed face; her eyes are lost in smile-lines. He's pointing at her, proud.

I smile and babble back. 'Yes, she's nice. She's like you – got your eyes. Her hair must be quite long to get it in that bun.' I sound stupid, insincere. I'm sure this isn't right – not mothers in a brothel, not family albums when he's paying for a whore.

He's produced another photo – a young girl this time, so young she's still in pigtails. His sister? Niece? I've got to stop him before he runs through the whole tribe. It's probably all my fault. I expect he sensed my nervousness and is trying to relax me, doing what I'm meant to do for him. I need a drink. We both do. It would kill two birds at once – relax the pair of us and help to swell Carl's profits. Do Koreans drink, though? Or are they mostly Buddhists or one of those religions which disapproves of booze? I'm so ignorant, I feel ashamed. I hardly know where Korea is on the map.

I return the photos, take Kyung's hand again, lead him to the bar. He can't be that strict or he wouldn't be with me. I point out the champagne, the best twelve-year-old malt whisky, leave the cheaper drinks to speak (softer) for themselves. He seems undecided, so I pick up the Krug, cradle the green bottle between my breasts, stroke its swollen belly, run my hands down lower to its base. It works. He's nodding, smiling. The next hazard is to open it without spilling all the fizz. (I've had lessons in that, too, but not with a client watching.) I pass Kyung his glass, clutch my own, knuckles white around its stem. Those scared hands should be working, taking off his clothes. I wish he had a few less on. He's dressed for a board meeting in a three-piece suit (yes, even a formal waistcoat in this heat), white shirt, silk tie, black laceups. Too many fiddly things – buttons, laces, tie-pin. I put my glass down, ease his jacket off, fight a private battle with the tie-pin, suck my bleeding thumb. He tries to help, but we're in each other's way, fumbling with buttons, knocking elbows. No wonder this profession's so well paid. There's a skill in all the tiny things – how to slide off socks or inch down trousers while keeping the erotic tension high, and not forgetting timing.

Already, I've gone too far too fast. I haven't checked him yet, and I'm meant to do that first, before removing all his clothes. If I find anything suspicious, any lumps or sores, redness or a discharge, then he has to leave immediately. It will be terribly embarrassing to buckle him back into all that pinstripe armour. And how will I explain? Yet equally embarrassing to start inspecting him cold-bloodedly. I wish I had the chutzpah of that ghastly Dr Bernstein who inspected me on Monday. *He* wasn't shy – far from it. By the time he'd finished, there wasn't any hole or slit he hadn't stuck his hands up. He took smears and scrapings, blood and pee; helped himself to bits of me without a by-your-leave; jabbed needles in my bottom, shoved hardware up my cunt, accompanied the whole process with a stream of stupid jokes.

All *I've* got to do is a quick check of a prick. The trouble is I can't see the sodding thing. Kyung's sitting on the bed again, with his legs pressed close together, looks rather like a girl – skinny back, no shoulders, pale and slender arms. His skin is very smooth, without a hair on it. I've got more down on my legs than he has on his whole body.

I kneel between his feet, stroke my hands slowly up his thighs, gently part them. No. He's not a girl, though his cock's so limp and tiny, it reminds me of a baby's. Peg's new grandson would have a little bud like that. I take it in my hands, feel him tense as I roll the foreskin back. Baby's crying, frightened, needs his mother's touch. I start to sing, very very softly. 'Rock a bye baby on the tree top . . .' He can't understand the words, but the tune is soothing, lulls us both. I feel him relax, even harden just a little.

'When the wind blows, the cradle will rock . . .'

I think he imagines it's some erotic song. It is, in its effects. He's stiff now, really stiff, and completely clear and healthy. I'm so relieved, I want to kiss him top to bottom. I can't. That costs more, has to be negotiated. He may not understand, refuse to pay the extra. I can see Carl's grey eye again snooping through the wall. We don't give favours here, okay? Every item is contracted and then charged. And get on with the washing, girl. You're slacking.

I fetch the Peter Pan. (Yeah, that's a joke – the pan they wash

389

the peters in. They have their little jokes here, the cutesy words and phrases which hide the blatant facts.) Kyung doesn't need a wash. He's so shining clean all over, it's as if he's had three baths already, scrubbed his nails, washed his hair, polished up his skin. I feel that I'm insulting him as I swab him down with water. The disinfectant's worse. He starts, looks quite offended, immediately subsides. I feel quite upset myself, want to make it up to him.

It may be unprofessional, but I rather like the lad. I'm so grateful that he's nice, disproves Naima's theories, that I long to give him everything. Angelique said not to go all out, not to get 'involved'; if I must respond, then fake it; not to waste my energies, and a lot of other 'not to's which I accepted at the time, but which now seem mean and grudging. She won't know if I try to make it memorable, stay a human being instead of acting like a robot.

I start to take my clothes off as sensuously as I can, repeating all the tricks I learnt at Ritzy's. Kyung makes no move to help, seems too shy even to watch, just snatches guilty glances at me, then eyes back to the carpet. At Ritzy's, I had cheers and adulation, thunderous applause. Here, just Kyung's nervous in-breath, countered by the out-breath of my zipper, the soft thud of a shoe. I remove my g-string, toss it over to him. He squirms with embarrassment, seems uncertain what to do with it. He looks so vulnerable, perched there on the very edge of the bed, hands torturing the scrap of scarlet lace, cheeks childish-plump against the thinness of his body. Once naked, I feel vulnerable myself, as if I've stripped off all my skin, as well as just my clothes. The silence makes it worse. I never really realized how useful conversation is, as psychological Polyfilla. If it were my first time, what would make it special? I remember Jon – me squashed into his sleeping-bag. He coaxed me out of it, told me I was wonderful, refused to put the light off so that he could keep gawping at my breasts, admiring my blonde bush. Those praises reassured me, made me feel all woman. Compliments won't mean much in a foreign tongue, but I can praise his body with my hands, my eyes.

I plump the pillows up, persuade Kyung to lie back and relax, stretch myself beside him. I feel too big, too fleshy, overlapping on to him. I wish he'd speak, even in Korean. I need compliments myself, or at least some reassurance. Does he like me? Like what I'm doing with my hands? Want to touch me too? No. Carl emphasized that we are to expect nothing back in bed. If we do enjoy the sex, that's fine, but purely incidental. (And pretty bloody rare as well, according to Joanne.) Our chief satisfaction comes later – with our pay cheque. He said I might find some problem with a few clients (very few) who are so conditioned into thinking of the woman, that they can't lie back and just give themselves to pleasure, without feeling guilty about not reciprocating. That's not Kyung's problem. He hasn't even touched me yet.

I guide his hand towards my breast. He strokes it, warily, as if it's something dangerous, which may blow up in his face. His prick is still quite minuscule, even when erect. I know it sounds ridiculous, but it makes the whole thing easier – as if it doesn't count as sex. He's just my little boy and we're cuddling up in bed. I never thought I'd be much good at mothering, but I rather like the feeling. I'm gentle loving Peg with a baby in my arms. I hold him close, try to comfort him. Perhaps he feared he'd never get a woman, feared he was too small.

I reach down again, use both my hands to measure. 'Big,' I say. 'Very big. I like it.'

I think he understands – not the words, my hands. I suppose I ought to guide him in. One of the problems of this job is timing. It's like stripping, in that way, so Angelique said. You mustn't go too far too quickly, yet can't overrun your time. It's all slightly schizophrenic. You have to appear abandoned, passionate, while all the time you're working out your moves, or have one eye on the clock. I can't relax at all. I'm still up in my head, wondering if I'm handling things all right. There's another conflict, too: I want to succeed, want to make him come, yet another part of me is shouting 'Stop! Stop *now*.' Up to this moment, I can still claim to be an innocent, a visitor, a friend of Angelique's staying at the brothel as a guest; maybe just helping out with Kyung, until she turns up herself, takes him over. But once he's actually entered me, there's no going back. I'm a whore – and that's official.

He must have sensed my struggle. He's losing his erection. I'm half relieved, half worried. Almost automatically, I use my hands again, try to pretend I'm only hands; force my mind to switch off, my conscience to shut down. I continue till he's stiff again. Now I'm hands and legs: legs opening, spreading wide, hands to guide him in. Now muscles: contracting, tensing, to keep him there, keep him stiff. I've done it. It's all right. I feel nothing. Not shame, distaste, remorse. Just relief.

Go on, then, woman, don't lie back. There's more to it than that. I close my eyes, make noises, shake my hair about. It's damned hard work, in fact – the acting, panting, the tensed and gripping muscles, but at least it stops me agonizing. I'm the professional now, controlled, in charge, with a job to do, a job I'm doing well. I even feel a certain pride. I've got out of my head; I'm pleasing my client, not thinking of myself; he likes me, he's relaxed. I tease my hands across his shoulders, then down beneath his balls, tongue his ears and eyes. He lets out a sudden gasping noise – the first sound he's made so far. I'm thrilled. Baby's first word. He's moving now, thrusting. I lie back, move in time with him. It's all pretend, except my sense of triumph.

'Great!' I shout. 'Wonderful. Go on. Yes, move. Go on!'

He stops. Stops dead. I must have scared him, yelling out like that, or perhaps he thought he'd hurt me. I can feel him losing contact, slipping out. I sit up, almost crying with frustration. Desirée told me her first virgin client came in just two seconds, before he'd even entered her. Desirée's more exciting, obviously.

Suddenly I freeze. He's still got one blue sock on. How could I have missed it – or he either? I mustn't laugh, though he does look quite ridiculous, one bare foot and one navy nylon one. We're useless, both of us. I can't undress a man and he's completely thrown by a woman's cry of passion. Except it wasn't passion, was it? He's so damned sensitive, he probably picked up my pretence. He's wet-sock limp, back to where we started, and I'm as jittery. I mustn't let him see it, must try to act relaxed. I use my hands as lightly as I can, just feathering them across his chest and stomach. He lets out a deep sigh. I stop holding my own breath, start humming the Dream Topping jingle, a silly catchy tune which has been trilling in my head since last night's commercial break.

Lighter, whiter, helps your weight . . .

I move my hands to the rhythm of the song, creeping lower, till I reach his balls.

Makes apple pie a winner,
Turns jello into dream . . .

It's working! He's responding. I stroke one finger round and round his slowly stiffening tip.

All the taste without the fat . . .

He's harder now, much harder. I've got to make it real this time – less pretence, more passion. I don't care what Angelique says. She's probably so experienced, she can fake and get away with it. I can't. I shut my eyes, guide Reuben in, not Kyung. He's huge, almost hurts me as he rams in deeper, deeper. I can smell his smell – aftershave and Gauloises, feel his hands, strong hands with dark hairs on the thumbs; dark hairs on his legs, his belly, back. He's booked me, paid Carl a fortune to run through the whole menu, hors-d'oeuvres to dessert. I move against him, whispering the vulgar words he taught me, words I can't pronounce, but which excite him. He's not listening. He's talking to some other girl – Desirée. His mouth is on Desirée's, his hands on Suzie's breasts. The bed is packed with bodies, all female save his own. Sudchit's giggling, that maddening tinkly giggle which grates on my nerves. Reuben loves it. He's tonguing her brown nipples, calling her his *bubeleh*, his *pushke*.

'Reuben, she's a *whore* – worked in some low bathhouse in Bangkok before she signed on here. You're just another nameless client who's bought her for an hour – and bought her with my money.'

I slam against him, furious. I never knew you could thrust with rage as wildly as with lust. I'm like an animal, teeth bared, talons clawing down his back.

'I loved you, Reuben, don't you understand? That's why I gave you all my winnings. I wanted you to have them for the things you cared about. I cared about them, too. Isn't that what love is?'

He doesn't answer, doesn't give a damn. His face is lost in Kristia's hair, thick blonde muffling hair; his hands round her fat arse. I jerk my body, try to force the filthy two apart. My movement just excites him more. He's coming. Far too soon. He never came that quickly, or so quietly. He always made a noise, heaved and groaned, shouted out my name. This come is shy and almost guilty, just a stifled bleat, a shudder. I open my eyes, stare into a small and childish face, soft cheeks filmed with sweat, tiny dainty features, grimacing now, screwed up.

'Kyung.'

He smiles, a sheepish smile, and suddenly he's talking, letting out a flash-flood of Korean. I can hear the triumph in it, the relief. I start to laugh myself, crazy hurting laughter which catches at my chest, makes tears run down my face into my mouth. The bed is shaking under me, as if Reuben is still thrusting. I try to stop it, fight to get control. I can't. Kyung will think I'm hysterical or mad. No. He's laughing with me, God knows why. Maybe just elation or politeness. We lie together for a while; me heaving, choking, he giggling like a girl. At last, I peter out, just a few weak final spasms and a dull pain in my ribs. He's subsided too, his prick a tiny foetus, the immaculate satin sheets stained a bit with sperm. I want to rip them off the bed, hang them from the window as a sign to Reuben.

'See, super-prick, I can do it too, betray you too. You're not so special, are you? This boy really likes me. And he's decent with it – sensitive and caring.'

I squeeze Kyung's hot hand. We're bonded now, not by sex, but by all that stupid laughing, letting-go. Mutual orgasm. I pad out of bed, pour us more champagne. Champagne to celebrate, not to boost Carl's profits. I clink my glass to Kyung's. 'Many happy returns,' I say, wishing he understood.

He takes two sips, then reaches for his shirt. He's going. It's all over. I ought to be relieved. Instead, I feel a stab of almost panic. Once he's left, I'll be alone again, alone with Reuben. Until this afternoon. Then two more clients, maybe jerks or bastards, Naima's sort. I was lucky with Kyung. I watch him do his waistcoat up, knot his quiet blue tie. He looks so neat and safe, I long to keep him here. If only we could talk, communicate. I'd like to ask him where he's staying, what he does, how he lives back home. I can see his grey-haired mother serving rice, that pigtailed niece or sister playing chequers with him. Nice to join their circle, be another sister, with a proper family, somewhere to belong.

'Don't go,' I whisper silently. 'You're special. You're my first.' Peg's got this baby-book with photos of her grandson pasted in – first tiny tooth, first curl. I want to stick Kyung in my own book, snip off a lock of hair, scoop up a drop of come.

Sentimental claptrap! This stranger doesn't even know my name. He's buckling on his watch, his mind already on his next appointment. There'll be a string of others after him who don't know who I am, don't care; who've picked me from the line-up as just a new and different cunt.

I replace my own clothes. The playsuit seems too tight now, as if I've spread and bloated. I pick up Kyung's jacket, help him on with it. The formal suit makes us both more solemn. He even bows to me, a little nervous bobbing bow, as I hold the door for him, then escort him to Carl's office. I have to report to Carl myself as soon as Kyung's left. Meanwhile, I slink along the passage to my own room, glad no one's around. Elation and revenge are like champagne – all fizz at first, then flat, then hangover.

I flop back on my bed, light a cigarette. It's odd to think that almost no one in the world knows where I am. I suppose I should be glad. At least I'm pretty safe, safe from the police, but it's a horrid frightening feeling all the same. My pants are damp with Kyung, slimy, leaking sperm. Am I really going to stick this life? I haven't got much choice. I've got to hide somewhere, make some money somehow. I'm responsible for Norah, for myself. If I give up now, we both could starve.

Kyung's taxi is pulling up outside. I hear a door slam, the engine starting up again. I seem to fade and dwindle with it as it drones away, fainter, fainter, fainter. Silence for a moment. I take a deep drag on my cigarette, feel the smoke burning in my throat. A baby cries. I jump. Is Peg's grandson still around? It feels as if years and years have passed, as if the kid should be grown-up now, not a wailing babe-in-arms. I'm surprised that Carl allows it here at all. Its crying sounds so desperate, so pleading sort of hopeless. Someone sings to shush it; not Peg this time, a younger voice. The lullaby's the same, though – a threatening violent song.

> *When the bough breaks, the cradle will fall,*
> *Down will come Carole, Norah and all.*

24

'If you have been raped, or sexually assaulted, then ring this number . . .'

The number is a long one. It flashes on and off the screen. I know what rape is. Angelique told me. She said not to leave the house. There's a doctor on the programme. He's not like Dr Bates. He's talking to six women who have all been raped. None of them is pretty. One of them is old.

'Every man is a rapist,' says the old one. 'In his mind.'

I suddenly feel frightened. I'm all alone with George. The maid has gone out shopping. Someone came to fetch her. A dark man on a motor-bike. She's never gone out before, or left us on our own. George sees me glance at him, stares back, keeps on staring. I look down, then up again. His eyes are on me still.

'In America alone, someone, somewhere, is being sexually assaulted every three and a quarter minutes . . .'

I'm not sure if George can hear. I switch the programme off, watch his face. It doesn't change. His eyes are following everything I do.

'Don't stare,' I say. 'It's rude.'

He takes no notice. He never ever answers if I speak. I still talk to him, just to be polite. Or because I hate the silence. It's not Death Valley silence. That was safe, and stretched for miles. Here, we're all closed in. There's a fence around the house and trees around the fence. The trees are bare, but tall. They shut out half the light. The windows don't open and there are three separate layers of curtains, the lacey ones stretched right across the glass.

We're both too old and shabby for the room. It's full of new expensive things, which don't like us being here. I'm scared to use the table, in case the glass top cracks, and the maid took the cushions off the chairseats, because she said we'd dirty them. The seats are very hard. There's a picture on the wall of a man with two heads but only one eye. The eye has no lashes, never closes. Whenever I look up at it, it's watching me. Three eyes watching me. His and George's two.

I don't think it's Angelique's home. Carole said it was, but she said that just to trick me. *They're* living in her real home. Angelique's her friend now. Angelique is prettier. And younger. They left together on the Monday morning, disappeared before I was awake. Carole didn't leave a note. She phoned me twice, but I don't think it was her. She told me she was phoning from a place called New Orleans, where she was working as a dancer in a club, but the maid said no, the call was just a local one.

George is still staring. 'Do you know where Angelique lives?' I ask him, very loudly. He dribbles in reply.

The silence seems much worse than yesterday's. I put my earplugs in, to block it out. The ones from Flyaway. I didn't steal them. I found them in the bottom of my handbag.

It's all I've got left, that old brown bag and Carole's wedding dress. I miss my green two-piece. It had my smell on it. I left it in the Gold Rush and the Gold Rush has closed down. So has Beechgrove. Carole didn't tell me. She's kind like that. She knew it would upset me. But I guessed it anyway. We were meant to fly home yesterday, but we didn't go. We couldn't. Beechgrove is just rubble.

I think we've moved to lodgings. Lodgings in America are very new and grand, but there are still a lot of rules. We sit in just one room all day, watching the TV. We can't go out, or make tea in the kitchen, and usually we're watched. The maid's in charge. She shouts a lot, like Miss Johnson in my other lodgings. Her name's Maria, which is Mary's name. That's wrong for her. God's mother never shouted.

I have to wear her clothes. I've got her dress on and her knickers. The dress is pink and shiny and smells of dead carnations, and the knickers have brown stains on. I don't like them at all, but Angelique's clothes won't fit and I'm scared of wearing George's any more. He's very ill and some illnesses are catching. I'd hate to never speak. It makes you feel more lonely.

I take my earplugs out in case he's talking now. He isn't, so I put them back. I can hear things with them in. Noises in my head. Conversations. Sometimes Carole's speaking. She says we're friends again, says she's coming back. She's only been away two days. It feels longer. Much longer.

I haven't seen the house yet, only this room and my bedroom and three toilets. I sleep alone, which you have to do in lodgings. When Carole was here (which was only one night), she slept in Angelique's room. I heard them laughing. I don't like it on my own. I'm frightened of the wolves.

I wish I could get up. I'm hungry. George and I have our meals on trays. They get smaller every day. It's probably because I haven't paid. I haven't any money. On Sunday night, we had proper cooked tea sitting round a table with Angelique and Carole, and the maid brought all the food in (lots of food) and called Angelique 'madam'. We may not get any meals at all today. Or drinks. I'm thirsty, very thirsty. I think I'll go and find a glass of water. Water's free.

'Would you like a drink of water, George?'

He's gone to sleep. He only sleeps, or stares. I have to ask him, though, in case he's listening in a dream. Some people are more real in dreams.

I creep out to the passage, stop outside the kitchen door. Not a sound. I'd like to see the kitchen. I push the door a crack, slip in. It's very big and clean and reminds me of the chocolate factory because of all the white machines. There's some food on the table. A loaf of bread with little bits of wood-shaving sprinkled on the top, some round red shiny apples and two big fat bananas. We never had bananas in the war. We don't have them at Beechgrove. Only tinned fruit in bowls, with custard, for Sunday evening tea. I'd like a piece of real fruit, fruit with skin on and a smell.

Eve stole an apple, which is why everyone wears clothes. They were naked in the Garden before she ate the fruit. I'd rather wear my clothes. You'd get raped if you were naked.

It's hard to eat an apple with false teeth. Bananas are much softer. Even babies eat them. Even George. I eat one in my mind. It's very soft and ripe. I can smell it through the skin. There's cream on top, and sugar, that damp and yellow sugar which looks like sand.

I miss the sand. I miss the walks with Bernie. Bernie liked me. Bernie was my friend. I was better in Death Valley. Here I'm worse, much worse. I must be. They've shut me up with George. George takes pills as well. More than I do. Yellow ones, and blue ones, and shiny red and purple ones at night. Mine are only white.

I pretend I'm very full. I ate both the big bananas, all the cream and sugar, and half the loaf of bread. Now I need a drink to wash them down. I drink some water from the tap. I don't know where the glasses are and even if I found one, I might leave germs on it.

I wipe my mouth, start back to the sitting room. Then stop. If Maria's out, I could look around the house, find out whose it is. There may be other patients, other lodgers. I'd like to talk to someone. I'd like to make a friend.

Carole was my friend. Friends always say goodbye, or leave a note. Perhaps she left the note upstairs, laid it on her bed. A letter with her name signed underneath. I could cut the 'Carole' out, keep it in a matchbox.

I creep upstairs to the room she slept in. The door opens with a groan, as if it's ill. Thirty, forty women turn to look at me, women with red steel lips and nails. They're pinned up round the walls. Some of them are naked; some are Angelique. She's dancing with a bear. She's shaking hands with people. A small bald man is staring at her bosoms. Another man is giving her a chalice. I don't think he's a priest.

I'm scared of Angelique. She doesn't like me. She doesn't like her brother, never smiles at him. She only likes people if they're pretty and not ill. She's smiling on the walls, smiling thirteen times. I count the smiles. Thirteen is unlucky.

The other women all look sad or angry. They don't want me here, don't like me in their room. I think they're cross that I came upstairs at all.

'I'm looking for a note,' I say. 'A letter from my friend.' I like to call her friend still. Sometimes if you say things, they come true.

The room is sad as well, very stiff and clean, as if it's died and someone's laid it out for burial. Everything is white. White walls. White curtains, drawn to keep the sun out, white shroud on the bed. I'll never find the note. The Death Men have cleared everything away. At Beechgrove, patients have old dolls, or dirty bits of rag, or knitting bags, or fruit drops, spread out in a jumble on their lockers. The chest of drawers is bare here. And the dressing table. There's just a vase of flowers standing on the sill. Pale green flowers which stare.

I go across and smell them. There isn't any smell. I'm not sure if they're real or not. Flowers are never green. I'm scared to touch them, scared to move at all. I stand there for a while, try to think of Carole. The thoughts don't work. I can only think of coffins and white shrouds.

There's a sudden cry behind me. The cat's walked in through the open bedroom door. Carole said it's Burmese, but she's wrong. It's a Russian Blue – Angelique told me so herself. It isn't blue, but a dirty greyish brown. I've never seen a blue cat. A lot of things are foreign here. The maid is Guatemalan. I don't know what that is, but most foreigners are cross.

The cat is snarling at me, drawing back its top lip, showing yellow teeth. I squeeze behind the bed, crouch down on the floor. There's something on the carpet, something small and coloured. I pick it up. It's a hairslide, Carole's hairslide. It's shaped like a butterfly with pink and purple wings. She wore it for her wedding. The Death Man must have missed it, which means Carole's still alive. I hold it in my palm, feel it flutter. The women on the walls are watching, muttering. I can hear them saying 'Thief!'

'It's not Angelique's,' I tell them. 'It belongs to Carole. And I'm going to give it back.'

They don't believe me. I think I'd better leave. They may be men, those women. They had women in the show like that, with long red nails, and jewels, and even bosoms, but the lady sitting next to me told me they were men in female clothes. Perhaps I didn't hear right. The pills affect my ears. I've started taking them again, but only half the dose; Carole said we're short of pills. Sister gave me enough for fourteen days. We've been here twelve. I think. We should be home in England with more pills. If you stop or start your tablets or change the strength, they can make you worse, not better. I feel much worse since Carole left. Since Monday.

I close the door as quietly as I can, walk on down the passage. I find another flight of stairs, just a short one, leading to a room all on its own. I walk up very slowly. I'm so hungry, there's nothing in my legs. I didn't take an apple. Eve stole just a bite of one and they had to leave the Garden and work all day instead of picking flowers.

I try the door. It isn't locked, so I push it and go in. I can see a pair of brown bare legs stretched out on the bed. Men's legs. Hairy legs. There isn't any head. The legs are jerking up and down.

'Are you all right?' I ask. If these are patients' lodgings, the man may be unwell, or epileptic. Some patients have bad fits and roll around.

There's a sudden shout and then two heads appear, one of them Maria's. No. Maria went out shopping with a man. A short dark man with curly hair. This one's short and dark. His hair is curly, wet with sweat. He's shouting. Both the mouths are shouting. It can't be Maria. She's always spoken English. This is something else, a very angry language. I may need stronger drugs. It happened once before: I couldn't understand what mouths were saying. I could see them moving, making faces at me, red and very rude, but silent rude. They gave me an injection and when I woke up, all the sounds came back again, though muffled.

It's happening now. The words are coming back. English words. Maria's foreign English. It *is* Maria. I recognize her voice. I think she was undressed. She's pulling on a skirt, banging things around while she searches for her shoes.

'I'm sorry,' I keep saying. I don't know what I've done, but it's something very bad.

She pushes past me, crashes down the stairs. I can hear her shouting still, slamming doors. The small dark man is zipping up his trousers. He slams his door as well, almost in my face.

I tiptoe down the stairs, hide in the toilet. I'm very frightened. I hate people to shout. She's yelling things at George now, awful things. I wait for a long time. There are blue roses in the toilet. Angelique likes blue. I like brown and green. I clutch my old brown handbag very tight. I'm glad I've got it with me. I never leave it anywhere, not now. I sleep with it beside me on the pillow. Sometimes I don't sleep at all. I'm frightened they may close the bedroom down, before I wake.

There are no windows in the toilet, only blinds. But I hear a motor-bike roar off. That's the dark man's bike. It sounds angry, like Maria. Maybe they've gone shopping. Really shopping.

I wait a bit longer, in case they both come back. They don't. The house is holding its breath. I can feel its heartbeat, pounding far too hard.

I go back to the sitting room. I won't leave it again. George hasn't any eyes now. They've disappeared and the skin around them is all swollen and puffed up. He's crying. Crying silently. I've never seen him cry before. His lips are opening, wriggling, but no words come out. Or perhaps they do, but I'm just too ill to hear them. We're both much worse, George as well as me.

If the maid reports us, I expect we'll have to move again. At least it's very clean here, with lots of room. The new place may be dirty, or so crowded they run out of sheets and blankets and we have to sleep on mattresses with just old curtains over us. Perhaps they've told George that we're moving and he's scared.

'You'll have me,' I say. 'I'll help you.'

Unless they separate us. They may send him to one place and me to somewhere else. I don't think he could manage on his own. He can't even dry his eyes. I dry them for him on a piece of toilet paper. I lost all my handkerchiefs. They were in my suitcase and those people on the plane confiscated it. They were angry because I stole the soap.

George is still crying, stretching out his hands to me. I don't know what to do. I take his hand, just one of them. It's very fat and hot. He holds mine very tight. His fingers really hurt me. I smile, to show they don't. His tears are falling on my dress, making shiny stains. The maid will say I've ruined it, shout again, slam doors.

'Don't cry,' I say.

He cries.

I'd like to make a cup of tea. It's not allowed and it isn't tea-time yet. I rummage in my bag. I might disturb a fruit drop at the bottom. George likes sweets, all kinds.

I find a picture postcard with the Gold Rush on the front and lots of coloured lights. On the back there's just one line in pencil. 'We've arrived.' The writing's very wobbly. I can't read the name at all. I don't know who arrived or where they slept. The Gold Rush has closed down. It's probably just a hole now, a big hole in the ground. You can't sleep in a hole.

I still can't find a sweet. The lining of the bag's torn, so I poke my fingers through and feel all round. There's something there. A pill bottle which rattles when I shake it. It doesn't sound like pills.

'MARY'S RING,' it says. I don't know any Marys. There were three once in the ward, but they all died long ago. Maybe it's Maria's and that's why she's so angry: I stole her ring.

I didn't. She doesn't wear a ring. Perhaps I know a Mary, but she's gone. People never stay long. Perhaps she sent that card.

I tip the other things out. Lots and lots of things. I saved all Carole's matchboxes and the stones from Bernie's dates, and some beetles from Death Valley which have died and lost their wings. I also find an Oxo cube and an empty powder compact which Nurse Sullivan threw out, and the two cartons of confetti I bought for Carole's wedding.

'Look, George,' I say. 'Confetti.'

I open up the boxes, shake some in his hand. His mouth is open. He tries to stuff it in.

'No,' I say. 'Not sweeties.'

He's smiling now and pointing. I think he likes the colours. I like them too, like the different shapes. There are little bows, and flowers, and wedding bells, and stars, and silver slippers. And horseshoes, lucky horseshoes, lots of them. I make a row of horseshoes, pink and blue, spread out on my lap, the open ends on top. That's the right way up for horseshoes, otherwise the luck falls out. Miss O'Toole said.

George chuckles with no noise, tries to grab them.

'Mustn't touch,' I say.

The confetti is so light, my breath makes it tremble when I talk. It wants to fly away. I wish we could fly with it. Both of us. I tip more out on my dress: yellow flowers, red hearts. I wouldn't be a horseshoe or a heart. I'd be a star. A star called Pegasus.

'What would you be, George?'

He doesn't answer, but I think he'd be a bell. He could ring then, all the time, make a noise. I put my earplugs in again, so I can hear the bells instead of just the silence. There's wedding music, too. Carole's wedding.

I unzip my bag again. I'd better find the hairslide. It's still alive, purple wings throbbing in my hand. George snatches.

'No. Give it back,' I say. 'That's Carole's slide, her wedding slide.'

I have to tug quite hard to get it from his fingers. He starts to cry again. I take my earplugs out to hear, but there isn't any noise. Silent crying's sadder than the normal kind.

'All right,' I say. 'You borrow it. I'll put it in your hair.'

I lean across. His hair is very fine, silky like a child's. It's hard to keep the slide in. It keeps slipping out, undoing. At last, I snap it shut, though it falls again, hangs low above one eye. His hair is mousy-pale, so the slide looks very bright. I show him in my little handbag mirror, hold it steady for him. He smiles. The smile gets slowly bigger until it fills the mirror. I think he'd like to laugh, but the noise is stuck inside him. He keeps pointing at himself, rocking to and fro, making laughing movements with his mouth.

I put my earplugs back. I can hear him laughing now, hear the bells again. I'm not frightened any more. He won't rape me. He's like an angel, doesn't have those men's bits, only wings. His wings are pink and purple, lifting off.

I pass him one box of the confetti. He opens it, starts to throw it everywhere. It's flying. The hearts are coloured kites kicking at the wind. The bows are little planes with shining wings. The silver horseshoes belong to flying horses. The stars are shooting stars.

Everything is flying – horses jumping stars; kites and petals bobbing in the sky. Pink and blue and yellow are spinning past my eyes. Silver pours like rain. Red is galloping.

I'm grey and left behind. Too solid, far too clumsy. I reach across, clutch my bridegroom's hand. He'll help me. His huge angel's wings are spreading out, unfolding.

'Fly,' I beg him. 'Fly. And take me with you.'

25

I need another order form. There's no room on this one. I've ordered eighteen items for Norah, all with her name on, or initials. She loves her name on things. I've chosen a set of squirrel bookplates ('From Norah Toomey's Library'), a pie dish ('Pies by Norah'), a Rolls-Royce car-plaque ('Custom-built for Toomey'), a shamrock butter cooler (''Tis a Blessing to be Irish'), a monogrammed gold-plated case to hold a packet of chewing gum, a plastic wine carafe ('*Vin Maison* Toomey'), and seven egg cups, all with legs. That's fourteen legs, which ought to be enough for anyone. I've already bought her a load of clothes – two pairs of men's pyjamas, some flesh-pink bras and bloomers, a decent coat, and the sort of safe and ample dresses she likes to lose her body in.

For myself, I decided on a cigarette box which plays '*O, Sole Mio*' when you open it, a set of miniature brass cowboy boots for stamping out fag ends, and a plastic unicorn whose horn conceals a ballpoint pen. That's just the fun stuff. Mail order is a craze here. All the girls swap catalogues or splurge their extra cash on silver-plated ice-cream cornet holders, or luminous plaster models of Michelangelo's masterpieces. Okay, call it crap, but I quite like buying useless things, feeling I can waste my money if I want, and don't have to rely on hard-slog competitions for a one-in-a-million chance of winning some small luxury. I know I should be saving, but what's the point? We can't go back to England without passports, and even if we got there, I'd no longer fit. I'd never manage on the dole – not now. Just a taste of wealth ruins you for normal life. And what about a place to live? I couldn't just return to Jan's, pick up our friendship where we dropped it, as if this last eleven days had never happened. And I could never ever tell her what I've done – the Four Girl Fantasia when I was fourth girl, and all for one five-foot-nothing Jap; my double act with Kristia when we played two dykes in bed together, to turn a client on; the Drag Party when I had to dress the guy in female gear, make him up with lipstick, eye gloss, blusher, then let him fuck me while he was still in his high heels.

Jan would be appalled, maybe never speak to me again. How could I explain that it isn't that important? The first time is a shock, of course, seeing some big wheel arrive, and change from martinet to mincing girl; or watching an axe-faced senator romp naked in the jacuzzi with half a dozen females. But once the session's over, you somehow block it out. There's no real contact anyway. The sex is just a non-event, something mechanical, impersonal. I cracked just once – with client number five. He wasn't brutish, didn't treat me badly. He was ugly, yes, with a paunch and sweaty hands, a boil erupting on his back. That's nothing. You get used to sweat and acne, fungus toes, psoriasis. No, it was the way he wanted me to sit on his lap, have me call him Dad.

'D . . . Dad.' I heard my voice crack. I had to keep on saying it all the time he screwed me: 'I love you, Dad,' as he humped and heaved and groaned; 'Yeah, I love you, Daddy,' as he came. There was silence after that. He didn't move, just lay wet and hot on top of me. Dead weight. Dead father.

'Dad,' I said. Last time. My voice didn't break. Not then. Not until he'd gone. Then I crept down into the bathroom, meaning to have a shower. I never got as far as even turning on the taps. I just lay down on the bathmat and sobbed for a whole hour or more, while my dead Dad's living sperm seeped and dribbled out of me.

Angelique found me in the end, told me off for spoiling my complexion, taking things too personally. After that, I made sure my plastic cover didn't slip. It envelops me completely now, clingy like a leotard, prevents anything or anyone from touching me too closely.

I suspect the other girls have their own different versions of my clingfilm. We don't discuss our work much. There's far more talk about what's for dinner, or which salesman's calling when, to flog us clothes. I've spent a lot on clothes – classy stuff – evening gowns and negligés, a nightie trimmed with marabou. Why not? There's not much else to do in our free time. It's easier for the others. Most of them have cars. We're stuck out in the desert here, so if I want to see a shop or cinema, or get a haircut or a takeaway, I have to cadge a lift. I'm not that keen on cadging. The girls accept me more now, but there's none I'd call a real pal, and you have to be quite careful. Adrienne made overtures, but it turns out that she's dykey. Angelique just shrugged it off, said a lot of hookers end up gay – searching for the tenderness they never get with men. I can sympathize with that, though I'm not convinced you'd get much more with women – not these women anyway. Some are too neurotic to make any real relationships, some too hard and bitter.

The trouble is, our pasts come with us here. If a father beat us, or a husband left us, or a boss fired us for incompetence, or an undeveloped country stuck us in the paddy fields, all those fathers, spouses, bosses, countries, are still fermenting in our guts, setting off old grudges and resentments, fuelling jealousies. I know that from my own case. I can't stand Suzie – not just because she's tough (and got hair down to her waist), but because she's got a doting (living) Dad. I don't deny that many girls have made good lives here, escaped dead-end jobs or clapped-out marriages, but it's still a ghetto, and the tensions still run high.

In one way, it's like Beechgrove. We're all shut up, labelled odd or tainted; shunned and feared by 'normal' people, locked away from them. And we still have rules and timetables; hostesses as strict as Sister Watkins; the chores and cooking done for us, but no real choice or freedom. And whores, like mental patients, have often had bad childhoods, or come from rotten homes, or landed in some mess. Some of the girls here could do with Dr Bates. Samantha's always gloomy, Marlee overeats, Kathy starves. They're all terrified of age, or operations, or anything which might take away their looks. That's why it's crap to call the place a happy family home.

409

Homes keep open doors, families stand by you, whether you're plain or sick or fading. Not here. Any girl not capable of bringing in the men is instantly orphaned and disowned. They all work hard, I'll give them that, but it's forced labour, in a way; a job they wouldn't do if they had some other means to make it rich, or hadn't found themselves in debt or trouble. Oh, I know Carl assured me they all love their work, and that he only takes on girls who are what he calls naturally sensual (which sounds like a commercial in itself), but that's just one of the house-lies – like the caption 'Nearest brothel to Las Vegas' (there are two nearer, one by twenty miles); or the 'Most beautiful girls in the world' thing, or the 'Cultured courtesans'. Okay, so Kathy plays the fiddle, and Kristia speaks four languages, but a lot of them are nothings and wouldn't know Bartok from Boursin.

God, listen to me! What a nerve I've got when I've done zilch myself and can't play middle C. Bitchiness is catching, I suppose. And my respect for men hasn't exactly trebled since I've been here. It's exhausting, actually, the constant pretending, the instant charm and switch-on sexiness, the perky smiles even for the sods. They're not all sods or brutes, in fact, whatever Naima says. Nor all moneybags. Some of them are decent guys with quite humble jobs and backgrounds. There was this grocery clerk with a stutter who'd been saving up for months, and a chicken farmer who was really sweet and gentle. I tried my best for those two. And even with the piggish ones, I'm not completely charmless. I don't want to get too bitter or too blasé, land up a Joanne.

Anyway, they're often more pathetic than perverted – losers, sexual failures: men with pricks just one inch long, even when erect; men with money but no friends; passive types who want to play the woman; men who brag and talk big, then come in just two seconds when they've booked an hour or more; religious maniacs dripping shame and guilt; Roman Catholics who see all women as the Blessed Virgin Mary, but can't wait to bugger her.

Most of them like you to respond, if only as a sop to their male pride, proof of their virility. Virility my arse! I've never met such duffers. Their pricks are wasted on them, half the time. Mind you, it's easy just to kid them. A moan or two, a spasm, and they're preening like prize bulls. There was this guy of forty-six, married twice, and who even had a mistress, yet he'd never managed to make a woman come, never actually seen a female orgasm, not once in his whole life. My fake one so excited him, he drove all the way from Vegas three more times that day. He couldn't come himself, not after the first time, but my own panting and grimacing really turned him on. Actually, I was working out my plans for the weekend, making mental lists, panting and grimacing through 'wash hair', 'buy talc for Norah'.

'Jeez!' he said. 'You're dynamite.' It always pays to please them. Repeat business is important in this game. And he tipped me fifty bucks each come.

I've learnt a lot in just ten days, and I'm loads more confident. The guys all seem to like me, choose me from the line-ups. Joanne was really bitchy – said they'd choose a frump or a baboon, so long as it was in its teens, like I am. Okay, so some of them are hung up on their daughters. I'm more hardened to it now – braced for it, expecting it, even ready to say 'Dad' again and not feel a single twinge. (I haven't had to, actually. It's more little girl in general – hair in plaits, bobby socks, silly lispy voice. One guy even asked me to wear braces on my teeth, though I drew the line at that.) But they're not all cradle-snatchers. Some of them treat me like their mother, need babying themselves. To others, I'm an auntie, handing out advice. I feel quite important sometimes. Other times, I'm just a bloody robot; a slave, a slag, a dustbin.

The slag picks up her pen, has a last check through the catalogue, adds a loo-roll holder with holly-printed toilet paper (a leftover from Christmas). That's a must for Norah when she spends so much time in toilets. I'm missing her quite badly. If anyone had told me just two weeks ago that I'd be counting the hours till I caught a glimpse of Toomey, I'd have laughed right in their face. It's true, though. Only sixteen hours to go. Thank heavens! I've been worrying about her. Angelique's so . . . so casual, almost callous. In fact, that famous heart of gold is just a thin veneer, I've come to see. Easy to mop up all the credit for looking after your retarded elder brother, then pay a maid to do the donkey work. It was the same in Death Valley; she hardly saw poor George at all, left him to the ranger.

Wasn't I as bad, though? I exchanged a dozen words with Norah that weekend – maybe less. I was so caught up in my own hurt pride and misery, nothing else existed. And even now, I'm only sort of buying her, using presents to say 'sorry' and 'I need you'. *I do* need her – even more, now I'm working here. She's a strange rare creature like my plastic unicorn, a virgin in a world of whores.

I can't wait until tomorrow. We're driving back to see her, first thing in the morning, me and Angelique. God! I'll really spoil her – food, presents, chocolates, flowers, the lot. I only hope I won't feel quite so lousy. It's that wretched Pill, makes me queasy all the time. My breasts are full and tender and my stomach's swollen up – though that may be Peg's cooking. I'm always hanging round the kitchen, drawn to Peg like all the other girls now; not just her shortcrust or her fudge-cake, but because she's the only one untainted by her work, the wholesome mother figure.

I wasn't all that keen to take the Pill, especially as we take it every day here, right on through the cycle, with no break for the curse. Periods are profit-stealers, make us unavailable. Every month, for six whole years, I've had my period. It's part of me, part of being normal. It will seem very odd to stop, make me feel I'm pregnant. It's a bit like that already – morning sickness, bloated breasts.

That greasy little doctor pulled my boobs around, didn't stop at those. I had another test today – more jabs and smears – and jokes. Carl's fanatic about tests, especially since the AIDS plague. It would be far safer, actually (not to mention cheaper), to make the men wear Durex. Most brothels do, in fact now, but rubbers are like periods – keep the guys away, turn them off, and Carl won't risk losing business. The girls seem to like them, not just as a protection from disease, but a sort of psychological barrier between the clients and their cunts – no

412

actual contact of skin and skin. Yeah, some of them are squeamish. I mean, Melanie admitted that she'll never mouth-kiss, ever, regards it as too intimate. She'll pee in some guy's mouth, no problem, but if he puts his tongue in hers, God help him.

Saliva's germy, mind you. Everything is germy – sperm, pee, cocks, mouths. It's a pretty risky business altogether. Not just AIDS and other vile diseases, but the constant threat of violence. It's far worse on the streets, of course, and I've heard some hairy stories from girls who've walked a beat, but even here a guy could pull a gun on you before you've had a chance to sound the alarm. Some girls like the risks, say it gives their life a sort of charge which they'd never get in dreary jobs like waitressing. Kathy claims that hookers are like gamblers. Both refuse to earn their living in some boring routine job; both hope to make a killing, then retire; and both accept danger, even court it.

On the whole, I'm far more fagged than frightened, though that's probably just the Pill again. It seems to make me tired as well as queasy. And I've had a lot of backache, which is an occupational hazard here, with so many heavyweights slumped on top of you, or frustrated sportsmen trying out contortions. My cunt itself feels numb. I never call it Abigail, not now. It's far too twee, too personal. It's just a hole – anonymous – which gets on with the job. I was scared it might get sore from over-use. I even half expected some ghastly retribution – inflammation, discharge, genital warts or blisters, swelling, itching, rashes, hives, the lot. None of that has happened. I was a little tender one day, when I'd had some oaf who wore a prick-extension and erection-booster in a rather rigid latex, followed by another guy who used a twelve-inch (gold) vibrator on me because he couldn't get it up himself. I thought that might excite me, but I didn't feel a thing – except intrigued about the gold. Was it real or plated, plastic or just paint? I never touch myself now, since going on the game, never use fingers or vibrators. It's as if my cunt's no longer mine: I've bartered it for cash.

I think I'll have a bath, try to soak the queasiness away. It's a treat to bath alone. A lot of clients book a bubble bath or spa bath as an appetiser, pay extra for the girl to get in too. It may sound daft, but I find sharing a bath somehow more invasive than sharing a bed. Or maybe it's just memories of Reuben. It's hard to have to soap a man, sponge his prick and balls, shampoo his body hair, and keep smiling, coolly prattling, when it's Reuben I'm remembering in the tub. Now I really relish it when I can lock the door, lard my face with cream, close my eyes and shut out every stupid bloody man, Reuben included.

I unpeel my jeans, slip into the old towelling dressing gown which Angelique threw out. I prefer to save my new clothes, keep them nice for work. I set my hair in rollers, disguise them with a plastic cap, slap on cleansing cream. I'm whistling as I walk along the passage. Only one more booking later on this evening, then I'm free, free the whole weekend. Actually, it's quite a special booking – my hundredth man. I've been keeping count of them, totting up my earnings. It sounds a lot, a hundred in ten days. It isn't. They were so busy over Christmas, Angelique said; had so many girls on holiday, that the few girls left worked through a hundred and fifty each in just a week. If I admitted that to anyone back home, they'd be absolutely horrified; see us all as lost – outlawed and depraved. I shrug, keep whistling, louder. Ninety-nine pricks, okay. So what?

Suddenly, I freeze. Suzie and a client are walking straight towards me. Clients never come this way. This plain and poky section of the house is out of bounds to them. I press myself against the wall, stare down at the floor. I'm breaking rules myself. We shouldn't really undress until we reach the safety of the bathroom, should never take the risk of being caught looking sloppy and unkempt. I can hear the couple talking. Maybe they won't notice me, will simply walk on by. Their footsteps slow, seem to hesitate a moment before stopping altogether. A voice says 'Jan', a man's voice, a voice I recognize, though it sounds quite stunned and shaky.

I look up, simply stare. I can't believe it.

His face has drained of colour. He clutches at the wall, as if to save himself from falling. 'J . . . Jan,' he says again.

Suzie corrects him. 'Adorée.' She gives the name a veneer of quiet contempt. She always thought it ridiculously pretentious, and for a fright in a yellow plastic bath-cap and a grubby bathrobe three sizes too big, it must seem quite inane.

'Are you two long-lost buddies?' She's enjoying my predicament. I can't even take the cap off, not with pink foam padded rollers underneath.

'No.' 'Yes.' Our two voices overlap.

What in God's name is he doing here? Perhaps he came to buy a tee shirt. Some men do − drive five hundred miles or more, just to waste their money on a trashy bit of merchandise: Silver Palm bumper-sticks, or a baseball cap with 'WHOREHOUSE' round the brim. No. Not him. Impossible. He always dressed so formally, would never sport a silly hat, or make himself ridiculous by appearing in a sweatshirt with 'LAY AWAY!' or 'SUPPORT YOUR LOCAL HOOKERS' on the front. And anyway, he was holding Suzie's arm, coming from the direction of her room.

'Jan, I . . . I've got to talk to you.' He moves towards me, slowly, like a convalescent in a state of shock.

Suzie steps between us, takes his arm again, as if to show who owns him. 'Well, I'm afraid you can't talk here, hon. If you've changed your mind and want to stay, then I'll take you to the bar.'

'No.' He raps it out, obviously alarmed, turns to me again. 'Is there no place we can talk, Jan? Somewhere private?'

Suzie answers for me. 'I'm sorry, Alvin, honey, but that's not on. You were booked with me, and our time's up anyway. I can't just turn you over to another girl. But if we go back to the office, you can have a word with Carl and . . .'

Alvin? So he's changed his name as well, bloody booked with Suzie. Rotten hypocrite! He always posed as the shrinking violet, the bashful modest guy with no interest in sex. And now I find him buying it − and from a girl whose speciality is whipping − walking through a brothel as bold as brass. Suzie is a toughie, deals with all the 'naughty boys', the ones who need strict discipline. She's also given tricky clients, guys with hang-ups or perversions. She's trusted to stay cool, handle anything, trusted not to tittle-tattle. So what's Alvin's special vice? I don't want to know, don't even want to talk to him.

'I'm afraid I haven't time, Alvin.' I give his name the same contemptuous emphasis as Suzie gave Adorée. 'I'm about to have a bath, and after that I'm . . . booked.'

I see him wince. The fraud! He's just had it off with Suzie, and he dares to look so pained.

'Goodbye,' I call, as I stride off down the passage, back the way I came. I sit trembling in my room. I don't know why I feel so overwrought. That man's nothing to me. I only knew him for a brief two days. Just a pick-up, a holiday romance – not even much romance. Okay, so he's discovered I'm working in a brothel. Is that any worse than my knowing he's a client? I snatch my bath-cap off, glimpse my naked face glistening in the mirror. God! I look a slut. And he's only ever seen me glamorous and gift-wrapped. Who cares? It was Suzie that he screwed and she looked good enough in that tight blue dress with side-slits. I start ripping out my rollers, scrubbing at my face. Someone knocks.

'Who is it?'

Suzie barges in.

'I didn't say "come in", Suzie. I'm not dressed or . . .'

'That didn't seem to worry you before. Jeez! I was embarrassed. You looked like shit. And that's a new important client you insulted. We try to grab new business here, not scare it off. Don't you know the rules yet?'

I brush my hair violently, tearing at the roots. 'I thought it was another rule that we don't bring clients down here.'

'Don't tell me my job. Alvin wanted total privacy, so I arranged with Carl to take him out the side way. You can always do that if your client's famous or concerned about not meeting anyone.'

'So your Alvin's famous, is he?'

'No, he's not, but if you really want to know, he's quite some guy. He . . .'

The phone cuts through her words, Carl's internal phone,

which starts hectoring me as well. Am I dressed? Is my room a tip? Alvin's paid for time with me. Yeah, Carl knows it's my free hour, but the crazy guy's paid double and he only wants to talk. Yeah, he's sorry, but I'll have to use my room. Nowhere else is free and the guy wants privacy.

Privacy. Privacy. What about *mine*, I'd like to know? Carl nabbed my one free morning just last week. Free for what, you might say, when I'm still trapped here without a car, but it's the principle which matters. Free to slob around, free not to smile; be sad, or bored, or frigid. And I don't want men in here. My room's become a sort of sanctuary, the only place I dare be really naked. I don't mean without clothes – that's nothing now – I mean without a mask. I can cry here if I want, or tell the walls I'm lonely or plain scared, or make up crazy crappy letters to my father, asking if he's more than simply ashes. All the other girls have to use their rooms for sex, unless the client's booked a special lounge or service. But this room's far too small. It used to be a boxroom before Carl took me on. There's just a bed, a wardrobe, and a makeshift dressing-table with a hard-topped kitchen stool. If we're going to sit and talk, we need two easy chairs. How *can* we sit and talk? The whole thing's quite impossible. If only he'd just left, pretended not to see me.

Suzie's picking up my clothes, playing martyr, like my mother.

'Look, piss off, Suzie. I like my knickers on the floor.'

She flounces out, still nagging, and I start tidying up myself, shovelling all the clutter into drawers. I strip my bathrobe off, spray myself with scent to make up for no bath, then rummage through my wardrobe. Suzie wears a lot of blue. Okay, blue then, Alvin – if that's what turns you on. The dress is halter-necked, shows my breasts almost to the nipples. I struggle with the zip. Another knock. Uncle Carl, no doubt, come to read the riot act. Suzie's probably played the sneak, reported me, like school.

It's Alvin. Shit! Not yet. I haven't done my face, which is still shining with the cream, haven't found my shoes or combed my hair.

'Come in,' I say. 'Sit down.'

He doesn't sit, just stands there by the door, looking horribly embarrassed. 'Jan, I don't know what to say. I . . .'

'I'm *not* Jan.'

'Honey, why pretend? I'd know you anywhere. I can't call you Adorée. That may be your name here, but I met you as Jan and . . .' He falters, shakes his head, as if still confused, incredulous. 'Jesus Christ! I've missed you.'

He sounds almost angry now, gazing at my face as if he's checking every detail, making sure that nothing's changed. I feel suddenly ashamed. I was so involved with Reuben, so mad for Reuben, mad with Reuben, so hurt, stunned, betrayed, I'd forgotten Victor totally – this greying nothing man with his pale tired face and boring clothes, who was so devoted and so kind, who listened to me, cared; who was always so sweet to Norah, generous to us both. Was it just two days we had together? More than that, it must have been.

I think back to the poker room, the tournament – blush as I remember sneaking out on him, flirting with Snake Jake, regretting it, escaping; searching for him everywhere, then landing up in Milton's bed, not his. And I'd hardly recovered from that galling non-event, when Reuben bowled me over. No wonder honest Victor got squeezed out. Yet now the memories are flying round my head again, fond and happy memories – Victor ordering extra strawberries for my strawberry daiquiris, Victor teaching Norah crazy golf, Victor driving me to Red Rock Canyon with a flame-red sunset as an extra, which he swore he'd laid on specially; Victor buying chocolates, Victor buying flowers; shy and awkward Victor telling me I'm beautiful.

He's *not* a nothing man. Okay, he's old, and not wildly handsome or wildly anything. In fact, you might well overlook him in a crowd. But his eyes are really beautiful and he's got a lovely generous mouth, and I'm somehow thrown by his solid stubborn presence. It's as if Reuben had erased him, faded him and shrunk him in my mind. I'd remembered him as smaller, even flimsier, without that straight strong back, those lean and muscly hands which seem too real, too male, for the effete and shadowy Victor I'd shrugged off.

He moves towards me, takes my hand in his. Yeah, it's real all right. His grip is really hurting, his laser gaze piercing through my skull-bones. His voice is less assured, though. 'I was stupid to . . . go off like that. I'm sorry.'

'Go off?' I was the one who'd buggered off, I thought.

'I was just destroyed when I saw you with that . . . that . . .'

'What d'you mean?' I try to play the innocent, though I'm all too certain what he means. He spotted me and Jake together – must have done. I'd feared that all along. That damned casino was far too small for any privacy; not a great anonymous ant-hill like Caesars or the Hilton, but a cramped and crummy hencoop.

'You know exactly what I mean. I saw the guy.'

I pull my hand away, try to sound offhand. 'It was nothing, Victor, honestly. I was just getting a bit bored, that's all. And you seemed so sort of . . . distant. I mean, once you'd sat down with those cards, you were like someone else completely and I just didn't exist.'

'Are you crazy? Not exist! I was only playing for you. Every hand I won, I was buying you a dinner – or a diamond. You were my luck, my inspiration, my . . . I've never played as well before – until I happened to turn round and you'd completely disappeared. I couldn't understand it. I asked the cocktail waitress if she'd seen you go someplace. Yeah, she had . . .' (another angry pause) ' – she'd seen the two of you sitting drinking Pepsis in the lounge.'

Sod the sneaky bitch. She sounds less like a waitress than a spy. I expect Victor tipped her well, to make it worth her while to track me down. He's still filling in the details, those jolt-blue eyes angry and accusing. He sounds passionate, possessive, as if I'm his steady girlfriend of five or ten years' standing. I'm astonished, almost speechless, yet I must admit relieved. I assumed he'd just lost interest, given me the brush-off. Now I realize he was jealous, madly fiercely jealous; seems steamed up even now. He's pacing to and fro, his voice reproachful, fraught.

'My game went down the chute then. I was hardly even

looking at my cards. I had this huge great stack of chips, but once I started losing, I just threw the last ones off, left the table. I went out via the lounge, thought I'd check your plans. But you looked far too snug and settled to want to be disturbed.'

Settled? Christ! With Jake? I was crawling up the wall, plotting murder.

'I went straight to my hotel, checked out, scorched back home at a hundred miles an hour. Okay, I overreacted, I admit it. It was childish, stupid.' He sounds angry with himself as well as me; suddenly swings round, voice gentler now, and pleading. 'Forgive me, Jan.'

'Please don't call me Jan.' This time I must be real. No masks, no false identities, especially if he feels so strongly. I almost wish he didn't. Oh, I'm glad he still fancies me – it's ghastly being ditched and I'd suffered agonies running through my faults: my bossiness, my boringness, my total lack of sex appeal. But to move so fast from rejection to devotion, I'm not sure I can cope – not so soon after Reuben. My own emotions are really bruised and raw. I need a rest from any new entanglement until I'm less demoralized, less drained.

'I must,' he says, voice tense still. 'I want us to be close again, friends again, not hiding behind trick names or playing silly games. Okay, I realize you're embarrassed, Jan, me stumbling on you here, but – Christ Almighty! – what d'you think *I* feel?' He breaks off, hands gesturing, as if searching for the words his voice can't find. 'I still can't quite believe it – to find you in this . . . this . . . What happened, for Christ's sake? You said you were on vacation.'

'Yes,' I say. 'I was.'

'I was imagining you back home by now – in England. I even went to the airport on the 5th, to see if I could find you, stayed there all damned day.'

'You what?'

'Yeah. From six twenty in the morning – that's when the first plane leaves – to ten past two the next morning. That's the last.'

I'm stunned. I don't even remember telling him the date of

our flight back. To have hung around that long for a girl who'd blanked him out, who was mourning someone else . . .

He's holding both my hands now, and I'm sure he doesn't realize quite how tightly. I feel almost honoured by the pain. I'm not used to such vehemence, such passion.

'Jan, I've got to know what happened, what went wrong – what you're doing here.'

I say nothing. I'm running back in time to the evening I last saw him; all the things which have happened since that night – Milton, Ritzy's, Reuben. I daren't mention any of them, least of all admit that I almost married a man who's now awaiting sentence in a prison cell. It will only quite appal him, and seems disloyal to Reuben, too. And yet I don't want to start the chain of lies again, not with Victor. I stare down at my feet, bare feet. Does he really think I'm beautiful, with grubby toenails and without a scrap of make-up?

He lets me go, still holds me with his eyes. 'Okay, honey, you don't want to talk about it. I respect that. But I've got to get you out of here. It's wrong, Jan, absolutely wrong – a lovely girl like you working in a . . .'

Again, he's stuck for words, can't seem to hit on one that's disparaging enough. I kick out at the skirting. 'Why come here yourself then, if it's such a lousy dump?' He's just another Reuben, getting all his thrills from hookers while posing as a faithful ardent type. Worse than Reuben, in running down girls who try to please him, condemning the whole set-up as a stews. 'It's okay for you, splurging all your cash here, then pretending you despise the place. I *haven't* any cash, Victor. I . . . lost it all, lost everything, even our tickets back to England.' I flop down on the stool, cringe at my reflection in the mirror. I've still got one pink roller in.

Two faces in the mirror now. Victor stands behind me, leaning down. His face is a grey against my tan, his brows drawn tight together. 'Jan – hell – I'm sorry . . .' He hardly needs words now. The whole mirror aches with his concern. His hands are clenched, a tiny muscle twitching in one cheek. I watch him watch me, his blue eyes fixed on mine and creased in horror.

'Was it . . . craps?' he asks. He puts a hot and tentative hand on my bare shoulder.

I nod. Nodding isn't lying. Victor warned me about craps, knew I found it tempting. As a poker player, he's wary of games with more chance in them than skill. I shrug his hand off. I feel some strange sense of loyalty to Reuben – even now – loyalty and fury.

'Jan, I've got money. You've got to let me help you. And Norah. What happened to poor Norah? Is she all right?'

I nod. I'm touched that he should ask, but somehow wary still. Why should he help, or care so much?

'I don't care what it costs, so long as you get out of here.'

I chew my thumb, which saves me from replying. Of course I'm flattered, grateful, but a bit pissed off as well.

He's still hot and damp from Suzie, just shot his sperm inside her, or paid to have her spank him, tie him up. Yet he can still play the puritan with me, the innocent who finds brothels quite distasteful and has to 'rescue' me.

'It's not that easy, Victor. I can't just walk out. Carl's been pretty decent on the whole, and we're busy at the moment and . . .'

'*I'll* deal with Carl. If you've got a contract here, I'll buy you off. Money's not a problem. I'll go see him now, explain you're . . .'

'No!' I shout. 'I don't want you interfering. I don't want you here at all.'

The silence seems louder than my yell. I don't know why I shouted, or even why I sounded quite so cruel. I'm so confused and somehow still suspicious. I can't explain it really, but it feels as if he's . . . buying me. He'll pay for me to leave, but what is he expecting in return? I line up my jars of make-up in a row. So many jars, so much paint and camouflage: lip-gloss, varnish, highlighters. Is Victor's kindness another sort of mask, concealing something sinister – the outward smiling face of some perversion?

He slumps against the wall; seems older, even haggard, face more drawn, frown-lines newly etched as he stares down at my sentry-line of pots. When he speaks at last, it's very flatly; a

dry brown shrivelled voice with no sap left in it. 'Okay, Jan,
I'll go.' He walks heavily and slowly to the door, stops, turns
round to face me. 'Would you let me do one thing?'

'What?'

'Send you two airline tickets back to London? Then if you
or Norah change your mind, or find you're missing England
or want to go back home, at least you're not stranded here
alone. I'll get them in the mail tomorrow, leave them open-
dated.'

I spring up from the stool. Can I be hearing right? This man
wants nothing in return, is willing to spend a thousand dollars
on a girl who shouts at him, a girl he'll never see again, a mean
mistrustful girl who thinks giving and taking are two joined
and hyphened words. Victor's knocked the hyphen out,
kicked aside the taking. This is giving for its own sake,
without strings or IOUs. And the saintly guy is leaving,
walking through the door. I can only see his navy back,
hunched and defeated, as he turns into the passage.

'Wait!' I shout, dash out after him, drag him back, close the
door and lean against it. We catch each other's eyes, look
down. Now I'm the one who's short of words. Thank you is
too feeble. 'I'm . . . not going back to England,' is all I manage
to blurt out. 'Not for ages, anyway.'

'No?' His whole body seems reprieved, as if someone's let
him go, stopped holding him bone-rigid on a string.

'No.'

'But you're . . . staying here to work?' The string tautens
once again, even the voice gruffer and more harsh now.

'I'm not sure. Let me think about it. It's such a shock, this,
Victor, meeting you again and . . .'

'I know. I understand. It's one helluva shock for me as
well.'

I edge away from him. This room is too damned small for
all the wild emotions whirling through it – shame, amazement,
gratitude, resentment still and fear, and some crazy new
excitement that the guy should care so much. I don't want
emotions, do I, don't want to feel at all. I've spent the last ten
days learning to be cool and tough, indifferent; not to have a

heart, or only just a plastic one. And now Victor reappears, churns me up again, reminds me that I *can* feel, that I'm not completely numb.

Numb? I'm boiling hot, and shaky; grope towards the windowsill. I feel short of space, short of air. The one small window is too high up to open. The walls are dizzy with flocks of flying birds which seem to flap towards me, hem me in. I've never understood why birds in a boxroom, especially this exotic breed, bluebirds from a fairy-tale with outstretched necks and golden eyes. Perhaps the wallpaper came cheap, or they used this room for children once. Wild blue wings are thrashing in my stomach, sharp beaks pecking down my spine. I steady myself against the sill, trace the outline of one V-shaped body. 'Did you . . . really miss me, Victor? I mean you're not just saying it?' I'm speaking to the wall.

Victor's voice is right behind my back. When I move, *he* moves, as if he can't bear being parted from me, even by an eight-foot stretch of carpet.

'I've been searching for you ever since. I've spent hours and hours hanging around the foyer of the Tropicana, watching everyone go in and out – everyone but you.'

'The Tropicana? Why?'

'That's where you were staying, wasn't it?'

Another invention, one I'd quite forgotten. So many lies. Will he ever know the real me? Do I want him to? I've been hurt enough with Reuben.

'Or were you working here already, Jan? Was the Tropicana story just a cover?'

'No, of course not. Well, yes, I mean . . .' God! It's so confusing. I mustn't lie to Victor. He's such a genuinely decent sort of person, my lies seem really shabby and unfair.

He turns me round, tries to search my eyes. 'Jan, that guy. The one I saw you with. Was he – well . . . important? I mean, things were really great between us – or so I thought until . . .' He swallows, tries again. 'I just couldn't understand what made you go off with some guy like that. What did I do wrong?'

I sink down on the bed, silent for a moment. I'm

remembering again: Victor feeding me his steak; buying me my trench coat; kissing all my fingertips when he left me late at night; still touching hands when he was halfway through the door, as if he couldn't bear to tear himself away. 'Nothing,' I whisper. 'Absolutely nothing. You treated me quite beautifully. The man was no one, worse than no one. I've never even seen him since that night. And I wouldn't want to, thanks.'

He lifts his head, as if I've removed some crushing burden from it. He doesn't speak – nor do I – just comes and sits beside me on the bed, links his fingers through my own, puts an arm around me. Minutes pass. I feel my breathing calm a little. I'd forgotten just how peaceful it could be with him, not wild crazy elation as with Reuben, just quiet content.

We both jump when the phone rings. It's Carl again. My customer's arrived – early. Will I get myself together and go greet him in the lounge.

'But Victor's here still.'

'Who?'

'Er . . . Alvin.'

'*I'll* look after Alvin. Danny's a big spender, I don't want him messed about. Fix him a drink first, then take him down to Suzie's room.'

'Suzie's?'

'Yeah. It's the only one that's free. She's in the jacuzzi with a bunch of Japs.'

'But . . .'

'No "buts", kid. Move your ass.'

Carl's slammed his receiver down. I'm still holding on to mine, clinging to it like an anchor while cross-currents surge and swell within my mind. Suzie's room, Suzie's bed, where Victor lay himself just half an hour ago; gentle Victor overlaid by big brash raucous Danny; Carl's peremptory orders when Victor's just offered me my freedom. The phone-lead kinks itself in tangles as I fidget to and fro with it, trying to decide what to do, what to even say. 'I'm . . . wanted, Victor,' I stutter out at last.

'What d'you mean?'

425

I try to explain, leave the sentence hanging. I've never seen Victor so distraught. He's striding up and down, ramming his fist against the wall, whirling round to face me. 'No, Jan, *no*. You can't. You mustn't.' He strikes his own palm, hard, sinks down on the stool, leaps up again. 'I'll go see Carl, explain you're leaving with me.'

'No,' I say with equal vehemence. How can I just walk out? It's all too sudden, too dramatic. I'm not sure I can trust him, even now. And what right has he to tell me what I can't do? He had Suzie. I'll have Danny. At least that makes us quits. Anyway, I need more time, time to think, time to weigh his offer up, including that offer of free flights back to England. I could always change my mind, move somewhere new and different: the Midlands or the North, even Scotland maybe, start again from scratch. My hundredth man – then out, back home to freedom. Well, maybe not quite freedom, but at least it might be simpler than trying to stay on here, without a proper permit and no medical insurance. Just one minor illness could set us back a hundred bucks, and I'm worried about Norah as it is. Angelique got her some new pills, but God knows what they are or if they'll suit her. And she can't stay there for ever, sitting on her butt all day with just a cat for company, and George. I dragged her out here; I ought to get her back. Perhaps I *should* walk out. I mean, now's the time to leave – leave Carl, leave the States – while I've got a guy to help me, not just with the air fares, but with the whole frightening business of reporting our lost passports.

No, impossible. How can I confess about the passports, admit the whole Reuben thing to Victor, when he's already so disturbed by some less-than-nothing client? He's crouching down in front of me, imploring. 'Jan, let me stay with you, extend my time. Can't this . . . this Danny' – he vomits out the name – 'have someone else?'

'There isn't anyone else. Fridays are like Clapham Junction here.'

'Well, let me try, for Christ's sake. There must be some way around it, something Carl can do. Won't you let me even ask?'

I nod. 'Okay, if you want, but . . .'

He's already through the door and down the passage. He isn't old at all, not now. He's shed twenty years in seconds. I'm smiling to myself as I watch him disappear. I've never been wanted quite so desperately – and just to talk. I suspect he'll offer Carl a fortune, outbid even Danny. Carl will haggle, obviously, take advantage of the deadlock. I can almost hear that iron-in-velvet voice. 'Yeah, sure I understand, sir, but this other guy's a highly respected customer. I can't afford to lose him. He booked Adorée specially. She's very popular.'

Adorée finds her shoes, her stockings, sits down at the dressing-table, lipsticks on her smile. Two men smile back dim wraiths in the mirror – jowly sun-scorched Danny on the left, pale devoted Victor on the right. She sweeps her cache of jars to the right side of the table – her pile of gaming chips.

Her money's all on Victor.

26

I lost. I'm lying under Danny, on Suzie's huge gold water-bed. Actually, we're almost through. He's come already, though it's no credit to me. I'm surprised he didn't kick me out, in fact. I was just a second mattress; could hardly feel my body for all the turmoil raging through my mind. I was really back with Victor in my room. He's in there now, alone. He arranged with Carl to take me on an out-date, an All-Niter – after Danny's left. I was furious at first. My free night gone, tomorrow's early start with Angelique simply shrugged aside. Victor's offer was obviously too high for Carl to worry about petty things like free time or prior arrangements.

All-Niters can be dangerous. Some brothels won't allow them, so those that do can charge the earth – up to two hundred bucks an hour. That won't stop a pervert who wants a girl all night, and all alone, just so he can strangle her, or fire a round of bullets up her cunt. Carl takes down all the details on the client's driving licence, makes sure he's got the name of his hotel, but it still remains a risk – another of the risks we run to swell his funds, keep his profits flowing. Okay, Victor's not a homicidal maniac, but there are other sorts of danger, and I still feel so mixed up. I mean, supposing he . . .

'You're kinda quiet tonight, doll.' Danny shifts his weight, tweaks my hair. I try to smile and flirt a bit, my words as damp and heavy as his naked torso slumped across my breasts. My hundredth man, and I've more or less ignored him. It's the next man I'm concerned with, the next few hours in front of me. Danny's just a hindrance. I listen for the pinger, will it to go off. I can only hear his fast and phlegmy breathing. He leans up on one elbow.

'You not feelin' good, sugar?'

'Yeah, I'm fine.' I stroke his hair mechanically. Victor was wonderful at stroking. We never did much more; I don't know why. I wish Carl hadn't left him in my room. It was a question of privacy again – Victor's privacy, of course, not mine. Supposing he's rifling through my things? No, he wouldn't dream of doing that. I feel uneasy, all the same. I've told so many lies, I suppose I'm scared he'll find me out, find some evidence against me – thief or mental patient, failed Zionist, failed bride. It's odd that I could feel so much for Reuben, lose everything for Reuben, and now be in a jitter because another guy, a completely different guy, different in age, looks, temperament, ideals, is about to take me out. Do I want to go or don't I? God! I wish I knew. I was rather looking forward to my early night – a really gluttonous supper with no big-hulk man lying on my groaning stomach afterwards; a giggle with Desirée in the cat-room, then off to bed, alone, with a glossy magazine. I'll have to warn Angelique that I won't be leaving with her in the morning, scribble her a note if she's otherwise engaged, tell her I'll join her at her house, as soon as I can get away tomorrow, book a cab or something. And she'd better take the clothes and stuff for Norah. I can't lug thick lisle stockings and armpit-high pink bloomers on my first romantic out-date.

'You sure are miles away.' Danny's sounding peeved. The pinger kindly blurs my lame excuses. We both get up. I help him with his clothes as a sort of extra-cum-apology – tartan trousers, two-tone shoes. He smells of sweat and aftershave; his skin is tacky damp. Both smell and dampness seem to have transferred themselves to me. It's as if I've lost my cover, or Victor's peeled it off. That makes me still more nervous. I keep inanely chattering as I pass his shirt and jacket. The jacket feels quite heavy, weighed down with wallet, bankrolls, silver cigarette case. I dress myself, smooth the frilled gold bedspread, retrieve the velvet cushions. Suzie's room is daunting. The ruched and pleated drapes exactly match the thick gold satin padding round the mirrors which reflect more silk and frills.

I usher Danny to the door, try to use the few remaining

minutes to blank out the last hour, so he'll leave with happy memories. There's also the small matter of a tip. Usually he stuffs a wad of dollar bills down each cup of my bra. It's a little joke between us, to keep my breasts warm, as he puts it. Lots of clients slip you extra. It's a way of saying thank you, a sort of bond between you. My breasts stay cold this evening. Danny says goodbye, but nothing else. I start to worry. Supposing he reports me? That could really lead to trouble, cost me my whole job.

I return to my room via Angelique's. She's not there, so I leave the note and a cartoon drawing of Danny with a massive body and a tiny cock. I open my door as quietly as I can. If Victor's snooping, he deserves to be surprised. He's not. He's sitting on the stool, head down, sad slumped back towards me.

'Victor.'

He swings round, relief and resentment fighting in his face. Neither of us speaks. The moment's too embarrassing. I'd like to scour Danny off, shower three times, soak in disinfectant. Impossible with Victor there. He clears his throat, mumbles something about leaving when I'm ready.

I'm not ready. I need a respite on my own, just to quieten down, change my knickers, change my mood. Yet it seems cruel to ask Victor to hang around outside when he's already had one agonizing wait, and is now hovering around me with that anxious hangdog look. So I simply grab a toothbrush and a sweater, let him lead me to his car. I'll wash in his hotel. He seems to have forgotten his pressing need for privacy, takes me out the front and public way, almost flaunts me as he settles me in front. The Jan who sat there just two weeks ago is dead and buried. All except her name. Every time he uses it, I feel a pang of guilt, but I daren't explain things now, when we're both so nervous still, so unsure of one another.

I'm surprised to see it's dark. It was only afternoon when I stripped off to have my bath, and the time with Danny could have been bright dawn or spooky midnight for all the notice I was taking of trivial things like time of day. We seem to have plunged straight from sunny daylight to black night, with no dusk or twilight in between. The powerful headlamps light up the dirt road. The rest is shadow; blurry shapes surging into focus, then disappearing as we swoop away. I've been closeted indoors every evening since I came here, confined to bluebird walls or cosy chintz. The dark gape of the night seems raw and threatening in comparison. Carl has failed to tame it, rig it up with spotlights, soften it with drapes.

Victor switches on some music, a cassette of marching tunes. I'm grateful. Talking isn't easy. Danny's come between us, is still there in the car. I'm leaking his semen, smelling of his Aramis, and I know how Victor hates that. He seems turned in on himself, driving too fast along the bumpy pitted track. The music lurches with us – oompah-oompah, angry clash of cymbals.

At last, we reach the main road with its decent concrete surface. A jaunty trumpet blares out my own relief. We're almost at the highway. Victor stops before we reach it, turns the engine off.

I tense. What now? He's changed his mind. I'm not worth all that cash.

'What's wrong?'

'Nothing. I've been wondering all this time where to go for dinner. I thought I'd take you somewhere special, Jan. There's this Persian place with a real unusual menu and little boys in turbans who bring you finger-bowls with flower petals floating on the top. Or there's a tiny French one, very chic, with a chef who trained in Paris, or there's always Caesars – the Palace Court or the Bacchanal. Except we've been to both of those. In fact, we've spent too much time in restaurants. What I'd really like is . . .' He breaks off, seems embarrassed.

'Yes?'

'To take you home to my place.'

Home? He used that word before – an hour or so ago 'scorching home at a hundred miles an hour', he said. I didn't even know he had a home. Everyone in Vegas is a tourist, staying in hotels, and Victor seems more rootless than the rest. He's never married – I asked him that, and he said 'no' rather sadly. He grew up in Kentucky as a country boy, moved to New York, where he lived ten years or so, then moved again when the firm he was working for merged with a competitor and poor Victor was bought out. I never quite discovered exactly what he does, or where he does it. He was always a bit cagey, as if he didn't like me probing, or there was something he was hiding; encouraged me to talk instead. I knew he'd trained as a construction engineer, working chiefly on state highways, but he doesn't seem to do that now, and he can't have retired yet, surely, at the age of forty-two. Perhaps he works for some big armaments firm, and is scared I'll disapprove. Nevada's full of bombs and things. They test them in the desert. Is that where home is? Some godforsaken rocket-launching site?

'Where do you live?' I ask.

'You won't have heard of it. It's tiny. Just a store, a gas station and a few small houses tucked beneath the mountains and sitting in a lot of empty space. I chose it for the peace and quiet, the solitude. I've always been attracted by the desert. I don't know why. I guess it's just so basic. No façades. I'm never all that happy in big towns. Okay, Vegas isn't big, but it's twenty-four-hour neon and a real suspicious city where no one trusts their own best friend and all the women are hookers . . .' He stops, embarrassed, realizes what he's said. I remember our first meeting, how he took me for an escort girl. I still suspect he's something of a hypocrite, pitching into hookers when he buys their time and bodies; running down Las Vegas where he wins all his spare cash.

'You can't play poker in a stretch of empty space.'

'No.' He grins, accepts my veiled rebuke. 'I like to be near Vegas for the cards, of course, even for the restaurants or a show or two – but not that near. My home's about sixty miles north-west. We're closer to it here, just twenty miles or so. The only problem is I can't lay on finger-bowls or frogs' legs. But if you don't mind scrambled eggs . . .'

'Sounds fine,' I say. I'm nervous. In a restaurant, there'd be lots of other people; bustle and distraction. In his home, just silence and the two of us.

He starts the engine, pulls away. 'At least it's early yet.'

'Yes.' It seems like the middle of the night. Time is rushing by like the frightened stretch of road bolting out of darkness just ahead of us. The sky is dark as well – bruised clouds swelling round the moon's already half-closed eye. I ought to be making conversation. Out-date means just that. I'm his date, his companion for the evening, a charming sympathetic ear, who'll relax and flatter him, listen to his problems. Always before, it was him who did the listening, me who got the sympathy, attention.

'Er . . . do you have a house, or just a flat?' I ask. It sounds lame and over-formal. Out-dates can be tricky, last too long.

He laughs.

'What's funny?'

'Flat. Your English words crack me up. No, it's not a flat. It's a clapboard house with three bedrooms and a garden.'

'All for you?'

'All for me. Are you a gardener, Jan?'

'No. I've never grown a thing. Except mustard and cress on Aertex vests at school.'

Victor's looking puzzled. Language again. They probably don't have Aertex over here, and vest means waistcoat in American. I'm too tired to do translations. 'Is your garden big?' I ask instead.

'No. Though even a small one needs a lot of work. The soil's real dry and sandy here, and the guy who owns the store said all he'd ever harvested were stones and tumbleweed. But I was kind of keen to be a country boy again, grow my own vegetables and fruits. So I really worked at it – bought bags of mulch and peat-moss and loads of fertilizer, made my own compost, fixed up a sprinkler system and invested in some hoses, then planted a row of athel trees, for shade. Now I grow zucchini, peppers, egg plant, maize, tomatoes . . .'

A sports car flashes past, pulps the other vegetables. A police car follows, sirens wailing. We're on the highway now, have joined the busy world again.

'What?' I shout. 'I missed that last bit, Victor.'

'I said, "Do you like fish?"'

'To eat, you mean? Not specially. I'd rather have the scrambled eggs.'

He laughs again. 'I couldn't let you eat my fish. They're

buddies. I built myself this salt-water aquarium. We're three hundred miles from the ocean here, at least, but I've got my own bit of brine, right inside my living room.'

I can hear the excitement in his voice as he describes his surgeonfish, his clown fish, his saffron-blue damsels, his ozonizers, corals, zebra morays. I feel just a trifle peeved. He's paid to spend the night with me, and what's he doing? Giving me an inventory of sea-snails, pointing out the dangers of pathogens in South Pacific seawater. I'd rather hear (again) how much he missed me, how beautiful I look in blue.

I let my hand stray over to his knee, feel him tense. He was always very wary about anything too intimate. I felt hurt before, rejected, because he never seemed to want me as more than just a friend. A special friend, admittedly. I haven't forgotten the cuddles and the stroking. But that's always where it stopped. I suppose I should be grateful that he's sensitive, respects me, appreciates my company instead of just my cunt. And yet . . .

'You need real patience, Jan, when you're building up a tank. It's best to start with hardy breeds, tough guys like my damsels. I started with just saffron blues – waited for a while before I bought my batfish and my angels. Then I got a second tank, just had to have some lionfish. They're a real majestic breed, with huge fins like lions' manes. Have you ever seen one, Jan?'

'No,' I say. 'I haven't.'

'Mine are beauts. We'll have a guided tour when we get in – first the garden, then the tanks, and then the cacti and the orchids. Or maybe supper first. You hungry?'

'No,' I say again, remove my hand.

I stare into the eyes of a sharp-spined Hawaiian lionfish. It seems to look right through me, disregard me. Its own body is transparent, striped brown and cream, with the most amazing showy fins like sword-edged lace – delicate and frilly, yet with these huge great lethal needles sticking up on top. Strange how Victor dotes on such a bully-boy. He said it stung him once and his arm swelled up to twice its normal size. He announced it with real pride, as if he were boasting of the ferocious creature's genius. Apparently, they gobble up all smaller fish – snap, gulp and they're gone. That's why he keeps two separate tanks: one for the peaceniks, one for the Huns.

Both tanks are colossal, seem to dominate the room. There's not a lot else in it – one armchair, a tiny portable TV, small bookshelf, smaller table. Victor's house is not a home, not really. No photographs, no clutter, nothing personal at all, unless you count the fish. The house itself is nondescript – just one storey, and rather flimsy-looking, as if it might blow away in the first bad storm. English homes have roots, deep and clutching roots which go down for miles and on for years. This place seems sort of instant and disposable, something from a supermarket which came with ten cents off.

It's his garden that's the showpiece. We saw that first, before we went inside. Victor switched the lights on, so everything looked sheeny and quite magical, a shimmering silver trellis on the green. We stood there breathing in the smells – musky hot-house scents from exotic flowers I'd never heard of and which were only blooming on account of Victor's skills. And then he showed me all his fruits and vegetables – which were like his brood of children, proudly introduced, their biographies fleshed out, their weights and heights and progress lovingly compared, their personal idiosyncrasies explained. I was really quite impressed. He'd created an oasis in a stretch of stony wasteland – turquoise water, green and leafy plants. Beyond us rose the brown and jagged mountains, above us soared the coldly distant clouds; everything dark and vast and barren save his own enchanted tiny patch. He saw me shiver, took my arm, seemed nervous as he fumbled for his key. I wasn't that relaxed myself, especially when the front door closed behind us and I felt a sudden twinge of fear.

It was the fish which saved us, actually, broke the tension. They were so dazzling, so dramatic; such brilliant neon colours – zingy yellow, violent orange, a really startling blue. It was as if they'd been enamelled for the latest Show Spectacular in Vegas. I left Victor at the door, rushed straight up to the tanks, stared in fascination. I've never seen breeds like this before, such amazing shapes and colours, never even realized they existed. If I say 'fish', the word conjures up dead grey hunks of flesh stinking on the market stall in Bristol; men in dirty aprons sharpening up their sales-talk as they slice off heads and tails. These heads and tails are real collectors' items – bewhiskered tawny mouths, striped or tigered snouts; rainbow-coloured tail-fins sweeping behind streamlined silver bodies; tails like muslin skirts.

I lean forward in my chair, tap my fingers on the glass as some swinger cruises past, zigzagged blue and beige with a gleaming turquoise underbelly; brushes bodies with a smaller spiky punk-fish. I can't remember all the names. Victor went too fast. Even the orchids and the cacti are all jumbled up together in my mind. But I was touched by his enthusiasm, the way he seemed to want to share it with me, share everything with me. He kept pressing me with coffee, cocktails, titbits, English tea; kept fretting that I was cold or tired or hungry; settled me in this chair with cushions at my head and a footstool at my feet while he went to fix our supper in the kitchen. He's still there.

'Can't I help?' I call, though I'm rather enjoying my role of pampered princess.

'You can come and keep me company.'

I dislodge the cushions, stroll into the narrow passage of the kitchen, stop in shock. Pots are bubbling on all four gases on the stove, every surface piled with food – fruits and salads, breads and cheeses, a luscious-looking gâteau – everything but scrambled eggs, in fact. Victor stopped en route to buy what he described as a few basics; must have bought the shop.

'Good God!' I say. 'Expecting company? I thought you said you couldn't cook.'

'I can't. Try this. Think it needs more salt?'

'No, it's great. What is it?'

'Victor's Standby Beef. There's chicken too, if you prefer. Oh, and I tried to make a soup, but it's gone kind of weird. Sit down, Jan. Want another drink?'

He sounds flurried, yet elated. He's no longer pale; cheeks flushed from the gases, jacket off, sleeves rolled up, tie askew. It's a feast he's preparing in my honour, the tiny table laid with plates and dishes, royal blue serviettes, enticing smells of sizzling butter, garlic.

'Oh, Victor . . .'

'What?'

'Finger-bowls!'

He shrugs. 'Just a joke.'

Not a joke. They're beautiful, a slice of lemon floating in each one and sprinkled with real flowerheads. 'You're quite an artist.'

'Well, you're my inspiration.'

Silence. We're both embarrassed by the compliments. Victor turns his back again, starts stirring vigorously.

'Is there nothing I can do?' I ask.

'Not a thing.'

Even after the meal, I'm not allowed to lift a finger, not wash a dish nor scrape a plate. We're both feeling floaty from the wine, so it seems entirely natural to move from kitchen chairs to sitting-room rug. Victor pillows my head with his arm as we stretch out on the floor. Still another treat – Godiva chocolates, which I know from the advertisements cost thirty bucks for just a tiny box. Victor feeds me strawberry creams and nougats. I've never seen him so relaxed. Shoes off, tie off, shirt flecked with butter where he sautéed onions too enthusiastically. The room is dim, just the subtle coloured lighting of the fish tanks glowing in our faces. The only noise is tank noise, the bubbling of the aerators, a sudden tiny plop as a batfish breaks the surface of the water.

I suck chocolate off my fingers, realize I'm happy. The last time I felt happy was early New Year's Eve, so the feeling's quite a shock, like swallowing food again after days and days of fasting.

The meal itself was great. Okay, so the soup sort of curdled and I've tasted better beef, but Victor took such trouble. Every course was homage to me, every dish precious because he lavished so much care on it. Jon would have sloshed baked beans in two chipped cereal bowls, burnt the toast. I've never met a man before who's so obviously devoted. I lapped up the devotion; lapped up cream and coffee, felt like a fat cat. I'm purring still. All my fears and conflicts seem to have been left behind with Carl. It may be just the wine, acting as a tranquillizer. I doubt it. Victor always had the gift of making me feel peaceful. He's like a happy-drug, with no dangerous side effects.

I close my eyes. His arms are wrapped around me. He holds me very carefully, as if I'm made of glass. He smells innocent; no swanky aftershave, no strong French cigarettes. I pull away a moment, touch his face. 'Alvin,' I tease.

'Adorée,' he counters.

We're giggling, both of us. 'It doesn't suit you, Victor.'

'No. Adorée does, though.'

'What, suits you?'

'No, you.'

'I've got something to confess.'

'What?'

'My real name's Carole.'

'*Carole?*'

'Mm.'

'Carole Jan?'

'No, Carole Margaret. Do you mind?'

'No. I'm just surprised. Any more names?'

'Only Joseph.'

'That's a guy's name.'

'No, a surname. Carole Margaret Joseph. Is your name really Victor?'

'Yeah. Victor Brown.'

'Brown?'

'Boring, isn't it?'

'No, I like it.' Brown's real and sort of solid, much safer than Ben Shmuel. I feel incredible relief that I'm Carole now at last. It may be stupid, but that Jan kept getting in the way. I was even jealous of her because she wasn't me. Now Victor knows the real me, or some of her at least. I daren't risk the rest yet – Reuben, the swiss-roll. I could admit my age, though. It hardly matters any more whether I'm twenty-one or not. We're not in Vegas, not buying drinks, or gambling. And it would be one less lie between us.

'Hey, Victor . . .' I try to make a joke of it. 'Carole's a bit younger than Jan was.'

'What d'you mean?'

'Well, I'm . . . eighteen, not twenty-one.'

He looks a bit bewildered. I can hardly blame the guy. All these sudden changes. 'I'm sorry, Victor, it's just that I thought they . . . you . . .' I fumble with the pronouns – 'wouldn't let me try the games or buy a drink or anything, if I admitted I was underage.'

He says nothing. Have I shocked him with my fabrications? They're only fibs, footling little fibs. 'I'm nineteen fairly soon. Well, not that long. My birthday's June – June 19th. I'm Gemini. What sign are you?'

He doesn't answer. He's staring at me, seems really quite upset. It can't be that important, surely – two and a half years?

'Victor, don't be cross. Please. It was stupid to pretend, I know. I was just scared I'd miss out on things, that's all.'

'It's okay.' He still sounds a bit uptight, but he offers me a praline, tries to force a smile. 'I'm Libra. Gandhi was a Libran, and Alexander the Great. Oh, and Brigitte Bardot. So I guess we can't be that bad. Are Gemini and Libra meant to get along okay?'

I've no idea. I've never met a Libra guy before. 'Oh, yeah,' I say. 'Terrific. They're made for one another.' I snuggle close, let myself relax again, lie back against his arm. He brushes one soft finger across my closed lids.

'Tired, darling?' he asks.

Darling? Perhaps it's just the easiest solution after Jan and Carole Margaret, but all the same I treasure it. I nod. I am tired. We've spun the evening out as far as it will go and it's now the wee small hours.

'Shall we go to bed?' I whisper.

He doesn't speak – I think he's nervous still – just helps me to my feet, removes our cups and glasses, then takes me down the passage to a simple whitewashed room with toothpaste curtains striped white and minty green.

'I'm afraid it's rather small, but that bed's real comfortable and you'll get a great view of the mountains in the morning.'

I stare at him. Surely he's not suggesting that we should sleep apart – when we've got so close, just weeded out the lies; eaten our supper holding hands so we couldn't cut our meat

439

up; shared our piece of gâteau – which meant I got all the cherries and the cream, and Victor just the stodgy bits. He ate nothing much himself, in fact; just consumed me with his eyes, hoarded all my words as if they were precious truffles or rum-soaked petits fours. So what's changed now? Oh, I understand he may not feel like sex. He probably had the works with Suzie, and older men need longer to recover. That's okay by me. In fact it's quite a treat these days to go to bed to sleep. But why not *his* bed? Wouldn't that be cosier, more friendly?

He's still cosseting me, lending me pyjamas, leaving cookies by my bed, offering me hot chocolate. But those are all child things. Is that the problem? He's still upset I lied about my age, thinks eighteen is too young. That's ridiculous. Most men like me young, choose me for that reason. Maybe he's annoyed and wants to pay me back for lying – bed on my own as a penance for deceiving him? No, Victor's not like that, and anyway, he's always played the suitor rather than the stud; the chaste and bashful suitor who wouldn't go too far. It's beginning to annoy me. It's great to be adored, but how can I be real with him if he keeps idealizing me, making me a nun? All through the evening he's avoided certain topics. If I ever mentioned Carl or Angelique, or any aspect of the Silver Palm, he'd tense and change the subject.

He kisses me goodnight, a child's kiss on the cheek, softly shuts the door. I feel banished and rejected as I listen to his footsteps fading away. I strip my dress off, stand naked on the little bedside rug, squeeze my breasts together so they look bigger than they are. Big or no, they're obviously not wanted. I shrug, lose them in his oversized pyjamas, climb into the chilly narrow bed.

Sleep won't come. The room feels strange and I'm suffering a sort of mental indigestion – dregs of happiness fermenting in my gut, along with confusion, disappointment, self-doubt (again), and even a touch of sheer contempt that any man should be so ludicrously old-fashioned. I mean, imagine paying Carl a fortune to keep me for the night, then shutting me in here alone. I just can't make him out. He seemed so jealous of

Snake Jake, so furiously possessive, yet now he's got me to himself, he doesn't want to know.

I fumble for my cigarettes. He bought me a huge carton. Whatever else, he does allow his little girl to smoke. Little girl. Is that it? Perhaps he wants me as a child, is glad I'm even younger than I said I was; has some hang-up about school-kids, like those weirdos at the Silver Palm. Except they were wild to screw me, and he's not; doesn't even want me in his bed. Okay, then, Victor, separate rooms. Goodnight, sleep well, and where's my teddy bear?

By half past five, I'm still awake and freezing. I'm tempted to wake Victor up as well, but it seems unfair when he looked so tired and drawn. And what's the point, when he's already made it clear he prefers sleep and solitude to any kind of contact? Perhaps I'll make a cup of tea, find a book or something, even watch TV. I creep out of bed and down the passage, put the kettle on, take my cup to the sitting room, where at least I've got the fish for company. They don't look all that thrilled about it. I think most of them were dozing and the harsh light woke them up.

I turn it off again, switch on just a lamp, trail over to the window, lift the curtain. With the garden lights turned off, everything looks completely blackly barren. This is still the desert – arid, ruthless, bitter cold at night. I shiver in my thick blue-striped pyjamas. I keep tripping on the legs, losing hands and fingers in the sleeves. The pyjamas are well ironed, very crisp and clean. Does Victor iron his clothes himself? I can't see him with a maid. He seems to have put himself in quarantine, bought a house which is miles from any neighbour, along a bumpy winding dirt track, and in a tiny hamlet which is too small to be even a dot on any map. He hasn't bothered much about comfort – things like scatter-rugs or cushions, and if his bedroom's much the same as mine, then there's nothing but the basics: bed and cupboard. All his care and skills have been poured out on the garden, the aquarium. That tiny square of lawn had been nannied like an invalid, and he spends two hours every day on just his tanks – cleaning them, testing the purity and balance of the water, preparing special feeds for faddy prima donnas.

I mooch back to admire them, lay my hands against the glass, which is really basking warm. That water must be kept at over eighty. Chilly for mere humans, tropical for fish. I'm getting almost jealous of these fish, the time Victor spends with them, the finger-flirting, pet-names. Some of them are ugly, even monstrous, with huge pouting lips or spiny beards. I've forgotten all their names now, except the clown fish, which I remember because of Norah. They're really comic and so bright they seem unreal – a show-off Day-Glo orange, which makes marigolds and tangerines look pale, with three wide bands of Persil-white gleaming round their torsos. I touch noses with one through the glass. It darts away, startled, conceals itself behind a piece of coral, itself a fiery red; stays there, shy and cowering.

'Better call you Norah,' I say out loud. I wonder when I'll see her. It all depends on Victor, how long he wants me, what he plans to do. Perhaps he was just tired last night. Men of his age are always better in the morning; fresher, recharged after sleep. I suspect he's also shy, or even scared. It's surprising how many men are nervous, even regulars, whom you'd imagine would be hardened. At first, it used to throw me, make me jittery as well, but now I've learnt to handle it. At least, I can with *other* guys. Victor's different, special, which makes me nervous too. I'm not sure how to deal with men I actually feel fond of. If he does want sex, will I be able to respond? I've faked so much, I'm no longer all that certain I can do the thing for real. Do I even want to? I let rip with Reuben – heart and soul and body, gave him everything, and look what happened there. Anyway, I'm still a bit on edge that Victor may be kinky in some way. Oh, I know he seems quite normal on the surface, in fact exceptionally sensitive and gentle, and he's never done the slightest thing to give me cause to worry, but I've learnt already that you can never tell. My most brutal client yet was wearing a tee shirt which said 'My second name is Love'.

I flop down on the carpet. There's not a sound outside. Victor's house is off the road, so you don't hear any traffic. The birds are still asleep, if any bird is fool enough to live here. Why did Victor choose a place like this? Okay, so he's keen on peace and quiet, but you can find those just ten minutes out of Vegas, without holing yourself up in the back of beyond.

I switch the TV on, tune into a party – couples dancing, chatting guests. Nobody alone. I loathe the early hours. Things seem so depressing then, and empty. Las Vegas solves the problem by outlawing the night – a twenty-four-hour city where nothing stops or fades. I wish we'd gone for dinner there, stayed out on the town. If Victor sleeps till nine or ten, that's four more hours cooped up here on my own. I'd feel more at home in my poky little boxroom at the Silver Palm. At least I've made it cosy. I glance around the room again. That one marooned armchair looks quite pathetic, as if Victor never shares his life, or has company or friends in. I keep wondering why he never married. Perhaps he's gay. No – gays don't go for Suzie. They've got their own special brothel, ten miles up the road. It's funny, but I can't get rid of Suzie. She keeps popping up to bug me, remind me she's had Victor when I haven't.

They're kissing on the box now – a stunning blonde with Suzie's nose. Funny how he didn't even kiss me, not on the lips, not even when we were lying on the floor. I switch the kiss off, check through Victor's bookcase. No distraction there. All fish manuals or gardening guides, or huge tomes on engineering. Nothing frothy, no romance. I choose a book on breeding axolotls (whatever they are), take it to the light. A moth got there before me, a small brown stupid moth which keeps fluttering round the lamp, falling back as if it's singed, then flapping up to burn itself again.

I force myself to concentrate. 'The female lays five hundred eggs, sometimes several times a year. At least threequarters of these will die after hatching . . .'

I slam the book shut. Suzie wouldn't be shivering here reading death statistics, with her client lying a few yards down the passage in a cosy double bed. I jump up from my chair, slip along to Victor's room, open his door a crack. He's not asleep at all, just propped against the pillows with the bedside light switched on. I start to giggle. Crazy. Both of us awake in separate rooms.

'Jan? Is that you?' He sounds wary, almost sharp.

'No, it's Carole.' I pad over to the bed, still giggling, lift the covers. 'Can I get in? I'm cold.'

'I'll . . . er . . . find another blanket.' He's trying to slip out the other side. I stop him, squeeze his hand.

'You're warmer than a blanket.'

'Look, Carole, I think it's better if we . . .'

I kiss him on the lips to stop him talking. Of course he's scared – it's obvious. I should have been less selfish, thought of him, rather than myself. I'm a professional now, with a few tricks up my sleeve: how to take the initiative myself without appearing dominant or threatening; how to coax a shy man, build his confidence.

'Let's just lie together, shall we? It's nice like that, relaxing.'

'I'll . . . make some tea.'

'I've had tea.'

'Well, breakfast then. I bought some sourdough muffins. Or there's . . .'

'Victor, darling, it's still not six o'clock. We don't want breakfast yet. Just relax.'

I undo my pyjama top, let him see my tits. He makes no move to touch them. He's lying there, absolutely rigid, trying to cover his body with the bedclothes. I coax them off again, lean over, so my naked breasts are poured out on his chest. He shuts his eyes, lets out a sigh so deep it's more a groan, starts to stroke my nipples. They love it, stiffen up immediately. I'm tremendously relieved to see I can respond, even down below. Yes, dead cold Abigail is slowly resurrecting, stirring into life. I unbutton my pyjama bottoms, slide my hand across to his, fumble for the fastening.

He's out of bed – just like that – blundering towards the door, reaching for his dressing-gown en route, clutching it round him, mumbling something about having to switch the immersion heater on, and how about some fresh-squeezed orange juice; using words to keep me at a distance. Actually, I haven't moved. I glance down at my silly eager nipples. This is more than shyness. He must have some real problem. Hundreds of men do. Impotence, premature ejaculation, are as common as the common cold. At the Silver Palm, we flatter both the

444

rockets and the squibs, tell them all they're wonderful, to boost their egos (and erections), keep them coming back. I probably handled Victor wrong, frightened him by stripping off like that.

I punch the pillows flat, collapse against them. Can't he talk, for heaven's sake, at least explain what's bugging him? He probably doesn't realize there are ways of getting round these things, and that Suzie's not the only one who knows them; slow-down techniques for young or inexperienced guys who can't hold it back (especially wealthy ones who can afford to pay for extra time); speed-up skills for when we're busy, short of girls. The ex-streetwalkers are pretty good at those – it's all speed-up on the beat; grab your cash in hand, then get the whole thing over as quickly as you can. Victor needs a different tack completely, something very subtle and low-key. I'd better go and find him, start again from scratch. Sudchit taught me an Oriental foot massage, which is specially good for problem men. It doesn't just relax them, it disarms them. Feet are safe, they think. Actually, it's surprisingly erotic, as if there's a hotline from the big toe to the prick. I'll have a shot at it. I owe him that, at least, when he's paid so much to keep me here all night.

He's in the bathroom. I can hear splashing, running taps. Perhaps he was just embarrassed about BO. I like him for that, actually. Too few men consider it.

I knock. 'Can I come in? I'd love a bath myself.' That often works as well – relaxing in warm water with the guy, letting him imagine that the bath is just a preliminary, then surprising him offguard.

'I'll run yours after mine, okay?'

God! He is a prude, can't even share a bath. I try the door. It's locked. That's the bloody end. To lock me out as if I'm some pesky little kid, instead of a skilled courtesan who's been trained to give men baths – French baths, Japanese baths, spa baths, fantasy baths. How can I try anything if he won't even let me in? I lean against the wall, see Reuben's cracked old tub again, feel his greedy soapy hands edging up my thighs. He was wild for me, betrayed me. Victor's honourable, devoted, and a wimp. No wonder Adrienne and co. find comfort with their own sex. I stomp into the kitchen, pour some orange juice. I've finished half the carton by the time he comes to find me. He's double-wrapped in pyjamas and a full-length stripey dressing-gown, which makes him look like some ageing Arab sheik.

'Water's running, Carole. I've put some bubble bath in and there are clean towels on the stool.'

I don't say thanks. I still feel irritated, maybe just dog-tired from lack of sleep. To hell with fancy massages. The sooner I can get away the better. I'll snatch a few hours kip at Angelique's, then devote the rest of this weekend to Norah. *She* won't lock me out.

The bathroom's hot and steamy, smells of pine. My bath is far too full. I try to turn the taps off, but the shower comes on instead – ice-cold. I twiddle knobs and dials. No good. Still that jet of fierce and freezing water. The water's ribcage high now, threatening to spill over. I dash along to Victor's room, burst in through the door. 'Victor, that dratted shower's gone crazy and . . .'

I stop, clutch the door handle. Victor's about to step into his underpants, wearing nothing but a shirt which is unbuttoned, hanging open. He freezes for one panic-stricken second. So do I. He sees me staring. I can't not stare. I feel sick, shocked, yet my eyes won't move from that horrifying sight. Suddenly he snatches up the dressing-gown, uses it like a shield.

'Get out!' he shouts. 'Get out of here.'

I'm out, pounding down the passage, unlocking the front door, dashing through the garden and along the dirt-track. It's still dark outside and fiercely cold. My feet keep sliding, tripping on loose stones. I even fall once, graze my knee. I don't feel any pain though. Nothing else will register, save that one first shock.

I keep on running, almost blindly, blundering into bushes, sweating and shivering both at once. I can hear my own breathing disturbing the dank silence of the night. It *is* still night, not a glint or chink of morning; dark and angry clouds racing overhead, as if I've set them off by my own ungainly pace.

At last, I stop. A dark shape off the path turns into the ruins of a house. I creep inside, slump against the damp and crumbling walls. I hear a sudden rustle. A mouse? A bat? I'm terrified of both, but I've got to stop and rest. My own pain is throbbing back, aching knee, sore and stinging feet. I close my eyes, but I can still see Victor's body, the lower half horribly scarred. The skin is gnarled and puckered, cobbled up as if someone's ripped it off, then sewn it back too tightly. It doesn't even look like skin. It's dry and dead with little raised and twisted ridges running down his stomach and his thighs, flat discoloured patches in between. His cock's affected, too, lumpy and thickened as if it's got some cover over it. I could never ever look at it again, couldn't bear to touch him. I've always been squeamish about things like scars or blemishes, even if they're tiny, and his are massive. It's bad enough seeing them on strangers, let alone a man you're involved with, almost went to bed with. Horrible. And the way he shouted, really yelled as if I were a dog. That was quite a shock as well, when he's never even raised his voice before. I felt utterly put down.

So what does *he* feel? Loved and wanted? Hardly. I let my back slide slowly down the wall till I'm sitting on the floor. I could have shown more sympathy, reacted less hysterically, instead of bolting out in pyjamas and bare feet, as if he were a leper. Poor Victor. What in God's name happened to him? Some ghastly car crash probably, like that poor sod Angelique described. Or an accident at work, maybe. Yet couldn't he have told me, warned me in advance? He's deceived me, really, posing as a normal guy, pretending he's like anybody else.

The floor feels damp and soggy. Christ knows what I'm sitting on – dung or shit or something, or the remains of a dead bird. I shudder, try to stop my mind racing round and round in circles, darting from pity to revulsion to resentment. What am I going to do? Stay here all day, go back and say I'm sorry, go back and say nothing, pretend I never saw a thing – or simply disappear?

Something runs across my foot. I jump, dodge across the rotting piles of debris to the door, blink as I emerge. The windows of the house were boarded up, so I couldn't see the first grey ghosts of light filtering from the east. Dawn seems reluctant and bad-tempered, not rosy-pink, but a sallow mauvish-grey streaked across the sky. The mountains are still blurred and bulky shapes, only their peaks shining spooky-white with snow.

I stand dithering on the path. One way leads to Victor, the other to the garage and the store. The garage has a public phone. I could call a cab, escape to Angelique's. He'd never find me there and he's far too decent to complain to Carl or make trouble for me at the Silver Palm.

Decent. Yes, he is. Kind, loving, honest; generous with his self and time and money. And no one's ever worshipped me like he does. It's marvellous being worshipped. All your bad bits simply seep away and you bask in being beautiful, inside as well as out. Can't I do the same for him, then, make him feel good, overlook the scarring? After all, it doesn't show, not in public when he's dressed. His arms and legs and face and chest are fine. It's just that middle band, only puckered skin, for heaven's sake. Is it really so important, so horrendous?

Yes, it is. I take the right fork, scramble down the dirt track to the garage and the phone. If I go the other way, Victor might want more than I can give. I'm prepared to be friendly, but not to go to bed with him – not now. No one could expect that.

I stop a moment. Suzie went to bed with him. I can see them suddenly, walking down that passage in the Silver Palm, chattering and laughing. She didn't seem disgusted. In fact, she praised him to me, called him quite some guy. It's easier for her, though. She's used to all the horrors – disabled men and perverts, wrecks in wheelchairs, amputees. It's just a job to her, a sort of social work which I could never face myself. Maybe I'm selfish, but you could also call it sensitive. Suzie's so thick-skinned it's as if she's scarred as well.

I lurch on down the path, trying to avoid the roughest of the rocks. God! I look a sight. Ripped pyjamas, bleeding knee and feet. These little hamlets are buzzing hives of gossip and the garage man knows Carl. Suppose he reports me, says a wild girl in men's nightwear came tearing in at dawn and asked to used his phone. All-Niters last past dawn, so Carl will know I've run out on my job. That could mean the sack.

He'll be pretty mad already. I forgot to call him, say I was okay. You're meant to phone once or twice on out-dates, so he can keep a check on you. It's a stupid rule, in fact. You could be phoning in at knife-point, or with a gun held to your back. That happened once, apparently, to a French girl called Thérèse. She was lucky to escape alive. Carl was pretty shaken, but he didn't stop the out-dates, just charged more for them.

I stumble to a halt, new resentment churning in my mind. Carl should have told me about Victor, warned me what I'd have to face. Perhaps he didn't know, though. Suzie did – that's certain – but I wouldn't be surprised if she concealed the fact on purpose, relishing the thought that I'd be shocked and couldn't cope. Oh, *can't* I, Suzie? Really? So feeble, am I, gutless?

I swing round, start charging back the way I've come. My legs ache, my noisy laboured breathing hurts my throat. I don't care. I'll show her. She's racing me, the bitch, her slimmer longer legs pounding past me, that waist-length hair flicking in my face.

'No, you don't,' I shout. 'Get back! He may have bloody fucked you, but he didn't take you home.'

27

I'm out of breath, jabbing stitch both sides. I clutch my middle, slow into a walk as I glimpse the house at last. I hadn't realized quite how far I'd run. The whole place looks different in the light. I'm still astonished by the change in my surroundings since that brazen sun first burst above the mountain tops, staining the sky a deep and gloating crimson. The stony hills are shining now, the clouds slashed and gorged with red. I almost hate that sun. It seems so heartless, so absorbed in its own glory, when drabber, feebler creatures are hurt or scarred or terrified. My heart is thumping, not so much from running, but from fear – fear of seeing Victor again, fear of what to say and how to be; fear of his anger or embarrassment, of making things still worse.

My pace slackens even more as I turn into the garden. The house looks hostile somehow, closed against me, though the front door is open still, the passage warm in contrast to the chilly air outside. I stop and listen. Not a sound. Is Victor there still? My bare feet make no noise, yet the house is so ominously quiet, they seem to startle and disturb it. I check the kitchen and the bathroom; one empty, the other semi-flooded; go on to his bedroom. The bed's unmade, a limp blue tie coils across the floor. I pick it up, feel a sudden sweaty panic as I stare down at the tiny monogram. Supposing Victor's disappeared, done the sort of bolt I was planning on myself? No, he mustn't. Can't. Suzie's right. Of course he's quite some guy. Didn't I feel happier last night than I've felt for years and years; notice how he put me first in every tiny way; how sane and wise and balanced all his views seemed? Jon never had opinions, except on snooker and hard rock, and

Reuben's were all fanatical and revengeful. I've got to find him: better grab a coat and shoes, go and search outside for him.

I didn't bring a coat, so I'll have to borrow his; find it in the wardrobe, stand a moment, motionless, holding just one sleeve. I'm remembering when we bought those two cream trench coats, how we strutted in the mirror, tried on silly hats as well; what fun he was, how generous. He asked me where my coat was when we were driving here last night, and I had to lie again. It wasn't easy. You don't lose coats at craps, yet how could I explain that it was shut up at the Gold Rush, or perhaps in the hands of the police? He didn't probe, or nag about my carelessness, just promised me another one. And when I mumbled something about expense, he said his own coat was mate to mine and hated being parted from it, so it was an act of simple mercy to replace it, not extravagance at all.

I smile, sling his lonely coat across my shoulders. I'll find this guy if I have to search the whole damn desert for him. I race back to my room to get my shoes, stifle a cry as I stop dead at the door. He's in there, sitting on my bed, fully dressed except for rings and socks. He hasn't seen me. He's staring at the floor, head down, shoulders sagging; seems somehow much more vulnerable bare-fingered and barefoot. I feel suddenly confused. Did I dream the scars? The skin that's showing looks so smooth and normal, can it really be so monstrous lower down? He's holding my blue dress, has it twisted through his fingers, lying on his lap. I clear my throat, see him start. I imagine he'll leap up, maybe dart away. He doesn't; simply shifts position on the bed. 'Sit down,' is all he says.

I can't bring myself to join him on the bed, so I squat down on the floor, his coat still round my shoulders. It's gloomy in the room, the curtains drawn tight shut, that gloating sun blocked out.

'Remember last night you told me when your birthday was?'

What's he on about? My birthday's five whole months

away. Is he just trying to pretend everything's all right, that the last hour hasn't happened, blank it out in small talk? That's fine by me. 'Yeah,' I say. 'I'll be nineteen on 19th June. Nineteen must be lucky.'

He shakes his head. 'No way. Though it's quite incredible – same date, same year. When I heard that, Carole, I felt real churned up inside. It seemed kind of . . . meant – you being born on the day that . . .' He breaks off, bites his lip.

'What d'you mean? Which day?'

He doesn't answer. The bedroom door is open and I can hear a sudden judder from the ancient fridge, filling in his silence. I lick my finger, try to clean my oozy knee through my ripped pyjama leg. My blue dress has slithered off his lap, fallen to the floor. I don't think he's even noticed.

At last he looks across at me. 'Let's go back a bit, okay? October '67.'

Pre-history. I wasn't even born then. I can feel the years slowly creaking back. My parents got married that year – two scared people in stiff clothes, yellowing on our front-room mantelpiece. Victor's picking at a nail, seems more remote from me than he's ever been before, as if he's moved into a past that can't include me. 'That's the date I joined Battery C in Bardstown.'

'Joined what?'

'The National Guard. It's a civilian reserve force, something like your Territorial Army. To be honest with you, Carole, I only joined in the hope of dodging the draft. I was twenty-two and a real live wire.' Suddenly he laughs. I jump. The sound is totally unexpected when he's been looking so anguished and intense. 'I wish you'd known me then.' He runs his hand through his thinning greying hair. 'I had a thick brown beard and hair to match and I was so lean and keen and hot to trot, I was like a jumping bean. I was determined to get ahead – and also save the world as well, just in my spare time. My Dad was a pretty humble guy, and Christ! was I going to make him proud of me. I'd already worked my way through college and landed on my feet as a site engineer in a small construction firm with big ideas. The last thing I wanted was to louse up my career, lose two years of my life to the regular army, which didn't really figure in my high ideals. But Battery C was like the perfect compromise – just six months training, and only weekend duties, and there was no way we could be drafted, or so we thought. Then in May '68 – May 13th, actually – my father said he'd heard something on the radio about Nixon activating a whole bunch of Guards units for front-line duty in Vietnam.'

'Vietnam? You mean you . . .'

'Hang on a second, Carole, let me finish. I told my Dad he must have got it wrong. "No way, Pop," I said. "If they send us anywhere, it'll be to Cincinnati, to help put down the race riots." Three months later, I was stepping off a military plane in Saigon.'

Saigon. I stare at him. I've heard so much about that war, seen films – pro the war, anti the war, revenge for the war, remorse for the war. Yet it always seemed remote. I'd never met anyone who's actually set foot there, not in Saigon.

'We were posted to Tomahawk Hill – that's near Phu Bai, the northern part of South Vietnam. We had to take another plane to Danang, then we drove our guns to Phu Bai, and from there we were choppered into Tomahawk. It was a helluva trip for someone whose foreign travels had been restricted to Miami and LA!' He allows himself a grin. 'There were worse postings, far worse. We had hot meals and dry beds, even ice-machines and electric cooling fans, donated by the loyal folks back home. It was a spooky kind of place, though, completely bare, not a tree or blade of grass in sight, just old abandoned cemeteries.'

He shivers, as if he can see the place again, rubs his eyes, perhaps to blot it out. 'Our year was almost up. It hadn't been too bad. We'd had a real good community feeling, almost like a family. We were all local boys who'd grown up together, trained together, and mostly damn good gunners . . .'

'You were a gunner, Victor?' I simply can't imagine it, can't imagine him a soldier at all, not Victor.

'Yeah. I was lucky. We gunners had it easy. It was the grunts who did the dirty work, out in the paddies and the

453

jungle. They slept in all sorts of shit – if they slept at all – while we reclined on bunk beds in the dry. And like all good artillerymen I could sleep through our own gunfire. So when I woke in the early hours of June 19th 1969 . . .'

'That's when I was born,' I interrupt. 'The early hours. About two o'clock I think it was. My Ma was most indignant. She's always liked to sleep late.'

He doesn't laugh, just gets up from the bed and comes and squats in front of me, takes my hands in his. 'You were born at two o'clock, Carole?'

I nod. His expression is so strange, so fierce, I feel quite scared. Another nervous rumble from the fridge, then silence closes over it again.

'What's the matter, Victor?'

'Nothing. It just seems so . . .' He leaves the sentence hanging, then gets up slowly, moves towards the door, seems to be almost talking to himself.

'It's still so clear, that night. I can remember every little goddamn detail, like I'm living it again. We'd seen a movie – *Bonnie and Clyde* it was – and a barbecue was planned. Oh yeah, they tried to keep us happy, give us lots of goodies, but it started pouring down with rain, the kind of icy sheeting rain you only get out there, so we all drifted off to our bunkers instead of broiling steaks and chicken. I went to sleep with the noise of the rain drumming down like crazy. I woke up to another noise – enemy guns.'

He pauses for a moment. When he speaks again, his voice is different – strained and tight. 'Fourteen of our men were killed, five of them from Battery C, all good buddies of mine. One guy – we'd been real close, Carole, grown up together, more or less, been to the same school, same church – he was burned so bad, his back just came away when I put my arm around him.'

Victor slumps down on the bed again, shuts his eyes. 'We . . . we were duty crew in the gun when it got hit. My buddy got the worst of it. He was still alive – just; wanted me to stay with him until . . .' He makes a gesture, a horizontal slicing of the hand.

I can't speak myself, feel too upset, too sick. Some tactless bird is squawking through the silence, singing about light and food and morning when Victor's friend is dying in the dark. I get up for a cigarette, try to keep my movements small and quiet. It feels wrong to move, disturb this solemn moment with matches which won't strike. The third one does, takes me by surprise. I jump with the flame, almost burn my fingers holding it too long. Victor's still sitting there in silence, mops his face with a corner of the sheet. It's quite chilly in the bedroom with the curtains closed, but I can see the sweat glistening on his forehead.

At last, he speaks again. His voice is flat, matter-of-fact. 'Then more gooks poured in, wearing just these jockstraps, with their naked bodies greased so they could slip through the barbed wire. They were firing grenades, spraying the place with machine-guns, shooting anything that moved. It was pandemonium.'

'You mean you stayed there, Victor, with all that going on?'

He shrugs. 'It wasn't long before I *couldn't* move. Some of our ammo started blowing up. We had these phosphorus shells piled nearby and I got caught by one of those. White phosphorus burns even worse than napalm, Carole. It kind of clings and then eats slowly through layers and layers of skin. And it's no good dousing it with water. It just ignites again, so the more water you pour on, the worse it burns.'

I clutch my stomach. Now I understand. Those are burn scars, skin-graft scars. I should have known. Jan's got this friend who used to come to supper, a trainee nurse, working on a burns unit. I couldn't bear even to hear her talk about it, and her text-books – God! – the pictures. She told us she had nightmares the first few weeks she worked there, woke up screaming, sweating. Yet Victor seems so calm, is speaking quite impassively, still fiddling with the corner of the sheet.

'It's kind of odd. Up to then, I remember everything, and in real strong Technicolor, but after that it all goes blank and black. Next thing I knew, I was waking up in base hospital in Danang – or half of me waking up. I guess God has a sense of the ridiculous – hit a guy where it'll really louse him up. It's okay, Carole, everything's still there, in working order.' He gives a forced and bitter laugh. 'But as you've seen, it doesn't look too hot. I understand how you felt just now. It was years before I could look at my own body without wanting to throw up, even after twenty separate skin-grafts.'

'*Twenty?*'

'Yeah. Once I was out of danger, they flew me back Stateside, then on to Louisville. I was lucky. I had one of the best plastic surgeons in the country, but it was a real slow business waiting for the scars to heal before they'd risk a new graft. And I kept getting infections, so it was like one step forward, two steps back. You're helpless as a baby in that state. My weight went down by nearly thirty pounds, and I had so many tubes and drips and wires, I felt like a sick computer.'

He grins. I'm still feeling sick and shocked, still remembering what Jan's nurse friend said. Some of her patients lay for months and months with their faces missing or half their bodies gone. And it wasn't just the physical pain, but the shock of being permanently deformed and having to live with it. They were sometimes quite alone. Their relatives couldn't face them, couldn't cope; made more fuss than the patients did, or simply stayed away. I'd have been like that, rushing off, more sorry for myself than the poor wretch in the bed. I take a deep drag of my cigarette, inhale the smoke right into my lungs. Even now, I haven't managed a simple word of sympathy, am more concerned with my stupid heaving stomach than with Victor lying maimed in hospital. Did people rally round, or was he left to sweat alone? He's an only child – I know that – and his parents are both dead now, had him late in life.

'Were your parents still alive then, Victor? I mean, did they help and visit you and . . .?'

'Oh, yeah, they were great, Mom especially. It was harder for my Dad. He was so upset and not in such great shape himself.'

'So why did you leave Bardstown, when that was your home town with all your friends and family and everything?'

He pauses a moment, tugs at the sheet as if he'd like to rip it end to end. 'I . . . er . . . couldn't stand living round the corner from my girlfriend – not after she married someone else.'

'You mean you were engaged?'

'Yeah, even bought the ring. It was a pretty ring – sapphires and diamonds.'

I'm suddenly furious and jealous, hate the girl, loathe her rotten ring. 'And she threw you over?'

'I don't blame her, Carole. She was loyal at first, waited a whole year, in fact. The trouble was, I guess I didn't seem much better at the end of it than I did at the beginning. They had to use the good skin on my thighs for grafting, so they were scarred as well. And I had these ugly rashes on my hands and feet and arms, which didn't seem to heal. The grunts called it jungle-rot, and I soon discovered why, once I'd joined them on a few patrols. I wasn't used to walking trails, and my soft and pampered gunner's feet began to fall to pieces, ended up corpse-white and kind of dead. It's a fungus thing which eats away the skin, makes it ooze and crack. It can go on for years. I was luckier than most, though. Mine was nothing compared with what I'd seen. All the same. . .' He shrugs. 'I guess I didn't look exactly the romantic bridegroom.'

'But you were a . . . hero, Victor, a war hero.'

'No way. I didn't even want to fight, went out there protesting.'

'That doesn't matter. You still went, and you stayed by your friend when you could have run for cover.'

'I'd have been hit most likely, whatever I'd have done. It was chaos, total chaos. The whole war was like that. You can't use words like "hero" for a war which fucked up three whole decades. We're still fighting it in one way, fighting its results. There was so much bitterness, it was like it poisoned the whole country. We *were* heroes when we first returned, at least in Bardstown, where our folks did everything they could to honour us and mourn the boys who didn't make it back. But a couple of years later, the media fucked us over, called us all drug-crazed dangerous psychopaths, who might explode at any moment and couldn't be trusted with a job or . . . I know that from my own case. Well, I guess I was crazy for a while, not on drugs, but real mixed up.' He stops, as if remembering, makes a gesture of contempt.

'I was living in a fog of pain-killers and fear and self-disgust, especially when my girlfriend returned the ring. The hardest thing was seeing her with her new guy. He was from Chicago and dodged the draft by staying on at school to do a doctorate. None of us Bardstown boys did that. In fact, several of my buddies dropped out of college because they felt their first duty was to fight. But who was I to criticize? I hadn't been the great patriot myself – far from it.' He traces the deep frown-line which runs between his brows. I can hardly see his eyes, their reassuring blue. 'All the same, I wasn't exactly wild about the guy. The first time I met him he was only wearing tennis shorts. That really rubbed it in. Those long brown legs and smooth expanse of back without so much as an acne scar.'

'I'd have murdered him, Victor. *And* her.'

'I didn't need to.' His voice is barely audible. 'She was killed in a four-car crash just six months after the wedding. She was . . . pregnant, Carole. I was in the hospital again when I heard the news – skin graft number seven. I couldn't even cry, not with all those tubes and stuff. I wept inside, though. I'd wanted my revenge, but now I had it, it was like I'd lost her a second time, maybe even . . . killed her.'

'Killed her? How could you, Victor? You weren't driving, were you?'

'No, I told you, I was lying on my back, half raw. But thoughts themselves are dangerous – more powerful than we realize, maybe.' A jet plane screeches through his words. He waits, silent, while it passes, its echo throbbing through my head. 'After that, I changed.'

'How d'you mean?'

'Well, revenge was out, to start with – all revenge, whether against the gooks or the government, or the growing bunch of draft dodgers, including rival Dougie, who was now a widower. I guess I just accepted things, stopped feeling so damned sorry for myself. I was alive, when all those other unlucky guys were dead – *and* the girl I'd loved. I could walk and talk and even earn my living, when thousands more were paralysed or crippled or missing arms or legs. To say nothing of the psychos and the junkies and those who snuffed themselves because they couldn't face the world after what they'd seen and done in combat.'

Victor's hands are locked together. I've always liked his hands, but now they look quite different: soldier's hands, hands which have loaded shells, fed huge and hungry guns, picked up stinking corpses. I realize that I've never really known him – only just the outside. He shifts one leg, leans forward.

'D'you realize, Carole, by the end of that damned war, the death-toll had reached fifty-eight thousand men, and I doubt if that included all the suicides. A load of guys had breakdowns or ended up as dope fiends. The media weren't so wrong there. You could buy drugs like candy in 'Nam. No one really cared if you were stoned, so long as you kept fighting. In the end, people acted kind of wary of you if you'd been out there at all – assumed you were a baby-burner or a raving sickie who might shoot up innocent women in the street. It wasn't so bad in Bardstown. It's a patriotic little place, and loyal to the hometown boys. All the same, I decided on a second move. I was still too close to home, still pitied as the poor wounded soldier, still labelled as Laura's ex-fiancé. I needed a new start, new friends who'd never met Laura and weren't wondering every time they saw me how bad I looked underneath my clothes.'

He pauses, grimacing at himself, as if seeing with their eyes. Silence in the room. I feel guilty, don't know what to say. Empty clichés about looks not mattering are not only untrue, but hypocritical. I ran away myself.

He looks up, breaks the tension. 'New York was quite a shock at first, after small-town living, but I survived, found a job of sorts, even found another girl. She was a nurse, so I figured she wouldn't be too thrown by all those scars. Even so, it was months before I told her, and longer still before I let her have a look.'

'What. . . happened?'

'Not a lot. She just stopped answering her phone, started being busy all the time, too busy to see me any more. After that, I lost my confidence. I kind of chopped myself in two and threw away the bottom half. I was just a head, a chest, two arms. Oh, there was plenty I could do – I worked damn hard, read a lot, improved my poker, raised orchids in my one-room bachelor apartment. It wasn't such a bad life – quite a wrench, in fact, when I was forced to change it. My firm was taken over. I told you that already, didn't I?'

I nod. Though it's only now I realize what a shock it must have been, coming after so many other losses.

'I took it hard, though it was really just tough luck, I guess. The new company already had an ace engineer. It was either him or me, and not much question which one would have to go. So now I had my financial compensation from the war and this new severance pay. I felt doubly on the scrapheap, a write-off with two pensions – nothing else. I sat at home feeling sorry for myself, just went out in the evenings to play poker – though I kept losing even there. I seemed to be unlucky, not just in my life, but in my cards. I had a run of really heavy losses. It became a vicious circle. The more I lost, the more I felt a victim. The other players sensed that, saw me as no threat. I was an easy mark and they jumped all over me. Psychology in poker's all important, Carole, but I didn't even see what I was doing. Well – not until one evening when I'd lost another grand, and this old guy, Mitch, who was always hanging around the poker room, parked himself beside me, ordered us two beers.

'"Vic," he said. "You sat in that game resigned to lose, expecting to, in fact. You've even started to root against yourself. I've watched you. Okay, you've had some bad streaks, and it's real tough running bad, but every deal affords you the same chance to be lucky or unlucky as any other deal – regardless of what happened yesterday, or the day before, or any goddamned day. Why don't you decide to be a winner for a change, instead of making yourself a target for the rest?"

'I was mad at him at first. He'd no right to just butt in, start giving me advice I didn't want. Now I'm very grateful to the guy. He turned me round, changed my way of thinking. I couldn't sleep that night for mulling it all over. I mean, he was only talking about cards, but what he said applied to my whole life. Did I really want to live it as a loser? Okay, I'd lost my job, but I was still alive, still had funds – and wits. And I kept remembering that phrase about every deal offering you another chance. It was obvious, even trite maybe, yet I'd been trying to deny it, refusing even to take the breaks I got.

'That next night at poker, I had a full house and a straight flush in just the first half hour. I took it as an omen.' He grins. 'We poker players are real superstitious, Carole, but I needed that good luck. It psyched me up, helped me change gear from unlucky guy to winner. The difference was incredible. Even when I had bad cards, I played them with a will to win. Sure I still had losses, but I didn't just accept them, sit there like a turkey, resigned to lose, like Mitch had said. And I was winning more than losing – much more. In fact, I even . . .' He breaks off. 'I'm boring you, I'm sorry, Carole. Poker freaks are the biggest bores on earth. Get us on to cards, and five hours later, we'll still be yakking away.'

Boring me? Good God no! That's the last word that I'd use. I'm shocked, admiring, humbled, and confused. So many emotions are churning through my mind, I hardly know what to say or think or feel. Victor seems a stranger. I'm awed by what he's been through, what he's seen and suffered; need time to take it in. And so many things he's said have a bearing on my own life. All that stuff about losing, failing, feeling sorry for oneself, letting go revenge. I light another cigarette, try to sort my thoughts out. The silence feels uncomfortable.

'Did you find another job?' I ask. I must say something, or he will assume I'm bored.

'No. I tried. It wasn't easy. My field was fairly specialized and I was already old in their terms. And when I went for interviews, people always seemed uneasy that I wasn't married.' He laughs. 'An ageing fag, I guess they thought. All the same, I got close several times – in the final group, in fact – but each damn time it was a younger married man who got the job. I was feeling rather sore about it, until I realized I didn't need to work. I could live off my two handouts and my winnings. I guess it was a question of attitude again. I could see myself as out of work and useless, or I could enjoy the fact I was free of any ties – which meant free to fly to places like Las Vegas, so I could play in tournaments, play a tougher game with pros. After that, it was Vegas every month. I never really planned to settle there, though I liked the climate, especially in the winter. As I said, it's not a friendly town, but I was used to living a private sort of life, presenting just a face to people, concealing all the rest; so that wasn't any problem. In Vegas, you're accepted as you are, no questions asked. A lot of guys end up there who have things to hide, or want to start new lives.'

He rubs his chin, reflecting. 'I had a real good start myself, a run of wins, soon found my niche in a couple of casinos where they knew me as just "Vic" – no past, no state, no surname. That suited me just fine. But I was getting tired of all the travelling – crowded planes, delays at airports. It seemed more sensible to buy a place, try my luck here as a native. I already knew this neck of the woods. I used to hire a car and drive out on weekends – explore the desert and the mountains. One day, I stopped to take a hike, admire the sunset, and I came across a house for sale – this house. Twelve weeks later, I'd sold up in New York and moved in here. So . . .' he shrugs. 'Now you know my story.'

A pretty bloody lonely one, I think, as I ease my aching legs, stretch them into life again. Victor's lost everything, not just a normal healthy body, but love, marriage, the chance of children, a proper family home. And he's still not bitter, not furious like I'd be.

'And you . . . never met another girl?' I ask him.

He grins. 'Dozens. But I didn't fall in love again until just this last December.'

I snap a match in two. 'In love?'

He picks up my blue dress, which has lain forgotten on the floor, smooths it out, handling it as gently as if it were precious antique lace. 'Carole, I shouldn't tell you this, but I fell in love with you the very first moment I saw you standing on that sidewalk, soaked to the skin with your wet hair dripping into those furious blue eyes.' He's talking to the dress, mumbling, nervous, yet incredibly intense.

'In love?' I say again. I need to play for time. I'm stunned. I suppose I guessed it really, but to have him spell it out, declare it formally, when I've still not recovered from the first shock.

'I vowed I'd never tell you. It wasn't fair. I'm twenty-one years older. No – twenty-four. Jeez! That sounds a whole lot worse. I've been worrying all this time about a twenty-one-year age gap, and now you've made it more.'

'D'you want me to be twenty-one again?' I feel much older, more than twenty-one. So much has happened in this last half hour – a whole war, twenty skin grafts, fifty-eight thousand deaths.

'No.' He grins. 'Forty-two's still double that. Even if you shot right up to twenty-five, I'd still be much too old for you, as well as being . . .' He stops, embarrassed, searches for the word.

'Scarred,' I tell him silently. 'Disfigured.'

'Well – not exactly Mr Universe. I just hoped we could be friends. Except it wasn't simply friendship I was feeling. Christ, no! In fact, it was only because of you I went to that damned brothel. I guess you must have stirred up all my hormones.' He gives a sheepish laugh.

'You mean, you've never been before – not to other ones? Not in all those years?'

'Never. Not even in Vietnam, where there were hundreds of girls available, and half the bars were brothels.'

'Loyal to Laura, I suppose?' I try to keep the resentment from my voice.

'Well, she was only just a kid, Carole, and always seemed so . . . trusting. And she wrote me every goddamned day out there. So,' he grins, 'I managed to resist. Not that it was easy. This may shock you, Carole, but war's a kind of turn-on. I guess it's the adrenaline which gives GIs the hots. The night before you're going into combat, all you want to do is screw your brains out. Otherwise, you just lie there on your own, shit-scared and keyed-up both at once, so it's impossible to sleep. And after it's all over, it's like you're extra horny just to celebrate the fact you're still alive, haven't lost your vital bits and pieces. You've got to try them out, to prove you can still function.'

He glances at me, as if he's afraid he's gone too far. 'All the same, I'm glad now I said no. I saw my pals buying girls with dollars, or softening them up with Lucky Strikes and bars of soap. It all seemed so damned casual – just throw your money down, do your stuff, wham-bam, then saunter out. It caught up with them later. I've heard guys say they couldn't handle women once they'd left the military – not emotionally – couldn't relate or feel, couldn't give themselves.'

I say nothing. That's hardly news to me. At the Silver Palm, we're just objects to be bought. It may be stupid, or even hypocritical, but I'm still upset that Victor ever went there. He seems to read my thoughts, or perhaps he's just defensive at my silence. Anyway, he starts explaining.

'Listen, Carole darling, I only went this time because I was so upset about the fact that I'd lost you, so turned on when I thought of you . . . Oh, I knew you'd never look at me, not in that way, but so long as you were with me, I felt the greatest luckiest guy in all of Vegas.'

'But it was only two days, Victor.' I try to haul them back, re-examine them. I can't. The Victor I knew then was not the same – not scarred, not a gunner, not a bloody hero.

'No. Two centuries. Except time went backwards then. I was twenty-one again, with thick brown hair and a bushy beard and not a mark on my lithe body. You mean to say you didn't even notice?' This time it's a real laugh. I don't join in; I'm still too overwhelmed.

'I felt just the same last night, when you were lying on the carpet in my arms. Though that wasn't meant to happen. I only took you home to tell you the whole story. I felt it wasn't fair to go on hiding things, and I couldn't broach the subject in a public restaurant with waiters breathing down our necks. It would be easier at home, I thought, more private and relaxed. Except it wasn't easy – impossible, in fact. Once I'd got you home, I longed to keep you there, not frighten you away with ugly stories. Losing you seemed worse than anything, worse even than the scars themselves. Then, once we'd had the meal, and wine, and we were stretched out on that carpet, the scars just disappeared. You'd healed me, Carole, and I was a normal healthy guy again, round about your own age and horny as all hell, who was wild to . . . to . . .'

'Screw me?' I suggest.

'The word's not good enough. Love you. Make love to you. Christ Almighty, Carole, you just can't understand how much I wanted that. I lay awake all night, feeling furious and bitter – all the things I thought I'd licked – and old again, old and grey and finished because you'd gone.'

'Gone?'

'In my mind you had. I'd told you in my mind, you see, and what else could you do but go? And if I didn't tell you, well, how could we continue avoiding one another, sleeping separately? As it was, I had to almost tie myself to the bedposts to stop me barging into your room.'

And I thought he was asleep, dismissed him as a wimp. I stub my cigarette out. The room smells smoky: acrid smoke from scorching flesh, burning villages. I sit in silence, scared of my own power; power to heal him – or blow his life to bits a second time. Being loved feels almost like a burden, a responsibility which I'm not sure I can handle.

He gets up from the bed, offers me both hands, scoops me from the floor. 'You deserve a medal for endurance, darling. I don't think I've ever talked so long before, and I've certainly never seen you sit so still. This must be a record. You're so full of energy – I love it. Even your face is always on the move. You've got so many expressions, do you know that? And you're so . . . so involved with everything. If I buy you chocolates, the whole of you lights up; if you're mad, you're really roaring mad. You should have been an actress, a star. You *are* a star. And I'm your fan. I love everything about you, Carole – your real cute English accent, the way you eat your strawberries – two tiny bites, as if you're scared they might bite back – then gulp, just like my lionfish; the way you love all food, never leave a morsel; the kind of crazy way you laugh, your kindness to Norah, your . . .'

'Kindness?' As far as I recall, I spent most of the time avoiding or resenting her.

'Yeah. That touched me. You're a real good person,

darling. I mean, the fact you came back now, had the guts to do that.'

I pull away. He's going far too far too fast, assumes I've accepted him, that the scarring doesn't matter. It does. It does. Okay, he loves me, but that doesn't mean everything's just fine. Yet how can I reject him like Laura and that nurse did, be another no-go in his life? He is a hero, brave and loyal and incredibly accepting. I'm still bitter about Reuben and my father's death and a host of other things, while he's moved beyond that; builds gardens, raises orchids, even charms the desert; can cry for the bitch who ditched him when I'd be glad she died. I love him for all that, and it isn't simply pity. He's far too good for pity. The problem is he thinks I'm good as well, doesn't realize what I'm thinking underneath, or understand the rotten selfish reasons why I slunk back here at all. It was more to do with Suzie than with him, a desire to do her down; plus abject craven fears about losing my job, alienating Carl. Yet he still thinks I'm wonderful, big-hearted.

He strides over to the window, pulls the curtains back. We both blink against the brilliant desert light.

'Carole, you're hurt. I didn't realize.'

'Hurt?'

'Your knee. And both your feet are bleeding. Gee, I'm sorry, honey. I've been rambling on for hours, while you're shivering in those damp pyjamas. You'd better take 'em off. I'll fetch some antiseptic.'

I'm the child again, the little girl who must be fussed and spoiled and petted. I can hear him in the bathroom, opening cupboards, running water in the basin. If I play the child's role, let him bathe my knee, that means removing my pyjama bottoms. Then I'm a woman, with a woman's body, a body which he loves, which turns him on. Already he's admiring it, standing at the door while I stretch and yawn, finger-comb my hair.

'Look, Victor, I think I'll have that bath now. It'll warm me up and clean my grazes at the same time. Don't worry' – I force a laugh – 'I promise not to touch the shower this time. 'And why don't you fix breakfast while I'm in the bath? I'm starving now, aren't you?' Toasting muffins will keep him busy, keep him off. I still need far more time, time to sort out what I feel, process his last twenty years.

The bathroom floor is damp still, though Victor's mopped the worst up; left me antiseptic, soothing creams. Can you love a guy because he's more concerned about your footling little grazes than the fact that half his body's scarred? I help myself to bath salts, flinging in several generous handfuls till the water turns a murky green; then strip off my pyjamas and climb in. It's heaven. I didn't realize how stiff and tired and achy I was feeling. The hot water lulls my body, but my mind is still racing round in circles. Victor's life – the hell of it, the waste, yet the way he's battled on, outlawed all self-pity.

I close my eyes, try to shut my mind off, but the pictures keep on coming. I can see his body bursting into flame as he sits beside the corpse of his best friend; see him sick and silent in the hospital, watch the dials on a life-support machine record each twitch and shiver of his illness. I can't see Laura – only the diamonds flashing on her hand, and all her letters, long and loving letters, written in a neat and childish writing, with red biro kisses at the bottom. He was loyal to her. That's rare. I've seen too many clients betray their wives and girlfriends, even two-time a fiancée the day they bought the ring. Oafs and rotters, all of them.

No, not all. I suddenly see Victor, young and bearded Victor, sitting in a bar in Vietnam. Half the bars were brothels, so he said. Sudchit's there as well, ogling him, haggling, trying to lure him in. He's smiling, saying no, saying no to Le Thi Sang, to Sun-Hee, to all those gorgeous Eastern girls. He can have hardly slept with anyone in all these years and years. While I've been through a hundred men in just eleven days.

I sit bolt upright in the bath, splashing water everywhere. It's as if only now I realize what I've done. I hear my own voice, stupidly offhand: 'A hundred pricks. So what?' How could I have shrugged them off like that, pretended they were nothing, believed that I was shielded by some footling plastic cover? I stare down at my body. I'm scarred – like Victor – scarred indelibly.

I reach out for the soap, a brilliant yellow bar in the shape of a whole lemon, lather it between my hands. I can't smell soap or sharp astringent lemon, only sweaty heaving bodies, unwashed underarms, the stink of men on heat. All one hundred of them are crowding round the bath, as if to prove exactly what I've done, really rub it in. 'No!' I whisper, horrified. 'Go away. Get out of here.' They don't. They only press still closer, digging in their nails, gasping, panting as they come, tugging at my hair. That Jewish guy, he's there again: not Reuben – Nathan – though I was angry with him just the same; his onion-flavoured breath only half disguised with peppermints, the long hairs in his nostrils, coarse hair in his ears; his bristly chin butting at my bum as I kneel down on all fours and he comes in from behind, ramming ramming ramming like a piston engine. Is he furious as well? It feels like it. We're hating one another as we make what he calls love.

Make love. Victor's word. I'm tainted for him now, tainted by a hundred pricks. Con-men's pricks and thugs' pricks; pricks which almost choke me as they hammer down my throat. Semen in my mouth, slimy adult snot. I smack my lips, pretend to swallow it, pretend to come myself, pretend to smile. Everything pretend, to make those jerks feel supermen.

God! I sound like Naima, angry and embittered, despising every client. A lot of whores are angry, get worse with age, tougher and more cynical – anti-life, anti-men, anti the whole human race. I was right in one way – a hundred men is nothing, not compared with Naima. A hundred in eleven days, three thousand in a year, fifty thousand by the time I've reached her age. I cling on to the bath. I'm trembling, shivering. Of course I wouldn't stay that long – except that's what all whores say. Naima did herself, and Joanne, who's forty. They all intend to quit, get out before they're lost, but the majority slag on, because there's nowhere else they'll fit, no one who'll accept them. So the spiral just continues. They're bitter, they're unlucky, so they keep on losing, losing, like Victor did at cards.

I must escape; I've got to, break the spiral now before I'm just burnt out. I pick up Victor's sponge, hold it in both hands.

Victor said I had the power to heal him, but it could work the other way. He's already shown me that men can still be caring – sensitive and gentle, that I can't dismiss them all as pricks and tricks, that at least there's one exception, one guy in the world who's got a heart, a conscience. He's already tried to buy me out, get me free of Carl, offered me a lifeline. The word's quite apt – it *is* a lifeline – a way to stop me becoming dead inside, dead and hard and toughened like his skin.

Instinctively, I flinch. That's the problem, though, the reason it won't work. I just can't accept that skin. I'm not as brave as he is, nothing like as decent. The age thing doesn't bother me. He's boyish, in a way, and so crazily in love with me, he's like an adolescent, bashful and passionate at once. But his body and his cock, those ghastly creepy scars . . .

Mind you, I could accept his help and bugger off. He offered me a let-out with no strings attached, not a quid pro quo. I don't have to sleep with him, or love him back, or save him. I stare down at his sponge, its tiny holes, its uneven squashy shape. It looks alive, as if it's breathing. I'm clutching it too tight, squeezing all the life out. I cradle it more gently, sniff its soapy sweetish smell. No, I couldn't just run off. Not now. He's showed me what love is – giving, not just grabbing, caring, staying loyal. Loyal like Norah. She can love as well. She's always put me first like Victor does, came to Las Vegas in the first place just to make me happy, when the whole idea probably scared her stiff; risked God knows what to buy my wedding dress. I've been pretty cool to her, used her when it suited me, ignored her other times.

Have I ever loved anyone, ever really given in my life? Oh, I use the word a lot. I loved Reuben, didn't I, maybe love him still. Sexy handsome Reuben, kissing me all over; lying faithless Reuben, grabbing all I had. *Do I love* him? Did I? Do I know what the word means? I'm better at the bad things – anger and revenge. I know what anger means. I'm furious with Reuben for taking all my cash. I could have used that money to start a different life, included Norah, set us up together in a decent London flat. And I'm furious with every guy who's bought me, even the pathetic ones. I can hear my silly voice again. 'Yeah, I love you, Dad'; see that raddled father whimpering 'Kay, my little Kay.' His daughter – Kay – was grown up now, he told me, never wrote at all, refused even to speak to him. No, wait – she's speaking now, lisping through my voice. 'Pop,' she's saying. 'You're the best Dad in the world.' He's preening, on cloud nine. His clammy flesh is squelching into mine, his clumsy hands with their bitten broken nails fumbling for my nipples. 'Dad,' I mouth again, as he pulls me on his lap, holds me closer, his stubble to my breast. My arms are round his neck. I can feel the boil swelling on his back; hot and lumpy, throbbing; its pus erupting, spilling over; pus inside me, running down my legs.

I slap them with the sponge, slap my eyes as well. What's the point of blubbing? He paid me, didn't he? They all paid bloody well, and I'm in this game purely for the cash – cash I've wasted, most of it. I sold my cunt to buy an instant wineglass-froster, screwed my father for an electronic Wonder Key Ring which finds lost keys, lights up in the dark.

I jump up, turn the tap on, just the hot one, let it run, hotter, hotter, hotter, till the water's almost scalding me. That's okay. I've got to burn away my pain and shame, sterilize my body, kill off all the germs. I snatch up the bathbrush, dig it in the soap, scour my naked breasts, scrub down my whole body, scrape off all those men – their nail-marks, tooth-marks, fingerprints, their sweat and sperm and slobber; dislodge festering little pockets of revenge, grimy coils of anger and resentment. I can smell lemon now, stinging cleansing lemon cutting through the reek of sweaty men. They're leaving, shuffling out, fighting through the door, elbowing and jostling one another, swearing, swapping insults. The last half dozen swagger off; last two, last one. I hear the door slam shut, let out a deep breath. I'm absolutely knackered, as if I haven't slept a wink for years and years, instead of just one night. My body feels quite raw, but at least it's clean now – gasping tingling clean, not even anger left.

I put the bathbrush down, let myself lie back. The water's tamed a little, still hot, but lulling hot. I'm too tired to go on thinking. My mind is raw as well. Too many shocks and problems, too many guilts and fears. I haven't any answers, but it doesn't seem to matter quite so much. I want simply to drift, float away in a haze of pine and steam. I close my eyes. Frightening things like wars and scars recede; dangerous things like love condense in tiny droplets on the walls. I'm falling, flowing with them, sinking even deeper in the water. Only water, only warm green water, the scent of summer pinewoods, lemon groves in flower . . .

I jump when Victor knocks. He's calling through the door. I think I'd just dozed off. His voice sounds very distant, as if it's coming from a thousand years away.

'What?' I shout.

'I wondered if you're nearly through? Your coffee's getting cold.'

'Bring it in, then. I'm too whacked to get out.'

He's never seen me naked. I reach across, tip in still more bath salts, stretch out flat so only my head and feet are showing. He can't see me now. The water's like a thick green coverlet.

My eyes keep closing. I open them to a second knock, a loaded breakfast tray. He's spoiling me again. Not just coffee, but bacon, muffins, fruit juice, and two melon halves with strawberries piled on top. I'm instantly awake. It's amazing the effect he has. I'm no longer an angry raddled whore, too fagged to move a muscle, but a precious guest who's hungry, even happy.

'I can't eat bacon in the bath,' I smile.

'Sure you can. I'll feed you. Want your melon first?'

'Yes, please.'

Soon, we're both giggling as I lose strawberries in the water and get juice all down my chin. Then he spills coffee on my breasts which shouldn't be showing, but somehow pop up from the water while he feeds me with hot muffin. I can see him trying not to look at them. He's eaten nothing himself, hasn't had a chance yet.

'Why don't you get in as well? Then I can feed you.'

'In where?'

'In the bath.' Why in God's name did I say that? Am I mad or something?'

'You mean, with . . . you?'

'Yeah, why not? There's room for two.' There isn't, 'course there isn't.

'I . . . I've had a bath.'

'Have another.' My voice sounds harsh and strained. 'You're not short of water, are you? Actually, I ought to let some out. Otherwise we'll flood the place again. I've filled it far too full.'

I spend longer than I need fiddling with the plug. He's taking off his clothes. I can't look, daren't. The room's so tense now, I can feel my breakfast burning in my gut. He's undressing very slowly. I can hear a shirt or something slither to the floor, a tiny creaking sigh as he unbuckles his belt. I keep staring down, staring down. Whole hours seem to pass. Then a large cold foot jabs against my stomach; a nervous voice says 'Sorry.'

'That's okay,' I mumble. 'Course it's bloody not. Those scars are almost touching me, that repulsive puckered skin pressed right against my own. I can suddenly see Reuben in the bath – his smooth unblemished stomach, his long but slender prick. I fight a whole tidal wave of feelings: regret, resentment, anger, fear, desire; force my voice to make some trite remark, concentrate on Victor. Reuben's gone. He went out through that door, with all the rest.

'Quite a squash,' I mumble. Victor's bent his thighs up, one each side of my legs.

'Yes.'

'That's the first time you've said "yes", Victor.'

'What d'you mean? I'm always saying yes.'

'No, you're not. You normally say "yeah".'

'Ah, but I'm learning English now, you see – while I take my *barth*.' He lengthens and exaggerates the a.

'Well, you can't have sourdough muffins if you're English. We don't have them back home.' My voice is doing well. I sound quite normal now, chatty and relaxed. 'Here, open wide.' I feed him with a soggy piece of one.

He chews and talks at once. 'That's weird. We even call 'em English muffins here. And what about your muffin man?'

'He's just a song, a dead one.' It's all right – I can't see the scars, not even when I look up. That green good-mannered water blanks out everything, especially now he's straightened out his legs. He's like any normal guy: nice face, smooth chest, strong and muscly arms. I'm so relieved, I burst out laughing.

'What's the joke?'

'Nothing. Just that silly muffin man. Let's sing it.'

'I don't know the words.'

'They're easy. I'll teach you. "Oh, have you seen the muffin man, the muffin man, the muffin man?" Right, that bit first.'

We sing together, though I keep breaking down in giggles. I don't know why. We go on and on, me laughing, Victor singing. I feel really quite peculiar – elated, almost drunk, pissed on juice and coffee.

He taps my foot. 'What's the next line, honey? We've sung those first two more than twenty times.'

'I can't remember.'

'You mean, that's all you know?'

'Yeah.'

'*Yes*.'

'Yes. Oh, Victor, stop me laughing. It hurts. By the way, what's an axolotl?'

'It's a kind of aquatic salamander.'

'Gosh! Have you got one?'

'No. But I can offer you something even more exotic.' He reaches behind him, floats a yellow plastic duck on the little pond of water between our two hidden stomach reefs. 'That was a gift from one of my poker-playing buddies.'

'Would it like some muffin?'

'*I* would.'

I lean over for the plate. 'They've gone all sort of hard now.'

'Doesn't matter.'

I feed him. I even let my hand brush along his thigh. Not so bad. The skin feels dry and rough, rather like a loofah.

'How about a strawberry muffin, Victor?'

473

'What's that?'

'A sourdough one with strawberries on. Damn! That's another strawberry gone. We'll turn bright pink if I drop any more in.'

'You're pink already, darling. This water's far too hot. We'd better get out now. I think we've had enough.'

'Okay, you first. I'll dry you.'

'No!'

I can feel the tension surging back again; hear it in that strangled 'No', see it in my stupid shaking hands. Why in God's name did I spoil things when we'd just relaxed?

'Yeah, I want to, Victor. I'd like that, really.' Of course I wouldn't. It's all a fucking lie. I'm terrified. I'll puke. I'll shrink away. He'll only be more hurt, feel totally rejected. I can see it now, the scarring, as he stands up, clambers out. God! It's horrible, revolting. I'll never touch it, never, not even through a towel.

'Is this your towel?' I ask.

He nods. They're all his towels, for God's sake, but I've got to keep on talking. 'We . . . er . . . never ate the bacon.'

'No.'

'We could have it cold in sandwiches, for lunch.'

'Yeah.'

'*Yes.*'

'You said "yeah".'

'Did I? When?'

'Just now.'

'Victor . . . ?'

'What?'

'I'm not drying you too hard, am I? I mean, it doesn't . . . hurt?'

'No. It's kind of dead, that skin. Like the muffin man.'

'It looks rather like a muffin.' I force myself to see not skin, not scars or horrors, but a cold dead hardening piece of muffin.

He laughs. 'One of the nurses in the hospital said it reminded her of a moonscape. With little craters.'

That's better still. A moonscape. Something very far away. Something almost abstract, dead grey lunar rocks. Death Valley

474

was like that – a warped and twisted landscape, dry and barren, but somehow still impressive. I trace the craters, let my fingers touch the fissured rock-face. Nothing dreadful happens. I don't throw up, or faint away. The earth keeps turning on its axis.

I pick up a second towel, dry his lower back. That doesn't look too bad. Or am I simply getting used to it? I let my hands feather down his spine from neck to coccyx, then stroke slowly up again.

'That's lovely, darling. You're spoiling me.'

'I like to.' It's funny, but I do. I'm good now, truly good. Kind and loving, like he said. I feel triumphant inside and glowing.

'You're shivering, Carole.'

'No, I'm not. I'm boiling.'

'Let me dry you now.'

'Okay.'

He takes the towel from me, swathes me in it, top to toe, then holds me close against him. I can feel my heart pounding into his, feel he's got a hard-on.

'Carole, I just can't tell you what . . .'

'Ssh,' I whisper, pull away a moment, release the towel, let it fall around my feet, then press close to him again. They're right against me now, the scars, the ridges, that thickened lumpy prick. I don't care. The feeling's quite fantastic. I'm brave. I'm a hero. I can love.

'Carole, you're still cold. Here, put this round you.' He wraps us both in his giant-sized dressing gown, sits me on the stool with him. I'm angered by that gown. He chose it so he could hide away, so nobody would ever see an inch of him. I slip my hands beneath it, rest them on his thighs.

'My Dad used to dry me after my bath. Years and years ago. And tell me stories. "Once upon a time . . ." No, he never said that, actually. I don't know why. Shall I tell *you* a story?'

Victor nods.

'It's a story about Victors. They're very special creatures, Victors are. They've got this very thin and delicate white skin. It's so sensitive, the slightest thing can hurt it, so they have to wear another skin on top. The second skin is tougher, to protect them, but when you peel it off, they're all white and soft and shining underneath, like . . . like . . . unicorns.' My voice is wobbling. Stupid voice. I force it to go on.

'Not everybody understands. Ordinary women can't – girls like Laura. Only fair princesses. Sometimes it's a long wait till the princess comes along – years and years and years. Then everything's all right. The princess and the Victor go to bed together and they wake up in the morning and . . . and . . .'

I'm crying. I don't know why. It's soppy, really wimpish, and embarrassing for Victor. But I'm so sorry for that skin, that poor, burnt, dead and shrivelled skin.

'Carole, what's the matter? What is it, darling?'

'Nothing. I'm just so . . . tired and . . .' I jump up, gulp some water from the tap. I feel quite ill again, sick and dizzy – side-effects from Victor, not the Pill. I keep my back to him, so he can't see my burning face. My voice is shaky still.

'Oh, Victor, I think I . . . sort of – love you and I'm terrified.'

28

The world is going to end. Very soon. Perhaps today. There's going to be a Bomb, the biggest ever. Lots of people have gone to hide in shelters. They're underground. Carole's gone as well. She was meant to come to see me. Saturday, she said, early in the morning. It's Sunday afternoon now and still she hasn't come. Angelique arrived alone, early yesterday. She said Carole would come later, take me out to lunch.

I had lunch all on my own. Angelique took George away. She told me he was going back to England and she had to drive him to the airport, put him on the plane. I think that was a lie. They were going to the shelter, but they didn't want to tell me. There's not much room in shelters, so they leave some people out — older folks, people without families or jobs.

I saw a programme yesterday about a farmer and his wife who gave away their farm and all the land. It was on the television. Both of them were crying. They gave it to the Church because the world was going to end in twenty years. The Godman told them so. The twenty years is up now, so they're waiting for the Bomb.

The Bomb's upset the weather. There's snow in Rome and storms in California. I'm not sure where Rome is, but it's somewhere where you don't have snow. Only when the world is going to end. Everyone will die except the ones in shelters.

You have to take your own food to the shelters. And special clothes. Carole sent me mine. She didn't know there wasn't room for me. She sent me lots of things. Food and chocolates, underwear and frocks, a real new winter coat, even some champagne. Angelique brought them in her car. I won't need them now if I haven't got a shelter, but they make me feel she's closer, help to fill the room up.

The room seems bigger when there's only me. George didn't say goodbye. I said it several times, slowly and quite loudly, but I don't think he remembered who I was. We were just becoming friends. We'd been talking in confetti. We used the second box. He'd spell out a bell or flower or slipper, and I'd reply with a horseshoe or a heart. It was very slow, the talking, and sometimes George would fall asleep before I'd even answered. But I preferred it with him here. He smiled at me three times. He hardly ever smiles.

The phone keeps ringing, ringing. It makes me feel even more alone. I'm not allowed to pick it up. The maid does that. Except she's gone as well. She said she'd see me later. She wouldn't be that long, she said, but today was her day off and she wanted to go out. I don't think that was true. I expect Angelique took her to the shelter, so she could clean for them, and cook.

She doesn't cook for me. She left me a roll and some brown stuff on a tray, but I was too upset to eat it. That was Saturday. The roll is very stale now, and the brown stuff has gone grey.

I start turning out my handbag. I haven't any sweets. I've looked before, several times, for George. But sometimes there are miracles. We had one at St Joseph's, forty years ago. A dead nun came to life again. I never saw her dead, but Reverend Mother did. We had to spend all next day in chapel to thank God for His goodness. I didn't like the nun.

There isn't a miracle, but I find a piece of newspaper folded very small. I unfold it, start to read. It's stained with something red. I know it's blood when I see 'FREE FUNERAL'.

I read some more. The words are difficult. You have to drink and drive. I haven't got a car. Angelique's gone off in hers and maids aren't allowed them.

The phone is ringing again. Perhaps I ought to answer it. I get up from my chair, start to walk into the hall.

I stop. It might be Sister. She'll be very angry with me. She was expecting us thirteen days ago. Thirteen is unlucky. Victor told me so. I liked Victor, but he disappeared as well. I walk back to my chair. Sister may be rubble. It's earlier here than England, so the world could have ended there already.

I clutch the sideboard, stand completely still. I can hear a dreadful roar. It's the Bomb. They've dropped it. I crouch down on the floor. The roar gets louder, louder. Then stops — just like that.

I hear a door slam, heavy footsteps tramping down the passage. Someone's walking in. It may be a Godman, or the man who drops the Bombs.

'Jeez! You scared me. What you doin' on the floor? Are you sick or somethin'?'

It's the maid's boyfriend, the dark short curly angry one, who rides a motorbike. He isn't hurt, or burnt, so that must have been a siren or a Warning. Which means I've still got time.

'I need a car,' I tell him, struggling up.

'Join the club.'

'Have you got one?'

He doesn't answer. He's glancing round the room, looking at my presents, fingering the champagne.

'If you get me one, I'll pay you.' Carole left me money as well as all those things. Lots of money. She didn't leave a note. I'd rather have had a note.

'You gotta licence?'

'No.'

'Then how you gonna drive?'

'I'll give you all my money. It's a lot.'

'How much?'

I've forgotten how to count, so I show him all the banknotes. He tries to take them from me, but I hold on very tight. Angelique warned me to be careful with the money. She said it was a lot.

'That's peanuts. You couldn't buy a car with that.'

'Could I hire one?' Carole was going to hire a car. To come here yesterday. Angelique told me that. I expect she hired one to take her to the shelter. It's a different shelter from Angelique's and George's. Shelters are quite small, so you have to all split up.

'Where d'you wanna go?'

'Death Valley.'

'Are you mad or somethin'? It's miles.'

I don't reply. It has to be Death Valley.

He's pacing round the room. He's wearing black, all black. The black looks wet and shiny. He takes a cigarette from Angelique's gold box. She doesn't know he takes them.

'Gotta light?' he asks.

'You can phone for cars,' I tell him. 'My friend did yesterday.' She *is* my friend. She must be. She sent me all those clothes. 'But I don't know where to phone. You can have the chocolates if you do it for me. And the clothes.' I hate to give him things which Carole bought me, but I think she'll understand. And once I'm in Death Valley, I won't need anything. I pick up the coat, press it into his arms. 'This is new, brand new. Not an old one from a jumble sale. It cost a lot of money. You can have it if you phone.'

'Can't help,' he says. 'I'm sorry.' He throws the coat back, still looking at my purse. 'I'm late already. Gotta meet Maria. She needs her other bag.' He dashes up the stairs. I can hear his feet crashing overhead.

'Don't go,' I say, to no one.

He's gone; down the stairs again, out through the front door.

He's late. We've had the Warning. If they drop the Bomb before he's in the shelter, he'll be blown to pieces in the street. There's a big white flash and all your skin peels off. Thousands die, and all the bits of body stick together. Even bones melt and squash like candles. I saw a film about it on TV. There were maggots eating people before they were quite dead, crawling on their flesh. They made the maggots very big, bigger than the Bomb. Then they made them small again, but showed a lot more corpses. Some corpses disappeared, they said; blown away in a cloud of dust and smoke. No one ever found them. Not a finger.

There are lots of Bombs near here. All waiting to go off. They keep them here because there aren't that many people and the land is dead already. They're staring at me now. Bombs are like God. You can't see them, but they see everyone. One of them will go off very soon. The biggest one, the one with the largest eyes. I'll die here. Alone.

I sit and wait.

I've been waiting a long time. I haven't got a watch, but I think several hours have passed. Nobody has come. They won't come now. They're all in shelters, waiting for the Bomb. Everybody but me.

It's dark now, really dark. You're not allowed the lights on. It's blackout in the war. In the other war, we had cocoa with Miss O'Something in the shelter. I'd like some cocoa now. I'm hungry, very cold.

My dress is far too thin. It's one of Maria's old ones which hasn't any sleeves. I'd like to change, wear the thick blue warm one which Carole bought. I've never had new clothes before. And I've never had so many – not at once. I won't be able to wear them all. There won't be time before the Bomb. We've only got today. Perhaps tomorrow. Carole chose them specially, picked out all the colours. She'll be sad if I don't wear them. She's my friend.

It's rude to take your clothes off in a sitting room, but nobody can see me in the dark.

'Dark,' I say. Sometimes I say words out loud to make sure I can still speak. I'm frightened of catching George's illness. Even after people go, they leave their germs behind. You can't see germs, Sister said. I saw them once, millions of them, marching up the inside of my cup. But nobody else did.

'Nobody,' I say. The word sounds empty, very cold. A draught is blowing on my naked skin.

I put all three pairs of knickers on, one above the other. There are three brassieres as well, pink to match the knickers. I hook each one up in turn, then struggle with the petticoats. It's not that easy dressing in the dark.

The stockings are the thick ones which don't show any leg through. I like those best. They're difficult to fasten. Only the first two pairs will fit in the suspenders, so I roll the others down. A lot of Beechgrove patients never wear suspenders.

Their stockings sag if they get up from their chairs. Mine are sagging now, the last two pairs.

I move towards the window where some light is seeping through. It may be a searchlight. You have searchlights in the war. It may be just the moon. I can't tell through the curtains.

The white blouse gleams a bit, so I put that one on first. Then the other two. I do up all the buttons. It takes me a long time. The dresses go on top – the blue one, and two green ones, and a thinner one with flowers. The last one is a struggle, splits along the seams. The pyjamas are men's large size, but it's still quite hard to fit them over frocks. The jacket on the second pair is pulling, hurts me on the shoulders. I leave it open, go and fetch the coat. Carole chose a loose one. She thought of everything. I feel better with her clothes on, though I wish they smelt of her. They smell of nothing, only new.

I'm not cold now. Just hungry. I'd like to eat a chocolate. If you're given such a big box, you have to pass them round, share them with the nurses. Sister says it's greedy to keep them for yourself.

There's a ribbon on the box. I take it off, put it in my bag. Ribbons are expensive. I lift the lid. Everybody's staring. It's usually Maltesers or tiny tubes of wine gums; cheaper things and smaller.

'Help yourself,' I tell them. All the hands reach out. Lil can't manage hers. It's a toffee and too hard. I go right up to the window, so I can see the chocolate names, pick her out a cream. I hold it while she dribbles. George is dribbling too. George loves sweets, all kinds. I feed him with two nut ones; read him out the names. He likes the names. He's smiling. Peanut Kisses. Butterchew. Tipperary Bonbon. That's somewhere in a song.

I clap my hands, beg them to be quiet. They're all whimpering for more, Ethel Barnes snatching without asking, Meg O'Riley shouting.

'Ssh,' I say. 'There's still another layer.'

Martha Mead can't hear. I put a nougat in her hand, take a fudge myself. Sister's got her mouth full. When she speaks, little flecks of chocolate land on people's clothes. Another nurse is standing by the door. The new nurse with the smile. There's someone just behind her. A pretty girl with fair streaked hair. She wears red shoes. She's smoking. Her eyes are blue with little darker flecks in them.

'This is Carole, Norah.'

'Hallo,' I say, and offer her a chocolate.

She takes two, then another two. She's standing very close. I can smell her hair. It smells of strawberries. She's going to be my friend.

'Would you like to see the library?' I suggest. Miss Barratt's in the library. Miss Barratt's very clever. And there are books with pictures, books with mountains in.

'Yeah,' she says and smiles. I like her smile. She only smiles for me. I take her hand, lead her to the door. A porter blocks our way, a short dark angry one with curly hair. He's switched on all the lights. My eyes hurt in the glare.

'You goin' out?' he asks.

'No,' I say. 'We're going to the library. Carole's new.'

'What you on about? And why you wearin' all that gear? You look dressed up for a snowstorm. I hope you're not plannin' on some disappearin' trick. I've got your car.'

'What car?'

'Shit! I just done you a favour, lady. Borrowed my mate's pick-up truck. I left Maria with him and came all this way back to drive you to Death Valley.'

Death Valley. That was in the library books. The mountains. 'Yes,' I say. 'I'm going there.'

'What d'you mean, you're goin' there? You got another car booked?'

'No,' I say. I wish he wouldn't shout.

'Good. You booked me first, see? Okay, I guess I'm late, but Murray had to use his truck to shift a load o' stuff. It took longer than he figured.'

'That's all right,' I say. I don't remember Murray. I keep forgetting things. I need more pills from Sister. Mine are all used up. Angelique got me some, but they're not the same at all. I think she must have stolen them, because the bottle's got someone else's name on. Morton, G. I don't know who he is, but he must be very ill. The pills are strong and gave me awful headaches. Things like walls kept moving; coming closer, then swinging right away. I don't take them any more, except when I forget. It's easy to forget. I've been taking pills for nearly forty years.

The man is speaking to me. He's chewing gum as well. He takes the gum out, peers at it, puts it back again.

'We gotta fix a price first. It's double Sundays, always is. And it's a long way, Death Valley – understand?'

I nod. He's picking at his teeth with one black nail. I think the gum has stuck to them.

'How long you gonna be there? I can't hang around, not if you don't pay. Waiting-time is extra.'

'You won't have to wait,' I tell him. 'Not at all. You can go straight back on your own.'

'What, you stayin' there or somethin'?'

I don't reply. I wish I could remember. I had it all worked out before.

The man edges a bit closer. 'Right. Where's the cash?' he asks.

It's in my bag. I made sure I put it back there straight away. Sister says you can't trust other patients. I go and fetch it, pass him all the notes.

'That's not enough,' he says.

'It's all I've got. I'm sorry.' I feel around the bottom and the sides. Sometimes things appear which you know you didn't have. I find a piece of newspaper with blood on. I also find a pill bottle. It isn't Morton G.'s. 'MARY'S RING', it says. Perhaps Angelique stole it and hid it in my bag before she left. I put it back again.

The man picks up the champagne. 'What about the bubbly?'

'No,' I say. 'I need that.' It's slowly coming back now. You have to drink and drive. That bit of paper says so.

'Oh, you need it, do you? Well, maybe we can split it. Let's take it anyways. You ready?'

I try to think. There are other things I need. The Dress. That's in Angelique's room, hanging in her wardrobe. There wasn't room in mine. I tell the man I'll be a few more minutes.

It's hard to climb the stairs with so many layers of clothes on. I can feel my stockings creeping down my legs, flapping round my ankles. They're trying to trip me up. I'm sweating when I reach the top. I think I probably smell bad. Not just of sweat, but other things. Nasty things. That's why they didn't want me in a shelter.

Angelique's wardrobe is like a room itself. I've never seen so many frocks, so many pairs of shoes. Coloured shoes – all colours – blue and green and red. *Red shoes*. I pick them up and smell them. They'd be too small, but if I squeezed my toes up tightly at the ends . . .

I carry them downstairs, float the Dress behind me. The man is staring.

'What the hell? You goin' to a ball or somethin'?'

'No,' I say. 'A wedding.'

He laughs. The noise sounds rude. 'So who's the lucky guy?'

I don't reply, just try to fold the Dress. It doesn't want to fold, keeps springing back at me. He disappears a moment, returns with a carrier bag, a black one with a Message on. I push the Dress in, drop one red shoe in each of the deep pockets of my coat. I can feel them hard and comforting.

I begin to feel excited. I can hear the Dress whispering in its bag. I collect up the confetti, put it in my handbag. Only half a box left. George dropped a lot and ate some.

There's nothing else I need. I follow the man out through the front door. There's no blackout on the moon. It's shining very bright. It's been dark so long, I thought it would be morning. I keep muddling things – the date, the time of day. It must be Sunday still. The day after Saturday when Carole said she'd come. She tried to come, I know she did. But the Bomb-men wouldn't let her.

The car is very big. It's not a car. It's a kind of lorry with an open back. The back is full of rubbish. I get in the front. The man gets in beside me. I wish I knew his name.

He lights a cigarette. I don't like smoke, but I'm going to Death Valley where no one smokes and the air is pure and clean.

I hold my bag, my Dress. I'm very lucky.

I'm going to wear red shoes.

29

I think it was a hundred years we slept – give or take a couple. I remember waking once or twice, and there was always that comforting warm shape beside me. Sometimes it was awake as well and whispered things and put its arms around me. Other times, it was very still and quiet. When at last we surfaced, it was Sunday afternoon, winter sun streaming through the window. Sunday. Day of rest. Blessed day with Victor.

We still haven't made love. We shan't yet. That may sound crazy when we've got so close, shared a bed, and when Victor's still paying for his right to screw me – all day, all night, if that's his wish. He calls the tune as client.

No. I hate that word, can't bear the thought of Victor being number hundred and one. It's as if I'm still in quarantine and daren't risk infecting him. I need time to heal, recover. I want to be a virgin for him, virgin to his unicorn. He's tainted, too, from Suzie, and also scared, I think – nervous that he'll never measure up. That's crazy. The very fact he understood, didn't rush me, override me, made me want him more. But something still said 'wait'. It must be very special when it happens.

We're sitting in the garden now, in recliner canvas chairs. It's like a holiday. Blue sky and suntan lotion. Imagine sunbathing in mid-January! I wish I'd brought a sundress or bikini. I'm dressed in an old blue vest of Victor's (which *he* calls an undershirt), and a sort of mini-skirt, improvised from one of his checked shirts, tied around my middle by its sleeves. It's a relief to wear old and comfy clothes. Okay, I like nice gear, but it was becoming quite a chore to have to look sexy as a duty; hoist my breasts in black lace push-up bras, totter round in three-inch heels, always wear suspenders. My legs are bare today, my hair's a mess. Yet Victor's told me, twice, that I look stunning. He's dressed very formally in grey trousers and a clean white shirt. I suspect he's so careful about his clothes to compensate for the problems underneath. He daren't look anything but conventional and neat, in case he draws attention to himself. And it was only today when I was sorting through his clothes to try to find a pair of shorts to borrow, that I realized that he can't have worn either shorts or swim trunks for nearly twenty years. He's still hiding from the world. It makes me furious that he should have to give up all those simple pleasures like sunbathing or swimming, in case stupid ignorant people shrink away. People like myself.

I start undoing his shoes, peeling off his socks.

'What you doing?'

'I want your feet to sunbathe.'

'Don't. It tickles.'

'You've got smashing feet.' He has. They're straight and very solid-looking, as if he's firmly planted on the world and won't ever trip or stumble.

'Aren't feet all the same?'

'Don't be silly. 'Course they're not.' I glance down at my own – small and rather chubby, the two big toes curving slightly inwards. 'Gosh! I'm thirsty in this sun.' I fill my glass with Victor's strawberry cooler, more lethal than it sounds. We've had a sort of picnic tea (which was also lunch and breakfast) spread out on the grass, and now I'm feeling flushed and fizzy, too content to move.

I reach out for a cigarette, remember that I've hidden them, pick a blade of grass instead. I've given up. Yes, really. It's my gift to Victor. He used to smoke himself, but they made him stop when he was having all those skin grafts and he'd caught a chest infection. He said the anaesthetist came and warned him, read the riot act, called him a bad risk. That was years ago, but I still don't want to harm him, when he's been through so much hell. Every time I smoke, he inhales quite a high percentage of all that ghastly nicotine. I read it in the Las Vegas *Sun*. I'd hate him to die of Rothman's, like my father did.

I 'smoke' my blade of grass, chew the top of it. Distractions help. It's really hard to quit. It makes me feel jittery and my hands are restless all the time, as if they've lost their role, but I also feel quite proud. I've never done something quite as big as that, not for someone else. I know it's only Day One and the worst is yet to come. I may even get the shakes or blinding headaches, but I'm still determined not to weaken. No one's ever given Victor anything, except a few fucking medals in return for half his skin. Norah will be pleased as well. She hates the smell of smoke and grotty ashtrays. I just wish I could tell her, find out how she is. I've been ringing her all afternoon, and several times yesterday before we went to sleep at twelve. (Twelve noon, not midnight. Falling in love is horribly exhausting.) But there's never any answer.

I force myself to get up, take my tumbler with me as I float across the grass. 'I'd better try Norah again. They may be back by now.'

They're *not* back. The unanswered phone quavers on and on.

'No luck?' asks Victor, as I flop back in my chair.

'No. I'm not worried, though. She'll be out with Angelique still.' I've been unfair to Angelique. She may be a bit hard on George, but you can rely on her to help you in a crisis. Well, it's not strictly a crisis, but she must assume it is. (Trouble with a clinging client, or Carl overbooking, then expecting me to bail him out.) Anyway, I couldn't lie here basking in the sun and Victor's love, without Nanny Angelique to keep an eye on Norah. I'll do the same for her one day, take George off her hands, maybe, next time he comes over. He's off them at the moment, flew home yesterday. They must have taken Norah to the airport with them. She'd love to watch the planes, and I expect they all had lunch out first. We'll hear all about it when we see her later on. We're driving over this evening – me and Victor. I like that: me-and-Victor – joined and one.

I gaze out at the mountains in the distance. They look so beautiful: white clouds snagging on white peaks. Even the bare brown slopes beneath the snow-line are shining in the sun. I soak up sun and silence, feel the peace seeping through my skin. Victor's peace.

'Oh, Victor.'

'What?'

'Nothing.' I reach down, help myself to grass, keep my fingers busy splitting each fine blade. I'd like to say 'I love you', but I daren't. I'm wary of the word. I used it with Reuben, even meant it. Yet I didn't know him; still don't quite know Victor, not the whole of him. And he knows less of me. I take a deep breath in.

'Listen, Vic, there's something I . . .'

He gets up from his chair, leans down over mine. 'It's at least fifteen minutes since I kissed you.'

'No, don't – not now. You've got to listen, Victor, otherwise you may be in love with the wrong me. I mean, could you love a liar and a thief? Please don't laugh. It's true. I was caught stealing from a supermarket just this last September. Oh, I didn't nick much, only a swiss roll and . . .'

'Swiss roll?'

'Don't you have those in the States – sort of sponge cake things rolled up with jam? No, you don't have jam, either, do you? Hell! It's like a foreign language. Thank God you're learning English. At least we'll soon be able to communicate.'

'Jelly rolls?'

'You have them?'

'Yeah. Only the word means something else as well.'

'What?'

'It's difficult to . . .' He breaks off, starts to demonstrate, making thrusting circling movements with his hips.

'Wow! Victor, you look like Elvis Presley crossed with Michael Jackson.'

He laughs, collapses on the grass. 'I guess that's where Jelly Roll Morton got his name.'

'Who's he?' I lie down next to him, curl into his chest.

'Forget him. Let's get back to your swiss roll.'

Victor's right. I can't chicken out now I've started. He's got to know the real me – and the real me's got to smoke. I can't blurt out all that heavy stuff without a fag to help me. I get up to go inside. That huge carton's in the sitting room, hidden in the bookcase behind a row of fish books. A hundred and eighty left. I counted yesterday. I'll have just one – less than one – just a few quick puffs to give me courage.

'Where you going, darling?'

'Only for a pee.'

I get almost to the door, turn back. Fool, I tell myself. Weakling. Selfish bitch. I should have thrown the bloody things away, except it seemed a shocking waste and I knew Angelique would love all those free fags. 'It's okay, I can wait,' I say, as I plump down on the ground. I sit on both my hands, clear my throat, and suddenly I'm telling him everything – my childhood and my father and Jan's bedsit in Vauxhall and the police and Dr Bates, and even Reuben and the wedding. Reuben is the hardest. I can feel Victor tense, hear the minefield in his voice.

'Did you . . . love him, Carole?'

I pause. If I say 'no', then I'm lying once again, denying what I truly felt: the excitement, the elation, the best sex I ever had.

'Yes,' I say. 'I did.'

'So you must be very hurt?'

'I was. Yes.'

Victor leans up on one elbow. His whole face is different now. 'Christ! You don't think . . .? I mean, what you feel for me isn't just a reaction, Carole? Love on the rebound?'

'It could be. Yes.'

'You're very honest.'

I tie his shirt more firmly round my middle, start fiddling with the buttons on the sleeves. It's easier not to look at him. 'I must be, Victor. Because the girl who almost married Reuben wasn't honest. She was a rotten little liar who deceived herself as well. This Carole is a new one, one who's going to tell the truth – or bloody try. And she's a virgin, like you want.'

'Carole, I don't want. I want *you* – all of you. The crazy kid who steals swiss rolls, and the poor screwed-up Carole in the hospital, and the complicated Carole who's called Jan and disappears.'

I'm chewing on a button, mumbling through it. 'And the Carole who landed in a brothel?'

He's silent for a moment. 'Yes. And her. Her especially, because otherwise I might never have met up with her again.' He leans over, kisses me. I can't respond. I'm too stunned by what he's said. It's only now I realize that if it hadn't been for Reuben, I'd have lost Victor for ever, been safely back in England, not working as a whore.

Victor strokes my foot. '*I* stole something once.'

'What?' I pull my foot away. The stroking tickles, and my mind is still on Reuben. The dregs of love and anger are leavened now by a crazy sort of gratitude.

'A diamond ring from the five-and-dime.'

'You're joking.'

'No. I'm not. Well, maybe not exactly diamonds. I was eight or nine at the time. I wanted to get married to this gorgeous girl in third grade and I couldn't afford the ring.'

'So you were always a romantic?'

'Always.'

I rip up a daisy, pull its petals off. Can one be jealous of a gorgeous girl in third grade? I glance at Victor's eyes. When I'm not with him, I forget how blue they are. Even when I woke him up this morning (afternoon), I was jolted by the fierceness of that blue again. He looks different now I know him. I keep noticing things I overlooked before – the fair hairs on his thumbs, the little indentation above his upper lip, which people always say is a sign of passion, the decisive ways he moves, his calm good-tempered voice. I turn over on my tummy. 'I was horrible at nine. Know what I used to do?'

He shakes his head.

'Well, you know fish and chip shops?'

'No.'

'Oh, you do, Victor. Don't be dumb. They've got these huge great jars of salt, up on the counter with the vinegar and stuff, and people help themselves. Well, I had this friend, Jackie, a real tomboy – tall with freckles. We used to go into the shop and unscrew the salt, so the top was just balanced on the jar. Then, when the next customer picked it

491

up, a whole pound or so of salt cascaded on his cod and chips.'

Victor laughs, refills his glass, as if the salt has made him thirsty.

'Another thing we did when we were older was to phone people up – just strangers – and tell them they'd won thousands on the pools.'

'Pools?'

'You know, like your lottery.' It almost scares me, the way we speak two different languages. Even with the same one, there are still misunderstandings and half-truths; thinking words mean what they don't, or can't – not words like 'pools' or 'vest', but dangerous ones like 'love'.

'So you were a cute little liar even then?'

'Mm. Does it put you off me?'

'No. I love you more.'

Victor's brave. He's used the word 'love' at least ten times already, whereas I still shy away from it. '*Yeah*,' I say, correcting him.

'I thought we were speaking English.'

'No. I prefer American, especially jelly rolls. Do it again – the Michael Jackson bit. It really turned me on.'

He does it, twice, then picks me up, feet right off the ground, whirls me round and round. He's strong. It's a funny combination – strong and doting. He spoils me so, I half believe he even chose the day for me today, drove miles and miles to pick me out a really bright and sunny one, paid a fortune to make sure the sky stayed blue. Only now is it beginning to fade, tarnish into twilight.

'Shall we go in? I'll make some tea.'

'It's dinner time.'

'No, it's not. We started late. That tea was really lunch, so now it's tea again.'

'Okay.'

I take more trouble with that tea than I've ever done before – not just teabags dunked in mugs, but a proper heated teapot (well, the nearest I can find to it, which is actually a flower vase with a saucer as a lid), and pretty cups, and milk in a jug and not the carton, and a white cloth on the tray. And I won't let us pig it in the kitchen. This is posh tea in the sitting room with side plates for our biscuits and paper serviettes. Jan wouldn't recognize me. Even the fish look pretty damn impressed. I get pleasure from Victor's pleasure, though, as I pour him out a second cup. He leans across to take it, lets his hand brush across my breasts.

'It shouldn't be allowed, you know, leaving off your bra like that. I don't know how I've kept my hands to myself.'

I push my vest up, take his hand, place it where I want it. 'You don't have to keep them to yourself.' I can sense him still uncertain, holding back. 'What's wrong?'

'I . . . I still feel it's just not fair, Carole. I mean, I've put you in a like . . . difficult position. You can't *not* respond, because you're scared to hurt me, and yet you may feel . . .'

'I feel good. All over. Especially my right breast. Now touch the other one.'

'Like that?'

'Mmm.' I am in a difficult position. I love him touching me, but I don't want to go too far. Oh, he says he understands, but I can't help worrying that he thinks I'm still revolted by his scars. It's so hard to balance everything – my fears, his lack of confidence, my feeling that we still need much more time, contradicted by my desire to reassure him. I lean across, run my hands across his chest, and lower. He's got a hard-on. I start inching down his zip.

'No, Carole.'

I keep my hands exactly where they are. 'Victor, I want you to believe me. I'm not put off at all, not now. It was just the first shock, and really more you shouting than anything I saw.' I'm lying. Yes, I know I said I wouldn't lie, but this is a good lie, a precious lie, the best one I've ever told. That scarred skin still upsets me, that lumpy roughened prick is still a shock, but they're part of Victor, part of his courage and unselfishness. And my lies are part of loving him.

He's got his eyes shut, as if he can't bear to see himself. I stroke him stiff again. 'There was this machine I saw, Victor. It was in some loo – I can't remember where now, and it sold these contraceptives with special raised spirals which gave the woman extra thrills and stuff. They cost a bomb – five dollars each or something. You've got them naturally.'

He kisses me: a brief kiss, but the fiercest yet.

I touch my mouth – it's hurting – slide my body down a bit so my breasts can keep him hard. 'Well, it's my special hero prick, you see, and I'm very proud of it.'

He's going limp again. God knows what I've said now. I have to be so careful.

'Don't use that word. Please don't.'

'What, "prick"?'

'No, "hero".' He fumbles for his cup, drains his tea.

I push myself against him. I'm feeling quite excited. That kiss! All the sex he hasn't had, all the excitement and frustration dammed up for years and years, seemed to flood and crackle into it. Christ! If it's like that when we actually make love . . . Are we mad to wait? Wasting precious time? I remove his cup, try to get his hands all to myself.

'No, Carole darling, listen.' He leans back in his chair, as if he needs to put a bit of space between us. 'Remember what you said just now about loving the wrong you? I've been scared of that myself.'

I tense. 'You mean, you do love the other me, the Jan?'

'No, no. I'm talking about me this time – all this hero stuff. You used the word earlier when we were lying in the garden.'

'I didn't.'

'Yeah, you did. It's a seductive word, I guess. Except all of us are cowards in the end. Heroism always cracks at some point, Carole. I've seen it happen loads of times, even with the so-called bravest men.' He takes a biscuit, a chocolate-coated cream, uses it to gesture with. 'There's another kind of heroism, the small and hidden kind that wins no medals – just the day-to-day business of getting on with life without bitterness or bitching; or putting up with poverty or sickness; or battling through the daily grind with a few kind words to spare for fellow sufferers. I guess that sounds really sentimental. It's hard to find the words for what I mean. But I've met more heroes digging dirt and shovelling sand, or lugging round the lunch trays in the hospital, or even commuting on the New

York subway, than I ever did in 'Nam.' He puts the biscuit down again, sucks a smear of chocolate off his thumb.

'I don't want to drag up Vietnam again, but you've got to understand – I was shit-scared out there, Carole – really *not* a hero. There were dangers all around us: not just the shelling, but mortars, snipers, booby-traps, maybe ground-up glass in a cup of coffee, or a tiny smiling kid with a gun behind his back. You relaxed for a minute, you were dead. You couldn't even look forward to the next hour or day or week, let alone to going home. That was tempting fate, when each day might be your last, and when so many of your friends had died already.'

Victor traps his hands between his knees. I copy him. I'm itching for a fag still, and all this talk of danger makes it worse.

'Okay, we were all scared. If you haven't been in combat, it's hard to understand – the constant stress, the shakes, the cold-sweat nightmares when you're wrestling in your sleep with bloody stinking corpses. It was far worse for the grunts, of course. They were in the thick of it. I had this friend in the marines who was out there several years. His nerves were shot to pieces. Even two years after coming home, he'd dive down to the ground if he heard a car backfire. I know just how he felt. I was in this restaurant when they were preparing steak diane – you know, the one they flame on a little charcoal burner at your table. They lit the match – I shot out of my seat. It was '69 again. White phosphorus . . .'

'Victor, that's not cowardice.'

'What is it then?'

Imagination. Sensitivity. Honesty. All the things I love him for. I kiss him for reply. His own kiss is half-hearted now.

'I'm not sure you understand, honey. It makes you real damn mean, that kind of fear. You see your best friend maimed or shot to pieces, and you're thinking thank God it's *his* smashed leg, not mine, or *his* corpse cold and stiff.'

'But we all think that, not just in wars. It's natural.'

'It's not. It's sick, inhuman. You get so you can hardly feel a thing for thousands dead. You're just scared out of your wits for your one puny little life.' He shakes his head. 'I don't care to be like that.'

'That's only because you're nicer than most people.'

'Yeah, I know — a hero.' He winces at the word, suddenly leans forward, takes my hand. 'Carole, honey, you ask me can I love a thief, but can you love a murderer? I *killed* men, Carole, and not just men — women, children, too — innocent civilians. I can't forget that, ever. It's left scars, worse than these.' He gestures to his thighs and stomach, as if dismissing them. 'Oh, I know it's not called murder in a war. They dress it up with other names: self-defence, patriotism, defeating the red menace. You shoot a little gook kid and they give you a medal for serving Uncle Sam. You burn down a whole village and . . .' He breaks off, shakes his head.

'We gunners were so out of touch. I mean, some of our guys never even saw the enemy. They just sat in their air-conditioned bunkers shooting at a map reference fifteen miles away. But this friend of mine in the marines was always needling me about having things too cushy — cold beer on demand and no dismembered corpses underfoot. So I joined him on a few patrols. I just had to see what was going on out there. I was really shaken, Carole, kept asking could I accompany him again, as if I couldn't quite believe it first time round — the heat and stench and rotting limbs, and whole villages destroyed. The rest of the guys thought I was crazy, but it was far too easy shelling all those targets without seeing the results, with no real blood on our hands or boots or consciences.'

He gets up, walks slowly to the window, stares out, frowning, as if at blood and carnage. 'I'll never forget it, never. Those villages were poor, dirt poor — just little shacks, with ducks and chickens in the streets, and old bent peasant women haggling for a banana or a cup of rice, and kids who could still smile, though God knows why.' He turns back to me, voice angry, both hands clenched. 'Often, we'd just smashed them to pieces — nothing left at all — no kids, no houses, not even any corpses, or none that you could recognize. Just fire and smoke and rubble. Those villages were their life, and we'd destroyed them. *I'd* destroyed them. That's hard to live with, Carole.'

I say nothing. War for me is just a word — or has been up to yesterday; something historical and abstract which always happened long ago, or miles away, not exploding in the present in a tiny charring room. Victor feels so passionately about it, even now, when all those years have passed. Isn't that proof he's not a brute, the fact he cares so much, feels so guilty still? I try to point it out to him. He interrupts.

'That's too easy, Carole. We *were* brutes, some of us. I've seen guys slice off ears and fingers from VC corpses, even . . . private parts, collect them up as souvenirs.'

I shudder. There's nothing left of our blue and golden day. It's grey outside, clouds and darkness building up, winter-time again. 'But *you* didn't do that, Victor. I simply don't believe it.'

'No-o.' He spins the word out. 'But I could have done. Those guys were normal decent men when they joined up – boys, not men – your age, Carole, barely out of high school, confused and scared and maybe trying to prove themselves. The training brutalized them. I saw one guy fire twenty rounds into a tiny kid of only twelve or so, and the look on that man's face – my God! I can't forget it. It was like he was enjoying it. Many vets admitted they got a kind of thrill from having power – power to rough up peasant women just for the sheer hell of it, or set fire to their houses and burn everything inside, even animals and babies who'd been left behind. The war turned them into thugs, taught them not to feel.'

I grip my cup. That's not so different from the Silver Palm. Young girls starting innocent, learning to be hard, becoming ruthless, callous, enjoying any chance to humiliate or even hurt the clients, relishing their power. Okay, it's not a war, and outwardly everyone's good friends, but I've still seen the equivalent of Victor's tough GIs – bitter female veterans, unable to adapt to the normal world outside.

Victor moves towards his fish tanks, stands between them, one hand on the glass. 'They made us still more brutish by trying to convince us we were fighting some lower form of life. I swallowed all that shit at first – that the VC weren't normal human beings with hearts and souls, just slant-eyed commie gooks who didn't value life or mourn their dead. All

Orientals were meant to be the same, not just inscrutable – inhuman. Then I saw a village funeral, and the grief was quite incredible. I cried myself, just watching.'

'And you call yourself a brute, Victor?'

He's looking at his morays, not at me, as if he still can't meet my eyes. 'I did become much harder, Carole. You had to. I felt I'd lost all touch with that idealistic boy of twenty-two who'd never used a gun except to shoot a rabbit or racoon. I guess that's why I've never been back home again – preferred to forget that kid, forget his high ideals.'

I reach my hand out. 'Do you miss your home town, Victor?'

'Sure I do. It's where my roots are, where I still belong. And yet I'm kind of nervous still. If I did go back, people might well gossip, maybe criticize, or . . .'

'Criticize? What for?'

'Well, some would say for fighting in a pointless war, but more would disapprove of the way I see things now, call me unpatriotic. And then they might object to my having run off to New York, cut my ties.'

I spring up, kick my chair away. 'God! They're all the same, Victor. They were like that back in Portishead – all petty tittle-tattle. Why had I gone to London, when Bristol was good enough for them, and what a louse I was to leave my poor sick widowed mother on her own. And when I landed up in court – jeez! the uproar. Jan's parents wouldn't even have me in their house.'

'Hush, darling, it's not like that back home – not at all. In fact, if I'm honest with myself, I guess most of it is simply in my head. I'm just embarrassed about the way I look, and everybody knowing.' He slumps down at the table. 'I hate that pity stuff.'

I hate it for him. I can suddenly see Laura, a stuck-up bitch like Suzie, walking out on Victor in the hospital. She probably had a doting living father, so she didn't need him, didn't value him. I'll show her, show them all. I'll have him walk down the main street in . . . in . . . tennis shorts, and if anyone so much as turns their head, they'll have me to contend with. He *will* be a hero and so will I. I like the word, whatever Victor says. I pull him to his feet.

'Victor, let's go back – together – you and me.'

He laughs. 'Come on, honey. Time to change. Shouldn't you try Norah again, tell her we'll be leaving soon, give Angelique some warning that you're bringing someone with you?'

'Okay, in a sec. But, listen, Victor, I'm serious. I want to see your home town. I'd even like to live there, settle down.'

He's staring at me, stunned.

'You don't belong here, Victor. It's not your home, not really. You're a foreigner, like your fish. Even half your plants were brought in from somewhere else. Everything's imported – lionfish, orchids, corals, flowers.' I trace the exotic lilies on the vase. They never grew in Vegas. And I'm even more a foreigner myself. I've been feeling really rootless recently. The fact I've lost my passport seems to have cut me off from England altogether. I'd never get a job there anyway, and I can't go back to Jan's now, and Beechgrove's closing down.

Beechgrove. I think of Norah, alone with Angelique, nervous of her, shy, maybe scared to ask if she needs the toilet; stuck with George for a whole two weeks before that. It's time she had a let out.

'Victor?' I nudge his arm. 'It's not a bad idea, you know. We all three need a home.'

'Three?'

'Well, Norah. I feel sort of responsible, since it was me who dragged her out here in the first place. Would you mind if she came with us?'

'N . . . no. Of course not. But . . .'

'But what?'

Victor's leaning against the wall, as if he can't support himself; looks rigid, almost paralysed. 'Carole, I've got to get this straight. Are you talking about us . . .' He swallows, seems to find the word impossible. 'Marrying?'

I don't answer for a moment. The word's difficult for me as well, full of dangerous memories, betrayals. 'Not necessarily. And certainly not yet. Not on the rebound, as you put it. I think we ought to wait. It's like the . . . sex thing. I want us to recover first. From everything. From Reuben and the brothel and Vietnam and . . .'

Victor's sounding dazed still. 'But marriage is for ever. You can't mean . . .'

'So you don't want me then, for ever?'

'It's not that.' His voice is suddenly cold, cold and even hard. He's moved away, right up to the door, as if he's trying to escape me. 'Look, Carole, we've been over this before. I'm twenty-four years older.'

'So? They can gossip about that, instead, in Bardstown. I'll have to move, in any case. Otherwise I'll never live my past down. If we stay on here, they'll tattle about you living with a tart. God! That reminds me – d'you realize you're still paying Carl a fortune to keep me here at all? Even yesterday, he was gloating when I phoned. You could almost hear him totting up the hours, working out his profit. I'd better phone again, tell him you drove me to Angelique's last night and I've been officially off-duty since then.'

'*I'll* call him, Carole.' Victor still sounds cool. His face is closed, defensive. He doesn't want me, obviously. He's not even looking at me, just staring down, as if regretting all the things he's ever said.

I march over to the phone, snatch up the receiver. 'I'll make my own calls, thanks.' I'm praying that he'll follow, tell me he still loves me, that he's thrilled by my idea. He doesn't speak, doesn't move at all.

'Damn,' I say. 'I misdialled.' There's a recorded message babbling on, some cheerful smarmy female I could murder.

'Carole, let me handle this. You could land yourself in trouble. Carl's a real tough guy. He may want you back immediately, insist you go on working there.'

I shrug. Who cares? Okay, so it's back to oafs and rotters, pricks and perverts, but rather them than bloody hypocrites who pretend they're crazed with love for you, until you actually let on you'd like to live with them. I steal another glance at Victor – face still shuttered, eyes not meeting mine. Fine for him to act the great romantic, so long as he imagined

500

it was all a fantasy and he could make his exit quickly if things became too real. Okay, so he still wants to 'save' me from the brothel, but nothing else, apparently, nothing permanent. And it's 'Carole' now, not darling, honey, sweetheart – 'Carole' twice.

I jerk back to the bookcase, lob out half a dozen heavy books, leave them scattered on the floor, retrieve my cigarettes. I ram one in my mouth, search round for a match. I threw away my lighter as a symbolic gesture yesterday. Symbolic bilge! All that stuff about love and sacrifice is just a load of claptrap. You're always disillusioned in the end. Better to stay tough, grit your teeth and accept that men are shits.

I can't find any matches. I push past Victor, slouch out to the passage, search the bureau there.

He follows me this time, asks me what's the matter, what's he done. As if he didn't know! I don't bother to reply, just doodle with my dead cold fag on the hard unfeeling wood.

'Look, why don't I phone Carl from my bedroom? Then you won't have to listen if it bugs you.'

I swing round to face him. 'Forget the bloody phone-call! If you don't want me yourself, Victor, I may as well go back to Carl. At least he values me. He was saying just last week that I'm . . .'

Victor grabs my shoulder. 'Don't want you? Are you crazy? I want you more than anything in the world.'

'Yeah, and the minute I suggest we might shack up together, you go all cold and distant, can't wait to get away. What d'you think I feel when you shy away from the very idea of marriage?'

He takes me back to the sitting room, sits me down, tries to calm his own voice as he crouches on the carpet at my feet. 'Of course I've thought of marriage. I've been dying to ask you if you'd be my wife, had to try and stop myself at least a dozen times.' He turns away, frowning, stares down at his hands. 'It simply isn't fair.'

'Not fair?'

'In terms of poker, I've got a dead hand. There's that great age gap to start with, and the . . . scars and . . .' He pummels

501

his thighs, as if furious with them suddenly. His voice is low, embarrassed. 'And I'm not sure I can have kids. You didn't know that, did you? It isn't certain. The doctors couldn't say. They just advised me to wait and see.'

'Who said I wanted kids? I'd be a rotten mother anyway.' I grin. 'Always blowing my top.'

'I'd love kids. *Your* kids.'

'So you expect me to have them out of marriage, then? Poor rotten little bastards.'

He shifts position on the floor, so that now he's almost kneeling at my feet. 'Carole, will you marry me?'

'No, I won't,' I say. 'I asked you first and you said no. Typical male pride.' I'm laughing, almost crying. 'Oh, Victor, d'you think we really dare?'

'It's settled.' He gets up, starts mixing two martinis. He needs a drink even more than I do. The gin's missing the glasses, spilling on the sideboard. 'We'll go back to Bardstown, like you said, and get married in the church where my parents had their own wedding. It's a lovely little church – plain wood painted white, with trees outside and . . .'

'No, wait. Don't go too fast, Victor.' I'm the one who's scared now, backing off. White dresses, wedding chapels, police cars, screaming sirens. 'I . . . I'm not sure.'

'Yes, you are. We both are. Absolutely sure.'

'Well, just a simple wedding.' I hear my own voice peter out. I'm remembering all my childish dreams: the big white fancy wedding, froth of pink tulle bridesmaids, six-tier cake, huge marquee; the young and handsome bridegroom, jet-black hair, tanned and muscly torso, film star looks. The pictures fade and shrink. The church is strange – and tiny. No marquee, no crowds. Not a soul I know. The groom is greying, lined; his lower body scarred beneath his neat and boring suit.

I get up, walk slowly to the window, keep my back to Victor. It's silent in the room; only the throbbing of the aerators, which seem to mock me with their contented steady purr. I could still change my mind, return to England, forget Victor and Las Vegas altogether. Better that than say what I don't mean, kid myself again. I haven't said 'I love you' all damn day. Deliberately. I've got to know exactly what I'm doing. No lies this time, no fudging, no rainbow fantasies. I find my crumpled fag, unlit. It's like a warning, proving just how hard love is, what guts it may demand. I squash it in my palm. I'm scared of my own weakness, the way I grab and winge, my stupid sulks and tantrums. I'm not one of Victor's 'heroes' – truckers and commuters, nurses with those lunch trays, battling on through thick and thin without a moan or groan. I grip the windowsill, stare out into black.

He's there, behind me, accepting me – moody selfish me – arms around my waist, refusing to let me go or let me fail, insisting we go on. 'We'll get married in our trench coats, his and hers, okay?'

'Okay.' I try to grin. 'And Norah can wear her new blue men's pyjamas.' I turn to face him. 'Victor, will you really not mind if Norah comes to live with us? I know you said yes, but you didn't sound that thrilled.'

He presses closer. 'I was simply stunned by the fact that I might actually live with *you.*'

'She's nowhere else to go, you see.'

'Sure she'll come. I'd like that. She can help us choose the house.'

I'm so choked I'm close to tears. Norah's never had a home before, and Victor's so damn generous. A lot of men would bitch about a threesome, close their hearts to Norah. 'Can we take the fish?' I ask, looking at them now with Norah's eyes; the magic rainbow colours, the paradise of plants.

'I wouldn't dream of leaving them. You can send them airfreight, in these special insulated cartons. It'll cost a bomb, but . . .' He shrugs. 'It's worth it. You're right, you know, honey. I have missed my home town. I was no one in New York – just half a line of print in the telephone directory and a social security number on the IRS's file. And Vegas is a mean town which rates you by your bankroll, not your personality.'

I walk over to the fish tanks, lure the shyest of the clown fish from its bolt-hole of green weed. 'If we have a garden, can Norah have a bit of it, a patch all to herself? She's never grown a bloody dandelion.'

503

'I'll teach her to grow orchids.'

I take his hand, put a kiss inside the palm, close his fingers over it. We glance at one another. 'Let's go and tell her. Now,' I say. 'This minute. Before we've even changed. I want to tell everyone.'

'But we're not formally engaged.'

'What d'you mean, formally? D'you have to nick another diamond ring from the five-and-dime before it's official?' I exchange grins with the lionfish.

Victor laughs. 'You'll have the best ring in Las Vegas.'

I don't say no. If I love his scars, then I'm allowed to love his money. I know I'm not a saint – I'm greedy for too many things. It would never have worked with Reuben. I'm not a Jew, couldn't be a Zionist, can't change the world, or save it. All the same, I'd like a cause.

'Hey, Victor?'

'What?'

'I've just had an idea. If we can't have our own kids, why don't we adopt a few from Vietnam – you know, as sort of . . . compensation?'

I'm slightly hurt when Victor laughs. I thought he'd tell me I was good again. I like it when he does that, feel capable of anything – Lady Bountiful dispatching crates of rice to shanty villages, or brave unselfish earth-mother breast-feeding hordes of slant-eyed commie orphans. I drain my dry martini. I guess I'll have to settle for a less dramatic cause – loving one man, taking in one dear and batty woman.

Victor takes my glass. 'You're far too young for kids yet. You ought to go to college first. My old one, maybe. I could drive you there and back each day.'

I pretend to bridle. 'I know – you just want me out of the house, so you can have some peace and quiet – you and Norah.'

'Yeah, that's right. And a wife with a Master's who can keep me in my old age.'

'You're not going to be old, Victor. I shan't allow it – ever. Well, not till I'm old, too. If we go back to Bardstown, you'll be twenty-two again, like you said you felt. We'll cancel all those horrid years when you were on your own and in hospital and everything.' I run my hand along his chin. 'I'd like you with a bushy beard. You could rub it on my breasts.'

He touches them, fingers circling across and round the nipples. I shiver. 'And I'll go back a bit as well, cut out that whole summer when I gave up my college place and nicked those things and landed up in Beechgrove.'

He smiles. 'You wouldn't have met Norah then.'

I say nothing for a moment. Norah's precious. I can't explain it really. To the outside world she's a pudding-brained old bat, but for me she's become a sort of relative – the nicest, most important kind, who loves you as you are and would give you her right hand without demanding something back, or playing martyr. And she knows things, deep things, which other people don't. She may not have the words for them, but that doesn't mean she's thick. And she's perceptive about people, liked Victor from the start, distrusted Reuben.

I pull at Victor's tie. 'I wouldn't have met you, either. If I'd gone to university, I'd have been probably far too busy to enter competitions – not sixty-three times anyway, all for the same one.'

'So you can't go back, you see. And nor can I. All we can do, as you limeys say, is simply soldier on.' Victor flicks his tie straight, as if he's about to be inspected by his sergeant, holds me with his eyes. 'Okay, so you gave up your college place in England, but that doesn't stop you applying here. In fact, we've got a lot more colleges. Not just Louisville, but the University of Kentucky in Lexington and several other good ones.'

I'm silent. My father was so eager that I had an education, got somewhere in life. Goals again, a purpose; Dad proud of what he called his brainy girl. I can see him in his baggy Fair Isle cardigan, sorting through prospectuses with me, stumbling over words like anthropology, worrying about grants and means-test forms. There won't be any grants out here. Only Victor's bounty, his support. I hug him suddenly.

'Oh Victor, I do wish you could meet him.'

'Who?'

'My Dad.'

'He'd disapprove – of me, I mean. You and me.'

Victor's right. He probably would. All the same, I'd like him there, in Bardstown, in that little white wood church with all the trees outside, giving me away. And Jan – I'd like her too. She could do the flowers, make up my bouquet. Suddenly, I'm missing her.

'Victor, we can visit England, can't we?'

'Sure.'

'And we'll still come back to Vegas sometimes?' I'm missing Angelique now, all the girls. If they're tough and hardened, it's only because they've never had my luck, a guy to bail them out, a second chance.

Victor laughs. 'I guess we'll have to, honey, if I'm going to pay for all those transatlantic flights. I'll need a run of wins.'

'Will you teach me poker?'

'Absolutely not. We'd wind up in Cardboard City.'

'So you don't think I'd make a gambler?'

'I'd prefer you as my wife.'

I get up, join him at the sideboard where he's replenishing the drinks. 'So when are we getting married, then?'

'Tomorrow morning, nine o'clock?'

'Don't be nutty, Victor. How about my birthday, 19th June? We can put my wedding flowers on your friend's grave – the one who died. Does he have a grave in Bardstown?'

Victor nods. 'They . . . sent his body back – all the bodies.'

'We'll put flowers on all the graves, then. And I want to see your house and where you went to school.'

'And we'll call on my old buddies and make our own new friends and maybe join the tennis club.' Victor recaps the vermouth, passes me my drink. 'I guess it may turn out to be another heroes' welcome, honey, especially with you there. The Kentucky *Standard*'s bound to run a piece on us. "Tomahawk Hill survivor returns with English bride."'

'We'll be in the paper, Victor? Really? With photographs and everything?'

'Sure. It's headline news. And everyone will envy me for

having such a beautiful young bride.' He puts his glass down, takes both my hands in his. 'Oh, Carole, my crazy darling Carole, can you really take me on – for better for worse?'

I grip his fingers. That ancient hackneyed phrase. It's only now I realize how serious it is, how absolutely terrifying. Not just 'I love you', which is hard enough to say and really mean, but a solemn vow to make and keep for ever. For richer for poorer, in sickness and in health. A gamble with no guarantees. My parents didn't make it. I think back to their years of co-existence, the endless nagging tension, no love, no give and take.

I reach out for a cigarette, let my hand fall back, wonder when it won't be quite so hard. 'Yes,' I say. I'm cold. I'm really shivering, though he's turned the heater on. 'I think I hope I can.'

30

We've arrived. Quite some time ago. I'm sitting on my own on
a piece of fallen rock. I still feel sick, a bit. The drive was very
bumpy, very fast. The man didn't understand that I had to drive
myself. I asked him several times, but he only laughed quite
rudely and said did I want to kill him. I said no, just myself. I
showed him the piece of paper about free funerals, but he
pushed my hand away and said if I didn't shut my trap and let
him listen to the radio, he'd drive straight back the way we'd
come.

I said nothing after that. I couldn't even think because the
music was so loud. Sometimes there was news. I listened very
hard, but there was nothing about the Bomb. I think they keep
it secret so the Russians won't find out. I've never seen a
Russian.

He dropped me at the ranger's house. When we first set out,
he asked me where I was staying and which part of Death Valley
did I want. I didn't know. It all felt very muddled and I can't
remember names.

I do remember one name: Jubilee. That's where all the
flowers bloom in the spring. Reverend Mother had a Jubilee. It
was the only day she smiled. They're not allowed to smile. We
had cake for tea instead of bread and marge and everyone was
happy. The ranger is happy all the time.

'I'd like to go to Jubilee,' I told the man. I still don't know his
name.

'Jubilee?'

'It's a mountain. Very high.'

'I can't leave you up a fuckin' mountain.'

He was getting very cross by then because I didn't know the

way. He said I must have an address, but the ranger doesn't have one. He lives all on his own in a very lonely place, far away from anyone without a street or number. I've never seen his home.

In the end, we found it. A house all on its own. I think it was the right one because it was hidden in the mountains and very dark and quiet.

'Let's stop here,' I said.

The man left me a torch. He was quite kind once we'd stopped. He asked me if the ranger was expecting me and I said yes, he was, and told him not to wait.

He did wait, quite a while. He gave me his Thermos and half a bag of sweets. Then he drove away.

The ranger may be dead. There are no lights on in his house and no one answered when I rang the bell. I've rung it seven times. He may be in a shelter.

I don't know what to do. I was going to ask the ranger if I could drive his car. You have to drink and drive if you want the funeral. I don't think I'll get it now. It had to be New Year. I'm not sure what the date is, but it must be nearly February, and after that it's spring.

Spring is when you get the flowers. I've never seen a flower here, not in all Death Valley. Sometimes they don't bloom at all, not even in the spring. Not if there's no rain. The ranger told me that. Sometimes, they wait years and years, too dry and parched to sprout. A million tiny seeds hiding in the dark.

This year, they'll all burst out. There's been rain this winter. More this winter than for over twenty years. The ranger said they'll be wonderful this spring. He told me all their names. The names were beautiful. I tried to lock them in my mind, but they escaped and got away.

The flowers only bloom a short time. Sometimes just a week, sometimes less. They wait all those years to flower, he said, then die in just a day or so. He said he hoped I'd see them. I think he liked me. I think I was his friend.

'Will you be staying through to March?' he asked.

I couldn't say, because I didn't know when March was. St Joseph has his feast in March. In the convent, we had two

509

Masses on his feast day, and you could buy Holy Pictures of him. They were very long, the Masses, and he looked angry in his pictures. St Joseph's never angry.

I'm not allowed to drink, so I couldn't drink and drive. It doesn't mix with pills. I haven't any pills. I forgot to bring them with me. And the man took the champagne. He said I owed it to him for the gas. I didn't use the gas. Maria wouldn't let me.

I'd like some nice hot tea. There's coffee in the Thermos, but I couldn't get it open. My hands don't seem to work. They're very cold and stiff. My body's cold as well. You can't be cold in deserts. People die of heat here. It's the hottest driest place in all the world.

I think I'll die of cold.

It's been dark for hours. It's still dark. It's meant to be full moon tonight. The man who drove me said so. I can't see any moon at all, not even just the peel of one. Only thick dark clouds. The clouds are black. Everything is black. It's a quiet and peaceful black. Not quiet like Angelique's house. That was frightening because people always listened, people with no bodies, only ears.

I'm not shut in, not here. The sky goes on much further than most skies. I keep looking up and up until my neck aches. I can see some stars between the clouds. Stars are saints, saints with silver eyes. I'm very near the saints here, near St Joseph.

Saints never need to go. I have to go a lot now, number one. I've been three times already, crouched down by the rock. And we had to stop six times in the car. The man got very cross. When I go, it stings.

You don't go when you're dead. When you're dead, you smell of flowers, not toilets. Stars don't smell, not ever, not even when they're old. I'd like to be a star.

I get up and ring the bell again. The ranger may be sitting with the lights out. I knock as well, but no one comes.

I didn't steal the shoes. I was going to pay, but the man took all my money. I'll have to leave my handbag in return. Then Angelique can pawn it. It's quite a useful bag. It isn't new. I've never had a new one, but I've always kept it nice.

The shamrock is for Carole. I hope she doesn't pawn that. It's silver, like the stars, and very special. My mother left it for me. It meant she loved me, left me all her luck. I'll leave it for Carole, leave her all I've got. I want her to be lucky and shamrocks bring you luck.

I'd like to wrap it up. I haven't any paper. Only newspaper, the bit about the funerals. It's torn now, but I make a little parcel, find a stub of pencil in my bag.

The ranger's name begins with B. Or D. 'Dear B,' I write, then cross it out. I can't see what I'm writing. I try to make the torch work, but it's sleeping like the Thermos. I shake it once or twice, but it keeps its eye tight shut. Everything is sleeping, maybe dead.

I go on writing in the dark. The writing is important. I'm asking if he'll give the Luck to Carole, say it's from her Friend.

I get up again, put it through his letter-box, knock and ring three times. No reply.

I sit down on another piece of rock. B or D doesn't have a garden, only stones. They may have dropped the Bomb here. When they drop the Bomb, grass and trees and plants all disappear.

I think that's why it's cold. It's always winter when they drop the Bomb. People scorch to pieces, but the flames are cold and black.

They've dropped bombs here before. The ranger told me. He didn't call them bombs, but everything exploded just the same. Flames flew out of rocks and huge mountains walked around. It was long ago, before anyone was born, even Miss O'Something and St Joseph. The earth was very young then, young and fidgety. It couldn't sit still, kept turning upside-down or jumping up.

The earth moves all the time. Sister Watkins said so. But in Beechgrove you can't feel it. I can feel it now. It moves like waves in seas. I saw the sea when I was thirty-nine. It was made of rock, dull grey rock which moved.

It's moving now. Underneath my feet. The whole mountain's heaving up. I think it's called an earthquake. They

511

had earthquakes here before. I saw the pictures in the ranger's book.

I clutch my piece of rock, shut my eyes against the flying sand. My head feels very strange. It's full of pictures, pictures from that book. They're moving too, leaping off the page.

I try to hold the ground still, cling on with both hands. No good. It's tipping, swinging, turning upside-down. I'm twisted, split apart. Bits of rock break off from my body, go crashing down the mountainside. My arms have gone. I haven't any feet. I'm thrown up in the air, tossed back again, broken into pieces.

The rocks are very angry. I hear them roar and roar. I can only hear, not see. Sharp-edged stones have got into my eyes, wedged right across the lids.

It's raining now, sheeting rain, turning the whole mountain into flood. Dirty water is gushing from my mouth, stinging down my legs. I'm swept into the flood, bumping over boulders, plunging down and down. I try to struggle up. Can't stand. Can't see at all. I'm spitting water, choking it; crying thick black mud.

I haven't got a face left. Wind and rain have ground it down to nothing, worn it smooth and flat. I'm old, I'm very old. I was born before the moon was.

I lie still. Nothing's still. Flames and ash spurting from the black hole in my head. Lava bursting out. I'm hot, I'm burning hot, so hot my rocks are melting, pouring down the mountains to the sea.

I'm waves, I'm only waves now. I can feel myself rolling up and over, white froth in my mouth and on my hands. I'm smashing against cliffs, wearing them away. Huge mountains worn to sand.

Only dust and sand.
Only soft black sand.
Soft.
And black.
Black.
Black.

I'm not dead when I wake. I don't think I was sleeping because

I've still got all my clothes on, far too many clothes on. I don't sleep in my coat. It's not my coat. It's new.

I can see the moon, or some of it. It's trapped behind a cloud. It must have come to help me. It makes the whole sky lighter, makes it easier to climb.

I feel quite faint, so I get up very slowly. I've got to get to Jubilee. Jubilee means happy all the time.

I can see it now, a tall black mountain standing just in front of me. It wasn't there before.

I leave my bag behind, tip out all the things first, put them in my plastic carrier. The bag is for someone else. I can't remember who.

I walk towards the mountain. It walks the other way. It's so big, it moves quite slowly, but still I can't catch up.

'Wait!' I shout. I'm tired. I'm very tired, not feeling well at all.

It stops, turns round. I clamber on its back, hold on tight. It's bigger than I thought, and still I've got to climb, climb right to the top.

It's very hard to climb. I keep falling, sliding, tripping on loose stones. I can't see far, even in the moonlight. My hands are made of silver, but the mountain's made of black.

'B!' I call. He may have come up here to see the flowers.

Silence. I think I've got his name wrong. I shout some other names. I don't know whose they are, or if I've ever met them. No one answers.

I call my Mother. I think she's waiting somewhere.

No. She doesn't hear. She must have gone.

I call my Father.

Nothing.

B (or someone) said all the little creatures come out in the night-time in the desert. It's safer in the night-time, not so hot. People die of heat in deserts, leave their bones behind.

I can't see any creatures, none at all.

It's very cold, not hot.

Mountains have black bones. I can see them sticking up, very tall and jagged in the sky. No flesh on them, no grass.

I stop a moment. I'll have to take my coat off. I can't climb in a coat. I fold it neatly, leave it on a rock.

There isn't any path, only stones and stumbles. I keep bumping into things, things that hurt a lot. My feet are very frightened. My legs ache at the backs.

I shouldn't wear pyjamas, not when I'm awake, and not so many pairs. Laundry is expensive. Sister will be cross. I take them off as well. It isn't easy. My hands are cold and clumsy and I keep overbalancing.

I'm making too much noise. I've woken sleeping things. I can hear them grumbling, snuffling, reporting me to Sister. There are black rags on the moon. The sky is getting bigger all the time. I must be close to God.

There are mountains all around me now, not just Jubilee. Nothing else but mountains, one above the other. They're climbing – climbing with me. I can hear them panting, feel their heartbeats pounding through my shoes. I look up into black. The moon has disappeared again. I think it must be busy like the nurses. They're always disappearing.

'Nurse!' I call. 'Nurse Clarke.'

I expect she's gone to tea.

I wish they'd bring my pills. I can't tell where the mountains end and where the sky begins. Both are dark and blurred. I feel quite dizzy because nothing will keep still. The clouds keep changing places, changing shape. I'm not sure if they're clouds, or only shadows. I step right on a shadow, hear it scream.

I don't know why I'm wearing all these frocks.

I stop again, try to drag them off. My head seems bigger than it was before. The last frock won't budge past it. I choke a while in tiny nylon flowers. I'm blinking flowers, eating flowers. In the end, it rips and lets me out.

Three blouses underneath. I can't undo the buttons. The buttons are too small, the hands too big. I think they're someone else's hands. Several buttons break and fall, like teeth.

I leave the blouses folded in my locker. We don't have hangers in the ward, not wire ones. You can undo the ends of wire ones and jab them through your eye. Tom Bryden did.

'Tom!' I call. 'Tom Bryden.'

I think he died at Eastbourne, jumped off a high cliff.

It's easier to climb in just my underclothes. I'm higher now, much higher. The moon's come out again. It must get very lonely. There's only just one moon, so it's always on its own. The stars all have each other.

I can see some white stuff shining just above me. It may be snow. It may be just the moonlight. The moon is very cold, slaps my naked arms. It's rude to take your clothes off in the ward.

They've dropped the Bomb – I know now. I didn't hear it, but it's colder all the time. Cold and very bare. All the trees have died. And all the birds. None of them are singing, not even owls, or night-birds. I'm treading on their bones.

I'm the only one alive.

There are a lot more fallen rocks now. I don't always know they're there. Sometimes they spring out at me. Sometimes I fall down.

I use my hands to help me climb. It's hard to hold the carrier as well. It's very heavy, keeps trying to drag me down again. It's the shoes which make it heavy, not the Dress. The Dress is made of air.

I didn't steal the shoes. I only stole a feather. Feathers fly.

I think my feet are bleeding. I sit down, undo my laceups, start to take my stockings off. It takes me a long time. I'm feeling stiff and shaky, so I rest between each pair. I'd like to see the doctor, but Sister says he's busy. Everyone is busy.

Both my legs are bare now. The wind blows up and down them. I'm not sure if I'm cold or not. My skin is cold, but the inside of me is hot. Very hot.

I struggle with my petticoats, claw and fight them off. It's getting hard to breathe. The brassieres are tight and make a thumping noise. I'd better keep those on. Naked chests are rude.

It hurts to walk barefoot, so I get down on my hands and knees. It's very steep, the mountain, tears my hands. I need to go again. The moon is watching, so I try to hide. It stings and burns a lot, worse than all the other times.

I leave all three pairs of knickers off. I expect they're full of germs.

I don't think I'll reach the top. However high I climb, it's always higher. There may not be a top.

I unhook my brassieres. Nobody can see me. They're all dead. Or gone to shelters. Even Sister. No point calling; nobody can hear. I call once more, to check.

Someone's answering.

Just my own voice, deeper. The mountains copy it.

It's peaceful when you die. You don't have to climb, or breathe, or call out names. Your feet don't hurt or bleed. You're cold, but you can't feel it. You can't feel anything. You don't wear brassieres. You don't wear clothes at all, just bare white skin.

My skin looks very white, shining in the moonlight. The ground looks white as well – silver-white below me; far below. I think it's salt, not snow. Salt embalms your body. That means it doesn't smell. Salt is made of tears.

I look down, then up, to see how far I've climbed. Very far. The stars are really close now. I can almost touch the moon.

I lie down where I am.

St Joseph wakes me, taps me on the shoulder. He's brought me to the top. There are mountains all around me, but I'm the highest now.

I'm lying on a ledge. Below me is just fall. Just black and dizzy fall. I hardly dare look down.

The moon is very bright. The clouds have gone, all gone. It's a full moon now. It wasn't full before, but St Joseph made it bigger. Full moons bring you luck.

I think it must be March. He wants me for his feast day. Jubilee means feast day when everyone is happy and there's cake for tea instead of sand and stones.

I'm not alone, not now. The desert creatures have come out of their holes. I can hear them breathing, rustling, all around me.

It's safer coming out at night. People can't see you if you take off all your clothes. It's cold without your clothes. I've never been so cold before. The cold is like a fire.

I try to put the Dress on. My body keeps on shaking, so I have to stop and rest. Nothing underneath. Carole wore nothing underneath. The Dress feels cool and silky against my burning skin. It's tight. It's very tight. I leave the zip undone.

I've never worn a long frock, or lacy petticoats. I haven't got a mirror, but I know I'm beautiful. My hair is fair and my eyes are blue with little darker flecks in them.

Carole wore a hairslide. It's broken now. George broke it, but I've still got the ribbon from the chocolate box. I tie it in my hair. I tip out the carrier bag, find a comb, a beetle. Then I find a pill bottle. I haven't any pills. I try to read the label, hold it very close. The moon is like a torch. 'MARY'S RING', it says.

I smile. St Joseph's bought the ring, bought my wedding ring. A ring means someone wants you. It's a very special ring. He bought it at that shop and put it with my pills. He knew I'd find it then. I take pills every day.

'MARY'S RING.' He wrote that on himself. Mary's beautiful. She always wears long frocks. I've seen her in the pictures. Long frocks and small red shoes.

My feet are sore and blistered, but I force the red shoes on, take a few steps up and down the ledge. The train floats and whispers after me. Only Queens have trains. I'm Queen. I'm Queen of Jubilee.

Carole carried flowers. I haven't found the flowers yet. It can't be spring, not yet.

I stare down at my Dress. There are white flowers on the skirt. Sprigs of orange blossom. That's for funerals. It means you'll have children and be happy. Reverend Mother had three hundred children.

At funerals, you have to say 'I will'. And you have to have a witness. I've got my witnesses, crowding all around me. Scorpions and pack-rats. Circus beetles. Kit fox.

I know I'm better because I remember all the names. I feel light and made of glass. Precious glass. There's more room in my head. Room for all the names. St Joseph made me better. He's my bridegroom, dressed in brown. I've got his wedding ring. I didn't steal it. I only stole a feather.

I open the pill bottle and tip the ring into my hand. It's

gold, it's solid gold. I slip it on my finger. Mary/Joseph, joined for ever.

I throw away the bottle. I shan't need pills again. Mary doesn't take them. And she never had a germ, not one on her whole body.

I sit down on the ground. Joseph's late. We'll have to wait our turn now. They've closed the chapel doors. They're marrying someone else. Carole's getting worried, pacing up and down.

'Of course he'll come,' I tell her. 'He said he might be late.'

I take my glasses off. I don't wear glasses. It's then I see the flowers, a million million flowers, blooming on the mountain-top – for me.

They've waited twenty years. More than twenty years. Waited in the dark. Waited for my wedding. Burst out just for me. They're wearing coloured frocks, bright expensive frocks. They're crowding round me, staring at the Dress.

I remember all their names. St Joseph made me better, so there's room for all the names now. Maidenhair and Lantern Flower. Blue-Eyed Grass. (That's Carole's.) Desert Star. I can almost touch the stars. Gold Carpet. Desertgold.

The flowers are mostly gold. I saw them in the ranger's book. Gold daisies, golden poppies, golden eyes and mouths. I've found my crock of gold. Before, I wasn't high enough, and it was cold grey winter still. Now, it's golden spring.

I can hear the buzz of insects. Heavy bees, insects with red wings. They're naked in the flowers, deep inside the petals, sucking up the pollen. St Joseph has red wings.

The moon is like the sun. Burning sun, so hot it hurts my eyes. Burning golden pollen.

I'm ready now, step right towards the edge. There's nothing underneath me. Only fall. Only black and plunging fall.

I pick up a handful of confetti, toss it into the air. It doesn't fall. It flies. A million million tiny bright balloons filling the whole sky on New Year's Eve. I knew they'd fly here for my party in the end.

New Year's Eve. I can hear the wedding bells, hear my bridegroom calling very softly.

I take a step towards him. There's nothing underneath me. Only sky. I'm falling into sky. Huge black shapes rush by me. The stars are very close and very cold. I see St Joseph smiling as I fall fall fly towards him.

'I will,' I say, and

Wendy Perriam

Michael, Michael

Oxford. May Morning. Pouring rain. Eighteen-year-old student Tessa Reeves has a close shave with death as Dr Michael Edwards comes hurtling round the corner in his scarlet MG. By way of apology, he treats her to a lavish breakfast in a country hotel, and over strawberries, steak and champagne, she first experiences his greed – a greed which later culminates in electrifying sex.

Tessa, from the wrong side of the tracks, brought up with no frills – and no father – by the irrepressible but decidedly uncultured April, feels overawed by the pressured mystique of Oxford. The charismatic Michael boosts her spirits and her status, and fires her own ambition. But it is darkness which descends as the affair turns sour, and Tessa searches in increasing desperation for her lost lover, and later for his surrogate and namesake, the suburban GP, Dr Michael Edwards. Spellbound, her love becomes an obsession, and her quest for Michael Michael takes over her whole life.

'Sex, retribution, madness . . . Wendy Perriam is back on characteristic form with guns firing'   Val Hennessy, *Daily Mail*

'Smooth, interesting, pacy . . . the prose is stylish and the blend of dialogue with narrative well-judged'   *The Times*

'*Michael, Michael* is an arresting novel . . . poignant and deeply affecting'   *Catholic Herald*

'A well-written and enthralling tale'   *Books*

ISBN 0 00 654670 6

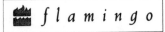